PEOPLE OF THE
SILENCE

KATHLEEN O'NEAL GEAR
and W. MICHAEL GEAR

TOR®

A TOM DOHERTY ASSOCIATES BOOK
NEW YORK

This is a work of fiction. All the characters and events portrayed in this book are either products of the author's imagination or are used fictitiously.

PEOPLE OF THE SILENCE

Copyright © 1996 by Kathleen O'Neal Gear and W. Michael Gear

Cover art by Royo
Maps and interior art by Ellisa Mitchell

A Tor Book
Published by Tom Doherty Associates, LLC
175 Fifth Avenue
New York, NY 10010

www.tor.com

Tor® is a registered trademark of Tom Doherty Associates, LLC.

ISBN: 0-812-51559-5
Library of Congress Catalog Card Number: 96-23402

First edition: December 1996
First mass market edition: September 1997

Printed in the United States of America

0   9   8   7   6   5   4

To Doug and Sue Morley
and
Lester and Ruth Hofer

For more than forty years of generosity and kindness

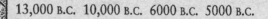

13,000 B.C.   10,000 B.C.   6000 B.C.   5000 B.C.

Paleo Indian

Early Archaic

People of the Wolf
Alaska & Canadian
Northwest

People of the Fire
Central Rockies &
Great Plains

People of the Sea
Pacific Coast &
Great Basin

People of the Lightning
Florida

Paleo Indian

---- *Archaic*

3000 B.C.	100 A.D.	800 A.D.	1300 A.D.

Archaic — *Woodland* — *Mississippian*

People of the Earth
Northern Plains
& Basins

People of the Mist
Chesapeake Bay

People of the River
Mississippi Valley

People of the Lakes
East-Central Woodlands
& Great Lakes

People of the Silence
Southwest Anasazi

Basketmaker — *Pueblo*

North

People
of the
Silence

TOWER
BUILDERS
STRAIGHT PATH
PEOPLE
MOGOLLON
HOHOKAM

the Canyon
Towns

Straight Path Wash

Spider Woman's
Butte

to Deer
Mother
Village

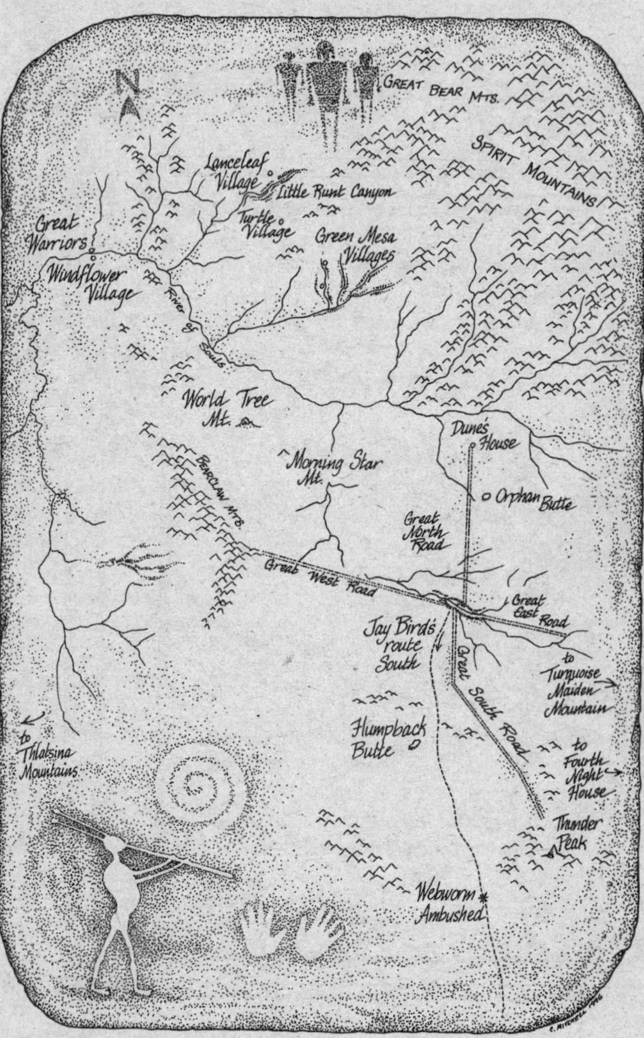

N
GREAT BEAR MTS.
SPIRIT MOUNTAINS
Lanceleaf Village
Little Runt Canyon
Turtle Village
Green Mesa Villages
Great Warriors
Windflower Village
River of Souls
World Tree Mt.
Dune's House
Morning Star Mt.
BEARCLAW MTS.
Orphan Butte
Great North Road
Great West Road
Great East Road
Jay Bird's route South
Great South Road
to Turquoise Maiden Mountain
Humpback Butte
to Thlatsina Mountains
to Fourth Night House
Thunder Peak
Webworm Ambushed

Acknowledgments

We would like to thank Dr. Jonathan Haas and Dr. Winifred Creamer for their outstanding work on Anasazi warfare. Dr. Debra Martin sent us a copy of her excellent unpublished paper, "Lives Unlived: The Political Economy of Violence Against Anasazi Women." We've also relied upon Dr. Linda Scott Cummings's work on Anasazi diet, and Dr. Ray Williamson's work on prehistoric astronomy.

Special gratitude goes to California State University in Bakersfield for a 1975 Humanities Research Award that sparked an abiding interest in the Chaco Anasazi, and to the National Park Service staff at Chaco Canyon, who have an impossible job and manage to do it extremely well.

Tom Doherty, our publisher, has supported us throughout this project, though we've often bored him glassy-eyed with the intricate minutiae of archaeology. Linda Quinton, associate publisher, deserves our sincere appreciation for her firm belief that the best way to bring the science of archaeology to the people is through this medium. And, as always, we owe a great deal to Harold and Sylvia Fenn, Rob Howard, and all the wonderful H. B. Fenn folks in Canada.

The debt we owe to Harriet McDougal goes beyond words. She is, simply, the finest teacher and friend that a writer can have.

Foreword

At a 6,000-foot elevation in northwestern New Mexico lies a high desert valley—a gash worn through the enduring sandstone by eons of sun, wind, and water. Only about ten miles long, defined by majestic sheer-walled sandstone cliffs, Chaco Canyon is characterized as Upper Sonoran desert. When the rain does fall, it cascades violently off the slick rock, and powerful torrents scour the washes. Temperatures soar to over one hundred degrees Fahrenheit during summer, and plunge to twenty degrees below zero in the winter. Periods of drought are common and severe. At the best of times, it is an inhospitable, if hauntingly beautiful, place.

Yet during the eleventh century this canyon became a cultural center for a people we call the Anasazi. The Chaco culture encompassed over 115,000 square miles and included approximately 100,000 people.

There are many reasons for what is called the "Chaco Phenomenon." By about A.D. 1050 Chaco Canyon had become the focal point for the manufacture of turquoise goods. Beads, figurines, and jewelry were produced in large quantities and traded to outlying communities. Archaeologists have traced the turquoise to mines over one hundred miles away, near the present-day town of Cerrillos, New Mexico. Those mines seem to have been under the direct control of the Chacoan elite. But finished turquoise goods were more than "money." They amounted to a ceremonial industry which maintained links between the Chacoan elite and the leaders in outlying communities.

During this period the Chacoans began construction of an elaborate road system that would be unequaled in North America for another seven hundred years. These were by no means "dirt trails," but carefully engineered roads. Thirty feet wide in places, the roadbeds were generally excavated into the ground and bordered by earthen berms or low masonry walls. Many of them appear to have been surfaced with crushed potsherds. In one location north of Chaco Canyon, the road becomes a four-lane "highway," where four parallel routes head north. When the desired routes encountered cliffs or steep hills, the engineers built wood scaffolding or earthen ramps, or carved stairs into solid rock. They are lined with signal towers, "way-stations," and shrines. The latter seem to have functioned as places of prayer and ritual reflection similar to the stations of the cross in the Christian tradition.

Chacoan architecture is stunning. The Chaco Anasazi constructed multistoried Great Houses: walled towns that would have awed Europeans of the same period. D-shaped, rectangular, or circular, the Great Houses contained hundreds of rooms—most of which were never lived in. The population of these enormous Great Houses probably hovered at between one hundred and two hundred people. The extra rooms were used for storage and may have acted as guest quarters when the canyon population expanded during major ceremonials. To support the weight of the upper stories, the lower walls were built three to four feet thick, and each story was set back at regular intervals to create a "stairlike" appearance. Such daunting edifices required the builders to quarry and dress tons of stone, haul it for miles to reach the building site, and carry enough sand, clay, and water to make the mortar. Interior and exterior walls were then plastered with bright clays and painted with colorful artwork.

Chacoans were also extraordinary astronomers. The elegant motions of the sun, moon, and stars were the very heart of their Great Houses.

Pueblo Bonito (called Talon Town in *People of the Silence*) demonstrates alignments with the cardinal directions and several solstice-monitoring stations. The axis of the large kiva—a subterranean ceremonial chamber—is on a true north-south line, as is the internal line of rooms that divides the pueblo in half. The long straight wall forming the front of the west half of Pueblo Bonito runs true east-west.

Pueblo Bonito also contains curious "corner windows." One of these windows, Room 228, begins charting the coming winter solstice forty-nine days in advance of the event. A thin beam of light strikes the room's back wall. This beam gradually widens as the winter solstice approaches, moving northward an inch a day across the wall. At dawn on the solstice, a full rectangle of light shines on the north wall.

Despite the grandeur of their culture, Chaco Canyon was a place of marginal resources. Water, wood, and productive soils were very precious. By the time the canyon reached its peak, at the beginning of the twelfth century, those resources were being strained to the limit. The Chacoans constructed dams and ditches to divert rainwater to their fields, and cultivated special gardens in the side canyons and on the mesa tops. But when the population reached around 2,000 people, the fragile desert ecosystems failed. The canyon could no longer feed its inhabitants.

The outlying communities—linked by the roads—brought a wide variety of goods to Chaco Canyon, in addition to food, timber, turquoise, and other rare minerals. The Chacoan elite also managed a trade network that brought seashells from as far away as the Pacific Ocean, and copper bells and macaws from central Mexico.

Even many utilitarian goods were imported. Up to one-third of the stone tools and half of the pottery cooking vessels found at Pueblo Alto (called Center Place in this book) were made from special stones and clays found in the Chuska Mountains fifty miles west of Chaco Canyon. Much of the finished pottery came from the Mesa Verde region in southern Colorado.

We know from tree-ring data that precipitation between A.D. 900–1150 was extremely variable around the San Juan Basin. One village might have received unusual rainfall and produced a food surplus, while another village, a few miles away, might have suffered both drought and famine. Many archaeologists have theorized that Chaco Canyon served as a central storage and redistribution center. Surplus food would have been hauled in from prosperous villages, then shipped out to needy outlying communities. This theory is not unreasonable, given that modern Puebloan peoples, such as the Hopi, still maintain a three-year food supply.

Around A.D. 1130, a new drought began. In a high desert environment even a short drought can be disastrous, but this one lasted twenty-five years. The springs and seeps dried up. Growing traditional crops of corns, beans, and squash became precarious. After decades of exploitation, every stick of wood had been collected, every clump of brush twisted out of the ground. When the scant rainfall did come, the exposed topsoil was vulnerable. Floods surged down the drainages, stripping the exhausted earth and uprooting the frail crops. Chaco Wash, the primary source of water for the canyon, reached its deepest point around A.D. 1150, cutting to a depth of thirteen feet and lowering the water table.

From skeletal material we know the people suffered increasing malnutrition. A bone disease called porotic hyperostosis—lesions in the skull—afflicted 65% of the adults, and 75% of the children. The disorder is caused by profound iron deficiency, among a lack of other nutrients.

These two events, the drought and the ensuing malnutrition, would have been enough to turn Chaco Canyon into a frightening place to live—but there's more.

It required approximately 250,000 trees to build the Great Houses in Chaco Canyon. Pueblo Bonito alone, the oldest and largest of the Great Houses, constructed approximately A.D. 920–1120, stood five stories tall and contained around *eight hundred* rooms. Analyses of pollen and seed records tell us that the Chacoans quickly consumed the building materials in and near the canyon. The count of tree pollens drops dramatically during the last one hundred years of habitation—meaning they cut down every tree they could find within walking distance. And remember, for two hundred years, the resident population had had to cook, fire pottery, light their kivas, and keep warm during the bitter winters.

Why, then, would an ailing people continue to congregate in such large numbers in an area of vanishing resources? The architecture tells us a great deal.

In the last years, the Chacoans began sealing exterior windows and doorways—actually walling them up with stone and mortar. They even plugged small vents designed to aid the circulation of air through the pueblo. Pueblo Bonito had originally been open in front, so that people could come and go as they wished, but during the eleventh century a string of rooms closed off that opening. They left only two entryways. Then one of those was walled up so that only a gate in the southeast corner of the western plaza remained. That single gate was then narrowed to the width of a door and finally walled off altogether. Just before the end, they sealed the town completely. The only way in or out of Pueblo Bonito was by ladder over the walls. The difficulties this would create, especially for the elderly members of the community, are obvious. But the Chacoans clearly believed they *had* to strengthen their defenses.

The evidence for warfare is overwhelming. Modern-day Pueblo peoples, such as the Hopi, Keres, Zuni, Tewa, and Tanoans—the most likely descendants of the Anasazi—tell of ancient and fierce wars fought by their ancestors. Some involve the destruction of entire towns. The archaeological evidence is also powerful: burned buildings, battered bodies, and crushed skulls.

Prior to the 1960s, archaeologists believed that the warfare arose from the influx of the nomadic Navajo, Apaches, and other "Athabaskan" peoples into the peaceful Pueblo sphere, but further research has severely weakened this theory. The best evidence now suggests that the Athabaskan peoples arrived in the Southwest in the sixteenth century—and then in such small numbers that they could not have been a significant threat to fortified pueblos.

The "enemy" may have been other Southwestern cultures: the Hohokam, the Fremont, or the Mogollon. It may even have been other groups of Anasazi. As the religious, economic, and social systems disintegrated, village may have turned upon village, clan upon clan.

By 1150 Chaco Canyon had been abandoned, and many Anasazi began building their houses on highly defensible hilltops, on pillars of rock separated from canyon walls, in hollows in sheer cliffs—all far removed from sources of drinking water and their fields, but sites where they must have felt a small measure of safety.

Yet for more than two centuries Chacoan culture had thrived. They built stunning edifices, engineered hundreds of miles of roads, established an elaborate ceremonial system, created magnificent art, charted the courses of the sun, moon, and stars. The abandonment of the great pueblos was a slow process, occurring over decades. But make no mistake, those grand prehistoric peoples did not "vanish," as some books and television shows would have you believe. Their descendants, the modern Pueblo tribes, continue to live and flourish in the American Southwest. Indeed, much of what we theorize about prehistoric peoples is based upon Puebloan oral tradition.

The myths, legends, and concepts of the sacred that you will discover in this novel come from those oral traditions. Spider Woman, the Great Warriors, and the *Katchinas* (whom we call *thlatsinas*) are still worshiped today. It is difficult to know from the archaeological record when the *Katchinas* first came into existence, but they probably originated during the latter half of the twelfth or early thirteenth centuries. The Humpbacked Flute Player—the subject of much Southwestern art, modern and ancient—is even older. Depictions of male and female flute players were etched into rocks, painted on bowls, even carved into kiva floors. The humpbacked flute player symbolized fertility, which means much more than human sexuality; it means that he or she embodied the creative power of the universe.

We encourage you to visit the prehistoric sites—Hovenweep in Utah; Chaco Canyon and Aztec ruins in New Mexico; Mesa Verde and the Crow Canyon Archaeological Center in Colorado; and Wupatki and Casa Malpais in Arizona, to name just a few—as well as the modern Southwestern pueblos, such as Acoma and Oraibi.

To really understand the majestic history of the North American continent, one must look for the point where the past meets the present.

Introduction

"Be careful, Grandma. The stones are slick from the rain."

Maggie Walking Hawk Taylor brushed wind-blown strands of short black hair out of her eyes and guided her sick grandmother toward the entry to the ancient pueblo. Though a fine mist continued to fall, golden shafts of light slanted down through the rain clouds, making oblong pools of bright gold on the cracked and weathered canyon walls that surrounded them. The sage-covered bottomlands glimmered and sparkled. The blocks of red sandstone that formed the walls of the pueblo shone a deep dark crimson, the color of old blood.

Slumber Walking Hawk puffed as she hobbled along, her purple skirt flapping about her legs.

"There's a step here, Grandma. Do you see it? It's that rock, right there." Maggie pointed.

Slumber stopped, but she looked up instead of down. Her gaze took in the huge semicircular structure. It had originally been five stories tall, but only four remained to tell the thousand-year-old story. Maggie followed her grandmother's gaze. No matter how many times she came here, she always felt dwarfed by the magnificence of the Anasazi, the ancient people who'd built this structure. The pueblo, a walled town, covered over three acres of land.

Slumber took a breath, and Maggie held her wrinkled arm tightly. Sometimes her grandmother tripped over imaginary rocks—and then swore they'd been there when she'd tripped. No one dared tell her otherwise, either, out of fear of being wrong. Her grandmother was a great Seer. She didn't always live in this ordinary world.

Slumber used a clawlike hand to point to the spot Maggie had indicated. "There? That's the step?"

"Yes, Grandma. Hold onto me. I'll help you."

Cautiously, Slumber lifted her right foot and placed it on the lip of stone, then allowed Maggie to support her weight while she rose on to the step. A small groan escaped Slumber's lips, and Maggie's heart ached. *She's so ill. Why did she insist on coming, today of all days?*

"This is going to be a bad day, Grandma. You know I have to meet with those two from the local hiking club. I wish you'd stayed home in bed."

Maggie had patiently explained how hostile the club president was, not that Kyle Laroque was a bad guy—he wasn't. Maggie actually liked him. When she'd first met him a year ago, she'd seen a light in his eyes that she'd come to identify only with Indian holy people. It had surprised and fascinated her. But, recently, that light had vanished. The new park plan had affected recreationists the way a match did a fuse. She expected the final grand explosion today. Yet Slumber had insisted upon coming, and she'd been so adamant that Maggie couldn't say no.

Slumber simply whispered, "I must be here. Saw it . . . in a dream."

"All right, Grandma. Let me take you over to the wall. You can sit down and rest while we wait."

Slumber's grip tightened on Maggie's arm, and they started across the plaza, but after only ten paces, Slumber stopped. She wheezed in and out, then took another two steps and stopped, breathing some more.

Maggie tenderly brushed loose strands of gray hair behind her grandmother's ears. Just looking at her made Maggie hurt. She resembled a knotted twig. Four feet seven inches tall, Slumber was thin enough to blow away if a powerful gust of wind came along. Wispy gray hair clung to her age-spotted scalp, and thick blue veins crawled like knobby worms across her arms and hands. She had the sort of classic "ancient" Indian face that photographers loved to shoot and put on postcards. Cadaverous, and criss-crossed by a thousand wrinkles, it acted like a magnet. People would smile in a kindly way at her wrinkled visage, then glance beneath the thick gray brows that jutted out over Slumber's eyes and stand transfixed. Maggie had seen it happen. People would just suddenly stop and go quiet. Slumber's eyes gave no evidence that she had witnessed the passing of ninety-two long, hard years—reservation years, filled with too much hunger, and cold so deep it settled in the bones until a person felt like they'd never get warm. Curiously clear and as black as midnight, Slumber Walking Hawk's eyes had *Power*. The Navajo called her, "That Crazy Old Keres Holy Woman," but her own people knew her as, "She Who Haunts the Dead."

And, gods help me to stand it, she will be among them soon.

Maggie put an arm around her grandmother's shoulders and hugged her. Slumber affectionately patted her hand in return.

"I'm all right," Slumber said.

Two weeks ago, the doctor in Albuquerque had given Slumber a maximum of eight weeks to live. The cancer had spread through her entire body. Maggie had been frightened and empty, uncertain what to say or do. Slumber had merely smiled and returned to the pueblo, going about her daily tasks as she had always done. No matter what she might be feeling inside, to the outside world Slumber kept up the appearance of being hale and hearty.

Maggie led her grandmother to a low wall, next to one of the *"Don't Sit on The Walls!"* signs, and gently eased her down.

Slumber gestured to the sign and grinned. "You're a big park ranger so it doesn't matter, eh?"

"I make these decisions on a case-by-case basis," Maggie replied in her best bureaucratese. "When I'm on duty, the elderly get special treatment."

The roar of a Jeep sounded at the parking lot and Maggie lifted a hand to shield her eyes from the rain. *Damn, they're here.* "Grandma," she said, "I have to go meet these people. Will you be all right?"

"Yes, you know I will. Go on," Slumber said, and waved a transparent old hand, smiling. "I just want to sit for a while and listen."

Maggie stroked her grandmother's hair again and turned away.

*　　*　　*

Slumber watched her granddaughter trot toward the trail that led down to the parking lot and sighed. *I'm almost done in. My soul's hanging by a spiderweb, floating somewhere high above my body.*

That pleased Slumber. She needed to escape. The pain was getting too bad. Every square inch of her old body hurt. Oh, the doctor had given her all kinds of pills to take, but she'd tucked them into a paper bag and tossed them in the trash. When the time came, Slumber Walking Hawk would stand up, greet whichever ancestor came to get her, and climb into the skyworld with a clear mind and an open heart.

She straightened her ankle-length purple cotton dress around her. The color looked startling against the fine red stones that formed the wall.

Two people came through the front entry with Magpie. Both had their brows furrowed, as if ready for a fight, and they spoke in dark tones. That tall man, though, he had some *Power*. Slumber could see it wavering about him like a faint blue glow. With the right teacher he could really be something. Too bad most Whites couldn't spot it.

Slumber gazed southward across the rugged canyon. A wavering veil of rain was sweeping northward. The damp earth smelled like perfume. She inhaled and held the blessing breath in her lungs while she silently thanked the *Shiwana* for the shower. The *Shiwana* were the spirits of the dead who'd climbed into the heavens and become cloud beings. The Hopi called them *Katchinas*, the Zuni called them *Koko*, the Tewa knew them as the *Okhua*, but most Whites used the word *katchina*, because of the dolls the Navajo made and sold in all the grocery and gun stores.

The storm edged toward the ruins, and Slumber tipped her face up, letting the first big drops splat on her forehead. A soft patter fell on the ancient walls, and on the tan dust of the plaza. Rain was life itself in the desert. As wind gusted through the ruins, Slumber's short gray hair whipped about, slapping her deeply wrinkled cheeks and forehead, tangling with her stubby eyelashes. Slumber turned her head away and let the wind gust by.

The sweet lilting notes of a wooden flute drifted through the ruins. Slumber cocked her head and looked around. Did anyone else hear? She looked straight at the tall blond-haired man. He had stopped talking—his mouth was still open. But he shook his head slightly, as though denying what his soul heard because his ears hadn't, and he went back to waving his hands. Slumber let her eyes trace the half-moon shape of the ruins, searching for the musician.

Magpie led the two people to the center of the plaza and stopped to talk, saying, "I understand your point, Kyle. I just don't agree. The regional tribes have been using this canyon for religious rituals for centuries. Our proposed plan only gives that fact official recognition. We—"

"You're planning on closing the park for a month, Maggie!" Kyle propped his hands on his bony hips. He wore khaki shorts and a white T-shirt. Sunglasses shielded his eyes. His blond hair ruffled in the wind.

Slumber squinted at his legs. *Roadrunner skinny and hairy as a bear.* If she had legs like that, she'd keep them covered up so nobody'd gawk.

"Just who funded that plan of yours?" the woman hiker demanded to know. "Taxpayers! People like me who've been coming to this park in June for twenty years! It's White recreationists you're trying to keep out! That's racism!"

"Easy, Marisa. That's out of line," Kyle admonished.

Magpie bowed her head and seemed to be collecting her thoughts. Tall and thin, with rich brown eyes and short black hair, she wore an olive uniform. Her pants were perfect, the crease like a knife edge. A black leather belt tooled in basket-weave snugged her hips. The badge over her left breast gleamed. A government patch adorned her left shoulder. Slumber couldn't read it from here, but she knew it for a park patch, telling the tourists that her granddaughter worked here, just in case they wanted to complain about something, or ask directions, maybe quiz her one more time on what "Anasazi" meant.

Slumber smiled. She'd heard that question at least a hundred times: *"Is it Ancient Ones or Ancient Enemy?"* She always gave the same answer, "You got me. If you ever find out, let me know." Her own people, the Keres, claimed to be the descendants of the people who'd lived in this canyon a thousand years ago, but they'd never heard the word "Anasazi" until the Whites starting using it.

"Kyle," Magpie said, "the park administration isn't planning to close the park. They're asking visitors to voluntarily avoid certain holy places around the summer solstice, that's all. Many Puebloan peoples come here to perform healing, renewal, and purification rituals. The tribes believe this canyon has spiritual power. I know that may be hard for you to understand, but—"

"No, Maggie." He shook his head. The dark lenses of his sunglasses flashed. "It's not hard at all. *I* feel the spiritual power here. That's why *I* come."

Though her granddaughter's real name was Magpie, she'd started calling herself Maggie when she'd gotten her first government job, Maggie Walking Hawk Taylor. That was all right with Slumber. So long as it made Magpie happy—and so long as she didn't expect Slumber to call her that.

"What does 'voluntary' mean?" the woman asked. "Will we be punished if we don't avoid those places?"

"No, of course not, Ms. Fenton. We are just hoping that you will respect the sanctity and privacy of the native peoples."

Ms. Fenton looked all business. She wore her long graying brown hair in a neat bun. The style accented the flat planes of her round face and made her blue eyes seem huge. Her tan jacket and pants hugged all the right curves. Of course, she probably never had a chance to get fat, not with hiking all the time.

"This is a bad plan, Maggie," Kyle continued. "Surely you must see that. Those holy places are holy to the people in our club, too, and this is *public* land."

Magpie spread her hands in a pleading gesture. "This isn't an easy issue, Kyle. In the old days, there weren't so many conflicts. But as the number of tourists has increased, it's become almost impossible for the tribes to hold ceremonials without forty flashbulbs going off a minute. Do you see what I'm saying?"

"Yes, of course, and that's wrong, but the solution isn't to ban Whites, Blacks, Hispanics, and Orientals from those places. There must be another solution, Maggie. Let's work together to find it."

Magpie shifted uneasily. "Let me try to explain something about Native American religions—and I'm not sure I can. I don't think there's a similar concept in White culture. You see, religious sites aren't just pieces of land: *they're sacred space*. They include the underworlds below, the surface of the land, and the skyworlds above. Some tribes believe there are openings at those places which lead between the worlds. They're considered very dangerous. The uninitiated have been known to fall through those holes and be eaten by the monsters that inhabit those realms. Because of that—"

"This is getting pretty wild." Ms. Fenton rolled her eyes. "Monsters? Come on."

"I'm saying that some tribes have such beliefs," Magpie continued. "Because of that, knowledge of the religious site is often considered sacred in and of itself, and reserved only for the holy people of the tribe. Talking about those places with outsiders, or having outsiders set foot on them, can so profane the site that it actually loses its sacredness. The *Power* goes away, Kyle. The openings close up and never reopen. Please try to underst—"

"You expect me to understand," he cut her off, "but you refuse to see that it's just as important to me to be here during the solstice! This canyon *rings* with power at that time. Listen, Maggie, I work an eight-to-five job in Albuquerque. By the time I take my summer vacation, I'm exhausted, mentally, physically, and spiritually. I come out here to touch the sacred, and to find myself. You and—" He waved a hand in Slumber's general direction, and his gaze accidentally brushed Slumber's. For several moments, he stood as if frozen. Magpie smiled. Finally, he tugged his eyes away and haltingly continued, "You—you want to deny me the right to worship in a place that my own tax dollars, and the tax dollars of every other American, go to maintain. We *pay* for the right to come here."

Slumber braced a hand on the ancient wall and eased to her feet. Her legs shook. That old Flute Player was coming closer, and she wanted to go out and meet him. The music floated around her like butterfly wings, soft and playful.

Slumber hobbled out into the plaza, past a tall young man and a moon-faced young woman. Dressed in beautiful red-and-black knee-length shirts, they knelt prodding a fire to life. They smiled at each other, and laughed gaily, and Slumber chuckled.

New love was always filled with dreams. The aroma of burning cedar wafted on the wind.

Slumber took a few more steps and stopped. Most of her tribe knew that she saw into other worlds; that's why they called her "She Who Haunts the Dead." Half-seen people walked around her all the time, making pots, weaving cotton, knapping out stone tools. Whether Slumber lived in their long-gone world, or whether they'd stepped into hers, here and now, she didn't know. Usually they just passed each other. Sometimes very powerful holy people would gasp and stare at Slumber, as if seeing her through a thick mist—a few even tried to speak with her. But that never worked. She couldn't understand their tongue, and they couldn't understand hers.

Magpie said, "Only a century ago, the federal government in this country was banning Native American religions. They said that the First Amendment guarantee of the freedom of religion didn't apply to Indians. That's what Wounded Knee was all about. The people were Ghost Dancing and they'd been told it was against the law. The soldiers shot down over a hundred men, women, and little children."

"I think," Ms. Fenton pointed out with exaggerated politeness, "there was more to it than that."

"Yes." Magpie nodded. "There was. My point is this: in 1978 Congress passed Public Law 95–341, the American Indian Religious Freedom Act. That law recognized past injustices and guaranteed that it would be the policy of the United States from then on to protect and preserve American Indians' inherent right to believe, express, and exercise their traditional religions—especially if native sacred sites were on public lands. And *that* is what our new park plan is attempting to do."

"Does that same law give the federal government the right to 'create' Indian sacred sites?" Ms. Fenton asked. "Because that's what you're doing every time you dig up some old burial and replant it here in the canyon. How many bodies did you rebury last year? How many more places are you planning on keeping me out of?"

"We reinterred one burial last year. Just one." Magpie folded her arms over her chest. "The burial was discovered in the process of a highway-widening project, down south near Gila Cliff Dwellings. It was obviously an Anasazi man, buried beneath a slab of rock. His clothing and jewelry were unmistakable. The tribes asked that we take him. We agreed because—"

"Because the more religious sites you have in the park, the more money you need to manage them, and the more land you can close off. Isn't that right? All of this is a ploy for more taxpayer dollars?"

Magpie threw up her hands. "I knew this was going to be a difficult discussion. Perhaps we should just table this for now, and let our tempers cool down."

Ms. Fenton sidled closer to Magpie. Her blue eyes gleamed with malice. "If you authorize Indians to practice their religion at this federally funded site, you will be violating the 'separation of church and state' clause. My kids can't pray in school, but Indians can close down sections of the park to perform sacred rituals? Come on! What are you trying to do? Establish one official religion for the national parks in America? Indian religion?"

"No, no, we—"

"I demand equal treatment! I want a section of the park set aside for my private religious usage during the month of June. And I don't want any 'outsiders' around bothering me. I need absolute privacy to perform my rituals—"

"Does that mean," Magpie said with a weary smile, "that I can't bring my flash attachment to photograph you while you meditate in the nude?"

Ms. Fenton's expression tightened, but Kyle actually chuckled.

"Hey," Kyle said. He held up his hands as if in surrender. "I think Maggie's right. Why don't we call it a day? We can talk more when we've all had a chance to . . ."

As Slumber rounded a corner in the gigantic pueblo, their voices faded. She'd had a dream last night that told her to follow this trail today. It wound between walls and around kivas. Slumber stopped when she reached the glass door. Pressing her nose against the pane, she looked inside. Ancient paintings adorned the wall. She'd first seen them many years ago. Slumber had stood with her mouth open, counting the beautiful green and blue diamonds that zigzagged over the white plaster. There'd been people sitting inside, a mother and daughter; they'd laughed and talked while Slumber gaped. No one sat inside today, but Slumber could see half-transparent belongings, willow twig sitting mats, black-and-white pots, rows of baskets. The ghosts must be out tending to chores.

Slumber started to walk away, but saw that something blue and shiny stuck out of the dirt at her feet. She bent over to look at it, prodded it with her finger, then smoothed the sand away. A magnificent turquoise knife emerged, broken in half. Slumber picked up the pieces and straightened to examine the stunning workmanship. No one in this day and age could work turquoise like this, it took a master—

"*I've been waiting for you.*"

Slumber looked up. Like many men she'd seen here in the past, he dressed in ancient clothing, black cloth decorated with white spirals. A turquoise pendant, in the shape of a wolf, hung around his throat. He held a flute in his left hand and seemed to be looking directly at her.

"Are you . . . are you talking to me?"

He smiled. "*Yes, She Who Haunts the Dead.*"

Slumber edged closer. Maybe he was real, and her eyesight was just getting sketchy. He was actually *beautiful*. She'd never said that about a man before. Tall, with long thick black hair, he had eyes the shade of mahogany furniture. A warm light shone in those dark depths.

"How do you know the name my people call me by? Do I know you?"

He extended a hand to her. "*Come. We must hurry if we're going to use the clouds as stepping stones to get to the skyworlds. The storm is blowing away.*" He took a step closer. "*It is your choice, She Who Haunts the Dead. You may stay for a short time longer, or go now. With me.*"

Tears welled in Slumber's eyes as understanding dawned. She hadn't expected to be frightened, but she was. A little. Instinctively, she turned to gaze at Magpie. Longing wrung her heart. She would miss her granddaughter. Magpie had been very good to her. Slumber's knees started shaking.

"*You may stay if you wish,*" the man gently reminded. "*You do not have to come today. I just thought you might wish to.*"

Taking a deep breath, Slumber turned back to look at him. "It's my time. I've been itching to get away from the sickness."

He extended his hand a little further and smiled. "When

you put your hand in mine, the pain will go away."

Slumber wet her wrinkled lips, stepped toward him, and reached out . . .

Maggie hugged herself as Marisa Fenton stomped across the plaza, then headed for her Jeep. Her tan jacket fluttered in the wind.

Kyle Laroque propped his hands on his hips. His white sleeves were splotched with rain. "She's not as bad as you think. She's just feeling stepped on."

"So am I."

"I apologize, Maggie. I never intended for this to turn into a shouting match. I hope we're still friends."

Maggie shrugged. "Kyle, I know the canyon is a sacred place to you. And maybe to some of the others in your group. I—I'll talk to the park administrator and the regional tribes. There must be a solution to this problem. A middle road we can all take."

"Thank you, Maggie," he said sincerely. "That's all we ask. I . . ."

A curious, alarmed expression creased his tanned face. He tilted his head, as if listening.

"What's the matter, Kyle?"

A swallow went down his throat. "Maggie, I . . . did you hear that voice?" He turned halfway around, peering toward the rear of the pueblo. "It was a man's voice, deep, beautiful."

Maggie suddenly noticed that her grandmother no longer sat on the wall where she'd left her, and panic ran like fire through her veins. She shouted, "*Grandma? Grandma, where are you?*"

She broke into a run, dashing across the plaza with Kyle close behind. They peered into one empty room after another, then headed for the trail that led . . . her steps faltered.

"Oh . . ."

Slumber Walking Hawk lay curled on her side on the damp ground, one arm extended in front of her as if reaching for something. Wisps of gray hair had fallen over her wrinkled face, but Maggie could see her grandmother's serene expression.

She forced her numb legs forward and knelt. A broken turquoise knife lay clutched in her grandmother's hand and, beside it, what looked like an ancient deerbone stiletto. Maggie tenderly took Slumber's wrist to feel for a pulse.

Her throat ached. "Oh, Grandma." She eased down to the wet ground.

Kyle knelt beside her. "Is she—"

"Yes."

He bowed his head. "I'm sorry, Maggie."

"She was dying, Kyle. She knew it. And though she never said so, I think she's been in a lot of pain. It's just that I—I loved her so much." Maggie gazed at him through blurry eyes. "I wish she could have stayed for a little longer."

He fumbled with his sunglasses, pulling them off so he could really look at her. He had soft brown eyes. That glow had returned, the one that made her go still inside, as if she gazed through a door that led between the worlds. "The man . . . the voice I heard?"

Maggie frowned. "Yes?"

Folding the glasses, he tucked them into his shirt pocket, and seemed to be struggling with how to say something. Beads of rain shimmered on his blond hair. "The man said, 'You may stay if you wish. You do not have to come today. I just thought you might wish to.'"

She stared at him.

Kyle looked embarrassed, as if he wished he hadn't told her.

All of Maggie's life she'd heard people tell stories about her grandmother and ghosts, but her grandmother had never talked to Maggie about them. Was that why Slumber had insisted on coming? Had a ghost told her she'd be free if she accompanied Maggie to this place today? Free from her sick body. Free from the pain. *Free* . . .

Maggie used her sleeve to wipe away her tears. "I'm sure she wanted to go. I don't blame her."

"Why don't you stay here with her? I'll run back to the Visitor's Center and get help."

Maggie nodded, but as he trotted down the trail, Maggie called, "Kyle?"

He turned. Wind ruffled his blond hair.

"Thank you. For telling me about the voice you heard."

He shrugged. "It's just the place, Maggie. *It talks to me.*" He lifted a hand to her, then trotted away.

Maggie's gaze followed him until he vanished from sight. Then she squeezed her grandmother's frail old hand. Wind fluttered gray locks around Slumber's peaceful old face.

"I guess the *Shiwana* just see the colors of people's souls, huh, Grandma?"

One

Sun Cycle of the Buffalo, Moon of Falling Snow

Sternlight's moccasins went silent behind her.

Young Fawn turned and saw him drop to his knees in the middle of the trail, his white ritual shirt aglow with starlight. Huge sandstone boulders surrounded him. Many sun cycles ago they had broken free from the towering canyon wall and tumbled into the valley to stand like monstrous guardians along the Turning-Back-the-Sun trail. Kneeling in their midst, Sternlight looked pitifully small. Long black hair fluttered around him as he rocked back and forth, his face in his hands, his necklace of copper bells jingling. His cries resembled a lost child's.

"No," he kept whimpering. "No, please . . ."

He had stopped twice in the past hand of time. At first, he had pounded his fists on the ground. Now he wept inconsolably.

Young Fawn knew little about the trials of priests, but even she could tell he was weary beyond exhaustion. He had been praying for sixteen days, eating only cactus buttons, and begging the ancestor Spirits to help him. Now, it seemed, the ghosts would not leave him alone.

Young Fawn leaned against a rock and folded her arms on her pregnant belly. Golden owl eyes sparkled in every hollow of the dark sandstone cliff, watching, wondering. To the south, fires gleamed. Fourteen large towns and over two hundred smaller villages lined the canyon walls. The priests would be rising, readying themselves for morning prayers on this critical day of the sun cycle. The fires cast a wavering yellow gleam over the massive sandstone bluff on the opposite side of the canyon. It looked dark and brooding this early, but when Father Sun rose, the sandstone would turn so golden it would appear molten.

Young Fawn sighed. The tang of sage scented the wind, but the fragrance did little to soothe her fears. Sternlight spoke softly to someone, and apparently received an answer he did not wish to hear.

"But why must I do it?" he wept. He lifted his head and looked to his right. As he shook his head, his long black hair flashed silver. "Why me?"

At the age of twenty-seven, Sternlight had been Talon Town's Sunwatcher for nine winters, and his reputation had grown with each one. Chiefs as far away as three moons' walk relied upon his advice. Young Fawn had seen their messengers arrive, packs filled with extraordinary gifts. Over the cycles, stories about Sternlight's wealth had become legend. It was said that twenty rooms at Talon Town brimmed with his fortune— and some dared to whisper that only witchery paid so well.

Young Fawn nervously smoothed her palms over her turkey-feather cape. The brown-and-white feathers glistened in the light. Witches—her own people called them sleep-makers— had great Power. By jumping through a hoop of twisted yucca fibers, they could change themselves into animals, and they used rawhide shields to fly about, spying on people. The most terrifying sleep-makers raided burials to gather putrefying corpse flesh, which they dried and ground into a fine powder. Once the soul had left the body, only corruption and wickedness remained. Corpse powder concentrated that evil, and when sprinkled on someone, could cause death or madness.

Young Fawn had been captured in a raid ten summers ago, but she remembered the sleep-makers among her own people, the Mogollon, who lived far to the south. The Straight Path people called them Fire Dogs, for the Mogollon believed that they had originally come to earth in the form of wolves made from gouts of Father Sun's fire. The Mogollon and the Straight Path people raided each other constantly, taking slaves, stealing food. Her father, Jay Bird, was the greatest and most powerful Mogollon chief. Sleep-makers had continually tried to kill him.

. . . And the earth had quaked each time, as if the ancestor spirits who lived in the underworlds were enraged by the foolishness of the witches.

Young Fawn reached up to touch the small bags of sacred

cornmeal she wore around her throat. On occasion, when she missed her family, she thought about those sleep-makers and wondered if their Power had grown over the long summers. Was her father still alive? The earth continued to quake, more often of late, and she took each tremor as a great omen that he had survived yet another attempt on his life.

The Straight Path people, however, took the recent rash of quakes to mean that their ancestors were growing more and more angry with the greed and malice that filled the hearts of their descendants.

Young Fawn glanced at Sternlight. Could he be a sleep-maker? She had to admit that strange things did happen around him. His older sisters had vanished before they'd turned fifteen summers, and no traces had ever been found. Though rumors persisted that they had been taken slave by the Mogollon, Sternlight's cousin, the great warrior, Webworm, had suggested a dire possibility. Sleep-makers lived very long lives—at the expense of their families. When a sleep-maker grew ill, or wanted to extend his life, he used a spindle to extract his relative's heart and put it in his own chest.

After Sternlight's second sister disappeared, Webworm spent days going from family member to family member, begging them to help him kill Sternlight. Both had been very young at the time, Webworm thirteen, and Sternlight fourteen. Webworm's accusation had been taken very seriously. Sternlight, it was said, had truly feared for his life. The penalty for witchery was death, and the sleep-maker's own family had to carry out the sentence. When they'd killed him, they would throw him facedown in a grave and cover his body with a heavy sandstone slab so that his Spirit could never escape. Alone, locked in darkness, the ghost would wail for all eternity. But no one could hear. No one could save him.

Young Fawn jumped when a flock of piñon jays soared over the canyon rim. Against the twinkling background of the Evening People, they whirled like windblown black leaves. Long ago the jays had lived among her people as sacred clowns, Dancing, bringing laughter, and teaching spiritual lessons. They had chosen to be reborn as birds to watch over the Mogollon people.

Keep me safe, guardians. I fear I need your protection on this day.

Sternlight whispered, "Don't tell me that! I . . . I can't."

Young Fawn glanced at him. He had his hand out to no one she could see. Clenching her fists over her belly, she waited. No matter how desperately she longed to run away, she could not. It would shame her master and bring terrible punishment upon herself.

Last moon, the wife of the Blessed Sun had selected Young Fawn as Solstice Girl. The choice had been a competition between Young Fawn and her best friend, Mourning Dove, a fact which had delighted them both. Ordinarily, much older, wiser slaves received the honor. Because of that, Young Fawn performed her tasks with great care. She washed the priest's ritual clothes with yucca soap and pine needles to give them a pleasant scent; held his sacred herbs next to her heart to keep their Spirits warm; made certain the blood of his meats never fell upon the ground, for that might offend his animal Spirit helpers. Despite her youth, she tried to be the best Solstice Girl ever.

But as the child in her belly grew, the work became increasingly difficult.

Sternlight pulled himself to his feet and stood on shaking legs. The turquoise and jet bracelets on his arms winked and sparkled in the silvery light.

She called, "Elder, are you well?"

He jerked around, and his copper bell necklaces jingled wildly. His eyes went huge. "Who—who are you?"

"I am Young Fawn. Don't you remember?"

As sunrise approached, the evil Spirit child, Wind Baby, raced through the canyon, bending the scrawny weeds, flicking dust about and whistling around boulders. He ruffled Young Fawn's turkey-feather cape and probed at her white dress beneath, his fingers frigid. She shivered.

"Young Fawn?" Sternlight came forward like a man picking his way through a field of rattlesnakes. "You are Young Fawn?"

"Yes, Elder."

A hollow sensation swelled her heart. What a beautiful man. He had a straight nose and full lips. When he was an infant, the back of his skull had been flattened by the cradleboard, shoving his cheekbones forward and accentuating his deeply set brown eyes. Each time his moccasins struck the ground, the seashells tied to the laces made music. His knee-length shirt, woven from the finest cotton thread, outlined every muscle in his tall body.

He looks like one of the sacred sky gods fallen to earth.

He halted a hand's breadth from her, and in a pained voice said, "I prayed you would not be here. Why are you here?"

"I am the Solstice Girl for this cycle. I go where you go. I do as you tell me."

Gently, she took his arm and headed him on down the trail. They entered a grove of stunted junipers protected from cutting by the Blessed Sun's decree. There, the light fragmented, scattering their path with pewter triangles and glimmering over the clusters of small purple berries among the green needles. Young Fawn proceeded with care. Deer had scooped out beds in the duff, and rocks thrust up along the way, both threats to safe footing. All around them, gnarled gray branches reached upward for the blessings of the sky gods.

Sternlight gazed at her anxiously, eyes focused on her swollen belly in disbelief. "You are Solstice Girl?"

"Yes, Sunwatcher. I have been serving you for a full moon now."

The trail swung around a large pile of fallen rock and entered the sun cove, a hollow worn in the canyon wall by eons of spring runoff. Sternlight took one look at the stairs cut into the stone, and utter terror masked his face. He threw off her hand and backed away.

"No," he breathed, "Oh, no. I can't go up there!"

"But," Young Fawn said, "we must hurry. We have barely two fingers of time before dawn. You know how frightening the drought and warfare have become. You must help make it right. This is your duty. You are Sunwatcher."

His mouth quivered. Behind him, the flock of piñon jays wheeled, their cackles wavering in Wind Baby's gusts. Sternlight balled his fists. "You . . . you go first. I will wait until you are at the top, then I will follow. Yes, I—I will. Now go." When she hesitated, he shook both fists at her. "*Go!*"

She hitched up her white hem and began the climb. Ice filled the rocky depressions, watching her like ancient glazed eyes.

The last rainstorm had washed sand and gravel down the steps. Her yucca sandals *shished* on the grit.

By the time Young Fawn reached the narrow ledge overlooking the canyon, she was panting. A gently undulating surface, the ledge extended about four body lengths by five. A sandstone wall, taller than Young Fawn, ran along the north side. Scraggly rabbitbrush struggled to grow on top of the wall.

A magnificent vista spread around her. Chunky buttes rose like square towers from the desert floor, their sandstone faces shading purple and pink in the newborn light. She could see two of the three sacred mountains. In front of her, Thunder Peak rose in the south; to her right, Turquoise Maiden made a black hump against the eastern horizon. Spider Woman's Butte hid behind a translucent lavender veil. The few shreds of cloud that clung to her face glowed a rich magenta color. Two thousand people lived in the canyon, and their breakfast fires sparkled like a huge overturned box of amber jewels. Wonder filled Young Fawn. Among her people, beauty was sacred, and appreciating it, a prayer.

Gingerly, she lowered herself to the cold stone and encircled her belly with her arms. She would catch her breath, and then, if Sternlight had not arrived, she would go looking for him.

An ancient painting adorned the sandstone wall above where she sat—a white circle with rays emanating from all four sides. The Straight Path people claimed that the symbol had been drawn by Coyote in the Age of Emergence, immediately after their ancestors climbed through the four underworlds and out into this fifth world of light. She knew the Straight Path story by heart:

> "*Look!*" Coyote had said. "*I have drawn a map of the Center Place and the four roads of life and death. Listen, now, and I will tell you what it means.*
>
> "*There is a Great Circle; it is so huge it holds everything, for it is the universe, and all that live inside the Great Circle are relatives. When you stand at the heart of the circle, in the Center Place, you can see that the circle has four quarters. Each is sacred, for each has a mystical Power, and it is by those powers that we survive. Each quarter also has its own*

sacred animals, objects, and colors—these make its power accessible to humans.

"When you pray, you must first look down the east road to the dawn place where all the days of humans are born. Its color is white like the snows. It has the power to heal. White clay will cleanse, and the white hide of an albino buffalo will drive away sickness. Only the very strong may run this road to ask advice or give aid to Father Sun. The weak will be melted.

"Then you must look down the south road. It is red-hot like the summer. The pepper pod is its plant, and the ant its animal. This road is only for the dead, or those tending ceremonial tasks. They may travel it to the sacred Humpback Butte, where they will find the ladder to the four skyworlds. Those who climb up will become rain gods, and have the Power to make things grow and flourish.

"Next you must look down the road where Father Sun dies, and all of the days of humans have gone and shall go. Its color is yellow. Its animal is the bear. It has the power to bring peace. The Evening People hold its wisdom. This road is only for the living. People may run it to talk with the Evening People, to learn to live as one.

"Last is the north road. Its color is blue-black like the thunder clouds. Its stone is turquoise. It has the power to kill. It leads to the sipapu, the tunnel of emergence, and the entry to the four underworlds where the ancestors live. Only the dead, and their helpers, may run this road. The entrance to the sipapu is guarded by a huge black badger.

"Where the blue-black road of the dead meets the white road of the living at the Center Place is very holy. There coils the Rainbow Serpent. Her symbol is the sacred lightning-spiral. For those who look upon the Rainbow Serpent with newborn eyes, she shall wake and arc across the face of the world, and they may climb onto her back and rise into the skyworlds without dying. And, if they dare, they may speak with the gods."

Young Fawn gazed to the northwest, toward the Center Place where the roads met. Talon Town sat at the base of the bluff just beneath it. Every morning she looked up, hoping to see the Rainbow Serpent sparkle to life, but she never had. Nor had anyone now living, though the elders spoke of a time long ago when the Straight Path people had seen her arc across the heavens often. But extraordinarily holy people had lived in the canyon then, men and women who ran the east road routinely—people whose profane eyes had been burned away by the brilliant white light. When they grew sacred eyes, and gained the courage to look again, the Rainbow Serpent uncoiled and leaped into the sky.

Young Fawn exhaled in longing. *I would give my very life to see that.*

Her gaze drifted to her right. In the southeast the sacred rock pillar punctured the heavens. Father Sun had risen over that pillar for the past fifteen mornings straight. On this cold dawn, the shortest day of the cycle, Father Sun would be very weak. If he could travel no further, he would stand still on the horizon. That would be a signal that Sternlight needed to perform the "Turning-Back-the-Sun" ritual: He would have to run the east road to help Father Sun.

Four winters ago it had taken seven days for Sternlight to turn back the sun. By then, he had lain near death, curled on the rock like an infant. He had offered his own strength to Father Sun, and it nearly cost him his life. But if the sun could not be turned back, the world would be cast into perpetual winter, and the Straight Path people would die.

This day, of all days, nothing must interfere with the Turning-Back-the-Sun ritual. Father Sun had to see how hard they were trying, how desperate they were for his approval.

Last summer, as the warfare intensified, Father Sun had ordered the sky gods to withhold the blessing rain during the growing season. The Blessed Sun, chief of Talon Town, had told people to pour every extra drop of water they had onto the corn, bean, and squash fields. But they had withered to dust. The springs had dried up. Children had screamed with hunger. And raiders had rampaged across the desert. Like the Straight Path people, the Mogollon and the Hohokam had been willing to kill for a single basket of food.

Horrifying rumors spread that some Straight Path clans had turned in desperation to cannibalism. They'd sought out the Fire Dogs, taking them as slaves during raids, then offered them in bizarre ceremonials to appease Father Sun's anger before cooking their flesh.

Young Fawn shuddered.

Sternlight himself had marched from village to village pleading for people to turn away from evil, to return to the Straight Path, reminding them that the world had already been destroyed four times. The First World had been scorched with fire, the Second World covered with ice, the Third World drowned by floods. The Fourth World had died when Father Sun sucked all the air away. And the Fifth World, the world they now lived upon, would die too, he said, if people did not cleanse their hearts.

Young Fawn's breathing went shallow. Sternlight said that Father Sun had told him he would split the Fifth World apart by hurling huge fiery rocks. . . .

Gravel scritched.

Sternlight emerged from the staircase. He stood absolutely still, staring out at the horizon like a man facing his own executioner, eyes enormous, jaw clamped. Dawn blushed color into his white shirt, dyeing it the rich yellow of bitterbrush petals.

"Ready?" she asked.

He stumbled, startled. "Who—who are you? What are you doing here? Why haven't you run away?"

"I am Solstice Girl, Elder. I carry the sacred cornmeal." She untied the four small bags she wore as a necklace and held them out to him. "Come. It is time."

Sternlight did not move. He stared at her in horror, as though she were an ancient beast stalking him.

Young Fawn took the bags, lifted his right hand, and deposited them in his palm. "Elder," she said, "you must face the east. Is that not right?"

In a voice almost too low to hear, he said, "Yes," and forced himself to turn away.

After a few moments, he began Singing. Yesterday, the handsome War Chief, Ironwood, had been along to play the drum; the day before that short pudgy Creeper, leader of the Buffalo Clan, had serenaded the dawn with majestic flute music. Today, the Sunwatcher Sang alone.

As Sternlight opened the first bag, he Sang, "In Beauty it is begun. In Beauty it is begun," and sprinkled a path of white cornmeal to the east.

He sprinkled the bag of red cornmeal to the south, yellow to the west, and finally the blue cornmeal to the north. Then he offered his meal-covered hands to Father Sky, and bent to touch Mother Earth, saying, "In Beauty it is finished. In Beauty it is finished."

The meals swirled upward in a luminous haze and sailed out beyond the rim of the canyon. Like fine summer mist, they sparkled and fell.

Young Fawn waited. It had happened the same way for fifteen days. Sternlight called out, and Father Sun appeared.

The Sunwatcher straightened, crossed his arms over his breast, and murmured, "Come, Father, arise and bring life to the world."

Awe prickled Young Fawn's spine. The first sliver of molten gold flared on the horizon, and the buttes and mesas shed their dark silhouettes and gleamed with a crimson fire. The drifting clouds blazed orange. Shadows sprang into existence, dark and long, stretching westward.

Sternlight used shaking hands to frame the image of the stone pillar and sun, then let them drop to his sides. Tears traced lines down his cheeks.

"Is something wrong?" she asked.

"Father Sun . . ." His voice broke. He kept silent for a moment, then finished, "He's too weak to go on. He rose in the same place today. I—I feared as much."

"Because it means you will have to run the east road, to give Father Sun the strength he needs to travel northward again?"

Sternlight bowed his head. Black hair tumbled over his shoulders, dancing in the wind. He didn't even seem to be breathing.

"Elder?" she pressed.

He put a hand over his eyes.

Young Fawn took a step toward him. "Sternlight?"

"Blessed gods," he choked out. "I *can't* do it!"

Young Fawn walked in front of him and gazed up into his handsome face, now stricken with horror. "You are the greatest Sunwatcher ever to live. There is nothing you cannot do."

"You do not understand! I . . ." He looked sharply to his right and seemed to be listening. His cries became pathetic.

Sobbing, he answered, "Yes . . . I know. For the sake of all, it . . . must be done."

Young Fawn glanced at the spot he'd spoken to. Nothing. Not even a ripple of light. Unnerved, she said, "I understand one thing, Elder: You are very weary. It will not hurt to rest for a time. Come. Lie down in the shelter of the rock. After you have slept you may attempt to run the road." She extended a hand to him. "Let me help you."

Sternlight squeezed his eyes closed and shook his head. "I— I'm afraid."

"But, Elder, you have run the east road many times. I'm sure Father Sun—"

He opened his eyes suddenly. "Do you really believe I'm evil? Isn't that what you were thinking earlier?"

A well of cold grew in her stomach. She swallowed hard. It was said that sleep-makers read thoughts like tracks in snow. That nothing could be hidden from them. "No. No, of course not," she said. "I was just—"

"But you do hate me." He tilted his head and peered at her unblinking.

Young Fawn's heart pounded. She deliberately misunderstood. "You mean because you weep out of fear? No, Elder. Anyone with sense would be frightened. Please. You will tire yourself even more, and Father Sun needs you to be strong."

Hesitantly, Sternlight reached out and slipped a hand beneath her turkey-feather cape to touch her pregnant belly. Young Fawn froze, uncertain how to respond. The heat of his fingers penetrated her dress, warming her skin. The open cape flapped around her.

"Precious," Sternlight said as he stroked the child. "So precious."

"Elder, I do not—"

As though on the verge of vomiting, he grabbed his stomach and bent double, gasping, "Oh, blessed gods, give this task to another!"

"Let me help you! That's why I'm here. Please, tell me what I may do to make the task easier."

A curious expression entered his eyes. Not fear, not apology, but a man bracing himself for a burden he could barely conceive. He took several deep breaths, then slowly straightened.

Wind Baby shrieked through the canyon, and Young Fawn thought she could almost make out frantic words. As though enraged that she did not understand, Wind Baby shoved her hard. Young Fawn staggered forward.

Sternlight rose and blocked her path with his tall body. He extended his arms and let them hover for a moment, then he embraced her and boldly drew her against him. "Let me hold you for just a moment. I want to feel you close to me."

Fear pumped in her veins. A curious smell clung to his white ritual shirt, musty, bitter, like the scent of a long-abandoned cave. "Sternlight, I do not think—"

He tightened his powerful arms, crushing her against his chest. "Stand still. Just don't move."

"But, Elder, you are hurting me. Please!"

He began sobbing again, terrible wrenching sobs that shook his whole body. He buried his face in her hair and his tears soaked her temple.

"I beg you," he said. "Don't fight me. I must do this thing quickly!"

He dropped his right hand to his belt. Against the gold of dawn, she glimpsed a deerbone dagger. "I need your baby, Young Fawn."

"What are you *talking* about? Let me go!" She twisted madly, watching him raise the dagger over his head.

Ducking and kicking violently, she broke free and dashed across the ledge, hair flying, racing for the stairs. The morning's gleam covered the dimpled sandstone like molten coral, shadowing every hollow and crack. She leaped over a hole and her foot slipped on ice, breaking her stride.

Sternlight's body struck her, slamming her to the ground. She cried out as pain lanced through her pregnant belly. The Sunwatcher flipped her onto her back and stretched out on top of her.

Tears beaded his cheeks. He held the bone dagger out to the east, the south, the west and north, then breathed a prayer as he lifted it to the glistening gold of the sky. He left it there, glowing in the sunlight, for a long moment.

"Sternlight?" she called in a shaking voice. "Please! I'll do anything you ask. Just let me go!"

"What?" he cried. Terror creased his face as he looked

around the mesa. "Who said that? Who *are* you? Boy? Boy, is that you?"

Like a man fighting to wake from a terrible dream, he shook himself and shoved back, straddling her, his wide eyes fixed on the north. After several moments, he sucked in a breath and blinked at Young Fawn, as if seeing her for the first time. Black hair danced about his broad shoulders.

"You are Solstice Girl," he whispered reverently, and with lightning swiftness, he plunged the dagger down, offering it to Mother Earth through Young Fawn's heart.

First Day

Sun Cycle of the Dragonfly,
Moon of Prayerstick Cutting

Sixteen Summers Later

I sit in a shallow channel carved into the mountain's side, my bare back against the cool limestone. I have been here since dawn, without food or water, or a companion's voice to serenade me with forgetfulness.

Walkingcane cactus dots the soil around me. It is spring, and purple blossoms cover the limbs and trunks, scenting the air with a delicate bouquet. Far below, the Gila Monster Cliffs wind eastward in a striking range of colors. Morning light lances yellow into the gorge, glitters on the white and yellow walls and plays in the mottled pine trees blanketing the highlands. Occasionally a flowering bush splashes the hills with red.

To the north, a hideous pall of smoke rises like black billowing thunderheads, driven by west winds across the blue sky. The underbelly of that pall glows orange, as if the fire is born in the clouds.

I narrow my aching eyes. Am I witnessing the end of the world? I can believe it. After the things I have seen . . .

I am not an old man, familiar with the ways of the world and the treachery of human beings. I am young, sixteen summers. This is not easy for me. Friends. Enemies. Both have betrayed me.

My grandfather's warriors have captured them and locked them in a room without windows or doors. A ladder thrust down through a hole in the roof is the only way in or out. They are under constant guard.

My people demand that I kill them.

But some of the captives . . . I love.

"All wounds are openings to the sacred," the great holy man, Dune the Derelict, once taught me. "You must crawl inside those chasms. Go alone, on your hands and knees, and sit in that terrible darkness. If you sit long enough, you will discover that the worst pain is the breath of compassion."

So I sit.

By day, I study the changing patterns of light that sheathe these *lofty mountains; by night the movements of the Evening People stir silver ashes in my heart.*

This wound is a doorway. I must be brave enough to go through it. And braver still to journey across the dark face of my familiar world and into a strange dawn land that can be grasped only with the hands of my soul.

Hallowed rain gods, I feel so empty.

Why couldn't the Blessed Sternlight have let me die? So many others would have been spared.

I tip my head back to rest on a shelf of stone and stare unblinking into the vast smoky distances, listening to the perfectly clear silences, thinking of all that I am, and am not, remembering all that has brought me to this place. . . .

Two

The Time of Gestation

Buckthorn knelt on a willow-twig mat before the low fire in his mother's home. The small square house, last in the solid line of the village, spread three body-lengths across. Dried vegetables hung from the rafters: corn, beans, squash, whole sunflowers, and red prickly pear cactus fruits. Rising smoke helped to keep insects and rot away. It also coated the plants with a shiny black layer of creosote. Through them, Buckthorn could just make out the pine ceiling poles. Swirls of soot marked the gray-plastered walls, covering the faded images Mother had painted there long ago. Since then, a collection of baskets had been hung over them.

In one corner stood a collection of reddish-brown glazed pots, storage for special possessions. In another corner, three big pots, their sides corrugated and rims weighted with sandstone slabs, held what was left of their winter corn and beans.

Smaller cooking pots sat to one side, the outer surfaces charred from countless fires.

How familiar and safe it all seemed on this long-hoped-for and terrible day.

Buckthorn's fingers tugged nervously at the fringes on his knee-length shirt. The white buckskin warmed his skinny body and reflected the firelight's wavering patterns like a pyrite mirror. His mother had painted the black-and-yellow images of the Great Warriors of East and West on the shirt's chest, and the Rainbow Serpent, a slithering line of red, yellow, blue-black and white, that encircled his waist. In the fluttering gleam of the flames, the Great Warriors blazed. The lightning lances in their upraised hands wavered, ready to fly across the face of the world in a great roar, to slit open the bellies of the Cloud People and offer life-giving rain to Our Mother Earth— or to bring eternal destruction to wicked human beings.

Buckthorn had not eaten in four days, a holy number, and he felt lightheaded and frightened. Soon, very soon, his life would change forever. He would no longer be the strange, lonely youth that the other children shunned and laughed at. His soul would tumble down the dark tunnel to the First Underworld, and he would either become a revered sacred Singer . . . .or he would be dead.

Buckthorn frowned down at the Great Warriors. *Do they already know which it will be?*

In the Age of Emergence, just after the First People had climbed through the four underworlds to get to this Fifth World of light; the Great Warriors of East and West had vanquished many monsters that threatened to eat the new people. In the last horrifying battle, the Warriors' bodies had been turned to stone, but their heroism had earned their souls special places in the skyworlds, sparkling on either side of Father Sun. Father Sun often told them about things that would happen in the world of humans. When necessary, the Warriors soared to earth as shooting stars and walked among men, advising, helping. Sometimes they even killed.

Buckthorn had once known a boy named Little Shield who had been chosen by the elders, as Buckthorn had been, to journey into the underworlds. He had died horribly. At the first sign of trouble, the elders had dragged the boy up from the kiva, the womblike subterranean ceremonial chamber, and stretched him out on the plaza while they raced about gathering herbs and Power bundles, anything that might help tie his soul to his body again.

Buckthorn had been six summers old at the time. He vividly recalled the way Little Shield had thrashed about and screamed that he saw the Great Warriors swooping from the sky to tear his flesh from his bones. It had taken half a day, but the holy twins had finally sunk their talons into Little Shield's soul and ripped it apart; then they had carried its pieces to the skyworlds and cast them loose in the brilliant light of Father Sun.

The elders said that Little Shield had not been strong enough to make the journey to the underworlds, and that the Great Warriors had killed him so his soul would not be lost forever in the darkness.

A shudder climbed Buckthorn's spine. Little Shield had died with his eyes wide open, staring in terror at the evening sky.

Will that happen to me?

A low drumbeat outside reminded him that his heart, that all hearts, beat in rhythm with that of the Creator, and that she alone had the Power to decide how long a boy might live.

Buckthorn tugged at his turquoise necklace, fighting vainly to loosen it so he could get more air into his lungs.

Just breathe.

He'd been choking since dawn, when he'd bathed in the icy river and his mother had twisted his wet black hair into a bun on top of his head.

He forced himself to inhale and exhale.

Beyond the door, Our Mother Earth slept beneath a soft blanket of snow, gathering her strength for spring. The Windflower Clan tiptoed about—so as not to wake her. Yucca sandals crunched the snow, and dogs padded by his door. During the Time of Gestation, the forty Blessing days, no digging, plastering, or wood chopping was permitted. No one could cut his hair. Women had to clean their houses only after sundown, and then very quietly.

The lilting voices of the Singers in the great kiva wafted to him on the west wind. The kiva nestled on the west side of the rectangular plaza, while two- and three-story buildings stretched eastward under the sheer face of the buff sandstone cliff. The Singers prepared the way for him. . . .

"They're coming," he whispered to reassure himself. "They'll be here soon."

He let out a taut breath.

To lessen his fears, Buckthorn counted the beautiful baskets that decorated the walls, large ones on top, smaller ones on the bottom. Black geometric designs and tan people adorned the weaves. His mother, Snow Mountain, had arranged them in order of descending height along the wall to his left.

"Oh, Spirits," he whispered, "I'm scared."

From the time he'd turned four summers, the great Singers of Windflower Village had looked at him differently than at other children. Their sharp old eyes had watched the other children tormenting him and noted the times when he'd sought the solitude of the canyons that cut down through solid rock to the River of Souls—and they were many. The elders had marked every fight he'd broken up, and every moment he'd sat with tears running down his face listening to them Sing. Those Powerful elders had seen in him more than an odd lonely child—a boy who had lost his father before he'd seen one summer.

At a Winter Solstice celebration at Talon Town when he'd seen ten summers, old gray-haired Black Mesa had come to sit beside him, his deeply wrinkled face mottled with firelight, and asked, "Why do you cry when you lift your voice to the gods?"

Buckthorn had looked at Black Mesa, but hadn't known the answer. His only reply had been that he couldn't help himself. But he knew better now. Deep inside him, he felt such agonized love, such longing to hear the gods speak to him, to feel their comforting touch that it manifested itself as despair.

Seven days ago, Black Mesa had entered his mother's home, and asked to speak with Buckthorn alone. Snow Mountain had bowed respectfully and left. Buckthorn couldn't conceive any reason why the elder needed privacy to speak with him. He'd shifted uneasily as Black Mesa placed a gnarled hand on his shoulder. The old man's seamed face had been somber.

"Buckthorn, I have been sent to ask you if you wish to give your life for love. For your people." Black Mesa had paused, then added, "You may say 'no' and no shame will come of it."

"Oh, but I do!" Buckthorn had answered with his whole soul in his voice. "I do."

He forced himself to inhale again. His stomach had knotted. *But what if I'm not strong enough? What if I can't travel into the underworlds and return alive?*

He frowned down at the two dead field mice lanced on the stick beside him. Black Mesa had instructed him to offer the mice as a tribute to the masked god who would come to drag him away to the underworlds. If the god refused, Buckthorn had been told to expect death.

Perhaps I should have shot a deer, instead? That would seem a far better tribute for a god than a couple of measly . . .

Feet pounded across the snowy plaza.

He whirled to stare at the door curtain. It fluttered gently in the cold breeze.

The feet stopped outside.

Buckthorn gritted his teeth so hard his jaw ached.

A rumble of voices rose, getting closer, louder . . . the whole house suddenly erupted in shrillness when the Dancers began scraping the exterior walls with what sounded like knives.

Buckthorn's heart nearly burst through is chest. *Blessed gods, what's going on?*

The Monster Thlatsina threw back the door curtain and stepped inside. Buckthorn gaped in horror.

She was *huge*. A red-and-white mouth dominated the bottom half of her jet-black mask, and a greasy gray beard hung to her waist. Long tangled black hair, dotted with tufts of cotton, fell over her menacing yellow eyes. Her mouth puckered in an eternal whistle. All his life he had been told that if he didn't listen to his elders, the Monster Thlatsina would sneak up on him and suck his brains out through his ears. In her left hand she held a crooked staff to catch her victims. Her right fist gripped a huge obsidian knife: for dismembering those who refused to obey her.

"*Here!*" Buckthorn yelled, and thrust the two dead mice at her. "These are for you!"

The Monster slapped them from his hand, and Buckthorn watched the mice fly across the room, strike the wall, and fall to the floor with a dull thump.

"*Get up!*" the Monster shouted. She slammed him in the shoulder with her crooked staff.

Buckthorn jumped to his feet.

The Monster pointed to the door. "Get out!"

He scrambled beneath the door curtain and into the late afternoon glare. His mother's room lay at ground level, on the east side of the building complex. Looking over his shoulder, he could see the twin knobs of rounded sandstone, the Great Warriors, that rose above the cliff.

The River of Souls cut down through sandstone here, and the Straight Path people had found the rich bottomlands perfect for growing corn, beans, and squash. Over the years the village had grown from several small square houses into a three-story structure that rose under the sheer north wall of the cliff, watched over by the ancient bodies of the Great Warriors.

Light snow had fallen last night and blanketed the village like a glittering layer of crushed gypsum. The high cliff dwarfed the gray clay-washed houses. To his right, southward across the mighty River of Souls, cornfields covered the floodplain. There, but a brief run from the village, the river flowed silver in the sunlight. Buckthorn could imagine those murky waters lapping against the cliffs that hemmed it on the south.

People perched on the flat roofs, wrapped snugly in blankets, smiling, happy for him. His mother stood by the ladder that led down into the great kiva. She looked radiant in her red dress with black and yellow triangles around the hem. Eagle down fluttered on the crown of her head. He had to step up onto the circular lip of the kiva. Only about two hands of the structure stood aboveground; the other twenty hands sank deep into the flesh of Our Mother Earth.

The Monster Thlatsina's staff came down hard on Buckthorn's shoulder. "Pay attention!"

He spun to look at her. What should he pay attention to?

At that moment his mother stepped back, and a long line of unearthly figures emerged from the black belly of the kiva. They trotted forward in a swinging gait, their feet kicking up sparkles of snow. Ruffs of pine encircled their necks, and their naked torsos gleamed with blue paint. They peered at Buckthorn with great bulging eyes. Their masks, part animal, part wondrous god, bore sprinkles of stars, zigzags of lightning, and dark ridges of sacred mountains. The slant of the sun threw their ethereal shadows across the plaza like leaping beasts. They shook gourd rattles as they came toward him in their loose-kneed shuffle. Their Singing resembled a breeze soughing through a thick stand of pines.

Buckthorn waited in nervous silence.

With each tramp of their sacred feet the Dancers wrested Power from the world, pulling shreds from all living things, and then drawing the Power about them like cloaks of iron—Power that could tremble the distant mountains and mold the thunderheads gathering in the deep blue sky.

The Monster pricked Buckthorn in the back with her obsidian knife and ordered, "Walk!"

He stumbled forward. People on the roofs lifted hands to him, their faces alight. Buckthorn tried to smile back, though he felt a little queasy. Two of the Buffalo Clan elders sat side by side, their legs dangling over the edge of the roof as they shared a pipe of sacred tobacco. Each puff of smoke that rose into the frosty air emulated the creation of clouds . . . of life itself.

They smoked for him, for his life. Silently, desperately, he prayed to the Great Warriors, asking that they help him find the First Underworld.

When he reached the middle of the snowy plaza, the Dancers split and veered around him. Linking arms, they formed two concentric circles with Buckthorn at the center. The circles of Dancers moved in opposite directions, kicking out their legs and trilling in voices as sweet as a mating piñon jay's.

Flute music rose from the kiva, akin to the fear and joy that filled Buckthorn. The melody twined across the village like a beautiful solitary vine, twisting through the air. The booms of a pot drum grew stronger, keeping time with the flute.

The Dance circles broke apart and veered outward, then reformed into one large circle around Buckthorn. With a ululating cry that prickled his scalp, they took off running for the kiva, forcing Buckthorn to run with them.

As they neared the kiva, the Bear Thlatsina climbed the ladder and stood beside Buckthorn's mother. A helmet of bear fur covered his head and draped down over his back and shoulders. Three black dots, for eyes and mouth, painted his white buckskin mask. Naked to the waist, the thlatsina had two blue lines running down his right breast and two yellow lines down his left. His forearms were painted blue, his hands white. Around his waist, he wore a plain white cotton kirtle, secured with a red sash. The frayed ends of his sash whipped in the icy wind.

The Bear Thlatsina lifted a white hand and dismissed Buckthorn's mother. He watched her walk through the middle of the plaza, smiling at the people on the roofs. She entered their home and vanished.

The protective circle of Dancers which had carried him this far split and retreated, leaving Buckthorn alone before the kiva. The sweet notes of the flute brought tears to Buckthorn's eyes.

Buckthorn's gaze riveted on the Bear Thlatsina. He had to stand by himself now. Either worthy . . . or not.

His knees shook.

The Bear Thlatsina took four steps toward Buckthorn, extended his left fist, and opened it to reveal a small sack covered with glimmering turquoise beads. The thlatsina opened the sack and sprinkled corn pollen to the four directions. He lifted it to Brother Sky, where his gaze lingered a long moment on the building clouds, then reverently touched the bag to Our Mother Earth.

Without a word, he lifted the empty bag over his head.

Two women, attired in white doeskin dresses, climbed from the kiva and shuffled through the snow in white boots, their cheeks painted with black spots. They passed very close to Buckthorn—but sacrosanct, untouchable. Two long eagle feathers adorned their freshly washed hair. The Deer Mothers circled Buckthorn four times, Dancing, moving through the dazzling white sunlight, supernatural beings that had just stepped from the haze of myth and legend.

The other masked Dancers drew back with strange haunting mutters, withdrawing from the divine Deer Mothers. Some hunched in terror. Others bleated like animals about to be slaughtered. The people on the roofs placed hands over their mouths, keeping silent.

The Deer Mothers took up their places at Buckthorn's sides. He clenched his fists and forced a swallow down his tight throat.

The Bear Thlatsina held out a pollen-covered hand.

Buckthorn walked forward and bravely put his fingers in the thlatsina's palm. Gazing up into that bizarre half-human, half-animal face, he nearly buckled at the knees.

The sky god led him to the ladder jutting from the kiva's packed roof and went down first, descending into the belly of the underworlds to announce Buckthorn's coming.

Buckthorn stood at the yawning mouth and peered into the firelit darkness below. The blessing scent of cedar wafted up through the opening. Juniper fires burned all year long in the kiva, in honor of the Grandmother of Life: flame. At the core of the universe and in the hearts of people a flame burned always—until the day a person's soul escaped and returned to the underworlds for good.

The flute stopped, but the pot drum continued to boom in its rhythmic bass.

With thuds and creaks his relatives on the roofs stood up, their blanket-wrapped bodies silhouetted against the translucent blue of Brother Sky, faces joyous. Little children stared at Buckthorn in awe. They would watch, he knew, until he vanished from sight completely.

The Bear Thlatsina's deep voice began:

> *The Creator calls you,*
> *The divine Mother has seen you*
> *   on your journey,*
> *She has seen your worn moccasins,*
> *She offers her life-giving breath,*
> *   Her breath of birth,*
> *   Her breath of water,*
> *   Her breath of seeds,*
> *   Her breath of death,*
> *Asking for your breath,*
> *   To add to her own,*
> *That the one great life of all might continue*
> *   unbroken.*

Buckthorn gripped the pine-pole ladder, the use-polished wood smooth under his fingers. Then, swallowing hard, and vowing to be brave, he climbed down into the warm firelit womb of the underworlds.

The ceiling represented the Fourth World through which the First People had journeyed, known as the Feather-Wing World. The Fog World, or Third World, was represented by the bench that encircled the chamber. The floor level, or Second World, was called the Sulfur-smell World; lastly, the masonry-lined hole in the floor, the *sipapu*, represented the tunnel to the First Underworld—the Soot World. Sacred cedar smoke purified him as he descended, bathing his frail human body, and stinging his eyes.

Two old men and two old women sat on the low Fog World bench that curved around the great circular chamber. A flute nestled on the bench between the men, a drum between the women. All wore long turkey-feather capes. Not one of them looked at Buckthorn. They had their gazes fixed on the four massive masonry pillars that supported the weight of the roof, which represented the four directions. For them, servants of the unseen Powers that hid at the corners of the world, nothing else existed.

The Bear Thlatsina stood silently beside Buckthorn.

Waiting. But for what?

Buckthorn's gaze took in the softly gleaming chamber. A fire burned in the middle of the floor; honeyed light danced over the breathtaking thlatsinas painted on the white walls. Some Danced around, bent forward, a foot lifted, ready to stamp down. Others stood with their feet planted firmly on the sacred earth, their awesome beaks and muzzles tipped toward the Blessed Evening People, howling their praises.

He tried to draw himself up straighter, but his stomach felt as if it were shriveling.

Twenty-eight wall crypts filled with magnificent offerings separated the thlatsinas, one for each day of the moon. Macaw and parrot feathers gleamed in the crypts, along with ritual pots and painted dance sticks. A wealth of shining black obsidian glittered around the base of each offering.

From the mouths of the elders, the most eerie of all the sacred chants began in a whisper: "*Hututu! Hututu!*"

Buckthorn whispered the name of the Rain God with them, knowing that by the end of this evening, that name would rise to a cry so hoarse and piercing it would sunder the skyworlds. Rain would fall tonight. It always did.

He had sat on the roofs through many long nights listening to this ritual, his heart aching to know how the young Singers-in-the-making felt.

Now I know. They all wanted to faint.

The Bear Thlatsina quietly pointed to the floor, his hand indicating the slender line of cornmeal. The Road of Life. It ran eastward, linking the firepit to the *sipapu*, the dark opening to the lowest underworld.

Buckthorn walked the Road, placing his feet carefully.

Hututu! Hututu! Hututu!

What would he see when he gazed down that black tunnel into the First Underworld? Legends said that all of his dead ancestors would be gazing up at him.

A well of disembodied eyes . . .

The Bear Thlatsina knelt on one side of the *sipapu* and indicated Buckthorn's place.

He sat cross-legged facing the god. Afraid to look into the opening until told to, he stared at the thlatsina's white mask. Through the black eye holes, he saw nothing staring out. Nothing at all. Just darkness.

The four elders, Keepers of the sacred directions, sat down around Buckthorn and the Bear Thlatsina, their wrinkled faces drawn.

Old Woman North removed a small pot, red-brown and painted with intricate designs, from beneath her turkey-feather cape. Cupped in her gnarled fingers, she held it out to the thlatsina. The god took it in pure white hands and blew down into the pot four times, adding his breath, bringing life to whatever resided inside.

Hututu! Hututu! Hututu! Hututu!

The thlatsina reached out with two fingers and closed Buckthorn's eyes. Buckthorn trembled. He couldn't help it.

A strange musty smell taunted his nostrils and he felt something touch his lips. He opened his mouth. A thin dry slice of something like desiccated hide was laid upon his tongue. Chalky bitterness coated his mouth. He shuddered involuntarily. Working it around, mixing it with his saliva, just made it worse. He chewed. Within moments, nausea began. Weakness prickled his muscles.

"I . . . I'm going to throw up," he said.

A pot was placed in his hands.

Buckthorn's stomach heaved and heaved until he felt like a quivering mass of bruised flesh. He set the pot aside and wiped his mouth with the back of his hand. Despite the effort, he had not opened his eyes. Nor would he, until told to do so.

Faintly, the drumbeat echoed through the gleaming chamber.

He *saw* the beat pulsing on the gold-tinged backs of his eyelids. The four sacred colors lanced out from each beat, soaring away like glowing arrows, flying to the farthest edges of his vision, and beyond into a shimmering haze.

The passing of time vanished until he might have sat there forever, but he jerked when fingers touched his eyes and gently pulled up his lids.

Buckthorn blinked lazily.

The flute joined the drum . . .

His balance fled. He fell forward, bracing his hands on either side of the tunnel to the underworld, looking straight into the *sipapu*. The darkness wavered. Ripples flowed out like windblown waves journeying across a lake without a shore. In the heart of that blackness, a crystal pillar took shape, rising, growing, shimmering like a thousand diamonds as it rushed upward, building crystal upon crystal.

Fear, bright and glowing, shot through Buckthorn. "It . . . it's coming too fast. It's going to lance right through me!"

The darkness around the crystal pillar changed from pitch black to deep blue. Then, as if the tunnel had been pierced by an unseen shaft of light, the blue turned a magnificent shade of turquoise, and a blue-green cave took shape. Light flashed. Thousands of falling stars cascaded down like points of white fire. In the heart of the cave, flame sparked, and the crystal pillar caught fire. The blaze roared out of control, devouring the cave, and in the midst of it he saw a young woman's face, beautiful, crying, with long black hair falling about her shoulders . . . and a jagged mountain peak sheathed in starlight.

"Ah!" Buckthorn cried out. "Help me! I—I'm falling! I'm falling in!"

A soft voice said, *You are going where the world is born, Buckthorn. Just let yourself go. Let go.*

The golden ceremonial chamber spun, and Buckthorn dove headfirst through breathtaking flame-colored skies, falling, falling . . .

Black Mesa stood beside Snow Mountain, watching Buckthorn, who sat in the middle of the plaza, making a drum. The snow had melted in the rain that had fallen for two days, leaving the sand clean and sparkling. Pools of water shone on the terraced fields stretching out from the base of the sandstone cliffs. Scruffy patches of saltbush and grass edged the fields with dull colors. Rivulets had incised the plaster covering the village's stone walls, giving them an aged look. They would have to be replastered.

Scattered around Buckthorn lay pieces of leather, stone tools, strips of sinew and rawhide, and a single perfect turkey feather.

The youth hadn't said a word in three days. Not since he had emerged from the kiva.

People moved around the plaza, enjoying the warm sun, weaving blankets on large looms, grinding corn, and attending to mending. They patted Buckthorn's head or shoulder and spoke to him in gentle tones as they passed.

Buckthorn only smiled in return. Silent. His narrow face glowing as if from an inner radiance. No one pushed him. Everyone knew he must return to them in his own time, that part of his soul still hovered in the First Underworld, walking among the ancestors, studying the strange plants and animals that lived there.

Black Mesa folded his aged arms across his breast. His black shirt hung to his knees and looked huge on his frail body. Over the long passing of the seasons, his muscles had evaporated to stringy masses, leaving a rickety bag of bones behind. He'd left his long gray hair loose today, and it fluttered around his wrinkled face.

Snow Mountain murmured, "He'll be all right, won't he?"

"Of course."

Worry shone in her dark eyes. At the age of thirty-five summers, silver had just begun to streak her black hair and lines to etch her forehead. Her short pointed nose rode over thin lips. She wore a red and black dress today. "Did he tell you?" she asked anxiously. "Did he tell you what he saw in the First Underworld?"

"It won't make much sense to you."

"But I wish to know. If you can tell me, perhaps it will help me to understand him better. He has always been a . . . a mystery to me. And my greatest joy. I'm worried about him, Black Mesa."

Black Mesa's gaze drifted to the twin knobs that loomed over the valley—the stone bodies of gods, eternally watching. He had long wondered what their souls did in the skyworlds. Did they make bows and recount their exploits? Did they hunt? Or just Dance continually to keep the world vibrantly alive? The blue-gray thunderheads that had been gathering all day had crumbled to ruins in the sky. Shreds of their glory drifted northward, tinged with the palest of blues.

Black Mesa looked down into Snow Mountain's worried face. "He saw his father," he answered.

Snow Mountain's taut expression slackened. "H-his real father?"

"Yes. His body was mumbling, telling what his soul saw as it passed through the worlds. He called the man 'father,' but I don't know if he truly realizes the man's identity in this world."

"He can't know, Black Mesa. I never told him anything! He has asked many times, but—"

"Snow Mountain," Black Mesa gently interrupted, "you must understand. Everything that leaves, returns. Everything that dies is reborn. Everything that is hidden is revealed. We humans live in an immense and naked universe, a universe we barely understand."

Life "moved," Black Mesa knew, as inconstant and fickle as Wind Baby, frolicking, sleeping, but never truly still, never solid, or finished. Seed and fruit, rain and drought, belief and reality, everything traveled in a gigantic circle, an eternal process of becoming something else.

Snow Mountain's gaze focused on her son. Buckthorn had

finished hollowing out his two-hands-tall section of cotton-wood log and had begun constructing the "heart" of the drum. He stretched a piece of sinew through the middle, tied it off, and attached the turkey feather to the taut strand. Black Mesa nodded when the youth bent forward and growled into the drum in the deepest voice he could muster, to give the drum a rumbling bass voice.

Without taking her eyes from Buckthorn, Snow Mountain asked, "What else happened to him in the Soot World?"

"His father taught him a Song. They Sang it together. While they were Singing, the earth began to tremble, and then rivers of fire consumed the earth. To escape, Buckthorn climbed into the sky, using the clouds as stepping stones."

"I don't understand."

Black Mesa shrugged. "The vision was not given to you."

"Did Buckthorn understand?"

He watched Buckthorn place two pieces of deerhide over the top and bottom, then lace them together by pulling strips of rawhide through holes he had punched around the edges. "No," Black Mesa said through a tired exhalation. "But he will. Someday."

"You will teach him?"

"I cannot. I have promised Buckthorn that the holy Derelict will teach him."

Snow Mountain's lips parted as she lifted a hand to her heart. Her eyes seemed to enlarge. "Dune? But I thought Dune never wished to see him again? That's what you *told* me!"

Black Mesa lowered his gaze, searching for the right words. "The Great Circle has shifted. There are many things Buckthorn must know. Perhaps even the identity of his real father."

"Should I be the one—"

"No." He reached out, placing a hand on her shoulder to emphasize his words. "There is great danger in this revelation. If he must know, Dune will tell him. It is, after all, Dune's right to decide if and when he is told."

Buckthorn tentatively beat his drum with his forefinger to test the resonance. Black Mesa glanced at him, a great weari-ness settling on his heart. A soft smile came to the youth's face. He looked up eagerly to see if anyone else in the village had heard the beautiful tone. Black Mesa gave him an approving nod, and Buckthorn's smile widened. He tapped the drum again. "You must trust me, Snow Mountain. Dune will teach Buckthorn."

Snow Mountain seemed to be digesting this news. "And does this mean my son will be a great Singer?"

"I can say only that he will be needed." He peered at Snow Mountain. "Which of us dares ask for more than that?"

Three

As the flames of sunset dwindled, the drifting clouds turned a somber gray, smudging the heavens like oily smoke. The shadows of the canyon lengthened until they blended with the night. Owls sailed over the sage, their calls echoing. The evening fires from fourteen large towns and over two hundred small villages gave the canyon an eerie glow and a pungent smell. The massive cliffs seemed to flutter and dance.

Ironwood, War Chief of Talon Town, paced back and forth within the confines of the rock shelter. A deep hollow in the sheer-walled sandstone cliff, the smooth buff-colored overhang rose barely a hand's width above his head. On the rear wall, the carved images of the Spiral, Evening People, and various gods watched him. This rock shelter lay midway between Talon Town and Kettle Town. When Ironwood looked to the east, he could just see the hanging porch that ran high along Kettle Town's second story. This late in winter, with the chill in the air, no one stood there.

A fragrant whisper of wind blew through the stubble of last summer's cornfields, across the cold dirt, and flicked the hem of his red warrior's shirt. Ironwood shivered. A muscular man, he had an oval face and flat nose. Unlike most of the Bear Clan, his eyebrows did not arch neatly over his eyes, but slanted upward as if with mischievous intent. He had lived forty-five summers, and gray had overpowered his once jet-black hair. He wore it in a single thick braid that fell to the middle of his back.

Ironwood glanced at Sternlight, who leaned on a chunk of fallen roof back in the shadows. Dust puffed from beneath Sternlight's restless sandals and coated his long white ritual shirt. His brown eyes held a strange light, as though Father Sun breathed inside his tall, lean frame. Ironwood's backbone prickled. Yet he trusted this man. Trusted him like no other.

"The Blessed Sun, Chief Crow Beard, is dying," Ironwood said.

Sternlight's beautiful lips pressed into a bloodless line. "Maybe. None of us can say for certain. He—"

"You know it."

"No," Sternlight corrected. "I *believe* he's dying. But he has fooled us so often in the past, I hesitate for fear he will prove us wrong again."

"I hesitate, too, my friend." Ironwood glanced uneasily at the carved gods behind Sternlight. They seemed to be watching them. "But if he is dying, we must act quickly."

Sternlight steepled his fingers over his lips. "This is not a decision I can make, Ironwood. *You* must make it."

"I know that, old friend. It is just as much my responsibility today as it was almost sixteen summers ago."

Sternlight glanced up, pinning Ironwood with sober eyes. Against the darkening sandstone, his pale face and white shirt seemed to blaze. "You truly believe the child is in danger?"

"Yes."

"Does this mean you suspect treachery?"

Ironwood needed to phrase his next words carefully. "No. But if the Blessed Sun dies, there is no longer a reason to hide the child. And Talon Town with its massive defensive walls and trained warriors is certainly safer than a little village."

"You just want the child close to you, is that it?"

"Sternlight, I—"

"That was not a reprimand, Ironwood. Just a question. If you truly mean to do this, be smart. I don't think it's wise to go and drag the child away from the only family—"

"I wouldn't do that." Though that was precisely what he longed to do. Ironwood folded muscular arms over his aching chest, as if he could protect his heart. "I was thinking about sending Wraps-His-Tail, my deputy, to the village with some story about how much I need Beargrass to return to Talon Town."

"And hope he brings the child with him?"

"Yes, and I think he will. If I tell him that the Mogollon are raiding and I fear for his family's safety, he'll come." Ironwood resumed his pacing, his yucca sandals soundless in the rock shelter's powdery soil. Far out in the desert a pack of coyotes yipped, then broke into a beautiful lilting chorus.

"But, Ironwood, the Fire Dogs have been raiding for many sun cycles." Sternlight used his fingertips to massage his temples, as though a headache had just started behind his dark eyes. "Why would such a message make him come?"

"I'll add that the northern barbarians, the Tower Builders, are slinking about like wildcats, just waiting for a chance to slip into Straight Path country and kill us all." Ironwood caught Sternlight's sidelong look. "It's true, you know. If Chief Crow Beard dies, the Tower Builders will look upon it as an opportunity to sweep down and steal whatever they can lay their dirty hands on."

"I suppose so."

"And they may be able to take advantage of our confusion. After all, Snake Head will become the new Blessed Sun when his father is gone. People are certain to feel despondent for a time."

Sternlight nodded. "I certainly will."

"It is a burden we must bear—at least for a time."

"Night Sun—"

"Snake Head's mother is not here," Ironwood pointed out. "She is off on one of her Healing trips, caring for the people in the neighboring villages. Cloud Playing, her daughter, is with her. Snake Head has no other relatives who will stand up for him. He is hated by everyone."

Sternlight looked up. The crow's feet around his eyes pulled tight. "We play a dangerous game, you and I. I fear we may tangle ourselves in our own complicated web of deception and forget why we're doing this."

"*I* will never forget."

Sternlight fell silent.

Ironwood lifted his gaze to the canyon.

Across the wash, hundreds of fires sparkled to life, sprinkling the flats like tangled necklaces of copper beads. Most gleamed around Sunset Town, which sat at the base of the western canyon wall, but many lit small villages where those of low status lived, enjoying their closeness to the elite First People of Straight Path canyon.

Several fires glowed on the mesas, including one on the summit of Spider Woman's Butte.

Ironwood studied it while he thought. Must be a priest. No one else would dare visit such a strong Power place.

On top of Spider Woman's Butte stood the Sun Stone. Etched with spirals, it allowed Sternlight to measure the exact cycles of the sun. When the summer solstice arrived, a dagger of sunlight lanced between two upright stones and split the spiral down the middle, enabling Sternlight to count the exact number of days until they could harvest the rice grass, corn, beans, and squash, and organize the communal hunts for deer and rabbits. Spider Woman herself guarded the Sun Stone.

The Straight Path people had long lived by rigid schedules. They planted and harvested, collected pine nuts and juniper berries, and ran their hunts on the days Sternlight said they must, for fear that they would offend Our Mother Earth and Father Sun if they did not.

But people had grown more disobedient over recent summers. When the rains fell and the crops grew, people believed in Sternlight's Powers and did everything he asked. But when no rains came and the crops withered in the fields . . .

Ironwood glanced at the empty cornfields, remembering the last poor harvest. Those plants that had born fruit had been stunted, the ears of corn short, with poorly formed kernels. It was as if the ground in this valley no longer nourished the plants that had fed the Straight Path people for generations.

People worried that the gods had turned against Sternlight—or he against the gods. Ridiculous rumors about Sternlight being a witch had become common.

"Are we finished?" Sternlight asked.

"Yes, for now. I will send Wraps-His-Tail to Beargrass tomorrow."

"And I," Sternlight said softly, "will pray for him. If anyone discovers—"

"No one will."

Sternlight braced a hand against the carved wall of the rock shelter and rose to stare at Ironwood eye-to-eye. His white shirt whipped around his legs. "Someday soon, someone will. We cannot keep this hidden forever. You realize that, don't you?"

Ironwood let his folded arms fall to his sides. "The vigil is almost over, my friend. I *promise* you."

Sternlight vented a tired breath, whispered, "Yes," and walked past Ironwood, following the deer trail that ran close to the cliff.

Where once sage had grown, weeds now raked their legs and snagged at their long shirts. The sage had long ago been twisted out to feed ravenous hearths. People needed to cook and heat their houses.

They dared not take the main road that ran between Kettle and Talon Town. Someone would mention that he had seen the War Chief and the Sunwatcher walking alone after dark. Snake Head's suspicions would wake. He would ask them what they had been doing. Why they couldn't speak to each other in town. He would suspect betrayal.

And he would be right.

"Sternlight," Ironwood murmured, "forget the trail. Let's walk as close to the cliff as we can. The overhanging rock and darkness should hide us completely."

The chill deepened as they passed the jumble of individual square structures—poorly plastered, the roof poles raggedly finished—set against the cliff. Dark now, the doorways were covered, awaiting the visitors who only came to the canyon for the solstice festivals. The Evening People woke to light the night sky. Ironwood's breathing created a misty blur in the starlit darkness.

Talon Town loomed ahead, gigantic even after summers of familiarity. The rear wall rose over one hundred hands tall. Propped Pillar, the giant sandstone column that leaned out from the cliff, tilted threateningly toward it.

On the fifth floor, Crow Beard lay dying like some ancient and malignant spider. Filaments of webs spun long ago whirled out of the past, drawing all of them into some hidden trap. Even now Snake Head might be looking out from his little square window. Ironwood's steps faltered, and he shivered.

But not entirely from cold.

Buckthorn's yellow cape billowed in the dawn breeze that gusted along the sandstone cliffs and whimpered through the village. An azure halo swelled in the east, throwing the canyon walls into silhouette. One by one the stars twinkled out of existence, and the clay-washed walls of Windflower Village turned a soft robin's-egg blue. Ladder legs extended from some of the roofs; pine poles poked out in lines along the ceilings, some hung with peppers and shocks of dried corn or yucca leaves. The square shoulders of the village seemed to dominate the beaten-earth plaza where he'd played as a boy. The sacred kiva on the rise west of the plaza still hid in its dark cloak of shadows.

Buckthorn gazed at it longingly. His old life, the life of the child he had been, had been eaten away in there. A new man had been born in that boy's place. He didn't know this man, yet. *But I want to, very badly.*

People began to wake. An infant cried, and a soft voice responded, soothing the child. Someone coughed. He could hear some elders now, their arms lifted as they Sang to greet the new day. Gentle wisps of smoke rose from the morning fires, lacing the air with the scent of burning juniper.

Buckthorn tipped back his head, raising his hooked nose, and breathed in the cool earthy air. He'd plaited his black hair into two braids that covered his ears, protecting them from the wintry chill. The ends hung down on his chest. A new pair of yucca sandals adorned his feet. His mother had made them for him, and just looking at their fine workmanship made his soul ache. The weaving over the toes was tight and perfect. The shell bells tied to the ends of the laces clicked pleasantly with each step he took.

Snow Mountain ducked beneath the door curtain of their house and walked across the plaza. Silver-streaked black hair hung loosely about the shoulders of her turkey-feather cape.

Her feet in their tall moccasins passed silently over the frozen sand.

She knelt on the ground at his side and tucked freshly-made blue corncakes into his top pack. In the soft gleam of dawn, she looked sad, but pride glowed in her dark eyes. Few youths received the village elders' blessings to become Singers, and fewer still were sent off to the holy Derelict for training.

Buckthorn couldn't believe he had been one of the chosen. At any moment, the dream would vanish, and he'd wake up the same skinny youth he'd always been.

His mother used a braided rawhide thong to tie his three packs together—one for himself, and two for Dune, the latter filled with gifts from Windflower Village. Buckthorn's breathing went shallow when he looked at those packs. His relatives had contributed their finest belongings: beautiful flutes; two of the renowned Windflower pots, with their reddish-brown slip; decorated baskets, so tightly woven they'd hold water; a few precious turquoise fetishes; a masterfully carved set of the Great Warriors; and other things. They had parted with these treasures willingly, believing that when Buckthorn became a great Singer, he would pay them back tenfold.

And I will. I'll learn every lesson the holy Derelict wishes to teach me. I will memorize every Healing plant and Song.

Dune the Derelict had a reputation for paradoxical instruction. Buckthorn had known two young Singers who had been sent to Dune and come running home after a single day of what they called "the holy Derelict's madness." Both of those young men had failed and taken up lives as farmers—but Buckthorn would not fail.

A yearning lived inside him. He *would* speak to the Cloud People in their own language. He *would* be able to recognize fiendish witches and cure the sick. He *would* Sing and Dance for his people, bringing rain and bountiful harvests, giving them life itself.

Hallowed thlatsinas, I promise to try very hard. I beg you to help me.

He looked south, across the misty waters of the River of Souls, beyond the line of sandstone cliffs that blocked the southern horizon. As if he could see the distant Thlatsina

Mountains rising against the sky, he visualized the gods there, leaping, spinning, their heads thrown back, voices rising like wings into the star-spotted dawn. Terrible longing filled him. *I'll see those mountains one day. I promise.*

He'd heard that leaden clouds clung to the tallest peaks, holding on for their lives against Wind Baby's torments. That's how Wind Baby had gotten his evil reputation: he blew away the clouds and sucked every drop of moisture from the land, leaving both Our Mother Earth and Brother Sky parched and thirsty. When that happened, the children of the Straight Path nation begged for food, and parents grew frantic.

During the summer, Singers Danced and prayed for days, but not just for themselves. They prayed for everyone who was thirsty: animals, plants, even the dry stones that rested in the drainage bottoms. Power lived everywhere, beneath cactus thorns, secreted in sparkles of dew, and hidden in the flecks of moonlight that silvered the sage. By calling upon that Power, Singers could pull clouds together and awaken the soaring Thunderbirds.

Snow Mountain stood up and peered soberly at Buckthorn. Her face was full of love for him. "Black Mesa drew you a map, yes?"

"Yes, Mother, last night. I know exactly how to find the Derelict." He knew she wanted him to repeat his instructions. "I'll follow the trail from the river crossing up through the cap rock and turn east until I hit the Tower Road. It's a good road that will take me south to the Derelict's canyon. Black Mesa said that if I run it is only four or five days away. I'll find it. Don't worry."

"I know you're a man, and protected by the gods, but there has been so much raiding this winter by those northern barbarians . . . Perhaps I should find a runner to go with—"

"Mother," he said with a smile, "I must go alone. That is the way of it. A Singer goes alone to his destiny."

"I know, but I—"

"Don't worry." He put a hand on her cheek and bent down to look directly into her anxious eyes. "If I cannot go by myself to Dune's house, Mother, how will I ever be able to make the lonely journey over the sacred roads to find the gods?"

Snow Mountain squeezed her eyes closed for several moments, and nuzzled her face against his hand. "Learn all that you can. I'll be waiting for your return, my son."

"I will make you proud of me, Mother. I promise. I *will* come back a Singer."

She smiled. "I know you will, Buckthorn. I've known that for many summers."

Buckthorn picked up his three packs and slipped his arms through the shoulder straps, testing the weight. Heavy. But not too heavy. Wood clattered against stone in one of the gift packs.

"Mother?" Buckthorn said softly. "May I . . ." He hesitated. "If I ask you a question, will you promise to tell me the truth?"

Snow Mountain wet her lips, as though afraid what he might ask. Wind ruffled through the feathers of her cape and tossed her long graying black hair about her face. "I will tell you what I can, my son. Ask."

The pain in her eyes told Buckthorn she had phrased that carefully.

He shifted the weight of his packs and gripped the shoulder straps, holding them to steady himself. "My father . . ."

She seemed breathless. "Yes? What about him?"

"Was he truly a Trader?"

". . . Yes."

"His name really was Sitting-in-the-Sky?"

In toneless words, she said, "Yes, my son."

Buckthorn frowned at the kiva where his vision had come to him. The Spirits had no reason to lie. That meant his mother did. She was a good, loving woman. The truth must hurt her very much. He couldn't twist it from her soul, like a rabbit from a hole. He would not even try. People had the right to keep secrets if they needed to. Besides, he knew that she would tell him someday, and that was enough.

Buckthorn kissed her on the forehead, and whispered, "Thank you, Mother. For caring for me. For loving me. You are the most important thing in my life."

Snow Mountain's eyes blurred, and she hugged him, awkwardly putting her arms around his heavy packs. Hoarsely, she said, "I love you, Buckthorn. I always have."

"I promise I won't disappoint you."

She released Buckthorn and gazed up through swimming

eyes. "Black Mesa asked me to give you a message."

"What?"

She spoke the words slowly: "He said to remind you that 'You must have the heart of a cloud to walk upon the wind.' "

A smile warmed Buckthorn's face. He touched a hand to his chest. "Please tell him I will not forget the many kindnesses he has shown me. I carry the words inside my heartdrum."

Snow Mountain nodded and stepped back. "Have a safe journey, Buckthorn. Save some of the blue corncakes for your first dinner with Dune. I put in extra pine nuts. I've heard he likes those."

"Thank you, Mother. I wish . . ." He stopped himself. "I wish I didn't have to go, but I will return as quickly as I can. Goodbye."

Time after time, he turned to wave at Snow Mountain as he followed the familiar path down to the river. Once he'd been ferried across, he'd really be on his way.

He glanced back at the Great Warriors, the twin pillars of rock. *Watch over me, please. At least until I reach the holy Derelict.* They jutted up in silence, stern guardians of Windflower Village, and of the lush bottomland they surveyed.

Buckthorn's next landmark would be World Tree Mountain. Her roots sank deep into the First Underworld, and her trunk twisted up through the other underworlds until it popped through Our Mother Earth's skin. The branches spread out through the four skyworlds, but they were too great and powerful to be visible to humans, though, now and then, a shaman claimed to have seen misty green limbs wavering through the clouds above the jagged peaks.

Buckthorn trotted past the waiting fields, remembering the sweet voices of the gods that had thrilled his soul. However this journey ended, it would be marvelous.

Four

Cornsilk knelt on the north side of the plaza with two grinding slabs, one coarse and one fine, before her. An empty black-and-white bowl and a plain clay pot filled with red corn sat to her left. She had been here for over a hand of time and hadn't made any apparent headway on the corn, though meal covered her hands and the skirt of her brown dress. As she studied the situation, it appeared that she had more cornmeal on her than on her slabs. Five paces away, a large pot tilted sideways on the hot coals of her firepit, reminding her of her duties. She leaned forward and pounded a handful of corn with the pointed end of her handstone, cracking the kernels.

Morning blushed gold into the rolling hills around Lanceleaf Village and glimmered on the green spears of yucca choking the slopes. It shone on the up-tilted blocks of tan sandstone rising over the patchwork of empty corn, squash, and bean fields that lay on every flat area around the village.

Billows of orange cloud burned swathes in the translucent eastern sky. Beneath them, the rugged peaks of the distant mountains were mantled in pristine white, and today they seemed to rip at the bottom of the clouds. At their base lay flat mesas, home of the Green Mesa clans who farmed the butte tops.

To the north rose the Great Bear Mountains, the home of First Bear, who had raised the high granite peaks to shelter him in hibernation. The claw marks of First Bear had ripped the land under the mountain, leaving long twisting ridges of canted rock. Ephemeral creeks ran at the bases of those ridges, flash flooding in spring, tumbling whole trees down into the basins, and trickling cool and clear after misty winter rainstorms. Those washes brought life to the land around Lanceleaf Village.

Generations ago, several families of the Ant Clan had come

to farm the alluvial flats and mesa tops around Lanceleaf. In the beginning they built an attached line of four houses to spend the summers in while they worked the fields. With the crop surplus, they'd stayed through the winter, and in the following years, other clan members came, and additional rooms were built onto the village. Several kivas were dug into the red clay soil.

Life hadn't been easy despite the rich bottomlands and water. The Tower Builders, barbarians who lived to the northwest, raided the Straight Path clans, killing, stealing food, and taking slaves that they drove northward to work their fields and clean their squalid houses. Sometimes wild peoples came down from the mountains, hunters who wore skins and worshiped animal gods. The wild hunters might trade, or they might raid. Then, like the beasts they were, they'd melt into the mountains without a trace.

Nor had all enemies been foreign. Lanceleaf had fought its share of wars with other Straight Path clans over the years. As a result, what had begun as a line of houses had been expanded with an eye toward defense. As the village grew, a second story had been added, then more rooms until the rectangular structure completely enclosed the plaza, providing a perfect corral. The only exit was a small gap between the walls in the southeastern corner, which they blocked with a pine-pole gate.

As long as the people had adequate warning, and could close the gate, the villagers could stand off any number of attackers by taking to the roofs with their bows.

But on this bright winter day, thoughts of war were far away. The men had left Lanceleaf Village to hunt at dawn, and most of the young women had gone to gather colored sand for sacred paintings. Dogs stretched out in the sunlight, sleeping. A few bold flies buzzed around them. Occasionally one would land, take a bite. The dog would wake with a sharp yip and go into a snapping frenzy, before flopping down again and drifting back to sleep.

Turkeys strutted through the village plaza, and they dipped their heads to examine every human activity, their brown-and-white feathers glinting in the wash of sunlight.

They had been bothering Cornsilk earlier, but now they tormented the seven old women sitting on the west side of the plaza. Her village rarely had meat, except on special occasions, so the turkeys were particularly prized. The young pullets pecked relentlessly at the strips of green yucca laid out for weaving baskets. Waving arms and harsh words split the morning. Matron Clover, the elder of Lanceleaf Village, reached out for a strip to weave into her sifter basket. As she started to lift it, one of the pullets leaped forward, grabbed the strip, and tugged.

"Stop that!" Clover yelled, her elderly face a mass of crisscrossing wrinkles. She tugged back. "Let go!"

With a great heave, she jerked the wet yucca strip away, and eyed the turkey malevolently. "Get away! Go find somebody else to bother." She used the yucca to smack the pullet on the back. It let out a sharp high-pitched squawk and bounded off. Clover mumbled something Cornsilk couldn't hear, but the other women laughed.

On the opposite side of the plaza, five hens dodged the flying chips from the eight old men making stone tools. Every time one of the men's antler batons struck a flake of stone from a chert core, the hens dove for it, squabbling and plucking feathers from each other, before one hen grabbed it up, contemplatively tasted it, and spit it out.

The fat gobblers had bedded down along the south wall where a line of cradleboards leaned in the shade. Infants wrapped in bright blankets gurgled, shrieked, and waved tiny fists at nothing. Cotton straps ran across their foreheads, tying them to the cradleboards, and shaping their skulls. Flattening the back of the head broadened the cheekbones and gave the face a more desirable triangular appearance.

Cornsilk's mother had not done a very good job on her head. Her face remained oval, though young men claimed she was still pretty—at least, they did after she threatened them. Cornsilk grinned to herself. The young warriors didn't like her much, but the feeling was mutual. She had a pointed chin, full lips, and large dark eyes. When her black hair hung loose, it draped in a thick wealth to her hips. Her mother, however, insisted she wear her hair in large whorls over her ears, a style which resembled the wings of a butterfly—to announce to all the young men that she had reached a marriageable age. And she did wear them . . . within sight of the village.

She wiped her sweating forehead with the back of her mealy hand and tipped her pot to check inside. Still full. Oh, what she would give to be out with Leafhopper.

Beyond the village, little children played. Cornsilk's best friend, Leafhopper, supervised them, ambling along behind while the children chased each other, threw sticks for their dogs, and laughed joyously.

Cornsilk sighed, reached into the pot for another handful of red corn . . .

Flapping wings split the air.

Cornsilk looked up. A huge raven fluttered to the ground ten hands away. His black feathers gleamed with a blue fire in the slanting light. Cornsilk glanced around the plaza. No one had noticed yet. She scowled at the raven.

"Brother, I swear you can smell the sweet scent of ground corn from half a day's walk."

The raven world was the first of the skyworlds.

"Go home," she hissed at the big bird, and pointed heavenward.

Placing a handful of corn on the grinding slab, she sat back on her heels and took the opportunity to stretch her aching back muscles. Her brown dress spread around her knees. Warm sunshine drenched her face and glistened in her butterfly whorls.

The raven leaped into the air and came down closer to Cornsilk, head twisting curiously.

Across the crowded plaza her relatives turned to watch, whispering behind their hands.

"Look, brother," she said, and gestured to the people in the plaza. "You have them whispering again. Do you wish them to think me a witch? We are Ant Clan. We don't like you raven people. That's why we always scare you away from our villages. From the instant the Creator breathed over us and brought us to life, the raven nation has been gobbling up Ant people. Why should I feed you when you have so many of my ancestors in your belly?"

The raven made a low pathetic sound and fluffed out his feathers, as if indignant at the suggestion.

"No," Cornsilk said.

She picked up her handstone and pounded the red corn kernels on the coarse slab. After each sharp bang she rocked her stone back and forth, crunching the kernels, to grind them to a medium-grained flour. It took forever.

The raven *thock-thocked* at her.

"No! I'm not giving you any. Now, fly away!"

The raven stretched out his black neck and cawed loudly. He flapped his wings.

Leafhopper's group of children trotted into the plaza and gathered into a knot near the kiva where the long-necked water jars sat. As they fought over who got to drink first, several pointed at her, their eyes wide. Leafhopper entered the plaza, herding the last children ahead of her, and stopped dead when she saw the raven.

Cornsilk glared at the big bird. "What's wrong with you? Every day I scare you away. I throw rocks at you. I scream at you. Nothing works. Are you certain you're not Trickster Coyote in disguise? Just seeing how much trouble you can mix up?"

Coyote had a bad reputation. After the First People emerged from the underworlds, Coyote had hidden in the grass with his long penis coiled in a basket on his back. He had stayed perfectly still until the first woman walked by, then he'd uncoiled his penis and sent it slithering through the grass after her. When she saw it, she thought it a snake, picked up a branch and proceeded to beat his penis half to death. Coyote had held a grudge ever since—for thousands of sun cycles. He got revenge whenever he could, tripping humans, fooling them, leading them off in the wrong direction on hunts.

Cornsilk eyed the raven. Surreptitiously, she tossed him several small bits of corn. "Now leave!"

The raven gobbled them down, rearranged his wings in satisfaction, and hopped closer.

"Hallowed thlatsinas!" she yelled. "Go away!" She waved her arms furiously, and shouted, "Go on! Leave me alone! *Get out of here!*"

The raven just hunched and waited for the tirade to be over. When Cornsilk's arms fell limply to her sides, he straightened again and took a tentative step toward her.

Glum, she scooped the corn flour from her coarse slab and placed it into the black-and-white bowl at her side. Then she rose and walked toward the fire.

The raven hopped along behind her, wings out for balance.

The children by the kiva shoved each other, then one let out a sharp shriek, and all of them raced through the gobbling turkeys, scattering them every which way. Feathers flew up and gently pirouetted down across the plaza.

Adults murmured worriedly. Cornsilk caught a look of condemnation on Clover's old face.

Crouching, she dumped her bowl of flour into the hot pot sitting on the coals and used a wooden paddle to stir it around until the cornmeal steamed, losing some of its moisture and browning slightly. Moisture led to spoilage, so this process assured that the flour would last longer and taste better. She stirred it for a time longer, then scooped the flour out with the paddle and refilled the bowl.

Every eye in the plaza rested on her as she rose and headed back to her grinding slabs, her moccasins soundless on the hard-packed dirt of the plaza.

The Ant Clan plastered their buildings with a rusty-hued clay that faded into the background of the rolling red and tan hills, but just over the roofs she saw yucca plants spiking up through the sage and heard their fist-sized seed pods rattling in the breeze. The fragrance of burning cedar encircled her.

Cornsilk's family didn't live in the main village complex, but in a small house on the hillside just behind it. Cornsilk's father, Beargrass, held the position of War Chief of Lanceleaf Village. For this reason their house had been built higher than the rest of the village, with a wide view of the cornfields and approaches to the village. From those heights, Beargrass could keep better watch for Tower Builders, or Wild Men.

At that moment, Cornsilk's mother, Thistle, walked into the plaza and caught sight of the raven. Thistle wore a white-and-yellow striped dress and carried a pot balanced on her head. She folded her arms, face sour as she watched the raven stride at Cornsilk's side.

Cornsilk leveled a kick at him.

The raven fluttered up and came down.

"Blessed Spirits!" she hollered. "What do you wish from me?"

She speeded up. The raven ran faster, keeping pace with her.

Dropping to her knees, Cornsilk dumped the bowl of flour

onto the fine-grained slab and got back into position. As she worked her handstone over it, grinding it to powder, it changed color, going from red to a pale rose-petal pink. After being browned, it smelled deliciously like popped corn.

The raven stuck his beak out, sniffing.

Cornsilk ignored him.

Leafhopper kept glancing at her as she worked her way across the plaza, smiling politely at the elders and speaking to each one. Though Leafhopper was Cornsilk's age—fifteen summers, almost sixteen—she stood a head shorter, and had a round face with a pudgy squarish body. She never belted her dresses, which meant they hung like bean-harvesting sacks from her squat frame. Her parents had died four summers ago, and she lived with her aunt, who insisted Leafhopper wear her hair trimmed even with her chin, because the style required less care. A red headband kept it out of her soft brown eyes.

They had both become women fifteen moons ago, but not one young man had courted Leafhopper. Cornsilk herself had seen only one suitor: young Stone Forehead. He'd babbled endlessly about how one day he would be the greatest warrior the Ant Clan had ever known. The topic of conversation hadn't varied after their first tentative coupling. But Stone Forehead had stopped coming to see Cornsilk after she'd gone hunting with him and shot four sage grouse to his one. She suspected she'd made her real mistake the night over supper when she'd casually mentioned that *she* planned to be the greatest warrior the Ant Clan had ever known.

Leafhopper bent over Matron Clover and made some comment about her loosely woven sifter basket. Clover patted her plump cheek.

Cornsilk took the opportunity to fling an arm out at the raven. He just pulled his head back momentarily and returned to his former attentive position.

"Oh, all right!" she growled in defeat.

Grabbing a fistful of coarsely ground corn from the other slab, she scattered it in front of him. The raven ate it up like a bird on the verge of starving to death.

"Now will you leave, *please?*"

The raven cocked his head, peered at her with one eye, and leaped into the sky. Cornsilk watched him circle the village, his black body striking against the deep blue of the winter sky, then wing southward toward the distant butte that thrust its square nose into the sky.

Cornsilk breathed a sigh of relief and went back to grinding the coarse meal.

Leafhopper hurried toward Cornsilk, her tan-and-black dress swishing around her short legs. She knelt, drew a handful of corn from the full pot, and placed it on the coarse slab. When she picked up a handstone, she whispered, "Great Badger, Cornsilk! This is the fourth day in a row that raven has pestered you. That's a *sacred* number. Everyone is muttering about it."

"It's not my fault," Cornsilk replied. She threw all of her weight into grinding the meal, crushing it to fine flour. "I think he's just hungry."

"Ravens move in flocks. This one comes to you alone. That's not natural." Leafhopper gave Cornsilk a sidelong glance. "He hasn't talked to you, has he?"

"*What!*" Cornsilk slammed her handstone down into the meal. Pink flour puffed up and swirled in the breeze. Ravens only spoke to Ant people who were witches. She stared disbelievingly at Leafhopper. "Of course not!"

Leafhopper lifted a shoulder and short black hair fluttered over her fat cheeks. "I was only asking."

"I am *not* a witch, Leafhopper. You know I'm not!"

Leafhopper pounded the kernels until they cracked and fragmented, then rocked her handstone over them and pounded some more. Eager to change the subject, Leafhopper tipped her head to the gray-haired women weaving baskets. "Brave Boy told me a story about old Pocket Gopher today."

Pocket Gopher sat next to Clover, her dress—gray and white in diamond patterns—clinging to her skinny frame. She had a perfect triangular face with a long beak of a nose and deeply set black eyes. Pocket Gopher had never borne a child, but made up for it by disciplining everybody else's. When Cornsilk had seen six summers, Pocket Gopher caught her hiding out in the bean field, eating the tender new shoots. The old woman had grabbed a dead cactus limb and beaten Cornsilk over the head all the way home. She *scared* Cornsilk—and every other child in the village.

"Brave Boy has seen only five summers. What could he know?"

Leafhopper whispered, "He said one of the young warriors standing guard saw her out in the burial ground at midnight on the full moon."

Cornsilk's handstone halted in mid-downward swing. "Doing what?"

"The warrior didn't say, but I'm sure the old hag is a witch. She's so mean to people, she must be. Do you remember what happened to Sand Melon?"

Cornsilk wet her lips nervously. "Yes."

Sand Melon had miscarried in her sixth moon, and when the birthing women came to care for her, they'd found corpse powder sprinkled all over Sand Melon's house. Sand Melon had accused Pocket Gopher, screaming that the old woman had been the last person in her house before Sand Melon had returned home. But no evidence could be found.

Still, people watched Pocket Gopher closely now, and if she had been seen in the burial grounds . . . Blessed thlatsinas! Perhaps she *was* a witch.

"I don't believe it," Cornsilk said. "People accuse me of being a witch, and I'm not."

"I know that."

Cornsilk pushed the flour to the side of the grinding slab and scooped more coarse meal onto the fine-grained slab. "It's just the weather. People are worried." She pounded the meal.

"The weather and the raiding," Leafhopper corrected.

"They go together. Each summer without rain makes things worse. More and more witches are being accused and killed. And I . . ." She tilted her head at the blasphemy. "I'm not sure they are to blame."

Leafhopper sat back on her heels and wiped her meal-covered hands on her dress hem while she gazed at Cornsilk. "Then who is?"

"I don't know! Maybe . . . maybe the First People at Talon Town. We send them corn and pots and everything else we make. All that, and they're supposed to talk to the gods so it will rain. They're the ones who always start the wars. Not only that . . ." Cornsilk leaned forward to whisper, "I heard that

Chief Crow Beard keeps corpse powder in his chamber to use against his enemies! Maybe he's the witch!"

Leafhopper set the black-and-white bowl at the bottom of her grinding slab and pulled the coarse red meal into it. She had clamped her lower lip between her teeth, thinking.

Cornsilk kept grinding.

There were two kinds of "people" in the world: First People and Made People. The First People were descendants of those who had bravely climbed through the four underworlds, led by a blue-black wolf, and emerged from the darkness into this fifth world of light. All First People lived in Straight Path Canyon. The four clans of the Straight Path nation were, on the other hand, Made People. The Creator had "made" them from animals to provide company for the First People after their emergence. The Bear Clan, the Buffalo Clan, the Coyote Clan, and Cornsilk's own people, the Ant Clan, had been the creatures their names implied. Through the miracle of the Creator's divine breath, they had changed into humans. But the First People saw them as inferiors because they had once been animals, while the First People had always been humans.

Outsiders, like the Mogollon, the Hohokam, and the northern Tower Builders, were not people at all. Despite their human bodies, the Straight Path people knew they had the souls of beasts. Why, the Mogollon's own legends said they had once lived as fiery wolves in Father Sun's heart and been cast out because they started chewing up his body. As they ran through the heavens toward earth, their blazing wolf bodies had transformed into human shapes. To this day the Straight Path people called them Fire Dogs, for their souls remained predators, watching, waiting for the right time to kill.

The Fire Dogs could not be trusted. They didn't think like humans.

Cornsilk wondered how the elders of the Made People clans got along at Talon Town. Each clan sent their greatest leader to live among the First People, to help and advise them on the ways of the world. The Made People had, after all, lived here much longer than the First People. But Cornsilk had heard that the First People routinely treated their clan leaders little better than Fire Dog slaves.

Sternlight, the legendary Sunwatcher, had the worst reputation. The Straight Path nation had been suffering from drought for sixteen summers, and where once the clans had looked to Sternlight for guidance, now they openly accused him of witchcraft.

Power flowed through everything in the world, from the smallest dandelion seed floating across the desert to the grandest of the Comet People. Priests and shamans called upon Power to help their peoples, to bring health, assure good crops, and influence the rains to fall. Witches used it to benefit themselves.

Two summers ago, a Trader had whispered that he had stumbled into one of Sternlight's private chambers at Talon Town by accident. He said he'd seen piles of exquisite blankets, fine pots filled with chunks of turquoise, jet, malachite, and coral, and baskets of priceless macaw and parrot feathers. He'd also claimed he'd seen a line of human skulls mounted on the wall.

Cornsilk suppressed a shiver.

Good people never accumulated wealth. They shared what they had with their families. Only witches amassed such "things" for their own pleasures.

Leafhopper shifted her squat body to lean over and murmur, "Do you think the First People would starve without us?"

Cornsilk cocked a brow. "Thinking of subtle ways to kill the witches?"

"Shh!" Leafhopper said. She glanced over her shoulder, and her bean-sack dress pulled tight across her flat chest. "No, I was just—"

"Yes, they'd starve. We provide them with almost all of their corn, beans, squash, and dried meat."

Made People hosted every major ceremonial at Talon Town, hauling in massive quantities of food to feed the attendants, and pay the priests, Dancers, and Singers who used their spiritual powers to call upon the gods. When the ritual cycle ended, the Made People stored the excess food at Talon Town. First People grew little of their own food; they survived on those reserves.

No one minded, not if the First People's voices reached the gods and rain made the crops flourish—but that had not happened in many cycles. The gods seemed to have abandoned the First People.

But they still ate the Made People's food.

"So," Leafhopper said, "if we just stopped bringing them food they would die?"

"Or go away. There aren't very many of them left anyway. It wouldn't take much."

First People only married other First People, and many of their children didn't live past the first two summers. As a result, their numbers had dwindled dramatically. The Blessed Night Sun, Matron of Talon Town, and her husband, the Blessed Sun, had two living children—all the others had died. The Sunwatcher, Sternlight, had never married, and many of the other First People at Talon Town had vanished mysteriously. In the other thirteen towns in Straight Path canyon, perhaps another three hundred First People lived.

"But if they all die"—Leafhopper glanced uneasily at Cornsilk—"how will we ever find our ways to the afterlife?"

"We'll just follow the north road to the *sipapu* and travel into the underworlds. We'll get there."

Because the First People had come up through the underworlds, they, and they alone, knew the correct path to the Land of the Ancestors. Legends said that unimaginable dangers, traps and snares, and bizarre half-human creatures, waited to leap upon the unwary soul. Fortunately, the First People knew each trap and hiding place. And, for a price, they would share their secret knowledge.

"Maybe we'd better not starve them," Leafhopper said. "I wish to see my parents again. Besides, I think it might take a lot of Power to starve them. And, as you said, Crow Beard keeps corpse powder in his chamber. I don't think we want to be witched as punishment."

Cornsilk smacked a new handful of meal. Pink flour wafted up around her face. "A really evil witch could beat him."

"Maybe." A smile came to Leafhopper's round face. She shoved up her red headband with a finger, leaving a streak of red meal across her forehead. "Wouldn't *that* be interesting to watch? Witches hurling curses and drowning each other with corpse powder. I'd give a Green Mesa pot to witness that."

Cornsilk absently glanced eastward, toward the Green Mesa clans. "You don't own a Green Mesa pot."

"Nobody does."

"Some of the First People do. They get them in exchange for those little turquoise figurines that guide souls down to the Land of the Ancestors."

"Great," Leafhopper said. "I'll have to steal a figurine to get a pot so I can pay to see witches kill each other."

Cornsilk smiled, grabbed the black-and-white bowl of coarsely ground meal and got to her feet. "I'm going to go heat this up."

"I'm coming with you!" Leafhopper jumped to her feet and stared wide-eyed at Cornsilk. "After all this talk of witches, I'm not going to sit here by myself. What if there's a witch watching from the bushes? He might shoot a witch pill into my mouth and kill me."

Cornsilk frowned out at the red hills, where birds chirped and membranous insect wings glittered in the sunlight. A nighthawk sailed over a line of up-tilted sandstone slabs and disappeared into a stand of prickly pear cactus.

"I don't see anybody out there," Cornsilk said, and started across the plaza . . . briskly. *Just in case.*

Leafhopper trotted at her side, craning her neck to examine anything that moved beyond the walls of Lanceleaf Village.

Five

When the sun sank below the distant mesa, glowing red spikes shot over the horizon, lancing the hearts of drifting Cloud People, turning them into blazing beasts as they lazily roamed the skyworlds. Southward, the tallest peak of Morning Star Mountain gleamed crimson. Shadows cloaked the rolling hills around the sacred mountain. As the light dwindled, birds found perches on the cactuses and scraggly limbs of brush, their feathers fluffed against the cold.

Buckthorn pulled his red-and-black blanket up over his chest. He had camped on a hillside in a fragrant grove of junipers. The branches twisted above him and created a spiky nest at his back. Faint traces of blue smoke from his supper fire had been trapped by the thick needles; they spun and curled as they poked for a way out.

In the spaces between the limbs, Buckthorn could see the early risers among the Evening People.

He yawned. He had run, off and on, all day, and weariness weighted his tall skinny body. As slumber came, his thoughts flitted like moth wings in torchlight. Where did his path lie? What did the Spirits wish of him?

He had traveled to the First Underworld and received a vision from the ancestor Spirits who lived there. A strange vision of his father. He'd been young, with jet-black hair and broad shoulders. He had worn a pure white buckskin shirt and a magnificent turquoise pendant. When the man had first spoken to Buckthorn, he had instantly recognized that voice—because it sounded so much like his own, deep, soft, with a wistful tinge.

A cold breath of wind shivered the juniper grove. Buckthorn tugged his blanket up to his chin. Fanned by the breeze, the gray charcoal in his firepit became a living bed of red winking eyes. He watched them, and yawned again.

If only he had understood what his father had been trying to tell him.

"There is danger ahead, my son. You must have the heart of a cloud in order to walk upon the wind."

"The heart of a cloud . . ." Buckthorn whispered. Deep blue puffs of cloud sailed overhead, their edges shining with starlight. Wind stirred the juniper branches. The gnarled trees creaked and moaned in complaint. "But what does that mean?"

His weary soul seemed to rise at the urging of Wind Baby and coasted on the current like corn pollen on a summer zephyr. His father's soft voice slipped into his Dream with the lightness of a bobcat's footfalls. . . .

"Come this way, son. Come this way."

Buckthorn seemed to float, breathing hard, and stared into the black eyes of the young man who had guided him through the First Underworld. The man bent over Buckthorn, smiling, his handsome face, with the straight nose and large dark eyes, glowing reddish in the glare of the wind-blown coals. He wore the same white buckskin shirt and magnificent turquoise pendant. His loose long hair flipped around his broad shoulders in the gusts. His white moccasins reached his knees and seemed to blend with his long shirt. Blue, red, and black beads chevroned the tops of his moccasins.

"I am happy to see you, Father." Buckthorn rubbed sleep from his eyes. Stargleam sheathed the junipers, and he spotted an owl soaring through the darkness overhead, its wings flashing as it circled.

"Get up, my son. I must show you the secret place where the Cloud People hide their hearts."

Buckthorn braced an elbow in the forest duff and sat up. "Do you know where it is?"

"Yes, my son. Come. I will take you there."

Buckthorn threw back his blanket and got to his feet.

His father walked up the hill to the sage-covered crest, where the wind whipped his long hair and the hem of his white shirt. He stood tall, silhouetted against a star-sprinkled expanse of deep blue.

Carefully, Buckthorn followed, avoiding rocks and the coyote holes dug into the slope. Marked only by black spots the size of his head, they were difficult to see. He joined his father and stood with his head tipped back, studying Spider Woman. She had already crawled to the middle of the sky. The three stars that made up her body angled westward, while her legs crept out in every direction.

His father turned to Buckthorn. *"Are you ready, my son?"*

"I think so. What do I have to do?"

"This place we are going is very far. You cannot run the distance in a human body."

"Then how will I get there?"

His father placed a gentle hand on Buckthorn's shoulder. *"I will help you. Get down on all fours."*

Buckthorn dropped to his hands and knees and saw his father do the same beside him. They looked very strange as fourleggeds. A tender smile curled his father's mouth; he lifted a hand and scratched Buckthorn's neck, as if to dislodge biting fleas.

"What are you doing, Father?" Buckthorn hunched uncomfortably. "What—"

"Now run," his father instructed. *"Down the hill. Run."*

Buckthorn scrambled forward through the sage and sand, feeling foolish. "Father, why am I doing this, I . . ."

A beautiful coyote with a thick glossy coat trotted up beside Buckthorn. *"You are doing this,"* the coyote said, *"so that you may fly like the wind. Follow me now. Run!"*

The coyote galloped away through the sage, veering around cactus.

"Blessed Spirits!" Buckthorn said sullenly. "You're very fast, Father!"

He scrambled down the slope as quickly as he could. His knees tangled in his long shirt, and his palms landed in dead cactus pads that lay hidden in the darkness. When his right hand suddenly sunk into a rabbit burrow and landed hard four hands below, jamming his wrist, he screamed, "Yeowww!"

His father lifted his shining muzzle and howled, too, yipping and whining. *"Come on, boy! We haven't all night!"*

Buckthorn picked himself up and tried again, crawling through the brush with his face tipped so as not to have his eyes clawed out by the twigs. Thorns shredded his shirt and tore at his arms and legs.

At the bottom of the hill, he saw his father loping far out ahead, winding down a deer trail, and Buckthorn's own labors seemed to grow immensely easier. He trotted after his father, then broke into a lope, moving with the swiftness of a swallow, leaping upthrust stones effortlessly. He caught up with his father in no time, and ran at his side with his black-spotted pink tongue dangling from the side of his mouth.

"Father?" Buckthorn asked as they angled down toward a deeply cut drainage channel. A thread of water glinted in the bottom. "Have I always had a coyote's soul?"

"Yes, my son. Always."

His father leaped forward. He splashed through the trickle of water and bounded up the opposite side of the drainage, his coat glinting as though netted with fallen stars.

Buckthorn glanced down at his furry coyote body and felt warm and happy. He raced after his father. The silvered trail sped by beneath his soft paws. Freedom, like cold fire, tingled through his veins.

As he splashed through the muddy water, he threw his head back and yipped . . . letting his father know he followed.

When he reached the lip of the drainage and trotted out across the grassy flats, the scent of pines and water rose powerfully. His eyes widened. *Where am I? What happened to the desert?*

Jagged pine-whiskered mountains thrust up around him. He ran through an alpine meadow, surrounded on all sides by winter-bare aspen trees. A few old leaves clung to the white-barked branches, quaking in the cold wind. Elk grazed in the shadows. Their eyes glinted when they jerked their heads up to watch Buckthorn pass. Through the heart of the meadow, a small crystal-clear brook babbled its way down the slope.

Awe filled Buckthorn. His father trotted in the distance, his bushy tail down, his fur shimmering in the brilliant wash of moonlight. *Moonlight!*

Buckthorn looked eastward. Sister Moon crouched full and bright on the horizon. She had just cleared a vast range of shining peaks that rose like gigantic ice spears. Clouds encircled the summits.

His father stopped at the top of the grassy meadow and waited. When Buckthorn loped up, his father used his black nose to point. *"There, my son. The turquoise cave is up there."*

"The turquoise cave? The one I saw in my vision in the kiva?"

"Yes, son."

Buckthorn looked. "It's up there?" His night-sharp vision searched the lofty peaks and he spied a black spot, round, like a dark womb that receded endlessly into the side of the ice spear. The opening faced east. Buckthorn's belly prickled. He nervously licked his muzzle and expelled a frosty breath. "It . . . it reminds me of the tunnel to the underworlds, Father."

The coyote peered at him unblinking, his shining eyes pale green in the moonlight. *"Come, let us go."*

Buckthorn trotted up the snowy slope after his father, his paws slipping. Snow clotted the fur between his toes and made them ache. As they climbed, freezing wind blasted their faces, sleeking their fur back and forcing them to squint.

His father stood at the lip of the cave with one paw lifted, his nose thrust forward. He sniffed the dank moss-scented air. As if from something threatening, he backed away, his tail tucked between his legs.

"What is it?" Buckthorn asked.

"*I will stand guard. You must go in alone, my son. The cave is not open to me.*"

"But . . ." Buckthorn peered into the cave and his front legs shook. "How do you know it is open to me?"

His father's voice echoed hollowly from the cave: "*Go now, hurry.*"

His father turned and trotted to the base of the slope, where he stood scrutinizing the meadow for movement.

Buckthorn took a tentative step forward. As he edged closer, he noticed that the cave sloped downward. Moonlight spilled inside, lighting a narrow strip of the interior like a torch. A thicket of creeping barberry bushes blocked his way. Their waxy holly-shaped leaves reflected the moon glow.

Buckthorn lightly stepped into the thicket and tested the wind. The cave smelled oddly musty. It looked tiny and narrow, but he couldn't really tell. The thin crescent of light only went back a few body lengths. Beyond that the darkness extended forever. He pushed through the thicket and walked deeper.

His toenails clicked on the stone, and he heard water dripping, a melodic *plop, plop*. His whiskers quivered. The deeper he went, the warmer it felt.

Buckthorn looked around. As his eyes adjusted to the dimness, he could make out the thin veil of moisture on the walls. Drops slid down and pooled in the undulations of the floor, shining blackly.

He walked faster, his body swinging down the incline. The floor of the cave warmed his paws, and melted the snow clotted in the fur between his toes. He shivered with delight.

He entered what appeared to be a large chamber. A black pool of water covered the floor, and he could locate the source of the drip, straight above, draining down through the rock and splatting into the pool. Mist hovered near the roof, tendrils escaping into the brighter corridor, floating upward until they reached the mouth of the cave, where they shimmered. As they rose into the luminous sky, they gathered the cold around them like a thick woolly coat and grew, and grew, expanding to become clouds.

Buckthorn watched in wonder.

Sister Moon cleared the lip of the cave, hanging like a huge silver ball in the sky. When he turned back to the chamber, he expected to see a flood of revealing light pour down, but as she rose higher, he saw a flicker, then a series of flashes, as if bolts of lightning shot back and forth across the interior. A blinding azure blaze built, and a low half-moan half-growl rumbled in his throat. Buckthorn settled on his haunches and whined in fear. Now he could see. . . .

Over thousands of sun cycles, percolating water had carved a rounded hollow in a thick vein of turquoise, and this hollow *was* the chamber. Sharp fragments jutted out everywhere, like crystals in a geode. The moon glow made them burn with a brilliant blue fire. As Sister Moon continued her climb into the sky, the light shifted and Buckthorn's jaws parted in awe as light streamed directly down the entrance. The cave transformed itself into a tumbling waterfall of ice-blue, sparkling azure, flowing across the roof and flooding the floor. The entire blue world seemed to be on fire, the sacred stone flaming, searing his eyes, and tingling like sparks in his veins.

The conflagration died.

Just died.

Sister Moon rose higher and diffuse pewter light filled the cave.

Buckthorn blinked.

Heart hammering, he gazed down into the pool. He could still see the turquoise lining the basin, but it shone dully, like chunks of common slate.

The pool wavered, as if pushed by a breeze, but Wind Baby could not penetrate so deep. Buckthorn's eyes narrowed. He glanced up at the drip; it continued its rhythmic fall into the water: *plop, plop, plop.* Not the cause. The pool began to whirl and rock. Water washed over the walls of the cave.

Buckthorn stretched out on his belly and rested his chin on his paws to watch.

Someone shouted, an agonized cry. Then a scream, a thin wavering thread of sound, made him leap to his feet and scramble, slipping and sliding, up the wet corridor as fast as his paws would take him.

Just as he reached the barberry thicket, sharp pain lanced Buckthorn's belly, white hot, like a war lance. He let out a ragged yip, and fell back, sliding on his side down the incline until he struck the wall and spun to a halt. Water soaked his fur. He lay panting, his gaze seeking his attacker.

Thunder roared through the cave, but from the depths he made out voices, hundreds, no *thousands*, of shouting, screaming people. Then . . . *he saw them.* They oozed from the very walls. The cave filled with running people and slamming fists. Like an enraged swarm of bees, they crowded up to kick him, beating him with war clubs, yelling in an unknown tongue. Buckthorn huddled into a ball and yipped desperately, praying his father would come and . . .

A tall beautiful woman stepped from inside the turquoise cave and the enraged people faded as though they had never been. He could just make out her face, with its turned-up nose. Waist-length black hair draped her shoulders. She wore a magnificent scarlet dress, a shade he had never seen, iridescent like sunrise. A little Power bundle hung from her belt, and a turquoise pendant from a cord around her neck.

"Who are you?" Buckthorn called. "What do you wish from me? Did you make the vision go away?"

"I make visions come and go." Her deep voice sent chills up his spine. She walked closer, almost too graceful to be human, and peered into his eyes, as if searching his soul. "You are Coyote Clan. Why are you here?"

Breath shuddering, he answered, "M-my father . . . he brought me."

She knelt down, so close that Buckthorn could feel the warmth of her body. Locks of her long hair brushed his fur. He gazed into the woman's huge coal-black eyes with the shock of a lizard who suddenly feels the wind of a swooping hawk. He couldn't move.

The woman studied his body in minute detail. She touched each of his paws and ran her fingers down his furry back. When she examined his pointed ears, her hand moved with such aching tenderness that it set Buckthorn's heart to pounding.

"What is your name?" she asked.

"B-Buckthorn."

She rose to her feet and stood like a slender pillar of scarlet flame. "Buckthorn of the Coyote Clan. Who is your father?"

"I—I don't know . . . really." With his muzzle he gestured to the moonlit cave entry. "Shall I call to him? He is in the meadow—"

"He was very bold to bring you here. Tell him I said so." Her stare bored into his face. "I usually kill curiosity seekers."

"*Kill?*" Buckthorn asked breathlessly. "Why? Who are you?"

"I am the Keeper of the sacred Tortoise Bundle. My clan is . . . was . . . the Hollow Hoof Clan."

Buckthorn rose on trembling legs. "Was? Your clan is dead?"

"Dead and gone. Its heart, the Bundle, was stolen twenty-two summers ago. The people lost faith, they married into other clans. They drifted apart. I am all that is left of the noble Hollow Hoof."

Sorrow animated her words. She peered back into the turquoise cave, slate gray now, as still and silent as a tomb. Her gaze fixed on the pool, and her brows slanted down. Perhaps she saw something there that he did not. Something that held her unwavering attention. The corners of her mouth twitched.

For a long while she did not speak. Then, very softly, she said, "Ah, I understand." She nodded. "I see now why he brought you here. He *really* believed I'd kill you. Hmm. For that reason, I think I'll grant you some advice. Study the ways of the coyotes, Buckthorn. They are quick and smarter than humans believe. They watch from a distance, in silence, until they know it is time to move. Always be smarter than people think. Never take action before you are certain of your goal."

Shadows filled the hollows of her eyes, turning them into huge black wells. "In the coming moons, there are many who will seek to cage you. You will have to be very quick and very smart, or . . ." A grim smile curled her lips. "Or the next time you return here, Buckthorn of the Coyote Clan, your world will be dying all around you. Be prepared to make an offering. Do you understand?"

"An offering?" He paused uncertainly. "You mean like two mice on a juniper stick?"

Her smile waned. "I will demand much more from you than the Monster Thlatsina."

"How will I know what it is you wish me to bring—"

"*You will know.*"

From the pool behind her a huge figure slowly emerged. Water cascaded from its body, shining with moonlight. Buckthorn's muzzle gaped as the creature dropped to all fours. It leaped and kicked like a prancing deer. Only when the creature looked straight at him did Buckthorn see its massive twisted face, coated with pink clay from the sacred lake where the thlatsinas were born.

Mudhead!

The sacred being extended his arms and began to Dance. He whirled like a leaf in the primal winds of creation, floating higher, the rhythmic stamping of his feet pounding out the heartbeat of the world.

When the Mudhead kicked and soared like an arrow for Buckthorn's belly, Buckthorn let out a horrified shriek . . .

And jerked awake sitting up in his blanket. Drenched in sweat, he blinked to clear his blurry eyes, searching the starlit juniper grove. His firepit had blown clean of ash. One lump of charcoal sat in the ring of stones, completely dead.

"P-Power Dream . . ."

Buckthorn looked down. The trembling fingers of his right hand had knotted in the fabric over his aching belly. It took an act of will to pry them loose. When he brought the hand up, he frowned at the blood, not understanding at first.

"It can't be!"

He jerked up his long brown shirt, and starlight shone on the shallow cuts that covered his stomach and legs. Frantic, Buckthorn pulled up his sleeves. He gazed wide-eyed at the bloody scratches.

Just as if he'd loped through brush!

. . . Or rolled into the spiky nest of dead juniper limbs at his back.

A pack of coyotes broke into song, serenading the silence with mournful cries. Buckthorn bit his lip. Their beautiful voices echoed through the desert stillness. He listened intently for a time.

"Whew," he finally breathed. "It's all right. I don't understand any of their words."

He snuggled into the worn softness of his blankets and watched the darkness. As his gaze roamed the sparkling heavens, his thoughts kept returning to the beautiful woman in the turquoise cave high in the icy mountains.

Six

Footsteps. Very faint.

Thistle turned toward the leather door hanging that kept some of the cold at bay. As she moved, thick black hair fell over her shoulders, framing her fine-boned face. Thirty summers old, she stood ten hands tall and slight of build. She cocked her head, listening.

The steps came up the dirt path slowly, as though her husband's soul drifted in one of the skyworlds, seeking answers he could not find. He placed his feet so lightly that his sandals barely crunched the gravel.

She knew that walk. Knew what it meant. She had dreamed of yucca root last night, a warning of the nearness of death. But whose?

Thistle wiped her sweating palms on the hem of her lichen-dyed yellow dress, and looked to her left at Cornsilk and Fledgling. The children slept beneath brightly colored blankets. Only the top of Cornsilk's head showed, but Fledgling had thrown off most of his covers. She listened to the deep rhythms of their breathing, letting the sounds comfort her fears.

From the woodpile beside the slab-lined firepit, she picked up a pine knot. When she placed it on the glowing bed of coals, flames crackled and sparks winked upward toward the roof's smoke hole.

Her gaze roamed their small house, four body-lengths square. They had built it from sandstone, then plastered both interior and exterior walls with white clay carried all the way from the sacred lake in the south. A small window with a leather curtain pierced the rear wall. In front of her, on either side of the doorway, a black long-necked water jug stood in a line with several plain pots which held red, yellow, white, and blue cornmeal, as well as a variety of Healing herbs. She and Beargrass had collected them on a trip southward. It had been a bright spring morning filled with laughter and tender touches: turkey mullein for heart ailments, screwbean for stomach distress, prickly pear cactus pads to use as drawing poultices for bruises and burns, and the roots of yucca to ease the pain caused by the knotted-joint disease. Mugwort leaves to induce miscarriages.

A ring of scalps encircled Beargrass' weapons, his bow, two bone stilettos, and a long obsidian knife, which hung on the wall to her right, over their bed. After being carved from the head, the souls of the enemy scalps transformed themselves into water and seed beings, and bestowed long life and great spiritual Power upon the warrior brave enough to have taken them in battle.

A flat basket of stone tools and a pot of dried juniper berries rested to her right. When brewed into a strong tea, the Spirit of the berries trickled into a person's soul and warded off witchcraft. She had been using these more often of late. Rumors ran the roads, saying that entire villages had turned to witchcraft to protect themselves from the ambitious First People at Talon Town—especially the Powerful priest, Sternlight, and the terrible Crow Beard.

Thistle wet her lips anxiously. Her gaze drifted to the right. At the foot of their bed sat a large, elaborately painted pot, the ceramic lid weighted down with a heavy stone. The pot held extraordinary trade goods: red and green parrot feathers, jet and turquoise jewelry, seashells brought all the way from the great ocean, two flutes made from the leg bones of large cats, and six intricately carved statues—alien gods, with long teeth and bulging eyes.

The statues had been gifts from the Blessed Sun, Chief Crow Beard of Talon Town, and neither she nor Beargrass could have refused them. They terrified her. When Thistle least expected it, the Spirits in the statues would suddenly wake and send Power rushing like melted rock through her veins. She was no Spirit Dreamer, not even a seeker of visions, so their message eluded her. She knew only that they, too, feared the future.

The steps halted outside the door.

A gentle voice called, "You should not be awake, my wife. The Evening People have walked from dusk until nearly dawn. Did I not tell you you should—"

"And I *begged* you not to attend the meeting!" She leaped to her feet and went to stand over the children.

Beargrass pulled open the deerhide curtain, ducked through the low T-shaped doorway, and entered the house. He had a narrow face with a round nose, and eyes the color of old cedar bark, an odd gray-brown that glinted in the firelight. His long black hair hung loosely about his shoulders. Though he had seen only thirty-three summers, lines etched his forehead and ran crookedly from the corners of his eyes. He wore a beautiful blue blanket over his shoulders. Beneath it, his long red-and-black striped shirt hung to below his knees.

"I regret that the meeting took so long," he apologized. "I hope you didn't worry." He removed his blanket and quietly folded it. "How is Cornsilk?"

Thistle looked at him, knowing that he was delaying. *It's worse than I thought.* "She's still weak, but her cough is gone."

"And Fledgling?"

Thistle knelt beside the fifteen-summers-old youth and gently tucked the blanket around his bare back. Her long hair fell over her shoulders, shielding her strained expression. "He asked me many questions about where you had gone, and what news the runners had brought. He . . ."

Her hands started to shake. Tightening them into fists, she got to her feet and walked to stand face-to-face with her husband. "Tell me. What did they say?"

The grim runners had arrived at sundown, drenched in sweat. They had run for three days straight, neither eating nor sleeping. They went immediately to the clan Matron and asked to speak with Beargrass and Thistle, saying they brought urgent news from Ironwood, the great War Chief of Talon Town.

Panicked, Thistle had refused to leave her house, using her daughter's illness as an excuse, and advised her husband to do the same. He had ignored her—as loyal to the Blessed Sun and his favored War Chief now as he had been sixteen summers before.

Beargrass walked to their willow-twig sleeping mats and

placed the folded blanket atop them. With his broad back to her, he murmured, "They say Crow Beard is dying."

"Are they sure? But how *can* they be after—"

"Please." Beargrass turned, and she saw the ache in his eyes. "Let us sit down and speak of this calmly." He gestured to the mats spread around the fire.

Thistle cast a terrified look at the children, but did as he'd asked. Legs unsteady, she dropped to the south mat, facing the doorway, drew up her knees and wrapped her arms tightly around them. "Do you believe it?"

Beargrass knelt on the north mat, across from her. The golden aura of the fire bathed his shirt with a curious orange color. "Wraps-His-Tail told me himself. He is the War Chief's deputy and dearest friend. He is bound to the truth. He would not lie, as I wouldn't have when I was the War Chief's deputy. Thistle, the Blessed Sun has seen almost fifty-five summers. Given his frailty and the many illnesses he has suffered, Spider Woman has been generous to give him so many. I pray she—"

"But what will become of us?" The desperation in her voice surprised her. More quietly, she asked, "Of our *family*? He can't die! Not yet. Besides, how many times have we heard his death proclaimed? At least five! I do *not* believe it!"

Beargrass shifted uncomfortably and his shadow leaped over the wall behind him like a silent dancing ghost. His wrinkles deepened. "I admit that Crow Beard may just be off on another Soul March to the afterworld, but I don't think so." He rubbed his hands together, warming them. "In any case, we'll know soon enough. Sternlight will place his body on the great foot-drum in the First People's kiva and instruct slaves to watch over him."

Thistle closed her eyes. "If War Chief Ironwood doesn't slit his throat first to make certain. He hates Crow Beard. The man is—"

"*Hush, wife!*" Beargrass glanced around anxiously. "You know Wind Baby is his Spirit Helper! He tells Ironwood every word he hears!"

Thistle leaped up and ran to the door to peer out into the predawn darkness. A pale lavender glow lit the mountainous eastern horizon, pushing up the indigo of night, making way for Father Sun's daily rebirth. From this hillside above Lanceleaf Village, she could see the broad plaza and most of the valley. Within the protective rectangle of the village, the plaza was gray and silent.

Wide-eyed, she studied the desert plants. Not even the barest of breezes moved the sagebrush. She let the door curtain fall closed. "I think we are safe."

As she walked back toward her husband, forbidden thoughts crowded her soul, old fears she had worked cycles to suppress. What would life be like without her children? Every vista, every flower or tiny bug, looked brighter and more beautiful when she looked at it with them. She put a hand to her face to cover her tears.

"Don't cry, my wife." Beargrass drew her down to the mat beside him. "We *are* safe. Not even Wind Baby would betray us after what we have gone through for the Blessed Sun."

"I wasn't crying for us, my husband, but for the child. Don't you see? Crow Beard wouldn't have sent runners to us unless he himself believed he was about to die, and he was warning us that . . . that we might lose our child."

Beargrass put a gentle hand on her soft hair. "That makes no sense, my wife. Crow Beard has other children to rule after he is gone. If Crow Beard had wanted ours to come to Talon Town, he would demand it outright. Not send messengers with news that he is dying. What purpose would it serve?"

"I don't know," she answered softly.

He nuzzled his forehead against hers. "Listen to me. The Chief abandoned his offspring out of kindness, and has compensated us well for keeping his secret. Look at the fine blankets we own. The magnificent turquoise jewelry. The copper bells from the Hohokam people far to the southwest. Each is worth more than the rearing we've provided. He'd never ask for the child back. He couldn't be so cruel."

Hope, light and sweet, sent tendrils through her. She looked up at Beargrass. "Do you think so? Truly?"

"Yes. Maybe the Chief only wished to warn us that if he died the payments would stop coming."

"Yes. Yes, of course!" A desperate laugh escaped her lips. She clutched handfuls of her yellow skirt. "That's why he asked Ironwood to send runners! We have nothing to fear. There will be no more payments, but what do we care? The secret will die with us and our family will be safe forever!"

Beargrass whispered, "Yes," but his gaze darted uncertainly over the clay-washed walls.

"What's wrong? What are you thinking?"

Beargrass rose and went to stand over the children, his gaze on Cornsilk. Long raven strands of her hair spread over the sleeping mat. Beargrass reached down to touch them, but stopped a hand's breadth short, probably because she'd been ill, and he didn't wish to wake her. As though it hurt not to touch his daughter, he drew back his open hand and clenched it into a fist.

"I was thinking that we are not the only ones left who know."

Thistle swallowed her response when she saw Fledgling rouse. Their voices had been too loud. He yawned and stretched his arms over his head. His round tawny face gleamed when he rolled on his back to look up at Beargrass. "Hello, Father."

Beargrass knelt by his side. "I'm sorry I woke you, my son. It is not yet morning. Sleep some more."

Sleepily, Fledgling asked, "Did you just return?"

"Yes. It has been a long night."

"What did the runners want?"

"Oh, many things, most—"

"Father." Fledgling lifted himself on one elbow. The flame glow made his dark eyes shine as if coated with pure copper. His bare chest looked skinny and very pale. "The ghosts in the afterworld told me that they had come to ask you to be a warrior for the Blessed Sun again. It scared me."

"No, no, my son." Beargrass cast a worried glance at Thistle. "Nothing so serious."

Blood drained from Thistle's face. A lie? Was he saving this news for the last?

For two summers Beargrass had served as one of the Chief's most loyal guards. On the last night of his service, Sternlight had come to Beargrass with the newborn child in his arms, a tiny mewling creature wrapped in a magnificent turquoise-studded blanket. The Sunwatcher had explained Crow Beard's shame: *"The Blessed Sun mated with one of his wife's slaves. An error in judgment to be sure—more so since this child came from the union. Crow Beard does not wish the child dead, but you know how Night Sun is. She will have the infant skinned alive before the entire town. Beargrass, Chief Crow Beard knows your wife recently bore a child. He values your loyalty and wishes to ask a great favor of you. Would you and your wife claim the child as your own? Compensation will be given, of course. You must only vow never to tell anyone. . . ."*

Beargrass had not even hesitated. The bargain struck, he and Thistle had taken the child and come here, to the northern frontier where Thistle had Ant Clan relatives. She had told people the babies were twins and struggled to suckle both. When her milk ran out, she'd found another woman to nurse Fledgling.

Fledgling squinted his right eye suspiciously, then looked back and forth between Thistle and Beargrass, as if judging their faces. "Then what news did the runners bring, Father? I heard Matron Clover when she came to announce their arrival. She said it was urgent."

Beargrass smoothed tangled hair away from Fledgling's face. "Always so many questions, my son. Well, the most important news was that the barbaric Tower Builders raided Turtle Village again. They took several women, burned a few houses. Turtle Village has promised revenge. The runners wanted to warn us that our village sits right in the middle of the squabble."

"But why did they wish to speak with you *and mother*, Father?" Fledgling turned to Thistle.

"Because," she answered, thinking quickly, "I am a master mason, my son. If we decide to buttress Lanceleaf Village's defenses, I will design and build the new walls."

His face fell in disappointment. "That was all?"

Beargrass shrugged and smiled. "I told you it was nothing. Now, I think it's time you dreamed your soul back to the afterworld, my son. There must be many Spirits there who want to run and hunt with you."

Through a wide yawn, Fledgling said, "Ruddy Boy and I were in the middle of killing Fire Dog warriors. He needs my help more than he'll admit."

Ruddy Boy had died from a broken arm three summers ago.

He'd been Fledgling's best friend—and still was, it seemed.

"Sleep, son." Beargrass pulled the blankets up over Fledgling's chest and he closed his eyes. "Tell Ruddy Boy I miss him."

"I will, Father."

Beargrass waited until Fledgling's breath grew deep before returning to the fire to sit at Thistle's side. They stared at each other. Beargrass gently ran his fingers down the curve of her jaw. "I am very tired," he whispered. "Let us speak no more of this tonight."

Thistle breathed the question: "Did the runners ask you to be a warrior for the Blessed Sun again?"

Beargrass' mouth tightened. "No, not . . . not precisely. Wraps-His-Tail said that War Chief Ironwood wished me to know that hostility was increasing between the clans and their allied villages. Ironwood asked if I would be willing to return as his deputy if warfare broke out."

"And what did you answer?"

Beargrass hesitated. "You mustn't be upset—"

"You told him 'yes!' "

"I said I would do whatever the Blessed Sun wished, and I put it that way for a reason. While Ironwood may want me to return to Talon Town, I do not believe Chief Crow Beard does."

Thistle clenched her fists. "And you think that the War Chief will understand this? That you do not really wish to return and will only out of loyalty to Crow Beard?"

Beargrass nodded. "I do. Despite what you think, my wife, Ironwood is a man of honor."

Thistle studied her hands. In all the summers they had known each other, she had never criticized men he respected—even if she knew far more about them than he did. "Go to bed, my husband. You may need the rest more than either of us knows."

"Are you angry?"

"No. No, just . . . weary." She reached out and gave his hand a squeeze.

"Please come to bed with me. You must be as exhausted as I am."

"Soon. I promise. I want to think for a time longer."

He stroked her back. "As you wish."

He pulled his long shirt over his head and draped it on the pot at the foot of the sleeping mats. The hard muscles of his naked body gleamed. "You must not worry. Not yet. Wait until we know for certain if Crow Beard—"

"I'll try, my husband. I love you. Rest now. I'll be there before you realize it."

He stretched out on his back on the bedding. "I hope so. I don't sleep well without you close." Pulling up the cotton blanket woven with strips of rabbit fur, he slipped an arm beneath his head and closed his eyes.

Thistle turned away. The fire had burned down to a bed of glimmering coals ringed by white ash. The house seemed to breathe and sway in the crimson radiance, like an amorphous Spirit animal going about its nightly duties, oblivious to the petty lives of humans. She pulled a piece of juniper from the woodpile and laid it on the coals. Flames spluttered, sending wisps of blue smoke upward.

For many summers cold fear had lain like a slumbering rattlesnake beneath her heart. Tonight, the serpent had raised its head and looked her in the eye, issuing a Spirit challenge. Would she ever face the truth about the child?

She had never believed Sternlight's story. How could she? She, Thistle, had worked as a mason in Talon Town, helping to construct the multistoried buildings. She had seen the Blessed Sun daily. Even now, so many summers later, she could recall every detail of his face, and in no way did the child resemble him. The arching brows and broad cheekbones were not Chief Crow Beard's, nor were the thin bones and pale golden skin. As well, at the time of the child's birth, the Chief had been gone for ten moons on a trading mission to the Hohokam. The child might have been a late birth, but she doubted it. She distinctly recalled the winter night when Beargrass had placed the child in her arms—she had remarked that it looked to be an *early* birth.

Thistle hugged her knees to her chest. Less than a moon after they'd left Talon Town, terrible rumors had reached them. Young Fawn, one of Night Sun's slaves, missing for over a moon, had been found dead in a trash mound, her corpse buried beneath a winter's worth of debris. She had been stabbed twice in the breast, then her belly had been slit open, and the child she'd carried stolen from her womb—no one knew why, or what had happened to the baby.

Curiously, the rumors said that the great Matron of the First People hadn't made a single inquiry about the murder of a valued slave. But the runners hastened to add that Night Sun had been deathly ill, locked in her chamber with a fever. She had thrashed about like a madwoman they said, refusing to see any healer. Old Dune the Derelict, the great seer, said that she yearned so for her absent husband that the Spirit had left her heart. And, indeed, just after Crow Beard returned, she recovered.

Thistle studied the faint movements of the deerhide curtain. Wind Baby had roused. It would not be safe to say anything aloud now, but the fabric of her soul remembered the day Young Fawn missed her first bleeding. It had been a gorgeous spring day. The blooming desert plants had scented the air with sweetness. The young woman had been proud and excited. For nine moons she had been secretly loving a very powerful man, a man whispered to be close to War Chief Ironwood. Young Fawn claimed he was a warrior, but dared not mention his name for fear both of them would be punished. She had not been bold enough to ask Night Sun's permission for the coupling, as was proper for a slave. Owners naturally wished to supervise mate selection, hoping for stronger, better slaves. Young Fawn had vowed she would tell Night Sun as soon as she mustered the courage.

The child would have been eight, or eight and a half, moons at the time Young Fawn disappeared. Even if Young Fawn had never asked permission, clearly Night Sun had seen her pregnancy and allowed it to continue. Unless . . . had she banned even her servant women from her chamber during her fever? Had Night Sun finally risen, seen her pregnant slave, and heard the rumors of the Chief's indiscretion? Had she ordered Young Fawn killed in vengeance?

The small sounds of the dawn became incredibly vivid. The log in the fire cracked and hissed, flooding the white walls with ruby light. An owl hooted as it sailed over the bluffs. Somewhere up in the pines a pack of wolves serenaded the dying darkness, their mournful cries echoing with haunting clarity in the desert silence.

She lifted her gaze to her children.

No, not Crow Beard's child. Those probing eyes, that skin the color of winter-brown cottonwood leaves . . . the father could only be one man. War Chief Ironwood.

Terror took hold of Thistle. She tiptoed to her tool basket and pulled out a hafted chert knife, then silently went to her children. Slumping down against the wall between them, she propped the knife on her knees.

Orders were given and carried out with painstaking accuracy at Talon Town. Lives often depended upon it. Perhaps Night Sun had discovered Ironwood's dalliance with her slave and ordered Sternlight to kill Young Fawn. But why would the Sunwatcher have taken it upon himself to rescue the infant from the young woman's womb? Had he owed a favor to Ironwood?

Cornsilk stirred. She reached for her mother's skirt, and when she touched the yellow hem, she exhaled contentedly. Thistle tenderly held her daughter's hand.

"Sleep, my daughter. You must get well."

"Love you, Mother," Cornsilk murmured. Weakly, she opened her eyes.

Wonder prickled the edges of Thistle's soul. The young woman had eyes like thunder, powerful, promising a storm. Some of the village children had accused her of having "witch eyes." Their parents had scolded them for saying such a terrible thing, but Thistle could see the fear on the adults' faces. Half of them believed it. And the raven that kept returning just made it worse.

The older Cornsilk grew, the less she fit in. How long would it be before she became a stranger to her own clan?

Wind Baby flipped the door curtain and crept inside to listen to them. The fire hissed and popped, sending out a wreath of sparks. Thistle waited until Wind Baby left before she even allowed herself to think about the subject again.

Ironwood had many enemies. Did any of them suspect he had a child?

She sank back against the wall. They had but one choice: to run, to take the children far away.

Tomorrow she would tell Beargrass her suspicions about Ironwood, try to convince him that Sternlight had lied, and show him the danger they faced.

Would he believe her?

She gripped her knife hard.

She had to make him.

A furious gust of wind whistled around Talon Town and flapped the leather curtain over Snake Head's doorway. He leaned back against the white wall of his personal chamber and snugged his tan-and-yellow blanket more tightly about his shoulders. Around the curtain, he could see Evening People sparkling like crushed quartz crystals tossed upon a soft black mink hide. The fragrance of burning sage drifted on the night. In the middle of his floor, his warming bowl sizzled and flared redly, the coals casting a crimson gleam over the gloriously painted walls.

The chamber spread four by five body-lengths across. On the northern wall, the Badger Thlatsina Danced, his black body encircled by a ring of enemy scalps. Snake Head had cut them from the heads of eight Fire Dogs himself, trophies of the battles he'd fought and won. He smiled at them. His people performed a Scalp Dance to transform the hairy prizes into water and seed beings, so that they might bestow long life and great spiritual Power upon the owner—but he'd never felt any. To Snake Head, scalps were dead human hides, nothing more.

In the southwestern corner of the room, a red macaw fidgeted in its large willow-stick cage. It slid back and forth on its foot pole, squawking softly. A bowl of piñon nuts and sunflower seeds sat on the floor of the cage, surrounded by cracked hulls. The big bird stretched six hands from beak to tail and had a magnificent white face with blue, yellow, and red feathers. The macaw watched him intently.

Snake Head kept his sleeping mats on the far side of the room, because the malevolent bird took any opportunity to bite him. Once, just after Snake Head had obtained the bird from a Trader, he'd slept near the cage and accidentally rolled into the bars in his sleep. He'd awakened when a taloned foot nearly clawed his ear off.

Bowls clattered behind Snake Head, and he turned to see Mourning Dove bend to collect his dirty supper dishes.

Tiny, delicate, she had a face like a chipmunk, with plump cheeks, wide eyes, and a pointed nose. When Snake Head stood, the top of her head barely reached the middle of his chest. She wore a beautiful red dress tonight—one he'd given her. Olivella shells from the western ocean decorated the fringes on her sleeves, clicking pleasantly as she went about her nightly duties.

She glanced up, saw him watching, and asked, "May I go now, Blessed Snake Head?" She returned her gaze to the coals in the warming bowl, but her voice shook.

Snake Head sipped the cup of tea she'd made him. It tasted sweetly of dried phlox petals. "No, let's talk for a time."

"But I—I promised Creeper I would—"

"Creeper is one of the Made People," Snake Head reminded. "I am one of the First People. My needs come before his."

"Yes, of course, forgive me." Mourning Dove set the pile of dishes on the white plastered floor and stood. "What is it you require, Blessed Snake Head?"

"Look at me."

She lifted her gaze, and Snake Head smiled. Her eyes fascinated him, drawing him as a wounded rabbit draws a mountain lion. Fear and hatred shone in those soft brown depths: for him, and him alone. The fire of her emotions stirred his passions. Though she had always been his mother's slave, she'd been assigned to take care of Snake Head since he'd been a boy. And he'd *used* her. At the age of ten summers, he'd first ordered her to lie with him. During the insanity of adolescence, he'd called her to his chambers as often as four times a day. She had serviced him without a word, speaking only when spoken to.

She'd become his only confidante, which he found very ironic. He had been a privileged child, and she had always been a slave. Well, not always. At the age of thirteen summers, her Fire Dog mother had been taken captive by the northern Tower Builders. Mourning Dove's father had been a Tower Builder. She'd lived among the barbarians for the first eight summers of her life, until she'd been stolen by Straight Path warriors. The strange mixture of traditions had given her curious notions. She believed in the prophecies of her Fire Dog mother's people, for example, but traced her descent through her father, as did all Tower Builders.

Snake Head smiled. He'd been a precocious child. He'd loved playing "tricks" on her, hiding, pretending to be hurt, shrieking and throwing fits to get her in trouble for mistreating him. Because Mourning Dove had been terribly afraid of what would happen to her if Snake Head really got hurt, she'd followed him everywhere he went, even when he'd sneaked off after grownups to study their forbidden actions away from town. As a result, she knew almost as many secrets about the elders of Talon Town as he did, though she could speak of those things only to him. If anyone else realized she knew so much, it would mean her life.

Over the last fourteen summers, Snake Head had watched her initial fear of him become an outright lust for revenge. It amused him. When he gazed into her eyes these days, he saw death looking back.

"You said you saw Sternlight leave town two hands of time ago," Snake Head said. "And Ironwood went out about a hand of time later?"

Mourning Dove crushed her red dress in nervous fists. "Yes."

Snake Head swirled his tea, watching the pale green liquid wash the sides of the clay cup. "I want you to stay in Creeper's room tonight, where you have a view of the town entry." He sipped the tea, watching her through narrowed eyes. "Wait until Sternlight and Ironwood return, and note the time. They've been leaving separately, but they almost always return together. I want to know how long they've been out scheming against me."

Mourning Dove's shoulders tightened. "What makes you think they're discussing you?"

"Oh, they are. Trust me. Both of them are terrified of what will happen when I become the Blessed Sun."

Mourning Dove watched him from beneath her long lashes. "And what will happen?"

Snake Head made a light gesture with his hand. "I will establish new alliances. My father loved to trifle with our enemies: He raided them, then let them raid us. The only way to turn the Fire Dogs into useful allies is to tame them. Perhaps I'll even send a runner to the northern Tower Builders. They're savages, but they might—"

"How will you tame the Fire Dogs?" Mourning Dove couldn't quite hide the note of defiance. He'd touched the enduring fiber that ran through her. The light from the warming bowl cast a fluttering red gleam over her taut face.

"The same way people tame any dog." Snake Head told her offhandedly. "I'll throw them some scraps from our tables, maybe send them a great prize, or a supply of raw turquoise. I might even free some of our Mogollon slaves"—she glanced up at him and hope flickered in her eyes—"then, once they start to wag their tails every time they see us, we'll mount an army the size of which they wouldn't believe, run straight into the heart of their countries, and slaughter them by the thousands. After that," he said with a smile, "they'll be tame." He sipped more tea.

Mourning Dove clenched her jaw. "My people will fight back."

"That's why we have to take them by surprise and wipe them out in huge numbers. The first rule of open warfare is strike fast and hard so you destroy your enemy's will to fight back." He propped his cup on his drawn-up knee. "Defeating a warrior is simple, Mourning Dove. You just kill all of his family so he has nothing left to fight for. To do that, you take a village when they least expect it. Kill all the women and children, burn it, and move to the next before anyone can raise the alarm."

"You would wage open warfare?" she said disbelievingly.

"Of course. No more of this annoying hit-and-run raiding. It's time the Straight Path nation—"

Mourning Dove blurted out, "I hope the gods strike you dead for it!"

"And for a great many other things, I wager."

When she looked away, he laughed. The olivella shells on her red sleeves flickered in the light.

Snake Head set his cup aside and rose to his feet, towering over her.

Mourning Dove hastily bent to pick up the dishes again. "I—

I must be going, Blessed Snake Head. I have to find Creeper, let him know I'll be . . ."

As she started for the door, he blocked her path. "Not yet." He ran his fingers down her throat. "I'll send word that you will be late tonight."

"Please, Snake Head, I *must* go. Creeper is preparing a special gift for the Blessed Featherstone, and he needs my help with the porcupine quillwork. He cannot do it alone."

"Is he still wooing my cousin? What an old fool. Doesn't Creeper realize she'll never marry him?"

"He loves her, Snake Head. Truly, he does. I think Featherstone reminds him of his dead wife."

"Featherstone is one of the First People." Snake Head ran his fingers through her black hair. "Creeper is less than a Fire Dog."

"How can you say that?" Mourning Dove's face might have been a mask, so well did she cover her loathing at his touch. "Creeper is a good, honest man. You know nothing about him."

"I know you think that. That's why I allow you to couple with him. It's a small gift from me to you." And, as it happened, coupling with Creeper seemed to lessen her hatred for Snake Head and made her more pliable.

Snake Head took the dishes from her hands and set them on the floor beside the door. The cups clattered against the bowls.

Mourning Dove made a final valiant try to escape. "Who will keep watch for you, Snake Head?" she pleaded, and glanced out the door. "Sternlight and Ironwood will return and you will have no way of knowing when they—"

"Lie on the floor in front of the door."

Mourning Dove closed her eyes for a moment, then did as he'd ordered, stretching out on her back on the cold plaster. Her red dress spread across the white floor.

Snake Head lifted and hooked the curtain over the peg. Starlight flooded the chamber, brighter than the crimson glow of his warming bowl. The walls shimmered with a pewter radiance. "From here," he said as he gazed out the doorway over Talon Town, "I can see the entry myself."

Mourning Dove propped herself up on her elbows. Her chipmunk face tensed. "But Snake Head, anyone who looks up will be able to see us—"

"Yes." He pulled his shirt over his head and tossed it to the floor, then stretched out on top of her and stared down into her blazing eyes. "Violating sacred laws is one of my favorite activities."

He chuckled and nibbled her ear. As he reached down to lift her skirt, the macaw squawked and shrilled, *"I hate you! I hate you! I hate you!"* in a fair imitation of Mourning Dove's voice.

Snake Head grinned at the big bird and used his knee to force Mourning Dove's legs apart.

Second Day

I stand with my bare back against a rain-scented pillar of stone, my feet planted in the ruins of an abandoned house. Gray rock soars high above me. Fluffy Cloud People crowd the sky. I can feel their floating souls—as though clouds live in my heart.

How strange this freedom feels.

All my life I have believed in a wall between inside and outside. "Real" things only happened inside. I alone possessed true awareness. Everything outside had a shadow reality. Other people, the stars and animals, seemed vaguely alive, but not fully.

That wall was a womb that nourished my pride and allowed me to turn my head. To escape responsibility and relationships.

As I gaze across the endless undulating mountains that spread around me, I see a landscape without walls. A place of utter freedom.

But when I look down, I see carefully smoothed stones. What a fine mason she was, the woman who built this house. She hewed the gray stones to the size of her palm, then rubbed them together until they fit so snugly no mortar was necessary to keep the walls standing. She used the curved base of the pillar as her back wall and built out around it, constructing three fine rooms. One for her immediate family, one for storage, and one probably for elderly parents or grandparents.

She made walls outside.

I make walls inside.

I use my bare toe to flip over one of the fallen stones, and wonder . . .

Do the stones in the hills crawl down at night to look at the enslaved stones? Do they howl, the way coyotes do, at dogs in cages?

Do the unfettered Cloud People howl at me?

Wind whimpers in my ears, bathing my face with the sweet fragrances of newborn flowers and grass.

I smile and gently pet the stones still imprisoned in the standing walls. Then I bend down and begin pulling them apart, one by one, breaking the stones loose . . . freeing them.

Seven

Buckthorn halted in the middle of the road on the crest of a low hill overlooking the canyon, and tried to catch his breath. Stumps of long-dead ponderosa pines covered the hill. With all of the building that had gone on over the past fifty sun cycles, the larger trees had been chopped down and laboriously carried to the towns and villages as roof supports for rooms or kivas. Even the branches were tied together and used as lintels for the windows.

As far as he could see, the slopes were barren of the big trees. The weather-grayed stumps looked melancholy, as if remembering the towering giants that had once shaded the slopes. Gray-and-white squirrels must have played there, and the deer lurked in those cool shadows. Even the duff had washed away to leave exposed yellow soil. Rivulets had begun to eat into the soil around the parched roots, cutting away at the last of their rotting memories.

Buckthorn rubbed the back of his hot neck as he looked into the canyon before him. The future lay down there, not among the fading ghosts of dead trees.

Cloud People trailed gauzy filaments of rain as they glided northward. The warp and weft of light and shadow wove a shifting blanket of color. As he watched, the rugged canyon walls went from the deepest crimson to a washed-out pink. He smiled. When the thlatsinas Danced they brought rain, and life.

His long black braid fell over his shoulder. He swore he'd grown skinnier over the past five days. He rubbed the sweat from his thin hooked nose and narrow face. His mother had once told him he should be glad he had fawnlike eyes, otherwise people would call him The Vulture Child. His lungs drew deeply of the damp earthy air. Wind Baby flew across the hilltop, whipping Buckthorn's long tan shirt around his legs.

It felt good to rest. He had been running all day, rushing to his destiny.

He bent forward and braced his hands on his knees, taking the weight of his three packs from his lower back.

"I'll be there soon," he said, and joy flooded his chest.

Black Mesa had told him, "Follow the holy road to the stairs cut into the cliff face. At the bottom of the stairway, you will find a small white house. I have sent a messenger ahead. The Derelict knows you are coming."

The thought of meeting the blessed elder left him awestruck.

Buckthorn got one last breath into his lungs and trotted forward again. His sandals clicked as they struck the gravel in the road.

He reached the edge of the canyon, and a precipice dropped before him, perhaps two hundred hands. Buckthorn stopped and looked around. For as far as he could see, ridges twisted across the highlands like the knobby spines of ancient monsters. Ropy braids of red, yellow, and white rock sliced through the spines at odd angles. Eroded stone pillars poked up everywhere.

He peered over the precipice. Steep stairs had indeed been cut into the face of the cliff. Excited, he trotted forward. He went down backward, using the steps like a pine-pole ladder. His packs suddenly felt feather-light.

When he jumped off the bottom step, sweat coursed down his face, stinging his eyes. He blinked them clear and looked around.

A tiny, dingy house, two body-lengths square, hid in a tangle of tall sage and bricklebrush. The flat roof sagged. The deerhide over the low doorway had been mouse-gnawed. Plaster flakes from the cracked walls sprinkled the ground. It looked abandoned. Frightened, Buckthorn hurried forward, shoving his way through brush until he found a winding path. Deer tracks dimpled the red dirt, but he saw nothing that looked human.

"Oh, no. He *must* be here!" he whispered to himself. "I can't have run all this way for nothing."

He stopped ten hands from the door. The scent of old juniper smoke sweetened the air. Windflower villagers considered it impolite to shout or make your presence known by stamping your feet, so he stood quietly, breathing hard.

After several moments, a reedy old voice called, "Is it you?"

He smiled his relief. "I am Buckthorn of Windflower—"

"No, you are not. You no longer have a name, or a clan. You are simply you."

A hunched old man drew back the gnawed curtain and squinted out at him. The Derelict had a deeply seamed brown face and white hair that hung in thin wisps to his shoulders. His small round nose sank into his wrinkles like an egg in a nest, and he had bushy white brows. His lips had shrunken over his toothless gums, but his eyes . . . his eyes shone as though the blessed Sun Thlatsina lived inside him.

The Derelict hobbled out, scratching his hip through his tattered brown shirt, and gestured to the packs on Buckthorn's back. "Which are mine?"

"Oh!" Buckthorn blurted in embarrassment. "These two." He slipped them off his shoulders and handed them over. "My clan contributed all their finest possessions, Elder."

The packs clanked as Dune took them and slung them over his own thin shoulders. Without a word, he took off down a trail that led westward, paralleling the canyon wall.

Frowning, Buckthorn removed his own pack and stowed it by the door, then followed.

The old man walked until his path intersected a well-traveled trail. There he sat down in the soft sand with the packs before him and leaned against a giant sagebrush.

Buckthorn knelt at his side. The wash glistened in the distance. A silver strand of water flowed down the middle. When Dune said nothing, Buckthorn ventured, "Black Mesa asked me to give you his warmest—"

"Shh! Listen to the divine musician. Hear his music?"

Buckthorn's gaze roamed the sage and red cliffs. "You mean Wind Baby?" he asked. "I hear—"

"You're listening with your ears." Dune shook a finger. "Listen with your *heart*."

Buckthorn shifted to sit cross-legged and concentrated. He heard the twittering of birds, saw a roadrunner darting through the brush, heard a far-off coyote yip. "The world's voice is speaking to me, but I don't know what you mean by—"

"Stop seeking the musician outside. He is here." Dune tapped his chest.

"Oh, *emotions!* Yes, I feel things all the time. Very powerfully. As a matter of fact, I—"

Dune lifted a clawlike hand. "Don't speak! Listen!"

Buckthorn bit his lip. What a harsh voice the elder had, like a braying buffalo in mating season. Buckthorn sighed and tried to do as he'd been instructed. He listened to the sounds inside him. His heart beat like a pot drum, blood *shished* in his ears, and his breathing hissed in and out—but he dared not ask the Derelict if he'd located the "divine musician" for fear he'd be rebuked again.

"Ah," Dune grunted as he rose to his feet.

Buckthorn stood, too. An elderly woman came down the trail, dragging a little boy by the hand. She wore a faded red dress and had twisted her white hair into a topknot. Her nose seemed to have grown out of proportion with her face, thrusting forth like a crooked thumb. Buckthorn barely glanced at her before his gaze went to the little boy, whose long black shirt had been patched in several places. His moccasins had holes in the toes, and he looked thin and pale. But he skipped happily at the woman's side, his chin-length black hair bouncing as he asked question after question. The woman answered each with a smile.

"These are very poor people," Buckthorn said to Dune. "Are they slaves? But what master would deny his own servants good moccasins? It hardly seems—"

"With all that chatter filling your brain, it's no wonder you can't hear the divine musician."

Buckthorn hushed.

When the woman came close to Dune, she bowed reverently. "Greetings, holy Derelict."

"A blessed day to you, Wolf Widow." His voice had softened, become rich and deep. "I have gifts for you." Dune picked up the two packs and handed them to the old woman.

Buckthorn gaped, incredulous. His clan had impoverished itself to provide gifts for Dune, not some stranger! "Elder," he started to object, "I—"

"One more word, and I will send you straight home."

The old woman gazed at the packs and her eyes widened. She clutched them to her breast like suckling infants. "My grandson and I thank you, Elder. We are on our way to visit his sick mother. These things will bring a smile to her lips."

"Give your daughter my blessings, Wolf Widow." He placed a kind hand on her shoulder.

"Yes, Elder, I will." But she waited, apparently seeing if Dune wished to speak more. The little boy huddled against her leg, looking back and forth between them, drawing a half-circle in the dirt with the holed toe of his moccasin.

"Be on your way, Wolf Widow," Dune said gently. "Your daughter needs you."

"Thank you, Elder."

The woman bowed again and continued northward along the trail with the boy feeling the packs and jabbering excitedly.

Dune turned to Buckthorn and said, "Love and charity. They are all that matter."

"Yes, I know, but couldn't you have given them just one pack? I mean, my clan——"

"Don't say 'yes' when you haven't the slightest notion what I'm speaking about!"

In morose silence, Buckthorn followed Dune back along the sage-choked path that led to his little house. He might have been passing through a tunnel, for the sagebrush grew head-high.

When they reached the door, Dune ordered, "Collect wood for the fire, but not close to the house. Walk for at least a finger of time, then begin gathering wood."

"But look at the sage right here, elder." Buckthorn gestured to the blue-green jungle that practically swallowed the house. "It needs to be twisted out."

Dune fixed him with a glare. "This sage lives here, boy. Go kill something that isn't my friend."

Buckthorn stared. In irritation, he said, "Why didn't you tell me back at the trail? It will be getting dark soon, and if I have to walk for . . ."

Dune ducked through the doorway and into his house. The deerhide curtain swung behind him.

Buckthorn swallowed his next words, stood uncertainly for a moment, then trudged away, kicking every sagebrush he passed. Did the old man yell at all of his disciples? Black Mesa hadn't mentioned this cruel streak. Nor had anyone else.

Maybe Dune just doesn't like me.

While Father Sun descended into Our Mother Earth's western womb, Buckthorn angrily ripped off dead sage branches and stacked them in his left arm.

"It's all right," he whispered to calm himself. "You can endure it. Think of the things you will be able to do for your people once you've become a great Singer. You'll be able to Heal the sick, and help lonely ghosts find their ways to the afterworlds. You'll be prepared to battle witches, and speak with the plants and animals in their own languages."

It didn't take long before he'd lost himself and his anger in sublime thoughts of his future. Why, when he'd earned the title of Singer, no one would ever shout at him again. He'd be revered, and not a little feared. He chuckled at the thought.

A breath of wind trailed over the sage like the hem of a woman's dress, soft and silken. Buckthorn looked up. The gust whipped the brush on its journey westward toward a distant butte that stood alone in the middle of the canyon, its rocky top gleaming. Brush-covered flats spread around the butte, running until they butted against the red canyon walls on the north and south.

At some point in his training, Dune would bestow a new name upon Buckthorn, and he longed for one that echoed the names of his greatest heroes: Wolfdreamer, Born of Water, and Home-Going-Boy. Maybe something like Going-Home-Dreamer or Born-of-Wolf-Water. Those would be very powerful names. He'd have to hint about it to Dune.

Buckthorn happily trotted back for the house.

The light had faded to a rusty hue that turned the cliffs dark vermilion. Desert fragrances intensified with the night, the sage more pungent, the juniper rich and savory.

As he thrashed through a clot of buckbrush, he saw Dune come out to stand in front of his door. The old man had his sticklike arms folded. White hair made a wispy halo around his shriveled face.

Grinning, Buckthorn hurried forward. "Isn't it a beautiful evening, Elder? Just look at the colors!"

Dune scowled. "What *is* the matter with you?"

Buckthorn stopped dead in his tracks. "W-what?"

"You don't carry sacred sage like that! What a jumble! Do you wish to offend the Spirit of the plant? Order the sticks. Lay each in the crook of your arm like a precious child. Gently. One atop the other. Well? Don't stand there staring. Drop the sticks and order them. Now!"

Buckthorn hastily dumped his load and began picking them up again, doing as he'd been instructed, one at a time, gently. But he wondered at this lunacy. What possible difference could it make to the Spirit of the sage how he carried her dead branches?

Once he'd finished, Dune held aside the door curtain, and Buckthorn entered the house. He laid the branches by the fire-pit in the middle of the floor and looked around.

What a bleak place! Dune owned almost nothing. A flat slab and handstone, for grinding seeds, lay near the door. Beside them sat a large water jar and two clay pots, one for cornmeal and the other for dried meats. Ears of corn, squash gourds, sunflowers, and other plants hung from the rafters. In the corner, to Buckthorn's right, a stack of colored baskets leaned precariously. Two plain gray blankets lay rolled up on either side of the house. But no floor mats cushioned the cold dirt floor; no paintings brightened the soot-smudged clay walls.

Dune entered and heaved a tired breath. He gestured to the wood pile. "Make a fire. There are hot coals beneath the ash bed."

"Yes, Elder."

Buckthorn used a stick to dig around, isolating the hot coals from the dead ones. When he had a mound in the center of the pit, he laid four small pieces of wood on top and blew gently. White ash fluttered. The coals slowly reddened and flames crackled up around the tinder.

Buckthorn kept adding wood while he watched the Derelict. The old man set up his tea tripod and hung a soot-coated pot in the middle, then slumped down on the dirt floor and sighed.

Buckthorn said, "Elder? Why is it that you have not painted images of the thlatsinas on your walls? You are their greatest messenger. You *should* have them around you, and it would certainly brighten your house. It would please me very much to do that for you, if you wish."

Dune squinted. "Paintings and possessions are for people who plan to sleep in the same house for a long time. I do not."

"Oh, forgive me." He paused, squinting. "I thought you had lived here forever. Black Mesa knew right where you would be, and so I assumed—"

"Forty-four summers."

Buckthorn looked at him. "You've lived here for forty-four summers?"

"Almost forty-five."

"Well . . ." Buckthorn blinked in confusion. "If this has been your home for so long, where do you plan to sleep if not in this house?"

The old man raised his bushy white brows. "Under a stone slab if I'm not careful."

"Elder! You mustn't jest about witchcraft!"

"Why not?" Dune scratched his side.

"Blessed thlatsinas! I was sent here by my clan to learn to be a Spirit Singer. It wouldn't do to have people whispering behind their hands that I was trained by a man who lopes across the desert at night in the body of a bobcat!"

The deep wrinkles of Dune's face twisted and contorted when he grinned.

Buckthorn got to his feet and nervously thrust a hand toward the door. "I—I left my pack outside. I have blue corn cakes in it. My mother made them for us for supper tonight. Let me get it."

The brightest Evening People had opened their eyes. They peered down at Buckthorn as he retrieved his pack from beside the door. Confused, he grimaced at the growing darkness, feeling as if he'd been maneuvered into studying with Trickster Coyote. Didn't anybody know what a crazy old fool Dune was? Then he remembered the other two Singers-in-the-making who'd returned to Windflower Village proclaiming exactly that. Why hadn't anybody believed them?

Grumbling softly, he ducked back inside. Dune watched him through half-lidded eyes.

Buckthorn knelt by the fire and unlaced his pack. Firelight fluttered over his hands like luminous butterfly wings. Just as he started to pull out a cake, Dune ordered, "Give it to me."

"I'm getting ready to, Elder! Here." He extended a cake.

Dune took it, then held out his hand again. "The pack. Give me the pack."

Buckthorn did.

Dune took it, rummaged around to find all the cakes, set them on a hearth stone, and began eating. Crumbs fell down the front of his brown shirt, dotting it with blue.

Buckthorn sat in silence, counting each cake the old man ate. Finally, when he feared the worst, he said. "Elder, I ran all the way here. I am very hungry, so if you don't mind—"

Around a mouthful of food, Dune said, "You should sleep." He pointed to the blanket rolled up on the floor on the north side of the house. "That is your place."

"Yes, well," Buckthorn said as he glanced at it. "After I've eaten. I'm starving, and I—"

"*Now*," Dune shouted. "Go to sleep!"

Buckthorn lurched to his feet, fists clenched. "You do not have to yell at me, Elder! I am human, not a soulless rock! I deserve to be treated with a little dignity!"

"Dignity?" Dune said. He lowered the cake to his lap and gazed at Buckthorn with those strange shining eyes. "Listen to me. Look deeply into your soul. Look hard. Find that man who thinks he deserves to be treated with dignity, and ask him why. He will give you many reasons." Dune's voice softened to the same timbre he had used with old Wolf Widow. "That man will tell you all of the great deeds he has accomplished in his life, how kind he is, how deserving, and how many people love and have faith in him." Dune took another bite of corn cake, working it slowly around his toothless mouth.

"Yes," Buckthorn said. "Then what?"

Dune squeezed his eyes closed as though in great disappointment. "Each reason that man gives you is a stiletto in your heart. If you collect enough, you will kill your ability to love. Now, do not argue with me. Go to your place and sleep."

Buckthorn went. Wrapping up in the blanket, he stretched out on the hard-packed dirt floor. He could still hear the Derelict gumming the corn cakes to mush, and his stomach growled.

Buckthorn tossed to his right side and faced the wall, concentrating on the flickers of firelight that danced across the smudged plaster.

Hallowed Spirits, what had he gotten himself into?

Cornsilk came up the southern trail and spotted Fledgling. He crouched behind a sagebrush three body-lengths ahead. The rise overlooked their house and the north half of the village plaza where children ran. Fledgling's rabbit-fur cape and loose black hair glinted in the afternoon sunlight.

Cornsilk studied him thoughtfully. He had tilted his head, listening intently to their parents' faint voices coming from within the house.

She cupped a hand to her mouth and softly called, "Brother? Fledgling?"

When he didn't turn, Cornsilk picked up a rock and tossed it at him. She missed. He didn't move. Disgruntled, she looked for a bigger one. A fist-sized chunk of limestone lay half-hidden in the sand. She dug it out, hefted it to test the weight, and heaved it.

It struck him in the middle of the back. Fledgling jerked around, startled, his thin-boned face pale, and saw her. As though relieved, he gripped the cape over his heart, then waved her forward.

Cornsilk grinned and walked to him, carefully avoiding clumps of prickly pear. She sank on her knees at his side. "What are you doing? Spying on our parents?"

A thin coating of dust sprinkled his broad cheekbones and dark eyebrows. She could see his pulse throbbing in his temple.

"Listen," he whispered. "Mother and Father are arguing."

Through the rear window, she saw them, standing face to face. Her mother had a black-and-gray blanket snugged over her shoulders. Her father wore a pale blue shirt. He'd crossed his arms, as if hugging himself.

Her mother said, "Beargrass, we've been quarreling for two days. Enough! If you will not come, I will take Cornsilk and Fledgling and go away!"

"Thistle, please. I am Lanceleaf Village's War Chief. I have responsibilities. The Tower Builders are raiding. How can I leave now?"

Cornsilk stared breathlessly at the house. The red clay plaster shone orange in the bright sun. Down the hill, children played in the village plaza, wrestling, throwing sticks for barking dogs. A broad square of two-story buildings bordered the plaza. Women sat in the sunlight on the west side, grinding corn, laughing. The lilting voices of men rose from the kiva dug into the middle of the plaza.

"Thistle," her father pleaded, "don't do this to me. I beg you. I love you and—"

"If you did, you would protect us!"

Cornsilk breathed. "Fledgling, why does Mother wish to take us away?"

He shook his head. "I'm not certain yet. Shh."

"Thistle," her father said. "Please. I know you are frightened, but I do not believe we are in danger. Even if Night Sun discovered—"

"I am not afraid of Night Sun! She was *never* as wicked as Sternlight said! I thought she was a good woman. Kind to everyone—"

"All right!" Beargrass clenched his teeth. More quietly, he continued, "I don't believe it, but let's assume that Crow Beard is not the father, and that Ironwood is. How could his enemies find out where his child is? Ironwood would have told no one, except, perhaps, Sternlight. And I cannot believe that Sternlight would betray Ironwood."

"Why not?" Thistle asked, on the verge of tears. Her mouth trembled.

"They have been friends all their lives. Besides—"

"Would that matter if—"

"*Besides*," her father interrupted in a commanding voice, "we have been safe for over fifteen summers, Thistle. Why, after all this time, would someone suddenly decide to betray Ironwood? What would he have to gain?"

In a choking voice, her mother answered, "I don't know, but I'm terrified. We must do something! Please, help me think of a way of keeping our son and daughter safe."

Panic threaded Cornsilk's heart. *Mother wants to take us away because she thinks we are in danger . . . Ironwood is the father . . . of whom?*

Cornsilk whispered, "Fledgling? What child? Who is Ironwood's child?"

Fledgling closed his eyes. "I think they mean one of us."

It took some time for his meaning to sink in. "One of us? . . . Us?"

"Perhaps," her father said softly, "we should separate Cornsilk and Fledgling."

Her mother stood very still, then slowly nodded. "If you think that's best."

"Cornsilk could go to live with my brother Deer Bird in Two Horn Village. It isn't far. A half day's walk. And I suspect she might enjoy it. She has always loved Deer Bird."

Cornsilk forced a swallow down her tight throat. Her heart pounded.

Fledgling saw her wince and reached out to put an arm over her shoulders, holding her. "Wait. We don't know anything yet."

"Oh, Beargrass," her mother wept. "I'll miss Cornsilk."

Beargrass drew her mother close and tenderly kissed her hair. "It should only be for a short time. If Crow Beard lives, I believe we are still safe. If he dies—"

Her mother looked up. "If he dies, we can leave Cornsilk there for a moon or so . . . just to see."

"Yes. Anyone who wished to harm Crow Beard's child would do it immediately, if at all. And Ironwood's child—"

"Yes, I understand." Eagerly, her mother added, "And after a moon, we can go and fetch her, and bring her home."

"Yes."

"Fledgling," she said softly. "They mean *me*. It's me they're—!"

"What of Fledgling?" her mother asked. "Where should we send our son?"

Cornsilk watched the muscles in her brother's jaw tense.

Beargrass said, "I believe it is our duty to stay with Fledgling at all times. We—"

"No, he's old enough now," her mother said. "As soon as he kills his first enemy warrior, he will be a man. What if we send him to stay with your father? That way we could remain here, arousing no suspicion, and our son and daughter will be safe. You may continue your duties as War Chief. We'll just tell people that Cornsilk and Fledgling are away visiting relatives. Oh, Beargrass, that's the solution!"

Beargrass didn't say anything for a while, but placed his hands on Thistle's shoulders and peered deeply into her eyes. "If I agree to this, will you agree to let me send a runner to Talon Town to see what's happening there? To keep us informed about the Chief's health?"

Cornsilk waited breathlessly for her answer. Her brother's arm trembled where it lay over her shoulders.

"Yes," her mother said, "all right."

Beargrass heaved a breath. "Thank you, my wife. Now, let us prepare. We must hire someone to go to Talon Town. Someone we can trust to rush back with the news if Crow Beard dies."

Fledgling lowered his head. "I think it's me," he said. "I'm not your brother."

"You will always be my brother," she began, but her mother's strained voice made Cornsilk hush.

"Who can we trust, Beargrass?"

Her father smoothed a hand over his chin. "Young Stone Forehead, maybe. At seventeen summers, he is already a respected warrior. Let me speak with him. The Blessed thlatsinas know we have enough rare trade goods to pay him well for his loyalty."

Her parents moved out of sight of the window, and Cornsilk turned to Fledgling. His face had gone dark.

"Why didn't they ever tell me?" he whispered. "I am almost a man, Cornsilk. They *should* have told me! I—I would like to know my real parents! Who is my mother? And where is she? If I knew, I would go to her now, this instant!"

Cornsilk's thoughts darted about like bees, landing here and there. Four turkeys waddled across the plaza behind a child dragging a yucca cord. They kept pecking at the cord and each other, and squawking in dismay. "Fledgling, do you recall three nights ago, when the runners arrived?"

"Yes. Father said they brought news of raiding."

"I know, but I was sick and not sleeping very well, and I heard him say something different."

He stared wide-eyed at her. "What? Something about us?"

"I think so. At the time, I paid it no attention, because it didn't make any sense, but now . . . Fledgling, I woke when Father said that the runners had come to warn him and Mother that if the Chief died, the payments would stop coming."

"Payments? What payments?"

"Well, consider the beautiful things in our house. We have many more blankets, rare pots, and magnificent jewelry than anyone in the village. Where did they come from?"

Fledgling's black brows pulled together. Behind him, a road-runner darted through the sage, its neck stretched out, trying to grab a bug. "I thought they were payment for Mother's work as a mason and tribute to Father as the War Chief of the village."

"I did, too. But, after that, Mother said she didn't care if the payments stopped coming, that the secret would die with them, and our family would be safe forever."

"Safe from what?"

She pinned Fledgling with her gaze. "Someone they think wants to kill either you or me."

"But if one of us is Ironwood's child . . ." Fear twisted his expression. "Cornsilk, why would Chief Crow Beard pay for our parents to take care of Ironwood's child?"

She gripped his wrist hard. "Perhaps that's it."

His face slackened. "You mean . . . I am not Ironwood's son, but Crow Beard's? And one of the Chief's enemies fears that I might become the next Blessed Sun?"

Cornsilk made a disgusted sound. "Only if you came from Night Sun's belly. She has a son much older than you. Snake Head must have seen twenty-three or twenty-four summers."

The Straight Path clans traced lineage through the female, so when a man or woman died, all of his or her belongings were equally divided among the living daughters. The daughters then administered the lands, houses, and slaves, and gave a share of the remaining belongings—pots, shields, weapons, clothing—to the sons. The Matron of the First People, as a result, owned nearly everything and made all decisions except those regarding warfare. Men generally possessed little, but a Chief from the First People . . .

"Unless his mother marries again. Then she may declare her

new husband the Chief. Though Snake Head would rule until Night Sun selected another."

Cornsilk released his wrist and fiddled with a twig, shoving it across the sand with her finger. "What if . . . maybe I am the Chief's daughter and will inherit part of the wealth of his kingdom, and someone wants to stop that from happening."

"You wouldn't inherit much," Fledgling pointed out. "Night Sun owns everything. Chief Crow Beard has almost nothing without her, a few weapons, some trinkets. If you are Crow Beard's daughter by another woman, you have no claims at all. Oh, they might feel sorry for you and grant you a pittance, but—"

"Crow Beard's 'trinkets' might amount to unimaginable wealth, brother."

Fledgling said, "No matter who my real mother is, a true son of Crow Beard would have a claim on his personal belongings. I would be a threat to Snake Head's inheritance." He swallowed hard. "Do you think he's the man who wants to kill me? The one our mother fears? I've heard he's very wicked."

"I'll tell you exactly what I think," she said. "I think we're both leaping off a cliff before we're sure we're being chased. We may have all of this figured out wrong. I think we should speak to Mother and Father."

She started to rise and he gripped her hand. "We've seen fifteen summers, Cornsilk. Almost sixteen. If they haven't told us by now, they never plan to. You know how they are!"

She sagged to the sand. Their parents loved secrets. She and Fledgling frequently heard them whispering to each other in the darkness at night, always about frightening or forbidden things. "Maybe we should begin making plans of our own, Fledgling. If you have to go to—"

"Let's pretend we are going where they tell us to, and . . . and then let's go somewhere else! Together."

She nodded. "All right, maybe. We'll think about it."

"Let's just do it. In a moon, we can come home. They might be worried for a time, but in the end, we'd be all right. They'd get over being mad at us. They always do. And then—"

"Listen! If we decide to do this, we can't tell anyone. Do you understand? Not even Ruddy Boy in the afterworld. He might tell one of the ancestor Spirits, and there's no telling who would find out after that."

"I promise I won't tell."

Cornsilk got to her knees again and brushed her sweaty hands on her leggings. The fragrance of crushed sage filled her nose. "Well, let's go in and let them tell us they're sending us away, then we'll wait until they're out of the house and gather the things we'll need."

"Thank you, Cornsilk."

She smiled confidently, but her stomach ached with doubts. Nothing made sense. Except . . . except that her parents had always treated them differently. An extra pat on Fledgling's shoulder, a special tenderness in their smiles when they looked at him. Until today, Cornsilk thought they loved Fledgling more because he was just more lovable than she. Her brother obeyed their commands without question, while she took it as a matter of honor to figure a way around directions she didn't like. Her parents told her not to fight, so Cornsilk waged one subtle war after another among her peers. She had to out-shoot and out-hunt every other child in the village—especially the young men. On many occasions her exasperated mother had joked that a wild strain of weasel blood ran in Cornsilk's veins.

But they never joked when Fledgling did something wrong. They punished him.

Because he was truly their son, and it mattered?

Through the window, she glimpsed her mother duck out the door and heard her call, *"Fledgling? Cornsilk? Where are you?"*

They leaped to their feet and ran.

Eight

As the chill of winter deepened, the sunlight grew feeble and pale; it fell through the drifting clouds in streaks of fallow gold and slanted across the canyon.

Night Sun clutched her black-and-white cotton cape closed with both hands and descended the winding deer trail that ran along the west side of Straight Path Wash. Small garden plots dotted the flats. Filled with the withered corpses of frosty bean and squash vines, they were also scattered with corn stalks and tiny immature corncobs. They'd had a very wet spring and autumn, but cold had come much earlier than normal. Many of their crops had frozen on the vines. It had been a hard winter for smaller villages. In another moon, when the last supplies disappeared, raiding would intensify. No matter how much peace men and women held in their hearts, when their children cried for food, weapons filled their hands.

She shook her head and said a soft prayer to Spider Woman, begging for spring to come early. When people could gather enough tubers and tender plants, it staved off violence.

Her daughter's steps pattered behind her. Night Sun turned to look at Cloud Playing.

Though she had seen only nineteen summers, gray already touched her temples, highlighting the two long braids she wore. Her life had not been an easy one. Cloud Playing had borne four children and lost all four. They had died, along with her beloved husband, Tassel, from a strange wasting sickness that had swept the canyon two summers ago. Night Sun diligently pushed her to remarry, but Cloud Playing maintained she hadn't the heart for it, not yet. But her daughter also said she had "prospects." When Night Sun had seriously said, "Not Webworm, I hope," Cloud Playing had replied, "He is my friend, Mother. Nothing more. Though I do love him. He has been kind to me since I was a little girl." Still, it worried Night Sun.

Her brow wrinkled as she recalled the argument Cloud Playing and Webworm had been engaged in the morning they'd left on this journey. Half of Talon Town had come running at the sound of loud voices just outside the walls. Night Sun had stood numbly, watching the disagreement progress to a shoving match—which Cloud Playing won by accident. She'd pushed Webworm backward and he'd tripped over a rock and fallen to the ground. As onlookers burst out laughing, Cloud Playing had stamped away. She'd been silent and moody for two days afterward. She'd only begun to brighten late last night as they'd sat around their campfire talking of old times—times when they'd both been happy. Why had they been arguing?

Six summers ago, Webworm had asked to marry Cloud Playing, but neither Night Sun nor Crow Beard had approved. Since the deaths of her family, Cloud Playing had been very lonely, accompanying Night Sun on her Healing rounds, carrying the pack of sacred herbs, roots, and tools. The argument hadn't been over Cloud Playing's other "prospects," had it? Webworm had a reputation for jealousy.

Hallowed Ancestors, I hope not.

Over the past two summers, Cloud Playing had become Night Sun's best friend and closest confidante.

Despite the fact that Night Sun possessed considerable power and wealth, for most of her life her soul had been completely empty. A cavernous darkness lived inside her—as it had all the women in her family. Her mother and older sister had both spoken of that darkness as if it were a terrible ghostly lover; a specter whose shadowy arms often tightened around them until they felt so alone they wished to die. When the daily misery of Night Sun's wedded life became too much, she understood—and feared—what they had experienced, because the desperation turned her into a violent stranger.

A tall willowy woman of forty-four summers, gray glinted in Night Sun's black hair as it fluttered about her triangular face. She brushed the hair away and tipped up her pointed nose to sniff the air. Cedar smoke rode the wind. Her black dress whipped about her red leggings, creating a pleasant sound.

As she rounded a bend in the trail, she saw Deer Mother

Village. The square dwelling had been built beneath the overhanging canyon wall. Just beyond, the canyon turned shallow, the rim sloping to sage flats. Few families dared to stay in such isolated areas. With the raiding, it took real bravery, but these people of the Coyote Clan had always been brave. They had survived here for centuries—though only about ten members remained.

For that very reason Night Sun visited here once every four moons—always during the full moon. She feared that this small village might not exist much longer, and despite her dislike of the village Matron, Sweetwater, she loved the five slaves. They always greeted her with such affection.

"Mother?" Cloud Playing called. "There's someone coming."

"Where?" Night Sun shielded her eyes against the slant of sunlight, but saw nothing.

"Wait. He just vanished around the base of the rise. You'll see."

A breathless silence had gripped the desert. Birds sat fluffed up in the spiny arms of cacti, or huddled beneath rock overhangs. Coyotes quietly loped through the drainages, hunting mice and rabbits. Eagles circled through blue skies.

An old man appeared on the hilltop and waddled toward her. He wore a tattered gray cape and worn moccasins. When he met her, he murmured, "May the Blessed thlatsinas look over you this day."

"And you also, Elder."

He dipped his white head and continued on.

Night Sun followed the trail up the low hill. By the time she reached the top, she was panting. She untied the water jug from her belt, removed the ceramic lid, and drank deeply. Each swallow went down crisp and cold. She silently thanked the thlatsinas.

Water was the most precious of all resources in this high desert country. People filled jugs from potholes in the rocks, or larger sinks in the canyon bottom freshened by rain and melting snows. In the heat of the summer, when no reliable surface water could be found, people scooped out holes along drainages. Sometimes, they filled. Sometimes they remained dry and dusty, as empty of water as the supplicants were of hope.

Night Sun tied her water jug to her belt again and gazed back down the hill.

Cloud Playing had stopped to speak to the old man. Wind Baby billowed her blue dress around her legs. Her voice rose in soft lilting tones. The man answered, but Night Sun caught only a few words.

Cloud Playing smiled at something he said. She was a pretty young woman, with brown eyes and red-brown skin. Four black spirals tattooed her pointed chin—the mark of all the women in their family. Night Sun had them on her own chin.

Cloud Playing patted the old man's shoulder and unslung her pack. She rummaged around inside and handed him something, then ran up the hill to Night Sun, the pack swaying on her back.

Cloud Playing said, "He's from Yellow Moth Village in the south. He says the Mogollon raided there three moons ago."

Night Sun looked down the trail after the elder. The fact that he walked alone, and his ragged appearance, told her a great deal. "Was his family killed?"

Cloud Playing nodded. "He says he thinks he has a great-granddaughter in the Green Mesa villages. He is on his way there. I gave him jerked venison for the trip."

Night Sun smoothed her daughter's hair. "Thank you. I should have asked. It's a long journey for such an old man."

"He has nowhere else to go, Mother. I pray his relatives are still living in the Green Mesas."

She didn't wish to dwell on sadness, not today. It would make her think of her despicable son, Snake Head, or worse, her husband Crow Beard. Crow Beard had been cruel to her the morning she and Cloud Playing had left—accusing her, once again, of infidelity with one of his slaves. She shifted the pack she carried and let out a breath. If Crow Beard so much as suspected her of smiling at another man, he punished her with silence. He couldn't cast her out, because she owned everything, his chambers, his lands, even his children. But he could make her feel like an outcast—and did it with great skill.

As she walked down the rise, she heard a shrill voice Singing the Mogollon Migration Song, the sacred Song about the Hero Twins' destruction of the second underworld.

> *They went out,*
> > *Now they went,*
> *They crushed, crushed, crushed it,*
> > *they killed all the people,*
> > *all the people are dead,*
> *Now they cry,*
> > *they cry and cry . . .*

A sharp voice split the silence: "Shut up that Singing! You hear me, Catbird?"

A sullen, "Yes, sister," drifted on the wind.

Night Sun saw the six-summers-old slave girl come from behind a fallen boulder; the stick dragging behind her was making wavy patterns in the dirt. As she looked up and saw Night Sun and Cloud Playing, her mouth gaped, revealing missing front teeth. The girl shouted: "Mite! They're here!"

"Who?"

"The Blessed Night Sun and her daughter! Just as Mother said!" Catbird threw down her stick and raced up the trail, her brown dress flying about her legs. She threw her arms around Night Sun's waist with such strength it made her stagger. "Mother said you were coming. She told us last night! Oh, she will be so glad to see you. She's having the baby!"

"The baby?" Night Sun felt weak. "But it isn't supposed to be coming—not for another two moons."

"Just the same, she's having it."

Night Sun disentangled herself from the child's grasp and hurried down the sandy slope.

Mite stepped out of the house. Sixteen, and plump, she filled her faded green dress. She had her black pigtails tied together at the nape of her neck. "Thank Wolf," she said. "I can't tell you how glad I am to see you."

"Is your mother all right?" Night Sun asked as she approached the low doorway. The dwelling had no more than eight contiguous rooms, including a granary, and storerooms built like human swallow's nests into the overhang. The layered sandstone construction of the wall could be seen through gaps where the plaster had spalled off. Two paintings of the Humpbacked Flute Player, one male, the other female, adorned the dwelling. The twin images of fertility added to the ironic neglect of fields, people, and structures.

A framed ramada stood in the flat that served as a plaza. Corn shucks and shreds of juniper bark rattled in the wind. Four young women sat beneath the shelter, grinding corn. To the right of the plaza, a small kiva had been dug into the ground, the roof sagging around the two legs of the ladder that stuck up from the roof entry. Soft male voices carried from inside. The familiar songs pled for health and well-being, imploring the female Flute Player to ease the labor and allow a healthy birth.

"I'm not certain." Mite's shoulders slumped, mirroring the worry in her plump face.

Night Sun ducked inside the living quarters. The sloping rock of the overhang itself served as the roof, leaving just enough space to stand up. The villagers mixed their clay with local dirt before plastering it on the face of the building, which made the village almost invisible. Except for the three small windows and single doorway, it seemed to be part of the golden canyon wall.

Night Sun blinked in the dimness. A fire crackled in the pit in the middle of the floor. The paintings covering the walls jumped out at her. Half-beast, half-man, the thlatsinas Danced around the room. The White Wolf peered directly at her, ears pricked, a rattle in one hand, a dancestick in the other. He had his teeth bared, warning all those who dared enter with evil thoughts to cleanse their hearts before taking another step.

Night Sun breathed deeply of the smoky air. A blue haze moved over the ceiling, crawling for the window, where it seeped outside. Next to the door on Night Sun's left sat a water jar, clay cups, pots of dried meat and cornmeal. A pile of juniper wood stood stacked along the wall to her right. And . . . an old woman. She crouched there on a folded blanket, her gray hair awry, eyes dark and foreboding.

"Sweetwater? Are you well?"

"I've been better." Perspiration matted her gray hair into tiny curls across her wrinkled forehead. Her black eyes glistened like obsidian beads. As Matron, she owned the lands and almost all the possessions in the village, including three of the five slaves.

Along the north wall, straight ahead of her, Star Hunter lay on bulrush sleeping mats, a red blanket covering her swollen belly. In her bloated face, her eyes had sunken into twin blue circles. Soaked black hair spread around her.

Night Sun leaned out the door, and called, "Cloud Playing, where is my pack?"

"Oh, Mother, forgive me," her daughter answered, unslinging it and handing it over. She and Mite had been speaking in low voices. Mite's expression had turned grave. "I was talking with Mite, and I—"

"Do as I say, quickly. Get a pitcher and fill it with water. Pour half into a pot and set it to boiling, then fetch me some fresh yucca roots. I don't care how far you have to go to find them, do it, and do it now."

Cloud Playing said, "Yes, Mother," and ran back to Mite and Catbird, relaying her instructions. All three split in different directions.

Night Sun ducked inside again, removed her cape and tossed it on the floor, then set her pack down beside the water jar and cups. She unlaced the pack's ties, pulled out a bag of dried mugwort leaves, dropped a pinch into a clay cup, and poured water over the top.

As she set the cup at the edge of the fire to warm, Star Hunter opened her eyes. "Hello, Blessed Night Sun." A soft smile lit her face.

"Hello, Star Hunter. I wish you'd sent word to me. I could have been here before dawn."

"Birthing always takes me so long, and I knew you would be here sometime today. You're never late."

"Besides," old Sweetwater's reedy voice broke in, "she doesn't need you! The child is going to die. It's too soon for it to be born. It should die. If it lives it will be a weak and worthless slave."

Night Sun glared at the old woman. Sweetwater knew better than anyone how much Star Hunter loved this unborn child. From the first moon she had realized her pregnancy, she had been convinced it would be a boy—her first son. She had been weaving blankets and clothing, tanning rabbithides and sewing tiny moccasins. Four moons ago, Star Hunter's husband,

Whitetail, had showed Night Sun the little bow and arrows he had constructed for his son.

Night Sun went to kneel by Star Hunter's side, feeling her fevered cheeks and forehead. Star Hunter leaned into the coolness of her hands. Firelight flickered over her face. "The child may die," Night Sun said straightly, "but I will try to save it. When did the pains begin?"

"Last . . . night. Late," Star Hunter replied.

"She took a fall yesterday," Sweetwater said. "A bad fall. The gods tripped her. It was twilight and she went to dip melt water from the cistern in the sandstone. She tripped over nothing! And toppled face-first across the stone. It's little wonder she's birthing today. The gods wished her to lose the child. It probably has a very bad speck of dust in its head."

Wickedness, bad dreams, and evil acts came from a tiny grain of dust that Spider Woman placed in the back of a baby's head just before birth. It remained there forever.

"Have you checked the baby's position?" Night Sun asked.

"Why should I? The sooner it dies, the better."

"My mistress," Star Hunter said, "will not even let my daughters touch me. I had a lonely night."

"Well, I'm going to touch you. Let me see how the baby is lying. Raise your knees."

Night Sun pulled the red blanket away from Star Hunter's bulging belly and gently probed inside. "The child hasn't turned. Its head isn't down," she said, and tried not to show her alarm.

"I know." Star Hunter reached out and clasped Night Sun's arm, tugging feebly. "I'm sorry. It's my fault."

"It's no one's fault. Your fall was an accident."

Sweetwater said, "The gods did it!"

"My gods are not so cruel," Night Sun replied. "I'm sorry if yours are."

Sweetwater's ancient eyes slitted. "Are you saying that you don't believe—"

"Please," Star Hunter interrupted, tugging on Night Sun's arm. "Tell me the truth. I am so tired. Is my baby going to die?"

"Not if I can help it," Night Sun said, gripping Star Hunter's hand firmly. "Stop thinking such thoughts. I need you to be strong."

"I'll try, but I . . ." Her body convulsed.

Night Sun watched and waited. When the contraction eased, she ordered, "Sweetwater, please come over here. Take Star Hunter's left arm. I'll take her right." Then to Star Hunter she said, "Your womb is wide enough. It is time you got into a birthing position."

Sweetwater folded her arms, refusing to move.

Night Sun snapped, "Get up, blast you, before I—"

"You do *not* order me!" Sweetwater yelled. "Not in this village. Your status means nothing here! What you are doing is forbidden! When a child comes early, no help should be given. We do *not* wish the baby to live!"

Night Sun shot a hot glance of promise into the old woman's eyes: *I'll deal with you later!*

Star Hunter held tightly to Night Sun's arm and panted, straining to rise. Her legs shook.

"For now, just sit up, Star Hunter. That's enough. When the next contraction strikes, I will support you so you can squat. The birthing will be easier. Mother Earth will be pulling while you are pushing."

Star Hunter smiled tiredly. "Yes, all right."

Cloud Playing ducked through the doorway with Mite and Catbird following. "I've brought the yucca roots, Mother. I cut them up outside first, and Mite has the boiling pot on the tripod."

"Good. Set the pot over the fire, then throw in the chopped roots. When suds begin to pour over the top of the pot, remove it from the heat and soak several lengths of cloth in it for me."

"Yes, Mother."

Cloud Playing tossed in the roots while Mite arranged the pot over the low flames. Catbird stood in the doorway, a finger tucked into her mouth. Her soft eyes followed her mother's every movement.

Star Hunter gave her youngest daughter a smile. "It's all right, Catbird," she said. "The Blessed Night Sun is here. You needn't worry now."

"But I heard our mistress shouting. You're not going to die . . . are you?" Her young mouth puckered.

Star Hunter glanced at Night Sun, eyes bright with worry, but she said, "No. I'm not," and bit her lip as the next contraction hit. Her face wrenched with pain.

"Cloud Playing, take Star Hunter's other arm. Help her up."

Cloud Playing hurried to obey. They lifted Star Hunter into a squatting position, where she wept and groaned through clenched teeth. Her grip tightened on Night Sun's arm until her fingers dug into Night Sun's flesh.

Catbird stood in the doorway, crying, "Mother! Oh, Mother!"

Night Sun craned her neck, anxious for any sign of the baby.

A violent hiss made everyone jerk around as the pot boiled over and great tufts of suds plopped into the fire.

Mite grabbed a folded cloth to move the tripod away from the flames.

Star Hunter twisted and moaned, then stared at Night Sun. "Don't let my baby die. It'll break Whitetail's heart. He wants this baby so badly. Even more than I do."

"You're doing well," Night Sun said. "Everything is fine."

Star Hunter collapsed weakly, breathing hard, when the contraction subsided.

Sweetwater leaned forward, her wrinkled face taut, and hissed: "Have you ever seen an early baby that was any good? To anyone? Why do you wish to burden our clan with a useless runt?"

Night Sun ignored her and turned to Mite. "Please, drop in four lengths of cloth, then use a stick to stir and remove them. While they cool, bring me the cup at the edge of the fire."

"Yes, Blessed Night Sun." Mite found a worn dress in a pile by Sweetwater's blanket, ripped off the sleeves, tore them in two, and grabbed a long stick from the juniper pile. She dropped the cloths in, stirred them, and brought them up steaming. Propping the stick against the wall to cool, she reached for the cup.

Night Sun took it from her hand and sniffed it. The mugwort leaves smelled pungent enough. To test the temperature, she dipped her finger into the brew. Very warm, but not too hot.

"Star Hunter," she said, "try to drink this. It will help hurry the birth." Slipping an arm around Star Hunter's shoulders, Night Sun put the cup in the slave's hands and held her steady while she gulped the liquid. "There, that's good." She took the cup back and set it on the floor behind her. "Now, rest for as long as you can."

Star Hunter nodded and hung her head between her knees, breathing in swift shallow gasps. A branch broke in the fire, throwing a wavering carnelian veil over the room.

Sweetwater rose to her feet and stood over Night Sun, peering down hatefully. "Why aren't you tending to the Healing of your own family? You're supposed to be the great Healer of Talon Town. Go home! Stop wasting time on a worthless slave baby!"

Night Sun spent part of every day Healing the people in Talon Town, but she truly needed the time away. "Other people need me, too, Sweetwater."

Sweetwater's eyes narrowed skeptically. "You would abandon your own family to Heal slaves?"

"What?" Night Sun said in confusion. "My own family?"

Sweetwater blinked. "You don't know? A Trader came by yesterday morning, from Talon Town. He told us Chief Crow Beard was very ill. He said that Sternlight told him the Blessed Sun might by dying."

Speechless, Night Sun could only stare. Crow Beard had been ill often in the past sun cycle, but—

Cloud Playing rose. Her blue dress shone purple in the gleam. "When did my father fall ill? We have only been gone for three days. He was fine when we left!"

"Do not shout at me, girl!" Sweetwater retorted. "That's all the Trader said. I know no more."

"Mother? Could this be?" Cloud Playing whispered, her eyes frantic. "Do you think Father needs us?"

Night Sun's pulse quickened. Despite all the things Crow Beard had done to her over the years, she still cared for him, but he hadn't let her touch him in summers. He shunned her cures, refused her his bed, tormented her at every opportunity. Still . . . she had been his wife for thirty summers. *How will I survive without him?*

"Yes," Night Sun said softly. "He needs us. But I cannot leave until Star Hunter and her baby are safe. Then we will go—"

"The baby's coming!" Star Hunter cried. She grabbed Night Sun's arm, struggling to get into position.

"Cloud Playing!" Night Sun said sharply. "Help me hold her up!"

Cloud Playing lunged to grab Star Hunter's left arm.

Star Hunter's whole body shook and her moans became helpless cries. She twisted to one side, then to the other, and rocked back and forth, tears trickling down her face. When she screamed, little Catbird put her hands over her ears, and shrieked, "Oh, Blessed Father Sun, don't let my mother die! Please don't let her die!"

"Sweetwater, for the sake of Our Mother Earth," Night Sun called, "take Catbird outside and away from here!"

The old woman grudgingly hobbled across the floor, grabbed Catbird by the hand and dragged her outside. A slap sounded. Catbird's wails grew shrill, like an animal with an arrow in its belly.

Star Hunter sagged back against her arm, gasping, "Please, make the baby come . . . please . . . please . . ."

Cloud Playing peered at Night Sun imploringly—did she, too, believe Night Sun could say a prayer and make the pain end? Cloud Playing's children had come into the world in less than a hand of time and she'd been on her feet in two hands. Such agony must terrify her.

"Cloud Playing," she said gently, "let us ease Star Hunter back to the sleeping mat. I must check the child."

Star Hunter groaned when Night Sun reached inside, rolling back and forth on the mat, saying over and over, "Help me, Wolf. Help me, Wolf. Blessed thlatsinas . . ." Then she cried out and grabbed for Night Sun's and Cloud Playing's arms, hauling herself forward.

"Good, Star Hunter," Night Sun said, watching the fluids that leaked from her womb. "The child is coming. I can see its bottom. It's coming out first. Cloud Playing, help me to lift her higher."

Star Hunter half-stood, legs spread and trembling, her whole weight supported by Night Sun and Cloud Playing. Like a boat riding waves, Star Hunter bobbed up and down, sobbing, clawing at Night Sun's arm.

The baby boy slid out onto the soft blankets in a pool of blood.

Night Sun said, "You have a son, Star Hunter. You were right." Night Sun examined the wet, blood-streaked infant and her heart went cold. "He's . . . he's very beautiful."

Star Hunter laughed and cried as they lowered her to the mats, and Night Sun reached for her pack. She pulled out a sharp obsidian flake, severed the baby's cord, and knotted it.

"Let me see him!" Star Hunter panted. "I—I want to look at him."

"Just one moment," Night Sun said. "Mite, hand me those pieces of damp cloth."

"Yes," she said and pulled them from the stick where they had been cooling.

Night Sun tenderly cleaned the gore from the boy, then lifted him by his ankles and shook him. Star Hunter, smiling, stretched out her arms, wanting the baby.

Night Sun shook him again. And again.

Cloud Playing put a hand to her lips. Mite edged forward, staring. As though time had ceased, both of their faces froze. Their expressions might have been carved from wood.

Night Sun slapped the boy on the back and buttocks, turned him right side up and shook him back and forth. His tiny head hung limply.

She held him by the ankles and shook him once more.

"Night Sun?" Mite asked. "Is he . . ."

Night Sun hesitated. "Yes." Biting back her own sorrow, she cradled the dead baby in her arms and rocked him gently. .

Star Hunter wept. The sound tore Night Sun's soul. She had lost three newborns herself: two boys and a girl. One of them had been taken from her before she'd even had a chance to see it. She had heard it calling to her for moons, calling and calling . . .

It was a woman's trial. Something no man could fully understand. After moons of speaking to the child, feeling it move inside you, seeing it grow up in your dreams, a powerful love, like no other, developed. The shock of losing that child, of suddenly realizing you would never look into its living eyes—it stunned the soul.

"Oh, Mother," Mite whimpered. She ran to kneel beside

Star Hunter and gathered her mother's drenched body in her arms, holding her tightly.

"Cloud Playing," Night Sun said, "soak these cloths again and wring them out."

Cloud Playing took the soiled lengths of fabric, dipped them in the warm yucca water and squeezed them out.

Night Sun washed the baby thoroughly and gestured wearily toward the folded blanket where Sweetwater had been sitting. "Fetch me that blanket. This little boy is getting cold."

Star Hunter suddenly put a hand on the floor and gasped, moaning as the afterbirth flooded out. Mite supported her during the contractions.

Cloud Playing brought the blanket and Night Sun carefully wrapped the boy, so that only his face showed, making certain his soul would stay warm over the long cold night ahead.

Tomorrow his clan would dress him and Sing over his body. Relatives would offer gifts and their finest blankets, then bury him beneath the floor of a room, a place where his mother frequently walked, in the hopes that his soul might someday wish to enter her womb again and be reborn.

Night Sun prayed it would be so.

She walked to Star Hunter and laid the dead baby in her arms, saying, "Hold him for a time, Star Hunter."

Star Hunter tenderly kissed her dead son's forehead.

Night Sun said, "Cloud Playing, please rinse those cloths out again. Mite and I will wash Star Hunter and clean up here. Then she must sleep."

The Singing stopped in the kiva outside. Perhaps the men had just realized that the birthing cries had ceased.

Blessed sky gods, Night Sun had forgotten about Whitetail, the father. He would be eager to know how his wife and child were doing.

A clamor rose, feet clacking on the kiva ladder, then soft thuds as a man ran across the plaza.

"*Star Hunter?*" Whitetail called. "*Sweetwater?*"

Night Sun ducked out the door into the glare of winter sunlight to meet him halfway.

Nine

Buckthorn dressed in the predawn glow, quietly slipping on his long plain-weave shirt, buckskin leggings, and yucca sandals, trying not to wake Dune. The holy man slept on the opposite side of the house, wrapped in a faded gray blanket. Just the white top of his head showed. He'd snored all night—the sort of snores that shook the very earth. Buckthorn had gotten little sleep.

As he laced his sandals, he yawned and looked around. The fire had burned down to a bed of charcoal. Leftover tea from last evening sat in a clay pot at the edge of the coals, probably still warm. But Buckthorn couldn't have any, just as he hadn't had any for three days now. Dune had ordered him to fast for four days and climb the mesa every dawn. And, to Buckthorn's amazement, he had found that hunger kept his mind clear and his heart open to the faint voices of the thlatsinas who lived on the mesa top.

Buckthorn reached for his yellow cape, dyed a rich hue with a mixture of sunflower petals and ground lichen. As he slung it over his shoulder, a field mouse sneaked under the door curtain and sniffed the air. Every mouse for a day's walk knew Dune left crumbs of cornbread at the head of his sleeping mats. The mouse bounded across the floor and began munching happily, its whiskers quivering.

Buckthorn watched in fascination as the mouse clawed through Dune's hair to get to more breakfast. Dune shifted, shoving his blanket down so that his toothless smile showed. Buckthorn had seen it before, but it continued to astound him. He'd concluded that Mouse must be the old holy man's Spirit Helper. That was the only reason he could see for not swatting the creature and throwing it into the stew pot.

Buckthorn tiptoed to the door and stuck his hand around

the ratty curtain, testing the air outside. Cold. Very cold. He would need his blanket. He tiptoed back and grabbed it.

"Shielding yourself against the light?" Dune asked sleepily.

Buckthorn frowned. "Are you awake?"

"No, this is my departed soul speaking to you from the underworlds. Of course, I'm awake! Answer my question."

"Shielding myself? Why, no. When I reach the mesa top each morning I stand with my arms open so I am vulnerable to the light, so I can feel it the instant it is reborn."

Dune rolled to his side. The field mouse kept eating, its eyes bright. "Is that your goal? To stand in the light all of your life?"

"Yes, Elder," Buckthorn said serenely, "that is why I came to you. To learn how—"

"Then you will be forever in the darkness. Alone. Troubled."

Buckthorn shifted. "What does that mean?"

Dune extended the tip of his finger to stroke the mouse's silken back. The little animal barely seemed to notice. Deep wrinkles criss-crossed Dune's ancient face as he smiled. In the faint light streaming through the roof's smoke hole his white hair had a tinge of lavender. "You cannot be reborn on your feet, boy. You'll never *be* the light if you insist on keeping your eye on it."

Buckthorn stammered, "But I—I don't wish to be reborn. I want to be a great Spirit Singer, like you. So that I may help my people."

"A *great* Singer?" Dune threw off his blanket and scowled at Buckthorn. His long tan shirt shone darkly. "What arrogance. Do you know where such pride leads? To the kind of selfishness that will make you a terrible Singer."

"But, Elder . . ." He spread his arms helplessly. "I'm a terrible Singer now. I can't even recall the words to some of our most sacred Songs! If I can't look forward to being a great Singer, what can I look forward to?"

"Scorn," Dune said. "Occasionally contempt." He rolled up his blanket and tucked it in the corner near the baskets. "And a good deal of disbelief."

"Scorn?" Buckthorn whispered in horror. "But, Elder, I can't accept that. Why would the very people I'm struggling to help—"

"You can't *accept* it?" Dune's white brows drew down into a solid bushy line. "Well, then, I must prepare you better. Let me see. I know!" He slapped his palms on his knees. "You wish to have a new name, don't you?"

Buckthorn's eyes widened. "Oh, yes, Elder. Very much. I've been thinking about something like—"

"As of this instant, then, you are *Poor Singer*."

"Poor . . . Poor Singer! But that's insulting! Why would you do that to me?"

Dune's reedy voice grew gentle. "Because we do not strive for greatness here. We strive to be so small that no one notices us at all. If you must strive for something, strive to be a rat's tail, or a bird's toe, or a slimy drip of buffalo spittle. That's why you are here, Poor Singer."

"To learn to be buffalo spit?"

"Yes." Dune waggled a knobby finger. "And it's not easy. The first thing you must do is hack away at your heart; it's filled with too much of you. Carve it down to a speck, then seek out all of the other infinitesimally tiny things in the world. Ants that live beneath rocks. Grains of sand. Worms on plant stems. Strive to be one of them. See life through their eyes. Forget the big things."

"Carve up my heart," Buckthorn said sarcastically. "I imagine that will be painful."

Dune grinned like Bobcat crouched before Packrat's nest. "You have no idea."

The old man rose on rickety knees and made a sweeping gesture toward the door. "Go outside where the blood won't make a mess all over things. I'll take the first chop. And I want you to start thinking of yourself by your new name."

"I think that *is* the first chop, Elder." He reached for his blanket.

Poor Singer. I am Poor Singer. It is my name now. I am Poor . . . How can I go through life with a name like that? Poor Singer. Poor Singer. Blessed gods, only an idiot would hire someone with that name to do an important Sing for them! Which means I'll starve, or be forced to throw myself on the mercy of my family. No woman will marry me. I'll never have children. Wolf, help me! I've been cursed!

Angry, he roughly swung his blanket over his shoulders and started for the door.

"No," Dune said. "Leave your blanket."

Poor Singer threw it down, ducked beneath the door curtain, and stepped out into the frigid morning. The cliff towered over the house, two hundred hands tall, casting a long cold shadow. Beyond the rim, Brother Sky glistened a deep translucent blue. Two ravens flapped and circled on the wind currents. Poor Singer rubbed his freezing arms.

And waited.

When the old holy man didn't come out, Poor Singer yelled, "Dune? I'm out here freezing! Where are you?"

"In here . . . sipping warm tea by the fire."

"I thought you were coming out."

"Eventually."

"How soon is that?"

"Plenty soon enough for a poor Singer."

Glumly, he studied the heavens. Crimson dyed the drifting puffs of cloud. The long mesa that curved around Dune's house gleamed as if fresh blood oozed from pores in the rock.

Poor Singer sighed. Had Dune not interrupted his morning ritual, by now he would have reached the mesa top. Father Sun's light struck there first, and Buck . . . Poor Singer liked to witness that timeless moment when the world glowed to life again.

Yes, get used to it. Your name is Poor Singer.

He feathered his long black hair around his shoulders, hoping it would help warm him up. Despite his shirt and cape, shivers taunted his body.

Why does the old man have to torture me so? He treats me worse than a slave.

To keep the shivers at bay, he trotted in place, his feet sinking into the red soil.

"Blessed thlatsinas, I'm turning to ice!" he shouted at the house, and a white fog of breath condensed before him. "If you're not out here in—"

Dune drew back the door curtain and stepped out stark naked.

Poor Singer's feet rooted to the ground. The old man resembled a walking skeleton. Ribs barred his chest, and his arms and legs might have been knobby sticks. Scraggly white hair hung to his bony shoulders.

Dune shivered.

"Cold?" Poor Singer smiled.

In answer, Dune walked to the corner of the house and urinated. He did it with flare, so that the stream spiraled out, amber drops glimmering in the dawn. When he saw Poor Singer watching, he smiled back. "Stupid?" he asked.

Poor Singer's smile drooped.

Dune finished and strolled out beyond the cliff's shadow to look eastward. A rosy halo enveloped him. "We still have time."

"For what?"

"For you to learn that you are truly Father Sun's child."

"I already know that."

"That's the problem. You know too stinking much." Dune propped his hands on his pointed hip bones. "Take off your clothes."

Poor Singer's mouth gaped. "How will my turning blue show—"

"Are you afraid to face Father Sun as a newborn?"

"A . . . a newborn?" Poor Singer thought about it. "No. I'm not afraid."

Timidly, he pulled off his cape and shirt and dropped them to the ground. He had to sit down to remove his buckskin leggings and sandals. Red sand sheathed his exposed skin. While he untied his last sandal lace, he watched his scrotum shrivel. "Now what?"

Dune waved a clawlike hand. "Go climb the cliff. Be there when Father Sun rises. But today, Poor Singer, face him as an infant. Do not speak, or stand, or walk. Pretend you know nothing. That you don't even know how to crawl."

"But if I'm going to get there, I'll have to *run*."

Dune gave him a sidelong look. "Given your pride, boy, I suspect you'll have to run a very long way before you discover there's no 'there' to get to. But," he sighed, "I'll be praying for you."

Dune turned and went back into his house. The teapot rattled.

Teeth chattering, Poor Singer broke into a run, dodging brush, leaping rabbit holes, until he reached the steps cut into the red cliff wall. One body-length wide, the steps felt smooth to the touch. Hundreds of feet had sanded them to a texture as sleek as kit fur.

Poor Singer concentrated on his climb. He took deep breaths and let them out slowly. Wispy blades of dry grass clung to each ledge, smelling brittle and earthy. Halfway up, his irritation with Dune dissipated. He loved this dawn ritual, the solitude, the stunning desert silence, the sensation of joy as the darkness ran away, secreting itself in deep crevices in the rocks.

He climbed out onto the barren mesa top just as the horizon turned from lavender to a gleaming gold.

"Be a newborn," he muttered. "An infant. How in the world do I do that?"

He considered the words a moment, then shrugged, lay down on the cold sandstone, and curled on his side into a fetal position, facing east. The chill ate into his naked flesh, but as he gazed out across the buttes and ridges rising from the sage-covered flats, he felt curiously calm. The land possessed an unearthly tranquility. He let the stillness soak into his soul.

"Hack away at my heart."

Dune thought him conceited and vain. He knew the old holy man was trying to teach him to purge himself of his self-love, but his own longings and dreams were all he had ever had to keep him company. How could he let them go?

A meadowlark's voice carried in the quiet, its flutelike call melodious. As wind drifted over the mesa, he caught strains of whispers and thought he heard softly placed steps.

"What do you think he meant, thlatsinas?" Poor Singer whispered. "How do I face Father Sun as a baby would? A baby with no knowledge of the world. He told me not to speak, or . . ."

Realizing he had already violated Dune's orders, he hushed, and fought to quiet his internal dialogue, focusing his attention on the luminous sky.

Bright white spikes punctured the horizon. Beneath them, quiet as mouse, Father Sun peeked, warily checking the world before rising. His gleam washed the land, driving away the last shreds of darkness, flowing over Poor Singer like warm honey. The black hair on his body prickled. Awe surged in his heart.

Never before had he experienced the suddenness of the transfiguration from coldness to warmth.

He rolled to his back and spread his arms and legs, baring himself to Father Sun. His head rested on a small rise in the stone, and as he gazed over his skinny body, past the mound of dark hair between his legs, and beyond to the sculpted red-gold land, he felt a joy he had never known.

His clothing *had* shielded him!

Euphoric at the revelation, Poor Singer laughed out loud.

The sky blued above him while he thought: *So this is what Dune was trying to tell me.* Newborns came from a solitary world of constant night, expecting nothing, comprehending nothing. When the sunlight flooded over them for the first time, it must have filled them with wonder—as it had him this morning. Indeed, the light felt as much a part of him as the warm blood in his veins.

"Blessed thlatsinas. That's what Dune meant about being the light. Oh, yes, gods, please. I want to be sunlight, too."

He filled his lungs with the chill air and the rich fragrances of juniper and dew-soaked earth.

I can't wait to tell Dune! I understand! I really understand!

The frail scratching of bird feet made him turn toward the cliff's edge.

A sage thrasher perched on a rounded hump of sandstone, its brown head cocked to scrutinize him. Love swelled Poor Singer's chest. Once, long before the First People emerged from the underworlds, before the Made People walked the earth as animals, the bird and he had lived as one in the brilliant star that formed Spider Woman's heart. Sparkles, they had laughed and twinkled together. Only when the Creator named them did they become different. The instant they knew their names, they had fallen to earth, and become bird and coyote.

"Brother," Poor Singer whispered as he slowly extended a hand to the sage thrasher. "Come with me. Let us be one again in the sunlight."

The bird uttered a sweet lilting call, and flew away.

Poor Singer smiled.

It took effort to rise to his feet. He tingled all over.

As he climbed down the rock steps, he Sang, *"Our daylight fathers. Our daylight mothers. It comes alive. It comes alive, alive, alive."* His words echoed across the canyon like soft thunder,

Sung in the deep voice that had brought him renown at Wind-flower Village.

When Poor Singer reached the bottom stair, he saw two men trotting down the trail that wound around the base of the cliff. Big men, burly and coated with sweat. They wore red shirts, belted at the waist, and had coral pendants around their necks.

Poor Singer loped for the house, calling, "Dune? Dune, two men are coming!"

Sunlight had driven back the cliff's shadow, leaving Dune's house sitting in a puddle of yellow. The sage growing up around the clay-plastered walls glimmered green.

Dune pulled the door curtain aside and stuck his white head out. "Who?"

Poor Singer trotted up, breathing hard. "I can't say. I've never seen them before. But they are important men. They wear beautiful coral pendants—"

"Coral?" Dune asked, and stepped outside, still naked.

Both of them stood staring down the trail.

The men trotted up, squinted curiously at their nakedness, and exchanged knowing glances. Then the taller man bowed respectfully. "A blessed morning to you, Elder."

"And to you, Wraps-His-Tail. What—"

"*Wraps-His-Tail!*" Poor Singer blurted. "The—the great deputy to the War Chief of Talon Town?"

Wraps-His-Tail inclined his head humbly, but Dune growled, "Great, great, great! Is reputation all that concerns you?"

"F-forgive me, Dune." Poor Singer hung his head in shame. Whatever his soul had learned on the cliff, his mouth had immediately forgotten.

Dune glanced at the other man, shorter, but just as stout, with a round face and small eyes. "You are looking well, Cone."

"And you also, Elder," the man said with a smile. "It has been a long time since you graced us with your presence at Talon Town. We have missed you."

"Umm," Dune said, and carefully examined Wraps-His-Tail. "What are you doing way out here?"

"The Blessed Sun is sick again, Elder," Wraps-His-Tail answered. "We have been carrying the message around."

Dune's bushy brows plunged down. "That hardly seems the

sort of duty Ironwood would give his two best warriors."

Wraps-His-Tail shrugged. "We were at hand."

Cone added, "Ironwood wished to ensure that we beat the rumors. You know how people panic when a Chief falls ill. They always say he is dying."

"Yes, that's true."

"Well," Wraps-His-Tail bowed again, "we must be going. We promised Ironwood we would be back by tomorrow."

"Be off, then." Dune waved a hand. "Tell Crow Beard I wished him well."

"Indeed, we shall, Elder!"

Both men trotted on up the trail, heading toward the main road which led south. Dune watched them go, his eyes slitted suspiciously.

"What is it?" Poor Singer asked. "Is something wrong?"

"Not according to them." Dune fingered his sagging chin.

The old man ducked back into his house and Poor Singer heard him talking to the mouse. The door curtain swung, flashing in the sunlight.

"Dune!" Poor Singer said. "I have something important to tell you! Wait until you hear what I did this morning. You won't believe it!"

Poor Singer pulled back the curtain and saw Dune slipping on a tan shirt. His white hair shone in the firelight. Crouching, he added more wood to the fire, and asked, "What?"

Poor Singer swelled his chest. "I learned to be a newborn! On my first try!"

"Did you?" Dune's bushy brows arched.

"Yes, but you were right," Poor Singer quickly added, "it wasn't easy. Not at all. I had to work *very* hard."

"I see."

Poor Singer shifted uncomfortably. "See . . . what?"

Dune got to his feet. The wrinkles around his small round nose twitched. "I see that you and your pride are still standing tall in the light."

Ten

Six body-lengths wide, the road shimmered with crushed potsherds. Not all roads had such a surface, but many did, particularly those near sacred sites, or towns. Night Sun hurried, her black-and-white cape flapping around her like bat wings as she trotted past Kettle Town. Just to the east of Talon Town, it rose in stepped layers, its famous colonnade shining in the sun. Behind its north wall with its hanging porch, the rounded tower rose to the ladders and hand-holds that led to the stairway and the road north to Center Place.

Night Sun's cousin, Moon Bright, was Matron of Kettle Town. When the people, who perched on the roofs of the multistoried building, yelled questions at Night Sun, she just waved and continued on. She could see Talon Town ahead, shining whitely in the afternoon sun. A nearly perfect half-circle, the flat east–west wall of the giant structure faced south, gleaning the winter sun's warming rays. Slaves clustered around the single entrance in the western half of the flat wall, grinding corn in the mealing bins, carrying out the refuse, weaving brightly colored fabric on large looms. Two deerhides were being stretched on wooden frames. Women labored over them, scraping them with stone tools.

Young Swallowtail—fourteen summers old, muscular, and very tall for his age—knelt beside them, butchering a deer with a long obsidian blade. He took short, expert strokes, separating out each muscle, laying it on a flat stone to the side. The pile of rich red meat stood four hands tall. Each slave had specific duties. Swallowtail tended to cutting up animals and dusting the ceremonial masks in Talon Town. Both he and his mother, Mourning Dove, were extremely talented and loyal slaves. As Night Sun trotted up, Swallowtail smiled and greeted, "It is good to have you home, Blessed Matron."

"Thank you, Swallowtail. I hope you are well."

He beamed. "Oh, yes, better now." The boy glanced at the bandage on his arm. "The poultice you placed on my cut is working. No evil Spirits have entered the wound yet."

Night Sun smiled. He'd slipped and fallen down a hillside while carrying a large pot of water. One of the jagged sherds had slashed his upper arm. "I'm glad. I will look at it again tomorrow, just to make sure."

"Thank you, Blessed Matron. I . . ." He looked up suddenly and pointed. "I think you are being hailed."

Night Sun turned to the mounds that thrust up in front of Talon Town. Long, square, and flat-topped, they'd been built over old trash mounds, squared off, and heightened to allow the commoners to see above the south wall and into the plaza. During the ceremonial dances, those mounds were packed with spectators. But they served as more than viewing platforms. An enemy would have to sneak through a narrow defile about five body-lengths wide—between the mounds and the south wall—to rush the entry. Anyone so foolish would find Talon Town's warriors raining arrows down upon him.

The burly slave master, Gray Wood, stood atop the eastern mound, his red shirt billowing in the wind. He was waving his bow to catch Night Sun's attention. He called, "Welcome back, Blessed Night Sun!"

"Good day, Gray Wood!" she shouted. "How is my husband?"

Gray Wood lifted a hand uncertainly. His shadow stretched long and straight, pointing eastward. His loose hair glinted blue-black. "Only the gods know. But surely he will get better now that you are home."

Night Sun smiled weakly and hurried on into the narrow portal. Through the entry, she could see the *Yamuhakto*, the Great Warriors of East and West, who stood painted on the curving rear wall of Talon Town, thirty hands tall, magnificent. The rich blues, reds, and yellows of their terrifying masks took on an unearthly light in the afternoon sun. The lightning bolts in their upraised hands were aimed down at the plaza, at anyone or anything that might dare disrupt the sacred harmony of the Straight Path people.

Over the past twenty summers, Sternlight had often

Dreamed that Power was abandoning the canyon, disowning the Straight Path people. He'd warned that if they didn't do something soon, they would see their world crumble to dust. Last summer, Sternlight had gone out into the desert to fast and pray, then had returned at a run, shouting at Talon Town's artists to paint everything—interior and exterior walls, pots, clothing, jewelry—anything that would hold an image, a shred of the vanishing Power.

Then he had broken down and wept for four days and four nights, until he'd had no more tears to give.

Suddenly frightened, Night Sun ran through the entry, passing, to her left, the slave chambers and the Cage where they kept prisoners locked up. Three large kivas dotted the plaza in front of her. Ladders thrust up from their roofs, allowing entry and exit. A long strip of rooms cut through the middle of the plaza to her right, dividing it in half. Ahead, five stories of rooms rose, each story stepped back, resembling a huge staircase. Ladders led from roof to roof.

She bowed briefly to the Great Warriors, then began climbing, gripping the pine poles, her feet working, scaling the next ladder, and the next, until she reached the fifth story. Though most chambers in Talon Town were entered by ladders through holes in roofs, this block of rooms had T-shaped doorways. The shape helped cool the rooms in the summer. The cool air near the floor was hindered from escaping by the narrow base of the "T," while the hot air vented through the wide top. Ironwood stood beside the doorway she sought.

Night Sun stopped, breathing hard, and peered into his eyes. Tall, sun-bronzed, he leaned against the white-plastered wall with his muscular arms folded. He'd braided his graying black hair into a single plait that draped over his right shoulder. Muscles bulged under the fabric of his long red shirt. He wore black leggings and sandals. At the age of almost forty-six summers, the War Chief's violent life showed in his face. Deep lines etched his forehead and curved around his wide mouth, accentuating the flatness of his nose. Even when he smiled these days, he looked sad, though deep inside her, he would always be the handsome laughing youth she had loved so desperately.

But that was a long time ago, wasn't it, Ironwood? Back when we were both young and outrageously foolish.

As she walked toward him, he straightened, and tenderness softened his dark eyes. "Forgive me," he said as he extended an arm to block the door. "Crow Beard left orders not to let you enter his chamber."

"That doesn't surprise me, Ironwood. He's never known what was good for him—or for anyone else, for that matter. Is he alive?"

"Yes. Barely."

"Then he needs me. Get out of my way." She gripped his arm and tried to force it down.

He held fast. "Blessed Night Sun, would you have me disobey—"

Night Sun swiftly ducked beneath his arm and stalked across the elaborately painted room toward her husband's bedside, where Sternlight knelt. Dressed in white, his long hair shone as blackly as it had twenty summers ago. He gazed at her solemnly.

"Aunt," Sternlight said, "you know that I am honor-bound to tell you—"

"I do know it, nephew," she cut him off. "Which means there is no need for you to say it. Besides, Crow Beard is asleep. He cannot punish you for something he does not witness."

Sternlight raised an eyebrow. "True."

Night Sun knelt opposite him and gazed upon her husband. What she saw frightened her. Thin gray hair clung to his freckled scalp in damp wisps, and his wrinkled face was flushed. His chest moved rapidly beneath the blankets.

She bent forward to touch his gaunt cheeks. "Hallowed gods," she whispered. "What have you been doing for his fever?"

Sternlight peered at her with clear brown eyes. "Nothing. He ordered us not to call any Healers. He said he hates them all, even—"

"That's demented! Part of his fever! You believed him?"

"No, not—not really. But it was an order, Night Sun. I had no choice."

She gripped the fabric of her cape near her throat and pulled to untie the bow. "Well," she said through a taut exhalation, "my husband is unable to give you any more orders, great Sun-watcher. Now you take orders from me."

"Of course."

She removed her cape and spread it over Crow Beard. "Where is my son?"

"Snake Head stayed up all night. He only retired to his chambers to rest two hands of time ago."

"Good. He won't be around to bother me."

Sternlight bowed his head obligingly. "What is it you wish me to do to help you?"

"Where are my slave women? Find them. Order them to bring bowls of hot coals and set them around Crow Beard. Tell them I want all the hides they can gather."

"Yes, Night Sun. Is there anything else?"

She forced her exhausted mind to think. "Just one thing. I left Cloud Playing and my Healer's pack at Deer Mother Village. A woman there took ill after her baby was born—born dead. Since I do not have my pack, I will need several things from my chambers. Tell my slave, Mourning Dove, that I need the pot of willow bark. . . ." She let out a breath. Weariness weighted her shoulders like a cape of stone. She had run almost all the way home. "Ask Mourning Dove to pour me a warm bath and bring my blankets here. I will sleep beside Crow Beard tonight."

Both Ironwood and Sternlight gaped at her, as if they had not heard correctly. It had been many summers since she had slept in her husband's chamber, or he in hers. Everyone knew it.

Night Sun glared at Sternlight. "Are you deaf? Or just defying me?"

"Neither, Aunt." He rose to his feet. "I am on my way to deliver your orders."

Sternlight crossed the room gracefully, his white ritual shirt swaying with each step. He exchanged a glance with Ironwood before he exited into the rusty gleam of late afternoon.

Night Sun glared at Ironwood, daring him to make a comment. As he approached, the light from the doorway threw his tall body into silhouette, highlighting the breadth of his shoulders and narrowness of his waist. He knelt beside her, searching her face. Night Sun longed to touch him, to ease the constant pain in his eyes—but she couldn't. Not now. Not ever again.

We change what we love, she thought. *We turned each other into lonely people.*

Ironwood's deep voice came softly. "What are your orders for me, Night Sun? I'll do anything you ask."

"Indeed? Is that why you wouldn't let me in—"

"I *did* let you in, my friend."

Their gazes held.

"Yes, you did. I thank you for that."

He lowered his eyes to Crow Beard. "Is there anything you can do for him?"

She shook her head. "I honestly don't know. If his fever has been this high for days—"

"It has."

"Then I fear for his soul. It may have already begun the journey to the afterlife. Even if I can save him, he may never be the same."

Night Sun's eyes narrowed as she gazed upon Crow Beard. She never should have married him, never should have yielded to her family's pleading. But there had been a catastrophe. Her older sister, Whitefly, then Matron of the First People, had been killed by raiders along with her husband, the Blessed Sun. Both of Whitefly's daughters had vanished before they'd turned fifteen summers. The daughter left by their oldest sister, Lacewing, had been captured by the Fire Dogs, and no one knew if she lived or had been murdered. That left Night Sun, thirteen years her sister's junior, to serve as Matron. But she could not do it, they told her, as a single woman. Though no clan laws forbade a single woman from ruling, the clan demanded that she marry. And she had, quickly, taking the man they'd selected for her.

She should have sent Crow Beard away and forced her family to search for another. If she had, she would not be torn in two now, terrified he might die—and yearning for the liberty his death would bring.

Liberty—but at such a price. Until she, or Cloud Playing, remarried, if ever, her only son Snake Head would rule as Blessed Sun, but his arrogant self-absorption would free Night Sun to do as she wished, to travel and to Heal. She could even have her fill of lovers. Despite her age, many men would gladly lie with her, just to be able to say they had bedded the great Matron of Talon Town, or to gain the Power it might bring. . . . *No, I don't want lovers. That time is past.*

An odd sensation, as if she tumbled through emptiness, dizzied her. She reached out, and Ironwood gripped her arm firmly.

"What's wrong?" he asked.

"I was just . . . thinking."

"Feeling guilty? You've always blamed yourself for far too much. His illness is not your—"

"No, no." She swallowed. "I was thinking that my heart is dead, Ironwood. I don't love anymore." She paused. "But, I don't cry either."

He squeezed her arm, then let it go, and rose to his feet. Looking down, he said, "You've made a resolution, eh? Like giving up squash for the Summer Dances? All you have to do is say, 'I don't love anymore' and the need is gone? You are Powerful, indeed, Blessed Night Sun."

She gazed up at him. A faint smile tugged at the corners of his wide mouth.

I gave you up "like squash," didn't I?

She had made the decision in an instant. The day their baby died . . . she had known what she had to do, and she'd done it. For six moons afterward she couldn't see him without longing to weep.

"I'm tired," she said. "Will you stay with Crow Beard while I bathe and eat? I will return as soon as I—"

"Sleep, too," he commanded gently. "I will be here."

"If anything happens you'll—"

"Let you know instantly. Of course."

Night Sun brushed hair behind her ears and got to her feet. "I *will* be back soon."

"As you wish."

She started to walk past him, but halted. Lightly, she placed a hand on his arm and met his concerned gaze. "Thank you."

"Your servant, as always."

She left swiftly.

Snake Head leaned against the doorway of his chamber, watching the eastern plaza far below him.

"Which one of you slave brats stole my pack?" the Hohokam Trader, Blunt Face, yelled. "I know one of you did it!"

Five slave children, dressed in brown rags, gathered in a circle around the burly giant, most looking horrified by the accusation. They stared up with wide eyes.

Blunt Face propped his hands on his hips. He stood fourteen hands tall and wore a doehide shirt covered with copper bells. His black hair hung level with his chin. "If you won't tell me, I'll call for the War Chief. You don't wish me oto do that, do you? He'll punish you far worse than—"

"*What's wrong?*" Gray Wood, the slave master, stalked across the plaza, a yucca whip in his hand, and a bow and quiver of arrows over his left shoulder. He wore a red shirt and sandals. "What's all the yelling?"

Blunt Face gestured to the pack of slave children. "One of these brats is a thief! I stowed my packs by the wall over there, just as I always do, and one of them is missing. It's filled with rare Hohokam Trade goods! And very dangerous things! Power amulets and fetishes and—"

"All right." Gray Wood bent forward and scowled at the children, ranging in age from three to fourteen summers. "Who took the pack?" he asked. "Tell me now, or all of you will feel my whip!" He shook it at them.

The three-summers-old girl put a finger in her mouth and started crying. She shrieked, "*I didn't do it! I swear it!*"

"Well, who did? Tell me now or . . ."

Snake Head's attention was drawn away when his mother emerged from his father's fifth-floor chamber and started down the ladder to the fourth story. Weariness seemed to weight the tall and willowy woman like a cape of granite; her movements were sluggish. Snake Head lifted a brow. His mother's eyes glowed.

But, then, she had just spent a finger of time alone with Ironwood.

Snake Head's lip curled with disgust. As a boy, he had followed her, tracked her like a wolf on a blood trail, so he knew a great deal about her "secret" life.

The macaw behind him churred softly and cracked another

pine nut. The fragments of hull tapped the floor.

Snake Head's gaze went to the south side of the plaza, where the War Chief always stood watch on the roof beside the entry. Seventeen summers ago, just after his father had left on a trading mission to the Hohokam, Snake Head used to see his mother there often. She would wait until the town slept, then sneak from her chambers and go to sit beside Ironwood, just to talk to him, to touch him.

"At least, that's how it started," Snake Head murmured to himself.

Their meetings had gradually grown more intimate. As War Chief, Ironwood had to inform Night Sun the day before he left Talon Town, telling her where he would be and for how long, in case a crisis arose. No matter where Ironwood went—to the signal towers to send messages to neighboring villages, to check on distant antelope traps—he always found Night Sun waiting for him.

At the age of eight summers, Snake Head had been fascinated by this strange behavior. His mother would dress beautifully and leave before dawn, carrying a basket of food and a jug of tea. She never returned until after nightfall—and she seemed to think no one noticed her absences, or connected them with Ironwood's.

"You were such a fool, Mother," he whispered to himself. "About that and so *many* other things. I came to hate you for betraying my father. I only wish I—"

The birds suddenly went silent. The dogs in the plaza yipped and ran off with their tails between their legs. . . . Then, with a low growl, the shaking began. Snake Head braced himself in his door frame to keep from stumbling and listened to the roof timbers groan and crack. Stones shook loose from the canyon wall and crashed down to roll across the ground. Sharp cries and shouts rang out. The tremor lasted only a few moments, but by the time it subsided, Snake Head was breathing as if he'd run across the canyon and back. His knees had gone suddenly weak.

Night Sun rushed to her chamber and disappeared inside. Snake Head stared after her.

"Did you feel the rage of our ancestors, Mother?" he whispered. "They're giving you just a taste of what will happen if I ever tell anyone about the things I witnessed as a boy."

He rose and, as he walked by the macaw's cage, thumped the bars until the bird squawked and flapped. Snake Head smiled and proceeded to his bedding. He stretched out on his back, trying to get some rest.

He would need it. The moment his father died, Snake Head would take over as the new Blessed Sun of the Straight Path nation.

Then, his life would truly begin.

Eleven

In front of their house, Cornsilk stood quietly in the morning light while her mother draped a red-and-white striped cape around her shoulders. Thistle had been fussing with Cornsilk's clothing and pack ever since they'd finished breakfast, over a hand of time ago, making certain she had enough food and water, that her extra clothing would equal any change of weather.

People watched from the roofs of Lanceleaf Village, shading their eyes against the morning sun. All were curious, but too polite to ask the real reason for Cornsilk and Fledgling's departure.

Thistle retied the laces on Cornsilk's pack—for the second time—and grimaced. Her mother always fiddled with things when she had something to say but hadn't yet decided how to put it.

Thistle wore a deep reddish brown dress; the color came from a dye made with ripe prickly pear fruit. A tan blanket draped her shoulders.

"You look beautiful, my daughter," her mother said. "Don't forget to tell Deer Bird that this will only be for a short time. Just until we know for certain whether the Tower Builders plan to attack us or not. When we know we're safe, we'll come and get you." She stroked Cornsilk's hair tenderly. "I miss you already. I must have you back in my life as soon as possible."

Cornsilk gazed into her mother's agonized face. Lines etched the skin around her dark eyes, and she looked as if she might cry. "Don't worry, Mother. I'll be fine. I should be going. Fledgling is already waiting for me on the trail."

"Yes, I know, but . . ." Her mother spread her hands the way she did when coming to an important decision. "Just a moment, Cornsilk."

Thistle ducked into the house, draping the curtain over its peg. Through the open doorway, Cornsilk could see her as she crossed to the big painted pot at the foot of her bed. She lifted the stone that weighted the top, set it on the floor with a solid thump, and dug around inside.

Cornsilk swallowed hard. She'd never seen anyone open that pot! From her earliest memories, her parents had forbidden her to touch it. For once, she had obeyed. Strange sounds came from that pot late at night, hisses and taps, as if something alive were trapped in there. Something dangerous enough to require that huge rock to keep it in.

Her mother pulled out a folded blanket and held it to her heart before ducking back outside. "Cornsilk," she said, "if something happens to you or Fledgling—and nothing will, but just in case—I wish you to have this. It's very precious to me."

Cornsilk watched in awe as her mother unfolded the blanket. Polished chunks of turquoise studded the centers of the red, black, and blue diamonds that had been woven into the cotton fabric. Copper bells jingled at each corner.

"Where did it come from?" she whispered. "It's beautiful."

Thistle carefully tucked it into Cornsilk's pack, then retied the laces once more. "It was a gift to me many sun cycles ago."

Cornsilk girded herself, carefully considered the question, then looked at Thistle. "A gift . . . from my real mother?"

Thistle's hands hovered over Cornsilk's pack. A difficult swallow went down her throat. "Cornsilk . . . forgive me. I always meant to tell you."

Tears filled Cornsilk's eyes. The admission was like a blow to her stomach. She couldn't speak. She stood there in silence, her mouth open, as the tears spilled hotly down her cheeks.

"Oh, Cornsilk." Thistle left the pack on the ground and rose to embrace her. Holding Cornsilk tightly, she kissed her hair and whispered, "I love you so much. You will always be my daughter, even if I am not your birth mother. I—"

"Who is?" Cornsilk gazed up at her. "Who is my mother? And my father?" Desperation tickled the base of her throat. She *had* to know this.

Thistle shook her head. "I don't know. Truly. I wish I did." Gently, she stroked Cornsilk's back. "When you return, I will tell you everything I know, and all the things I suspect. For now, remember that . . . that I did not tell you before because I feared for your safety. If my suspicions are true, you would make a great prize, or a target for some ambitious warrior, Cornsilk. Tell no one about this. Promise me." When Cornsilk just stared at her, Thistle demanded, "*Promise me!* You must not even tell Fledgling. No one! Do you understand?"

Cornsilk managed to nod. "Yes."

Thistle lifted the pack and held it out for Cornsilk. Numb, she slipped her arms through the shoulder straps and knelt to retrieve her bow and quiver from where they leaned against the wall by the door. She slung her quiver over her left shoulder.

"Mother, I wish you to know that I love you more now than I ever have. For . . . for all the kindness you have shown me. I promise to take very good care of that blanket."

Thistle put her hands on either side of Cornsilk's face and said, "There is one more thing, my daughter: if you are ever in trouble and need help . . ." Words seemed to have evaporated from her lips. Finally, her gaze hardened and she continued, "If you are ever *desperate*, take that blanket to Talon Town and present it to the great priest Sternlight. Tell him that I gave it to you. He will understand."

"But isn't he a witch? Why would—"

"*Don't* ask me, my daughter. I can tell you only that I believe he will help you."

Questions plagued Cornsilk, and things she longed to say. Was Sternlight her father? Where was her mother? Still at Talon Town? Why had neither of them ever come to see her? Even secretly, just to get a glimpse of their little girl? . . . Didn't they care about her?

She hugged Thistle's shoulders. "I love you, Mother. I'll see you soon."

In a strained voice, Thistle answered, "I know you will. I love you, too."

With their arms around each other, they looked down over the familiar sights of Lanceleaf Village—the square of buildings that enclosed the plaza, the kiva that made a circle on the ground to the left. Two old men leaned against the ladder that stuck up through the roof of the holy structure, smiling, talking. A group of laughing children raced across the plaza with dogs barking and leaping at their heels.

Cornsilk turned to the road where Fledgling stood with their father. Beargrass wore a long gray shirt and red leggings. His black braid hung down his back.

"Fledgling is very frightened by all this," her mother said as they walked. "You are braver than he is, Cornsilk. Please, try to ease his fears as you walk him toward the split in the road."

Cornsilk squinted against the sun. Her heart had gone dead in her chest. "Should I walk him all the way to Grandfather Standing Gourd's village?"

"No, just to the split in the road. Deer Bird expects you to arrive before dark tonight. He'll be worried if you're late."

"All right, mother, I—"

Her mother suddenly hugged her so hard it forced the air from her lungs. Cornsilk jumped in surprise.

"Oh, my daughter," Thistle said as she nuzzled her cheek against Cornsilk's. "You are my joy. Never forget that."

Cornsilk kissed her mother's temple. "I love you, Mother. Don't worry. I'll be fine. And so will Fledgling. I won't let anyone hurt him. He is like . . . he *is* my brother. We'll see you when the threat of war is over."

Thistle released Cornsilk, her dark eyes moist. At that moment, Leafhopper ran from the gate with little Brave Boy sprinting at her heels. Five summers old, Brave Boy wore a perpetual grin. Leafhopper, however, looked sad. Every time one of her feet hit the ground, her chin-length black hair flapped over her ears like wings, and her chunky body jiggled.

"*Cornsilk!*" Leafhopper cried as she threw her arms around her. "You were leaving without saying good-bye?"

"I'll only be gone for a short time, Leafhopper."

"I know, but I'll miss you."

"I'll miss you, too. Try to stay out of trouble."

"I will . . . if you'll promise not to let any raiders catch you."

Cornsilk forced a smile, remembering what her mother had said about her being a prize or a target. "I won't. I promise."

Brave Boy grabbed Cornsilk around the leg and squeezed. "Goodbye, Cornsilk."

She brushed tangled hair away from his round face and smiled at him. "Try to be good, all right?"

He looked up with wide eyes. "I will. And I won't play hoop-and-stick with anyone else while you are gone!"

"I will miss you, Brave Boy."

He grinned, said, "Good-bye, Cornsilk," and raced away toward the village.

Leafhopper reached out to touch Cornsilk's arm. "Come home soon."

"I will, Leafhopper." Cornsilk indicated the watching people with a jerk of her head. "No matter what they think about me being a witch, that's not why I'm leaving."

"I know," Leafhopper said in a disbelieving voice. Then she backed away, turned, and ran for the plaza. Cornsilk watched until her friend disappeared through the gate.

"Ready?" her mother asked.

Cornsilk nodded and turned away.

Thistle held Cornsilk's hand tightly for the rest of the walk. Fledgling and Beargrass were standing where the trail led off toward Deer Bird and Standing Gourd's villages. From the looks of it, they'd been having a father–son talk. Fledgling clenched his fists nervously as they neared. Wind tousled the hem of his tan-and-brown cape. His brows, usually arched with mirth or curiosity, were drawn down above his pug nose.

Her father smiled. "Are you ready, Cornsilk?"

"Yes, F-father. Don't worry about us." When the word "father" stuck in her throat, Beargrass frowned.

He leaned down, cupped her chin with his hand, and looked at her with love in his eyes. "I'll worry every instant you're away. Protect yourself for me."

Cornsilk hugged him hard. "I will, Father. You and Mother take care of each other for us, too."

"We will."

Her father patted Cornsilk's back, rose, and cocked his head at Fledgling. Her brother looked miserable. He fumbled with the quiver over his shoulder, then ran his hand down the smooth wood of the bow tied to his belt. Tears filled his eyes.

Cornsilk winked at him. They had planned well. They would run straight past the fork in the road and head for the rock shelters that hollowed out the cliffs a half day's walk to the south. They had camped there with their parents last summer, and knew it to be a beautiful place. A cool spring bubbled up from the sandstone, and fragrant juniper trees blocked Wind Baby's evil antics.

"Come on," she called to Fledgling. "I'll race you to the split in the road!"

Cornsilk took off like a fleet-footed antelope, dust puffing beneath her sandals. She ran with all her heart, ran until the ache in her breast was overwhelmed by the panting of her air-starved lungs.

Fledgling pounded behind her, but she could hear him crying.

They turned around only once, on the crest of the hill, to wave to their parents. Then they sped down the other side toward the juniper grove that marked the split in the road.

Beargrass put his arm around Thistle. As though his attempt at comfort brought pain, she wept, but her eyes never left the horizon.

Tiny clouds of dust sprouted from the opposite side of the hill. Thistle's gaze clung to each one. In the crystal blue sky above, two golden eagles soared, their wings glinting in the sunlight. Beyond rose the cliffs of Little Runt Canyon. At this time of day, shades of mauve, violet, and deep red glimmered. Ghosts Danced there, whirling and shaking human fingerbone rattles.

Beargrass rubbed his chin over Thistle's dark hair. "It's all right. While you fed them, I spoke with Stone Forehead. He'll check on both of them tomorrow on his way to Talon Town.

If anything is wrong, if they got lost or hurt, he's promised to let us know."

Thistle slipped arms around his waist and embraced him. "I thank the blessed thlatsinas for you. Did you know that? Every day of my life."

Twelve

The scent of death permeated the air, coiling through Crow Beard's room as if alive.

Bone weary, Ironwood leaned his shoulder against the clay-washed wall of the Chief's chamber and closed his eyes. Just the illusion of sleep helped. His taut muscles relaxed, and he could finally pull a deep breath into his lungs. His buffalo cape warmed his torso, but his long black shirt and leggings couldn't block the cold.

Sandals creaked on the plastered floor. Ironwood turned to his left and saw Sternlight standing over the sleeping Night Sun. Rolled in a single black blanket with white diamonds woven around the edges, she looked frail and thin, her beautiful face serene in the red light cast by the bowls of glowing coals.

Sternlight adjusted her blanket so it covered her exposed right arm, then rose and went to his mats in the southwestern corner. His white ritual shirt swayed about his legs as he picked up his red blanket and swung it around his shoulders. He gave Ironwood a sympathetic glance before he sat down, propped his forehead on his knees, and tried to rest. Waist-length hair draped around him.

The great priest could sleep, but the great warrior had to remain on guard.

Ironwood's gaze drifted over the magnificent thlatsinas painted on the walls. Larger than life, they wore bright feathered masks and carried rattles in their hands. Four terraces of black thunder clouds adorned their chests, and red streaks of falling rain striped their kirtles. As heat rose from the bowls of coals brought in to warm the dying Chief, the gods blurred and wavered. . . . *Dancing*. Subtly, but Ironwood could see it. The thlatsinas seemed to spin, kirtles billowing, their hallowed feet pounding out the rhythm that had created the universe. If he concentrated, he could hear their voices. . . .

Ironwood shook himself. Sleep taunted him at the edges of his soul, beckoning like a lover's arms.

He pushed away from the wall and walked toward the low doorway in the corner. Before he'd fallen asleep, Crow Beard had ordered the curtain lifted, so that his soul might wander about the canyon, saying good-bye. Ironwood crouched in the entry, shivering in the icy breeze.

A light dusting of snow had fallen. The roofs and plaza of the huge town shone silver. Talon Town contained eight hundred rooms, but most of them served as storage. Crow Beard and Night Sun always strove to have a three-cycle supply of food stored, in case of crop failure.

Many other rooms became guest quarters during solstice ceremonials, when the population of Straight Path Canyon swelled to tens of thousands. A few rooms had been built for ghosts. Talon Town—like the other great towns in the canyon—was holy ground, and clan elders and priests from distant places occasionally wished to be buried here, so that they might be close to the gods.

The practice provided a third kind of afterlife. Made People followed the north road to the blessed *sipapu* and traveled to the underworlds to live with their ancestors, while the First People became thlatsinas, but elders of the Made People who could afford to be buried in Talon Town continued to live in this world. Their souls walked about, mingling with other ghosts, speaking to all of the gods who regularly visited here.

Ironwood shook his head. He could imagine no more dismal an afterlife. What would a man talk to a god about? He would run out of topics in a matter of days and be stuck in the company of divine beings for eternity. A horrifying thought.

What had rich Made People with such aspirations done before Talon Town became sacred ground?

Legends said that many cycles ago the fourteen towns in the canyon had been occupied only seasonally. People came and

went for ceremonials, but they didn't stay—alive or dead—
except perhaps by accident. Only in the past few generations
had a constant small population of chiefs, priests, clan elders,
and slaves lived here, caring for the ghosts, maintaining the
sacred shrines and producing the magnificent turquoise figurines used for trade with outlying villages.

Because the First People had emerged from the underworlds,
they possessed secret knowledge of those worlds that the Made
People did not. Stories had been passed down from generation
to generation, describing the trip through the underworlds, the
traps laid by wicked monsters, the landmarks which guided
traveling souls on the right path. For a price, the First People
shared their stories, and might even provide the seeker with a
turquoise wolf Spirit Helper to guide him on the journey.

The First People at Talon Town traded their knowledge for
almost everything. Their beautiful black-on-white pottery
came from the Green Mesa villages in the north, their hides
and meat from plains hunters, their turquoise from Fourth
Night House to the east. They grew some of their own crops
through extensive water control projects—canals, reservoirs,
dams, and the careful maintenance of farming terraces—but
most food came to Talon Town as gifts from the faithful villages
of Made People.

Each Made People clan had a specific role. Ironwood's clan,
the Bear Clan, provided warriors to manage the labor force,
guard food reserves, and conduct offensive and defensive warfare when necessary. Buffalo Clan controlled agricultural activities. They were responsible for planting, harvesting, designing
irrigation projects, and preparing food for storage. Ant Clan
did all of the building. They cut trees, quarried stone, built the
irrigation projects designed by Buffalo Clan, and constructed
the multistoried towns. The majestic stonework of Ant Clan
masons was esteemed even by the Fire Dogs. Coyote Clan provided hunters and Traders.

Almost unconsciously Ironwood's hand lifted to the turquoise wolf pendant that Night Sun had given him. The first
time they'd consummated their love, she'd told him how to get
to the underworlds. They'd been lying on a hilltop under a
blanket, staring up at a wealth of spring stars . . .

Ironwood rubbed his eyes and stared out at the night. Sound

carried to this highest row of rooms. He could hear Singing from the kivas, the voices weaving a soft background for the night. In the distance, dogs barked, and a child shrilled angrily.

Many lesser clans of Made People existed: the Red Bird, the Buffalobeard, the Canyon Wren. But each allied itself with one of the four great clans, and so was considered part of it. Clans came and went, depending upon the strength of their hands, the productivity of their lands, and the faith in their hearts. Ironwood had witnessed the death of six clans: The Blue Bead had been hunted down and slaughtered by the Hohokam; the Mogollon had wiped out the Butterfly Shield Clan; Two Stone Clan had been destroyed by Ironwood's warriors—their village burned, their bodies crushed with stones—when it was discovered they were witches.

And then there was the Hollow Hoof Clan, which had lost its sacred bundle to strange tattooed warriors who had come out of nowhere, stolen their Tortoise Bundle, and kidnapped a little girl . . . what had her name been? Yarrow and Red Cane's daughter. Three or four summers old. Nightshade? He couldn't recall for certain, though he had been in the plaza watching the sacred Dances that night. When the attack came, he'd dashed inside for his weapons and missed all but the last moments of the battle. He'd shot two arrows at the backs of fleeing men.

Over the years, Talon Town had lost many children to raiders. They stole them for slaves, then beat them half to death. Sometimes, an enemy warrior took children to make them part of his family. Perhaps his wife had not been able to give him a daughter, or his son had died from a childhood illness.

The Straight Path nation did the same.

Slaves moved about in the dark plaza below. Ironwood's eyes followed them as they built fires, carried water and food, and prepared for the feast to be held later in the day. He could hear them talking in their strange Fire Dog tongue. Two women delivered wood to the Buffalo Clan's kiva, carefully placing their armloads near the ladders that thrust up from the roofs.

From Ironwood's fifth-story perspective, the kivas resembled huge rings on the white plaza. Inside, the Buffalo Dancers Sang, their voices rising like smoke into the frosty darkness.

He leaned out the doorway to check the stars.

Spider Woman had one spindly leg extended over the eastern horizon. When she had climbed fully into the sky, the Dancers would emerge from the kivas, to try once more to save the Blessed Sun's life.

Behind him, Night Sun sighed. He turned. After a long yawn, she shoved back her blanket and got to her feet. Her bright blue dress clung to her slender body. She smoothed her mussed hair away from her face. When she twisted it into a bun on top of her head, as she did now, and secured it with turquoise-inlaid bone pins, she looked breathtaking.

Sternlight wakened at her movements, and called, "Night Sun?"

Without answering, she lit one of the torches from the glowing coals in the warming bowl. Made from shredded juniper bound together with cotton cord, the torch end gleamed with smoking red eyes. She blew them to life, creating a gold bubble of light in the room. Then she stepped over to her husband.

The Blessed Sun lay in the middle of the floor, covered with deerhides. The blood seemed to have drained from his wrinkled face, leaving it curiously pale in the wavering light. His eyes rested in bruised wells of flesh.

Sternlight rose. The copper bells on his white sleeves tinkled when he put a hand on Night Sun's arm. "Why don't you try to eat one of the blue corncakes the slaves brought? You've taken nothing in two days."

Night Sun knelt at the Chief's side, her blue dress spreading around her. Torchlight made the gray in her dark hair shimmer.

Ironwood glanced away and concentrated on the chamber. He couldn't stand to think about her, about the freedom Crow Beard's death would give her. Dared not.

Prayer feathers hung from the roof, and he watched them twist and flutter in the breeze. Every day clan leaders brought more. After Crow Beard's death, each Made People clan would assign a representative to escort the Chief's corpse down the south road to the sacred Humpback Butte, where his soul would climb into the skyworlds and become one of the thlatsinas. There, in the sky, he would bring rain and happiness to the people.

Ironwood's mouth hardened. How strange that after death

the Chief would bring happiness, when he had brought nothing but misery during his life.

For three days, memories had haunted Ironwood . . . voices of children begging him not to kill their parents . . . men and women screaming as they ran from burning villages. He had served Crow Beard for eighteen summers, faithfully and efficiently carrying out each insane order.

Because of that loyalty, hollow eyes crowded Ironwood's soul, staring at him, cursing him—sparing Crow Beard the anguish.

"Night Sun?" Sternlight tried again. "May I bring you something? A cup of hot tea, perhaps?"

"No," she murmured.

The frail sound of her voice struck Ironwood like a physical blow. He walked outside, hoping to lessen the pain.

The interplay of light mesmerized him. A yellow blur of reflected firelight tinted the smoke that hung over Talon Town. While starlight illuminated the barren fields in the canyon bottom, the snow that frosted the rimrock outlined every ledge.

Night chilled his skin as he raised his eyes to the sky.

Spider Woman had almost cleared the horizon.

"Sternlight," he called. "It is almost time."

"Is she up?"

"Soon."

"I'm coming."

The Sunwatcher picked up his conch shell horn. Conch shells came from the faraway ocean, a place Ironwood could barely imagine. Traders said the water went on forever. Ironwood had spent his entire life in the desert. Could such a place truly exist?

Sternlight swept by Ironwood. Just outside the doorway, the ladder to the roof leaned against the wall. He climbed it and stood on the highest point in Talon Town. The priest's weight made the roof creak. A dark shadow against the starry sky, Sternlight lifted the shell to his lips. A shrill high-pitched blast split the darkness. Then another. Four in all.

At the call, people emerged from their chambers. Some filtered into the plaza. Others perched on rooftops. The elderly gathered to his left, along the eastern wall, sitting with blankets over their white heads for warmth. To his right, along the western wall, children huddled in their parents' laps, eyes wide.

Sternlight descended the ladder. He stood beside Ironwood, his conch shell tucked beneath his arm.

Neither said anything for a time, then Sternlight whispered, "Have the runners returned from Lanceleaf Village yet?"

"Soon. I expected them today. Perhaps tomorrow."

"You posted warriors at the signal towers, so we would know in advance—"

"Of course, Sternlight." He exhaled wearily. "But with the snow, Blue Corn may not have seen the fires. He . . ."

Ironwood's voice faded as, one by one, the Buffalo Dancers climbed from the kiva's subterranean warmth and ghosted out into the cold plaza. They moved in the loose-limbed gait of dominant bulls, tossing their shaggy heads. Wisps of eagle down fluttered from the tips of their horns.

A buffalo's skull was hollowed out to fit over the Dancer's head, leaving the long bushy beard to warm his naked chest. Below that, the men wore kirtles and moccasins. As they trotted in front of the fires, their shadows bounced over the white walls like dark giants, and their feet kicked up puffs of snow.

When they reached the center of the plaza, the Dancers split into four groups and marched to the places marking the cardinal directions. They stood in silence, shaking their horns, their bodies swaying gently as if blown by the wind. The great Power of the buffalo banished illness and brought snowstorms to the mountains. In the spring, the snow melted, flooded the ephemeral creeks, and Brother Desert opened his eternal eyes. Buffalo gave life to the world, as they had since the emergence into this Fifth World.

"Sternlight!" Night Sun shouted.

Ironwood spun and saw Crow Beard lift a hand, as though to summon one of them.

Sternlight did not turn. Ironwood said, "He's awake."

Sternlight bowed his head. "I know."

The Buffalo Dancers began the sacred Songs, cleansing, pleading with the Spirits for help. As though he had just enough strength to do it, Sternlight tugged his gaze away and plodded inside to kneel beside the Chief.

Night Sun smoothed a hand down Crow Beard's wrinkled jaw. "Hello, my husband," she said softly. "Are you—"

"Go . . . away," the Blessed Sun ordered, and feebly glared at his wife. "Sternlight? I wish . . . only Sternlight."

"I am here, my chief."

Crow Beard's head lolled sideways. He squinted as if having trouble discerning the Sunwatcher's features in the pale glow. "Find Dune . . . bring him." He coughed weakly. "He must be . . . here . . . before I die."

"Yes, my chief. I will see to it." Sternlight drew one of the deerhides up to Crow Beard's chin. "Night Sun is here, too."

"No," Crow Beard hissed, and closed his eyes.

Night Sun's jaw trembled. She reached out and gently placed her fingertips on her husband's hair. "Crow Beard, I have been waiting for—"

"*Go away!*"

She sat so still she might have been carved from wood. Ironwood's fists clenched. He longed to say something to comfort her, but speaking would make matters worse.

Sternlight reached across the dying Chief, lightly touched Night Sun's cheek, and rose. He walked to Ironwood. When he passed the bowl of warming coals, his white ritual shirt took on a bloody hue. "Do you know where old Dune the Derelict lives?"

"Yes."

"Dispatch a runner immediately, and tell him . . ." Sternlight gestured awkwardly. "Warn him that Dune is odd. The old hermit may refuse to come."

"Even if Dune knows the Chief is dying?"

"Oh, yes. Dune will know instantly why he has been summoned. Make sure the runner tells Dune this is not a request; it is a command from the Blessed Sun."

"If you foresee such problems, perhaps I should go myself?" *I would do almost anything to be away from this chamber.* "Dune knows me. My presence might make the chore easier."

Sternlight glanced at Night Sun. She fussed with the Chief's blankets and hides, making certain every portion of Crow Beard's body stayed warm. "While Crow Beard no longer needs you, I fear that Night Sun might."

They exchanged a knowing glance, and Ironwood lowered his eyes. "She doesn't need me, Sunwatcher. She is a remarkably strong woman."

Ironwood turned to go, but Sternlight gripped his shoulder, stopping him, his expression serious. "My words were not an accusation. I meant them sincerely."

"I know that."

Sternlight murmured, "I will prepare a mixture of ground turquoise and blue corn for you to take to Dune. But if he shows any reluctance to come back with you, Ironwood, don't give it to him."

"You mean that you wish me to deceive one of the most Powerful shamans in our people's history?"

Sternlight's dark eyes seemed to expand. "Exactly. And hurry. I will expect you in two or three days."

"Three. Dune is old and frail. He will need the time. Keep a lookout for my runners."

"Of course."

Ironwood ducked through the doorway and strode out into the cold. He glimpsed Sternlight leaving after him, heading in the opposite direction, probably to prepare the turquoise and blue corn.

Ironwood climbed down four ladders, set foot on the snowy plaza, and veered wide around the shuffling Dancers. He made his way through the spectators. His own chamber lay to his left, on the southeastern end of the U-shaped structure.

Adults dipped their heads respectfully as he passed, and a few children reached out to touch the hem of his long shirt. Just a touch, nothing disturbing. When they brought their hands back, they stared at their fingers, young eyes worshipful. Two women smiled. Ironwood nodded politely in return, but the effort made his heart pound.

Silently, he cursed himself. How could memories sixteen summers old still be so vivid?

Night Sun had asked him once "to forget." As if it were as simple as walling up . . .

A man's hoarse scream split the darkness.

Ironwood whirled and pulled his bone dagger from his belt in one smooth movement.

Stunned silence fell over Talon Town, then chaos erupted. People ran in every direction, shouting orders, hurrying children inside. Infants wailed shrilly. Several old people stood up to get a better look at the commotion.

Five warriors dashed through the gate that connected the halves of the plaza.

"What's happened?" Ironwood demanded.

"Come quickly!" the lanky, square-jawed man in front replied. In the ruddy glow of the plaza fires, Webworm looked as though he'd just witnessed the rebirth of the Monster Children. "Creeper found a dead man."

Ironwood sprinted past his warriors.

People flooded toward the gate and the western plaza entry, shoving and shouting at each other. Frightened gasps carried on the wind. Ironwood had to force his way through, yelling, "Move. Move!"

When he made it through the gate, he turned left and raced for the entry. He found Creeper, leader of the Buffalo Clan, kneeling over a body, dressed in his magnificent ritual costume. His headdress lay on the ground beside him, the long buffalo beard shining in the amber gleam cast by the town. The body lay sprawled between the two mounds. The fourteen-summers-old slave boy, Swallowtail, crouched behind Creeper, a horrified expression on his face.

"Who is it?" Ironwood asked. "Is it—"

"It's Wraps-His-Tail," Creeper answered, and used the back of his hand to wipe sweat from his eyes. Short and fat, Creeper resembled a bear. Thick black hair covered his bare chest and arms. His white kirtle and moccasins shone eerily in the dim glow. "I sent Swallowtail out to fetch more wood for the fire. Swallowtail almost tripped over him, and came running to tell me. When I saw the blood, I yelled for Webworm."

Ironwood's closest friend lay curled on his side, his face turned northward toward the road that led to the sacred *sipapu.* The Evening People's radiance glinted in his blood-speckled eyes.

A hollow ache spread through Ironwood's gut. My *friend, gone. . . .*

Brains showed through the crack in Wraps-His-Tail's skull. Clearly, he'd been taken by surprise. His bow and his quiver of arrows were missing, but the slip knot securing his hafted stone knife to his belt remained intact. An eerie smile had frozen on his face—as if he'd seen his attacker and thought him a friend.

Who would kill him? And why? What purpose would his death

serve? People killed out of hatred, fear, self-preservation—but behind all of those lay desperation. What could have driven a man to be desperate enough to kill Wraps-His-Tail?

The murderer knew what news he carried.

But what part? The child? No. Not even Wraps-His-Tail knew the truth about that. He had instructed Wraps-His-Tail to ask if Beargrass would return to be his deputy if open warfare broke out. Did the murderer fear what Ironwood would do when he heard Beargrass' answer?

He raised his eyes to Webworm. The man's square jaw tightened in response. *I would have demoted you and put Beargrass in your place.*

But Webworm and Beargrass had been great friends. Webworm simply didn't have it in him to murder a friend over a question of status. Did he?

Ironwood returned his gaze to Wraps-His-Tail.

"What's that in his hand?" Ironwood pointed.

"What?" Creeper asked. "His hand?"

Creeper reached out and tenderly uncurled Wraps-His-Tail's cold fingers to pick up the object. A moment after he did, he let out a small cry and threw it on the ground. Furiously, he scrubbed his hand in the dirt.

The crowd surged forward, murmuring and craning their necks to see better.

"Blessed gods," Creeper whispered. "It's a badger's paw. But . . . what's it sprinkled with?"

"Corpse powder," Ironwood answered, and shivered involuntarily. Powdered corpse flesh had a distinctive silver sheen that clung to the skin. In the light cast by the town, it glowed with a bizarre brilliance.

Harshly, Ironwood ordered, "Webworm, find Sternlight!"

Night Sun lay wrapped in two blankets at Crow Beard's side. Through the pinned-back doorflap, she could see Ironwood and Sternlight standing outside the chamber, their tall bodies dark against a canvas of glittering stars. Ironwood had his arms folded across his broad chest. Sternlight stood against the wall.

She only caught a few of their words, but Sternlight spoke calmly, patiently, while Ironwood's deep voice had a bite to it.

". . . *why Wraps-His Tail?*" Ironwood asked. ". . . *murder has reasons . . . who could possibly have known . . .*"

Sternlight replied softly, and Night Sun did not hear his answer.

Her thoughts drifted. Thinking about Ironwood. About the first time they'd been alone together.

Blessed Spirits, what a long time ago . . . it seemed another life.

It had happened late in the Moon of Greening Grass.

Night Sun had spent all day supervising a difficult slave birth and had felt weary beyond exhaustion. As she'd crossed Talon Town's moonlit plaza, desperate for sleep, she'd looked up and seen Crow Beard standing in the doorway to their chamber, silhouetted blackly against the golden glow of torchlight. He had his fists clenched at his sides and his legs spread as if bracing for a fight.

He'd been acting strangely for moons, growing more and more frightening with his sudden emotional outbursts, punishing the children for no reason at all—especially their two-summers-old daughter, Cloud Playing, which enraged Night Sun. And worried her.

Night Sun had climbed the ladders to the fifth story, and when she stepped off onto the roof, called, "Crow Beard? Is something wrong?"

Night Sun hurried forward, her Healing pack in her hands. As she neared the door, Crow Beard turned and walked inside. Night Sun followed, dropping her pack by the door, untying her turkey-feather cape and hanging it on a wall peg.

"What's wrong this time?" she demanded.

Crow Beard slowly crossed the chamber and stood over their bed, staring at the rumpled red-and-black blankets. He wore a thin sleeping shirt. "You were out with one of my warriors, weren't you?" he said in a tight voice. "While I slept, you—"

"*What?*" Night Sun blurted. "I was down helping with the birth of Running Doe's daughter! You knew that. I told you!"

"You *told* me," he mocked. "Yes, you did. But I know better. You were with one of my warriors!"

She stalked across the room, eyes blazing. "Crow Beard, what is wrong with you? You've been acting like a madman for moons! Accusing me of betraying you, slapping your daughter for no reason—"

"When I ought to have slapped you!" he shouted, and shook both fists in her face.

Night Sun took a step back. He wouldn't dare. As Matron of Talon Town, she could divorce him and leave him with nothing. "You have no right, my husband, to disgrace me by making such charges. You are the only man I've ever been with. The only man I ever wish to—"

"*Don't lie to me!*" Crow Beard grabbed her by the shoulders and shook her until she thought her neck might snap.

"Stop! Crow Beard, stop! *Stop it!*" she yelled. When he didn't, Night Sun drew back and slapped him with all the strength she could muster.

He gasped, startled, and gazed down at her—eyes wild with struggle and despair. "I'll kill you before I'll let someone else have you! Do you understand me? *I'll kill you!*"

Frightened, exasperated, Night Sun had run from the chamber, hurrying down the ladders, then across the western plaza and out into the moonlit desert. She followed the curve of the towering canyon wall eastward toward Kettle Town. Sister Moon hung directly overhead, wavering through wispy clouds like an oblate silver shell. Her gleam tarnished the massive cliffs, glittered off the corn plants lifting their first leaves, and lit Night Sun's way as she strode down the road.

Despite the time, dozens of fires sprinkled the canyon bottom, twinkling and flashing as the wind blew.

Night Sun hugged herself. She should have grabbed her cape. The spring chill ate at her flesh.

This nonsense had begun last summer. Crow Beard had suddenly started following her, showing up unexpectedly at Healings, or birthings, staying just long enough to assure himself she was indeed where she'd told him she would be. When she returned to their chamber later, he'd be lying with his back to her, and no matter how she tried to soothe him, he refused to discuss it.

And she'd noticed other things. His hair had started to thin. Every time she cleaned his juniper-bark hairbrush, black strands came out in handfuls. Worse, he'd told her he could no longer "be" with her beneath the blankets. Night Sun assumed he must be going through the Calming that men experienced at his age; he might wobble for a time, but would soon find his footing again, and everything would be all right. If she just pampered and petted him, all would be well.

But he seemed to be getting worse.

She'd seen him trifling with the slave girls, touching them intimately . . . and said nothing.

Night Sun broke into a run, her yucca sandals padding down the moonlit trail as breath tore in and out of her lungs. Wind-blown gravel grated beneath her feet. "Blessed sky gods," she called in a choking voice, "tell me how to make it better! There must be a way to fix this!"

She thought she heard faint footfalls behind her, but saw only wind in the new corn. A coyote howled on the canyon rim high above her, and she looked up. Twinkling Evening People peered down at her.

Night Sun ran faster, trying to drive the misery from her soul. When she reached Kettle Town, the colonnade—like huge teeth—seemed to be leering at her. She veered right, taking the trail that led down to Straight Path Wash. Rain had fallen two days ago, and a silver ribbon of water flowed in the bottom of the ravine.

She ran headlong for it. Nothing she did pleased Crow Beard. There had actually been a time last moon when Crow Beard had looked at her with hatred in his eyes. Since that moment, her loneliness had been growing, eating holes in her soul.

A stone thrust up in the middle of the road, but Night Sun didn't see it until too late. She tripped and toppled into the fresh green grass that lined the way.

"Ah!" she grunted as pain lanced her ankle.

Moccasins sounded on the path, and she saw a tall man running toward her. "Blessed Night Sun," he said in a deep voice, "did you harm yourself?"

He knelt in front of her, his eyes looking over her face and body, in concern. It was the new War Chief, Ironwood. She had barely noticed him at the ritual installation a summer ago, but she knew his reputation. He'd led a strange life. He'd married at the age of fourteen summers, but his wife and son had both died in childbirth less than a sun cycle after the ceremony. In his grief, he'd vowed never to touch a woman again. And he'd kept that vow, dedicating himself to the arts of war. He'd become a legendary warrior. People in small villages whispered that Ironwood was really one of the Great Warriors in disguise, come to save the Straight Path people from destruction.

Night Sun smiled. God or not, he was a handsome man. He wore his long hair in a braid, and the style accented the oval shape of his face, the high arch of cheekbones, and the strong line of his jaw.

"It's my ankle." She leaned forward to touch it, and groaned. "I twisted it badly, I'm afraid."

"I'll carry you home—" He reached for her.

"No, just . . . please . . . I wish to sit here for a time. You may return to your duties. I'll be along as soon as I'm able."

"But"—his brows slanted down—"Blessed Night Sun, it is not safe for someone of your status to be out alone at night. The Mogollon dogs are raiding. They might be anywhere."

"Yes, well," she said in exasperation, "if they kill me tonight, at least I won't have to go home."

Ironwood peered at her a moment, then looked away. "May I escort you to another town? A—a more pleasant place?"

He must have overheard her argument with Crow Beard. But then, who hadn't? As War Chief, Ironwood would have been standing guard on the roof near the entry. Not only must he have heard the argument, he'd doubtless seen her run away . . . and followed, staying far enough away to grant her privacy, and close enough to help if she unwittingly found danger.

She rubbed her ankle. "No, thank you."

He sat down in the grass beside her. Apparently, try as she might, he wasn't going to leave.

Ironwood stared off into the distance, examining the flickering fires and the uneven line of the dark cliffs, gazing anywhere but at her. She saw him wet his lips nervously. He looked a little frightened.

"Scared?" she asked.

"Hmm?" He turned to frown at her.

"I'd be scared if I were you."

"Would you?"

"Why, yes. You're in a bad position out here. My husband

accuses me of dallying with one of his warriors, and then you wind up in the middle of nowhere with me—alone."

"But I can't just leave you out here, Blessed Night Sun. Much better that I stay to protect you than run the risk of having you killed by our enemies."

"That would reflect badly on you, wouldn't it?"

A wry eyebrow lifted. "I believe there are some who might hold it against me."

"But if my husband finds out—"

"People will be Singing about my courage long after I'm dead."

Night Sun blinked, then she laughed. Ironwood grinned in response, his white teeth shining in the darkness. How good it felt to laugh. She hadn't really laughed in a long time, not since before this insanity with Crow Beard began. She felt deeply grateful to this young man for a few instants of relief.

"Thank you," she said.

"Your servant, Matron."

Night Sun's smile dwindled. She expelled a worried breath. Though she wished to stay, she knew she'd better not. For *his* sake.

"Well, if you will help me up, I'll try to walk home." She struggled to get her feet under her.

Ironwood rose, slipped his hands beneath her arms, and pulled her to her feet. Her injured ankle gave way the moment she put weight on it, and she fell against him with a small cry. He clutched her tightly, holding her up.

Perhaps it was the comforting strength of his arms, or just the feel of another human body against hers, but all of the weariness from the long birthing, mixed with the worry about Crow Beard, flooded to the surface, and she started to cry. She buried her face against his shoulder to hide her embarrassment.

He said nothing, just stroked her back until her weeping subsided. Then he stepped away and laid a gentle hand against her hair, anxiously studying her face. "Are you all right?"

"Of course not," she said sharply. "I can't walk!"

"Here," he said, and turned sideways. "I think if you'll slip your left arm over my shoulders, I can get you home without too much trouble."

Night Sun did. He gripped her left hand with his and slowly

started forward. On the way, they'd laughed . . .

"No, Ironwood," Sternlight whispered harshly, the sound of his voice cleaving her from those sweet memories. "*Don't you . . . witches fly about spying on people! Perhaps . . . saw something . . .*"

Night Sun drew her warm blankets up around her throat and shivered, struggling to return to seventeen summers before, concentrating on the feel of Ironwood's body against hers.

Sleep lurked just beyond the edges of her awareness. She let it creep into her thoughts, twining itself around her soul, drowning out the external voices.

Across a gulf of time, Ironwood smiled at her. Happy. Laughing . . .

Third Day

Misty rain falls.

I lift my face and open my mouth, letting coolness coat my tongue. Gray clouds huddle above me. As sparkles fall from their bellies, they twist in the wind, flash and tumble. Their voices are silken. The fragrance of damp stone and earth encircles me. I was desperately hungry earlier, but now my body seems to float above this shallow wash like a wisp of cloud.

I am not alone anymore.

Over the past two days, I have found a strange world of endless horizon, where silence is the voice of forgiveness. I talk with the plants, and they answer in lilting tones as warm as a buffalo's undercoat.

"We hunt silence not to know freedom," Dune once told me, "but to know relatedness. From all living things, something flows into you all the time, and flows from you into them. Silence teaches us our dependence. By doing so, it washes the face of our soul clean, so we can see it better."

The walkingcane cactus beside me whispers as Wind Baby shakes its blossom-laden arms. I study the delicate purple petals. When raindrops pat their faces, they nod.

And I know what they are saying.

Just as the rain started last night, I had a Dream.

I stood at a walled-up doorway, knocking gently at first, then slamming my fists against the stones, demanding answers, wanting reasons, screaming: "You can't hide! Let me in! Tell me the truth! Let me in!"

In a deafening roar the wall crashed down, the stones crumbling before my eyes. Dust boiled up, and for a moment I could not see. Then . . .

I stood stunned, my raised fists trembling.

Because I had been knocking from the inside.

* * *

I sit very still.

And look out across the drenched land. Light winks on the surface of each wet pebble. The cliffs below are wavering sheets of silver. Sinuous threads of muddy water shine in the drainages.

I stretch out on the damp stone and open my arms to the weeping heavens. These tears are immaculate. I want them to soak clear to my bones.

Thirteen

Poor Singer straightened and winced. He'd been twisting gnarled sage out of the ground, and the small of his back stabbed him as if yucca leaves had been driven into it. His arms ached, and thirst plagued him. He glanced at Dune. The old holy man lay in the middle of the road, his mouth open in a toothless grin. Wind Baby playfully blew sand over his tan shirt and into his gaping maw. Dune didn't seem to notice.

Poor Singer wiped the sweat from his forehead and gazed up at the crimson cliff and the large rock painting that hid beneath the jagged rim. The painter must have lowered himself by ropes and hung suspended while he'd created his design. Two Humpbacked Flute Players adorned the wall, one male, the other female. The male had an exceptionally long penis. The female's blue head nestled beneath a large white spiral. The red paint came from crushed hematite, the white from gypsum, or maybe chalk, and the blue might be dried larkspur petals. Poor Singer smiled. If so, the female flute player would soon be headless—plant pigments didn't last nearly as long as minerals did.

His gaze moved over the rest of the cliff face, searching for other paintings, then drifted southward.

Weathered sandstone ridges receded into infinity, glowing lavender and purple in the morning light. Gray shadows pooled at the bases. On the distant horizon, an unearthly golden gleam sheathed the spire of rock that Dune called Woodcutter's Penis.

Poor Singer turned. Far to the west, the Thlatsina Mountains wore a misty crown of clouds. His eyes tightened with longing. Did a glimmering turquoise cave hide in that breathtaking blue?

Fragments of that Dream returned to him every night, and he relived the screams, the angry kicks, the strange woman . . .

He looked back at Dune. What a slave master the Derelict had turned out to be. He wouldn't listen to any of Poor Singer's stories about himself. He'd eaten all the food Poor Singer had brought, apparently without the slightest remorse. He'd ordered Poor Singer to go for days without eating or drinking, while he worked him brutally. Then the old man had smiled and claimed he was attempting to teach Poor Singer how to forget himself.

It was both annoying and amazing.

Only yesterday he'd been telling Dune how many Sings he'd been to, and how much he'd learned from them, and Dune had cocked an eyebrow and pleasantly observed, "It must be difficult to fill yourself up with divine Power, when you're so full already."

Poor Singer throttled another sage and twisted it, grunting, until it popped from the ground. He threw it on the huge pile to his left. As he bent for another, he spotted a dust cloud coming up the road from the south. He shielded his eyes against the morning glare.

Dune had ordered Poor Singer not to speak, not even to think. "Just gather sage," he'd said.

The man sprinted closer, until Poor Singer could see his red shirt, belted at the waist, and the magnificent turquoise pendant around his neck.

Poor Singer squinted at the sleeping Derelict. He tried mouthing the word, *Dune.*

Nothing.

Poor Singer edged closer and whispered, "Dune?"

Still nothing.

He stood at Dune's feet and rubbed his toe in the sand, making noise. Dune's smile didn't even dim. "Uh . . . Dune? There's a man coming."

Dune opened one eye. "You are such a stupid boy. Didn't I tell you a Singer's purpose is to *see*, not to babble?"

"Yes, well, I thought I'd better babble before you got trampled." Poor Singer pointed. "He's coming fast."

Dune lifted his white head and squinted at the man running toward him. "Ah," he breathed. "Bad news."

Poor Singer frowned skeptically. How could he know?

Dune sat up and waited.

When the visitor arrived, he bowed deeply. "I hope I find you well, holy Derelict."

"You do, Ironwood. What—"

"*Ironwood!*" Poor Singer spluttered. "The—the great War Chief of Talon Town?"

Dune yelled, "You *imbecile!* Ironwood is a man like any other! Except you. You're dog urine!"

Poor Singer winced with embarrassment. You couldn't be certain that what Dune said was truly what he meant. He'd called Poor Singer "slimy packrat dung" last night, and then explained his joy that Poor Singer had decided to become a part of the cleansing process of his people.

Poor Singer edged forward and asked, "Was that an insult?"

Ironwood was a broad-shouldered muscular man, his face hardened by years of weather, worry, and war. Dust sheathed his red shirt, and his moccasins were grimy from travel. The stout black bow over his shoulder gleamed as if waxed, however, and the arrows in his quiver looked newly fletched. A slim bone stiletto hung from his belt next to a stone-headed war club. The large turquoise pendant had been carved in the shape of a running wolf.

The warrior peered at Poor Singer as though he might be dimwitted, and said, "Dune—"

"What's wrong, War Chief?"

"The Blessed Sun is dying, and he wishes you to be there."

Dune scowled. "In what capacity? I see you offer me no mixture of ground turquoise and blue cornmeal."

Poor Singer listened intently. When a person was dying the

family sent such a mixture to the Singer they wished to attend the dying. If the Singer took it, it meant he or she accepted the dangerous physical tasks of washing, dressing, and handling the body of the dead, as well as the spiritual tasks of Singing the soul to the afterworld. The mixture would later be sprinkled over the corpse to sanctify it before the burial procession left for the journey down the sacred road.

Ironwood hesitated, apparently judging Dune's expression, then responded, "I do not, Elder. The Blessed Sun demands only your presence. That is all."

"Are you certain of this?"

"My orders come from his lips, holy Derelict."

Dune rubbed his wrinkled chin, as though considering. "But he's not dead yet?"

"Very close," Ironwood said. "When last I saw him—"

"Then go away." Dune waved a translucent old hand. "There's nothing I can do until he's dead. Tell Crow Beard I said so." He flopped back on the sand, clasped his hands over his stomach, and closed his eyes. Sunlight flowed into his wrinkles.

"Elder," Ironwood said, "the Blessed Sun is *dying*. This is not a request. He orders you to be present."

"He's just worried about his relatives. Tell him that when he's dead, I promise to bring my Bashing Rock. I will personally smack him in the face to free his soul. Unless, of course, his relatives have already thrown him facedown in a hole and dropped a slab of sandstone over him."

Poor Singer gasped. *Great Monster Slayer!* Suggesting such a thing about a Chief would have gotten most men whacked in the head and unceremoniously left for the coyotes. And Dune had just said it to the greatest War Chief alive!

Ironwood propped his hands on his hips. "Gather your things, Elder. We must leave immediately."

"You must leave immediately, War Chief. I—"

"But, Dune!" Poor Singer said. A swallow went down his dry throat. "You've taught me that we must be generous and kind. If the Chief needs you—"

"He doesn't. Not yet."

"Dune," Ironwood said, obviously choosing his words carefully. "If you will not come for the dying Chief, will you come for the Sunwatcher? Sternlight may need you more than Crow Beard does."

Dune braced himself up on one bony elbow. His expression changed. For the first time he looked sincerely worried. "Why? What's happened?"

"One of my runners, Wraps-His-Tail, was murdered last night. He had a badger's paw in his fist and corpse powder—"

"*Witchcraft!*" Poor Singer blurted, and took a step backward.

Ironwood shot him a glance. "Yes. The town has gone crazy with fear. They—"

"And your other runner?" Dune said.

"My other . . ." Ironwood's expression slackened. "How did you know I'd sent—"

"Is Cone dead?"

Ironwood gestured lamely. "All we know is that he has not returned to Talon Town."

Dune grunted as he got to his feet and walked off.

Confused, Poor Singer trotted after him. Ironwood brought up the rear, his footsteps light.

When they reached the sagging white house, Dune ducked under his door curtain. Poor Singer and Ironwood stood outside, glancing uneasily at each other. A single flute note blared, followed by the thump of a pack hitting the dirt floor.

"He's packing," Poor Singer said.

Ironwood ignored him, his hard gaze on the swaying curtain.

Awkwardly, Poor Singer added, "He's a very holy man. I'm sure he'll help in any way he can. He . . ."

Dune emerged from his house dressed in a clean brown shirt, his walking stick and pack in hand. He tossed the pack beside a sagebrush and headed straight for Poor Singer. He fell on his knees, bowed his head, and instructed, "This is going to be a grim journey. Sing for me."

"Wh-which Song?"

"Sing! Before I lay a curse upon you and all your unborn children!"

Poor Singer's arms shot heavenward, and he Sang the first Song that came to his mind:

> "*Far away in the north,*
> *Lies the road of emergence*
> *Cloud flowers blossom there.*

> And . . . uh . . . *lightning flashes*
> *Something . . . else . . . happens,*
> *and*
> > *Raindrops fall—!"*

"And," Dune said as he got to his feet, "they have Singers who know all the words."

Horrified, Poor Singer bit his lip.

Dune glared at him, grabbed his pack, and shouldered past Ironwood, saying, "Let's hurry."

"Don't worry about anything, Elder!" Poor Singer called after them. "Have a safe journey. I'm not going home. I promise! I'll be right here when you return!"

Over his shoulder, Dune yelled, "Remember what I have told you. Keep your tongue from waggling and practice being a bug. And don't forget to feed the mice!"

Poor Singer muttered, "I hate mice," but yelled, *"I won't!"*

Fourteen

Father Sun had vanished from the sky, but echoes of his brilliance lingered, reflecting from the flat faces of the cliffs, turning the juniper-filled hollow where Cornsilk and Fledgling sat into a luminous mosaic of purple, deep green, and the palest of golds.

Cornsilk pulled her red-and-white cloak tight about her shoulders. They couldn't have found a more perfect place. Water bubbled up from the sandstone and trickled down a pine-choked crevice in the rock. A small pool glistened at the base of the slope, surrounded by deer, rabbit, and bird tracks. It made hunting easy. They had already snared a rabbit for dinner.

While Fledgling skinned and rinsed the animal in the cool water, Cornsilk removed a handful of charred cotton from her pack, along with two chert cobbles. A shallow depression in the sandstone had old charcoal in it. She cleaned it out and mounded up her cotton, then carefully sprinkled dried pine needles and twigs over the top. You couldn't add too many, or the tinder would smother the cotton and it would just smoke, rather than catching fire. She reached for her cobbles and struck them sharply against each other. They sparked. After several attempts, the cotton smoldered, then flared. Cornsilk quickly put her cobbles aside and bent to blow on it.

Orange flames crackled through the pine needles and licked up around the twigs. She added larger and larger pieces of wood until she had a good blaze going, then moved their tea tripod to the edge of the flames to warm. She had collected shriveled rose hips and juniper berries and added them to the water earlier. The gut bag swung, creaking.

"Fledgling?" she called. "How is the rabbit coming?"

Fledgling held up the skinned carcass, smiling. "Almost ready."

His stubby hands caught the sunset gleam as he lowered the rabbit to the pool and rinsed it one last time. He had their mother's broad cheekbones and their father's eyes, but his own pug nose. Long black hair fell down his back, blending with the charcoal diamonds woven into his tan shirt. *He looks so much like them. I don't. Why have I never seen that before?*

Uncertainty gnawed at her soul. Cornsilk surveyed their camp. Junipers, she decided, could grow anywhere. The smallest dirt-filled gap in the stone held a tree twice her height. As the cool of evening deepened, they released their sweet scent and set it loose on the wind.

Fledgling walked back and knelt beside her. "Where's that sharp blade you had?"

"Here, in my pack." Cornsilk drew out her obsidian blade. As long as her hand, it was only a finger-width across.

"I'll hold the rabbit," Fledgling said, "if you'll butcher it." He pulled a back leg straight and held it out for her.

Cornsilk carefully sliced through the pink muscles and down to the leg joint. She had to work her blade through the tough tendons to get inside the joint, pop it loose, and continue through the meat on the opposite side of the joint.

The leg came off in Fledgling's right hand and the remainder of the rabbit swung in his left. "Let's cut off the other hind leg, and save the rest for breakfast."

"All right. Here—let me skewer that leg and get it started. Then I'll cut off the other one."

Cornsilk pulled a long thin stick from the woodpile by the firepit and slid it through the leg. She propped it near the edge of the flames and picked up her blade again.

As she cut, Fledgling looked up at the twilight sky. "It might be a clear night. If so, it's going to get very cold."

"Hard frost by morning." She watched her blade to make certain she didn't slice off any of her brother's fingers. "After we eat, we'll gather more wood, then we'll move our blankets close. We'll be all right." She glanced up and saw Fledgling's brows draw together in worry. "What's wrong, brother?"

The leg came off in Cornsilk's hand and she reached for another stick from the woodpile. Fledgling watched her slip the stick through the tendons on the lower leg and lean it close to the flames. The first piece of rabbit already sizzled, dripping fat onto the gleaming coals. It smelled delicious.

Fledgling rose and took the rest of the rabbit carcass to the nearest tree. Removing the cord he wore as a belt, he tied it to the rabbit's forelegs and looped it around a high branch, to keep the meat from hungry animals. After he'd knotted the cord, he turned. The carcass swung behind him. "You've been very quiet," he said. "Is something wrong?"

Cornsilk longed to tell him how confused she felt, that *she* was the hidden child, but she'd promised her mother. She looked away, tucked her chert cobbles in her pack beneath the magnificent turquoise-studded blanket, then leaned back against the pack to watch the fire glow flicker over the towering cliff. The light moved like silent golden wings, fluttering, swooping. "I'm just tired, Fledgling."

"Cornsilk?" Fledgling returned and sat cross-legged beside her. His hair fell over his skinny chest. "I've been thinking."

Cornsilk reached for their clay cups, sitting close to the tripod, and used hers as a dipper. She filled her brother's cup first, handed it to him, then dipped out her own. The rich fragrance of rose hips encircled her face as she sniffed the steaming brew. "About what?"

Fledgling looked at her over the rim of his cup. "Do you remember much from when we were little?"

Cold leeched up from the rock, biting at her legs like tiny teeth. She shifted to a new position. "No, not very much." *And how I wish I did.*

"Do you remember that Mother and Father said we were born at Talon Town?"

"Yes. What about it?"

"I remember many things," he said, "but nothing of Talon Town."

"Why would you? Mother said we left there right after we were born. It would be stranger if you did remember it."

Wind Baby barely breathed tonight, tenderly touching the juniper and pine needles, fanning the flames of their fire. The scent of faraway rain carried on the breeze.

"Do you think people there remember us?" Fledgling asked.

"Somebody must."

The gleam of the fire tipped his lashes as he looked over at her. "I was wondering if Ironwood would recognize . . . one of us."

Fear prickled her veins. "And I wonder if any of Ironwood's enemies would recognize us."

Fledgling fumbled with the fringe on his blanket. "I know it's dangerous, but I—"

"You or I could end up dead."

A pained look creased Fledgling's face. "Cornsilk, I *must* know who my parents are. I—I want to go. To ask Ironwood myself."

Cornsilk turned both rabbit sticks, taking her time so she could think. "Fledgling, I have been asking myself many questions over the past two days, and the scariest question of all is about Ironwood. I mean, haven't you wondered why he would give up his child?"

"Yes."

"He was War Chief, even then. Such a powerful man could have kept his child if he'd wished to. Couldn't he?"

"You mean he wanted to be rid of me, don't you?" Fledgling looked miserable.

Cornsilk used her charred poker to draw slithering black

designs on the sandstone around her feet. They resembled a nest of baby snakes. "You or me."

"Maybe he didn't wish to give me up, but someone told him he had to."

"Who?" Cornsilk scoffed. "Only an idiot would dare to tell the War Chief to get rid of his child."

"An idiot or someone more powerful than the War Chief."

Cornsilk had to fight to keep from pulling the pack from behind her back. The turquoise-studded blanket had been filling her dreams, as if it had a soul, and were struggling to speak with her. "Who?"

Fledgling leaned toward her to breathe, "Crow Beard. Ironwood would have done anything the Chief ordered him to."

"It's possible, but why would the Blessed Sun demand such a thing?"

"Incest?"

Fear fluttered in her chest. "No." She shook her head. "If incest were involved, they would have just killed the child. Or—"

"Maybe it wasn't incest," Fledgling said. "Maybe Ironwood mated with one of the First People. A child from such a union would bring great shame on the First People."

Cornsilk studied the roasting rabbit legs. That actually made sense. She turned and squinted at her brother. "Which of the First People at Talon Town would stoop to coupling with a lowly Bear Clan man?"

Fledgling frowned into his cup. "I've only met one of the First People in my life," he said. "Do you remember him?"

"Who?"

"The Blessed Webworm. He hasn't come in many summers, but he used to stop at Lanceleaf once every other spring. I remember because Father laughed a lot at the stories Webworm told."

Cornsilk searched her memory. Many old friends, both male and female, surprised her parents with visits. "Wait . . . was he a warrior?"

"Yes."

Cornsilk's thoughts soured. She *did* remember him. He used to look at her very strangely—as though she were a grown woman instead of a child. He had frightened her. When Webworm visited, Cornsilk had always stayed very close to her mother. "Perhaps he came to keep an eye on you, or me?"

"I don't know, but—"

They both jumped when a man stepped out of the shadows, tall and muscular, with two short braids that fell to his broad shoulders. He took another step toward them, and firelight gleamed along the yellow threads in his long shirt, as if he were netted all over with a web of flame.

"Stone Forehead!" Fledgling yelled as he leaped to his feet. "What are you doing here?"

The warrior trudged forward. "I have been tracking you since early yesterday morning." Dirt caked his face.

"Why?"

Stone Forehead crouched by the fire and extended his hands to warm them. "I am on my way to Talon Town, and your parents asked me to check on you, to make certain you had reached your relatives' villages. At the split in the road, I knew you'd had other plans." He shook a finger at no one in particular. "Which one of you decided to climb through every rock outcrop on the way here? I nearly broke my ankle!"

Fledgling glanced at Cornsilk.

"Well," she said, "we didn't wish anyone to track us. How did you?"

Stone Forehead smiled. "Every so often the yucca bottoms of your sandals left a light-colored scratch on the sandstone. But it took me forever to work out your trail."

Cornsilk grumbled, "I knew we should have worn our moccasins."

"They don't turn the cactus as well as sandals," Fledgling said, "and we waded through a thorny sea today."

"Are you hungry, Stone Forehead?" Cornsilk asked, and gestured to the half-butchered rabbit in the tree. "We could cut off another leg for you."

"No." He held up a hand. "I have been chewing jerky for the past hand of time. But I could use some of that delicious-smelling tea."

Cornsilk said, "Where's your cup?"

He shrugged out of his pack, unlaced the top, and dug around until he found it, then bent forward, filled it, and drank. Steam bathed his face. He refilled his cup and drank some more. "This is very good," he said.

Fledgling smiled.

Cornsilk, however, watched him glumly. Her parents had said they wanted to hire him to go to Talon Town to monitor happenings there and notify them if Crow Beard died. Her parents must also have feared Cornsilk might do something unpredictable—as was her habit. On the one hand, their concern warmed Cornsilk's heart, and on the other . . .

"Stone Forehead." An unpleasant tickle taunted her stomach, as if doom had walked in with him. "Now that you've found us, what are you supposed to do?"

He stretched his stocky body out across the sandstone and gestured with his cup. The glow of the fire sheathed his dark eyes with a sunrise sheen. "Your parents said to make certain you got to your relatives' villages. Tomorrow morning that is what I will do. We will walk back to the fork in the road, then I'll—"

"You're going to drag us away, even though we don't wish to go!" Cornsilk said indignantly.

Stone Forehead grinned, his white teeth flashing in the firelight. "Exactly. At the point of an arrow, if necessary."

Cornsilk reached over, took the two sticks with rabbit legs, and thrust one into Fledgling's hand. He took it sullenly.

She sank her teeth into the hot meat. As she chewed, she glowered at Stone Forehead. "It's a good thing you brought your own food."

Stone Forehead grinned. "You've always been a problem. I expected—"

"And a good thing you brought your bow," she added, "because I'm not going."

The twinkle vanished from Stone Forehead's eyes. "What are you talking about? You have no choice."

"You mean you're going to kill me? Perhaps beat me into submission? I can't wait to see the look on my parents' faces when they hear the news."

"Cornsilk," Stone Forehead warned, "don't force me—"

"Go ahead." She smiled evilly at him. "*Try* to force me to go."

Stone Forehead jumped to his feet. "So help me, Cornsilk,

I swear, you've . . . Ever since that time you shot those four grouse when I only shot one, I knew you were impossible!" He threw up his hands. "By the Blessed Ones! You are the most stubborn woman I have ever known!" He glared at her through weary eyes, shoulders slumped in defeat. "What did I ever see in you in the first place?"

She lifted a shoulder.

"Cornsilk, you will shame me! Is that what you wish? To make me look bad before our entire village?"

She smiled and took another juicy bite of rabbit.

Fifteen

The sacred road, which had been heading due south, veered off at an angle toward Center Place. Ironwood studied the land while he waited for Dune. A thick coating of frost caught the slanting sun, striking sparkles from each leaf and blade of grass. Behind him, the ancient holy man hobbled along, placing his walking stick with great care.

Spider Woman must have smoked her pipe all night long to create the shimmering layer of fog that rolled through Straight Path Canyon. As the mist crept over the tan cliffs, it changed from golden to the palest of pinks. The brush glittered with a coral hue.

Ironwood propped his foot on a sandstone boulder, unslung his pack, and drew out a juniper stick and an obsidian flake—a thin palm-sized piece of stone. When honed and fire-hardened, the stick would make a deadly stiletto.

They had crossed the flats north of the canyon, where scrubby sage and wispy grasses fought for existence in the clay-heavy soils. The occasional small dunes they'd passed, little more than shadows of thin sand, supported here and there some rabbitbrush or greasewood, but little else.

Ironwood longed for the pines, but few of them grew this

close to the canyon, and those that did survived by sinking roots along the steeply eroded cliffs. Ironwood had often stopped to wonder at them. They survived by clinging to any crack in the stone where soil and water existed. Their squat trunks twisted back and forth, seeming to wallow before they gained enough strength to send up stubby branches. There was something Powerful about an old, old tree that refused to die. Something deeply sacred.

Dune came alongside and gazed out over the mist. His long brown shirt and tattered buckskin leggings contrasted sharply with his sparse white hair. He leaned on his walking stick for balance, breath puffing whitely.

"Give me a moment," Dune said, "to catch my wind."

"Take as long as you wish. We've kept a good pace, Dune. We'll be at Talon Town by midafternoon."

Ironwood shaved off a curl of wood and watched it spiral to the ground. The rich fragrance of juniper encircled him.

He had been thinking of Night Sun all morning. The Blessed Sun's impending death had opened a door inside him that he'd walled up long ago—and he couldn't seem to close it again. Though he had not touched her in many sun cycles, his hands remembered the softness of her skin and the mink's fur texture of her long hair. Sometimes late at night, just at the edge of sleep, he heard her joyous laugh and reached out for her . . . to touch only empty air.

"Ironwood," Dune said in his reedy old voice. "Is that a runner?"

"Where?" He straightened and peered down the road. At this time of morning, the surface of crushed potsherds glittered with blinding intensity.

Dune lifted his thin arm and pointed. "There."

Ironwood squinted. "I see nothing."

"Well, he'll be here soon enough. It will give me time to rest."

He hobbled off the road and sat on a gnarled old tree stump. It had once been a huge ponderosa pine, but like so many of the tall trees, it had been taken for building and firewood. The early morning sunlight struck Dune's face on the right side, shadowing his deep wrinkles and accentuating the age spots on his scalp. "I can't see well up close, but I can see with the clarity of an antelope at a distance." He gestured with his walking stick. "That runner is a boy."

In frustration, Ironwood looked again. Two ravens flapped overhead, cawing, but he saw no other movement. He shook his head. "My eyesight is not what it once was."

Dune tipped his ancient face to the warming sun and sighed. "You have seen forty-five summers now, haven't you?"

"Yes."

Dune grunted softly. "That is not so very old, War Chief— though it's true most people are dead by your age. And I fear they will die much earlier, and with greater frequency, after Crow Beard's death."

"You mean because Snake Head will take his father's place."

"The boy's a fool."

"Well . . . he does have a passion for battle," Ironwood said noncommittally. He had taken Snake Head on four raids, and prayed he'd seen the last. The youth's black eyes gleamed with an inhuman light at the first glimpse of blood. He wasn't much for the actual fighting, hanging back until the battle was won before charging in. Then he seemed to lose himself in the killing of the wounded. Ironwood had witnessed many horrors, but on several occasions Snake Head had sickened him.

But he will *be the new Blessed Sun.*

Dune's expression went sour, as if he'd bitten into something bitter. "Unfortunate. Violent raiding is on the increase. Villages no longer fight for women and food, but out of sheer hatred. I fear Snake Head's arrogance may fan the flames to outright war."

Ironwood whittled on his juniper stick. "I expect it, Dune."

He could not serve Snake Head. Would not. Considering Ironwood's age, the boy might even dismiss him. His forty-five summers had indeed taken a toll, and on more than just his eyesight. On cold nights—like the one just past—Ironwood's bones ached miserably, and he admitted he had trouble breathing on long runs. His strength *had* begun to fail.

Dune's bushy white brows lowered. "You won't continue as War Chief, will you?"

A faint smile came to Ironwood's lips. He looked down at his stiletto-in-the-making. "There are younger men whom Snake Head will wish to be at his side."

"Like Webworm?"

"Yes. He's a fine warrior—brave, thoughtful. And he's one of the First People." He sighed. "It's odd how life works out. I'd assumed Wraps-His-Tail would follow me. Or perhaps Cone. Now, one is dead, the other likely so."

"Webworm is only four summers younger than you, Ironwood."

"But he is still strong. I—I am not." Ironwood examined the road again. The fog had begun to dissipate as the sun warmed, shredding into patches, floating upward to cling to the canyon rim. "Webworm has served me well. I believe he deserves my position."

"But he doesn't have your head for things. He doesn't think his actions through." Dune kicked at an old sun-bleached pine cone that had rolled against the stump where he sat. The cone bounced off the low masonry wall bordering the west side of the road. "He used to pull the feathers out of baby birds when he was a boy. Did you know that? In the spring, when the babies were just learning to fly, he would run after them as they bounced about trying to escape. When he caught them, he carried the birds back to Talon Town, called all his playmates, and plucked the babies' feathers out one-by-one. The birds died, of course. Webworm has a cruel streak. I've never liked him."

"Then you and Sternlight have something in common." Ironwood lifted a shoulder. "Priests judge men differently than warriors."

"If Snake Head dismisses you, where will you go? What will you do?"

Visions of the forested canyons in the north flitted through Ironwood's mind. Deer and grouse flourished in the foothills under the high mountains. The creeks ran clear, fed by the melting snows in the high country. He had gone there as a boy, but few people would remember him. He might be able to live in peace.

"I don't know. It will take some thought."

Seeing the glum look on Dune's ancient face, Ironwood changed the subject. "I was surprised to see the youth at your house. You haven't had many apprentices in the past few cycles, have you?"

"Too many," Dune snorted. "They come in droves, but few stay for more than a day or two."

"Well, the hermit's life is not easy, especially on young men. They have needs. At their age, *pressing* needs. Their bodies are just ripening—"

"Learning to be a Singer has its own pressing needs. Far more pressing than a penis against a breechclout, Ironwood. A Singer must become a world in himself for another's sake—and it is a great undertaking."

Ironwood sliced another curl of wood from his stick. "At Poor Singer's age, I was a world in myself for my own sake. I wished to live, and love, and . . ."

"Many who come to me do, too. Remember the lessons taught by the Humpbacked Flute Players? Male and female are two halves of a whole. I try to show young Singers that our creativity, our fruitfulness, our very ability to love, are one. Fertility is sacred. It is the Creator."

"The Creator?"

"Of course. The needs of the body and the needs of the Spirit aren't different, Ironwood. Power is Power."

"They feel different."

Dune smiled toothlessly. "That's why humans wage constant war upon themselves—and why you are at war with yourself. You must befriend fertility. Stop using it like a tool. The Creator only befriends those who befriend her first."

Ironwood turned his flake over to use the sharper side. "I know of no god that I wish for my friend."

"Well," Dune sighed, "do the best with what you have. A god you hate is better than no god at all."

Ironwood cocked a brow. What a strange statement! He did hate a few of the gods—especially those he'd prayed to in battle, begging them to take his life instead of one of his friends' lives. But they'd let his friend die anyway. What sort of gods were those? "Is it really possible to end that internal war over fertility? We are humans, after all. Vain, boastful—"

"To truly love is hard work. And a lonely struggle. But it is possible. Singers understand that there is a mysterious fruitfulness in solitude."

"Solitude?" Ironwood propped his stick on his knee and frowned out at the tendrils of mist rising above the canyon rim to become clouds. "I'm not sure I could stand that. I enjoy the company of others too much."

"Solitude is a necessary preparation for living with others, War Chief. People, especially young people, get in trouble because they lack a foundation of solitude. Solitude, you see, is the heartbeat of the soul."

"Hmm," Ironwood grunted. "I thought they got in trouble because they lacked a foundation of themselves."

"That's what I said."

Ironwood glanced at him. "Poor Singer is new to the shaman's life. Aren't you afraid he'll get bored and leave while you are away? I would."

Dune smiled sadly. "The only thing I fear, War Chief, is the pride lurking in his heart."

"You mean he is too proud to be a good Singer?"

"I mean that pride is Poor Singer's worst enemy." Dune placed his walking stick across his knees. "For some Singers the villain is wealth, for others it's the devotion of their people. For Poor Singer it is pride. Every time he speaks kindly, or touches gently, he feels very good about it. In fact, it makes him feel quite superior. He's proud of himself for being kind." Dune gripped his walking stick as if trying to wring the life from it. "If Poor Singer isn't diligent and careful, that enemy will gouge out both his eyes and blind him to the real needs of others."

Ironwood raised his stiletto again, but stopped with his obsidian flake hovering above the wood. He squinted at the road. A blurry form dressed in white raced toward them. "A messenger from Sternlight; he wears white." He tucked his flake and stiletto into his pack and slung it over his shoulder.

Dune stood. "Coming for us?"

About fourteen summers old, with shoulder-length black hair and a moonish face, the boy had large dark eyes and was unusually tall and muscular for his age. Snake Head had given the boy to Sternlight just after Mourning Dove had given birth to him.

Ironwood called, "Greetings, young Swallowtail. Do you search for us? Or others?"

The boy stopped and bent over to brace his palms on his knees while he breathed deeply of the crisp morning air. He kept his dark eyes averted from Dune, as though afraid the legendary Straight Path holy man would steal his Fire Dog soul. "War Chief, you must . . . come quickly. The Chief . . . he's almost gone. My master wishes Dune to be there when it happens, so that the great Derelict might take over . . . and carry out the physical tasks of caring for the Blessed Sun's body and soul."

"*What!*" Dune shouted.

Ironwood reddened. He still carried the unopened pot of ground turquoise and blue cornmeal in his pack.

"Dune," he said as he turned, "if I had presented the sacred mixture to you, you wouldn't have come, no matter what I told you, and I had strict orders from Crow Beard to bring you."

"You lying son of a weasel! You disrespectful dog drool!"

The Derelict, holy man to four generations of Chiefs, hobbled across the sacred road, gazed at him sternly, and whacked Ironwood in the back of the head with his walking stick.

Young Swallowtail let out a shocked shriek and took off in the direction he had come from, his legs pumping like a terrified coyote's. He glanced over his shoulder repeatedly, as if to make certain neither of them followed him.

Ironwood rubbed the knot forming at the base of his skull. "I had my orders. It was your own fault, Dune. You forced me to deceive you when you kept asking if Crow Beard was dead."

Dune sucked his wrinkled lips over toothless gums. Glaring, he lifted his walking stick and pointed to a pink sandstone pillar which stood in the distance. "Do you know what that is?"

"Of course I do," Ironwood responded. "It's called Woodcutter's Penis."

Dune slitted an eye. "Woodcutter was the last man to deceive me." He planted his walking stick and headed toward Talon Town. Sunlight glittered through his wispy white hair as he hobbled away.

Ironwood's gaze riveted on the pink pillar.

"Dune!" he yelled. "Wait! I am innocent! I was under orders . . . Dune? Dune, *wait!*"

Poor Singer knotted his gray blanket around his shoulders, picked up Dune's long-necked water jug from beside the door, and ducked beneath the door curtain.

Sunset sheathed the canyon. The cliffs threw long cold shadows across the flats and exuded the dusty scent of evening. Luminous patches of gold lay like dropped scarves on the tallest buttes. A single brilliant pink cloud hovered above the western horizon.

Poor Singer walked with his shoulders slumped, head down, kicking every sage that leaned into the trail. He'd kept his fast. The gnawing hunger pangs had receded to leave a terrible craving for food. Even the winter-dry stems on the four-wing saltbush had started to look good. A floaty halo hung at the edge of his vision, and his thoughts wandered even more than usual.

"I'm morose," he muttered. "Why am I morose? I shouldn't be morose. This is one of the great moments of my life. I'm studying with the renowned Singer, Dune the Derelict. Why, there are young men who would give their very lives to be where I am today."

He kicked another sage. The fragrance of crushed leaves surrounded him. He knew better than to eat sage leaves; they gave a man a terrible headache. Finches twittered in the brush, hopping from branch to branch, eying him curiously. A finch, on the other hand . . .

"I'm probably morose because I haven't eaten in so long. How many days has it been?" He squinted down at the narrow slash of wash where the trail ended. "I had my last corncake for lunch on the day I met Dune. What's that? Six days?"

He'd lost track of the physical world and begun doing some very strange things . . .

"Ah!" He tripped over a big black rock in the trail's deepening shadows, and fell on his face. Sage raked his cheeks and stabbed him in the chest. The water jug, by some miracle, didn't break, but rolled to one side and rocked mockingly on its curved side.

As he pulled himself to his feet, he cried, "Blast you, rock! Do you have to do that to me every night?"

After all the times he'd tripped over it, he still forgot where it was. Out of frustration, he kicked the rock, picked up the water jar, then limped on down the trail.

"Give their very lives, ha! All I'm studying is Dune's house. I'm not studying with Dune. He's two days' walk away!" Anger and sorrow boiled in his empty belly. His clan expected him home in a moon or two—home, and transformed into a real Singer. "I can see it now. I'll go home and someone will ask me to do a Sing, and I'll get up, open my mouth, and nothing will come out because I still can't recall the words! Nobody will believe me when I tell them I arrived, and Dune left and never came back. Or if they do, *that* could be worse!"

The little wash zigzagged along the base of the cliff and had, over countless summers, carved out a rounded pool in the red sandstone. Water collected there, pure and sparkling.

Poor Singer knelt and dipped in his jug, letting it gurgle full while his gaze roamed the stillness of the desert. He really ought to eat. Though the fasting kept his soul clear, he couldn't be certain he wasn't doing crazy things. He'd been having elaborate conversations with the white pieces of plaster that cracked off Dune's house and the sage that grew up around the walls. Only that morning, he'd spent a hand of time accusing the firepit of sabotaging his efforts to make tea because the charred cotton he used as a starter would never catch. He'd placed the cotton over the red coals, as he did every morning, and blown on it until he thought he'd faint. When all he got was a pitiful smolder, he'd become convinced the firepit had evil intentions. Though, naturally, the pit denied it.

Poor Singer pulled his full jug out of the pool and rose to his feet. Water dripped from the curve to spatter on his toes. The damp ceramic felt cool and gritty. Twilight had deepened, turning the sky into a dove-colored dome. The red canyon walls had shaded purple. The shallow pool would be covered by a thin sheet of ice in the morning.

Poor Singer took a deep breath. The damp scent of water increased as darkness grew. Soon, the mountain lions, bobcats, and coyotes would be following the scent to drink from this shallow pool.

He started home.

A supernatural quiet came over the desert as evening fell. Birds perched on the cactuses, soft gray feathers fluffed out for warmth, their songs hushed. Wind Baby, who had been puffing unpredictably all day, had gone still. Poor Singer's moccasins, patting on the dirt trail, gave a lonely voice to the night.

Perhaps, if the firepit would let him, he'd boil some venison jerky and make a nice broth for dinner. He'd add a little salt and maybe throw in some dried onions. He doubted his stomach could handle any blue corn dumplings, though the idea . . .

He tripped over the black rock and let out a howl of dismay as he staggered to catch his wobbly balance. The pot seemed to weigh half the world. "What's the matter with you?" he demanded of the rock. "Look at this! My toe has a big bruise! Why can't you live somewhere else? You're ugly and have sharp edges! I hate you!"

While he sucked in a breath, preparing to get really nasty, Poor Singer *heard* a voice, not words exactly, more like wind through dry grass:

Why do you insist on kicking me in the belly every day?

Stunned, he stood silent, mouth open.

"Bless the Spirits! Did you just say something to me?"

The rock glared at him, and Poor Singer blinked and straightened.

"I—I'm sorry," he whispered. "I didn't mean to hurt you."

He continued up the trail toward Dune's house, wondering if a lack of food produced delusions, or if it opened his soul to voices he would not otherwise hear.

The latter, stupid. That's why shamans fast.

Poor Singer grinned and trotted through the darkness, trying to stroke each sage he'd ruthlessly kicked on the way to the pool. Unfortunately, they all looked alike, so he couldn't be certain he'd apologized to the right ones. Well, no matter, tomorrow he'd Sing for them, and then they would all know.

As he approached the shabby little white house in the jungle of sage, Poor Singer spied a small round pebble glowing in the trail. He picked it up, and put it in his mouth, to remind him that if he kept his own tongue from waggling, he might hear some of the voices that called from the depths of the Silence.

He suspected Dune would approve.

Sixteen

Webworm knelt in the doorway of the Blessed Sun's chamber, keeping guard, his gaze drifting over the land beyond Talon Town. Frost coated the fallow fields and lay upon the golden ledges of the canyon. Every flat rock shone. Down near the wash, the people bustled in Streambed Town. Like Talon Town, Streambed Town curved in a huge half-moon shape, but it was much smaller. About eighty people lived there. Priests dressed in white stood in the plaza, along with several brown-clothed slaves. Cottony tufts of cloud hovered just above the canyon rim.

What a magnificent morning—not that he could enjoy it. The Chief's chamber overflowed with whispering dignitaries, all waiting for the Blessed Sun to breathe his last. Webworm secretly wished the Chief would just do it. Then he and everyone else in Talon Town could get back to their normal lives.

His gaze drifted to the empty plaza, where slender coils of smoke rose from the kiva roof entries. The smell of burning juniper wafted up to him. He inhaled deeply and shivered against the chill. What he would give to be down there.

Sternlight said something soft, inaudible. Creeper asked, "What? Is he waking?"

"No," Sternlight answered. "It was just a moan."

Creeper glanced at Webworm and they exchanged an exasperated look. Webworm liked Creeper, despite the fat little man's peculiarities. Creeper had a bad habit of overhearing private conversations and repeating every word. But he had always treated Webworm with kindness and respect, probably because Creeper was in love with Webworm's mother, Featherstone.

Badgerbow, of the Coyote Clan, leaned against the south wall, a blanket over his shoulders. His knee-length kirtle had been painted with thunderclouds and mountains. He had brought twelve bunches of prayer feathers to hang from the ceiling.

Webworm watched the sacred offerings trembling in the air currents of the room.

Creeper hunched forward like a small black bear, hissing in Badgerbow's ear. Badgerbow nodded. He had a long misshapen face, deeply scarred in battle, and only half a head of black hair. He had been poorly scalped by the Mogollon many sun cycles before, leaving the pitted bone of his skull naked on the left side of his head.

On the walls, the thlatsinas watched and listened, their painted bodies reflecting the sunlight that flooded the room. Webworm studied them warily. People said they were holy, but Webworm felt only evil coming from those masked figures. The Wolf Thlatsina had his fangs bared, his ears pricked, his yellow eyes wide and alert. No matter where Webworm moved in the chamber, Wolf tracked him, as though distrustful of Webworm's presence.

He glared at the gaudy thlatsina. Though the bestial figure had a wolf's head, his body was human, the lower arms and legs painted black with white spots. His chest shone pure white. *If I were Chief, false god, I would replaster the walls over the top of you, burying you forever. You would never look at anyone that way again.*

Wolf's eyes glimmered, and a faint smile seemed to turn up the corners of the thlatsina's muzzle. Or a snarl?

Webworm's fingers tightened around the deerbone stiletto tied to his belt.

"In beauty it is begun," Sternlight softly Sang. "In beauty it is begun."

Sternlight walked around the dying Chief, sprinkling cornmeal to the four directions. Despite his forty-three summers, the priest looked remarkably young. He had bathed at dawn and left his waist-length hair loose. Against the pure white of his long shirt, it glinted blacker than black.

Soon, Webworm promised. *Very soon. I will expose you for the witch you are, cousin.*

After Wraps-His-Tail's death, Webworm had searched everywhere for Sternlight, without success. The Buffalo Dancers had seen him leave the Chief's chamber, but he had not been in his room when Ironwood ordered he be found. Half a hand of time later, Sternlight had walked up the trail from the wash, humming pleasantly, his white shirt blazing in the starlight.

And had the audacity to say he had not even heard the commotion!

"He's waking," Night Sun said.

She sat in the northwestern corner, her graying black hair twisted into a bun on top of her head. Her triangular face with its long eyelashes had gone deathly pale. She wore a scarlet dress fringed with seashells.

"No, he's not, Mother." Snake Head sat on the floor beside her. Starkly handsome, he had a perfect oval face, large dark eyes, and full lips. A priceless purple shirt decorated with copper bells and macaw feathers draped his tall body. "It was just a deception of the light. A cloud moved across the face of Father Sun. That's all."

Webworm had to bite his lip to keep it from twisting in disgust.

Snake Head's haughtiness grated on him like sandstone on raw flesh. The man had never suffered, not in his entire twenty-four summers. He had been treated as delicately as a precious Green Mesa pot. Because of that, he remained a boy in a man's body. He was intolerant and quick to judge. As Snake Head gazed upon his dying father, he showed no emotion at all. He might have been gazing upon a dead rabbit—or been a dead rabbit himself. The youth cared for nothing. No . . . Webworm shook his head. That wasn't quite true. Snake Head cared very much about his own enjoyment. More than anything, Snake Head relished watching people die.

Webworm peered out the doorway at the sunlit plaza and fervently prayed for Ironwood's return.

People had emerged from their chambers and begun their daily duties. Slaves with water jugs walked down the dirt path that led to the wash. A few women had tumplines around their foreheads, bearing the weight of the cradleboards they wore on their backs. The whimpers of an infant carried on the air, high and breathless. Two old men, white-haired and hunched over, crossed the eastern plaza with small square looms and balls of cotton yarn under their arms. Webworm could hear their laughter.

Then he saw his own mother, Featherstone, roaming around outside the town. Wearing her best cape, made of buffalo fur and macaw feathers, she looked regal—like a woman on her way to a grand ceremony. And, perhaps, that's where she thought she was. Webworm's heart ached. Dark gray hair lay tangled around her withered face. She used her walking stick to tap the dusty ground, then hobbled around in a circle, her lips moving in words too distant to hear. At times, she could be completely lucid, loving, and funny . . . but she had bad days. Days when she didn't even recognize Webworm, and begged over and over for him to tell her his name.

Love swelled within his soul. Featherstone had once been very Powerful. At the age of ten summers, she had been chosen by the priests of the Straight Path nation to be Sunwatcher. Then she had been captured by Fire Dog raiders, and they had clubbed her in the head so often that many of the cords which tethered her soul to her body had been severed; it hung by a thin thread now—sometimes in her body, other times gone.

Featherstone tripped over a rock and staggered. Webworm went rigid, fighting the impulse to rush to her, but she did not fall. She had fallen two summers ago and snapped a bone in her wrist. It still hurt her on cold days.

Sternlight knelt and placed his ear close to the Chief's mouth. "His breath is about the length of my finger. He must be on the road to the skyworlds."

Webworm glared at Sternlight. *If my mother had not been captured and beaten by the Fire Dogs, she would be Sunwatcher now, and you would be nothing.*

Creeper blinked his wide black eyes and whispered, "Look, Crow Beard's moving!"

The Chief groaned.

Badgerbow sucked in a breath and edged forward expectantly. Night Sun rose to her feet, but did not approach. She stood in the corner with her hands clasped tightly in front of her, her beautiful face tense. Snake Head remained sitting on the floor, eyes half-lidded. He watched his father like a warrior standing over a wounded enemy.

Sternlight leaned forward, and his long black hair framed his beautiful serene face. "Good morning, Crow Beard."

"Dune? I wish . . . Dune."

Sternlight answered, "The Derelict is not yet here. But he will be, soon. Swallowtail just returned to say they are coming, and the watchers in the signal towers reported two men on the north road. Give them perhaps another two hands of time. Dune is old."

The bruised circles around the Blessed Sun's eyes had turned black, making the rest of his face seem very pale. "His Bashing Rock . . . do you think he brought it?"

"Of course," Sternlight replied in a comforting voice, and tucked the corners of the blanket around Crow Beard's throat. "He promised you he would on your eighteenth bornday, didn't he?"

"He's getting old. Sometimes, he forgets." The Chief's head lolled sideways, and he squinted at Sternlight, as if trying to make out his features.

"He hasn't forgotten about this, my chief. Now rest. They will be here before you—"

"My wife," Crow Beard whispered. His age-spotted fingers fumbled at his blankets. "Where is . . . my wife?"

"Oh, Crow Beard." Night Sun hurried forward like a woman who had just heard her death sentence commuted. She knelt by Crow Beard's side and gripped his hand. "I am here, my husband."

The chief seemed to be struggling to find the strength to speak. His eyes drifted before he could focus on her face. When he did, the lines of his forehead deepened. "Before I . . . I die," he said. "I wish you to know . . . I—I forgive you."

Tears filled her eyes. "I love you, Crow Beard. Don't leave me."

Breath rasped in his lungs. "Tell me . . . will you?"

Night Sun leaned closer to him. "Anything. What is it, my husband?"

"Almost seventeen . . . summers ago . . . I went to trade . . . with the Hohokam. When I returned . . . ten months later . . ."

Night Sun's face suddenly went gray, and Webworm feared she might be about to faint. He got to his feet, preparing for the worst—and saw Snake Head smile grimly at his mother's back.

She gripped her husband's hand tighter. Against the brightly colored background of Dancing thlatsinas, Night Sun looked as still and grave as a corpse. "Yes? What about it?"

"I knew . . ." Crow Beard's head dipped in a nod. "Could tell from the marks . . . on your belly."

"W-what?" Night Sun exchanged a panicked glance with Sternlight, and Sternlight's jaw set. "I had been sick, I—"

Crow Beard shook her hand weakly. "Do not lie . . . not now. Tell me . . . the child?"

"There is no child, Crow Beard," Night Sun insisted. "I swear to you! That is the truth."

The blanket over Crow Beard's chest rose and fell rapidly. His breathing had gone shallow. "The child . . . where did you . . . put it?"

Webworm stared at the elders, but they appeared as stunned as he. Creeper's round face had slackened until his mouth hung open. Badgerbow stood rigid, the bare half of his skull sickly yellow in the sun. Had Webworm understood correctly? A child? Night Sun had birthed a child nearly sixteen summers ago? While her husband had been gone? And Crow Beard knew nothing of the child's fate? At the terrible implications Webworm's muscles contracted, bulging through his red warrior's shirt.

In a shaking voice, Night Sun said, "You are ill, my husband. You should sleep."

Night Sun tried to rise, but Crow Beard's fingers dug into her hand with a strength Webworm would not have thought he possessed. The Blessed Sun pulled his wife to the floor again, and Night Sun let out a small cry.

"Crow Beard, listen to me. Please! You do not know what you're saying. There is *no* child. Let me go. Please, I—"

"A boy?" the Chief rasped. "Or a . . . a girl?"

Sternlight stepped forward with the silent grace of a deer. He dropped to Night Sun's side. "My chief," he said softly as he gently tried to pry Crow Beard's fingers from Night Sun's hand. The Chief fought him, tightening his hold. "Night Sun is tired. She has not left your side—"

"I must know!" Crow Beard demanded. "*Tell me, Night Sun,* or gods help you . . . I—I will never leave this place. I will walk at your side every day for the rest of your life. I will kill you . . .

over and over . . . in your dreams. You'll never sleep without me beside you, never look upon the world without seeing me. *I promise you, I will never give you peace—*"

"Crow Beard!" Night Sun sobbed. "I beg you—"

"You must answer me, my wife. The child . . . may have a claim. If so, I have last duties . . . to perform."

Snake Head suddenly lurched to his feet. The macaw feathers on his purple shirt shimmered in a rainbow of red, blue, and yellow. "A claim? On my pitiful share of the wealth! Father, are you saying my mother betrayed you? I mean, we've all heard the rumors, but I never believed them!"

Sternlight lifted his head and in a silken voice said, *"Didn't you?"*

Snake Head's eyes slitted. "What are you saying?"

Webworm stood awkwardly, not knowing what to do. Adultery was punishable by banishment—even death. The clans would go mad. A woman of the First People had *never* been found guilty of such a crime!

As though his strength had failed, Crow Beard's hand fell back to his blankets with a soft thud. Night Sun quickly got to her feet and backed away, breathing hard, rubbing her wrist.

"Mother?" Snake Head demanded.

She shook her head. "He's ill, my son. He doesn't know what he's saying."

"Then you deny having a child by another man?"

"Yes, of course, I do!"

Crow Beard's hands knotted in his blankets. "Ironwood? Must tell . . . Jay Bird's brood. Where is Ironwood? I want my War Chief! Ironwood? *Ironwood?*"

As though terrified, Night Sun placed a hand over her mouth.

Snake Head chuckled darkly, and Night Sun jerked around to stare at him.

Webworm gave her a questioning look as he walked by, but she would not meet his eyes. He bent over the Chief's bed. Crow Beard's nostrils had pinched, as though he could not get enough air. "Ironwood is bringing Dune, my chief," Webworm said. "I am Webworm, his deputy."

"Closer . . ." Crow Beard's eyes wandered, as if seeking him through some growing mist. "Closer."

Webworm knelt. "What do you wish, my chief?"

An eerie gleam entered Crow Beard's eyes. "My sister-in-law's grandson . . . yes, I remember. You have always served me . . . loyally. Do you . . . do you realize that if . . . if a savior rises now . . . you have Fire Dog blood. Do you understand?"

Webworm frowned. "No, my chief. Try to tell me what you require of me. I will do anything you ask."

Crow Beard reached out feebly and touched Webworm's moccasin in trust. "I wish you to . . . to find the child," he said. "Do you hear me? Find the child?"

"Yes, find the child. And after that?"

"K-Kill it."

Night Sun blurted, *"Crow Beard, for the sake of the gods! There is no child!"*

Crow Beard fumbled at the leather fringes on Webworm's moccasin. "Find the child," he repeated. "You—you must . . . kill the child."

Webworm lifted his head and fixed Night Sun with a hard look. "Where is the child?"

Night Sun folded her arms and hugged herself. "I have told you the truth, grand nephew. No child exists."

Snake Head grabbed his mother's sleeve and spun her around. His purple shirt contrasted with the deep red tones of her dress. "My father says you bore a child while he was away Trading. Where is it? Answer me!"

Night Sun's expression changed from desperate worry to rage in less than a heartbeat. She slapped her son with all the strength in her slender body. "Do not *ever* speak to me that way again, my son."

Snake Head's mouth puckered into an enraged pout, but he backed away.

Webworm propped his hands on his hips. "What do you wish, Snake Head? If there is a child, we must learn where it is, or we cannot carry out the Blessed Sun's order."

Snake Head seemed to be weighing possibilities. "Creeper?" He turned to the fat little man with the jet black hair. "You are Elder of the Buffalo Clan. What are the wishes of your people? Whom do you believe?"

Creeper gave Webworm a pleading look. For many summers, Creeper had been like a father to Webworm, teaching him the things a boy should know, telling him the ritual stories. Creeper was the only other person in the world who understood and loved Featherstone. And Featherstone loved Night Sun. Webworm knew this was a terrible trial for Creeper—deciding the fate of Featherstone's aunt.

Creeper flapped his arms helplessly. "We must know. If there is a child, then we—"

"We must force her to tell us!" Badgerbow shouted. He clenched his teeth and glowered at Night Sun. She met his gaze squarely, her eyes blazing. Badgerbow said, "The order to find the child may have been Crow Beard's last. We are obligated to carry it out!"

Webworm said, "When the people discover this, they will go wild. No woman of the First People has ever been caught in such a crime. Oh, some will demand her execution, but most—"

"Most will defend her," Sternlight said as he walked in front of Night Sun, standing between her and her accusers. Shining waist-length hair draped the front of his ritual shirt.

Night Sun placed a hand on his shoulder. "Don't," she whispered to him. Sternlight turned halfway round to look into her eyes. As though exchanging some silent secret knowledge, they stared at each other for a long moment, then Night Sun hoarsely murmured, "Don't endanger yourself. I never meant for this to happen. Not to you. Not after all you have—"

"Hush!" Sternlight ordered. "Do not speak another word!"

Creeper and Badgerbow edged forward, breathlessly awaiting the outcome of this private conversation. Snake Head, too, seemed rapt. He stood like a stone statue, his large dark eyes wide. One of the copper bells on his right sleeve caught the sunlight and projected a tiny gleaming star on the wall.

Night Sun returned to Crow Beard's side and sat down, hugging her knees to her chest.

Timidly, Creeper asked, "Sternlight? We are waiting. What should we do? You are Sunwatcher. It is your duty to advise us on moral matters. If Night Sun is guilty, she must be punished. Banished, or—"

"Or *killed*," Snake Head said. "And if there is a child, it, too, must be killed, as my father ordered."

"Perhaps—" Sternlight's voice came low, insistent. He

seemed to be searching desperately. "Perhaps, Night Sun might be spared, if you knew the location and identity of the child."

Night Sun jerked around. "What are you talking about?"

Snake Head shot her a glance, then tipped his chin toward Sternlight. "Possibly, but I doubt she will confess—"

"I will tell you." Sternlight swallowed hard and closed his eyes.

"*You?*" Webworm asked. "How would you know?"

No one seemed to be breathing. Creeper and Badgerbow both peered unblinking at Sternlight.

Only Night Sun moved. She rose on trembling legs and said, "Sternlight? What are you saying?"

"Please," Sternlight hissed, "trust me."

"But what are you saying? You told me—"

"Yes, I know I did, but—"

"She's guilty!" Snake Head pointed a condemning finger. "I knew it! My mother betrayed my father! She deserves to *die* for this! This will shame all First People! Hallowed gods, the taint will last for generations. Even *my* children will bear the blame! Oh, Mother, how could you do this to me?"

Sternlight's face mottled with rage. He stalked to stand face-to-face with Snake Head. Snake Head leaned backward slightly, obviously frightened.

Webworm's spine tingled. Not once in forty-one summers had he seen his cousin angry. No, Sternlight moved through life like dandelion seed held aloft on a breeze, looking down at people and events, never becoming involved. What had happened those many summers ago that would evoke such behavior today?

In a hoarse whisper, Sternlight said, "I will tell you only once, Snake Head. The boy lives at Lanceleaf Village. He is the son of—"

"A boy?" Snake Head shouted. "He *will* demand a share of my wealth! In Lanceleaf Village? Isn't that where—"

"Yes," Sternlight answered, "where Beargrass, son of Black Rock Woman, took his wife and children almost sixteen summers ago."

Night Sun shook her head, apparently just as stunned by the words as everyone else in the room. "No," she said. "No, Sternlight. You—you're lying! Why are you saying this?"

Webworm glanced back and forth between them. Stern-light's expression silently begged Night Sun to say no more, and Webworm's hand crept to the deerbone stiletto on his belt. He had not seen Beargrass in summers, but he still considered him a friend. They had fought many battles together. "Blessed gods," he whispered.

"Do you know this man?" Snake Head demanded. He took the opportunity to step away from Sternlight and seemed to breathe easier as he turned toward Webworm.

"Yes," Webworm answered. "Beargrass was Ironwood's dep-uty long before me, and I—I have visited his house in the past, whenever I ran the road that goes by Lanceleaf Village."

"Good," Snake Head said. "Then you know what his chil-dren look like—"

"No! No, I don't. I haven't seen the children in many sum-mers." Well, he remembered Beargrass' beautiful daughter very well, but truly he couldn't recall the boy at all.

Snake Head irritably waved a hand. "Doesn't matter. Find the boy. Kill him and be done with it."

Night Sun had broken out in a sweat. Beads of moisture dotted her straight nose and forehead. She stared blankly at Sternlight. The priest simply stared back.

"Sternlight?" Night Sun said.

At a soft gasp everyone spun around.

Crow Beard's head rolled to the side, and he lay very still.

"Oh . . ." Night Sun whispered.

Snake Head rushed over and placed a finger over the large vein in the Chief's neck, checking for a pulse. After several moments, he announced, "My father is dead. As the only male in my lineage, I rule now. I—"

"Wait," Sternlight said. He knelt beside Snake Head and examined the Chief's face, touching his temple, then picking up one of Crow Beard's hands and pressing on the thumbnail to see if the blood retreated and did not return. "He may be dead, but we can't be certain. He has done this five times in the past sun cycle. He may be on another Soul March to the afterworld. We must put him in a kiva for a few days to see if he returns to us."

Snake Head's lip curled. He turned to Webworm. "Regard-less, he looks dead, so I am in charge. My first act is to name this man, Webworm, as the new War Chief. I have *always* wanted my cousin Webworm at my side."

The abrupt advancement staggered Webworm. At first, he didn't understand, and then, in a moment of sheer terror, he realized the meaning. A sick feeling settled in his gut, as if he'd stabbed Ironwood in the heart. A new Chief with even a thread of respect would have allowed Ironwood the chance to step down on his own. Dismissing him as War Chief would dishonor Ironwood, and the brave warrior did not deserve such treatment.

Snake Head gestured imperiously at Webworm. "Go, War Chief. Carry out my father's wishes. Find my mother's wretched spawn and kill it."

"Yes, my chief."

But as Webworm backed away, he noticed that neither Sternlight nor Night Sun had moved. They continued to stare at each other like frozen corpses.

Seventeen

Wind Baby tormented the hem of Ironwood's red shirt as he and Dune hurried for Talon Town. In the sky, a moisture-spawned halo encircled the flaming face of Father Sun. Eerie light filtered through the halo, turning the shadows from gray to a smoky azure. Before him, the land descended toward the rim of Straight Path Canyon in layers of pale slickrock.

Center Place perched near the canyon rim just ahead, its white walls gleaming in the diffuse light. The large town contained over one hundred and thirty-three rooms and was ruled over by a diminutive old woman named Weedblossom. Few people lived there, however. All of the inhabitants were holy people, guardians of the legendary Rainbow Serpent.

The sound of voices Singing and pots shattering carried in the air.

Ironwood watched a young priest leave Center Place carrying a handful of sherds to the sacred Broken Pottery mound in front of the town, where he tossed the fragments down, lifted his arms to the sky and Sang.

"I always feel uneasy up here," Ironwood said. "They free so many souls every day—which means I'm surrounded by ghosts, and I don't even know it."

Dune's mouth widened in a toothless grin. "Be glad you're blind to them."

Ironwood cocked his head. "Why? Are they cursing me to my face?"

"And to your back," Dune said. "Especially your victims."

Ironwood plucked a piece of pottery from the road and turned it in his hands, studying the black-and-white geometric designs. "Tell them I regret the sorrow I caused them."

"I already have, War Chief."

Center Place served as the spiritual crossroads to the afterworlds. All souls began their journey from this point, even those born at great distances.

To make certain their relatives found the afterworld, caring families used a "soul pot" to capture and hold a dying relative's last breath. Then, during major ceremonials, they brought the pot to Center Place, paid the priests, and left, knowing that the holy people would, someday soon, shatter the pot and free their relative's soul to run the road to the afterworld.

Ironwood glanced about, studying every shadow, but he saw no ghosts, just swaying spikes of yellow grass and eroded slickrock.

Holy roads angled off in every direction, intersecting each other, sometimes running parallel courses, but all converging at the heart of the town.

Dune stopped suddenly. "Listen. Do you hear it?"

Ironwood turned his right ear to Wind Baby. "Yes. It sounds like . . . shouts . . . eddying on the gusts of wind. What—"

"Run ahead! Hurry!" Dune waved his walking stick. "I'll catch up!"

Ironwood's sandals pounded as he trotted down the road past Center Place to the canyon rim.

For several moments, no sound except Ironwood's footsteps and a muted roar like faraway thunder came to his ears, but as he neared the rim, threats and shouts rose above the general frenzy. A woman screamed, *"Let her go! Crow Beard . . . a witch! We all know it! How many innocent people . . . murdered in the past sun cycle?"*

An explosion of voices answered.

Ironwood peered over the edge. Two hundred hands below, Talon Town's plaza writhed with people shoving each other, shouting. Slaves moved among the crowd, their tattered brown clothing contrasting sharply with the brilliant reds, blues, and yellows of the elite. Curious. But they wouldn't be there if their masters had not given them permission.

Ironwood clenched his fists. What could have caused . . . ? *Crow Beard is dead.* Yes, it must be. People always panicked after the death of a Chief. If not handled quickly, their rampaging emotions could lead to hysteria, violence, and killing.

Anxiously, Ironwood looked back down the road. Dune seemed to be trying to hurry.

Ironwood waited.

Dune wheezed as he stopped at Ironwood's side and peered over the edge. Wind flipped his white hair over his ears. "So . . ." Dune said quietly. "He's finally dead."

"That's the only answer."

"What are they saying? I can't make out any words."

"They're shouting that Crow Beard was wicked."

"Well, that's true enough." Dune raised a bushy white brow. "I'd throw a slab over him myself if . . ." An unnerving intensity entered Dune's faded eyes.

"If what?"

"Hmm?"

"You said you'd throw a slab over him if—what?"

Dune took Ironwood's arm and guided him along the rim toward the stairway cut into the canyon wall just above Kettle Town.

"If I hadn't promised that I wouldn't."

"But he deserves it, Dune. Why would you help an evil man ascend to the skyworlds to become a god? I shouldn't think that you would wish—"

"Because." Dune squinted down at Kettle Town, east of Talon Town, and almost as large. People crowded the roofs, working, talking. Many stood peering anxiously at the turmoil in Talon Town. "On his eighteenth bornday I told Crow Beard I would free his soul after his death. He was a good man, then. The promise made sense. Despite the monster he's become, I must keep my word."

Ironwood led the way eastward along the canyon rim to the stairway cut into the cliff face above Kettle Town.

Dune halted at the stairs and took a deep breath. "I'm ready. Let's climb down."

"I'll go first," Ironwood said, and climbed over the edge, descending as quickly as he could. Dune eased over, taking the stairs with care. When the cliff face grew too steep for steps, a ladder, coupled with handholds, let Ironwood down onto the rounded tower that supported the ladder's butt.

Voices rose from Kettle Town. People shielded their eyes to stare.

"*Look!*" a woman shouted. "*It's Ironwood! And the holy Derelict! Dune! It's Dune and Ironwood!*"

A roar of adulation went up, and people ran to the hanging balcony on Kettle Town's north wall, others flooding out of the entries to gather at the base of the ladder Ironwood was climbing down.

The instant Ironwood stepped off, an old woman, Moon Bright, the Matron of Kettle Town, pushed through the crowd, her silver brows a solid line across her wrinkled forehead.

"Come," she said, and gripped Ironwood's arm. She led him through the crowd to a place where they stood alone, and whispered, "I have terrible news. Before he died, Crow Beard forced Night Sun to admit she had given birth to a child sixteen summers ago. He—"

"*What?*"

"Let me finish!" Moon Bright's eyes blazed. "Snake Head ordered his mother confined in the Cage."

"The Cage?" Ironwood whispered. The room had neither windows nor doors. The only light came through a small opening in the roof, which was sealed when prisoners were being held there. "Hallowed gods."

Moon Bright gazed intently at Ironwood. "After his father's death, Snake Head appointed Webworm as his new War Chief." Her grip on Ironwood's arm tightened. "His first order was that Webworm find Night Sun's misbegotten spawn and kill it."

Blood throbbed in Ironwood's ears. "What . . . what did she tell Snake Head? Did she defend herself?"

"No." Moon Bright's ancient head shook. "Night Sun insisted that there was no child!"

"Then how—"

"Sternlight claimed that the child lived."

Ironwood's mouth opened, but words refused to form.

"Webworm gathered his warriors and left immediately for Lanceleaf Village. They followed Straight Path Wash north. He had orders to—"

"Thank you, Matron." Ironwood patted her hand and turned to watch Dune. The holy man had made it halfway down the ladder. "When the Derelict arrives, please tell him the news. I will meet him in the chief's chamber later. But, now, I must go."

He had to speak with Sternlight, find out what he'd told Webworm—it couldn't have been the truth. Of that, Ironwood was certain. And he had to see Night Sun. Locked in the Cage by her own son's order! Her heart would be breaking.

Moon Bright gave Ironwood a shove. "Go on. *Hurry.*"

Night Sun sat alone on the dirt floor, her head leaned back against the wall. A terrible darkness closed in around her, pressing on her ears and eyes until she longed to scream. No sound penetrated the gloom, though earlier she had heard the cries of the people in the plaza, some demanding her release, others her death.

Moisture dripped from the ceiling and ran down the wall behind her like forlorn tears. She had no blanket, and the dampness clawed at her bones. She had loosed her long, graying black hair and feathered it over her shoulders for warmth, but she'd been shivering for a long time. How long, she did not know. Time had ceased.

The room spread two body-lengths square. She had walked it over and over. It had no wall benches, no hearth, no ventilation shaft, only a hole in the roof through which a ladder could be lowered. A red clay pot, for her bodily wastes, sat in the southwestern corner. She had received neither food nor water since her imprisonment, and thirst plagued her, as if a dry root had lodged in her throat.

Those things, she could stand.

It was that other darkness, the sick despair, that sucked away her strength.

For the first time in her life, Night Sun was truly alone. Crow Beard had left her, and no matter how much she tried to convince herself she was better off, her soul wobbled for balance, as if she'd broken a leg. She and Crow Beard had grown used to each other over the summers. That familiarity had brought some measure of comfort to their strange lives. She had counted on him, not for emotional support, or love, but for advice on clan bickering, an occasional approving smile, discussions about their children. Things no one else could provide.

Night Sun drew up her knees and braced her chin on them, staring into the darkness. Her people wouldn't condemn her based upon rumor or gossip, but if proof of her infidelity could be found, they might decide she deserved to die, or be banished. It would be the same. Banishment would tear her from her home, throw her into the desert to slowly waste away. None of the Made People clans would dare take her in. And her relatives among the First People—shamed by the revelations of her conduct—wouldn't give her refuge.

A raven cawed outside, loud and raucous, perhaps engaged in a battle over food, and her mind wandered. Could there truly be a child? How? Had Sternlight lied?

For three moons before Crow Beard left on his trading mission to the Hohokam, he had tormented her and mistreated Cloud Playing. Night Sun had been so distraught she had actually contemplated divorcing him, which would have disgraced them both.

She'd found herself in the monster's belly before she realized what was happening. A smothering blackness had swallowed her soul, and she'd become a stranger to herself. At that point she hadn't even recognized the face of the woman who stared back from her pyrite mirror. Those haunted eyes could not be hers. . . .

Desperate, she had focused on the nearest human face with any kindness in it. She'd fought to cling to that person long enough that she could follow the awl prick of light and crawl out of the blackness.

That face had belonged to Ironwood.

She had turned to him—and he'd loved her with all of his soul.

When her pregnancy had begun to show, Night Sun had locked herself in her chambers and forbidden even her most faithful slaves, Young Fawn and Mourning Dove, to enter. The only one she had trusted had been her nephew, Sternlight. He had brought her food and water, played the flute for her, and talked in gentle tones to soothe her fears.

Her contractions had begun before dawn. At sunrise Sternlight had picked up his conch shell horn, climbed to the roof above Crow Beard's chamber, and called the people out. He'd announced that he'd had a horrifying Dream. Everyone had to leave Talon Town! The gods themselves had commanded it! He would send word when it was safe to return. Terrified, the people had gone. Ironwood had led them to Kettle Town for the day.

Night Sun had been free to cry out all she wanted. Only Sternlight and the empty town could hear her.

Sternlight had never left her side. At dusk, the baby had slid out. Sternlight had wrapped it in a beautiful blanket and disappeared. On his return, he told Night Sun that the baby had never made a sound, that it must have died in her womb.

Ravaged with guilt, certain the gods were punishing her, she had been very ready to believe him. By the time Crow Beard had returned from his trip to the Hohokam, Night Sun had recovered and could greet her husband as if nothing had happened.

But her life had crumbled.

Frightened and lonely, she had longed for Ironwood. They had shared each other's hearts, begotten and lost a precious child, and only in his arms could she find comfort for her grief . . . a comfort she dared not seek.

They passed each other every day without a word or a glance.

As the moons swept by, that "dead" baby had called her name endlessly in her dreams, drawing her into a netherworld of doubt and pain.

Night Sun folded her arms over her chest and hugged herself. Sternlight's words had opened a door in her soul that she couldn't seal again.

Could the child be alive?

"Blessed thlatsinas," she prayed. "If my son is alive, I beg you to kill him." Tears traced warm lines down Night Sun's cheeks. "Kill him before the warriors get there."

Sunset flamed across the sky and lit the high mountain peaks to the north and east with fire. The brassy gleam penetrated the window behind Thistle, coated the white walls, and dyed her yellow dress a deep rich amber. Beargrass, lost in thought, sat opposite her. His expression seemed curiously calm.

She bent over the line of pots along the west wall of her small house, removed the lid on the buckwheat, and scooped a handful into the bowl she held. Next she dipped out dried currants and beeweed leaves, and added a dash of ricegrass flour.

Outside, robins jumped from cactus to cactus, uttering lilting mating calls. The shrill cries of a red-tailed hawk carried on a cool wind that blew through the window. Damp mossy smells wafted up from the creek below Lanceleaf Village.

Thistle returned to the fire, set her bowl down, and poked the low flames with a juniper stick. Sparks rose and blinked out before they reached the soot-encrusted ceiling poles. A pot of boiling water sat at the edges of the flames.

"They must be all right," she said to Beargrass, who was sipping from a cup of dried yucca petal tea. "If they weren't, we would know by now, wouldn't we? I mean—"

"Thistle, they're fine," Beargrass repeated for the fifth time that afternoon. Exasperation lined his narrow face. He wore a long red shirt and had twisted his black hair into a bun at the base of his head. "Stone Forehead would have come back to tell us if anything had gone wrong. I'm certain he found Corn-silk happily chattering to Deer Bird, and Fledgling driving my father crazy with questions about making stone tools. You must stop worrying. You'll wear yourself out."

She wet her lips anxiously. The fringes on the hem of her yellow dress swished on the bulrush mat as she sat down. "I've been annoying you, haven't I?"

Beargrass smiled gently. "Both children have never been away at the same time before, and never for such a length of time. Your worry is understandable. But you seem to be tearing yourself apart. There's no reason for it, Thistle. They're safe. That's what we wanted. And it's only for a moon or so."

Thistle dumped her bowl of currants, flour, and beeweed into the pot of boiling water and stirred the mixture with a horn spoon. A pleasantly tangy aroma rose. The currants would add sweetness to the buckwheat stew, while the ricegrass flour would thicken it. The soup would go well with the squash roasting in the coals. Perhaps later she would take some of her hoarded store of popcorn, place it in the popping pot with a little fat, and salve her worry with the treat.

Thistle's nostrils flared as she leaned over to smell her bubbling stew. Her stomach growled in anticipation.

Placing her spoon on a hearthstone, Thistle sat back and lifted her own cup of tea. As she sipped, her gaze went to the stacked sleeping mats on her left. Fledgling's personal basket sat beside them, holding every precious thing he owned. The antelope hoof rattle—the one he'd received after his first kiva initiation—stuck out on top. Cornsilk's basket sat on the right side. Two beautiful olivella-shell necklaces lay coiled on a bed of colored waist sashes. Terrible longing swelled in Thistle's chest. She missed them so. They'd only been gone for four days, but it seemed . . .

High-pitched shrieks split the dusk, rising and falling on the wind. Surprised shouts, then screams, rang from Lanceleaf's plaza.

Simultaneously, Beargrass and Thistle lunged for the door, throwing back the curtain to look outside.

Warriors flooded through the village gate below, their faces lurid in the red flames of sunset. They kicked turkeys out of the way, slammed barking dogs with war clubs, shot arrows into fleeing people.

"*Blessed gods, what's happening?*" Beargrass whispered.

A tall warrior grabbed Matron Clover by her frail old arm, swung her around, and struck her head with his club. When she staggered but didn't fall, another warrior shot her in the belly. She slumped to the ground, rocking back and forth, her white hair matted to her head with blood. Her screams pierced the din.

"Who *are* they?" Thistle cried. "They're not Tower Builders! They're—"

"*Ours.*" Beargrass almost choked on the word. "They're Straight Path warriors."

She couldn't speak.

Beargrass turned, gripped Thistle by the shoulders, and looked her in the eyes. "I must fight. And you must run."

"But there are so many of them, Beargrass! Twenty or thirty warriors! We can't fight so many! We must—"

"I will join you at Father's village. Run!"

"No, please, I want to—"

"*Run!*"

He grabbed his bow and quiver of arrows from where they lay by the door and charged outside, running down the hill for the village, his red shirt flying about his legs.

Two men ran around the plaza, smearing pine pitch on the plastered walls, preparing to fire them.

Thistle took her pack, threw in some food, an obsidian knife and bone stiletto, and ducked outside. The billowing clouds to the west had begun to shade gray with night. She fled northward, skirting cornfields. At the rim of one of the small gorges feeding into Squash Blossom Canyon, she took the trail off the caprock and down into the rock-tumbled depths, praying the darkness would shield her.

Screams rose to a terrifying cacophony behind her.

She didn't turn around. Thorns ripped at her legs and shredded her yellow dress as she shoved through a greasewood thicket down by the drainage and pounded along the wet soil, following the canyon to its mouth. Water-smoothed stones in the drainage bottom slipped beneath her moccasins, almost tumbling her.

From out of nowhere, a crackling roar split the twilight. Like thunder, it rose to swallow the screams and shouts.

Thistle turned to look.

Even from the depths of the canyon, she could see. Flames leaped into the darkening sky, dancing like monstrous blazing beasts, licking at the bellies of the clouds.

For a moment, just a moment, she thought she heard Beargrass . . . screaming . . .

And she turned.

Three black forms raced down the hill toward her. Friends fleeing the catastrophe?

Thistle fell to her knees and crawled into a dense tangle of head-high sage. Through the fragrant branches, she watched the enemy warriors dash down toward the creek.

A short while later, someone cried out.

Thistle clenched her teeth. And prayed.

Eighteen

Cornsilk tramped her way to the crest of a juniper-and-piñon-studded hill and slowed to catch her breath. Shocks of ricegrass, wheatgrass, and winter-dried lupine madé patterns on the yellow soil and bobbed in thé breeze.

Stone Forehead had whined all night, declaring that he'd never be a great warrior if it got around that he couldn't even get a young woman home—and it would be all her fault.

More than a little disgusted with herself for giving in, Cornsilk raised her bow over her head and stretched her aching back muscles while she waited for Stone Forehead and Fledgling. They hiked up the hill slowly, talking. Both carried bows in their right hands and quivers of arrows on their backs, waiting for dinner to run from behind a bush.

Though only two summers separated them, Stone Forehead stood a head taller than Fledgling and had shoulders twice as broad. Fledgling had left his hair free to blow in the breeze; it flapped over his gray shirt. Stone Forehead wore a yellow shirt belted at the waist. A pack hung lopsided on his back between his two short braids. He gestured with his left hand, probably entertaining Fledgling with war tales again.

It had been irksome having Stone Forehead around for a night and a whole day. Once she'd given in, he jabbered nonstop about his battle exploits. While it thrilled Fledgling, Cornsilk had been bored to the point of contemplating murder. She'd run ahead all day just to escape.

Dusk settled across the desert in a cool lavender veil and flowed into the spaces between the buttes, dyeing the sky a deep purple. From the crest of the low rise, she could see vast distances. Square-topped buttes jutted up across the broken country. Slanting rays from the dying sun cast their long shadows across the sage-covered bottoms and mingled with the dark slashes of drainages zigzagging down the slopes. To her right, the territory of the Green Mesa clans rose toward the sky in cool, green layers, the ragged foothills giving way to pine-covered mountains.

Ahead of her, billowing black clouds hovered above Lanceleaf, their bellies tarnished by an amber glow. Perhaps it was some odd shaft of evening sunshine through the clouds?

Cornsilk let out a taut breath. She missed her parents and Leafhopper. All day long she had been hearing her mother's beautiful voice and teasing laughter, and they had wounded her soul. To be frustrated in her plans was irritating enough, but she was also homesick.

Her dreams last night had been bizarre and tormented. She'd found herself tumbling through a flaming sky, and a huge white-faced bear had run around and around her, trying to save her from crashing to the earth. He'd finally told her to climb onto his back. Cornsilk had grabbed the fur around his neck and ridden him as he'd leaped from cloud to cloud. When he landed on the ground, she'd climbed off and petted his neck softly. She'd loved that bear deeply for all he'd done for her. . . .

Walking over the crest of the hill, she could see where the tan trail forked in the juniper-furred valley below. She scrutinized it. If she took off running, she could be home in less than half-a-hand of time. She wouldn't stay. She knew her parents did not wish that, but if she could, she . . .

Stone Forehead would just run you down. You've raced him before, and he's much faster than you are.

So was Fledgling, for that matter. She watched the two young men as they topped the hill and walked toward her. From the smiles on their faces, they'd become fast friends. Fledgling would probably help Stone Forehead tackle her and drag her kicking and screaming to Uncle Deer Bird's house.

"We should camp here tonight," Stone Forehead said as he hiked up beside Cornsilk. His yellow sleeves flapped in a sudden gust of wind. "This is a good place."

Fledgling looked around and nodded. "All right, I'll gather wood for a fire, then we'll—"

"You dimwits," Cornsilk said disgustedly. "Oh, yes, this is a fine place. Why, up here on this hilltop enemy warriors will be able to see us for half a day's walk. A fire here will be seen as far south as the Fire Dogs! Not to mention the Tower Builders and the Wild Men. Besides, up here, Wind Baby will scour our faces raw." She thrust her bow toward the split in the road. "I'm camping down in the junipers."

Fledgling grinned and his pug nose crinkled. "She's right, you know. It would be safer. Finding wood will be easier, too. We might even be able to ambush a deer, or net some birds in the trees."

Cornsilk and Fledgling stared at Stone Forehead, awaiting an answer.

The young warrior stood stiffly, his dark brows lowered, peering unblinking at the northern highlands. A flush crept into his cheeks, as if his heart had begun to thunder.

Fledgling said, "What is it? What do you see?"

Cornsilk turned, frowned, and glanced northward. Father Sun's radiance had completely died, so the golden gleam could not be a strange reflection of the light. Had Lanceleaf Village built a huge bonfire, or—

Stone Forehead breathed, "Oh, Blessed gods," and ran, his legs flashing as he raced down the hill.

A cold pit opened in Cornsilk's belly. She flew after him, her pack flopping on her back. A pitiful voice whispered in her soul, *No, it can't be . . .*

Fledgling caught up with her and shouted, "It's happening, Cornsilk! Just as our parents feared!" He pulled out ahead.

She squinted against the dust his feet kicked up. The dirt trail cut through the junipers and climbed the opposite slope.

Stone Forehead leaped a log in the trail before she lost him in the trees.

Fledgling darted past the split in the trail and vanished into the deep green, following Stone Forehead.

Cornsilk briefly glanced at the trail which led to her uncle's home, and forced her legs to run harder. She panted up the slope, ducking beneath the low juniper branches, and continued on.

When she reached the top, Stone Forehead was way out ahead. He'd hit his stride, and his long legs ate away at the distance. Fledgling ran behind him.

As the evening deepened, they became black silhouettes, and the gleam in front of them turned savage. What she had earlier taken for clouds hovering over the village metamorphosed into great billows of smoke. Tormented by Wind Baby, they lengthened, becoming thin charcoal threads as they blew eastward. The glow rose into the night like a fiery blister.

Cornsilk ran with all her heart, powered by panic. *Mother! Blessed thlatsinas . . . not Mother!* The need to feel her arms around her again grew overwhelming. Cornsilk prayed as she had never prayed before, "If anything's happened to her . . . thlatsinas, don't let her die! Please, *don't let her die!*"

Stone Forehead and Fledgling pulled further and further ahead. Breath tore in and out of Cornsilk's lungs. She blinked her tears back as she vaulted dark spots in the trail. They might have only been shadowed depressions, but brush and rocks often tumbled into such hollows. She couldn't risk a fall.

Her father had said that anyone who wished to harm the hidden child would do it immediately after the Chief died. Did that mean the Blessed Sun was gone? Or had the vicious Tower Builders or the cursed Fire Dogs attacked Lanceleaf?

"Mother?" she called. "Father?"

Maybe her parents weren't even in the village. They could be out gathering cactus pads, or hunting rabbits.

Mother's sad eyes formed in the darkness before her, filled with love and worry. "*Oh, my daughter. You are my joy. Never forget that.*"

Sobs choked Cornsilk as her sandals pounded over a hump in the road and down the other side.

The closer she came to Lanceleaf Village, the more the

crackling flames swelled and roared. Thin cries wavered above the cacophony.

Panting, her lungs fevered for air, Cornsilk crested the last rise . . . and her legs went weak. She stumbled, catching herself just before she fell.

An inferno of flame rose from the village, earth trembling as one burning roof after another collapsed and fell into the houses. Torrents of sparks whirled into the sky and drifted lazily through blood-colored clouds of smoke.

Willow and bulrush mats had been thrown onto the blaze. Cornsilk locked her shaking knees. Black pitch streaked the walls. The warriors must have dragged out people's bedding, tucked it around the bases of the walls, then thrown the pitch over the buildings and set them on fire.

Stone walls remained standing to outline the square of buildings that had surrounded the plaza, but the interiors of the houses blazed in fiery heaps. Charred pine poles, all that was left of the ceiling, thrust up against the orange glare like burned arms imploring the sky gods for help.

A whimper lodged in her throat. She pulled an arrow from her quiver, nocked it in her bow, and bent low, trotting along the tall dead grass that edged a cornfield, praying for a glimpse of her family's home. Had it burned, too?

She drew closer—and saw her home.

Three of the walls still stood, blackened with soot, but the wall facing the village had toppled into a mound of rubble.

Frantically, Cornsilk's eyes searched for people. No one stood beyond the halo of light. Where had they all gone? Where were her parents? And Leafhopper? Had the villagers seen the raiders coming and fled before they arrived?

She scrambled for the rise behind her home which overlooked the village. As she crept closer, she heard voices. An old woman wept bitterly; a man gave gruff orders.

Cornsilk got down on her belly and slid through the sand until she reached the big yucca where she had lain only a few short days ago and seen her brother eavesdropping on their parents. *Oh, Fledgling, where are you?*

Heart throbbing in her ears, she inched forward and stopped suddenly. The rear window of their house, which had originally been blocked by the front wall, now opened onto the plaza and people huddled there.

Little Snail, seven summers old, wailed, a soft and shrill sound, as she struggled to drag a small body away from a burning building. The body flopped onto its back and Cornsilk covered her mouth with her hand to stop its trembling. *Brave Boy!* One of his eyes was open and stared blindly at the sky.

Little Snail sobbed breathlessly as she dragged her brother away by the feet. His arms had spread and scooped sand every time she tugged. Throwing all of her weight into the struggle, Little Snail moved Brave Boy less than a hand's breadth, then sank to the ground, sobbing. She buried her face against her brother's chest.

When Little Snail dropped, Cornsilk saw her father . . . *and Fledgling!* They sat on the ground in the middle of the plaza. A tall, square-jawed man stood over them. He wore a warrior's helmet, a close-fitting cap of buffalo hide. He swung a war club in his right hand, the stone head blood-shiny in the firelight.

Cornsilk squirmed to the left. Where was her mother? What had happened to her mother? Had she escaped? Blessed thlatsinas, let it be so! And Stone Forehead? Where had he gone?

Her stomach knotted. Stone Forehead would have run straight into the battle, firing arrows as quickly as he could, trying to defend his people. Was he dead? Perhaps he had known the battle hopeless and run away.

Her father put an arm around Fledgling, holding him close, and the act seemed to enrage the lanky warrior. His red shirt whipped about his legs as he paced in front of them.

"You must know, Beargrass," the man shouted over the roar of the flames, "that I will kill you if you do not tell me."

Her father's hold on Fledgling tightened. He yelled. "I know that, Webworm."

Webworm! What is he doing here?

"Who is this boy's real father?" Webworm demanded.

Fledgling squeezed his eyes closed, his expression one of sick fear.

"I am." Beargrass tried to straighten his leg and choked a cry. Was that blood mottling the skin of his thigh?

"Don't lie to me! I know his mother is the whore Night Sun!

She will be punished for her crime. But we must find the father, too. Answer me! Is it my cousin Sternlight?"

Cries of outrage rose from his warriors. Such a mating would be incest! They glanced at each other uneasily.

Webworm paced back and forth, smacking the bloody war club on his palm, bellowing, "I know that Sternlight slept in Night Sun's personal chamber while Crow Beard traded with the Hohokam! He *must* be the father!"

"Fledgling is *my* son," Beargrass insisted angrily. "His mother . . ." His voice broke. "Was . . . was my wife, Thistle. You know this, Webworm. From the nights you sat at my fire, sharing my hospitality. I am telling you the truth!"

Cornsilk's heart cried out in terror, *No!* Mother couldn't be—

Webworm pointed at Beargrass with his war club. In the lurid glare, it shone amber. "You are calling the Blessed Sun a liar?"

"What *is* this madness?" Beargrass shouted. "Webworm, you know me! By the Blessed thlatsinas, I swear on my soul, I'm telling you the *truth!* This boy is my son by my wife! If the Blessed Sun says otherwise, he's *wrong!*" Beargrass glared up through pain-slitted eyes, voice strained. "Even now, Webworm, after this atrocity, I'll not call the Blessed Sun a liar— but I'll say he's *mistaken!*"

Sobs caught Cornsilk by surprise. She smothered the sound as best she could. Tears blurred her eyes and ran hotly down her face. The Blessed Sun had told Webworm to find a *boy.* What did that mean? Had her mother lied to her? But why would she?

Beargrass glared up at Webworm. "In all the years you fought at my side, shared cold and fatigue, did you ever see me act dishonorably? Did you ever question my loyalty, or courage?"

Webworm shook his head. His mouth moved, but Cornsilk couldn't hear his answer.

Beargrass rose unsteadily to his feet, limping painfully on his bloody leg, and glared at the warriors in the plaza. "I risked my life to save many of you! That man who fought beside you, the warrior who shared your fire, and cared for you when you were wounded, tells you that you are wrong! This is my son, as the gods bear witness! You have murdered innocents! Do you wish two more murders on your souls? Any of you?"

Webworm slapped his war club into his palm. "I must do this, Beargrass! I have no choice. I have orders to leave no witnesses!"

Her father collapsed to the ground again and hugged Fledgling so tightly his arms shook. Cornsilk saw that Fledgling was crying. "Then for the sakes of your own souls, do it quickly!"

Webworm lifted a hand to someone outside Cornsilk's vision, and shouted, "Gnat! Do . . . do it!"

The ring of warriors closed in, until six warriors stood framed in the window, blocking her view. Cornsilk blinked to clear her eyes of tears. Webworm tramped out of sight, then reappeared outside the square of burned buildings. He winced as he massaged his shoulder—the way a man would to soothe a wound—then sank to the ground, removed his buffalo helmet, and dropped his sweaty head in his hands.

Her father cried out sharply, a hollow smack sounded, and Fledgling screamed, high and clear—the sound cut off as if by a sliver of obsidian.

The group of warriors milled around for several instants, then one man cursed loudly, and they all began to back away.

Cornsilk raised herself on her elbows, shaking, eyes searching.

As the warriors filed out of the plaza, she glimpsed her father lying on his back. Blood soaked the front of his shirt, and across his stomach . . .

"Here!" Gnat walked up to Webworm and threw him something that resembled a hide ball.

Cornsilk thrust her sand-encrusted fist into her mouth to stifle the scream.

Webworm caught Fledgling's head and tucked it beneath his good arm. "Gnat, take your men and finish this. Let no one live to tell this story."

Gnat gestured to his warriors and returned to the smoke-stained village plaza.

Webworm looked at another warrior and cried, "Let's go! That man was my friend." He got to his feet. "We will make camp at the split in the road."

He took off at a trot with ten or twelve men running after him.

Cornsilk watched them lope into the darkness.

She barely breathed.

More hideous shrieks split the night. Gnat and his men raced in front of the window. The howls of the killers mixed with the screams of her clan in a sickening roar. Old man Fat Cob stumbled in front of the window, his hands over his head, sobbing. A warrior ran up behind him with a club . . . and they disappeared from view. Little Snail's childish voice shrieked, *"No, please, I haven't done anything wrong! Please, don't hurt me! NO—"*

She saw a firelit war club lift and slam down, and heard the meaty snap of a skull.

Cornsilk rolled to her back and gasped for breath. The Evening People glimmered and twinkled. Her muscles began to spasm, limbs twitching like a wounded animal's. She chewed her sandy fist while tears streaked her face.

Inside the shell of her body, her soul let out a silent scream.

Nineteen

Ironwood stood in the doorway of Snake Head's personal chamber, arms crossed, watching Swallowtail deliver the new Chief's supper. The Mogollon youth set the long wooden platter down beside the bowl of warming coals in the middle of the floor, then checked to see that the teapot suspended from the tripod was heating properly. As he backed away, he laced his fingers before him, awaiting instructions. He stood almost as tall as Ironwood. When Swallowtail gazed at Snake Head, hatred glinted in his dark eyes.

Snake Head stood with his back to them, preening before a pyrite mirror. Every now and then the mirror would flash and

Ironwood would catch Snake Head watching him with a gloating smile.

Arrogant young fool. He knows the people have been talking to me. That's why he's keeping me waiting, as a reminder that I no longer have the right to speak to him of these things.

A torch of shredded cedar bark burned on the wall to Ironwood's right, casting a wavering amber glow over the chamber. Four-by-five body-lengths across, the room had a high ceiling and gloriously painted walls. Swallowtail's gaze was riveted on the northern wall to his left, where the dangerous Badger Thlatsina stood. The god had a black body, long muzzle, and sharp teeth. A circle of enemy scalps—mostly Mogollon—encircled him. Now that they were water and seed beings, these scalps gave Snake Head more Power than any young man his age deserved.

In its large cage, a bright red macaw walked back and forth on its foot pole, plucking piñon nuts from a small clay bowl and cracking them noisily with its big sickle-shaped beak. It had blue-and-yellow wings, a white face, and a long blue-and-red tail. Six hands from the tip of the tail to its head, it shimmered in the wavering torchlight. The bent willow cage stretched from the white-plastered floor to the ceiling and covered a space about fifteen hands square. Cracked nut hulls littered the floor of the cage.

Ironwood kept an eye on the macaw. Slaves whispered that it could speak in a human voice, but he had never . . . The bird cocked its beautiful head, gave Ironwood a malevolent look, and let out a low screech. Swallowtail went rigid, and Ironwood's eyes narrowed. The macaw threaded its way back across its pole, picked up a sunflower seed and crushed it—but it watched Ironwood the entire time.

Swallowtail's chest rose and fell rapidly beneath his shirt. Ironwood knew that the Fire Dogs believed macaws had human souls. Was the boy wondering whose?

The Straight Path people, on the other hand, feared that macaws *might* have human souls. Though gods occasionally adopted bird form to soar down from the skyworlds and check on human activities, witches frequently flew about as birds. Only the greatest shamans could tell the difference.

The macaw made a soft mournful sound, and Snake Head

turned to see the bird watching Swallowtail through one eye. He said, "Even my bird hates you, boy. Get out of here. Go back to the slave chamber. And tell your mother I want her. *Now*."

Swallowtail hesitated, his nostrils quivering, but said, "Yes, Blessed Sun," ducked past Ironwood, and ran away.

Snake Head wore a buckskin shirt decorated with dyed porcupine quills. The flattened quills had been sewn down the sleeves in zigzagging lines of red and yellow lightning bolts. Shell bells clicked on his sandals. A bun of black hair decked the top of his head.

Snake Head studied Ironwood through slitted eyes, then walked across the floor and dipped himself a cup of pine sap tea. The sweet tangy scent filled the room. It had become a rarity. Once, many summers ago, there had been so many pines in the canyon that all of the First People could enjoy the treat every day. But now only a few could afford such luxuries.

Snake Head straightened, took a drink of his tea, and smacked his lips appreciatively. In a cold voice, he said, "What are you doing here, Ironwood? You are no longer War Chief. What business could you possibly have with me?"

Ironwood dropped his arms to his sides. "I had hoped, out of consideration for my many summers of loyal service to your father, that you might help me to understand what happened while I was away. People tell me that you sent Webworm—"

"Yes, I did." A small gloating smile touched his lips. "And I gave *my* War Chief instructions to find my mother's wretched spawn and kill it. I think that's all you need to know, warrior. Now, if you've nothing more pressing, I'm very busy."

"But I don't understand why you would wish the boy dead. How could he possibly be a threat to you?"

Snake Head swirled the tea in his black-and-white cup. "My 'wishes' were not considered, Ironwood. It was my father's last order."

"And what of your mother? How long do you plan on keeping her imprisoned?"

"That is none of your concern."

"I live here, Snake Head. Of course it is my concern. Don't you realize that—"

"I realize everything that I need to, Ironwood!" Snake Head

spun and crouched, suddenly looking like his namesake. "Now, *leave!*"

Ironwood impassively crossed his arms again. "Every moment that she's locked up, the people grow more restless. I don't believe you're prepared to put down a revolt, Snake Head—not with your War Chief and thirty of your best warriors away on a raid."

Snake Head glared.

"Please," Ironwood pleaded, "listen to me. The people have stopped protesting in the plaza, but all that means is that they are at home, whispering over supper, telling each other everything they know and wondering what the truth is. If you don't end this soon, the people will fill the gaps with speculation and create a whole new story. One that could tear this place apart."

Snake Head brusquely sat down on the mat before his supper platter. He picked up a horn spoon and half a melon, and began eating. Their people buried melons, eggs, and certain types of gourds in deep piles of sand to preserve them through the cold winter. The melons grew sweeter, and the flesh of the gourds didn't dry out as fast. Eggs would last seven or eight moons kept that way.

Ironwood shrugged. "If it comes to that, they'll tear you down along with Talon Town. Is that what you want?"

Snake Head spooned more of the melon into his mouth and chewed, making no attempt to answer.

Ironwood sighed and gazed out the doorway.

As darkness settled over the desert, the jagged edges of the cliffs smoothed, and the color drained from the world. Evening People crowded the clear sky. Ironwood studied them and inhaled a breath of the cool breeze that roamed the canyon. It smelled of dry grass and dust. Once, it would have been tinged with the perfume of sage. The far-off whimpers of coyotes drifted in with the wind. No wonder the land was tired and refused to produce anymore.

"Did you know that my mother was a whore?" Snake Head asked.

For a long moment, Ironwood refused to take his gaze from the Evening People, then he looked back at Snake Head. The youth had finished his melon and picked up his teacup again. He had an odd expression on his face, curious, or testing.

"I pay no attention to gossip, Snake Head. I never have."

"Well, it's just that I know how often you talk with the slaves of Talon Town, and such vile people chatter. I thought perhaps you had overhead one of them—"

"No."

Snake Head rose and walked toward Ironwood. A silver sheen of torchlight flowed into the folds of his buckskin shirt. The shells on his sandals clicked. He stopped one body-length away and cocked his head. "So you really have no idea who the father of my misbegotten half-brother is?"

"No idea."

A secret smile, taunting and promising, curled Snake Head's lips. "That is all I have to say to you, Ironwood. For now." He walked back to his supper platter and picked up a cold corn-cake. "You may go."

"Your new War Chief will see that the child is killed. You will have fulfilled your duty to your father. What use is it to keep your mother imprisoned? It only stokes the anger—"

"And what do you suggest I do, former War Chief? Let her go? She *betrayed* my father!"

Ironwood clenched his fists and stepped toward Snake Head. A crawling sensation had invaded his gut. Fear flashed in Snake Head's eyes before he regained control of himself, and the new Chief haughtily lifted his chin.

"If that's true, Snake Head, then your duty now is to decide her fate quickly. For the sake of your people. Either banish her, or kill her. But be done with it."

An odd gleam lit Snake Head's dark eyes. He bit into his corncake and chewed while he searched Ironwood's face. Looking for . . . what?

"I think I shall kill her," Snake Head announced emotionlessly, crumbs sticking to his lips. "Yes, that will resolve the problem."

"Then do it."

Snake Head held Ironwood's fiery gaze for several instants. "I've never trusted you or your judgment, Ironwood."

"That's unfortunate. Your father did."

"Yes. I know." He laughed softly. "But then he never knew about my mother's *fondness* for you."

Ironwood's stomach knotted. "Are you suggesting—"

"I'm suggesting she was fond of you at one time," Snake Head answered through a mouthful of food. "That's all." He finished his corncake and brushed purplish blue crumbs from his hands onto the floor.

"Snake Head—"

"I have *finished* with you. I am the Blessed Sun. Leave, now! Or I shall call the guard and have you removed!"

Snake Head turned his back and walked to the macaw cage. He spoke softly to the bird. It answered him in a low hostile squawk.

Ironwood ducked out into the sharp night air and strode across the fourth-floor rooftop, his sandals rasping the plaster surface. He knotted and unknotted his fists as he went, jaw clamped tightly.

What could he know? Nothing . . . nothing at all. It's a bluff, a baiting game, a way of toying with people to see what he can flush from cover.

He climbed down the ladder to the fourth story and walked warily to Sternlight's chambers. Every nerve prickled, the way they did on a high ridge just before lightning struck.

He ducked beneath the door curtain. Sternlight glanced up from stirring the hot coals in his warming bowl. His white shirt flowed around his feet. Crow's feet pinched the skin around his weary brown eyes, and loose black hair draped his hunched shoulders.

The room was painted with thlatsinas, and one of the beautiful masks—the Badger Thlatsina, with its raven feathers—hung over Sternlight's bedding, as if gazing down fondly on him. Baskets and beautifully painted pots stood along one wall. Overhead, sacred herbs hung from the roof poles, bathed now in the dry incense of cedar smoke.

"Well?" Sternlight asked softly. "Does he know?"

"About the child? No. I don't think so."

Sternlight slowly rose to his feet. He had known Ironwood for far too long not to hear the unspoken words. A frown lined his brow. "But he knows about . . . what?"

Ironwood exhaled hard. "Perhaps about his mother and me."

Sternlight's facial muscles went slack. "Hallowed thlatsinas, then he might be able to guess the rest."

"He shoved me into his warming bowl!" Mourning Dove turned to look over her naked shoulder at Creeper and damp black hair framed her round face. "He was like one of the Wild Men, throwing things, shouting, beating me!"

As soon as she'd been released by Snake Head, she had begged the warrior standing guard over the slave chambers to bring Creeper. He'd thrown on a blue shirt, gathered some Healing supplies, and run across the plaza.

Ten slaves in tattered brown clothes sat on the floor encircling Creeper and Mourning Dove, watching in silence. A few small bags, containing their pitiful belongings, rested beside their sleeping mats on the floor. In its wall holder, a single cedar bark torch sputtered, coating their worried faces with reddish light, highlighting knitted brows and clamped jaws. One old man, Lark, buried his face in his hands.

Swallowtail sat to Creeper's left, hugging his knees to his chest, rocking back and forth like a wounded animal. The tall boy's face resembled a wooden mask, but the look in his eyes, which had fixed on his mother's injuries, was like a bludgeon. Creeper kept glancing at him. He could see the hatred growing darker, more violent by the moment; it was probably eating the boy alive.

"You're safe now, Mourning Dove." Creeper smoothed a salve of mallow and fat over the burns on her back. The fist-sized blisters oozed. He had to fight to keep his hands steady. Rage ate at every nerve in his body.

Snake Head is becoming more and more unpredictable and arrogant. For the sake of the Straight Path nation, someone should . . .

Mourning Dove flinched when Creeper suddenly rubbed too hard. "I'm sorry! I'm sorry, Mourning Dove." He patted her shoulder.

She hung her head and sighed. "It's all right. Thank you."

Creeper concentrated on gentleness, covering each blister, each open wound.

The faces around him had gone dour, hopeless. These were slaves. They knew the futility of objecting to brutality. As did

Creeper, as one of the lowly Made People. Creeper would bring this incident up at the next council with the First People elders, but it would do no good. Someone might chastise Snake Head, or mention in passing that he shouldn't have hurt Mourning Dove. Snake Head would just laugh—Creeper had seen it before. Many times.

Swallowtail leaned back against the white wall and serenely closed his eyes, appearing to have gained control of himself. His face was slack. Then Creeper saw his arms. The knotted muscles bulged and twitched beneath the fabric of his brown shirt—as if he were dreaming of beating someone to death with his bare hands.

As his own indignation built, Creeper nodded. He smoothed more salve on a particularly bad burn where the blister had burst and left raw meat beneath.

Mourning Dove moaned through gritted teeth.

"I'm sorry," Creeper repeated. "Did I hurt you again?"

"Oh, Creeper," she whispered hoarsely, "why would he do this to me? I know he was upset about something, but I did nothing wrong! I swear it! I obeyed his every order, I—"

"He did this," Creeper said in a shaking voice, and clenched his fist to still it, "because he's one of the First People, *and he could.*"

When the flames died and the cloak of night wrapped the hills, Thistle crawled out of the sage thicket and stood, trembling, looking up toward Lanceleaf Village.

Black smoke curled into the air. Wind Baby dragged it over the desert, stretching and tangling the smoke like slender lengths of rope. The stench of burned pitch stung her nose.

As silent as Hawk's shadow, she took three steps up the hill, then stopped to look and listen before taking another three. She dared not watch her feet. She kept her eyes on the dark shapes that surrounded her: brush, rocks, juniper trees. Prickly pear punctured her moccasins and stabbed her feet. Blood warmed her cold toes.

And all the while, her heart thundered with fear. *Beargrass?*

Occasionally smoldering wood cracked and hissed. Other than that, deathly quiet had settled on the hills like a smothering embrace.

Thistle climbed up to the scorched shell of her house and her throat constricted. "Blessed gods . . ." she whispered.

Movement caught her attention in the blackened remains of the village below. Faint whimpers carried.

Cautiously, she edged down the slope, trying not to lose sight of the person moving in the plaza. She found she could see him better if she didn't look directly at him, but slightly to the right. Squat and short, the individual walked as if hurt, favoring the left foot. The cries grew clearer.

Thistle entered the plaza through the ruined gate, stepping around fallen roof timbers and stone rubble. A live turkey huddled in the shadows, but when Thistle stepped near it, the bird let out a squawk and darted away in a flurry of wings.

"Who's there?" a girl called frantically.

"It's Thistle."

"Oh, Thistle . . ."

"Leafhopper?"

"Yes. I found my aunt." The whimpers became suffocating sobs. "She's dead."

Thistle stopped. All across the dirt, bodies lay sprawled. The coppery scent of blood clung to the back of her throat. She steeled herself and walked toward Leafhopper, but her eyes searched every corpse. Her terror mounted as she whispered their names, "*Clover. Birdtail. Old man Blackruff* . . . "

Leafhopper gathered her aunt's body into her arms and rocked pathetically, crying, "She's gone. My aunt's gone."

Thistle knelt and stroked Leafhopper's short hair. "I'll help you bury her. We'll make certain she finds the way to the underworlds. . . . Leafhopper, have you seen—"

"Yes," she answered, and nodded. "Over there." Leafhopper pointed with her chin and her voice grew shrill. "*Both of them.*"

Thistle gazed into her round face uncomprehending. As though moving in a nightmare, Thistle slowly rose to her feet and turned.

She saw Beargrass' red shirt . . .

And the entire world went cold and gray around her. Leafhopper's cries no longer shrilled in her ears. The reek of scorched wood vanished. She saw Beargrass' wide dead eyes, shining with starlight.

Her legs moved with cold efficiency. They lay so close she only had to take seven small terrible steps. She stood over them, staring down. A bloody puncture wound ripped her husband's shirt over his heart. They'd carved off most of his scalp, and an arrow, the feathers broken off, transfixed his blood-caked thigh.

For an eternity, she tried to fit what she saw on the ground with an image of Beargrass, but the pieces, like sherds from two different pots, didn't fit.

Then it occurred to her that the headless body sprawled across Beargrass' stomach was that of a youth. . . .

Her ears heard the insane scream that split the night, but she did not realize it had come from her own throat.

From an incredible distance, Thistle heard running feet, then vaguely felt arms go tight around her waist. Some detached part of her soul saw Leafhopper staring at her and talking—the young woman's mouth moved—but Thistle couldn't understand the words. Had she taken a sharp blow to the head?

Leafhopper led her a short distance away and sat her down gently. Then she vanished for a time and returned with a blanket, which she draped over Thistle's cold shoulders.

Leafhopper sat beside her, put an arm around her, and leaned her head against Thistle's shoulder. As if from another world, tears dropped onto Thistle's hand. Cool, so very cool on her skin.

The trembling began in Thistle's jaw and spread to her whole body.

"Oh, no," Leafhopper whispered.

She got to her feet and ran. Thistle saw her go down the ladder into the kiva. She emerged carrying some blankets. She draped another two around Thistle's shoulders and sank to the ground again. Hunching forward, Leafhopper Sang softly. The Death Song. . . .

Thistle watched unmoving: a woman in a Spirit trance. After several moments, she pulled Leafhopper against her.

Thistle rocked the young woman in her arms.

. . . Rocked and rocked.

Twenty

A clatter on the roof woke Night Sun. She slitted her eyes, preparing for an onslaught of light. Every time one of the slaves entered, the sudden brightness blinded her. She sat up—and stiffness shot pain through her muscles. The cold had eaten into the very marrow of her bones. As the pine-pole roof cover slid back, stars blazed. The ladder descended. It struck the ground with a dull thump.

"Night Sun?"

"Ironwood?" she blurted.

He climbed down, carrying a pack. "I mustn't stay long. Too many people know I'm here."

"I understand." She swallowed to ease the ache in her throat. "How did you get past the guard?"

"I still have the loyalty of many of our warriors. In the case of Blue Corn, who's guarding you tonight, I rescued him from a Fire Dog raiding party once."

The gleam of starlight after pitch blackness made the room seem as bright as daylight. Ironwood had braided his hair and coiled it into a bun at the back of his head. The silver sheen highlighted the planes of his oval face, falling across his high cheekbones and flat nose, playing in his slanting brows. His bright red shirt, turquoise pendant, and blue leggings glowed dully in the starlight. She noticed grimly that he had a bow and quiver over his shoulder and that his war club hung at his waist.

"I brought you two blankets," he said as he knelt beside her and opened the pack. "And food and water."

"Snake Head *let* you?"

"No. He's gone. I don't know where."

She grabbed for the first blanket and snugged it around her

shoulders. "Oh, this feels good. Did you warm it before you brought it?"

"Yes, I knew you'd be cold," he said as he draped the second blanket around her shoulders. "I hung them beside my fire while I spoke with Dune and Sternlight, then I folded them and came straight over."

Night Sun clutched them closed at her throat and delighted in the prickly sensation of heat seeping into her body. "Dune is here? In Talon Town?"

"He came with me." Ironwood sank to the floor beside her and sighed. He looked very tired. Deep lines grooved the skin around his eyes.

"I know you're not all right," he said, "but are you well enough to talk?"

Night Sun ran her slim fingers through her long hair. "Do you believe him, that the child is alive?"

Ironwood bowed his head. "I knew the child was alive, Night Sun."

"You . . . ?"

"Yes."

A dull thudding began in her chest, followed by a hollow sickness in her gut. All these years, her child had been alive. "Sternlight . . . he helped you hide the child?"

He nodded. "He's the best friend I've ever had. He knew how frightened you were, what Crow Beard would do to you if he found out. Sternlight made certain he was the only one present at the birth so that he could sneak the child away and see that no one—not even you—knew that it lived."

She propped her elbows on her knees and gripped handfuls of her thick graying black hair. Thoughts tumbled over each other in her head.

"I have been paying for the child's rearing," Ironwood said softly. "The family has taken very good care of her."

Night Sun stared dumbly at him. It took several moments for his meaning to dawn. "*Her?*" She scrambled to her knees facing him. "But Sternlight told me—"

"I know he did. But it was a girl."

Hallowed Spirits, have I seen her? My eyes passing over her as if she were a stranger?

"Is she here, Ironwood? In the—"

"No. I sent her away. It was the best way to keep her safe."

She fumbled for words as the horror became clear. "Then . . . oh, no. Blessed gods, no! Then an innocent boy is going to die! Is that what you're telling me? Sternlight lied to protect our daughter, and condemned—"

"That's what I'm telling you." He met her probing gaze. "Give me a few moments to explain. You don't understand, I—"

"I do understand! You and Sternlight—"

"No." He held up his hand and slowly curled the fingers into a fist. "Please!" Anguish twisted his handsome face. "This is hard, Night Sun, after all these summers."

"Yes, it is, Ironwood. For you . . . and me." She sank back against the wall, lowered her head and tugged at her blankets.

Ironwood shifted to sit cross-legged before her, his knees less than a handsbreadth from her sandals. They had not been this close in many summers. "Night Sun, you were all I ever wanted—and were worth everything to me. But I knew you well, my friend. Long before you told me, I realized I had lost you. That little girl was the one thing I had left of 'us.' I couldn't take the chance that Crow Beard might kill our daughter."

He frowned at the moisture running down the wall to his left. His shoulder muscles contracted from the strain, swelling beneath the thin red fabric of his shirt.

Night Sun stared at him.

Their gazes held, his pleading, hers stunned.

Night Sun tried to swallow, and it hurt. "Ironwood, would you hand me the water jug?"

He drew it from his pack, removed the wooden stopper, and handed it to her. The black-and-white lightning spirals decorating the base blazed in the stargleam.

Night Sun took a long drink, and then another. The liquid tasted earthy and cold. She sank back against the wall and drank more. *She's alive. After all these summers of mourning.*

"Does . . . does she know about me? I mean, that I'm her mother?"

"It was better that she knew nothing about either of us. As far as I know, she thinks the people she grew up with are her parents."

"Will you . . . ?" Night Sun set the water on the floor. "Ironwood, I have something I wish to ask of you."

"What?"

"In my personal chamber there is a blue-and-white basket. It is filled with things that I cherish. Please, speak to Cloud Playing. Explain to her that I wish all of those things to be divided equally between her and . . ." She blinked. "What is our daughter's name?"

"Cornsilk."

"Cornsilk." She tried it on her tongue. My *daughter*. . . . "Between her and Cornsilk. And of course the lands must be divided. I will leave the rest to Cloud Playing. She's generous and kind. She will know what to do."

Ironwood's jaw hardened at her defeated tone. "Have you given up already? Without even a fight? I have a plan, Night Sun. We must think of how to—"

"Wait," she interrupted. Reluctantly, he closed his mouth and sat back, listening. "You know as well as I that the child will be proof that I betrayed the Blessed Sun."

"Yes, but—" Ironwood reached out to touch her shoulder.

"No, don't touch me! Don't make it harder for me than it already is! I—I don't need . . . hope . . . from you. I need your promise!"

His hand hovered a moment, then drew back. "I will speak with Cloud Playing."

Night Sun saw the hurt in his eyes. "I'm sorry, Ironwood. I'm frightened and confused. I don't know what I'm saying."

"I know."

"Thank you for agreeing to speak with Cloud Playing. And now . . . you should go. You've been here far too long. Even your loyal Blue Corn may grow suspicious."

Ironwood rose and looked down at her, arms hanging limply at his sides. Starlight flowed into the wrinkles of his face. "Before I leave, I have something to ask of you, Night Sun."

She looked up. "What is it?"

His turquoise pendant flashed as he took a breath. "Promise me . . ." He paused as though uncertain how to say it. "Promise me that you won't take her away from me. You have had so much, Night Sun, and I have had so little. I *need* my daughter."

He stood poised between silver walls and shining stars, his

graying hair glinting; it occurred to her how much he must have suffered for nearly sixteen summers, knowing he had a child, longing to hold her and never able to. That little girl must have grown up in his heart and imagination—while she'd been dead to Night Sun.

"I will do whatever you wish, Ironwood."

"Thank you, Blessed Night Sun."

Then he turned and climbed the ladder. When he replaced the roof cover, he left it slightly ajar. Night Sun stared at the starlight that arced across the far wall like a slash of blue-white paint.

He spoke quietly to Blue Corn, then his steps faded.

She leaned her head back against the wall and breathed.

Warm rain fell.

Ironwood pulled his red cotton cape closed and tipped his face to the drizzle. He crouched in his old familiar place outside the dead Chief's chamber where, over the summers, he had worn a hollow in the sun-hardened clay plaster. His soul hurt from seeing Night Sun. He could not get her out of his thoughts. He had to do something, but had no idea of what. Though some warriors obeyed his commands, he had no real power here. Not anymore.

Misty silver veils wavered over Talon Town, shifting and twisting in the wind. His gaze fixed upon them. If it would only rain like this during the growing season, perhaps some of the tension would ease. The Straight Path people would begin planting corn, beans, and squash in a little over a moon, depending upon Sternlight's solar observations. He prayed the thlatsinas would send the rains then.

Inside the chamber, Dune and Snake Head spoke in low, strained voices. All day they had been arguing over Crow Beard's dead body, and Ironwood had grown tired of it. He was here because Dune had asked him to stand guard, and Snake Head had agreed—but only until Webworm returned.

Wind Baby gripped Ironwood's cape and flapped it around his shoulders like red wings. He tugged it closed again. Long ago, Wind Baby had been his Spirit Helper, but many summers had passed since he'd heard whispers in the wind.

In a voice too low for those inside to hear, he said, "I need you, Spirit Helper. Come. Speak with me. Advise me. I beg you."

In the stormy sky, Thunderbirds growled and soared, leaping from cloud to cloud. Lightning flashed and Ironwood saw a group of slaves huddled in the plaza five stories below. Ordinarily, at dusk, all slaves were confined in the circular windowless chambers on the edges of the plaza. For them to be caught outside at night, without the permission of a clan leader, or one of the First People, was a crime punishable by death. Snake Head must have assigned this group a special task. They sat in a small circle with blankets pulled over their heads. A tiny fire burned before them.

Ironwood wondered what they discussed. He knew so little about their lives. Slaves were taken by warriors during raids. As one of the spoils of victory, warriors could keep as many as they could guard, though most were given away to First People. In exchange, the warriors received the blessings of the gods, and curried the more secular favors of their rulers.

Slaves almost never spoke a civilized tongue, and they worshiped alien gods. Ironwood had owned as many as thirty slaves at a time, but he'd found that the expense of feeding, clothing, and guarding them required more than he gained in status. And, if the truth be known, as he grew older, slavery became more than his heart could bear. He often heard little children weeping in their chambers, and knew without needing words that they cried for home and their lost families. As a matter of honor, he still took slaves. But he sold them all to pay for Cornsilk's protection.

He gazed down at the Cage, where Night Sun remained imprisoned. The slaves worshiped her. Once a sun cycle, generally during the holy days of summer, she freed her most loyal slave and sent her home with a pack of riches. Cloud Playing had always done the same. It made them heroes to the captives. It also made Snake Head indignant. Crow Beard had never seemed to care, but Snake Head stamped about every solstice celebration, grumbling and complaining about *his* share of the wealth they were throwing away! He'd been especially adamant when Night Sun had wanted to free Mourning Dove.

Ironwood remembered the day well. Snake Head had been a boy, eleven or twelve. He'd thrown a tantrum so violent he'd lost consciousness and collapsed in the plaza. The event had shaken Night Sun, and she'd given Mourning Dove to Snake Head as his own personal slave.

Ironwood had always wondered why Mourning Dove didn't strangle Snake Head in his sleep.

Dune's reedy old voice rose from within the torchlit chamber. "*What was that, boy?*"

Ironwood leaned into the room and saw Dune hobbling across the chamber swinging his walking stick. Snake Head backed before him, hands thrown out for protection. His long purple shirt glimmered in the orange gleam. On the floor, Crow Beard's body lay under his blankets. His lips had drawn back into a strained grin that exposed the few stubby incisors left in his mouth.

"I meant only," Snake Head defended, "that you are old! Age affects the memory!"

"Not mine it doesn't." Dune backed Snake Head against the wall and cracked the boy on the elbow with his walking stick. Snake Head yipped, and Dune said, "I remember very well what your father wished of me. And I plan on doing it, whether you like it or not!"

Snake Head's large dark eyes and full lips pinched. He'd coiled his black hair into a bun. "If you smash my father in the face with your Bashing Rock, here, in this room, then his soul will fly free before it is ready! We must carry him to the sacred Humpback Butte and the ladder to the skyworlds! Surely my father would not have told you he wished to have his soul floating around Talon Town rather than climbing the ladder to become one of the thlatsinas!"

"Surely your father would have . . . and did." Dune scowled menacingly.

It made a strange picture. The tall handsome Snake Head in his regal purple clothing, trapped by little white-haired Dune dressed in a threadbare brown shirt. Dune's deep wrinkles looked cavernous in the pale torchlight.

"Dune," Snake Head said, "I am the new Chief. As Blessed Sun, I order you to carry out *my* wishes, not my—"

"What have you got planned, boy? Hmm?"

Snake Head's handsome face went rigid. "I wish my father's body to travel unharmed to the Humpback Butte. Don't you realize that there will be hundreds, perhaps thousands, of people who will wait alongside the road to see his body pass? Worshipers who will wish to look upon the glorious face of the Blessed Sun? But not if he doesn't have a face, Dune!"

"You slug!" Dune jabbed his stick into Snake Head's belly. "I didn't come here to be ridiculed by a mere boy who has just discovered the hidden life of his private parts!"

Snake Head's mouth gaped, and anger flashed in his eyes.

Ironwood rose and entered the room.

Snake Head glanced at him apprehensively. "I did *not* intend to anger you, holy Derelict. I only wished to show you the error—"

"Error!"

"That was—that was perhaps the wrong word." Snake Head squirmed against the wall. The thlatsinas behind him seemed to be peering down with great curiosity. "Let me try putting it another way."

Dune's busy white brows lowered, and he raised his walking stick into striking position. "What way?"

"I was wondering if it would be possible for you to smash my father's skull after we reach the sacred butte? That way anyone who wishes to see his face can do so."

Dune cocked his head warily. "Why do you want your father's soul in his body when we walk the road? Why is that so important to you?"

"Because," Snake Head said through gritted teeth, "I—"

"You're planning on hiring raiders to steal your father's body, aren't you?"

"*What?*" Snake Head blurted.

"It would make you a big man with Crow Beard's enemies, wouldn't it?" Dune glared up at Snake Head. "Who are you trying to establish an alliance with? Surely not the Tower Builders. They have nothing to offer but moldy pine cakes and ugly pottery. The Mogollon Fire Dogs? Now, there's a traitorous possibility."

"You've lost your wits, old man!" The veins stood out in

Snake Head's neck and his fingers worked as if he were on the verge of strangling the holy Derelict.

Ironwood's blood went cold. Could it be true? The Mogollon despised the Straight Path nation, though they exchanged goods with them through neutral Traders. Why would Snake Head wish to forge a relationship with such insolent predators? They couldn't be trusted. And they had enough cold-blooded warriors that when the alliance fell—and it would—they could use the event as a justification for full-scale war.

When Snake Head saw Ironwood's livid face in the doorway, his hands dropped to his sides, and he said, "You don't believe that, do you? It's ridiculous! Those people are our enemies! I would never—"

"It would be extremely dangerous, Snake Head." Ironwood threw his red cape over his shoulders and propped his hands on his hips. "We presently have an uneasy agreement with the Fire Dogs. We raid each other, take slaves, disrupt communication and trade, but none of us wishes outright war—and such an alliance would surely lead—"

"I don't want war!"

Ironwood tilted his head apologetically. "I'm sure that's true. Forgive me for interfering in your conversation."

He bowed, and walked away, bracing his shoulder against the doorway to look out at the storm. The bellies of the clouds had turned silver. He studied them, and wondered. Dune never said anything by chance. What had his purpose been?

"Dune," Snake Head began again, voice reasonable, "what may I give you to allow me to take my father's body to the Humpback Butte in one piece?"

"Nothing."

"Nothing?"

"No."

"Not even a dozen beautiful slave women? Perhaps a hundred baskets of precious jewels, turquoise, jet, malachite, coral?"

"Especially not jewels."

Snake Head spread his arms wide in a placating gesture. His hair shimmered blue-black in the light. "Tell me what you wish, and I will provide it. You have only to name your price!"

Dune's eyes narrowed. "And where would you get the goods?

Nothing belongs to you. Not yet. By imprisoning your mother, you've taken away her right to distribute Crow Beard's meager possessions. That means the duty falls to Cloud Playing. Until she gives you something with which to bribe me, you're hardly worth my time, Snake Head."

"Dune, this is silly—"

"No. You're silly. I'll keep my promise to your father, boy." Snake Head dropped his arms. "My father is doomed, then."

"Your father is saved."

"His soul will be wandering—!"

"His soul will be free."

"But, Dune, you—"

"*Enough!*"

"Dune, I'm the Blessed—"

"Do you truly wish to cross me, Snake Head?" Dune's eyes had taken on a frightening gleam.

Snake Head glared for the briefest of moments, then he swallowed hard and turned away.

The fire went out of Dune's faded eyes. His shoulders hunched forward. As if each step hurt, he slowly made his way back to Crow Beard's side and slumped to the floor, staring at the dead Chief's emaciated face.

"You haven't heard the last of this," Snake Head promised as he stalked from the room, passing Ironwood without a glance. He ducked through the door, glared up at the rain, and climbed down the ladder to the fourth story.

Ironwood watched the rain fall.

It splatted the roofs and stippled the wet plaza where the slaves sat before their spluttering fire. A pleasant whisper of raindrops filled the night, and the fragrance of soaked cedar wafted on the wind.

Ironwood turned. "Did you mean what you said? About Snake Head and our enemies?"

"I mean everything I say." Dune pulled Crow Beard's blanket up and tucked the edges around his throat.

"Did you Dream it? How do you know that he—"

"I don't have to have visions to know the boy is treacherous, Ironwood. All I have to do is draw up the worst possible thing I can imagine, and surely Snake Head has thought of it."

Ironwood stared somberly at the dead Chief. "Is Crow Beard

truly dead? Or on another Soul March to the afterworld?"

Dune braced a hand on the floor and met Ironwood's eyes. White hair blazed orange around his head. His deep wrinkles rearranged themselves. "Dead as a soulless rock."

Ironwood exhaled hard. "Do you really think you can free Crow Beard's soul against his son's wishes? Snake Head is, after all, the new Chief, and he has warriors to enforce his . . ."

Dune reached for his pack, pulled it close and rummaged around inside. He drew out a big chert cobble. With a grunt, he lifted it and slammed it into Crow Beard's face.

The crunching of bone made Ironwood jump.

Dune hefted the rock again and brought it down hard a second time. Bone snapped and grated. He left the cobble in the pulped hollow where Crow Beard's nose had been. "There," Dune said as he wiped his hands off on the blanket. "That ought to do it."

Ironwood studied the rock in the caved-in face. "Yes." He nodded. "I wager it will. One way or the other."

Dune rose on rickety knees and hobbled across the room; the holes in his brown robe revealed patches of wrinkled skin. "Tomorrow, I'll need to send a messenger to Poor Singer. Since you never managed to tell me I'd be responsible for caring for Crow Beard, all of my burial herbs and tools are at my house. Someone will need to bring them to me." He thumped his walking stick on the floor. "Can you arrange a runner for me?"

"At dawn, if you wish."

"I do wish, Ironwood."

"I'm sure Sternlight will allow us to use his slave Swallowtail. He's a reliable boy."

"Good."

Dune placed an aged hand on Ironwood's arm, squeezed weakly, and ducked outside into the misty shower.

Anxiety gnawed Ironwood's nerves. Somewhere close by, Crow Beard's ghost walked.

Ironwood exited the chamber and turned right, walking westward across the rooftop. Pools of water glistened in every irregularity in the plaster. The cliff rose like a black wall to his right, and above it, thunderheads billowed, blotting out most of the stars. Another dove-colored veil of rain swept down into the canyon. The little fire in the plaza wavered and hissed. The slaves huddled closer together, extending their blankets to protect the flames.

Ironwood climbed the ladder to the fifth-story roof and sat cross-legged in the rain, peering at the fires that flickered across the lowlands. Hundreds of them. Straight Path Canyon had neither the farmland nor the water to provide for the masses who had migrated here to be close to the sacred First People. Still, they came. He gazed down at the silver stream of water slithering through the wash. When the wind gusted just right, he heard flute music—faint, lilting. Perhaps it came from Kettle Town.

Ironwood held his cape closed around his throat and blinked against the raindrops. He longed to sit here until the cold lanced his bones. Maybe when his flesh felt as icy as his soul, he'd be able to think straight again. He'd been stumbling around like a fool, not knowing what to do or how. Feeling lost.

He inhaled deeply of the damp night, and his thoughts returned to Night Sun.

. . . Remembering the first time they'd had days alone together.

Before Crow Beard had left on his trading mission to the Hohokam, he'd given Ironwood specific instructions: *"She is to go nowhere alone. Do you understand me, War Chief? Nowhere. Not on a walk to a nearby town, not to visit relatives, not even down to the wash to fill a jug of water. Do not let my wife out of your sight—ever!"*

The words had been delivered with such utter gravity that Ironwood had vowed he would obey. He had escorted Night Sun everywhere—to her dismay.

Crow Beard had been gone for half a moon when Night Sun packed for one of her Healing trips to the neighboring villages.

The day before she planned to go, she and Ironwood had been standing in the middle of the plaza, surrounded by people weaving blankets, making pots, and knapping out stone tools, when he'd informed her that he would be accompanying her. Night Sun had grabbed three greenware pots from a potmaker and thrown them at Ironwood. He'd ducked the first one. The second had struck him in the shoulder. The last had missed—after which she'd called him unpleasant names.

She'd tried to sneak out   Talon Town⚞⚟the middle of the night to avoid him.

Naturally, he'd anticipated her, and followed.

For three days, she'd refused to speak to him. Then, on the fourth day, they had been walking along the eastern end of the canyon, Night Sun in front, Ironwood guarding her back. He' been studying the swirling patterns in the cliff. As though sanded by the hands of the gods, the designs felt as smooth as combed cotton. He ran his fingers over those he could reach, and marveled.

Night Sun strode along the trail, oblivious to the majesty, her tan-and-black dress dancing in the wind. She'd plaited her long hair into a single braid that hung to the middle of her back. Every so often, when she gazed into the distances, he caught sight of her triangular face with its pointed nose and large dark eyes. Her beauty stoked a hollow longing inside him.

As they rounded a bend in the trail, storm clouds rolled over the rim and engulfed the sky, rumbling and spitting rain. Thunderbirds roared. Ironwood jumped. Spring thunderstorms were common, but could be very dangerous.

"Blessed Night Sun?" he called. "We should find cover!"

Lightning slashed the heavens, so brilliant it blinded him, the roar almost deafening. Ironwood fell back against the cliff, his gaze glued to the sky. A searing web of light stitched the tortured heavens.

Night Sun also leaped back against the cliff, breathing hard, her eyes wide.

Ironwood started toward her, and a bolt of lightning lanced down, blasted a juniper tree less than two hundred hands from them, spraying wood and striking fire. Flames burst to life in the branches. Sparks blew, and grass and brush flared. Junipers torched as the wildfire rushed through the grass.

"Come on!" Ironwood yelled and ran for Night Sun. "We have to find cover! There's a rock shelter up that talus slope!"

Grabbing her hand, he dragged her up the slope. Loose rocks and gravel made the climb difficult, but they reached the shelter, which sat about a hundred hands above the raging prairie fire. Smoke boiled into the air as the flames leapt and roared.

"We should be safe here," he said as he sank to the floor of the shelter and leaned back against the cool sandstone.

The clouds opened and rain poured down in a shimmering opaque wall of water. The air smelled of burning cedar and rain. Blue smoke curled in the wind.

Night Sun sat down as far away from him as she could, which wasn't far given the size of the rock shelter. The stone hollow stretched two body-lengths across and less than half a body-length deep—but if Wind Baby kept blowing from the north, it would keep them mostly dry.

Ironwood unslung his pack and pulled out his gut water bag. Tipping his head back, he took several swallows.

The rock shelter had a lovely view of the surrounding country. To the east, grassy flats stretched for half a day's walk, punctuated by square buttes and weatherbeaten ridges. Far away, the Bearclaw Mountains etched a jagged blue line against the sky. Snow lay heavy on the peaks. Southward, and curving up toward the northwest, the cliffs of Straight Path Canyon gleamed wetly, as if washed with fresh blood.

Ironwood handed his water bag to Night Sun.

She looked at his extended hand, then into his eyes, and said, "I don't like you."

He shrugged. "You don't have to like me to drink my water."

Ironwood leaned closer, the bag almost touching her arm.

Night Sun took it and drank, but she glared at him.

She looked beautiful, slender and willowy in her sand-matted dress. She drew up one knee, but the other leg, long and tanned, lay exposed to the gray stormlight. Windblown rain beaded her skin.

"Well, we might be here for a while," he said. "Let's make the best of it."

He pulled a fabric pouch of venison jerky from his pack, unlaced it, and handed her a piece. As she reached for it, their fingers brushed, and a curious tingling sensation went through him. He drew his hand back. How strange that her touch would stir such sensations. Or perhaps not so strange. He hadn't been alone with a woman since before the death of his precious wife, Lupine. His body remembered the texture of a woman's flesh, despite his soul's diligent attempts to forget.

He concentrated on his jerky. Smoky richness coated his tongue.

The Thunderbirds took the storm to the southeast and waving tendrils of rain blotted out the Bearclaw Mountains. Lightning continued to flash as the fire burned out beneath them. The downpour lessened to a steady patter. On the opposite rim of the canyon, a small herd of buffalo ran. From here they resembled black dots against a sage-sprinkled background.

"Buffalo," he said reverently. "It's been a long time since I've seen them so close to the canyon."

Night Sun followed his gaze and frowned.

"When I was a boy," Ironwood said, "my father used to take me out to watch the herds. We never hunted them, because there were so few left around our home; we just sat on the hilltops and watched. During mating season, they touch each other very tenderly—did you know that?" She didn't respond, and he continued, "The bull nuzzles the cow with his head, and she rubs her shoulder along his side. And they play all the time, running and leaping and twisting in midair." He laughed. "Even when they butt heads, it's rarely combat, but more an enjoyable contest of wills." He chewed another bite of jerky.

She gave him a sidelong glance. "Do you miss them?"

"Oh, yes, very much. I miss their loose-limbed walk and the way they toss their shaggy heads when they run." Ironwood paused. "Most of all, I miss looking into their eyes."

"Their eyes?" The anger had faded from her voice, but she still sounded hesitant.

Ironwood nodded and bowed his head. "It's not easy to explain, but . . . the Creator lives in their eyes. I always saw Her looking out at me."

Night Sun frowned down at the smoldering desert. Wisps of smoke struggled against the rain.

Ironwood took another drink of water, washing down the last of his jerky.

Night Sun sat silently, perhaps wondering at her War Chief's sentimentality. Unease stiffened his spine. He barely knew her. Perhaps he should not have revealed such . . . softness.

When she folded her long legs under her and turned to face him, Ironwood immediately glanced up. Night Sun gave him an apologetic look.

"Forgive me," she said. "After the past three days you must think me cruel, but I—"

"No, not at all. I think you're angry with your husband for

ordering me to spy on you." He gestured awkwardly. "I would be, too, if I were you."

She scooped a handful of sand from the floor, letting it trickle through her fingers. Wind gusted into the shelter, and a lock of black hair worked loose from her braid and fluttered over her large eyes.

Ironwood's gaze traced the smooth line of her jaw before coming back to her eyes. He found Night Sun watching him—and something in her expression made his stomach muscles go tight. She looked . . . determined, as though she had decided something and was silently asking questions about it. Questions he did not understand. . . .

As though in a dream, she bent forward and pressed her lips to his. Confused, in shock, he just sat there. Thunder rumbled over the canyon and lightning glittered across the sky. Night Sun slid closer and slipped her arms around his waist.

"N-Night Sun, please don't—"

She covered his mouth with hers, and her kisses grew insistent. A warm tide coursed through his veins. The sheer intensity of it frightened him. Ironwood lifted his arms and left them suspended uncertainly in midair. Blood pounded deafeningly in his ears. Night Sun's embrace tightened, and her breasts against his chest left him shaking.

Leaning forward, she pushed him to the floor of the rock shelter, and he felt her tears running warmly down his cheeks as she stretched out on top of him. Her whole body shuddered from silent sobs.

He took her face firmly in his hands and forced her to look at him. "Why are you doing this? To hurt your husband?"

Night Sun sank against him, burying her face in his long hair. "More to hurt myself, I think."

Her tears trickled down Ironwood's neck. The answer went straight to his heart. Gently, he wrapped his arms around her back. A friendly gesture, nothing more. "Why would you wish to do that?"

"Because I can't be what he wishes me to."

Against her hair, he murmured, "People must be who they are. That is the way the Creator made us."

"Not me." She shook her head violently. "My duty is to— to be who people wish me to be. I've never been who I am, I—"

"Then perhaps it's time to start."

She pushed up and searched his face. "I'm afraid the First People will throw me out."

"Well," he said with a tilt of his head, "these are the chances we take."

She arched one graceful brow. "You think that it's worth it to give up all that I have to be all that I wish?"

"Of course." Ironwood wiped the tears from her cheeks, letting himself drown, if only for a moment longer, in the softness of her skin. "I know I'm irresistible," he said with a grin, "but I think we should stop this."

"Oh, yes, I suppose we should. Forgive me." Night Sun nuzzled her cheek against his palm before she sat up. It was such an intimate loverlike gesture that Ironwood's grin evaporated.

He pulled his hand away and closed his numb fingers.

His expression must have startled her, because she went still and gazed at him nakedly, as though afraid of what he might say.

. . . The squawking of a turkey in the enclosed room below drew Ironwood's attention back to the present, and Talon Town. He looked down at the rain-slick plaza. Another squawk erupted, then a flurry of wings.

Ironwood leaned his head back, staring up at the falling rain, as if it could wash the memory from his eyes.

Despite the long lonely summers—and a daughter born and taken away from him—Ironwood had never regretted loving Night Sun. If he died tomorrow because of those brief moons of joy, it would be a small price to pay.

Loving her was the only thing he'd ever done that meant anything.

Twenty-One

Cloud Playing walked swiftly down the darkening trail, trying to reach Talon Town before the storm worsened. A half a hand of time ago, black clouds had rushed in and blotted out the first Evening People. Misty rain had fallen for a while, then stopped. But it would return. Lightning flashed over the eastern horizon.

She broke into a trot. The canyon wall loomed like a brooding giant across the drainage, mottled with silver patches of moonlight. In front of her, Straight Path Wash carved a deep jagged ravine. The trail dropped down into it through a still, wet world.

Cloud Playing descended, her footsteps as silent as in a dream. A trickle of water burbled in the bottom. She leaped it effortlessly and started up the opposite side of the drainage. The fragrances of soaked stone and earth twined into a rich perfume.

As she neared the top, an eerie sensation possessed her. Her pace slowed. Just beneath the crest, she found herself at a dead stop, breathing hard. Shafts of moonlight penetrated the clouds and threw odd shadows. She stared at one that resembled a crouching monster. She would have sworn it had eye sockets, huge and empty, and focused solely on her. But it didn't move.

"You are almost home," she whispered, irritated with herself. "Stop being silly."

She continued up the trail, peering about uncertainly as she strode out onto the mud-slick flats several bow shots from Kettle Town. In the flash of lightning, the pillars in the front stood out like ugly square teeth in a fiendish grin.

Talon Town glittered in the distance. Torches lit the plaza, casting a fluttering amber glow over the white walls and the

Great Warriors. They had their heads up, anxiously gazing out across the night. Cloud Playing smiled and—

Movement caught her eye.

A nightmare feeling swept over her so strongly the world went out of focus for an instant.

A voice spoke from the shadows, "Who—who are you?"

"I am Cloud Playing, daughter of—"

"Cloud Playing? You are Cloud Playing?"

"Yes! Who are you? What are you doing out here skulking around in the shadows?"

A man stood up, his black-painted chest and arms almost invisible. But as he stepped toward her, she could see the colors of his mask: red, blue, and yellow. One of the sacred thlatsina masks! Very few people had the right to touch them.

Cloud Playing's nerves hummed as she backed away. "Are you a priest? Out offering prayers to the full moon? What is your name?"

"You . . . you are really Cloud Playing?"

"Yes, I told you!"

"Oh," he said in a strained voice. "Oh, no. I prayed you would not be here. Why are you here?"

She unslung her bulging pack, where she had crammed both her things and her mother's, and held it like a weapon before her. The four black spirals painted across the front glowed darkly. "I am the daughter of Night Sun, Matron of Talon Town! My father is Crow Beard, our Blessed Sun. I am on my way home! You *will* let me pass!"

He spread his eerie black arms like a bird preparing to soar, and leaped at her, lifting his knees high in some perverted imitation of an eagle hunting on the ground.

"Don't you know who I am?" Cloud Playing screamed. "Stop it! Leave me alone!" and swung her pack with all the force she could muster. It struck his shoulder, knocking him sideways.

She sprinted back down the trail into Straight Path Wash and up the opposite side. Hearing no one pursuing, she risked a glance over her shoulder . . . and saw nothing. Nothing at all. A beam of moonlight briefly struck the wash, shadowing every undulation.

Terror drew a noose about her throat. She stopped and fought for control. Cocking her head, her ears strained for the sound of breathing or carefully placed steps. Could it have been an obscene joke?

"Doesn't matter. I'm not walking that trail!" *And as soon as I can send word to War Chief Ironwood, he'll have his warriors scouring every square hand of this country until he finds the culprit and brings him in.*

She looked westward. If she headed down the drainage, she would find the cut in the bank where the slaves came to fill water jugs and wash clothes. For a woman of her status to walk a slave's trail would create a stir, but better that than the black apparition.

Slinging her pack over her left shoulder, she proceeded stealthily, clinging to the deep shadows cast by the overhanging bank. All around her, golden owl eyes winked. The birds burrowed holes into the banks and lived there until the spring runoff cracked their homes off the drainage walls and washed them downstream. Her terror retreated. She braced a hand on the bank and continued cautiously.

A huge black cloud sailed over, and just as Cloud Playing looked up, Thunderbird bolted through the Cloud People, using his sharp talons to rip open their bellies. Sheets of rain gushed out, shining whitely in the moonlight.

Cloud Playing huddled beneath the overhang. The lower half of her dress quickly became sodden, clinging to her legs like a second skin, but her torso stayed dry.

That morning she had passed a Trader on his way to the Green Mesa villages, and he'd told her rumors that the Blessed Night Sun had been accused of adultery and imprisoned at Talon Town. Cloud Playing had stared at him mutely, too shocked to believe it. But after they'd parted, she'd started running, trying to get home as fast as she could.

When she'd been a little girl, there had been gossip among old women with nothing to lose—gossip about a child born and hidden away. Those old women had believed that someday the child would return to Talon Town with an army to avenge his abandonment. Cloud Playing had never thought much about it . . . until today.

The rain lasted barely thirty heartbeats.

When the cloud passed, moonlight slanted down, and a long

shadow stretched across the wash, cast by someone standing right above her.

Cloud Playing froze.

Unable to breathe, she longed to flee, but her good sense told her to stay put. He could not possibly see her from where he stood. The slave's trail cut the bank less than twenty body-lengths ahead. If she did not move, did not give him any sign—

"*I see you,*" he whispered, and his tall shadow dipped and swayed like a Dancing ghost. "What are you doing here? Why haven't you run away?"

"I am Cloud Playing! Daughter of Crow Beard and Night Sun! I'm trying to get home. I—"

"In Beauty it is begun," he Sang in a deep and haunting voice. "In Beauty it is begun."

A white haze showered down before her eyes, and she saw that it was sacred cornmeal. Three more handfuls fell, shimmering.

"What are you doing?" she demanded. "*This is sacrilege!*"

"In Beauty it is finished," he Sang. "In Beauty it is finished."

Terror shot through her soul—and she burst from cover like a hunted animal, stumbling over rocks, racing blindly for the cut in the bank. Rainwater ran down it, turning it into a silver swath. Just as she neared the crossing, black arms spread above her.

He leaped down the slave's trail, swaying from side to side, his mask shining, and stood ten hands from her. In an agonized voice, he repeated, "I prayed you would not be here. Why are you here?"

She shook her fists. "I am just trying to get home!"

"I—I'm afraid."

"Why? I'm not going to harm you!" Did she recognize that voice? It brimmed with such pain she couldn't be certain. She glanced at the trail that sloped up out of the wash. "Let me go! Please, it's important that I get to Talon Town. I *must* see to my mother."

He tilted his head curiously. "Are you Solstice Girl?"

"S-Solstice Girl?" she asked in confusion. "What are you talking about? We won't select a Solstice Girl for another three moons!"

He reached over his back and pulled up a bow and an arrow, which he calmly nocked.

"Wait . . . I—I'll do anything you want! What is it you wish from me?" She backed warily away from him.

He gestured to the trail with his bow. "You . . . you go first. I will wait until you are at the top, then I will follow. Go!"

She flew by him, struggling up the slope.

Behind her he cried, "Oh, no! No!"

When she hit the top, she ran full speed across the muddy flats, gibbering in terror, her wet dress tangling about her legs as she headed for the torchlit brilliance of Talon Town.

She hadn't made it twenty paces when the sharp sting lanced through her chest. She heard as well as felt the thumping impact, and staggered, almost losing her footing. Then the sting grew into a searing pain that burned white-hot through her lungs and left breast. After four more wobbling steps, she fell to her knees. Stunned, she didn't understand at first. Then she looked down.

The translucent obsidian point had sliced through the fabric of her dress. It glittered just beneath her left breast. Confused, she reached up, fingering the razor point, surprised by how firmly it was planted in her body.

"I beg you," he called. "Don't fight me! I must do this thing quickly!"

Steps pounded on the wet sand. He crouched in front of her and peered at her through the eyeholes in the glorious sacred mask. *It's the Badger Thlatsina.* Blue slashes rimmed the eyeholes, and a white line, bordered in red, ran down the center of his black face. Raven feathers fringed his head. The white teeth painted on his long black muzzle glowed. He carried a bow in his left hand and another arrow in his right.

The violent strength of the North lived in Badger's bones. . . .

A terrible weight had grown in her chest, and blood bubbled on her lips. She coughed, and pain speared her.

Cloud Playing stared into the blue-rimmed wells of his eye sockets as he raised another arrow. The shaft hovered against the background of moonlit clouds.

He whispered, "You *are* Solstice Girl."

Fourth Day

Magenta veils of light sheathe the peaks as sunset creeps across the face of the land. The shallow wash where I sit has turned still and quiet. The only sound comes from a piping piñon jay in the pines far below me.

I had a vision today.

It came upon me while my eyes were wide open. At first, I saw the images as if at a great distance. I squinted, trying to make them out. Faint voices punctured the quiet. Suddenly, the images sped toward me, growing larger, opening like a maw, until that alien world consumed the desert.

I found myself wading through a lake of blood. The Wolf Thlatsina waded beside me, his tall moccasins sending out bobbing silver rings. He had a wolf's head with pricked ears and a long black muzzle. His human body had been painted with white clay.

In front of us, a strange creature appeared, dark and feathered, chasing sparkles of morning sunlight reflecting from the red lake. She ate each one she caught, gobbled it down, and cried out in a voice that sounded very much like a woman's scream. Abruptly, she stopped chasing the sunlight and turned on us. Mouth gaping, she shrieked, spread her feathered wings, and flew at the thlatsina.

"Help me!" the thlatsina cried.

I shouted for her to go away, then dove for her legs, bringing her down. She struggled. I had to fight to keep her down until she drowned. But as her blood flowed out into the lake, a new creature took shape. Beautiful and golden, a human boy rose and floated on top of the blood.

The sea grew violent. Waves rolled in, crashing over us, hot and steamy, like molten rock. The lake grew deeper and deeper until it devoured the land and the people and nibbled at the belly of the sky.

The thlatsina drowned.

I saw order disintegrate into chaos. Nothing remained. Nothing, except blood for as far as I could see.

When the vision faded, I gazed wide-eyed across the sunny vista.

Finches twittered as they winged through the cloud-strewn heavens.

I had a curious sensation that I had not been seeing through my own eyes—but someone else's. A man. Powerful. Filled with despair.

But I do not know what the vision means.

Since I turned six summers, I have plagued every Trader with questions, and I have discovered that Dreamers everywhere speak of an End of time.

Did I see it?

Was that my own death?

. . . Or my own birth?

In the Dream, they seemed the same.

I blink wearily at the expanse of land and sky. Twilight has turned the forested peaks purple, and shadows stretch long and dark across the rumpled folds of mountains. Layer upon layer. Ever more distant.

Evening is coming fast.

Against the blackness, one image lingers: a golden boy, tiny fists waving, melting to a shriek.

I am suddenly afraid of the dark.

Terribly afraid.

Twenty-Two

The white walls of Talon Town shimmered with starlight as Dune made his way across the plaza. The slave who had wakened him had run ahead, leaving Dune to follow as he might. He tipped his head to check the positions of the Evening People; it had to be almost midnight. The clouds had long since scudded off to the east. He clamped a hand around the collar of his cloak, pulling it tightly closed. An icy breeze wandered the canyon, ruffling his white hair and batting at the hem of the long brown cape Sternlight had given him. Woven of dyed cotton and strips of rabbit fur, it kept his frail old body warm.

A faint red light penetrated around the door curtain of Crow Beard's chamber. Propped Pillar reflected the wavering light. Dune nodded. Someone had left a bowl of warming coals for the lonely thlatsinas who Danced on the walls. Sternlight, probably. It would never occur to Snake Head that the gods, too, might need light and warmth. Few other people had access to that chamber. After Snake Head had discovered his father's smashed skull, he'd even ordered Dune to stay away.

Dune sighed. No doubt Snake Head needed privacy to pillage his father's possessions before his sister returned and claimed them.

He kicked at a pebble and continued on his way.

He passed through the gate that connected the plazas and emerged in the western plaza. Three kivas sank into the ground to his right, leaving two-hand-high white plastered circles on the hard-packed dirt. Ladders thrust up from the entries.

As he passed beneath the Great Warriors he heard their soft voices, whispering to each other. Dune craned his neck to look up at them. The sacred Brothers peered down ominously, their thirty-hand-tall bodies shining as though they had run through the heart of Sister Moon and stolen some of her radiance.

"I know," Dune murmured. "I'm just as worried as you are."

To his left, near Talon Town's entry, the sacred stump of Spider Woman's Tree stood. A hundred sun cycles before, the Tree had lived there. Bright prayer fans encircled the stump. The white hawk feathers on one of the fans blazed. During the first frenzy of building, the Straight Path people had cut down every pine they could find, to shore up roofs, make ladders, and use for firewood. But no one had dared take that ancient conifer. It had been planted by Spider Woman herself, right after the First People emerged from the underworlds. When it had finally died, the very foundations of the world had shaken. The First People said that the Creator herself had wept.

Dune walked straight across the plaza, heading west. As he neared the slave chambers, someone moaned. Then a woman's angry shout pierced the night. He hurried. To enter this chamber, he had to climb the ladder to the roof, then climb down another ladder into the small circular chamber. He prayed his aching knees could stand it.

Gripping the rungs on the pole ladder, he began slowly hauling himself up. He stepped off onto the roof and caught his breath. From here he could look out across the barren flats to the south side of the canyon. A fire sparkled at Sunset Town. The cliff shone blackly, but some of the angular boulders on the talus slope caught the starlight and gleamed silver. Darkness cloaked the rest of the canyon.

Yips and howls erupted from three different locations, coyotes calling to each other. Dune smiled toothlessly. He loved their voices. Sometimes the coyotes hit notes so pure and beautiful he could swear he listened to a master flutemaker's prize instrument. One female who hunted the desert near his house sang like one of the gods.

Dune sucked in a breath and walked to the ladder that led down into the firelit chamber. Inside, he could see three people: Creeper, the short fat elder of the Buffalo Clan; the woman who had brashly wakened Dune from a sound sleep; and a prostrate old man. The old man lay on his back beneath a ragged tan blanket bordered with yellow and red designs. Dune put a foot on the ladder and descended. Sweet sage smoke bathed him.

"Oh, Blessed Elder, thank you for coming," Creeper said, and waited anxiously while Dune climbed down.

"May I help you, Elder?" the kneeling woman asked.

"No. I'm fine. It just takes me some time."

As slender as a willow pole, with delicate bones, the woman had a face like a chipmunk, with bright shining brown eyes and fat cheeks. Short black hair hung to her chin. Dune had seen her around Talon Town for many summers, but didn't know her name. She looked to have seen around thirty to thirty-five summers, and the hissing tones of the Tower Builders' language seeped into her words.

Creeper stood and took Dune's arm to help him step to the floor. "Are you well, Elder?"

"As well as can be expected at my age, Creeper. And you?"

"Well enough. Thank you."

The small fire in the middle of the floor smoked badly. Sage burned hot and fast, the leaves igniting in a wild blaze, then gobbling the wood. A thick bed of red coals remained. Sporadic tongues of flame licked up, flashing light over the soot-streaked white walls. Two brown blankets lay rolled on the south side of the circular chamber. Beside them sat a few possessions: a long-necked black water jug, two plain clay pots, one filled with yellow cornmeal, the other with red-spotted beans, a basket filled with roasted squash seeds, and one speckled grouse egg in a small bowl.

At the sight of the egg, Dune's lips pulled in over his toothless gums. *So . . .*

Creeper gestured to the woman, and said, "Elder, this is Mourning Dove. She is one of the Blessed Sun's slaves."

Dune nodded to her and gazed at the old man on the floor. "And who is this?"

"He is Lark."

Dune knelt by the gray-haired man and studied his skeletal face. Sweat beaded his long hooked nose and ran down his wrinkled throat. Gently, Dune pulled down the blanket to examine the man's chest. He could count Lark's ribs. "How long has he been ill?"

Mourning Dove knelt on the opposite side, her eyes tense with worry. "This morning. He . . . he fell down in the plaza and could not rise again. We—Creeper and I—carried him here. Lark is so light, it was easy."

Creeper knelt beside Mourning Dove and added, "Before his soul started to waver, Lark told us he had been witched. We didn't know what to do. We thought perhaps you, being a great holy man, might—"

"Of course I'll care for him." Dune's bushy white brows lowered. "But why would a witch harm Lark? Witches are clever; they select their victims with great care. What could Lark have done to anger a witch?"

Mourning Dove and Creeper looked at each other, then lowered their eyes. Creeper picked at the spatters of mud on his moccasins, as if suddenly embarrassed. Mourning Dove tenderly pulled the blanket back up to keep Lark's chest warm. "He . . ." Her voice had gone hoarse. "Lark belongs to Snake Head, Elder."

"So?"

Creeper nervously creased his black shirt with his fingernails. "It's all right, Mourning Dove. Tell him."

Mourning Dove nodded, but when she lifted her gaze to Dune, he saw sheer terror there.

"You may trust me, Mourning Dove," Dune promised. "I'll never repeat what you say to me."

"Creeper told me that you would use your powers to protect me, but I . . ." Mourning Dove glanced up at the hole in the roof, assuring no one stood there, then she leaned closer to Dune and whispered, "Snake Head left last night before sunset. He took his blanket and a big pack with him."

Dune frowned. "Perhaps he needed time to be alone after his father's death."

Mourning Dove shook her head. "No, Elder. Lark saw him, down by the wash. Snake Head was talking to another man. He gave the man that big pack, and—"

"And when Snake Head returned to Talon Town," Creeper broke in, obviously longing to tell the story himself, "he saw Lark hurrying across the plaza, and must have suspected he had been seen."

"How do you know? Did he call to Lark? Did he question him?"

"No," Mourning Dove replied, "but Lark said that Sternlight stepped out onto the roof of his fourth-story chambers and lifted a hand to Snake Head, and Lark felt a sudden sharp pain at the back of his throat. Lark feared that Snake Head had commanded Sternlight to shoot a witch pill into his mouth. Then today, when he fell in the plaza and could not rise . . ."

"You believed it, too," Dune finished for her. He nodded to himself. Sternlight seemed so strange and forbidding to the slaves that they feared him more than the gods themselves. For many summers Dune had fought to dispel the rumors of Sternlight being a witch, but his efforts seemed to inflame the situation, so he'd stopped. "Well, let us help Lark. We will worry about Snake Head later. Bring me the egg, please."

Mourning Dove hurried to obey. Very carefully, she picked up the egg and the bowl and carried them to Dune. He set them on the floor at his side.

Creeper hunched forward like a bear preparing to leap. Red mottled his cheeks. "Holy Derelict, Lark is a friend to me, and has been for twenty sun cycles. Please, I know he is only a slave, but he is a good and loyal man. I—"

"I will do my best, Creeper. Now, please, be silent. I have duties to perform."

"Yes, I—I'm sorry." Creeper sat back on his heels and folded his hands in his lap.

Mourning Dove knelt beside Creeper—close beside. It did not require keen eyesight to see their attachment to each other, and Dune wondered at that. Though many of the Made People coupled with slaves, it was considered unseemly for clan leaders to do so. Well . . . it mattered little to him.

Dune picked up the egg and held it in his hands a moment to warm it, then pulled Lark's blanket down to his waist. As he rubbed the egg over the old man's stomach, he Sang:

> Arise! Awake!
> Look beyond the knotted road,
>   to the Straight Path,
> Look beyond the tangle,
> Make it straight, straight, straight,
> Follow the Straight Path,
> Arise! Awake!

Lark moaned. His arms moved weakly.

Creeper leaned over his friend and gently murmured, "It's all right, Lark. The holy Derelict is here. He is cleansing you."

The words seemed to soothe Lark. His arms fell to his sides again and he heaved a satisfied sigh.

Dune took the egg, cracked it on the floor, and poured it into the clay bowl. The purity of the egg would draw the witch's evil—if there was any—from Lark's body. He set the bowl above Lark's head.

"Someone must stay with him," Dune said. "When an eye appears in the egg, he will be Healed, but he may spit up the pill that was shot into his mouth. If so, keep it. Witches often mark their tools. We may be able to identify the witch from it."

Creeper nodded and patted Mourning Dove's hand. "Mourning Dove will stay through the night, and I'll watch over Lark tomorrow."

"Good." Dune's knees crackled as he got to his feet. "I'm going back to my blankets. Let me know if you need me again."

Creeper gazed up gratefully. "Thank you, holy Derelict. I will."

Dune climbed the ladder step by step, and walked to the edge of the roof, watching the twinkling Evening People. Spider Woman had just stuck one spindly leg over the dark canyon rim, crawling her way across the sky after Father Sun. Dune exhaled, and his breath fogged before him.

His gaze drifted over the white walls of the town and down to the wash, a black zigzagging line. Dune's eyes narrowed.

Why would Snake Head, the Blessed Sun of Talon Town, meet with anyone in secret?

"Because he's doing something his people won't approve of," Dune murmured to himself. "Probably selling out the Straight Path nation to the highest bidder."

What had the big pack contained? Bribery? Payment for services?

Dune climbed down the ladder and hobbled across the plaza, his brow furrowed, wondering.

Poor Singer stood on top of the mesa, facing west. Afternoon clouds, like tufts of cattail down, hovered over the sunlit canyon. Their bellies glowed bright yellow, as if the gods had dipped each one in a strong lichen dye. He smiled. Not a breath of wind stirred. The skeleton of the land lay exposed. Red, gold, and white bones stretched in every direction, broken by slithers of drainages, speckled with pale green brush and dark green trees.

Far away in the southwest, the Thlatsina Mountains floated above the desert. Poor Singer could imagine them in his soul's eye. The Ancestor Spirits must be joyous. They huddled around the peaks in the form of clouds, conversing with the gods, advising them on the curious ways of humans. Shining blankets of rain slanted down.

Mountains served as the ribs of the universe. On their journey through the underworlds, the First People collected seeds from the mountains they saw. When the First People emerged into this Fifth World, they planted those seeds in the exact positions they had occupied in Our Mother Earth's womb, knowing that the roots of these mountains would sink deep and touch the peaks below.

The thlatsinas had done the same thing, except in the sky-worlds. They had collected seeds from the mountains on this Fifth World and replanted them in the clouds.

Sometimes, when the light was just right, humans could see the sky mountains. They looked like sculpted sunlight.

Poor Singer spread his arms, letting the sun beat life into him, offering his naked body to the beauty. A strange light-headed euphoria had possessed him. As if his flesh had awakened from a long slumber, he felt tender and vulnerable, like a new shoot of corn that had just pushed up through the soil.

An ancient juniper tree clung to the rock beside him, growing out of the red sandstone. Its limbs twisted and curled, and long roots stretched out over the bare rock like ropes, running for five or six body-lengths, but each had managed to find for itself a tiny depression where windblown dirt and water collected. Poor Singer marveled. Every moment of its life, this tree had fought for survival. The sight brought tears to his eyes.

He thought of old Black Mesa. One spring, many summers ago, he had been helping Black Mesa in his garden. While Black Mesa weeded, Poor Singer carried pots of water for the young plants.

Black Mesa had watched him for a time, then sat back in the dirt and said, "Don't water so much, boy. These plants are like people, they need to be a little scared."

"They need to be scared?"

Black Mesa had nodded. "If the seedlings aren't scared, they won't sink their roots deeply into Mother Earth. Then when the droughts come they'll blow away without a fight. If you want to save them, don't make their lives easy, force them to prepare for the worst." He'd nudged Poor Singer with his elbow. "Hurting makes everybody stronger."

Poor Singer reached out and gently stroked one of the gnarled juniper limbs, full of respect for all the hurts this old tree had endured.

Poor Singer's life had been easy. His mother had loved him very much. Granted, he'd been a lonely little boy, but even then, adults had praised and petted him. He had always had enough to eat and been warm through the long winters. He admitted now that he had no real understanding of suffering.

And it worried him, because he suspected he should. Every great Singer he had known had suffered terribly.

In the back of his soul, he could hear Dune shouting, *Great, great, great!* and squelched the thought.

Two hawks circled lazily out beyond the rim of the mesa. He watched them climb into the blue vault of sky and smiled. Sweat beaded on his hooked nose and soaked the black hair that clung to his narrow face. The thlatsinas played, one day sending freezing weather, and the next blazing sunlight.

He shifted the pebble in his mouth to his other cheek. He'd been carrying this stone under his tongue for two days, but it still tasted sweetly earthy.

Poor Singer turned his attention from the lazy dances of the hawks and ambled along the cliff's edge, searching. Since he had managed, as Dune had instructed, to keep his "tongue from waggling," he thought that today he would practice being a bug.

But which one? Did it matter? On warm days like this many appeared out of nowhere—and their presence proved a grave torment. He had an almost uncontrollable urge to slap each one and feel it crunch between his teeth. Probably because he hadn't eaten in six, or was it seven, days?

He'd lost track of time. The eternity of the desert had swallowed him up, and he . . .

A beetle!

The black bug crept along a jagged crack in the sandstone, plodding over nests of grass and old juniper needles, its bulbous body gleaming in the afternoon light.

Poor Singer contemplated the beetle, then put his hands on the stone, spread his legs wide, and began a beetle-walk, his hind end high in the air, while his hands delicately probed the way and his body swung from side to side.

When the beetle stopped to touch a gray pine cone with its threadlike arm, Poor Singer reached out and smoothed his fingers over the closest cone he could find, one gnawed down to its fibrous heart. The chipmunks had stripped the cone, leaving a slender cob covered with a haze of glistening hairs. The softness amazed him.

The beetle crawled around the cone and into a pile of dried juniper berries. Its tiny mouth worked.

Poor Singer scrutinized the shriveled berries, picked one up, and tasted it. A vaguely sweet, moldy flavor coated his mouth. His face puckered. He put the berry back in the crack.

The beetle continued on its way, apparently unconcerned that Poor Singer mimicked its movements. The warm stone felt gritty beneath his palms. Dust filled his nostrils. As more and more blood ran to his head, he feared his face might explode. But he stuck to his task, seeking to learn, sense, and feel the world as beetle did.

The beetle crawled up out of the crack and headed purposefully across the sandstone.

Poor Singer followed.

The bug broke into a run, its face low to the ground, as if sniffing out a trail. It nearly leaped over the rock.

When the beetle scrambled into the shadow of a boulder, halted and began working furiously with its arms and mouth, Poor Singer frowned. He bent down to get a closer look. The cool shadow enveloped him as he peered at the bug.

It had found a splatter of sage grouse dung and was gleefully rolling it into a ball.

Poor Singer rolled the pebble around his mouth. It no longer tasted sweet or earthy.

Dejected, he flopped down on the warm stone. Dune had told him that if you looked long enough at a dew drop, you would see the entire universe in it.

Poor Singer looked long and hard at the sage grouse feces. The beetle worked with great care, legs shaping, rolling.

He ran a hand through his black hair.

Maybe it would be all right if I was a butterfly?

"Dune? Dune the Derelict? Please, wake up!"

At the woman's voice, Dune braced himself on one elbow and pushed his blankets down around his waist. The beautiful white chamber gleamed pale blue in the predawn light. Covered with four blankets, he slept on soft bulrush sleeping mats.

A water jug and cup stood within reach, and pots of food lined the wall.

"Who's there?" he asked, looking up at the roof entry.

"It's Mourning Dove, holy Derelict! Please, come. Creeper sent me for you!"

"Give me a moment, Mourning Dove."

"Yes, Elder."

Dune wearily threw back his blankets and reached for his tattered brown robe. Slipping it over his head brought a groan from his throat. He didn't know which hurt worse, his shoulders, his knees, or his hips. Gingerly, he picked up his rabbit fur cape and tied it beneath his chin, then smoothed his sparse white hair back with his hands.

As he rose and reached for the rungs of the ladder, he noticed how the veins knotted and crawled over the backs of his hands, distended like fat blue earthworms. Age had ravaged his body, and weariness always made it worse.

"You can rest when you get home," he murmured to himself, and climbed the ladder one blasted step at a time. "May that be soon."

He'd begun to worry about Poor Singer. The boy filled Dune's dreams—saying incomprehensible things about a turquoise abyss and his father, the coyote. He could sense that Poor Singer needed him, and that added to his frustration. He prayed Poor Singer would arrive soon.

He stepped out onto the first-story roof. Frost coated the grass and sparkled on the winter-brittle weeds that lined the paths and the edges of the fallow cornfields. Despite the warmth of the days, night still held a bite. The blue gleam had dyed the cliffs a rich purple. Propped Pillar shimmered as though sprinkled with amethyst dust.

Mourning Dove stood before him, her chipmunk face swollen, eyes red-rimmed. She clutched a yellow-and-brown cotton cape about her shoulders.

"I'm sorry to disturb you, Elder." She glanced around fearfully, searching the white rooftops as if to assure herself that no one else was up.

"It's all right, Mourning Dove. What's happened?"

"Creeper . . . he sent me." Tears filled her eyes. "Lark died. But before his soul left his body, he spat up this." She held a small piece of cloth out in trembling fingers, as if it contained something loathsome.

He reached out and took the cloth, opening it to spill an object into his palm. It felt cold and smooth. Dune squinted his far-sighted eyes for a moment, identified the tiny black object, and murmured, "Oh, no."

"Do you know what it is?" Mourning Dove asked. "Creeper didn't. We thought perhaps—"

When had he ever felt this tired and worried? "Yes, I do. Return to Lark's chamber, Mourning Dove, before anyone sees us together. I will be there shortly. There are—things—I need to gather. Both you and Creeper must be cleansed. Now, go. Hurry. I'll be along."

Mourning Dove backed away. "A sleep-maker fashioned it, didn't he?"

"I'm afraid so."

Mourning Dove nodded. "I will tell Creeper you are coming."

When she had climbed down the ladder and Dune saw her running across the plaza, he opened his fist again and looked upon the horror.

Purple light flowed over the flawless jet, showing every detail of the terrible creature. Dune studied the extraordinary workmanship of the spiral serpent coiled inside the broken eggshell. The snake's red coral eye had been inlaid. How many members of the Straight Path nation would know the symbolism? Perhaps a handful of the Made People, and the highest leaders among the First People.

"A snake born from an egg laid by a cock."

The Hohokam believed that one look from the monster's eye could kill.

Dune closed his hand, shielding himself from the serpent's gaze while he scanned the town. Turkeys strutted across the plaza. Dogs played, biting at each other's ears. People had begun to rise. The orange gleams of cedar bark torches lit many windows and cast a muted amber gleam on the massive cliff behind Talon Town. Soft voices filled the cool morning air.

Could a Hohokam witch be moving unseen among them? One of the slaves? But where would a slave get such a rare and priceless object?

"He could have made it with his own hands, you old fool," Dune reminded himself. "Plenty of jet passes through this town."

But how could a slave purchase jet? Or steal it without notice?

Only the most wealthy of the First People could overlook losing a piece of flawless jet.

Dune shook his head to clear it. If Creeper and Mourning Dove did not undergo the cleansing ritual soon, they would sicken. They might even die.

He turned to the ladder.

Twenty-Three

Cornsilk trotted south on the hard-packed dirt road, her heart racing, breath tearing in and out of her lungs. Webworm and his bloody warriors had run down this very road, bearing their grisly trophy. Her feet touched the same soil theirs had. Her eyes gazed at the same wind-sculpted buttes and ridges, the same endless expanse of stumps that poked up from the waving amber grass. Ax marks were still visible on the desiccated wood.

Over and over, she kept reliving the last moments of her father's and Fledgling's lives, seeing their faces. The firelit darkness, the stench of pine pitch and smoldering bedding, Little Snail's wrenching cries, all had been carved into her heart.

"Why didn't I stay to search for my mother's body? To bury father and Fledgling?"

Tears blurred her eyes. She kept hearing her mother's voice: *"If you are ever in trouble, and need help . . ."*

She ran harder.

The road took her to the top of a scrubby saltbush-covered hill. Ahead, Wind Baby and Thunderbird's gigantic claws had ripped the surface of the land. Bands of red-and-white sandstone twisted through the basin like ribbons of finely dyed cloth. Groves of junipers and pines outlined the drainages with green.

She had been running, sleeping, running for a night and a day. Her lungs burned from gasping for breath, and fear ate at her empty belly. Exhaustion weighted her shoulders like a pack of stones. She *had* to get to Talon Town.

Cornsilk forced herself to think. She had been too dazed to do anything but flee, but as her wits slowly returned, she realized she couldn't just walk up and present herself and the blanket to Sternlight. First, she had to figure out what had happened.

Sternlight may have been my mother's friend over fifteen summers ago, but he may be my enemy today.

Someone had ordered those warriors to kill Fledgling. Probably the new Chief, but Sternlight was Talon Town's greatest priest—he must have known! And done nothing to stop it.

On the night of Lanceleaf's destruction, the warrior, Webworm, had said many frightening things. He had come hunting a boy—the Blessed Night Sun's boy—and he'd called Night Sun a "whore." He'd demanded to know the name of Fledgling's real father and seemed convinced it was Sternlight. The only thing Cornsilk knew for certain was that Webworm had replaced Ironwood as War Chief of Talon Town, and no one—not even Chief Snake Head—knew the true identity of the hidden child's father.

All of the arguments her parents had had, all the whispers late at night, made sense now. Night Sun had birthed a child in secret and given it away. She must have paid Cornsilk's parents to raise Fledgling . . . or Cornsilk. She was so confused, she couldn't think straight. Who did she believe? Her mother? Or the War Chief of Talon Town?

Her father had said, "I believe it is our duty to stay with Fledgling at all times." Because they were being paid to protect him? Or because he was truly their only child?

Who had revealed the location of the hidden child? And why?

Someone must have divulged the secret when Crow Beard died, perhaps thinking it safe to, or perhaps out of malice, but why had Snake Head, the new Chief, wanted Fledgling dead? By lineage, Fledgling posed no threat to Snake Head—at least not so far as the rulership of the Straight Path nation went.

"Oh, Fledgling." She pounded down the hill to drive the ache away, forcing one foot in front of the other, lungs aching, legs trembling. "Father? Mother? Was I really your daughter? Or did you just raise me?"

In the distance Turquoise Maiden Mountain glistened as the midday sun struck its snow-shrouded peak. Drainages cut the slopes and crept out across the arid flatlands like tree roots searching for water.

Ironwood might be Fledgling's real father, as Cornsilk's mother had suspected. But it meant nothing now. Ironwood had no obligation to offer Cornsilk aid just because she had been raised with his son.

I'm alone. I can't depend on anyone except myself.

Except, perhaps, the great priest, Sternlight. The tone in her mother's voice, the worry on her face, everything she had done and said that last day had convinced Cornsilk that Sternlight had given the magnificent turquoise-studded blanket to her mother.

Perhaps *he* had been the one sending the payments, not Night Sun? Had the blanket been another moon's worth of care for *his* son? As Webworm suspected?

I can't know for sure. It's impossible.

Despite her mother's confidence in Sternlight, Cornsilk would trust no one. Not after what had happened to Lanceleaf Village.

The road came to an abrupt end on the lip of a cliff. Cornsilk slowed, panting for breath.

From the cliff's vantage, she could see a vast expanse of folded ridges speckled by juniper and piñon, and sage-mottled flats. Green lines of trees marked the drainages. Here and there sharp pillars of stone thrust up, like dozens of cactus needles straining to poke holes through a rumpled red, yellow, and white blanket.

Cornsilk walked carefully to the cliff's edge and peered over. Stairs had been cut into the stone. Two hundred hands below, a young man stood stark naked in the brilliant sunlight. Tall and skinny, he had waist-length black hair that fluttered as he spun and flapped his arms. He seemed to be Singing, but it sounded more like a zizzing hum.

Was he dangerous? Cornsilk scanned the canyon for signs of a village, people, or even a campsite, but saw nothing. What could he be doing out here?

The young man laughed, threw back his head, and flapped his arms quickly.

Bone-weary, Cornsilk pulled her bow from her back and got down on her belly to watch him. Wind Baby breathed softly across the rim, cooling the sweat on her face. The scent of dust curled up around her. He looked harmless enough. Cornsilk guessed his age at about her own: fifteen or sixteen summers.

The youth started spinning around, stumbling through the sage as if he'd drunk a potful of juniper berry wine. He laughed. The sound echoed off the canyon walls. He didn't really look dangerous, though he might be slightly deranged.

Hunger gnawed at her belly. She'd eaten everything out of her pack and hadn't stopped long enough to hunt or collect more food. Even as she watched, her stomach gurgled and growled its displeasure. He might share a meal with her—but not if she greeted him with a nocked bow.

With the caution of a hunting cat, she stood, slipped her bow over her shoulder, and climbed over the edge, using the stairs like a ladder.

The youth didn't seem to notice. He just stumbled through the sage, grinning.

She stepped silently to the ground and saw the little white house with the cracked plaster nestled in the tall sage. His home? He lived way out here alone? With all the raiding going on, he *must* be deranged.

She stepped closer. Blessed Spirits! He was nothing but skin and bone. And his skin! It glowed an angry red. The sunburn covered his entire body, including his penis and testicles. Blisters bubbled over his shoulders and the hooked arch of his nose. Had he stood naked in the sun for days?

Crossing her arms, she asked, "Are you a hummingbird, or a bumblebee?"

His body came to a sudden stop, but his eyes kept spinning, and he crashed face down in a tangle of sagebrush. "Who *are* you!" He rolled over and struggled to prop himself up. His head wobbled. "Are you . . . don't I *know* you?"

"Lie flat until your balance returns."

"I—I think I'm going to throw up," he said, and shifted a round object from one cheek to the other.

Cornsilk crouched a body-length from him and studied his roasted body, his long black hair. "What were you doing? Spinning around like that and flapping your arms?"

His eyes roved about as if trying to fix on something. "I was learning to be a moth. You know how they're always whirling and fluttering, especially near fires." He paused to take a breath, and added, "I tried being a beetle and a cockroach, but they eat some really foul things. Did you know that?"

Cornsilk lifted a brow. "Why are you learning to be insects? Are you being taught by a shaman?"

He propped himself up on his elbows and his mouth quirked. "Look around. Do you see a shaman here?"

"I already looked. No."

"That's because he abandoned me." Gingerly, he sat up and took a deep breath, apparently feeling better. He shifted the round object back to the other cheek; it clacked on his teeth as it passed. "But before he went he told me to practice being a bug."

"As punishment?"

He blinked. A curious expression came to his narrow face. "How strange that I never thought of that."

Cornsilk gestured to his blistered shoulders. "You had better get a salve on that burn soon, or you'll scar."

"What?" he said, looking down at his skinny body. "What burn?"

Cornsilk stood up. "Maybe that spinning addled more than your sense of balance."

He grimaced, got to his feet, and staggered into her. Cornsilk grabbed his arms to steady him, but his feet kept weaving, as if dancing without his brain's consent. He stumbled into a thorny thicket of brush and almost toppled over backwards. Cornsilk gasped and tugged him firmly toward her. He braced his feet and blinked, as if not certain why she'd done that.

"Are you all right?" she asked, aware of the fevered heat rising from his sunburned flesh.

"Oh, it's just that I haven't eaten in many days, and my eyes go black when I stand up too soon."

"Haven't eaten? Then what's that in your mouth?"

"A pebble."

"You have a rock in your mouth?"

"Umm." He smiled and nodded happily.

She let go of his arms and studied him. "How many days have you been fasting?"

"I really can't say. I've lost track. Perhaps seven or eight?"

Cornsilk's expression slackened as her eyes took in his emaciated carcass. "Blessed Ancestors. You've been drinking water, though, haven't you?"

"Oh, yes. I figured I'd die if I didn't."

"Well," she said pointedly, "once you start to feel that burn, you might wish you had."

He held his arms out and examined himself, curiously frowning at the blisters on his chest, thighs, and arms. "You really think it's that bad? I don't feel anything. Except my skin feels tight, as if it's stretched out on a drying frame."

"You should see your back."

"Bad?"

"Raw meat."

Cornsilk glanced at the dilapidated little house. Big flakes of white plaster scattered the jungle of sagebrush that engulfed three walls. Only the front side had been cleared to allow entry and exit. There was a dangerous dip on the left side of the roof. The ceiling poles had rotted out until it looked as if it might collapse in upon itself at any moment.

She narrowed an eye. "If you'll share a meal with me, I'll tend those burns for you."

He gave her a startled look. "I've forgotten my manners! I should have invited you for supper. Please, come. It's not my food anyway, so it really doesn't matter."

"Uh . . . fine."

She gestured him ahead and followed him up the narrow trail. Prickly pear cactuses clotted the way, their thorns as long as her fingers. A wren had made a nest in one of the larger trunks of giant sagebrush. Dried grass and old feathers protruded from the hole.

Cornsilk leapt backward as the young man lost his balance and stumbled.

"Let me help you," she said.

"Oh, I'll be all right. Really, you don't have to—"

Cornsilk took his arm and led him to the door. The leather curtain had been mouse-gnawed. Where the plaster had cracked off, the red sandstone masonry showed. "Is this your house?"

"No."

"Well, if this isn't your house, or your food, who do they belong to?"

"My teacher, Dune the Derelict. He's a great Singer. A very holy . . . What's the matter?"

Cornsilk gasped and swung him around. He almost fell over the top of her. She put her hands in the middle of his chest to prop him up so she could stare into his soft brown eyes. "Great gods! This is where old Dune lives? *He's* your teacher?"

"He was. For a few days."

Fear prickled her spine. Dune had a reputation for doing unpredictable things, like changing people he didn't like into packrat urine or a sticky fly's foot. She gave the young man a suspicious look.

"How does your soul feel?

"Hmm?" he said, peering at her with the surprised curiosity of a roadrunner. His waist-length black hair billowed in a puff of wind, fluttering over Cornsilk's shoulders. "My soul?"

"Yes, does it still feel *human*? Maybe Dune gave you a moth's soul before he left, and that's why you've had the uncontrollable urge to be an insect."

The youth thought about that. "He does have an odd sense of humor, and I must admit I have been feeling very floaty and fluttery—"

"Like your soul has wings!" Cornsilk leaped back, and he crumpled. His knees struck the ground, then he sprawled face-first across the trail. When he struggled to get his knees under him, his bright red buttocks thrust up. That effort proved too difficult, so he gave up, rolled to his back, and squinted at Cornsilk.

After a few moments, he filled his lungs with air, and through a long exhalation said, "No, more like a cloud in a windstorm."

Cornsilk leaned over to peer down at him. "Oh, well." She shrugged. "Then maybe you're still human after all."

He sighed and extended his hand. "Could you help me up? I don't think I can make it by myself."

Cornsilk gripped his arm and hauled him to his feet. Weaving, he headed for the door, held back the curtain, and waited for her. Inside, she saw a firepit in the middle of the floor and a rolled-up gray blanket to the right of it. A stack of baskets, sat in the rear. Nothing looked sinister . . . and she longed to rest and eat. Her legs had begun to tremble again.

"Thank you," she said, and ducked under the curtain into the house.

He draped the curtain over a peg in the wall, leaving it open, and followed her. "With evening coming, we'll need the light to get the fire going."

She stood awkwardly while he scraped the long-dead coals to the side of the pit, arranged a nest of dead juniper bark, and pulled kindling from the woodpile to lay atop the bark. Her eyes took in the new surroundings.

Soot splotched the white walls and created a shiny black ring around the smoke hole in the roof. The dried corn, squash, beans, and prickly pear fruits hanging from the rafters bore a coating of creosote and ash. A grinding slab, water jug, and a few plainware pots sat by the door. Five tattered baskets leaned in the corner ahead and to her right. Not even a thin sleeping mat separated the gray blanket from the cold floor.

"Hallowed Ancestors," she murmured. "It had never occurred to me that a great Singer like Dune would be poor."

"He's a very holy man. He gives away everything he gets." The youth picked up his fire cobbles and began striking them together over the bark. They sparked, but nothing happened. He kept striking and mumbling, and after ten or twelve attempts, said, "This firepit *hates* me! I don't know what I've done, but—"

"Here," Cornsilk said, "You're weak, let me try."

He slid aside and handed her the chert cobbles. Cornsilk knelt, unslung her pack, and pulled out a small tuft of her remaining cotton. She tucked it into the midst of the shredded bark.

"While I start the fire, why don't you fill the boiling pot with water and bring over the tripod."

"I can do that," he said as he rose. "The boiling pot doesn't hate me." He went to the door where the water jug sat, and she heard water gurgling and splashing as he poured it into the pot.

Cornsilk leveled the fire cobbles over the cotton and smacked them together several times. Sparks flew, and a tiny red eye caught in the charred cotton. Cornsilk blew softly. The spark reddened, smoked more, and finally crackled to life. Flames greedily licked through the shredded bark. She kept blowing until the twigs caught, then added larger pieces of wood from the woodpile.

"The firepit likes you." He smiled as he knelt beside Cornsilk and arranged the tripod and boiling pot so that the bottom of the pot sat directly over the flames. His legs trembled as he sat back down. "I'm sorry, I didn't realize how feeble—"

"Rest," she said. "I'll make us supper and tea. Where are the cups and bowls?"

"Over by the door. Dune puts the small cups and medium-sized food bowls inside the larger bowls. Just lift up the top bowl and you'll find everything you need."

The rich fragrance of burning juniper encircled her as she rose and walked to the pots. She drew out cups, bowls, and two horn spoons, then examined the coarse pottery. It was plain and red; the potter had not even bothered to smooth away the coil marks. When a potter began a pot, she rolled out long snakes of clay, then coiled them on top of each other until she'd finished the basic shape of the pot. Next she took a piece of wood or stone and smoothed the surface to erase the coils so the pot could be decorated. This potter had not cared much about her work.

"Does Dune only keep the worst of everything?" she asked.

"Oh, yes. He distributes the rest of his belongings to the needy."

Cornsilk tilted her head curiously. She lifted the lid off the meal pot and examined the contents. Blue cornmeal. Good. It would give a sweet richness to the dumplings she planned to make. Another contained ash from the four-wing saltbush, which would make the dough rise. She carried the pots to the fire, along with the cups and supper bowls.

The young man was watching her with an unsettling intensity, as if seeing right through her. She ground her teeth a couple of times, then asked, "Is something bothering you?"

"Are you sure I don't know you? I would swear I've seen you before. What's your name?"

Cornsilk hesitated. *Trust no one!* "My name is . . . Spidersilk. But everyone calls me Silk."

"I'm Poor Singer."

She wrinkled her nose distastefully. "You are here studying to be a Singer—and you have a name like that? I'll bet you're eager for the day when old Dune gives you a new name."

"That is my new name."

Cornsilk cocked her head sympathetically and reached for a stick from the woodpile to prod the flames. "Maybe Dune thinks punishment is good for you."

"But I just don't know what I've done to deserve it!"

"Maybe it's something you haven't done."

Poor Singer stretched his naked body out across the dirt floor and Cornsilk winced, imagining how the grit felt on his singed flesh, though he didn't seem to notice. His long hair fell over his skinny chest and belly. He wasn't handsome by any standard. In fact, he resembled a bird of prey. But something in his round doelike eyes touched her.

"Where are you from, Silk?"

"F-from Turtle Village." Her voice shook, but she didn't try to stop it. "My family . . . they were killed by . . . by raiders, Tower Builders, and I . . ." A sob lodged in her throat. She prodded the fire again. Sparks shot out and winked upward toward the smoke hole.

Poor Singer's eyes tightened. "I'm sorry. I lost my father, too. But I was less than a summer old. I don't even remember him. How long ago was the raid on your village?"

"Half a moon," she answered, which was correct for Turtle Village.

"Blessed thlatsinas. You've been alone since then?"

She laid the cups, horn spoons, bowls, and pot of cornmeal out in a line in front of her. "Yes."

"But you must have other family. In another village?"

"I—I think maybe in Talon Town."

She stared at the flames that licked the bottom of the boiling pot and wondered what her Uncle Deer Bird and Grandfather Standing Gourd would be doing tonight. Had word of Lanceleaf's destruction reached them? Were they even now rushing to the charred ruins in search of their family?

Before she could stop it, all of her terror and anguish flooded up and she sobbed aloud. Her chest ached. Clamping a hand over her mouth, she sat there, fighting, until she could get a deep breath into her lungs.

Poor Singer's expression softened. "Is there something I can do to help, Silk?"

She shook her head. Rising swiftly, she went to the door, picked up the small grinding slab and handstone, and brought them back to the fire.

Poor Singer watched her remove several prickly pear fruits from their ties on the rafters. He said, "I tried to be a dung beetle a few days ago."

"What?" She looked down at him.

His eyes shone. "A dung beetle. I tried very hard to learn to be one, but I just couldn't." Firelight danced over his narrow face, highlighting the arch of his hooked nose. "I think it's because humans live in dung so much of the time that I couldn't bear the thought."

Cornsilk crouched to place the fruits on the grinding slab. "Maybe it isn't so bad for beetles. They seem to like dung." She used her brown sleeve to wipe her wet cheeks.

"Then again, maybe they don't have any choice."

Cornsilk thought about that. She hadn't had any choice. Nor had anyone else at Lanceleaf Village—especially not Fledgling.

She met Poor Singer's shining eyes as she picked up the handstone and began mashing the fruits on the grinding slab. "I think you're becoming a Singer. And not a poor one."

He grinned suddenly. "I want to be, very badly, so I can help my people."

"What is your village?"

"Windflower. I am of the Coyote Clan."

Cornsilk mashed the prickly pear fruits to a fine red mush, then leaned over to peer into the boiling pot. Tiny bubbles fizzed on the surface. For really good dumplings the water needed to be at a full boil, but she didn't care tonight. She dipped up two full cups of blue cornmeal and emptied them into her supper bowl, then added two cups of hot water. Pulling a flat juniper stick from the woodpile, she ran it along the edge of the firepit, until she'd scooped up enough white ash, and added it to the cornmeal. Finally, she dumped in half of the prickly pear fruit mush and stirred. A soft purple dough formed.

"Almost ready," she said. "But we should make tea first. There won't be any hot water left after I drop in the dumplings."

She dipped both of their cups full of hot water and added what remained of the prickly pear mush. As it steeped, the tea smelled delicately sweet. She handed a cup to Poor Singer.

He took it with a grateful smile. "Thank you. I'm still feeling like a cloud in a windstorm."

"I ran out of food yesterday. If you hadn't been willing to share with me, I would have had to hunt tonight. Hunting is always a chancy thing, and I was really too tired."

"I wanted to share. When I become a great Singer, I'll be able to share much more than food with people."

He sounded happy and eager to help his clan. She studied his luminous brown eyes. "What will you do first?"

"Hmm. Well, I'll either Heal the sick, or kill a few witches. Maybe both." He grinned.

A smile came to her lips, and Cornsilk sat for a moment, savoring the joy. Poor Singer seemed to understand, for he gazed at her with his whole heart in his eyes.

Cornsilk rolled the dough into beautiful purple balls and dropped them one by one into the boiling water. A lavender froth swelled and leaked over the edge of the pot. As bubbles plopped on the burning logs, they sizzled wildly. Steam gushed toward the roof.

She sat back to wait for the dumplings to cook. The first Evening People glittered through the smoke hole. "It must have been hard for you, having your father die before you saw one summer. How did it happen?"

"Well . . . I . . ." He looked like he wasn't certain. "My mother told me he broke his leg, and it became infected. She said it took three moons for him to die. She had loved him very much and refused to remarry. After that, all we had was each other." He frowned into the pale red liquid in his cup. "Everything I am, I owe to my mother, Snow Mountain."

Cornsilk sipped her prickly pear tea. It tasted deliciously tangy. "You don't believe your mother?"

He lifted his head and frowned at her. "Does it show?"

"You looked uneasy when you told me the story."

Poor Singer toyed with a pebble on the floor. "It doesn't really matter. If she's not telling me the truth, it's because the truth brings her too much pain. I love her with all my heart anyway."

Secrets. Did all parents keep things from their children?

Cornsilk sighed. "She must be very proud of you becoming a Singer."

"Oh, yes. She is." He took a small sip of his tea, and his stomach squealed so loudly they both stared at his sunburned belly. A nest of tiny black hairs filled his navel. It shimmered in the firelight.

"Are you going to throw up?" Cornsilk asked.

He squinted one eye as if in discomfort. "I hope not."

"Sip slowly, Poor Singer. I think you need to keep it down."

He burped, looked terrified, and cautiously said, "I think you're right."

Cornsilk used the flat juniper stick to dip out one of the dumplings. It had swelled into a fluffy pale blue ball. She put it in her bowl and cut it open. "They're done."

Poor Singer braced a hand on the floor and sat up as Cornsilk scooped the steaming dumplings into their bowls. Placing Poor Singer's on the floor at his side, she gave him a horn spoon.

She cut her first dumpling in quarters, blew on it, then spooned a piece into her mouth. The prickly pear fruits added a flowery sweetness to the nutty flavor of the blue corn. She ate as if she'd been the one fasting for days, chewing and swallowing as quickly as she could. As her stomach filled, her desperation began to lessen. The knots in her shoulders eased. But her weariness deepened, weighting her limbs. She yawned, set her bowl aside, and lifted her cup of tea, drinking as she watched Poor Singer.

He took the shiny pebble from his mouth and held it in his hand while he used his spoon to mash his dumplings up. He poured some of his tea into the mixture to create a thick soup. Gingerly, he ate.

"Are you feeling better?" Cornsilk asked.

"More cold than sick." Bumps prickled his skin.

Cornsilk rose, took the gray blanket from the floor, and carefully draped it over Poor Singer's blistered shoulders. Fevered skin was always more sensitive to cold. "Does that hurt?"

"No. Thank you. It feels good. That was very kind."

"You were kind to me," she said matter-of-factly. "I can be kind to you."

His eyes narrowed, and he seemed to be examining the air around Cornsilk, his gaze drawing a line around her hair and shoulders. "I think you would be kind to me anyway. You have a—a bright blue light around you. A Healing light." He dipped another spoonful of his dumpling soup and swallowed it.

Cornsilk sat down, picked up her teacup, and scrutinized him over the rim. Her mother had told her about Singers who could see the colors of the soul, but she'd never met one. "Have you always been able to do that?"

"Hmm?" he asked, startled. "Do what?"

"See the colors of the soul."

"Oh, no, not me." He shook his head. "Not until today. Yours is the first soul I've ever seen. I mean, other than my own. And I only saw mine just before I saw yours."

She lowered her cup to her lap. "What color is your soul?"

He smiled. "Yellow. Brilliant blinding yellow. That's why I was laughing earlier."

"Why?"

"Because it's yellow!" He leaned toward her, his eyes wide. "Don't you see, Silk. I've been sunlight all along. Of course I couldn't *stand* in the light, not when I *am* the light."

Cornsilk's brows drew down. "Well, if you are sunlight, then what am I?"

"You," he said, and looked at her with such love that she recoiled a little. "You are the sky at dawn."

"You mean my soul comes from there? That it's a part of the dawn sky, like a chunk cracked off, or something?"

Poor Singer bit his lip. "I'm not really a Singer yet, so I don't know for sure. All I can tell you is that when you live inside your soul, it doesn't feel like a chunk of sunlight or dawn sky, it feels like . . ." He stopped, as if he required concentration to speak correctly. "Well, I felt like I *was* sunlight, touching everything, shining everywhere all at once."

Cornsilk smiled. He bowed his head as though embarrassed, and dark hair fell around him, framing his thin hawkish face.

His mouth tightened. "I'm sorry. Did that sound prideful? Dune says I have a problem with pride. I—I don't mean to be vain, I—"

"You didn't sound prideful at all. In fact, you sounded"— she gestured uncertainly—"innocent. I used to have a friend, a little boy . . ." Tears beaded on Cornsilk's lashes. "His name was Brave Boy. He had seen five summers. He would laugh and—and the sound always made me ache inside, from happiness. Your voice sounded a lot like his. It made me ache, too."

Poor Singer smiled and ate more soup, slowly ladling it into his mouth and waiting after each spoonful to see what would happen. Finally, he said, "So, you are on your way to Talon Town? To find your relatives?"

"I've nothing left. Nowhere else to go."

"That's where Dune is. When you get there, please tell him I'm well."

"I will. If I find him."

"Oh, you can't miss him. He's about this tall"—he lifted a hand to show her—"with no teeth and a bad temper. When you see him, I'm sure he'll be bullying someone."

As evening descended upon the canyon, the cold deepened, nipping at her skin. She finished her tea, untied her blanket from her pack, and wrapped herself in it. Warmth seeped into her, and her eyelids suddenly felt as heavy as stones. Firelight fluttered over the walls like a flock of golden butterflies. She had not slept since . . . since the night before last. She stretched out beside the fire and pillowed her head on her pack. The precious turquoise-studded blanket inside it cushioned her ear. A faint whisper filtered up through the pack, and Cornsilk strained to hear what the blanket was saying, but she couldn't. She wondered if Poor Singer could, and looked at him.

He didn't seem to. He just ate the rest of his dumpling soup and lay down an arm's length away. Just before he pulled up his blanket, he put the pebble back in his mouth.

"Aren't you afraid you'll swallow it?"

He gave the matter careful consideration. "No. At least, I'm not afraid the pebble will hurt me. But it does worry me that

I might accidentally hurt the pebble. I wouldn't wish to do that. This pebble has been very good to me."

Cornsilk snugged her blanket around her throat and looked at him askance. "Tomorrow, I'll make a salve for your sunburn."

He yawned sleepily and tossed more wood on the fire. Crimson threads of light spattered the ceiling. "Perhaps by then, I'll be concerned. Right now, I just want to sleep, too. Have a good visit in the afterworld, Silk."

"And you also," she said, and closed her eyes.

Tears pressed hotly against her lids. Her dreams would be barren because her family wasn't in the afterworld. She hadn't cleaned and cared for their bodies. She hadn't Sung the proper ritual Songs, or led the burial procession to the sacred *sipapu*, as was her duty. Her parents and brother would be homeless ghosts, wandering the earth, lost and wailing.

When sobs racked her chest, she squeezed her eyes closed.

A hand, large, but very gentle, stroked her hair. She shifted, and saw Poor Singer staring at her. His gray blanket lay open, revealing his bare chest. Concern sparkled in his eyes. "Are you all right?"

Cornsilk braced herself on one elbow and tried to breathe deeply. Hoarsely, she answered, "Poor Singer, I . . . I didn't bury them, my f-family. I was too afraid. There were dozens of warriors running through the village. People were screaming. I couldn't move. I couldn't do anything except hide on top of the hill, and—and—"

"Shh," he whispered, and pulled away the hair that had fallen over her eyes, so he could look at her. He smiled gently. "They will be waiting. If you want me to, I'll go back with you."

Her lungs shuddered as she exhaled.

He searched her tormented face. "We will find them and care for them. We can make travoises to haul them along the sacred roads. It might take a few days, but we'll manage. Then we'll Sing their souls to the afterworld. I'm a new Singer, but I think I can remember all the words to the Death Songs."

Cornsilk eased back to the floor and pillowed her head on her arm. Her throat ached. "Thank you, Poor Singer."

He smoothed her hair again. "Everything will be all right.

Don't worry. Ghosts understand more than people think they do." He drew back his hand and pulled his blanket closed. "Sleep well, Silk."

Cornsilk listened to his slow, even breathing and sank into an exhausted sleep.

Twenty-Four

The pink glow of dawn streamed down through the east-facing doorway, lighting Cornsilk's face where she lay curled before the firepit. She inhaled a deep breath of the cedar-scented air and stretched her legs and back. The long run had taken more of a toll than she had realized. Twinges shot through her muscles.

She rolled to her back and blinked at the soot-smudged walls; the small house appeared truly dreary this morning. The baskets in the corner seemed to have edged another finger closer to toppling. They leaned so precariously, the slightest breath of wind would surely do it. The door curtain flapped in the breeze and she glimpsed birds perched on the frost-silvered sage outside.

She rubbed her eyes. Horrifying dreams had tormented her sleep. And through them all, the big white-faced bear had been there, advising her, trying to help her, nudging her with his nose when she took the wrong path and shrieking ghosts had her surrounded . . .

Cornsilk propped herself up on one elbow and caught movement from the corner of her eye. She turned slowly. A tiny brown-and-white field mouse hid between the pots by the doorway. The little beast watched her with shining eyes, ready to bolt, but too interested in the pile of corn crumbs by the largest pot. Its whiskers wiggled as it ate. Odd that she hadn't noticed the pile of crumbs last night. Poor Singer must have left it there.

Poor Singer huddled in his gray blanket, snoring softly. Just the top of his head was visible. The light pouring through the door made his tangled black hair sparkle with pink highlights. He didn't seem to have moved during the night. No doubt his body needed all of its energy after such a long fast.

Cornsilk shook her head. How could he and Dune sleep on this cold hard floor? She had tossed and turned all night, trying in vain to find a comfortable position . . . and trying not to hear the voices of her ancestors drifting up from the underworlds.

They had called and called to her.

And she had not known what to tell them. Cornsilk drew in a halting breath. In the middle of the night, she had scooped ashes from the firepit and rubbed them over her face, arms, and legs, to blind the ghosts who hunted her. Off and on for the rest of the night, she had scooped ashes and wished she had listened more closely to her mother's teachings about how to appease angry ghosts.

At the thought of her mother, Cornsilk closed her eyes. . . . She would be one of those angry ghosts.

Quietly, she rose and rolled up her blanket. The mouse's eyes never left her—but it did not run.

Cornsilk picked up the stick she had used as a poker last night and dug around in the firepit, isolating the hot coals by raking the ash aside. When she pulled out a larger piece of juniper, the woodpile shifted, sticks falling and clattering—the mouse flinched, but didn't flee, and Poor Singer kept snoring. Cornsilk gently laid several twigs on the coals, then bent to blow on them.

Flames crackled. As they licked through the tinder, she added larger sticks until the fire burned steadily.

Untying her bow and quiver from her pack, she slung them over her shoulder, then dug around inside and pulled out her hafted obsidian knife, which she tied to her belt. Lastly, she unhooked the rawhide thongs which held the boiling pot to the tripod. She stepped wide around the mouse, still nibbling busily, and ducked under the door curtain.

Sunlight glazed the frosted brush and grass with dazzling sparkles. Her breath puffed whitely. The majestic cliff loomed above the canyon like a sleeping beast, silent, massive. The stairs cut into the stone carved a dark gash down the face.

Mourning doves perched on the rim, cooing melodically. Their voices soothed her. The males uttered those soft melancholy sounds while in search of a mate. She hoped the females were listening.

Cool shadows clung to the bottom of the canyon, but spikes of pale yellow shot across the sky, and the tallest buttes had sunlit tops. Far to the south, Orphan Butte stood like a lone sentinel. Beyond it, the land rippled into an infinity of red, gold, and green. The deeply eroded highlands looked gnawed, as if ravaged by the sharp teeth of ancient monsters. In every gash, a twisting green line flowed.

Cornsilk walked around the side of the house and poured last night's dumpling water on the tall turquoise sage. She figured that must be what Dune did or the plants wouldn't be so huge. After she set the pot down, she hitched up her green dress and emptied her night water.

Then she ambled out through the sage, down the well-worn path that wound along the base of the towering cliff. The world smelled damp and fragrant. Frost patterns glistened on the leaves and cactus thorns. All heavily used trails led to water. From the time she had been a child, her mother had taught her that she had only to follow a good game trail to find a drink.

She swung the pot as she walked. Faint warmth oozed from the sunbathed cliff, making her shiver with pleasure.

Cornsilk stepped over a big black rock . . . and halted. Red corn kernels nestled in an indentation in the top. An offering? To the Spirit of the stone? Or to an animal that frequented this trail? She looked around. How odd that the mice and pack-rats hadn't gobbled up the offering during the night. Had Poor Singer asked his Spirit Helper to keep them away?

A narrow wash cut a jagged swath near the cliff. Cornsilk smiled when she saw the catch basin, a crystal clear pool about one body-length across. It had been hollowed out of the sandstone. Beautiful swirling rings of red, gray, and tan adorned the rock.

She placed the pot beside the pool and slowly lowered herself to a ledge of stone. Her legs shook. Beyond the faint apron of ice at the edges, not a breath of wind stirred the water. It reflected the undulations of the cliff, a small triangle of blue sky, and a wisp of cloud. Cornsilk drew up her knees and propped her bow on them, letting the silence of the morning seep into her.

Two canyon wrens fluttered through the sage. Brown above with a rust-colored rump and pure white breast, they blended so well with the shades of the desert they almost disappeared. Cornsilk cocked her head as they whistled softly to each other: clear descending notes, *tee-tee-teer*. *Tee-tee-teer*.

Cornsilk exhaled softly.

Sage and winter grasses blanketed the canyon bottom, creating a mosaic of gold and turquoise. Taller clumps of snakeweed, yucca, and rabbitbrush thrust up here and there.

Such beauty. It made her ache deep down.

She ran her fingers along the smooth wood of her bow and remembered the day Fledgling had helped her make it. They had been laughing . . .

A vague stinging sensation pervaded her body, as if every nerve hurt to the touch. Despair had become her constant companion. It breathed in her lungs, ran through her veins, gazed through her eyes. She had spent half the night fighting to recall the name of the warrior who—who'd killed Fledgling. *Gnat. His name was Gnat.*

More than anything, Cornsilk longed to curl up in a warm blanket and sleep forever. If only she could. . . .

At the soft padding of paws against stone, barely audible, she froze, every muscle still. Sand spilled from a ledge above her, drifting down in a fine red mist. The pool rippled.

Cornsilk reached up, her movements agonizingly slow, and quietly drew an arrow from her quiver. She placed it across her bow, and inched her gaze upward.

On the ledge thirty hands above, a bobcat crouched. Black spots dotted her tawny coat, and she had two black rings on her stubby tail. Her tufted ears lay flat at the sight of Cornsilk.

She must hunt here every morning, crouching on the ledge overlooking the pool, waiting for smaller animals to come and drink.

Eyes locked with Bobcat's, Cornsilk carefully nocked her arrow in her bow. The cat growled and arched her back, as if she understood perfectly well what Cornsilk had planned.

Cornsilk lifted the bow, pulled back the arrow . . .

An inhuman groaning, like a bear caught in a trap, sounded

behind her, then something thrashed through the sage. She jerked around. The bobcat scrambled down the ledge, leaped into the brush, and bounded across the desert. Cornsilk sighed in defeat and lowered her bow.

Poor Singer stood in the sage just to the right of the offering rock. His long black hair draped his chest. He had his arms lifted away from his sides and his legs spread. The horror on his narrow face sent a chill through her. The nostrils of his thin hooked nose quivered.

She ran to him. "What's wrong? Are you all right?"

"I tripped over the rock," he said, and hurried by her in a stiff-legged gait, swinging his legs wide.

Wading into the pool, heedless of the ice, he stretched out on his back, and leaned his head against the ledge where she had been sitting. His long black hair swam around him. Beneath the wavering water, his sunburned skin glowed a lurid reddish purple. "Blessed gods," he groaned as if in relief.

Cornsilk sat down cross-legged on a stone, facing him, and laid her bow aside. "You're just doomed to suffer, Poor Singer. I had that bobcat in my sights when you groaned. My chance for grease to salve your sunburn ran due east. Not that the bobcat would have had much fat this time of the sun cycle, but I thought anything would help."

He sank deeper into the pool, letting the cold water wash around his pointed chin. "I am more sorry than I can tell you."

"I'll make a salve from crushed prickly pear instead. It won't last as long, but it will ease the pain. Does old Dune have a supply of Spirit plants? Red dock root would really help."

"Some plants are hanging in amongst the corn, beans, and squash. There might be some red dock root up there. I don't know." Poor Singer let out a pained breath. "What does red dock root do?"

"It cleanses and quickens healing."

He turned to look at her. "How do you know so much about plants?"

Their gazes held. She couldn't speak for a moment. "My—my mother was a Healer. She taught me."

When her eyes blurred, he murmured, "I'm sorry, Silk. If you'll give me a day or two, I really will travel back to Turtle

Village with you. We'll find your family and take care of them. I promise."

She bowed her head.

What would he do when they didn't go to Turtle Village at all, but to Lanceleaf? Would he know the difference? Most clans knew the general locations of other villages.

She got to her feet. "While you soak, I'll collect prickly pear pads. Then, when I've tended your burn, I'll make us breakfast. How are you feeling today? After eating last night?"

He smiled wearily. "My soul is floating, but I have one foot on the ground again."

"Are you happy about that?"

Poor Singer shifted and sinuous locks of hair snaked around his skinny chest. "How strange that you would ask. No. Not completely. I've never felt so free in my life as I have the past quarter moon. Hunger purifies and sets the soul loose from the cage of the body. But why did you ask?"

Cornsilk lifted a shoulder. Her mother's smile, the tenderness of her touch . . . "My mother always fasted before a Healing. When the patient was truly ill, she would go without food for eight days—twice the holy number of four. And after the Healing she would come home, eat a single bluecorn dumpling, then sleep for a full day. When she woke, she said she was always deeply sad—because her soul had lost its wings."

Poor Singer exhaled and his breath sent silver ripples across the pool. The reflection did an ethereal dance over the red cliff. He nodded. "At least now I know my soul has wings. I didn't before. Though I thought I did." He smiled. "I thought I knew a lot of things."

Cornsilk untied her knife from her belt, picked up an arrow and headed out into the sage, hunting prickly pear, not far from the pool. "And you don't know as much now?"

She knelt down, said a soft prayer, begging the cactus to forgive her, asking that it allow her to use a few of its pads to help Poor Singer. She waited until she felt the prickly pear give its permission and gently cut off a juicy pad. Long thorns spiked up from the cactus; she carefully skewered the pad with her arrow.

"I don't know anything, Silk. I . . . I suppose I never did." Poor Singer splashed at the water. Rings bobbed out in every direction again, melting against the stone walls of the pool. Trailing green glimmers speckled the surface.

Cornsilk sawed off another cactus pad. "Don't you think every new Singer feels that way?"

"Well, if Dune were .ere I could ask, but he's not, so I have to guess. It's very frustrating."

Cornsilk moved on to the next cactus and repeated her prayer. You couldn't cut too many pads from a single plant or the Spirit would become angry, and prickly pears had a nasty reputation for afflicting people with the knotted joint disease. When she sensed that the cactus had assented, she began a careful process of pruning.

"Didn't you feel the same way when you went through your kiva initiation?" Many young men whispered about it, but she knew very little. It wasn t a thing for unmarried women. They had their own special rites and kiva ceremonials. "I have heard that the journey to the First Underworld humbles young men."

Poor Singer's expression turned somber. "It does." He looked away.

She took the hint.

The next plant stood half as tall as Cornsilk and had pads the length of her forearm and twice as wide. This time, she got no answer to her prayer, only a faint sensation of hostility. She moved on to another cactus, where she cut four pads and slipped her arrow through them. "I think ten pads will be enough. If not, I'll cut more later."

"Thank you."

A breeze rustled through the sage and blew over the surface of the pool; it winked and glimmered. Poor Singer frowned. "Silk? Did your mother ever speak about feeling empty inside after fasting?"

"Empty? Empty of what?"

"Everything—thoughts, emotions. I even feel empty of myself. As if I am not really here."

Cornsilk tied her knife to her belt again and considered his question. A piñon jay trilled high above her and she tipped her head back to look. The blue bird floated on the warming air currents above the rim, its wings wobbling against the glistening gold of morning.

"In my tenth summer, Mother did a Healing for a very old

woman. It took half a moon. I remember that Mother fasted, and Sang, and slept for no more than a few hands of time. But the woman died anyway." Cornsilk pictured her mother's haggard face, and heard her tearful voice explaining the woman's lingering death. "When Mother came home, she said that her soul had fled to the skyworlds, that it floated in nothingness, alone, waiting for the world to change." She made a lame gesture with her hand. "I don't know if she meant that she felt empty, but it sounds similar to what you're feeling."

Poor Singer closed his eyes. He didn't say anything more for a time. "How long did it take before her soul returned to her body?"

"A while. Four or five days, I think."

Poor Singer dipped his hand in the water and smoothed it over his sunburned face. He sighed as if in relief. "When mine returns, I—I'm not sure I will know who I am, since I don't right now. I feel . . . different."

Cornsilk propped her arrow against a rock, bent forward, picked up the boiling pot, and rinsed it out. As she refilled it, she thought about how much of herself she had lost. Where a child had played inside her a few days ago, now a frightened young woman crouched, breathless, confused. She responded, "I'll understand, Poor Singer."

She lifted the pot by the thongs and took the arrow in her opposite hand.

Poor Singer gazed up at her. "Should I rise?"

"It's up to you. I just thought I'd walk back and start peeling the prickly pear pads."

"But the sooner we salve my burns, the sooner they will heal."

Rising, he stood dripping in the pool. Water beaded on his cold-pimpled skin, and slicked his long hair down over his chest. "Here." He extended his hand. "Let me take the pot. You have your bow and the cactus pads to carry."

Cornsilk handed it to him.

He started up the trail in his stiff-legged gait, holding the pot out to his side. When they reached the black offering rock, Poor Singer cautiously bent forward and smoothed his fingers over the gritty surface.

"I'm sorry," he whispered. "I didn't mean to hurt you." He

picked up the kernels of red corn he'd knocked off earlier and carefully replaced them in the niche on top of the stone.

Cornsilk said, "Who is the offering to? The rock or something else?"

"It's to Silence," he said, and gently patted the rock.

Cornsilk frowned. An offering could be a request for help, or a gift in gratitude. Occasionally offerings simply symbolized the offerer's love for the Spirit. Her mother had made an offering every day to the Spirits of the drifting Cloud People. But to Silence?

She followed Poor Singer up the trail.

When they reached the little white house, Cornsilk held the door curtain back for Poor Singer. He grunted softly as he ducked low to enter, and Cornsilk draped the curtain over the peg, letting the morning sun into the room.

Poor Singer hung the boiling pot on the tripod, then hastily backed away. "I'm sure I'll go into convulsions if I stay near the fire, Silk." He looked around uneasily and said, "I think I'll sit next to the wall by the door. It's cooler there."

"Good. I'll scrape the pads and be there in a moment."

Poor Singer walked over and lowered his naked body to the hard-packed dirt floor, sighing, "Oh, that's better."

Cornsilk selected a large pot and set it beside the grinding slab. Propping her arrow beside her, she slid off the first cactus pad and took her obsidian knife from her belt. She had to be careful of the long thorns. They contained a very painful stinging poison. She slipped her blade through the pad like a stem and held it over the fire to burn off the thorns. Then she placed the pad on the grinding slab and skinned off the outer peel. She scraped the pale green pulp into the pot and started on another.

Poor Singer watched her with shining eyes. Despite his pain and self-doubts, he seemed oddly serene. He might have been looking upon the blessed face of the Sun Thlatsina, rather than Cornsilk scraping cactus pads. It made her feel peculiar, as if he looked through her, rather than at her. Was he looking at the color of her soul again?

As his waist-length hair dried, it fluffed into a black halo around his shoulders.

"Silk?" he said. "Can you . . . I mean, I don't wish to pry, but can you tell me about your family? Do you wish to?"

Her hand hovered. "What do you wish to know?" She finished the pad and reached for another.

"Did you have brothers and sisters?"

"A brother."

"What was his name?"

"F-Fledgling. He was my age."

"You were twins?"

". . . Yes."

Cornsilk's hands shook. She concentrated on burning off cactus thorns.

"I have heard," Poor Singer said in a soft voice, "that twins are especially close, that they live in each other's souls."

Cornsilk scraped the pulp into the pot. "Fledgling was my best friend."

"How did he die?"

Grief cut off her air. She struggled to fill her lungs. "I—I can't speak about that . . . not yet."

All night long, she had seen Gnat thrust Fledgling's head at Webworm. The bloody clouds, the stench of charred pine pitch, the coppery odor of blood . . . they had been as real last night as on the night they had happened. An icy mixture of hatred and rage chilled her. *Gnat and Webworm. They will be at Talon Town. I will find them.*

Poor Singer awkwardly toyed with a lock of his hair. "I'm sorry, Silk. I thought it might help you to talk about them. When I was small, I used to beg my mother to tell me about my father. She would recite story after story, because I needed to hear them."

Cornsilk laid her knife down. Pulp coated her hands. She spread it over her forearms. It felt luxuriously cool. "What did you say his name was?"

"Sitting-in-the-Sky. He was a great Trader. He used to visit the Hohokam many times a sun cycle."

"Today, it would be too dangerous. If the Hohokam didn't strike him down for bringing the wrong Trade goods, the Mogollon would ambush him on the trail and steal everything he carried."

Poor Singer shoved the lock of hair over his shoulder. "True. No one is safe these days, not even an innocent Trader."

Cornsilk dipped their cups full of boiling water and looked at the rafters, searching through the dried plants. She saw fans of juniper berries, saltbush seeds, lamb's quarter and purslane, globe mallow, milk vetch, pigweed, ricegrass, spears of yucca, and several limp sunflowers that had been picked fresh, the stems slipped between the roof poles.

She gently plucked a handful of crumbly sunflower petals and put them in their cups to steep. A savory scent wafted up with the steam. "I don't see any red dock root. I guess the prickly pear pulp will have to do. Tonight I'll go hunting again. Before we sleep, I'll make a grease salve, so your skin won't feel so tight."

"I'm sorry I spoiled your bobcat hunt."

"It's all right. I doubt she would have had much fat. I'll look for a rabbit this evening, or maybe a badger."

Cornsilk carried their cups over and set them on the floor by Poor Singer's side. "We can sip tea while I apply the salve."

He smiled, watching as she went to pick up the pot of pulp and bring it back.

Cornsilk knelt at his side, dipped her hands in and squished the pulp through her fingers until she had a watery glue. "Are you ready?"

Poor Singer sucked in a fortifying breath. "Yes, I think so."

"I'll start with your arms and chest." She gently spread the pulp over his ropy muscles.

He shivered. "It feels very cold."

"Good. It will take the burn out and help prevent scarring. Although"—she pulled his hair away from his left shoulder and frowned at the broken blisters —"your shoulders might be beyond help."

Poor Singer twisted his neck to look and grimaced as she smeared the salve on. "That stings!"

"These are open wounds, Poor Singer. The blisters are all broken. The flesh beneath is raw."

Poor Singer gritted his teeth as her hands moved gently over his tall skinny body. She coated his arms, chest, neck and face, but halted when she reached his groin.

"Here." She shoved the pot over. "I don't want to be responsible. If you thought it stung on your shoulders, just wait."

Poor Singer gazed down at his penis and testicles. They had

swollen from the burn and appeared, well, a little deformed. "I should have worn a breechclout, I suppose."

Cornsilk gave him a skeptical squint. "Weren't you afraid to expose yourself like that? Father Sun is the greatest creative Power of all. If he'd thought you boastful, he might have killed your semen to teach you a lesson."

He picked up his swollen manhood and squinted at it. "Maybe he did."

Cornsilk squinted, too. "Better salve it quickly. Just in case some is still alive."

Poor Singer dipped his hand into the pot. "You think it will hurt worse than my shoulders?"

"I think you might have glimpses of the afterworld."

Poor Singer gave her a dubious look, scooped up a handful of pale green salve, and smoothed it on. It didn't feel so bad. In fact, it . . .

"*Great gods!*" he screamed as he nearly leaped through the roof, doing everything he could to distance himself from his testicles.

Cornsilk sat back on her heels and sipped her tea as she watched him squirm. He'd clamped his lower lip between his teeth and squeezed his eyes closed until tears escaped to trickle down his cheeks. Against the sooty white wall he looked like a tortured warrior.

"Want me to finish your groin for you?" she asked dryly.

He looked at her. "Silk . . . you, you're a woman."

She set her cup down and gaped at him. Was this shame? Embarrassment? She could scarcely believe it. In her village, the differences between male and female bodies were hardly a secret. "Of course, I'm a woman. And my mother was a Healer, Poor Singer!"

"Its just that I—I have never *been* with a woman, and I'm afraid . . ." His voice trailed off.

The horrified expression on his face made her swallow her disbelief. He was almost sixteen summers old and still inexperienced? Quietly she said, "Why is that, Poor Singer?"

"Well, first of all, I was too scared to ask. And, second, well . . ." He lifted a shoulder. "No woman wanted me." He looked nervously down at his sun-wounded genitals, and added, "I suppose that won't change."

Cornsilk smiled. "I *can* salve your sunburn, Poor Singer. No matter where it is. If you wish me to."

"I—I'd rather do it. Thank you."

He dipped his hand into the cool salve and shut his eyes. As he spread it over every tender pore, he gritted his teeth. Finally, he slumped against the wall and panted.

Cornsilk sipped more of her sunflower petal tea. "You'll have to stand up so I can do your backside, Poor Singer."

"S-soon." His voice was toneless. "I'll stand up soon."

"Is the pain lessening? How are you feeling?"

Poor Singer slitted his right eye. "You don't think . . . I mean . . . I've seen people with frostbite lose toes."

"I watched my mother sever two frostbitten fingers once. Don't worry. It just takes a very sharp knife. With fingers, you've got to slice the joint just right. That takes time and a steady hand. Since there's no bone down there, it'll be so fast you'll hardly feel a thing."

Poor Singer sat unmoving, his expression frozen. He didn't blink. "That was *not* funny, Silk. Not one bit."

Cornsilk smiled anyway.

Twenty-Five

Purple thunderheads marched eastward, trailing iridescent tendrils of rain across the rumpled desert. Against the golden undercoat of sunrise they seemed to be long-legged giants striding to meet Father Sun.

Gnat stopped in the bottom of Straight Path Wash to watch them. The cool morning air carried the scent of wet earth and sage. He took the fragrances into his lungs and held them for as long as he could before releasing his breath. As he did, the sun rose higher and peeked through a gap in the clouds, and a spectacular orange glow bathed the land. Gnat stood still for a moment, immersing himself in the beauty.

Webworm walked up and Gnat fell in step beside his lanky leader, heading up the wash again.

They had been marching for less than a hand of time, but already the War Chief seemed preoccupied. He had been tripping over nothing and cursing: back stiff, jaw clenched, a black braid draped his right shoulder. He resembled a man walking to his death. Blood had leaked from the severed head in his pack and soaked his red shirt.

The thirty warriors behind them muttered, no doubt wondering, as Gnat did, what ailed their new leader. The raid had been easy, the deaths quick. They had carried out their orders—though not one man had liked them. But what difference did that make? They had done much worse under Crow Beard's command. Gnat ached for Beargrass, too. Murdering a friend . . . well, it wounded the soul. But it had been a disgrace that the War Chief had been unable to carry out the order himself.

Gnat had awakened twice in the night and both times Webworm's blanket had been empty. Once, he'd seen Webworm out in the sage, cradling his wounded arm and kicking at brush.

Gnat veered around a head-high pile of mud. Saturated walls of earth had slumped off the steeply eroded banks and blocked half the drainage. Thirty summers ago, this wash had been a broad shallow stream. Now the sheer walls rose two bodylengths over his head. Here and there lonely roots hung out, dangling in the breeze, their long-dead plants not even the ghosts of memory. A babbling brook of rust-colored water flowed by. Gnat slogged through it.

Yuccas spiked up along the bank, their bulbous seed pods rattling like old bones in the cool breeze. Bleached stems of rice grass quivered.

Gnat's gaze drifted southward, and he frowned, and stopped. His moccasins sank in the damp sand as he lifted a hand to shield his eyes from the glare of the rising sun. Puffs of smoke drifted among the clouds. "What's that?"

Webworm looked up suddenly, as if Gnat's voice had awakened him from a nightmare. His broad face lined with concern. "What?"

"Smoke. See it?"

Webworm squinted against the glare. "Yes. From the signal

tower near Center Place. Three puffs . . . followed by two long strands, then a single puff."

"If we saw the entire message. Let's wait."

They watched as the signal began to repeat, the gray smoke floating up among the Cloud People. At night the message would have been sent by draping a hide curtain over the window of the tower and building a fire inside. Three short flashes would have been followed by two longer bursts of light, then another short flash.

Webworm shifted the pack on his back. Gnat had wrapped Fledgling's head in lengths of cloth to absorb the blood; it must feel like a granite boulder on Webworm's shoulders.

"May I help with your pack?" Gnat asked.

"No, no, I . . ." Webworm shuddered lightly. "All night long I heard strange shrieks. I have an eerie feeling, as though the boy's soul rides my back like an enraged eagle, just waiting to sink his talons into me."

"Beargrass was your friend, and the boy . . . the boy was perhaps just Beargrass' son. But we did our duty, Webworm, what more—"

"But why did I believe Sternlight?" Webworm demanded as he swung around. "Never in my entire life have I trusted my cousin! He's a stinking witch—and a murderer! Why did I believe his story about Beargrass?"

Gnat's brows drew together. Webworm looked panicked, ready to flee for his life. "It doesn't matter," Gnat said. "Snake Head gave you an order, and you carried it out. What is *wrong* with you? You had no choice. None of us did."

Webworm shook a clenched fist in Gnat's face. "Didn't you see the look on Beargrass' face?" he hissed. "I knew him well! He told the truth when he said Fledgling came from his own body. Gnat . . . don't you understand? I murdered a dozen innocent people! Many of them children!" Webworm's eyes went wide and round. "Blessed Ancestors, I pray the gods forgive me."

So their men would not hear, Gnat gripped Webworm by the good arm and pulled him closer, murmuring, "Many of the gods were warriors. They understand duty."

"Do they?" Webworm shook off Gnat's hand and seemed to be struggling for control. He fixed his gaze on the smoke signals again. After several moments, he said, "Something's wrong. They are warning visitors to stay away."

"Then we should get back soon. It is, perhaps, nothing, but—"

"But it may be." Webworm pointed to the cut in the bank ahead. It had been packed down by thousands of feet, and the tan soil shone darker than the surrounding drainage. "Let's take the slave crossing. It'll be faster." Webworm turned to the warriors who trailed behind them. Heads went up. "Come closer!"

The men crowded around Webworm and Gnat. Fearful murmurs ran through the ranks. They had all seen the signals. Many men lifted hands to the Power pouches strung around their necks, small leather bags filled with sacred items, and offered silent prayers to their Spirit Helpers.

Webworm said, "Be ready! This may be nothing more than a few people ill with a fever, but we must prepare. Perhaps Talon Town is being raided."

The warriors pulled arrows from their quivers and nocked their bows. Against the background of the placid wash and slow-moving clouds, their movements seemed chaotic, their worried voices a muted roar.

Gnat drew an arrow from his own quiver and nocked his bow, then trotted toward the slave crossing with Webworm at his heels. The smoke signals repeated the silent warning.

When Gnat reached the crossing, he thrust out a hand to stop Webworm and pointed to the ground. Tracks dented the sand. "Look! Two people. A big man. He was heavy. See how his moccasins left deep impressions? The other is—"

"A woman," Webworm finished. He began carefully walking up the south side of the trail, working out the tracks.

Gnat took the north side, eyes narrowed as he read the footprints left in the ground. "She was running when she ascended the earthen ramp. Her heels almost never hit the ground, she must have—"

"Blessed Father Sun," Webworm whispered as he followed the man's tracks up the slope. "Gnat . . . do you see this? Look, here and here."

Gnat tilted his head in confusion. Not running. Not even walking. *But Dancing.* Despite the blurs caused by the rain, the prints clearly showed a man spinning around, his toes pointing one direction then another, as he climbed the ramp.

The warriors followed in single file, all studying the tracks intently.

At the top, Webworm crouched down and touched the knee print in the soil. Gnat looked over his shoulder. The man had knelt here, his right knee on the ground. Only the toe prints of his left foot showed, so he'd been leaning slightly forward, probably bracing . . .

Gnat jerked his head up and sighted along the direction the man must have been aiming. Pale green fabric caught the light, contrasting to the winter-brown of the weeds.

He trotted forward cautiously, until he saw the long black hair that haloed the person . . .

Blessed thlatsinas!

He broke into a run.

Gnat dropped beside her. She lay on her face, an arrow protruding from her back. Blood drenched her green dress and splattered the crushed weeds where she'd fallen.

Webworm trotted up beside him and bent over, frowning. "Who is it?"

"I don't know, but one arrow through the lung wouldn't cause this huge pool of clotted blood." It soaked the soil around her. She had to have been killed yesterday, or perhaps last night, because it had dried and blackened.

Gnat gripped her by the shoulder and flipped her onto her back.

Webworm sucked in a sharp breath.

"What sort of savagery is this?" Gnat's fist clenched.

Her belly had been slit open from her groin to her breasts. But with great care. Not a single intestine had been pricked, and the diaphragm and internal organs remained in place, but a curious shine coated the insides of her thighs. Semen? Had she been raped? Gnat recoiled, wondering if the murderer had taken her while alive, or after he'd killed her. The smooth places in the sand, and the dirt on the back of her hair and dress . . . it looked as if she'd been on her back when she'd first fallen. Had he turned her over after he'd finished with her?

"Oh, Cloud Playing," Webworm whispered. He knelt and every muscle in his strong body knotted.

Gnat clutched his weapons more tightly. Her pretty face bore streaks of blood. But her eyes had been closed by her attacker. Muddy fingerprints smudged her lids.

When Webworm's shoulders started shaking, Gnat looked away. Webworm had once loved her. Perhaps he still did. It had nearly killed Webworm when Crow Beard had ordered Cloud Playing not to see him again. Gnat didn't know all the details, except that she had married another, and Webworm had left Talon Town for three moons. Despite their parents, Webworm and Cloud Playing had always been friends. After her husband and children died, Gnat remembered seeing the two of them sitting on the banks of this wash, talking. She had been lonely. It had seemed to comfort her to have Webworm close.

Her name ran through the ranks: *"It's Cloud Playing!"*

"Blessed thlatsinas! Cloud Playing? Who could have done this?"

"Snake Head will be enraged! What will happen when he finds out his sister—"

"Quiet!" Gnat ordered. "Spread out! Look for more tracks! Raiders could have done this!"

The men trotted away in all directions, shoving sagebrush aside to peer under the branches, searching for mashed grass, or a thread torn from the murderer's clothing when he'd fled.

The first shock subsiding, Gnat took a closer look. First, he turned his attention to the arrow, and his gut soured. Mogollon Fire Dogs, Hohokam, and Straight Path people, each had their own distinct style of point. A man also marked each of his shafts with his personal colors, clan markings, or perhaps the cut of the fletching.

The arrow that had killed Cloud Playing was nondescript, made of plain willow, perfectly straight and smooth, but unpainted. The split turkey-feather fletching had been tied with sinew, and the obsidian arrowhead was a simple triangle, its flat base fitted into a slit in the willow shaft, glued with pine pitch. Behind the base, the sinew had been wrapped tightly to hold the point in place.

The skin on the back of Gnat's neck prickled. He took a deep breath and rocked back on his heels. Whoever did this had deliberately made an arrow that couldn't be traced. Her death was not the result of a raid, or an accident. This was murder. *But who? Why?*

Webworm bent forward to peer into Cloud Playing's open belly and throttled a cry. "Blessed gods . . ."

"What?" Gnat steeled himself and peered inside. At the first pungency of human entrails, he held his breath and studied the way the intestines looped, and the umber-brown lobe of liver. Dirt clung to the viscera, and they'd begun to wrinkle as they dried.

And then he saw it, down low, just above where the cut ended in the tangled thatch of pubic hair. Gnat swallowed hard and used the handle of his knife to hold the abdominal wall back. His hand trembled. The murderer had deliberately sliced into her womb, cut it wide open, and . . .

He whispered, "That's . . . *that's corpse powder!* Inside her. Do you see it? In the shadows, it shines!"

A shudder went through Webworm. "Yes."

Gnat got to his feet and stepped away from the body, far enough to take a clean breath of air and stare up at the clouds he'd thought so pretty. Now, despite the effects of sun and shadow, they seemed colorless, leached. He blinked and stared at the abandoned cornfields. Life was ebbing away, the land, the drainage channel, everything was drying up before his eyes. As if the world were bleeding to death, and no one knew it was happening.

Webworm rose unsteadily and came to stand beside him. "This . . . this is not the work of raiders."

"No," Gnat agreed.

Webworm slowly lifted his gaze to Talon Town, following the killer's tracks. The Great Warriors stood tall on the rear wall of the plaza, lightning bolts aimed directly at Gnat and Webworm. Their brilliantly colored masks shone in the early morning sunlight. "This," Webworm added softly, "is the work of a madman."

"A crazy witch."

"Gnat," Webworm's voice sounded frail. "I—I argued with her the last time I saw her. I begged her to marry me. She told me she couldn't. I started shouting like a maniac."

Gnat frowned. "What does that matter now?"

Webworm shook his head. His fists clenched. "I don't know." He turned, slung his bow, and shoved his arrow back in his quiver. Tears beaded on his lashes as, heedless of his wounded arm, he slipped his hands beneath Cloud Playing's shoulders and knees and clutched her to his chest. Blood ran from her stomach cavity and drenched his shirt.

Webworm began walking toward Talon Town as if in a trance.

Gnat kept pace at his side until he saw Webworm's arms shaking, and heard him say softly to Cloud Playing, "*Forgive me . . .*"

Gnat fell back, letting Webworm go ahead. He didn't know if Cloud Playing's soul could hear, but he knew Webworm considered the conversation private.

Gnat looked from the Great Warriors of East and West to the human warriors scattered through the ragged weeds, and back to Webworm clutching Cloud Playing's limp body in his arms.

Both Wraps-His-Tail and Cloud Playing had been First People. Both had been returning to Talon Town after a journey. Each had been sprinkled with corpse powder. Who could be responsible? He tried to recall who had been standing lookout on the night Wraps-His-Tail died. And who had been there last night.

Gnat shook himself. A feeling of impending doom slithered around his belly.

He studied Webworm's broad back. The War Chief had his forehead pressed against Cloud Playing's. Mournful sounds drifted on the morning wind. Gnat prayed none of the other warriors could hear. When a War Chief showed weakness, it sapped every man around him. In the past twenty cycles, Gnat could not recall one time when Ironwood had broken down. Ironwood had always been the rock against which men could brace their backs and fight the whole world, if necessary.

Gnat took up the trail again, weaving through the ratty patches of grass. Perhaps Webworm would not be War Chief very long. Idly, Gnat sifted through the names of men who might replace him. Wraps-His-Tail would have been next, then Cone. But Cone had been missing for half a moon. Everyone believed him dead.

Gnat scanned the trail, surveying the other warriors.

Perhaps, if he watched himself, even *he* might have a chance.

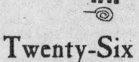

Twenty-Six

Poor Singer and Silk walked westward, hunting the drainages for the first slender leaves of wild onions. Banded humps of red-and-tan earth rolled around them, whiskered with green grass, rabbitbrush, and the tall golden shocks of last summer's foxtails. In the distance, Poor Singer counted twelve spires of rock. Twisted and eroded, they thrust up like knobby warning fingers. Far to the north, the jagged blue peaks of the Spirit Mountains hovered above the desert, suspended on a current of hot wavy air.

Poor Singer swung his half-full basket. The savory tang of onions filled his nostrils. After the fast, he couldn't seem to eat enough. They'd shared a big breakfast at dawn, but his stomach had started reminding him that Father Sun had more than passed his midday point. "Silk?" he called. She walked ahead of him on the trail, her loose long hair shining blue-black. "I'm getting hungry."

"So am I." She stopped to wait for him.

She wore a pale green dress that hugged her slender body and highlighted the golden tones of her skin. Perspiration beaded her pointed nose and broad cheekbones. If it weren't for the despair in her large dark eyes, she would be breathtakingly beautiful, but desperation always glittered, like tears, just beneath the surface.

Poor Singer trotted to catch up. "How many do you have?" He swung his basket around to place it beside hers. "Oh, you have more than I do. Where did you find so many? I thought we'd been hunting in the same places." Had he been eating *that* many?

Silk brushed hair behind her ears. From this side view she appeared all the more frail and willowy. "I know where they grow. My . . . my mother taught me."

He heard the ache in her voice, and it wounded his heart. "I know many things about animals, but not much about plants. I guess I spent my whole life working to be a Singer instead of a farmer. But if I'm going to Heal people, I really need to know more about wild plants. Will you teach me, Silk?"

She smiled suddenly. "I'd like that."

They walked down the slope into a low spot filled with prickly pear, patches of green grass, and a knot of scrubby juniper trees.

Silk glanced to the side and stopped. "Wait, Poor Singer. There are several more onions here. Let me get them. These will be the last, I promise."

She knelt, took her fire-hardened digging stick from her basket, and worked it into the ground under the delicious roots. As she levered the stick back, white bulbs popped up. With agile brown fingers she plucked them from the dry gray soil.

Poor Singer's gaze wandered. High above them, a red-tailed hawk circled lazily on the thermals, wings flashing with sunlight. Her hoarse screams pierced the quiet. The smaller male perched on a dead pine tree ahead; the male watched the female for a time, then gracefully lifted into the air and flapped toward her.

"I love hawks," Poor Singer said. "I always wanted a hawk as my Spirit Helper."

"And did you get one?" Silk dug for more onions. The fragrance of earth and the uprooted plants filled the warm air.

"No. Winged creatures just don't seem to—"

At that very moment a huge black raven soared down like a black arrow, its wings tucked. It pulled up right in front of Silk and fluttered to the ground. Its bulbous black beak had to be as long as Poor Singer's middle finger.

"Blessed Cloud People!" Poor Singer cried, stunned. "Look at the size of that bird."

Silk watched it with slit-eyed suspicion. The raven cocked its head first one way, then another.

Poor Singer grinned. "Isn't that odd? That the raven would show up just when I mentioned winged creatures?"

The raven hopped close enough to Silk to peer into her basket of onions.

"I don't believe it," she said.

"Believe what?"

She sat back on her heels and waved a hand at the raven. "Go away. Go on! Get out of here! Shoo!"

The raven hunched down and waited, as if it knew this harsh behavior wouldn't last long.

Silk studied her digging stick for a moment, shifted her grip, as if on a club, then shook her head and sighed. "This *can't* be the same bird that used to drive me crazy at home."

The sound of her voice emboldened the raven. It strutted around the side of her basket and peered at Silk through one black eye. Then it lifted its thick beak and *thock-thocked*.

Poor Singer cocked his head. "Turtle Village is three days' walk to the north. How could it have followed you so far?"

"I don't know, but it looks like the same bird."

"What did it do to drive you crazy?"

Silk gestured uneasily. "Whenever I was outside grinding corn, this raven would come and beg until I gave him some."

"Doesn't sound crazy to me. Sounds smart."

"Yes, well . . . that may be—but he got me in a lot of trouble. People started to fear that I might be a witch."

Poor Singer chuckled. "You? A witch?"

Silk wet her lips nervously. "It's not funny when people talk about you behind their hands, Poor Singer. When it happens, you take it seriously." She paused. "If you don't, they sneak up behind you, whack you in the back of the head, and throw a big rock on you after they drop you in a hole."

"Your own clan would call you a witch because a smart raven came to steal corn?"

Her gaze ate into him like cactus juice on clam shell. "When people are frightened, Poor Singer, they see witches everywhere."

The raven fluffed his feathers, head up. Poor Singer stared into its beady black eyes. From many days watching ravens and crows he knew they could be extremely clever.

"Poor Singer," Silk said, "you're learning to be a holy man. Can't you make it go away?"

He folded his arms, and considered. "You mean like Sing it to Windflower Village?"

"I mean like Sing it to one of the afterworlds."

Poor Singer smiled at the raven. Its feathers shimmered blue-black in the slanting afternoon sun. The bird had a strangely human look in its eyes that sent a sudden chill up Poor Singer's backbone. "Silk? Tell me something. How many times did the raven come to you at Turtle Village?"

Silk groaned. "I hate to tell you."

"How many?"

"Four. This is the fifth—"

"*Four*," Poor Singer said softly, and looked down at her in astonishment. "You know that's a holy number. Didn't it occur to you that the bird might be trying to warn you?"

Silk's lips parted. "What do you mean? Warn me? You mean . . . about the attack?"

The raven hopped to within pecking distance of Silk's knee and uttered a soft sound.

"Silk? Have you ever been on a vision quest? Or gone through a kiva initiation—"

"No." She knotted her fists around the use-polished digging stick. "Never."

"Well, regardless, I think you have a Spirit Helper."

"But they say that ravens are wicked, that—"

He blurted, "Who says?"

"My clan. The Ant Clan."

Poor Singer made an airy gesture with his hand. "He doesn't look wicked to me. Has he ever tried to peck you, or claw you with his talons?"

"No, he just pestered me. Why would a Spirit Helper be so annoying?"

The raven eyed Poor Singer as though waiting for his answer. Sunlight glinted in its left eye.

"Power is always annoying. Terrible and wondrous." Poor Singer paused. "Black Mesa—he's a holy man in my village—told me once that I had better listen to the Helpers who came to me in Dreams, or they would be forced to walk up to me in broad daylight to give me their news." He scratched his cheek thoughtfully. "Which is all right if your Helper is Raven, but if Rattlesnake or Grizzly Bear happen to be your—"

"I don't ever remember a raven coming to me in Dreams, Poor Singer." Silk studied the raven, no longer looking irritated, but frightened. Her pulse had begun to throb in her temple. "If this bird really is a Spirit Helper . . ."

Her voice faded as the raven leaped to the rim of Silk's basket, plucked up an onion, then spat it out and cawed his distaste while ruffling his wings angrily.

"Well, I don't have any corn," Silk apologized. "If I did, I'd give it to you. You know I would."

The raven hopped to the basket's handle and perched there, tilting its head to listen.

Silk chewed on her lower lip. "Are you sure about this, Poor Singer? I've never sought visions. Why would a Spirit Helper come to me?"

"Someone in the afterlife must have known you needed help."

"Who?"

He shrugged. "A dead relative?"

"Which one?"

"How should I know? Does the raven's voice remind you of anyone? An uncle or an aunt? Maybe he has your grandmother's eyes?"

Silk leaned toward the raven and scrutinized it. "He looks like a bird, Poor Singer."

"Well, maybe he's not a relative. Maybe he's one of the thlatsinas. Then again, the Great Warriors occasionally take flesh to communicate with humans."

Silk gave him a skeptical look. "If one of the gods wished to communicate with me, why wouldn't they speak a human tongue?"

"Maybe they have things to tell you that can't be said in a human tongue."

"Then how am I supposed to understand? I don't speak raven. Any god should know that."

Poor Singer's mouth quirked. "Have you no sense of divine mystery, Silk? Gods don't always wish to make things easy. In fact, they seem to enjoy making things difficult."

The raven stuck out its neck and cawed right in Silk's face, *four times*, then it leaped from the basket handle and flapped away, skimming the rolling badlands.

Silk clutched the fabric over her heart. "Great Ancestors. My heart is thundering."

Poor Singer watched the big black bird until it disappeared into a red fold in the land. "The raven flew toward the Great North Road."

Suddenly, his eyes widened. Puffs of dust drifted over the canyon rim, red against the deep blue of Brother Sky. "Silk . . . look."

She rose and stood beside him, shielding her eyes against the harsh afternoon glare. "You think it's a runner? Coming for you?"

"More likely for Dune. Few people know that he isn't here. Come on, let's go."

Poor Singer picked up his basket and trotted down the trail, veering wide around dense clumps of cactus and leaping dangerous rabbit and coyote burrows. Silk pounded behind him.

By the time they reached the road that ran near Dune's small white house, the man, dressed in dusty white, had climbed halfway down the steps cut into the cliff face. Wind billowed his long shirt so that it resembled wings. He might have been a snowy owl perched on the red sandstone, rather than a man.

I don't have my strength back. Poor Singer started to pant and slowed to a quick walk. The fast had sapped all of his reserves. Silk dashed on down the trail, reaching the house before the man set foot on the ground.

Poor Singer arrived, panting and near stumbling, as the man stepped out of the winding path through the sage.

"Here," Silk said. "Let me have your basket of onions, Poor Singer. I'll take them inside and get supper started. No matter what the runner wishes, we still have to eat tonight."

"Thank you." He slipped the basket from his arm and handed it to her.

Silk ducked beneath the shabby door curtain. He heard her set the baskets down with thumps, then pots rattled.

The man stepped out of the high sage and came forward. Poor Singer could see him clearly now. Red dirt stained his long white shirt. He looked even younger than Poor Singer, perhaps thirteen or fourteen summers, but he stood a good head taller, and had a moonish face—his mother had not been very good with the cradleboard. He had large black eyes framed by black hair that had been cut level with his muscular shoulders. It appeared he'd been doing hard labor for many summers.

"Good day to you," Poor Singer called as the youth neared. "Have you come to see Dune the Derelict?"

"You are Poor Singer?"

"I am." A tingle of foreboding went through him. "What's wrong?"

The boy stopped before Poor Singer, breathing hard, and bent forward to shift the small pack he carried on his back. Sweat matted strands of black hair to his jaw. "I am Swallowtail . . . of Talon Town. The holy Derelict asks that you bring his burial herbs and tools so that he might care for the dead Chief's body properly."

"The Blessed Sun is dead?"

Swallowtail nodded. "So far."

Poor Singer knew the stories of Chief Crow Beard's marches to the afterworld—just when everyone thought he was dead, he always woke up. No wonder Swallowtail hedged his answer. "Burial herbs and tools? I don't know where Dune keeps—"

"The Derelict said to tell you that his ritual bundle is hidden in the bottom basket in the corner."

Silk ducked beneath the curtain and stood awkwardly by the door, peering at the boy. "My name is Silk. You said you are from Talon Town?"

"Yes." Swallowtail had caught his breath and some of the flush had begun to drain from his round cheeks. "I am slave to the great Sunwatcher, Sternlight."

Silk gave the boy a strained smile. "Come in. I put on a pot of beans this morning and just added fresh onions. We have some leftover fried cornbread from yesterday. We would be happy if you would share supper with us."

The boy grinned. "Thank you! I'd be very happy to. Then I must go."

"You can't spend the night?" Silk asked. "But you must be tired after your run."

Swallowtail nodded. "I am, but my master told me to be back within six days. It took me four to get here—two days longer than it should have. The rain turned the drainages into roaring rivers and I had to run far out of my way to find safe crossings."

"Why must you make it back exactly on time? With the weather, anyone would understand——"

"*No.*" Swallowtail shook his head vehemently. "My master would not understand. While I am away, my mother is locked in the slave chamber. If I don't return on time, she could be killed."

Poor Singer's brows drew together. He had wondered why a slave, suddenly set free, wouldn't run directly back to his own people. Though slaves were rare in the smaller villages, they were closely guarded, never allowed to go anywhere alone, and separated at night so that they could not conspire against their masters. The First People of Talon Town, it seemed, had found a very effective way of assuring obedience.

Silk walked over and held up the door curtain. "Please, go in and sit down. You must rest and eat first."

"Thank you for your kindness." Swallowtail ducked into the dingy little house, unslung his pack, and slumped down by the crackling fire. He leaned over to sniff the fragrance rising from the bubbling bean pot. "This smells wonderful!"

Poor Singer glanced at Silk as he passed. A frightened, almost panicked expression touched her face, though she tried to hide it from him by smiling.

He mouthed, *Are you all right?*

Silk closed her eyes and nodded. "Go on in, Poor Singer. The beans should be ready."

He touched her green sleeve gently, then ducked inside and went to his place on the opposite side of the fire from the boy. Silk had already laid out three bowls, horn spoons, and teacups.

Poor Singer sat down cross-legged and noticed how pale Silk looked as she entered and let the door curtain fall. Firelight flowed over her, accentuating the narrow waist and shadowing her small breasts. Her long hair swayed about her hips as she bent to pick up the basket of cold cornbread.

She brought it back to the fire and knelt between Swallowtail and Poor Singer. "I'm sorry to hear of the Blessed Sun's death," Silk said. "I heard he was a generous ruler." She handed the basket of bread to Swallowtail.

The boy slid out two pieces of the flat round bread and bit into the first ravenously.

Gesturing with his bread, the boy said, "Not to slaves. The

first time he beat me with a yucca whip I had seen only two summers. I had knocked over a pot of ricegrass seeds. I still have the scars—" he pointed to his back "—if you want to see them."

Silk's gaze returned to the bean pot. She filled each of their bowls and set them down, then dipped their cups full of sunflower petal tea. As she handed Swallowtail his bowl and cup, she asked, "Is . . . is Sternlight a better master? Kinder?"

Poor Singer could tell from the tone of her voice that the question had not been idle. Silk *needed* to know the answer.

The boy grabbed up one of the spoons and began ladling food into his mouth. Hadn't he eaten in the entire four days? He took a bite of beans, ripped off a hunk of bread and repeated the process as quickly as he could. Finally, when he'd gobbled half his bowl, he sighed in relief, and slowed down.

"Sternlight," he said around a mouthful of cornbread, "is a witch."

Silk's spoonful of beans quavered. She lowered it back to her bowl with a clatter. "I have heard that. But I never really believed it. Why do you?"

"Oh, he's a witch, all right," Swallowtail said, and took a gulp of his tea. "Both of his sisters vanished before they had seen fifteen summers."

"Accidents happen. Someone goes off hunting and gets caught by a mountain lion, or bitten by a rattlesnake. Others die of thirst. Why would you believe—"

"He witched them," Swallowtail said in a low, frightened voice. "Even his own cousin, Webworm, says so. Not only that, more than forty summers ago, his mother and father were murdered, and his cousin, Featherstone, was taken captive by my people—the Mogollon. Many say that Sternlight caused the disaster."

"But he must have been just a baby at the time," Silk protested. "How could he have caused it?"

"Oh, he had great Power even then," Swallowtail said. "On his cradleboard, he used to point at birds, and they would fall dead from the skies." He gave Silk a confident nod and slurped another spoonful of beans. "And, once, when Sternlight had seen twelve summers, he witched a deerbone stiletto and sent it after a man named Walking Hawk. That stiletto hunted the man down for three days, and all Walking Hawk heard before it lanced his heart was a whistling noise." Swallowtail pointed with his spoon. "I heard that story from Walking Hawk's brother. He was there at the time it happened."

Silk took a bite of bread, before asking, "Well, perhaps Walking Hawk had done something bad to Sternlight. But why would he kill his own sisters and parents and cause his cousin to be captured?"

Chewing noisily, he answered, "So he could become Sunwatcher. Featherstone would have been Sunwatcher if she hadn't been captured. When she escaped fourteen moons later, her soul wasn't right. It still wanders all the time. Sometimes she knows who I am. Sometimes she doesn't. Sternlight became Sunwatcher instead." Swallowtail looked up suddenly, as if worried he might be talking too much.

"It's all right," Silk said. "We come from outlying villages. We hear almost no news. We're grateful that you're willing to share yours with us. Please, go on."

Swallowtail used his cornbread to clean the last beans out of the bottom of his bowl, then ate the bread with his eyes closed, as if greatly enjoying the mix of flavors.

Poor Singer sipped his tea and studied Silk and Swallowtail. The boy seemed to be genuinely enjoying being able to tell stories about the First People of Talon Town, and Silk ... . she hung on every word. Very interesting. Though he had known her for only a short time, he had never seen her look so profoundly serious. Not even when she spoke of her dead family, or the attack on Turtle Village. She'd said she might have relatives in Talon Town. Perhaps that explained her distress? He'd be worried, too, if a powerful witch lived in the same town as his last living relatives.

Swallowtail tipped up his cup and drained it dry, then wiped his mouth with the back of his hand. "It was very gracious of you to share your meal with me, a slave. I thank you." He pushed to his feet. His head almost touched the ceiling. "But I must be going." He grabbed for his pack.

"Oh, wait just a moment."

Silk laid out the last four pieces of fried bread and spooned beans into the center of each, then rolled them up and handed them to the boy. "Take these with you, Swallowtail. That way you won't have to stop to hunt tomorrow."

He looked stunned. "Thank you. You are very kind. I hope to see you when you arrive at Talon Town. Good-bye." He stuffed the cakes in his pack, slung it over his shoulder, and ducked through the door.

They listened to his feet trotting down the trail.

Poor Singer ladled more beans into his bowl. "These are delicious, Silk. The onions added just the right taste."

"I'm sorry I gave away our last bread, Poor Singer, but I thought he needed it more than we did. He's been running hard for four days. They must not send food with slaves."

"Probably not. I'm glad you gave him the bread."

Silk picked up her bowl again and began eating, but slowly, as if her thoughts had wandered far away. She stared at the flickering flames.

"Is something wrong?" Poor Singer asked softly.

She glanced up. "No. Why?"

"I just thought . . . I mean, you looked frightened when you were talking with Swallowtail."

She finished her bite of food and turned to him. "Do you think Sternlight is a witch?"

"If so, he's very clever. To hide your wickedness for more than forty summers . . . well, that's almost unbelievable."

"Yes, it is." She set her bowl down and drank her tea.

Poor Singer used his spoon to swish his beans around, trying to decide how to ask his next question. "Silk? I—I know I promised I would return to Turtle Village with you—"

"Of course you must go to Talon Town first. I understand. Dune needs his burial herbs and tools."

Guilt settled onto his shoulders like a great weight. "Will you go back alone? It might be dangerous. There are raiders everywhere."

She looked down into her teacup, as though gazing at her own reflection in the pale yellow liquid. "Could I . . . would it be a burden if I came with you to Talon Town?"

"Do you wish to?" he asked a little too eagerly.

"If I find relatives there, they might be willing to return to help me bury my family. That would be much easier than you and me trying to do it by ourselves."

Poor Singer patted her arm affectionately. "I would be very happy to have you along on the journey. When we arrive, if you want, I will help you search for your relatives."

"I'd be grateful."

She finished her beans and tea, and put her cup inside her bowl. "Well, I'll wash the dishes, if you'll gather things for the trip."

Poor Singer handed her his dishes and got to his feet. "I'd better find Dune's ritual bundle. Then I'll lay out our things. We should probably leave before dawn. Is that all right?"

"The sooner the better, Poor Singer."

But as Poor Singer studied her jumping jaw muscles, he didn't think that was true. She looked like a woman going out to slay a grizzly with only a deerbone stiletto.

"Silk?"

She turned, still holding the curtain up. "Yes?"

"Do you think the raven was trying to tell us about the runner? That the boy would be bringing bad news?"

The dirty dishes in her hands clattered as she shifted them to get a better grip. "He might also have been warning us about something that will happen in Talon Town." She glanced at him and ducked beneath the curtain.

Poor Singer watched the curtain swing, thinking about that. Then he nodded to himself and went to the stack of baskets to hunt for Dune's ritual bundle.

Twenty-Seven

The loud voices shocked Featherstone from her nap. She choked on a snore and blinked the sleep from her dim old eyes. The red designs on her tan dress shone in the light streaming down through the roof entry. Yes, she was here, in her room, surrounded by her painted pots and familiar white walls. This was Talon Town. Her soul was home.

"Oh, dear gods," a woman cried from outside, "what happened?"

"Quickly!" Ironwood's voice answered from beyond Featherstone's door. "Someone fetch Snake Head! And—"

A roar of voices drowned out the rest. The town dogs started barking and howling like wounded coyotes. Rushing feet pounded by outside.

"Where is Dune?" Ironwood yelled. "And Sternlight? . . . Well, find them!"

Featherstone combed her shoulder-length gray hair with her fingers and grabbed her crooked walking stick. She grunted as she rose to her feet. Her knees wobbled, but propping both hands on the polished knob of her stick, she managed to steady her ancient legs. Her prominent nose had spread and grown longer over the summers, taking up half her face now. No matter where she looked, she saw it. Which annoyed her. She had been such a beautiful child.

She had two chambers all to herself. One she used for storage, and the other served as both a living and sleeping chamber. She had been dozing close to the bowl of warming coals and her pot of steaming spruce needle tea. The chamber spread three body-lengths square. A thick layer of deer hides covered the floor, given to her by her blessed son, Webworm. Across the walls, masked thlatsinas leaped and spun, Dancing beneath a dark blue roof painted with gleaming white stars. Just looking at them brought serenity to her weary heart. Here, in this room, they Danced for Featherstone alone. They were her gods, no one else's.

She smiled and ran her tongue through the gap where her front teeth had been. Once, a long time ago, she had known many gods. But that was before the Mogollon Fire Dogs captured her and clubbed her in the head so many times that they'd wounded her soul.

Strange, that she recalled her childhood with such clarity. She had been a very Powerful little girl. Everyone had expected her to grow up and become the Sunwatcher. At the age of ten summers she had flown to Sister Moon on the back of a dragonfly, wheeling and soaring. The dragonfly had fluttered higher and higher, until it alighted on the tallest silver peak on Sister Moon's face. Featherstone had walked that shining dusty land.

She had spoken to Sister Moon in the sparkling voice of a meteor, and when she laughed with joy, the sound had twinkled across the luminous sky like crushed turquoise cast to the wind. Though poor eyesight now prevented her from seeing many things in this world, in her soul that laughter still twinkled—the dragonfly's glinting membranous wings still beat across the heavens.

"Yes, sometimes my memory is as clear as a quartz crystal, and other times I don't even recognize my own son. Thank the Spirits that he understands."

Webworm had always understood. He had been born right after she escaped from the village of the Fire Dogs. Featherstone had run every step of the way home with that infant boy in her arms, starving, praying she would reach Talon Town before her milk dried up.

"How long ago was that, old woman? Hmm?" Her mind mulled over the passing seasons as she rubbed her aching left hip. The fiery pain had grown much worse in the past cycle. She could not lie down for more than a hand of time without rising to agony. "I was fourteen. Yes. Just barely a woman, not that the Fire Dogs cared."

For more than a sun cycle they had used her cruelly, forcing her to quarry rocks for their buildings, beating her with clubs when she fell or faltered in her work, and raping her often. She hadn't the slightest notion who Webworm's father had been, nor did she wish to. She had certainly hated him. Besides, the Straight Path people traced descent through the women. Webworm belonged to her.

She reached for her turkey-feather cape and pulled it around her hunched shoulders. "You haven't had such an easy life, have you?" She chuckled at herself. Hardships built character, and she certainly had enough of that.

Her mother, Lacewing, had died shortly after giving her birth, and her father had gone home to his family in the Green Mesa villages in the north. Featherstone had been raised by Sternlight's mother, her Aunt Whitefly, until that fateful attack by the Fire Dogs when Whitefly and her husband, the Blessed Sun, had been killed and Featherstone taken captive.

"Thank the Ancestors that Sternlight and his two sisters were so young. Let me see . . ." She pondered a moment.

"Sternlight was three moons old, I think, and his sisters had seen fifteen and thirty moons. Yes, that's right. If Whitefly had not left them in Talon Town, they would have been taken captive, too. Or killed."

The ladder to the roof entry always took such effort that her heart sank. But curiosity had the better of her, and she had to go see what was happening outside.

Tucking her walking stick beneath her arm, she gripped the pine poles and climbed, one step at a time. Her old joints popped and hurt, but she emerged into a brilliant glare.

Noon sunlight burned through wispy clouds, pouring over the desert in streams of molten amber and reflecting blindingly from the white plastered walls of Talon Town. The hard-packed dirt of the plaza shone a dull tan in contrast.

Featherstone hobbled to the edge of the flat roof and looked down at the milling knot of people in the center of the western plaza. Children and curious dogs ringed the adults.

Barks and shouts rang out. Someone wept inconsolably. The slaves had gathered into a cluster of tattered brown garments near the entryway.

Featherstone squinted against the glare, trying to make out who was who, but when she couldn't, she reluctantly went to the ladder that led to the plaza and climbed down. Her knees cracked like green firewood.

Breathing hard, she stood for a time at the bottom of the ladder, hanging onto a rung. Wind Baby billowed her tan-and-red dress about her aching legs and slapped her gray hair, tangling it in her stubby eyelashes.

When a child raced by, she reached out and grabbed the back of his brown shirt. "Hold up!"

He craned his neck to look at her. Mud clotted his black hair. He must have just come up from the wash.

Featherstone eyed him. "Which one are you?"

"I'm Eagletail, Blessed Featherstone. What is it you wish?" He sounded anxious.

"What's your clan?"

"What?" he asked. "Coyote!"

"Ah, I remember you." She released him. "You're Leafcat's boy." Featherstone pointed her walking stick at the people. "What's going on?"

"Haven't you heard?"

"If I'd heard, I wouldn't have to ask, would I?"

He wet his lips and said, "The War Chief found Cloud Playing. She's dead!"

Featherstone stood stunned for several instants, unable to believe, then she sank back against the ladder and sat on the closest rung. Her heart thudded dully against her ribs. Softly, she said, "Was it Fire Dog raiders?"

The boy flapped his arms. "No one knows! Everybody is scared it was a witch! May I go now? My mother sent me to fetch—"

"A witch? Why?"

"Because Cloud Playing's belly had been split wide open, and corpse powder was sprinkled inside! Blessed Featherstone, I *must* go, before my mother—"

"Oh, very well! Leave!" She waved him away.

The boy dashed off, and Featherstone's gaze returned to the crowd. Her son must be out there somewhere. And he must be tearing himself apart. He had loved Cloud Playing with all his soul.

Six summers ago Crow Beard and Night Sun had called her to their chamber to inform her that they were refusing Cloud Playing's request to marry Webworm. Featherstone's anger had been stirred, and she demanded to know why. She had never told Webworm their answer. It broke her heart, and the knowledge would have just made things worse for her son.

"*He is half Fire Dog,*" Crow Beard had said with his chin held high. "*That would not bother us, but you know the stories. We cannot afford to fuel our enemies' legends. You must understand.*"

"The legends," she whispered to herself. "The Fire Dog legends about a stolen boy child?"

She had heard the prophecy over and over when she'd been a Fire Dog slave, at both their summer and winter ceremonials—the story of a stolen child who would one day return, conquer the Straight Path nation, and free his people from bondage.

Crow Beard's words had left her bereft. As if her son—a loyal Straight Path warrior—might fit that description! The Fire Dogs also traced descent through the women! They would never consider her son as one of their own. But Crow Beard had feared someone else might. The northern Tower Builders traced descent through the men. They hated the Straight Path nation. They would, truly, use any lever to destroy the Blessed Sun.

But many other Straight Path women had been violated by Fire Dogs! Why would the Tower Builders choose her son?

Featherstone frowned out at the plaza. Webworm had never married. So far as she knew, he'd never even courted another woman. Featherstone suspected that Cloud Playing would always fill her son's heart—even in death. She knotted her hands around her walking stick as her soul ached for him.

Taking a deep breath, she braced herself, stood, and slowly plodded across the plaza. After fifty-seven summers, she had to be careful. Even the smallest undulation in the ground might cause her to stumble and fall, and her hips couldn't stand it.

As she neared the crowd, Creeper stepped away and came toward her. Featherstone smiled. He had been a faithful friend for the past thirty summers. He visited her often to laugh and talk. She suspected he wished more from their closeness, but Featherstone could not contemplate marriage to one of the Made People. It would be degrading, both to herself and her son, especially now that Webworm had become War Chief. It would not do for his mother, one of the First People of Talon Town, to wed a lowly Buffalo Clan man.

Though she did enjoy Creeper's company.

Short and fat, he waddled when he walked. His black shirt whipped about his legs. "Good day to you, Blessed Featherstone," he greeted. "Have you heard the news?"

"Yes, I have," she answered sadly. "How did it happen? Does anyone know?"

"No. Webworm found her down by the wash." Creeper looked in that direction, and fear strained his expression. "Do you know about the corpse powder?"

"Yes. Leafcat's boy told me."

"There were also strange tracks, Featherstone. The man—"

"Tracks?" Featherstone took a step closer. "What tracks?"

Creeper heaved a breath, and explained, "The murderer was Dancing as he came after Cloud Playing."

"Dancing?" The color drained from Featherstone's wrinkled

cheeks. She gripped her walking stick with both hands. The killer had purposefully profaned the sacred ways. "Hallowed Ancestors, that's all we need. A witch in Talon Town. I thought it was just talk." A painful, swelling sensation began in her chest. "And the arrow, Creeper? Whose arrow?"

"It was unmarked, undecorated. Even the arrowhead was plain. Just a triangular sliver of obsidian. It could have been anyone's."

A fragment of legend rose from the dark caverns of memory, but just as she was about to reach out and grab it, it flittered away. The swelling in her chest had begun to suffocate her, and she teetered for balance.

Creeper put a gentle hand on her arm. Concern tightened his plump face. "Are you well, Blessed Featherstone? Do you wish me to escort you back to your house?"

"No. Thank you." She patted his hand as her balance returned. "I'm all right."

"Perhaps I could take you to your son? He's on the other side of the crowd."

"I would appreciate that, Creeper. I'm not as steady on my feet as I once was. If a dog runs in front of me, the wind of his passing might knock me over."

Creeper slipped his arm through hers and led her around the ring of gawking children. He took slow even steps to make it easier for her, and she held tightly to his arm. It felt good to have him close, to feel his warmth flowing into her and his hard muscles bulging beneath her hand. Creeper could be such a comfort.

Sternlight trotted through the front entry, his white shirt gleaming. Long black hair streamed over his broad shoulders. People behaved as though the witch himself had just flown down from the heavens. They hushed, and faded back, clearing a lane for him as he rushed forward and dropped to his knees, disappearing from Featherstone's view.

Sternlight said something too low to hear.

Dune's distinctly gruff voice answered, "What! Burn her? That's not necessary! I'll do a ritual cleansing for everyone involved. Let's just place her in the kiva, beside her father. We will decide what to do after speaking with Snake Head and Night Sun."

A pack of three dogs loped up to sniff Featherstone's freshly washed dress. They liked the scent of yucca soap. "Get away!" she shouted, and jabbed at them with her walking stick.

"Go on!" Creeper yelled. He leveled a kick at the curs.

The pack leader deftly dodged the moccasined foot, and the dogs regrouped, skulking behind with their tails between their legs, sniffing the yucca soap from afar.

Featherstone looked up at the golden cliff that rose behind Talon Town. Despite the springlike weather, frost clung in the shadowed crevices, tracing the sandstone like icy veins. Rock doves perched on the rim, cooing and strutting in the sunlight. They had just began mating and uttered the sweetest sounds to each other. Propped Pillar seemed to tilt precariously toward the town. Someday it would crash down and demolish dozens of rooms. Featherstone just hoped she wasn't here to see it. They had built a wall around its base to strengthen it, and every morning and evening, clan leaders placed prayer sticks on the wall, hoping to appease the pillar's menacing Spirit.

The crowd split suddenly. People shoved each other as they backed away, muttering. Dogs scampered and yipped, trying to evade the recoiling tide of people.

Ironwood carried Cloud Playing's body toward the First People's kiva, which lay inside the line of rooms that separated the halves of the plaza. Steps light, weather-beaten face somber, Dune followed behind him. Sternlight brought up the rear. They entered the doorway to the altar room, the aboveground antechamber to the kiva, and disappeared.

Featherstone frowned. She searched the crowd. "Where is Snake Head? I heard Ironwood call for him earlier."

Creeper's mouth tightened into a white line. Creeper hated Snake Head. So did everyone else, including Featherstone. She suspected, however, that Creeper's dislike ran deeper than her own. She just longed to knock the arrogant young Chief to his knees and bash him in the head with her walking stick a few times, to help straighten him out. Creeper, she feared, wanted to see Snake Head dismembered before his eyes. What had Snake Head done to rouse such emotion in a man so gentle?

Creeper said, "The slaves couldn't find him. He may have gone to one of the nearby towns for the day."

"Without telling anyone? That doesn't sound likely."

Creeper looked down at her through dark worried eyes. ". . . I know."

They peered at each other in silence, then Featherstone glimpsed Webworm and her attention shifted.

Her son broke away from his warriors and solemnly strode toward her. He seemed to be favoring one arm. Blood soaked his red shirt. It clung to his chest like a second skin. Red streamers had dried on his long legs. Misery lined his face.

Featherstone let go of Creeper and hobbled to meet her son. In a quiet voice she asked, "Are you all right?"

"Oh, Mother," Webworm whispered. "I can't believe it."

Featherstone reached out and touched his bloody hand. "She would not have wished you to suffer. She loved you too much."

Tears blurred his eyes. He quickly cast a glance at his men and forced a deep breath into his lungs. "Mother, I—I must find Snake Head. Forgive me, I have duties to perform." He bent down and kissed her forehead. "I will see you soon."

"I'll have supper waiting when you return."

Webworm smoothed his fingers down her cheek, nodded respectfully to Creeper, then trotted across the plaza. She watched him until he went out the entryway, and the slant of the afternoon sun struck her eyes painfully.

She turned. Creeper stood where she had left him, hands clenched at his sides.

Featherstone made her way back. "I have some spruce needle tea steeping in my chambers. Would you like to share it with me?"

"Of course I would. Thank you. We must talk anyway."

"Must we? What about?"

Creeper took her arm and headed her slowly across the plaza, taking care not to rush her. He knew each of her aches and pains by heart—she'd complained about them enough, he ought to. "There is talk . . ." He lowered his voice and cautiously looked around. "About who the witch is."

"Is this Made People talk?"

"*Slave* talk."

Featherstone narrowed her eyes. The worst rumors began with the slaves. After all, they worked in nearly every chamber, overheard dozens of conversations a day, and usually knew enough facts to piece together some very unsettling fictions.

On occasion, they pieced together even more unsettling truths.

"What name are they bantering about? Sternlight again?"

People seemed to enjoy making up stories about the great Sunwatcher, despite how much they hurt him, or perhaps because they did. Though Webworm believed every bad thing said, Featherstone refused to. Many summers ago, when Webworm accused Sternlight of witching and murdering his own sisters, she had urged him to let it go. When she'd lived among the Fire Dogs, she'd seen many Straight Path girls—girls who'd supposedly "vanished" without a trace. Featherstone strongly suspected that both of Sternlight's young sisters had been captured by enemy raiders.

Creeper leaned down and whispered, "*Snake Head*. They say he's the witch."

Featherstone squinted at the five stories that loomed above her. People sat cross-legged on several roofs, whispering behind their hands. For days people had been walking about like ghosts, frightened to breathe lest some witch snatch their breaths and drag their souls from their bodies. Snake Head had ordered all visitors to stay away, out of fear that they would spread the witchcraft rumors, and everyone in Talon Town would be charged with witchcraft.

She tapped her walking stick on the ground. "Snake Head's warning to visitors might be fuel for those rumors. I wouldn't pay them much attention."

"It doesn't matter what I believe." From the corner of his eye, Creeper shot her a worried glance. "Imagine what would happen if the Made People villages thought the new Blessed Sun was a witch."

Featherstone stopped dead in her tracks. She gazed into Creeper's strained face. "That is too terrible to conceive. The First People would have to support the new Blessed Sun, and that would give the Made People a reason to accuse all First People of being witches, and then—"

"The Made People would be terrified."

". . . And terror has always been a good reason for murder."

Creeper clutched her arm tenderly. "I will protect you from my people, Featherstone. You mustn't worry—"

"Then you don't have a single brain in your head, Creeper. You ought to run like a jackrabbit and save your own hide."

"You didn't"—a smile warmed his round face—"when the Fire Dogs grabbed my wife and son. You tried to fight them off. And you were just a girl."

Creeper's wife had fought like a caged mountain lion, trying to protect their two-summers-old son. Featherstone had run to protect them, firing her bow until her quiver was empty, then waded into the battle with her deerbone stiletto. Two of the cursed Fire Dogs had fallen to her skill before the others grabbed her and forced her to the ground. Knowing that death awaited her, Featherstone had braced herself. But the tall muscular Mogollon War Leader, Crooked Lance, had been so impressed by Featherstone's courage he'd claimed her as his personal slave.

She lived today because she'd fought for Creeper's family.

Creeper leaned down and peered into Featherstone's eyes, probably wondering if she'd gone "vacant" again; sometimes she lost herself in the past. "Blessed Featherstone?" he called softly. "Are you here with me?"

She ran her tongue through the gap where her two front teeth had been and sighed. "Yes, I was just thinking, that's all. Did I tell you your wife, Red Mask, fought like a lion? She was a brave girl, Creeper."

He patted her hand in a very gentle way. "Yes, you told me. I have kept your words in my heart for many summers, Featherstone. They warm me on cold lonely nights."

Featherstone clutched his arm tightly and said, "Well, come along, let us go and sip some of that tea I promised you."

Night Sun woke in blackness.

Silence breathed all around her. For a long frightening moment, she didn't know where she was, then understanding returned. Without a smoke hole to let in light, the darkness became a living monster. She felt it moving around her, gliding along the curve of the walls, ghosting close enough to stare her in the face from a hand's breadth away. The monster sucked at her eyes and ears until she feared it might drain the life from her body.

Pulling the blanket over her shoulders, she sat up and leaned against the cold wall. The dampness had vanished, which meant the days had warmed, though she could feel no change in here. This bleak room remained cold, night or day. Longing filled her heart. The first sprigs of grass and wild onion must be up. It took only a few warm nights to coax them to sprout. What she would give for a thick turkey and onion soup filled with blue corn dumplings.

Her beloved son had ordered that she be fed nothing but a single bowl of watery corn gruel a day. It had grown very unappetizing.

Moccasins thudded on the roof, and the covering over the hole slid aside. Night Sun looked up. The scarlet fires of sunset blazed through the drifting clouds and pierced her eyes like daggers of ice. She quickly closed them, but just that moment of vision had filled her with desperation. In a few more days, she would be willing to kill to get out of here—even if it meant walking to her death.

The knowledge had dawned slowly: Her son intended to kill her. *He is Blessed Sun now. He might be able to do it.* She prayed to the thlatsinas for just a few moments of freedom, so she could grab the first man who walked by and marry him—just to knock Snake Head off that pedestal.

She shook her head. Too late, much too late now.

The ladder's foot thumped the floor in front of her. She slitted her eyes as tiny cyclones of dust whirled in the reddish gleam.

Ironwood climbed down.

Night Sun had seen no one but slaves for the past three days. She smoothed her long silver-streaked black hair away from her triangular face.

"What's happening?" she asked, and wondered when her voice had grown so hoarse. "Has Snake Head decided my fate?"

"No," Ironwood answered softly. "I'm sorry."

Ironwood stepped to the floor, unslung a small pack from his shoulder, and knelt in front of Night Sun. From the pack, he removed a small buckskin bag and a jug. His pale golden skin looked pink in the dusky glow. He had tied his long graying hair back with a cotton cord and wore a clean red shirt. He smelled of soap. He must have just finished bathing. But sweat beaded on his flat nose and across the deep furrows in his forehead.

Night Sun frowned at the taut muscles bulging beneath his shirt. "What's wrong? Why are you here?"

"You must have heard the commotion in the plaza today, and I thought you might be worried. Webworm returned from his raid on Lanceleaf Village."

There was a terrible pause. The nostrils of Ironwood's flat nose flared.

Blood surged in her ears. "And?"

"I just finished speaking with him." Ironwood filled his lungs. "He killed Beargrass and Beargrass' son."

"And our daughter? What of Cornsilk?"

Ironwood pulled a piece of turkey jerky from the bag and handed it to her. She ate it ravenously, relishing the smoky flavor.

"I honestly don't know. Webworm says he left no witnesses, as he was ordered to do. I . . ." The bag of jerky in his hand wavered. He lowered it to his lap. "I can't believe she's dead, but I must know."

"What are you going to do?"

"Go to Lanceleaf Village as soon as things have settled down here. Someone may have escaped the raid. Maybe I can find—"

"Do you know what she looks like? Have you ever seen her?"

He shook his head. "But Beargrass had relatives in the nearby villages. I'll find them. Surely, they will know."

As though he'd suddenly lost his appetite, he set the jerky bag aside, slumped to the floor, and slid over against the wall beside her. He smelled clean and faintly flowery. After studying the floor for a long moment, he opened his mouth to say something else, then closed it. When he turned and looked at her, Night Sun's blood went cold.

"What is it?" Suspicion swelled like a black bubble in her chest. "Tell me."

Ironwood laid a gentle hand against her hair and anxiously searched her face. "Night Sun . . . Cloud Playing is dead."

She sat perfectly still. An azure glow suffused the room as twilight shrouded the canyon, and she saw for the first time how deeply the wrinkles etched the skin around his eyes, and how silver his temples had turned over the long summers.

"My—my Cloud Playing?"

His face tensed. "Yes, Night Sun."

"She . . . she's . . ."

"Yes." His words came slowly and softly, as though she might not hear him if he spoke too quickly. "No one knows for certain how it happened. I checked the tracks myself, just to make sure Webworm didn't miss anything. She was almost home. The man shot her from behind. Used an unmarked arrow. Apparently her attacker had been waiting for her down by the wash. Webworm's warriors scoured the area and found the man's campsite, little more than a shallow firepit and a scooped out place in the sand where he'd lain. He had obviously slept there the night before."

Dumbly, she looked up at Ironwood. Her eyes blurred, and his face contorted in shared pain.

"There's more, Night Sun."

"Tell me."

His jaw hardened. He stared at the floor a moment. "She had corpse powder—inside . . . her . . . her wounds."

"Witched?" she asked in shock. "My daughter was witched?"

"Apparently. Dune held a purification ritual tonight to cleanse Cloud Playing, and anyone who might have touched her."

The sobs started as a tightness in her throat, then built until they racked her entire body. "Oh, Ironwood, my daughter . . . she's gone."

She reached out for him, needing him like a freezing animal drawn to the warmth of a fire, and Ironwood wrapped his arms around her shoulders and drew her close. A warm rush of feeling flooded her. It had been so long since a man had held her . . . since he had held her. He murmured something soft, soothing, and kissed her hair.

As sunset faded, a feeble wash of dusk filled the room, graying the white walls, and shining darkly on the drops of blood that spotted Ironwood's moccasins. *Cloud Playing's blood?*

Night Sun buried her face against the soft fabric over his chest and closed her eyes.

When he shifted, as if to speak, she whispered hoarsely, "Don't let go."

His arms went tighter. "I won't."

Twenty-Eight

Ironwood sat on the bottom step of the stairway that led down into the First People's kiva, his head in his hands. Wind Baby raged outside, shivering the bones of Talon Town and breathing cold down his back. The worn softness of his red cotton cape did little to block the chill. A fire burned at the opposite end of the kiva, one hundred and four hands away, but almost none of the heat reached him.

He pulled his cape more tightly closed and gazed around the beautiful chamber. Four square pillars, painted red, supported the pine log roof, and three levels of benches ringed the kiva; the lowest was painted yellow, the next red, and the highest level blue. On holy days they seated all of Straight Path Canyon's three hundred First People. Thirty-six small crypts sank into the white walls, holding bowls of cornmeal and precious ceremonial objects such as dancesticks, yucca whips, and antelope hoof rattles. Above each crypt hung a magnificent thlatsina mask.

He should have felt safe here, surrounded by the gods, with two great holy men, Dune and Sternlight, standing in front of him, and the sacred scent of cedar filling his nostrils. But as he listened to their low voices discussing Cloud Playing's murder, deep weariness settled in his muscles.

"Why would someone do this?" Sternlight said in an agonized voice. "I don't understand."

The light of the flames dyed Sternlight's taut face orange, and reflected from Dune's faded old eyes. Both men wore white ritual shirts and knee-high white moccasins.

Dune said, "Killing is a form of mourning, Sternlight. It is an expression of grief. To find the murderer we must discover the source of the pain."

On either side of the chamber stood large rectangular foot

drums. Hollow masonry structures, fifteen hands long and eight hands wide, they had been plastered and painted white, then covered with rawhide. During ceremonials musicians sat on the edges of the masonry boxes and beat the drums with their feet.

Cloud Playing's body rested on the drum to Ironwood's left, Crow Beard's on the drum to his right. Turquoise-studded Death Blankets covered them.

Dune and Sternlight had removed Cloud Playing's blood-soaked dress, and washed her flesh and long hair with yucca soap. Her silver temples shone. The four spirals tattooed on her chin looked very black against her pale face.

"Here," Dune said as he handed Sternlight a wooden comb. "Let us finish this last task, so we can both rest. It's been a long day."

Sternlight took the comb and carefully separated Cloud Playing's hair into three parts, then began braiding it.

Dune's white bushy brows knitted. "The source of the pain," he repeated.

Sternlight glanced at him. "You mean an old wound?"

"Yes. One that has never stopped bleeding."

"But this is not simply murder, Dune," Sternlight said. "She was mutilated! This was a terrible, violent—"

"Everything violent is, in its heart, something helpless, reaching out for help." Dune's eyes drifted to the thlatsina masks. "Our task, Sternlight, is to offer help."

"Help the murderer?" Ironwood asked too loudly. His voice seemed to ring in the firelit stillness. Both Dune and Sternlight turned to stare at him. "Why would we wish to do that?"

Dune gave him a quizzical look, then put a hand on Sternlight's shoulder. "Would you mind if I sit down for a time? I—"

"Please, go and rest, Dune. You have been a great help to me today. I can finish this by myself. Thank you for all you have done."

Dune smiled and hobbled toward Ironwood. He slumped down on the yellow bench ten hands away. A sheen of sweat filled his wrinkles and matted his white hair to his cheeks. He bent forward and breathed deeply for a time.

Finally, he turned to Ironwood. "I wish to help because that is the only way we will ever catch her killer. To draw him out we must—"

"Her killer was a madman and a witch. I don't want to help him. I want him in range of my bow!"

Dune held up a crooked finger. "Think about this, Ironwood. Cloud Playing had no enemies. Even her slaves spoke well of her. She was a gentle, kind, and honest woman. She had no power. She owned nothing."

". . . Yet," Ironwood answered.

Dune braced his elbows on his knees and propped his chin with one knobby fist. "You suspect she was killed because she would one day have been matron of Talon Town?"

"It occurred to me."

After a pause, Dune asked, "Who would have cared? Snake Head, despite being the Blessed Sun, can't control her property. All of Cloud Playing's wealth would go to her nearest living *female* relative. Snake Head had nothing to gain by her death."

"Yes, he did, Dune. Snake Head only became the Blessed Sun because his father died, and neither his mother, nor his sister, had husbands. Some day, Cloud Playing would have remarried. And when that happened—"

"She would certainly have deposed Snake Head and put her new husband in his place." Dune sighed. "Yes, but that is not a wound, Ironwood. That is a reason. And not reason enough for this *kind* of killing."

Ironwood looked away, thinking while he watched Sternlight gently coil Cloud Playing's braid into a bun. Sternlight performed the task tenderly, stroking her hair, whispering to her. His long hair swung about him as he worked.

Ironwood said, "Cloud Playing's mutilation is not a single event, Dune. I've seen a belly slit open like this before. Sixteen summers ago. It was after the Winter Solstice . . ."

Sternlight dropped the shell hairpin he'd been holding. As he knelt to retrieve it, his hand shook, and Ironwood frowned. Sternlight picked up the pin and secured the bun, but his breaths had gone shallow, his chest rising and falling swiftly beneath his white shirt.

For a time, only the groan of wind disturbed the quiet.

Ironwood looked back at Dune. "Do you recall? The slave girl? What was her name?"

"Young Fawn," Dune answered, and grimaced at the floor. "I remember."

"Yes," Ironwood said. "Young Fawn. Webworm found her body in the trash mound. Her belly had been slit open just like Cloud Playing's. Except . . ." He searched his memory. "Young Fawn had been pregnant. Isn't that right, Sternlight?"

Sternlight put one more pin in place, then lifted his head. His cheeks had flushed. "I don't really recall."

The fire ate into the heart of a log and light leaped, dancing over the chamber, shading pure orange where it lay upon the red bench and four red pillars. As the light flowed into the small pits in the white walls, it created a pale yellow-and-gray mosaic, like exquisite beadwork.

Ironwood's brow furrowed. Sternlight had started wiping his hands on his shirt, over and over, as if to rid them of some sticky substance. *What's wrong, old friend? Why does this discussion disturb you so deeply?* As Sunwatcher, Sternlight would have been a party to the First People's private conversations about the event, but ordinarily the War Chief was informed of such discussions. Perhaps, there were things the elders had elected not to tell him.

"The child," Ironwood continued, "had been cut from her belly. We never found it. Or Young Fawn's murderer."

They had just finished Winter Solstice celebrations. There were still thousands of people at Talon Town, busy storing the extra food, carrying soul pots to Center Place, and visiting relatives. *And Night Sun was very close to giving birth to our daughter.* He'd had little else on his mind.

"No, of course not," Dune said. "You know how many fights break out after celebrations. People are always exhausted, and irritable. A murderer would have blended right in."

Ironwood shook his head. "I remember thinking that Young Fawn must have gotten into some kind of trouble. But after today, after seeing Cloud Playing's injuries . . . I'm not so sure."

Dune waved a hand. "There's no connection, Ironwood. Trust me."

"You had a Dream about it, eh? The gods told you there was no connection?"

"I have always suspected that Young Fawn died because she was Jay Bird's daughter, and somebody realized—"

Ironwood blurted, "*Blessed thlatsinas, that's right!* I had forgotten. Yes, and she was serving as Solstice Girl. Isn't that right, Sternlight?"

Sternlight groped for the bench behind him and sank down. "Yes. That's right."

Cold wind blew down the staircase and breathed over Ironwood's back. He shivered and saw Dune rub his sticklike arms.

Ironwood untied his red cape and draped it over Dune's hunched shoulders. "Here, Elder."

"Thank you, Ironwood." Dune fumbled to tie it beneath his chin. "The fact that she was Jay Bird's daughter would have been reason enough for any member of the Straight Path nation to kill the girl. Let's forget about her and concentrate on Cloud Play—"

"To kill her *and* her child," Ironwood said. "Especially if the baby had been a girl. The next matron of the Mogollon people? Blessed gods. Holding that child slave here in Talon Town would have been very dangerous. How is it that Young Fawn's pregnancy went unnoticed for so many moons? I never knew about it. Did you, Sternlight?" He paused. "If Young Fawn was Solstice Girl, you must have—"

"No." The answer was barely audible. "No, I—I didn't know."

"How could you *not* have known? She—"

"It was winter," Dune said brusquely. "She would have been wearing many layers of clothing. If she'd wished to keep her pregnancy hidden, she could have."

"But—"

"Let it go, Ironwood!"

Heat flushed Ironwood's veins. He glanced between them. "What are you two hiding from me? What's—"

"Ironwood," Sternlight said, his voice suddenly cutting, "I had far more important things to worry about at the time. Let us concentrate on Cloud Playing, and who might have wished *her* dead."

The tone stunned Ironwood. He'd never heard Sternlight speak in such . . . and then he understood.

Hallowed Ancestors, of course he'd had more important worries. Cornsilk was born less than a moon after Winter Solstice. Sternlight wouldn't have taken notice of a slave. Except for attending to ritual mandates, he spent all day, every day, with

Night Sun, caring for her, talking with her, trying to ease her fears . . .

"Forgive me." Ironwood tilted his head apologetically to Sternlight. "You're right. Let's worry about Cloud Playing."

Sternlight seemed relieved.

Dune let out a breath.

They all sat in silence for several moments.

"Yes," Dune said softly, as if to himself, "we must help him end the pain."

Ironwood gave the old holy man a sidelong glance. "I would be happy to, Dune. Swiftly. And forever."

Dune scowled. "Are you tired?"

"Very."

Dune nodded. "I think we're all tired. Why don't we discuss this tomorrow. When our souls can see more clearly." Dune braced his hand on Ironwood's shoulder and rose to his feet with a grunt. "Can both of you meet me here at dawn?"

"I can." Ironwood rubbed his grainy eyes.

Sternlight nodded. "I'll be here."

"A pleasant night to you, then." Dune climbed the stairs.

Ironwood waited until his footsteps died away, then fixed Sternlight with an inquiring look. Sternlight didn't look at him. Firelight coated the left side of his face and shimmered in his long black hair.

Ironwood opened his mouth to ask his friend some pointed questions . . .

But Sternlight said, "How did Night Sun take the news? Is she all right? I know I should have been the one to tell her, but I had so many religious responsibilities—"

"I'm glad you asked me to tell her." Ironwood inhaled a breath, left off balance by the sudden change of topics. His thoughts returned to Night Sun, to the haunted look on her beautiful face, the terror in her eyes. "She's reeling, Sternlight. I held her until the guard forced me to leave, but by then she was fast asleep. She needs time to work through the past half moon. First she loses her husband, then her daughter . . . she's soul-sick."

Sternlight exhaled hard. "Tomorrow will make it worse."

"How is that?"

The wind had risen to a constant shriek outside, and Ironwood could hear sand rattling on the buildings. Sternlight looked up the staircase, as if dreading the cold that awaited him when he emerged from this warm, firelit womb.

Sternlight said, "Snake Head caught me just before I came here. He told me that he will decide his mother's fate tomorrow. He's calling a gathering of the Straight Path elders. Be ready, Ironwood. There is no telling what that angry young man has in mind."

"Will I be invited to the proceedings? I'm not one of the First People, nor am I War Chief. I have no authority to ask."

"I will request that you be Night Sun's guard. Snake Head may accept. He may not. If he does not, you will accompany me, as *my* guard."

"I'll be ready."

"Good. Until then." Sternlight rose, touched Ironwood's shoulder as he passed, and climbed the stairs.

Ironwood sat quietly.

Too many things had happened for him to sort them out.

He needed to lay his own plans. The elders might condemn Night Sun to death, and if they did, he had to have a way of getting her out of Talon Town. . . .

Sternlight's white ritual shirt gleamed as he walked across the empty plaza in the starlight. Talon Town curled around him like a gigantic embracing arm. The sounds of people coughing and snoring, infants whimpering, and dogs growling at unusual night sounds filled the air. In one of the chambers, someone played a flute. The sweet lilting notes wavered over the town like the glitter of fine jewels. He tried to concentrate on the soothing melody, but failed. Though a cedar-scented wind caressed his face, he smelled only the blood on his clothing. Coppery. Sickening.

No one stood outside, not after seeing Cloud Playing's mutilated body this afternoon. They didn't dare. Witchcraft! The slaves had performed their duties and dashed for home. The Made People had spent most of the evening in their kivas discussing the horror.

He could feel the fear, like a palpable, breathing thing.

As Sternlight reached the first ladder soft voices drifted up from the roof holes of the kivas. Someone mentioned his name, then: *"Did you see . . . corpse powder? . . . everywhere. Witches hide . . . come out to steal peoples' souls."*

Sternlight climbed faster, trying not to think, not even to breathe until he reached his chamber.

When he ducked beneath his door curtain, he quickly dropped it and sank against the wall. Sweat stung his eyes. Starglow streamed through the window on the rear wall and threw a long silver rectangle across the floor. Absently, he focused on the tiny shadowed undulations of the plaster, not really seeing them, seeing only the horrifying sights of the day he'd just lived through.

In a whisper, he asked, "Oh, Cloud Playing, what happened?"

With frightening tenderness, he touched each spot of her blood that dotted the lower half of his shirt.

"My friend . . ."

She had been kind to him, treating him more like a brother than a distant cousin.

Though he'd washed his hands a dozen times, red crescents curved beneath the fingernails. The nauseating smell of yucca soap mixed with old blood burned his nose. Clenching his hands to fists, he shook them at some inner foe.

"Blessed gods, *what happened?"*

Voices called to him. The thlatsina masks that crowded the walls had been plaguing him for days, calling and calling, but he could not make out their words, as if their voices traveled over a great distance. He noted that dust coated their faces. One of Swallowtail's duties was to dust the masks. The youth had not been doing his job.

Sternlight frowned at the masks. Dark-furred muzzles and beaked faces gazed back, eerie, somehow haunting. "Can you speak louder? I've been trying very hard to understand you, but I can't."

The Badger mask seemed to be screaming at him. He shook his head. Dogs made sounds that humans couldn't hear, he knew, because he'd watched them closely all of his life. A dog would stand up, lift its head, and its throat muscles would move silently, but a sleeping dog across the plaza would wake and prick its ears. Were the thlatsinas calling to him in voices too low for him to hear?

"A truly Powerful priest would be able to hear you," he whispered.

The Badger Thlatsina's blue slits of eyes seemed to glow. Sternlight swallowed convulsively.

"Please, can you speak to me in a human tongue?"

Closing his eyes, Sternlight concentrated on *listening*. A tingle shot through him, and he jerked his eyes wide to stare at the Badger mask. . . . Not words, but a hoarse guttural cry of rage.

"What *is* it?"

His belly threatened to empty itself. He had walked into his chamber two nights ago, returning from performing a Healing on Featherstone's aching hip—which he did about once a moon—and surprised Mourning Dove. She'd let out a shocked squeak, dropped the tray of corncakes she'd been carrying, and breathlessly explained, "Forgive me, Blessed Sunwatcher. Creeper thought you might be hungry after Singing for Featherstone."

The Badger mask had been lying on the floor behind her, canted sideways, peering at Sternlight with hollow eyes.

"What happened?" he'd demanded, quickly going to the mask to rehang it on its peg in the wall. The wood felt damp.

Eyes huge, she'd exclaimed that she'd noticed how dirty it was and tried to clean it with a wet rag. In the process, she'd accidentally knocked it to the floor. The heavy wooden mask weighed as much as a small child. Mourning Dove apologized that she hadn't had the strength to lift it back up.

Sternlight shook his fists in frustration. He walked to his sleeping mats, not bothering to undress, and stretched out on top of his blankets, staring at the rectangle of starlight that stretched across the white plastered floor.

"Thlatsinas, please, help me to understand."

When he closed his eyes and curled on his side, sweet inaudible voices whispered in his ears . . . like butterfly wings brushing against his soul, just barely there, not quite real.

Strange images flitted through his dreams: Cloud Playing Dancing with the Badger Thlatsina . . . a fiery blue cave filled with black water . . . a beautiful young woman . . . her face coated with blood.

Twenty-Nine

Webworm stood in the doorway of Chief Snake Head's chamber, waiting for Mourning Dove to leave. She knelt near the macaw's cage, her tan-and-white dress dragging the plastered floor as she gathered and folded the Chief's soiled clothes, then tucked them into her black wash sack. The macaw kept an eye on her while it ate sunflower seeds. Each time the bird cocked its head, its magnificent red, yellow, and blue feathers flashed wildly. The sound of cracking hulls grated on Webworm's frayed nerves. He clutched his bloody pack against his chest and shifted to brace his feet. Heart sore, aching from the bruises he'd acquired in the battle, and desperately weary, he wished this were over. He wanted to go home and speak with his mother. Perhaps they would tell stories about Cloud Playing . . . and he could hear her laughter again in his soul.

Webworm straightened when Snake Head whispered something. The Chief stood on the far side of the room, stroking the Badger Thlatsina's muzzled face. The black painted figure contrasted eerily with the white wall; its red-and-white striped muzzle gleamed in the crimson light cast by the warming bowl. Snake Head murmured, "Yes, I know . . . it's all right."

Webworm and Mourning Dove exchanged a glance, but neither said a word.

Mourning Dove finished putting clothing in her wash sack and rose to her feet. The macaw let out a low menacing whistle, but she didn't look at it. "Is there anything else you require of me, Blessed Snake Head?"

Snake Head let his hand fall to his side. "No," he answered

without looking at her. His long yellow robe swayed with his movements. "Not tonight. You may go."

Mourning Dove bowed respectfully and rushed by Webworm. He saw her dash across the rooftop for the ladder, probably wishing to get away as quickly as possible, in case Snake Head changed his mind.

Webworm inhaled a breath and held it in his lungs to fortify himself.

Snake Head turned and gave Webworm a haughty, irritated look. "What is it, War Chief?" When he tilted his head, his long eyelashes threw shadows over his cheeks. He wore his black hair loose tonight, and it hung to the middle of his chest. As though a fine patina of copper coated his straight nose and large dark eyes, they shone with an orange hue.

Webworm carefully removed the grisly prize from his pack and unwrapped the layers of bloody cloth. The fabric had mashed the boy's nose to the side and pressed his mouth into a frozen cry. Blood clotted tangled hair to his cheeks. "As you instructed, Blessed Snake Head, I killed the boy. Here is the proof."

Snake Head crossed the room with a smirk on his handsome face. He scrutinized the severed head. "He doesn't look anything like my mother. Odd, isn't it?"

Webworm longed to blurt out his suspicions that Sternlight had tricked them all, but he merely nodded and extended the prize to Snake Head. "He is yours, my chief."

Snake Head took a step backward and flicked a hand uncomfortably. "Put it on the floor. I don't wish to touch it until it's been cleaned and purified."

Webworm knelt and eased the head down. Memories floated in his mind—happy times around Beargrass' fire, the wide-eyed little boy listening to the exploits of warriors. *Forgive me, little one. My fault . . . all my fault.*

"And what did Beargrass have to say for himself?" Snake Head asked.

Webworm stood. "He maintained until the very end that the boy was his son. He—"

"Well, that's to be expected," Snake Head interrupted. "I assume you taught him the price for betraying the Blessed Sun?"

"He is dead, yes."

"And the rest of the village?"

"Burned. I left no witnesses—at least none we could catch. A few people escaped, but not many."

Snake Head laughed gleefully. "Oh, I can't wait until my mother hears the news. Perhaps I shall tell her myself, just to see her face. Do you think she truly believed she could hide the child forever?"

Webworm shrugged. "I cannot say, my chief."

"Well, she will also pay the price for her treachery." Snake Head narrowed his eyes like a hawk about to sink its talons into prey. He glared down at the boy's head. "I'll see her *dead* for this outrage."

"But . . ." Webworm's mouth gaped. "She's your *mother*, Snake Head."

"Yes, well, of that I'm certain, but as to who my father was, I'll probably never really know."

Webworm's gaze went over Snake Head's face in detail, tracing the arching brows, straight nose, and oval shape. Snake Head looked so much like Crow Beard that, if thirty summers had not separated them, they might have been twins. How could he make such a ridiculous statement?

Snake Head must have sensed Webworm's incredulity, because he lifted his chin and ordered, "Go away, War Chief. I have many things to think about besides you."

"Yes, I—I know." Webworm bowed his head. "My heart aches with you over the loss of your sister. She—"

"Yes, yes, of course it does." Snake Head turned on his heel and walked away to kneel before the glowing coals in his warming bowl.

Webworm backed out of the chamber. Starlight, reflected from the white walls of Talon Town, threw a pale bluish gleam over the cliff. He walked toward the ladder. Every muscle in his body hurt. He rubbed his tender shoulder. Beargrass had struck him with a war club before Webworm could lift his arm to deflect the blow. Deep fiery pain throbbed in the swollen lump; Webworm feared the blow might actually have cracked a bone. As he climbed down the ladders to the first-story roof, he inhaled the rich scent of frying corncakes.

Webworm walked around the curving roof line until he reached his mother's chambers. The ladder thrust up through the roof hole. He stepped onto the first rung, and heard Creeper say: "Oh, Blessed Featherstone, let me help you with that."

Webworm knew that tone. He couldn't help but close his eyes briefly before he climbed down into the soft red light and stepped to the hide-covered floor.

Thlatsinas danced around the walls, leaping and spinning in time to some eternal drum that Webworm had never been able to hear. A tripod held a pot of tea suspended over the bowl of coals in the middle of the floor. The sweet fragrance of spruce needle tea rose. Corncakes and a bowl of pink-spotted beans sat near the coals, keeping warm.

His mother leaned in the northwestern corner, to his right, wearing a turkey-feather cape over her dress, her jaw slack, eyes focused on nothing. Gray hair straggled around her shoulders and framed her wrinkled face. Her prominent nose shimmered with beads of sweat.

Creeper sat next to her with a bowl of beans in one hand and a horn spoon in the other. Judging from the bean juice dribbling down Featherstone's chin, he'd been trying to feed her.

Webworm looked away. Seeing his mother like this always brought him pain. How could a woman who had spoken to Sister Moon in the sparkling voice of a meteor have come to this end? Webworm would have given anything to go back to that time when the Fire Dogs had ambushed her. He would have killed every one of them with his bare hands—though it meant he'd never have been born.

"How long has she been like this?" he asked.

Creeper said, "Two or three hands of time."

"What brought it on?"

"Who can say? We were speaking about witches and witchcraft. Featherstone was telling me about the witches Jay Bird executed when she lived among his people as a slave." He made a helpless gesture with the spoon. The red glow coated Creeper's plump face and flickered through his chin-length black hair. Short and pudgy, Creeper wore a buffalo cape around his shoulders. The kinky fur glittered with crimson highlights when he moved. "She just . drifted away."

Webworm sank to the floor near the bowl of coals and gestured to the food. "Is this mine?"

"Yes. I made supper right after I brought Featherstone back. I hope the corncakes are still warm."

"Doesn't matter. Thank you, Creeper." Webworm picked up the bowl and spoon and began shoveling the delicious beans into his mouth. The image of Cloud Playing's face drifted in his soul, seeking to break loose and drown him with grief.

No, not yet. Keep it at bay, just a little longer. Weary relief filtered through his empty belly as it filled.

Creeper put another spoon of beans into Featherstone's open mouth. After a few moments, she chewed and swallowed, though her unfocused eyes never moved. When her mouth gaped again and bean juice ran down her chin, Creeper lifted a piece of cloth from his lap and wiped her chin, saying, "That was good, Featherstone. Try to eat another bite." And he lifted the spoon to her lips again.

Webworm finished his beans and picked up a corncake. It was cold, but good, flavored with dried bits of prickly pear fruit. He leaned back against the wall and extended his muscular legs across the soft deerhides. Webworm had watched Creeper feed Featherstone hundreds of times. Why did it still disturb him?

"You spoke with Snake Head?" Creeper asked as he ladled another spoonful into Featherstone's mouth and waited for her to chew.

"If that's what you call it." Webworm finished his corncake and reached for another. Chewing slowly, he swallowed and added, "He didn't have much to say. I gave him the boy's head and he . . . he laughed, Creeper." Webworm let his head fall back against the wall and stared up at the stars visible through the roof entry. He lowered the cake to his lap. He'd yet to change clothes, and old blood stiffened the fabric of his red shirt. He felt dirty—in many ways.

"It's not your fault." Creeper glanced sympathetically at Webworm. "You are the new War Chief. You had no choice."

Webworm's eyes tightened. "Maybe," he murmured. "I'm not so sure. I think Ironwood would have asked for more proof before he went off to slaughter an entire village. I—I didn't even consider questioning the order."

And had I been here, perhaps Cloud Playing would still be alive. He struggled to force his thoughts away from her torn body. He should go to her, be there for her through the night. He pinched his eyes closed, afraid tears would betray his attempt at self control.

Creeper dabbed at the juice on Featherstone's chin again. "When the great priest Sternlight tells people that something is true, who dares to doubt it?"

"*I do!*" Webworm replied sharply, happy to strike out. "He's a liar, Creeper. You know it! Why did we believe him? My cousin is wicked! He's never told the truth in his entire life. Yet all he has to do is say Night Sun's child lives in Lanceleaf Village and warriors go to find the boy and kill him. . . . What's the matter with us?" In a frail voice, he asked, "Have we all lost our souls?"

Creeper placed the horn spoon in the empty bowl and set them aside. His calm brown eyes peered at Webworm. "No one has ever found evidence of Sternlight's wickedness, or he would have been killed for witchery many summers ago. Until such evidence comes to light, most people will continue to revere him as a great priest—and believe him."

Exhausted, disheartened, Webworm smiled and bowed his head, resting his chin on his chest. "Yes, yes."

Creeper leaned forward and dipped up two cups of tea. He handed one to Webworm, who took it gratefully.

"I'm sorry, Creeper," Webworm said. "I know you do not relish hearing me complain all the time, but I—"

"You have good reasons." Creeper leaned against the wall beside Featherstone and drank his tea. "May I ask you a question, though?"

Webworm looked up. "Of course."

Creeper's bushy black brows drew together over his small nose. "Do you recall the rumors in Talon Town about sixteen summers ago?"

"You mean about Night Sun being pregnant? Yes, I recall, but I never believed them."

Creeper frowned down into his cup of tea. "I didn't either, not fully. But after the accusations Crow Beard made just before he died, I began asking questions."

"Of whom?"

"The slaves." Creeper looked up and gave Webworm a stern look. "Mourning Dove was one of Night Sun's chamber slaves when the Matron became 'ill' while Crow Beard traded with the Hohokam."

Webworm shifted to lean his right shoulder against the wall, taking the pressure from his aching left shoulder. The pain had grown fiery. "So?"

Creeper glanced at Featherstone, as if worried that she might hear their conversation. He lowered his voice and said, "Mourning Dove told me that Night Sun had not bled in four or five moons. One of Mourning Dove's duties was to wash and dry Night Sun's bleeding cloths."

"And there weren't any during that time?"

Creeper shook his head. "None."

"Perhaps she asked another slave to take care of them."

Creeper glanced at Featherstone again. "Perhaps, but I suspect Night Sun *was* pregnant, and that she bore a child."

Webworm massaged his forehead. The ache behind his eyes pounded in time to his heartbeat. Weariness, mixed with his grief over Cloud Playing, had drained his strength. He longed to sleep. "I don't care anymore, Creeper. Even if she did—"

"Do you think it might have been a girl?"

Webworm glanced up. Deep lines carved Creeper's plump face. He looked almost . . . frightened. "You mean you think Sternlight lied to shield the real child?"

"I think he might have." Creeper set his teacup down on the deerhides and laced his fingers over his ample belly. "The only thing I can't figure is . . ."

Featherstone suddenly leaned forward and heaved a tired sigh as though she'd been running for moons, and only just found a resting place. "You know why, don't you?" she asked.

Webworm's soul sank. Her eyes were still vacant. Only her voice spoke.

"No, Featherstone," Creeper said gently. "Why?"

"He's doing it for me."

Webworm fumbled with his hands. Sometimes she droned on and on, speaking nonsense for hands of time without stopping.

Creeper brushed gray hair away from her face, and said, "Why is that, Featherstone?"

"Because!" she shouted. "He knows I am the rightful clan Matron!"

"I see," Creeper said with a smile.

"No, you don't!" she spat. "None of you do! But *he* does."

Something in the way she'd said it made Webworm go cold inside. He stared at his mother. As though the words had taken every bit of her energy, she wilted, her muscles going slack. Creeper grabbed her before she could topple sideways and helped her to lie down on her sleeping mats. He pulled the blankets up around Featherstone's throat and gently kissed her forehead.

"Sleep well, Blessed Featherstone," he whispered, and patted her shoulder.

In a curiously detached voice, Webworm said, "Snake Head told me he's going to kill his mother."

Creeper jerked around to look at him in shock. "Even if she did bear a child, none of the First People leaders will wish her dead! I know it!"

Webworm rubbed his aching shoulder, feeling sick to his stomach. "I pray you're right. But which of them will have the courage to defy the new Blessed Sun?"

Creeper shifted to sit cross-legged on the hides and his shoulders slumped forward. After thinking for a time, Creeper said, "Why don't you sleep, Webworm. There's nothing we can do about any of this tonight. And you've had enough blows in the last few days. I'll sit up for a time and watch over Featherstone."

Webworm gave Creeper a warm look. During her "vacant" episodes, she often choked after eating. At these times, she couldn't raise herself to swallow or get a breath, so someone had to be there for her. "I thank the Spirits that you came into our lives, Creeper. I don't know what we would have done without you."

Creeper smiled. "Get some sleep, War Chief."

Webworm nodded and stretched out on his side on the soft hides. His limbs felt like granite.

He heard Creeper rise and felt a blanket being draped over his shoulders. Webworm could not count the number of times Creeper had done that . . . and no matter what troubled him, that kindness always eased the pain.

Creeper returned to sit at the head of Featherstone's sleeping mats, and pulled an exquisite malachite figurine and a quartzite graver from beneath his cape. He sat there in the crimson glow, carving quietly. But worry creased his forehead.

Sleep overwhelmed Webworm almost immediately.

. . . And he found himself back on the mesa top. Morning sunlight slanted down, splashing the tan stone with warmth, waking him where he lay rolled in the blanket with Cloud Playing. At his movements, she woke and smiled up at him. Love and joy filled her eyes. They had loved each other for the first time that night. Black hair spread around her beautiful face in a dark halo. He touched it reverently and bent to kiss her . . .

Creeper sat beside Featherstone long into the night, as he had a hundred times, listening to the broken words she spoke—words that left him numb:

"Voices shouting . . . pain. Pain in my heart. Young woman . . . village burning . . . coming . . . to hurt me . . . she brings such pain . . . on the back of a bear. She's riding a huge bear!"

"The same girl?" he asked softly. "The one you saw last moon?"

Featherstone's dark eyes opened wide, staring at something Creeper could not see. It terrified her. She started to shiver. Tenderly, he pulled the blanket up and tucked it about her wrinkled throat.

"I won't let her hurt you, Featherstone," he said softly. Then he glanced at where Webworm slept and cupped a hand to Featherstone's ear to whisper, "And what about me? Do you see anything about me?"

Her lips moved.

Creeper bent down, leaning so close his ear almost touched her mouth.

". . . *The dead,*" she murmured. "*They're calling for you.*"

Fifth Day

The dead do not go away.

I sit cross-legged on the flat stone, my naked body cold in the dawn wind that whispers through the stunted pines. Father Sun sleeps below the eastern horizon, but a soft blue gleam sheaths the world. I gaze out across an infinite vista of purple ridges. They twist across the land like knotted lengths of cloth. As I watch, the silver Traders of the Evening People—the last falling stars—fly down to bargain with Our Mother Earth.

All day I have been desperately lonely, missing my mother and father, my friends, and I fear loneliness. It is not Silent. Loneliness overflows with the wrenching cries of my own suffering and the suffering of the world.

For a time, I thought I might go mad from those cries.

Then I heard my name whispered. Softly. Barely audible.

The dead did not call to me from the underworlds, but spoke to me from the rustling pine needles. They did not gaze down upon me from the skyworlds, but smiled up at me from a bead of dew trembling precariously upon a blade of grass.

They told me I have never been alone. Not for one instant.

Every soul is a thread in the fabric of the world. All I must do to see my relatives is gaze into the shining water that sleeps, and the grasses that weep. The Dances of the dead are motes of light, their voices sighing rocks.

My loved ones are all around me.

As I turn to face the east, I see the dead in the light that is coming alive. They climb over the rocky horizon like a sparkling golden tribe, and run across the face of the land, ruffling the grass, playing in the swaying pines.

I shiver and wonder at my own blindness.

Death is a silent, attentive partner in everything alive.

Of course the dead do not go away. They are the cloth that binds up the wounds of the world.

. . . My wounds.

Thirty

Cornsilk walked the rocky mesa rim with her arms out for balance, placing her yucca sandals carefully to avoid the thorny patches of cactus. Father Sun slipped behind a butte in the west, and a glistening halo engulfed the red tower of stone. The Cloud People blazed, brilliant orange puffs that glided through a sea of turquoise blue. Shadows lengthened across the rumpled land, cutting through brush-filled drainages and twining with the eroded rust and yellow beds of clay. Cornsilk smiled and hugged herself. Wind Baby gusted out of the north, whimpering and fluttering her long hair over her shoulders. Poor Singer said they would reach Talon Town tomorrow. She wanted to enjoy this evening of freedom. She might not have many more.

Basking in the warmth of the fading sunlight soothed her. She took her time, picking up sharp flakes of chert and obsidian left by a man who'd sat on this rim and knapped out stone tools sometime in the past. The exposed sandstone ledges made good places to sit and watch the surrounding country. A seep of water glistened at the base of the mesa, filled with cattails and three stunted pines. Poor Singer crouched in their camp at the edge of the water. He had a fire going and a teapot and boiling pot set up.

She would go down soon to help him with supper. But not just yet. For a while longer, she wanted to feel the wind through her hair and let the infinitely scoured vista beat life into her veins. She wanted to think.

Over the past few days, she had been struggling to piece together the things her mother and father had said, and the things she'd heard Webworm claim on the night of Lanceleaf's destruction. She could look at the events a little more clearly now and see the flaws to her original conclusions. Webworm *had* come looking for a boy, and he *had* said that Night Sun was the mother. Then he'd accused Sternlight of being Fledgling's father. In fact, Webworm had sounded convinced of it. But as the great Sunwatcher of Talon Town, Sternlight would have known about the order to kill Fledgling. He could have sent a messenger to warn Beargrass. Or hired someone to send signals down the roads. But he hadn't. Why would Sternlight have let his son die? The First People had great resources. He *could* have intervened.

The only answer that made sense to her was that Sternlight had not feared the outcome of the battle. Someone, somehow, had managed to deceive Webworm into killing a boy . . . to protect a girl. That's why no warning had come. Her mother had told her the truth.

And it left her weak and reeling.

If Sternlight turned out to be a witch, what would she do? She couldn't reveal herself to a witch. And what of Night Sun? Dead? Murdered for the crime of incest? Or banished?

She rubbed the toe of her sandal over a brightly colored rock. Perhaps Night Sun would wish her dead because she was the child of an incestuous union. Maybe that's why she'd sent Cornsilk away in the beginning. She'd hated the sight of her misbegotten child. . . .

Poor Singer watched her from camp. Silk walked with her head down, hair flying, her long tanned legs shining in the amber dusk. Her green dress was sleek upon her slender body, but she looked sad.

"She needs time alone," he murmured to the pines that swayed around him. "Time to heal."

She might put up a brave and courageous front, but deep in her eyes lay a terrible desolation of the soul that worried him. Only a moon had passed since the destruction of her village. It would probably take several more before the grief dimmed.

I pray she finds family in Talon Town. That they give her a place and a new family. Though he had to admit, he would miss her very much when they parted ways. Despite her inner turmoil, she managed to keep him smiling. But he was attracted to more than her beauty and sense of humor. Power lived inside her, hidden deep, like Thunderbird sleeping in a billowing nest of clouds, and Poor Singer had the feeling that when the Power woke . . . it would tremble the skyworlds.

He stretched out on his side in the red sand. He'd thrown their blankets out on a moss-covered area beneath the largest pine, but built the fire two body-lengths away, in a scooped hollow in the sand, to shield the flames from the wind. Pine needles scattered the ground and glinted in the bottom of the tiny pool. Cool, clear water gurgled up from a crevice in the red sandstone, and created a tiny marsh about ten hands across. The cattails had just sprouted. Green leaves poked up through the water.

The three pines leaned eastward, slanted by the prevailing winds. No wonder the western face of the low mesa had a scrubbed look. Jutting knuckles of stone tipped skyward, and deep furrows sliced down through the tan-and-red soil. On a flat sandstone face above the seep, a water being watched him. Carved into the stone by an expert hand, the being had a spiral face with a headdress of sunbeams and a square body. Its jagged arms imitated lightning bolts.

Poor Singer picked up a stick and prodded the fire. Sparks jumped and twisted away in the wind. Spirits lived here. Poor Singer could sense them breathing all around him.

He lowered his gaze to the struggling flames and said a silent prayer, thanking the Spirits for allowing him and Silk to spend the night. Pine boughs shished and rocked in response.

With a deer scapula, Poor Singer scooped more hot coals around the charred base of their boiling pot, then reached for his pack and removed the small bag of beeweed mixed with dried onions. He dumped the contents into the pot. When it started to bubble, he added a handful of cornmeal and stirred the gruel with a wooden paddle. He'd laid out their cups, bowls, and two horn spoons in preparation for supper.

He'd been feeling oddly—like a bit of eagle down whipped by gale force winds. During the long days of his fast, something had happened inside him. Though he could not say exactly when the change had been accomplished, he'd grown whole and unafraid. As if, in the blink of an eye, his soul had aged and ripened. He wondered if he'd grown the heart of a cloud without realizing it—and if he could now walk on the wind. He rubbed his fingers in the warm sand, thinking, wishing he knew what that meant. His father had not visited him in his dreams for half a moon, though he had run the sacred trail to the lip of the turquoise cave and bravely peered into the darkness. He'd respected the Keeper of the Tortoise Bundle's wishes and stayed outside . . . but he wanted to smell the high mountain pine trees, and watch the tiny clouds puffing from the entrance and floating up to join their relatives. Once, he had even dared to call to the woman inside, but she had not answered.

Poor Singer dipped himself a cup of pine needle tea, and braced himself on one elbow to drink. As he tasted the tangy brew, he saw Silk descending the game trail that slithered down the side of the mesa. She walked slowly, as if deep in thought. Long black hair flew around her beautiful face. Her golden skin was lavender in the twilight glow. She ducked beneath the limbs of a pine and smiled at him, but he could see the haunted look in her eyes. Her vulnerabilities lay as exposed as the rocks on the scoured mesa. No woman had ever looked at him the way she did—as though he were the only friend she had in the entire world. It made him feel strangely good.

Poor Singer smiled back. "The gruel is done. I hope you're hungry. I made enough for five people." He leaned forward to stir the thick corn mush with his paddle.

Silk knelt before the teapot and dipped her cup full. "I'm hungry enough to chew bark off a pine. We walked a long way today." She sat down cross-legged on the sand beside him and sighed. In the flickering light of the flames, her green dress turned a dark orange. "How are you feeling?"

"Pretty wobbly. Exhausted, actually."

"It takes time to get your strength back after a fast."

Poor Singer nodded agreement and used his horn spoon to fill their bowls with gruel. His fingers brushed hers lightly as he handed her one. "It came out thick. I hope it tastes good."

Silk sniffed her bowl. "It smells delicious, Poor Singer. Thank you for fixing supper while I was up walking in the wind.

I know I should have been down here helping you."

"I'm glad you took time to walk. You looked happy up there."

She gave him a soft smile that touched his heart. "For a few moments, I was."

"Besides," he said, "I like cooking. At home, in Windflower Village, I used to cook supper for my mother. I miss it—and her."

Silk picked up her horn spoon and began eating, but her eyes tensed. She chewed slowly, her gaze on the fire's brassy reflection where it danced among the green cattail stems. Old pine cones littered the bottom of the pool, canted at angles on a bed of shining white, black, and tan pebbles.

She's thinking about her own mother. Poor Singer suffered a pang of guilt for reminding her. He spooned corn gruel into his mouth and watched the clouds change from orange to dark grayish purple. The beeweed and onions gave the cornmeal a savory flavor.

As evening deepened, Wind Baby calmed down to a faint whisper, soughing through the pines and rustling the grass. Ripples bobbed across the firelit surface of the pool.

They ate in silence, Silk staring at something he could not see. Poor Singer watched her from the corner of his eye.

She finished her gruel, set her bowl aside, and drew up her legs. Wrapping her arms around them, she propped her chin on her knees. Long hair draped around her like a shining black curtain.

To take his mind from the longings she stirred within his traitorous body, Poor Singer said, "You seem far away."

"Um . . . I guess I am."

"What are you thinking about?"

Silk rubbed her chin on the fabric covering her knees and tilted her head to look at him. Her broad cheekbones and pointed nose caught the gleam of the fire. "Poor Singer, do you miss your friends?"

He used his spoon to scrape the last gruel from the bottom of his bowl. After he'd swallowed, he sat quietly for a time, then answered, "I didn't have any friends, Silk. At least, not my own age."

Her graceful eyebrows lifted. "Not even one?"

"My mother and Black Mesa were my friends. But—but that was all." Poor Singer picked up his teacup and turned it in his hands.

Silk's gaze searched his expression. "But you're so likable, Poor Singer. It doesn't make sense. Why didn't you have friends your own age?"

"Oh, I don't know. Black Mesa said they didn't understand the Power in my eyes, but I always believed it was because I couldn't do anything the other children considered important." He frowned at the dregs in his teacup. Actually, he couldn't do anything anyone considered important, except Sing. His deep resonant voice had brought him renown . . . but not friends.

Silk shifted, and he looked up. Behind her, dark clouds sailed over the pointed tops of the pine trees, silent as the shadows of the gods. The night animals had begun to prowl. The lilting howls of hunting coyotes echoed.

"What couldn't you do?" Silk asked.

Poor Singer smiled, amused at himself. "Well, first off, my stone tools resembled the fumbling efforts of a five-summers-old boy; every girl in the village could outrun me; I couldn't hit a quail with a rock if I was standing on top of the bird; every time I got into a fight, my opponent beat me senseless. And I was trying to win, Silk." She smiled, and he went on, "But more than that, I think the other children didn't like me because I was such a loner. I always preferred the company of insects and prickly pear to that of people."

Silk's eyes seemed to grow deeper and darker, shining like huge black moons. A young man could lose himself in those eyes, and never wish to be found. A tingle ran through Poor Singer's body and settled in all the wrong places—at least wrong according to Dune's teachings. He could hear the little tyrant's voice in his soul, "If you ever wish to be a wellspring of hope for your people, you must let go of your body. Flesh may feel soft and warm, but it is the most Powerful cage in Creation. Stronger than stone walls twenty hands thick. Let it go. . . ."

Feeling awkward, Poor Singer smiled and looked away. Perhaps that's why he'd been lonely most of his life: he needed to be.

Silk's gaze drifted to the sky. The first Evening People had wakened, and silver sparkles filled the night. From this side view, she looked all the more delicate and beautiful. A log snapped in the fire, and the flash threaded her face and hair with crimson light.

Silk's toes curled against the soles of her sandals. She continued to look up at the starry sky. "I like being alone, too."

"Do you?"

"Well, not all the time. Usually I like being close to people, but when I need to be alone, I need it like a starving woman needs food."

It had never occurred to him that anyone else in the world had ever sought solitude with the same single-minded passion that he had. "It's hard, isn't it?" He met her eyes. "To really *be* alone. I mean, even when you are by yourself, you are generally thinking of other people and so you're really not alone in your soul."

A breath of wind fluttered her long black hair against her back. "It's hard. Mostly because clans discourage solitude. There are so many people that someone is always trying to get you to gather another basket of ricegrass seeds, or fill a pot with water, or grind more corn. If you ever escape to sit on a hilltop just to listen to the canyon wrens, people scold you for wasting time. They tell you you've been bad, that you're shirking your duties and should be ashamed." She gazed at him solemnly. "That's why a friend is so important, Poor Singer. A friend acts as a shield for you. She makes sure you get to sit on hilltops now and then."

"I've never thought of it that way. It never occurred to me that another person could understand my soul so well. Did you have a friend like that, Silk?"

Tears welled in her eyes. "Yes, I did."

Poor Singer longed to touch her to ease that pain, but instead he gripped his teacup hard. "What was her name?"

"Leafhopper. I—I miss her."

"Was she killed in the attack?"

"I don't know. Leafhopper lived with her aunt at the corner of the village near the gate. The enemy warriors would have struck there first—wouldn't they?"

Poor Singer bit his lip. "I can't say, Silk. I've never been on a raid."

"I think they would have." Silk wiped her eyes with the back of her hand . . . and a warm wave of fear eddied through him.

Poor Singer sat up, his mouth open. As though he were falling into the first underworld again, lightheaded nausea tormented him. Fatigue from too much exertion after his fast? Or something else? A horrible premonition?

He sipped more tea to settle his stomach. "Silk? Do you remember when you first climbed down the stairs by Dune's house and I said I thought I knew you?"

A frown incised her forehead. "Yes."

"I know where I saw you."

She tucked hair behind her ears and tilted her head. "We've never met, Poor Singer. I would have remembered."

"No . . . not in this world."

Their gazes held.

Silk said, "You saw me in another world?"

He swallowed the lump in his throat. "When I went through the kiva initiation to become a Singer . . . you were there with me. I still don't understand it—but as I fell into the flames, you fell with me."

"Flames?"

Poor Singer nodded. Uneasy, he turned and sat cross-legged facing her. He leaned forward, peering directly into her soul, and said, "In the First Underworld, the Soot World, I saw a crystal pillar. It changed from black to blue, then, as if the tunnel to the underworld had been pierced by an unseen shaft of light, the blue turned a magnificent shade of turquoise. Thousands of falling stars cascaded down like fiery white sparks. Then the crystal caught fire and blazed, devouring the sky. But . . . but in the midst of the flames, I saw you, Silk. You were crying." He lifted a hand to touch her silken hair. "As you were just now. Long black hair tumbled over your shoulders. And behind you—" Poor Singer stopped suddenly as understanding dawned. A strange hollowness invaded his breast. "Blessed Ancestors, the jagged mountain peak that I saw behind you was the peak where the turquoise cave hides." Stunned by the realization, he sat perfectly still, his gaze locked with hers.

"What is the turquoise cave?"

"Oh, it's beautiful, Silk. It's . . . well, I don't know how to describe it, but it's like being inside a turquoise geode in a lightning storm." His brows arched at the inadequacy of the description. "When the storm is inside the geode with you," he added lamely, "it's *magical.*"

Silk folded her legs under her and shifted to face him. She braced a hand and said, "Was I in the cave with you?"

"No." He shook his head. "Just in the fiery pillar."

"Did we burn up?"

"No. The next thing I knew, we were walking through the Soot World together. . . ." His voice faded as the memory returned. Now that he knew Silk had been the young woman in the vision, it changed everything. "We were holding hands. Walking among giant trees, talking with the ghosts. . . . Until I found my father. Then you vanished." Poor Singer lowered his hand to his lap. "I never saw you again in the vision. The rest of the time I spent walking and talking with my father."

"I vanished the instant you saw your father?"

"Yes," he said, perplexed. They'd been walking along a winding deer trail that led between two huge cedar trees, and on the other side of the trees, the trail had forked. Silk said, *I don't want to go that way. . . .* Then his father had stepped out, dressed in his beautiful white hide shirt, and Silk just disappeared. "It was very strange."

Poor Singer drifted off, remembering how much his father had looked and sounded like him, recalling the things his father had said. . . .

Silk touched his ankle softly, and Poor Singer jerked back to this world. "Poor Singer, why do you think I was in the vision?"

"I don't know." Against his better judgment, he reached down and twined his fingers with hers. As darkness gathered about them, the air grew sweet with the fragrances of damp pines and mud. The wan starlight lay like a hazy veil over the desert. Poor Singer tightened his grip, and his heart started to pound. "Silk, I honestly don't know why you were there, but being with you made me very happy."

She looked down at the ground, and it took all of his strength to hide the dread that surged in his chest.

"W-what happened with your father?"

"Oh," he said, "something I still don't understand. We were in some kind of fight . . . and the ground began to quake, then

I climbed into a flaming sky, using the clouds as stepping stones."

Silk's gaze jerked up. "You saw a flaming sky?"

"Yes, a hideous orange color, filled with smoke. And rivers of fire poured over the earth."

Her beautiful face slackened. "Hallowed Ancestors." Her eyes seemed to enlarge. "I've been dreaming of a flaming sky, too, but I have a bear there to help me, Poor Singer. Whenever I'm in a dangerous situation, that bear keeps me alive."

Wind Baby gusted through the camp and blasted them with stinging sand. They turned their heads and closed their eyes until it passed. The pines creaked and groaned. When Poor Singer looked up again, he found Silk staring into the dancing flames, her expression contemplative.

"Thinking about the bear?"

She nodded, and firelight glimmered in the wind-blown locks of her hair. "I think that I've always dreamed of that bear, but I didn't remember until recently. If I could recall each of those dreams, do you think I'd discover the bear has always been there helping me?"

"Like a Spirit Helper, you mean?"

"Yes."

Poor Singer threw another dead branch onto the fire and orange flames licked up around the wood. Sparks whipped away in a blinking veil. "It's possible. Spirit Helpers can be mysterious. Maybe the bear doesn't wish you to know that he's your Helper."

After thinking about it, she nodded, and replied, "That's how it feels. He's never spoken to me. But he's always there when I need him."

"Have you tried talking to him?"

Silk's brow lined with a frown. "No. How strange. I never have."

"Maybe you should."

"Perhaps . . ."

Poor Singer waited for her to say more, and when she didn't, he said, "If we get up before dawn, I think we can make it across the flats to Talon Town by midmorning. Which means we should probably get some sleep."

Silk rose to her feet. "Yes, we should. I'll wash our cups and bowls if you'll kick dirt over the fire."

As she collected the dishes and went to dip them into the small pool of water, Poor Singer smothered the flames. What wonder this night had brought him. And trepidation.

In the Soot World, he had loved her with all his heart.

Thirty-One

Thistle and Leafhopper secreted themselves behind a thorny wall of greasewood and peered down into the drainage channel that cut through the rolling hills like a jagged wound. People walked below. They moved like black ghosts, their bodies consumed by the lengthening evening shadows. Not one of them so much as looked up as they slogged through the trickle of water in the drainage, seemingly too weary to hurry or to care about the mud, and so silent that had it not been for the steady hiss of their breathing, each might have been a weightless earth spirit. Clothing hung in tatters from their bodies. Heavy packs bent their backs. Many walked barefoot and, here and there, a dirty bandage wrapped an arm or leg wound. Guards marched beside them, hemming them in.

Thistle brushed her dark hair away from her fine-boned face and crawled closer to get a better view through the screen of branches. She bumped Leafhopper's arm. Despite being twice Leafhopper's age, Thistle stood about her height. They looked strange lying side-by-side, Thistle's thin childlike body next to Leafhopper's squat pudgy frame.

"They must be slaves," Leafhopper whispered bitterly.

Dirt streaked Leafhopper's round face and green dress. Twigs and old leaves tangled with her chin-length black hair. The hatred in her eyes chafed Thistle's heart. Where once a little girl in a woman's body had looked out, now a crone glared. Leafhopper had grown up in a single night of horror—and

Thistle didn't have the heart to try to find the girl and bring her back. Nor did she think it wise. Hatred had a way of giving purpose to even the most defeated person. With the difficulties ahead, Leafhopper might very well need that resolve.

Hatred had, after all, become Thistle's nourishment. It gave her strength and fed her will to survive, allowing Thistle to smother her overwhelming desire to lie down in the sand and weep. For the past four days, as they'd headed south, she'd been fighting with herself, forcing her feet to walk, struggling against the sobs that lodged like a white-knuckled fist in her throat. Without hatred to feed that fire in her soul, she knew she would yield to grief and be no good to anyone.

"Yes," Thistle murmured. "When the next guard goes by, look at the tattoos on his right wrist—a red star, a crescent moon, and a handprint. These warriors are from Starburst Town, northwest of Talon Town. They're Straight Path warriors."

Southward, in the direction of Starburst Town, the towering sandstone-capped walls of Straight Path Canyon butted against the clouds. Though shadows cloaked the lowlands, Father Sun's fading rays flamed over the highest cliffs and ignited the drifting Cloud People. A luminescent red-orange halo arced over the western horizon. Buttes stood like dark blocks in the distance, their shadows stretching across the desert. Eastward, behind broken slabs of uptilted sandstone, lavender hued the sky. It would be night soon. And cold. Already the chill ate at Thistle's bones. She needed to find a campsite for them.

But she didn't move. She only stared down at the despairing slave women. How strange. A few days ago, she would have run down into the drainage with open arms, seeking shelter and food among the Straight Path warriors. Now, they were her enemies. Her *own people* were her enemies.

Her fingers tightened on her bow. *I couldn't carry them down the sacred road, so I buried my husband and son with my own hands. I piled rocks on their graves. I Sang their souls to the underworlds . . . and I will never forget who killed them, or why.*

"Stay down!"

Thistle grabbed the top of Leafhopper's head as she lifted it above the greasewood for a better look. Leafhopper grunted when her chin struck the dirt. Her eyes widened. "Sorry," she whispered.

"Wait just a moment. They're almost gone."

As the last women and children passed, a little girl, dragging her injured left foot, stumbled. Dirty black hair framed a thin starved face. She stopped and stared at the people in front of her like a sleepwalker. Tears traced lines through the dirt on her sallow cheeks. "Mother . . ." the girl cried weakly. "Mother?"

Slowly, the girl's knees buckled and she crumpled to the dust. Her torn yellow dress flared around her skinny body. Without making a sound, two older girls turned and walked back. One, tall and slender with a beautiful triangular face, silently handed her pack to the other shorter girl, who had a long hooked nose. Kneeling, the tall girl slipped her arms under the child's body and lifted her.

Leafhopper stayed so still she did not seem to be breathing.

The little girl whimpered, "Where's my mother? Moth, have you seen my mother?"

Not new slaves. They speak the Straight Path language. These women have been slaves for generations. They must be moving them from one work location to another.

It was time to begin preparing the fields for the planting moon. First the fields had to be cleared, then they were usually burned, and the soil turned with stone hoes. In the outlying villages, the clans completed these chores, but the First People—who could afford them—used slaves.

Moth patted the child and exchanged a look of mourning with the shorter girl. "Shh, Lambtoe. Your mother has gone ahead. It's all right. She's just up ahead."

Thistle's heart clutched up. She knew from the tone of Moth's voice that Lambtoe's mother would not be up ahead, not ever again. Many slave women died from blows to the head, or broken bones. Thistle had seen it. When the time came to leave a work location, the guards rounded up the slaves, killed those too slow, and trotted the rest off as quickly as possible, leaving the dead where they had fallen. By now the coyotes had shredded the remains and hauled the bones off to their dens. Ghosts would wail tonight, roaming the earth, alone and frightened.

Thistle's fingers dug into the soft tan dirt of the hillside. *Cornsilk? Where are you? What happened to you?*

The ache in her chest made breathing difficult. Her daughter should have been with Fledgling. Thistle had searched through the smoldering remains of Lanceleaf Village, and Cornsilk's body had not been there. What had happened that night? Had Fledgling seen the flames and come running home, leaving Cornsilk behind somewhere? Or had the Straight Path warriors brought Fledgling with them and kept him outside the village until they'd captured Beargrass? Had they found Fledgling in Standing Gourd's village and dragged him back to use against Beargrass—to force Beargrass to give them information about Cornsilk?

Thistle gripped her bow harder and let her rage swell until it quashed the despair. Perhaps all of her fears about the identity of Cornsilk's father were misplaced. Had Crow Beard sent out warriors because he'd discovered the identity of Cornsilk's *grandfather?* Of course, Beargrass had told them nothing. He'd loved Cornsilk with all his soul. Fledgling had probably died first, as a warning to Beargrass. Blessed Spirits, watching his only son die before his eyes . . .

But if the Straight Path warriors had captured Fledgling to use against Beargrass, Cornsilk was still free. Somewhere. *Alone and aching.*

Thistle's gaze wandered the sunset sky, the dark hills hemming them in, and Leafhopper's strained expression. She studied the new lines in Leafhopper's young face; her fears had coalesced and stared out from the depths of her soul like dark hunching monsters.

"They're gone," Leafhopper said as the slaves and warriors disappeared around a curve in the drainage. "We should go."

"Yes," Thistle whispered. "We *will* go."

Leafhopper sensed the double meaning. "You mean to find a campsite?"

Thistle sat up, put her arrow back in her quiver, and slung her bow over her shoulder. "No, to find Cornsilk's grandfather."

"We're going to Standing Gourd's village? I thought you said we had to go to Talon Town, to speak with the great priest Sternlight, and try to—"

"I've changed my mind."

Thistle rose to her feet, made certain no one could see her, and started down the hill, veering away from the road that led to Straight Path Canyon, heading southeast instead. As she walked, the Evening People twinkled to life. The Road of Light which led to the highest skyworld dusted the belly of Brother Sky.

Leafhopper followed dutifully until it grew too dark to see, then stopped dead in her tracks. "Thistle, shouldn't we make camp? Where are we going?"

Thistle turned. Leafhopper stood ten paces away, silhouetted blackly against the choppy gray desert. The fragrance of damp earth carried on the cool night wind.

Thistle walked back and gently touched Leafhopper's tangled hair. "We'll camp here. Then, tomorrow morning, I'm heading for Gila Monster Cliffs. I think I can make it in five days, if I push myself and don't—"

"Why?" Leafhopper's mouth hung open. Her white teeth gleamed in the starlight. "The Fire Dogs will kill you! They'll know you're Straight Path and they'll enslave you and—"

"No, they won't." Thistle stroked Leafhopper's hair to calm her. The young woman had started clenching and unclenching her fists. "Not if I can reach their Chief. And it may be the only way I can protect Cornsilk—if she's still alive. You see, Chief Jay Bird and Matron Moondance's only daughter was Young Fawn—and I'm almost certain Young Fawn was Cornsilk's true mother."

"Cornsilk's true mother? But, I thought you were?"

"No, Leafhopper. I'm not."

"Why didn't Cornsilk ever tell me!"

"She didn't know. It's a long story. One I'll tell you on the way south, if you wish to go with me. You don't have to. As a matter of fact, it might be better if I leave you at a small Straight Path village along the way. You'll be safer—"

"I—I don't know," Leafhopper stammered. "I'll think about it tomorrow, but finish telling me what you are thinking. . . . You plan to tell Chief Jay Bird that his granddaughter is alive?"

Thistle unslung her pack and dropped it silently to the sand. "I do. Jay Bird married Moondance's sister, Downy Girl. That union only produced sons. If I'm right, Cornsilk is heir to Gila

Monster Cliffs Village and all its surrounding lands. Jay Bird won't be happy that the Blessed Sun is holding his granddaughter captive at Talon Town." She left the threat dangling.

Leafhopper whispered, "Is Cornsilk being held in Talon Town?"

"That's where I told her to go if something happened and she needed help. If she did as I told her—" Thistle took a deep breath, praying that for once Cornsilk had obeyed her "—she's there and safe."

"Not a captive, then?"

Thistle massaged her aching shoulders. "I don't think her real father would allow such a thing. I suspect he's the one who paid for her rearing for so many summers. But maybe not. And her father may even be dead by now. I can't be sure of anything, Leafhopper."

"Yes, you can. There is one thing you know."

"What?"

A tiny dagger of flame entered Leafhopper's eyes. Her voice cut like finely flaked obsidian. "If Jay Bird thinks that his granddaughter is being held in Talon Town, he'll want to get her back."

"If Jay Bird and Downy Girl believe me. And they've no reason to. I just think I can—"

"Many of the warriors who attacked Lanceleaf Village will die in the war." A grim smile curled Leafhopper's lips. She lifted her face to the heavens and closed her eyes. "I want to be there. To see it."

Thistle stared at her. Could this be the same fun-loving young woman who had romped with her daughter only a half moon ago? Thistle's soul turned cold.

Kneeling, she pulled her blanket from her pack and drew out two lengths of pemmican: meat, fat, and berries stuffed into a tube of deer intestine. They'd killed a yearling fawn two days ago, eaten as much as they could hold, and made pemmican from the rest. She handed a length to Leafhopper. The girl took it.

Thistle wrapped up in her blanket and curled on her side, facing south. As she untied one knotted end of the tube and squeezed pemmican into her mouth, wind flapped her blanket about her feet. She caught the waving corner and pinned it beneath her ankles. The delicious tang of venison and juniper berries soothed Thistle's raw nerves. She snuggled deeper into her blanket, ate more, and listened to the night. Wind Baby whistled as he skipped through the drainages. Sagebrush rustled. Almost too far away to hear, a lone coyote yipped.

She pictured Jay Bird's village. Though she'd never been there, she'd spoken to Traders who had. It sat near a pine-covered mountain and a river. Cottonwoods choked the water.

Cries of outrage would go up when she and Leafhopper boldly strode into a Mogollon village. It would be a miracle if they lived long enough to find someone who spoke their language. But if they did, Jay Bird would have to see them, out of curiosity, if nothing else.

Then, my husband and son, your brutal murders will not go unpunished.

Images of Fledgling's headless body tortured her. Thistle's throat suddenly ached. She lowered her pemmican to her blanket and closed her eyes.

She didn't want Leafhopper to hear her crying.

Thirty-Two

As Night Sun slipped the clean blue dress over her head, the copper bells on the hem and sleeves jingled pleasantly. She had washed and twisted her gray-streaked black hair into a bun at the nape of her neck and put on turquoise eardrops. She looked very thin and pale, but she felt ready. Two hands of time ago, a slave had brought her wash water, clothing, jewelry, and the cedar bark torch that flickered on the wall. She'd told Night Sun to prepare for the gathering of First People elders.

The moment had come: judgment. Fear and relief vied for control of her senses. At least the waiting would finally be over, and she would see Cloud Playing. Of all the cruelties she had endured, Snake Head's order that she not be allowed to see her daughter's body until tonight had hurt the most. And she hated him for it.

But she hated herself more for bringing them all to this terrible place. Had she kept a tight hold on herself seventeen summers ago, this would not be happening. She had yielded to the joy Ironwood brought her, and now they both stood on the brink of destruction.

By now everyone in Straight Path Canyon would know she had been accused of adultery, and half of them would be glorying in her downfall. In the outlying villages, clan Matrons would be whispering, taking a malicious glee in the troubles of the First People at Talon Town. No matter what happened to her tonight, the story would grow and grow. Nothing could stop it. Speculation about the father of her child would run rampant. It terrified her.

If Snake Head should decide to banish her, she would manage, somehow, to stand the slights, the curses, the loss of old friends, but if Ironwood's identity were known he would certainly be killed. The First People could not let such a scandal go unpunished. A member of the Bear Clan bedding the Matron of Talon Town! Unforgivable. Better that Night Sun had lain with an enemy chief, like Jay Bird, than one of the Made People. And it had not even been a powerful clan elder, but just a young warrior!

Night Sun's hands curled into fists. The torch spluttered and cast a fluttering orange glow over the white walls, highlighting the black-and-white water jug and her folded gray blanket. A grim smile came to her lips. In all likelihood, she wouldn't have to worry about any of this, since she suspected her son planned to execute her.

Night Sun bent to pick up the shell bracelet the slave had brought, and as she slipped it on her wrist, the covering over the roof hole slid back slightly.

Ironwood called, "Night Sun? May I enter?"

"You may, War Chief."

The ladder dropped. Ironwood climbed down. He wore a beautifully dyed tan shirt with blue and red porcupine quill chevrons sewn across the breast. Fringes adorned the arms and covered his knees. His graying hair hung in a single long braid. His oval face with its slanting brows and flat nose looked oddly serene. "I am no longer War Chief, Night Sun."

"To me, you always will be. As Matron of Talon Town, I can call you whatever I wish."

"Your son—"

"Can leap off a cliff, for all I care." She took a breath. "Has everyone arrived?"

"Yes. They're in the kiva, waiting."

Night Sun dried her clammy palms on her dress. "Then let's have this over with."

As she walked past him, Ironwood took her arm to stop her. It was the grip of a careless stranger, strong, painful. But as he peered down into her eyes, fear strained his expression. "Don't say anything that isn't absolutely necessary. Do you understand me?"

"You mean don't give them any information unless I have to."

"Exactly. Let Sternlight say all of the hard things. He is prepared to defend you."

Night Sun frowned at him. Had Ironwood and Sternlight planned something? A plot to save her? She clasped Ironwood's hand. "I promise I won't admit my guilt."

"Good." He stepped away from the ladder. "I am to be your guard tonight. Please stay close to me."

"You'll be there?" she asked hopefully. "At the gathering?"

"Snake Head resisted at first, then, to Sternlight's surprise, he relented. Sternlight said Snake Head almost looked satisfied with himself and muttered something about 'twisted justice.' I will take up my position at the foot of the stairs."

"Thank the Spirits." Just knowing he would be present gave her strength.

Night Sun climbed the ladder and stepped onto the roof. A din of whispers erupted. The plaza stood empty, but people crowded the white roofs, wrapped in blankets, watching. Night Sun's heart ached. She lifted a hand to them, and hands went up everywhere in response. They dared not speak to her, but she saw their concerned expressions and took some comfort.

A dust-scented breeze rustled her blue hem and whipped up plumes of tan dirt in the plaza. The familiar half-moon shape of Talon Town spread around her, beautifully white. Father Sun had just sunk below the horizon and flames burned through the drifting clouds, but dusk had already settled over the canyon. Hundreds of fires sprinkled the bottomlands. She could hear faint flute music drifting from Streambed Town.

Ironwood climbed up, glanced at the people, and said, "They started gathering four hands of time ago. The elders from all of the Made People clans are out there."

"And the slaves?"

"Snake Head wouldn't permit it. He said they would cause mayhem. Many of them tried to sneak out anyway, to show their support for you, but Webworm and his warriors discovered them and drove them back to their chambers."

"I wish I had strangled Snake Head at birth," she said bitterly.

"Please, walk ahead of me, Night Sun. I will follow."

She strode for the ladder that led down to the plaza, taking the rungs two at a time, rushing to the confrontation.

Ironwood walked behind her across the plaza, as a good guard should.

Propped Pillar shone purple in the twilight gleam, leaning over the eastern half of Talon Town where Night Sun's chambers stood. Oh, how she longed to be sound asleep, curled in her blankets on a pile of soft sleeping mats. But that might never happen again.

When Night Sun reached the altar room connected to the kiva, she ducked low to enter through the T-shaped doorway, then bowed reverently to the thlatsinas painted on the walls. They looked fierce, their fangs bared, the bows and arrows in their hands poised to kill. Their gaudy inhuman masks shone dimly in the firelight streaming from the kiva.

She turned to the staircase that led down and fought the desire to pant. She forced herself to take deep even breaths.

Ironwood came up behind her shoulder and whispered, "Face them as an innocent woman. You *can* do it. You must. Go on, Night Sun."

She descended the stairs with her chin up, her expression inscrutable. Voices murmured below. Night Sun stepped into the firelit warmth of the ceremonial chamber and turned to the elders sitting in a line on the lowest bench, the yellow one. Only the leaders had come: hunch-backed Moon Bright from Kettle Town, old man Whistling Bird from Streambed Town, diminutive Weedblossom from Center Place. A tiny, white-braided woman, Weedblossom suffered from the knotted-joint disease, and her hands looked like gnarled claws. She sat between Moon Bright and Whistling Bird.

Moon Bright's silver hair hung loose over her yellow dress. Beautiful red-and-black geometric designs covered the bodice and sleeves. Despite her deep wrinkles, her sharp eyes missed nothing. She tenderly patted Weedblossom's leg and said something softly.

Whistling Bird frowned at them. His bald head shone orange in the firelight. Polished circlets of clamshell shimmered over his blue shirt. He didn't hear very well and wore a perpetual frown as a result of concentrating so hard on people's voices.

Night Sun heard Sternlight's distinctive steps on the stairs, followed by several other people.

He entered wearing a fresh white robe and a turquoise pendant. He had pulled his hair away from his face into a bun at the back of his head. He glanced briefly at Ironwood, who stood to the right of the stairs, then bowed to the esteemed elders and strode to the pillar, which stood twenty hands in front of Ironwood, where he turned and clasped his hands.

Snake Head came down the stairs next, thumping a stick on each step. He emerged with a gloating smile on his handsome face. A boy's severed head had been impaled upon the shaft. The sight sickened Night Sun. The boy's eyes had desiccated and sunken into the pits; his mouth hung open, the jaw set askew. But his face and long black hair had been freshly washed and glistened in the firelight.

Snake Head paraded back and forth in front of the elders, before going to stand by the northwestern pillar, the one nearest Ironwood. The copper bells on his black shirt tinkled as he spread his legs. His black braid draped his left shoulder.

Dune plodded down the stairs, grunting each time his feet landed. When he stepped to the hard-packed dirt floor, he took Ironwood's arm to steady himself and looked around. His bushy white brows plunged down over his round nose.

Night Sun smiled. All of the other holy people had dressed in their finest jewelry and garments, but Dune wore the same tattered brown shirt he'd worn for many summers. How like the old hermit to comment on these shabby proceedings without saying a word.

Dune's sparse white hair gleamed as he glanced at Night Sun, then hobbled over to sit beside Whistling Bird. Whistling Bird leaned over and said something, and when Dune answered, Whistling Bird's lips moved in time, trying to keep up with the words.

Night Sun did not wait to be instructed. She crossed the chamber to the body lying beneath the turquoise-studded blanket on the eastern foot drum.

"Mother!" Snake Head exploded. "I did not give you permission to look upon my dead sister!"

"I didn't *ask* your permission."

Night Sun gently turned down the blanket to look at Cloud Playing. Her pale face had been rubbed with oil and shone in the firelight. Someone, probably Sternlight, had carefully braided and coiled her hair on top of her head. Tears constricted Night Sun's throat. She lifted a trembling hand to touch her daughter's cold cheek. "Oh, my baby," she whispered. "I miss you so much."

"Mother—!" Snake Head began.

"Wait," Sternlight broke in. "Give her a few more moments." His turquoise wolf pendant gleamed against his white shirt.

The elders whispered.

Night Sun kissed Cloud Playing's forehead and tenderly pulled the blanket back up.

You mustn't let them see your grief or fear.

Turning, Night Sun strode across the chamber and reached out to greet each elder, the corners of her eyes crinkling as she smiled. "Hello, Moon Bright. It's so good to see you."

"I feared you might have withered in that Cage," Moon Bright said sympathetically. "I am heartened to see you so well."

Night Sun reached for the great holy woman of Center Place. "Weedblossom, you look very lovely tonight."

The little old woman took Night Sun's hand in a gentle grip and said, "I'm here for you, girl. I want to hear your side."

Night Sun bent and lightly kissed Weedblossom's wrinkled cheek, murmuring, "Thank you."

When she reached for Whistling Bird's hand, he patted her fingers affectionately. "Are you well, cousin?"

So that he would hear, she answered loudly, "I'm much better now, thank you. It warms my heart to see you."

"And mine to see you," Whistling Bird said.

Before she could move to Dune, Snake Head ordered, "Come over here, Mother! Sit down." He pointed to the floor.

"I will stand," Night Sun said. "Ask me your questions."

Snake Head's mouth widened a little, but it could not have been called a smile. The coldness of the expression struck Night Sun like a blow to the stomach. How could he gaze at his own mother that way?

Night Sun lifted her chin. "Well? You have kept me imprisoned for a quarter moon. What charges do you bring against me?"

Over Snake Head's shoulder, she saw Sternlight's face. Ethereal. Beautiful. He might have been sitting alone on a mountaintop watching a gorgeous sunrise, rather than here. Her gaze slid to Ironwood at the foot of the staircase. Muscles bulged through his tan shirt. Sweat ran along his jaw and trickled down his throat.

He looks almost as frightened as I feel.

Snake Head ceremoniously paced in front of Night Sun, thumping his staff. The dead boy's long hair fluttered and a trickle of liquid ran down from the punctured brain. "Is what my father said about you true?"

"Are the things people say about you true?"

Soft chuckles broke out from the elders. Each knew the rumors of Snake Head's brutality, and even cowardice, in the face of battle.

Snake Head smiled coldly. "Did you betray my father? Did you bear *this* child"—he pointed to the severed head—"and hide him away?"

"No, and no," Night Sun answered.

"You are calling my father, the former Blessed Sun, a liar!"

Night Sun turned to the elders. "Please, hear me. When Crow Beard lay dying, he said many things that made no sense. I think his soul was wandering in and out of his body, and he could not tell the difference between things he imagined and real memories. I—"

"You must take us for fools!" Snake Head shouted. He whirled and pointed to Sternlight. The priest gazed back calmly. "What about the things Sternlight said? He told us the boy lived at Lanceleaf Village! That you had borne a son—"

"That is not what I told you," Sternlight murmured.

The elders went silent, waiting breathlessly.

Snake Head glared in disbelief. "You did so! I heard you! Creeper and Badgerbow heard you, too!"

"What I said," Sternlight clarified as he walked to stand beside Night Sun, "was that the boy lived in Lanceleaf Village. I did not say Night Sun had borne the child."

Snake Head pounded his staff into the floor like an angry child. The dead boy's head wobbled. "Are you trying to tell me you did not mean—"

"That's precisely what I'm telling you."

Struggling to regain his advantage, Snake Head said, "Then . . . then you had me kill an innocent child! I ordered Beargrass' son murdered because you made me think the boy was my mother's misbegotten spawn! You *filthy* murderer!"

Night Sun clenched her hands so hard her nails dug into her palms. What game did Sternlight play? She couldn't fathom it. He stood so still, so calm. Against the red pillar, he looked ghostly. Only his eyes moved. He glanced at each of the thlatsina masks on the walls, searching the gods' faces as if he were listening to their voices.

The elders muttered to each other for a time, and then Moon Bright looked up.

"Is this true, Sunwatcher? Did you deceive Snake Head?"

"I did, Blessed Moon Bright," Sternlight answered straightly. "Of that, I am guilty, and . . ." He drew breath and paused. "And perhaps I am also guilty of the boy's murder." He lifted his gaze to the severed head and anguish lined his handsome face.

A din of confused questions erupted, all of the elders talking at once.

Dune lifted a hand to still the outbursts. "Tell them why, Sternlight. It is time they knew."

"Time we know what?" Snake Head blurted. "I can't believe—"

"Listen, boy," Dune said, "you *will* believe."

Snake Head's jaw set indignantly. He glowered at Dune, then turned to Sternlight, who stood with his head bowed, hands clasped before him in a prayerful posture. "Well, Sunwatcher? Tell us!"

Night Sun searched Sternlight's face. He looked perfectly composed. The elders sat quietly, firelight dancing over their taut expressions.

Sternlight's white ritual shirt swayed in the cold breeze that puffed down the stairway, and a shiver went through him before he could suppress it.

"Go on," Dune urged.

Sternlight nodded and took a breath. He spoke slowly, clearly. "I took it upon myself to protect the Straight Path nation. I realize how presumptuous this will seem. But I did it alone. No one else is to blame."

"You did *not* do it alone," Dune objected. The deep wrinkles of his face rearranged themselves into gentler lines. Dune swiveled on the bench to look at the other elders. "It was my fault. I begged Crow Beard not to kill the child."

Night Sun stood riveted. *What child? Is this some trick?*

Snake Head shook his staff and the dead boy's hair fluttered. "Tell me what you're talking about!"

Sternlight peered soberly at Snake Head. "You did have a brother. But he was not your mother's son. He was your father's son."

Like a punctured deer bladder, Snake Head deflated, breath rushing from his lungs, "What?"

"The boy Beargrass raised."

Snake Head craned his neck to look up at the severed head. The boy's desiccated eyes seemed to gaze back with malevolent intent. "He really was my brother?"

"Yes, and I feared he might fuel the legends of our enemies. You see, his mother was Young Fawn. Jay Bird's daughter."

Whistling Bird yelled, "That war-loving Mogollon Chief?" Red mottled his face. "You mean, the legends about the child born and hidden away?"

Weedblossom gasped. "The boy who would return to destroy us? Great gods! His survival could have been disastrous!"

Sternlight laced his fingers together. "I am very much aware of that."

"But . . ." Weedblossom lifted a clawlike hand and held it out to Sternlight. "Why did you not simply tell us of this, Sunwatcher? Why the deception?"

Sternlight's lips pressed into a white line. "I promised Crow Beard I would tell no one. He was ashamed of what he had done. And he knew how very dangerous it was."

Weedblossom frowned as Dune rose to his feet. His threadbare brown shirt hung off his frame as though covering bare bones. His freckled scalp gleamed orange beneath his wispy white hair.

Night Sun had gone numb. She watched the proceedings like a battle-dazed warrior, not certain anything happening around her was real. She remembered Crow Beard standing in the plaza, touching the slave women suggestively. But more than that, she sensed that Sternlight and Ironwood played some desperate game, and they expected her to play along. Either she was their partner in this deception, or they were all dead.

"But that isn't the whole story," Dune said. "When Crow Beard discovered that Young Fawn carried his child, he called me in for advice. *I* am the one who asked Crow Beard to let the child live. I considered it a great gift when he said yes. But I also suggested to Crow Beard that he leave—that he find some excuse to be gone until after the child was born."

"Why would you have asked my father to allow the boy to live?" Snake Head demanded. "That's ridiculous. He should have been killed before birth!"

"I have never believed the Mogollon legends," Dune said. "And I thought it more prudent to avoid the embarrassment of having to admit the Blessed Sun had lain with a Fire Dog slave. That—"

"Did you ask Crow Beard to go away for ten moons," Night Sun's thin voice penetrated the gloom, "out of fear of what I might do?"

Dune's ancient head tottered in a nod. "Yes. You would certainly have divorced Crow Beard, wouldn't you?"

Night Sun's brows drew together. She considered the question. "Yes. I suppose I'd have had no choice." She folded her arms tightly over her breast. "I remember seeing him flirting with the slave women. But if I'd known that it was Young Fawn he was courting, I'd have been furious—because of the legends."

And it would have broken Cloud Playing's heart. We forbade her to marry Webworm because of the legends, then her own father had lain with Jay Bird's daughter!

Sternlight spread his arms to the elders and walked closer to the bench where they sat. His ritual shirt rustled softly. "And even if the Fire Dog legends are true," Sternlight said. "Dune and I decided it would be more just to fight a man than murder an infant."

Snake Head scoffed, "Then why did you tell me to murder him now?" He tipped his staff lower to peer into the sunken eyes.

"I had no choice," Sternlight said softly. "It was Crow Beard's last order."

"It was not!" Snake Head objected. He pointed an accusing finger at Sternlight. "His last order was to kill my *mother's* child."

Sternlight shook his head. "That is what he said, but Crow Beard was confused, babbling. I pieced together his intent from the phrases 'if a savior rises now,' and 'Jay Bird's brood.' Do you recall your father saying those things?"

Grudgingly, Snake Head admitted, "Something like that, yes."

"Don't you see?" Sternlight addressed the elders. "Crow Beard knew that in the summers since the boy's birth, the situation with the Mogollon has steadily worsened. We have knocked them back time and again. If a savior rose now, they would leap to follow him. Crow Beard's last order was to kill *that* child. And I knew what he meant." Sternlight exhaled hard. "But I could not reveal the secret, not while Crow Beard was alive. I had given him my promise."

The beauty of his deep voice seemed to have cast a spell upon the gathering. The elders sat transfixed. Night Sun looked at Ironwood and he held her gaze for so long that her heart slammed against her ribs. Could any of this be true?

Snake Head glanced at Night Sun, then Ironwood, and his eyes narrowed. "So, Sternlight. You lied to me."

"I did."

"And, thereby," Weedblossom said in a reedy voice, "may

have saved us all. I have heard enough. Moon Bright, what do you say?"

Moon Bright's silver hair glistened as she nodded. "I have no more questions."

"And you, Whistling Bird?"

The old man shouted, "What? Speak up!" He twisted around to stare at Weedblossom's lips.

She put a hand on his shoulder and leaned toward him, bellowing, "I asked if you had heard enough?"

Whistling Bird scowled at her. "No need to shout. I think she's innocent, if that's what you mean."

Weedblossom sighed. "Well, then, let's go. I'm very fatigued, and my joints ache." She stood and waited for the other elders to join her; they headed for the staircase.

"Wait!" Snake Head shouted. "We are not finished! *I* don't believe Sternlight's story! How can you—"

Weedblossom pushed by Snake Head as she led the way out. The elders filed by, whispering to each other.

Snake Head stalked from the chamber and hurried up the stairs, not bothering with the drama of thumping his staff this time. Night Sun could hear him calling, *"Weedblossom? Weedblossom, wait! You can't seriously think . . ."*

When their voices faded away, Sternlight reached for the bench, sank down, and dropped his head in his hands. He was trembling.

"Sternlight?" Night Sun called, and took two quick steps.

"No, I'm all right." He held up a hand. "Just . . . exhausted."

Night Sun knelt at his feet and gently touched his knee. "You kept that a secret all these summers, my nephew? Even from me?"

"I keep my promises, aunt. To you, and to your husband."

"Yes," she said softly. "I know."

Dune grunted as he rose. He hobbled over to pat Night Sun's shoulder. "You're free." Damp wisps of white hair matted his temples. "Snake Head knows he cannot win now. But watch him. There's no telling what he might try next to destroy you."

She gripped his knobby fingers. "Thank you, Dune, for helping me."

He smiled toothlessly. "It took a lot out of me. I'm too old for such bantering. I'm going to find my blankets. We'll speak more when you and I are both rested."

"If you don't mind," Sternlight said, "I'll walk with you. I'm very tired."

Dune nodded. "You must be. You were *extraordinary*, Sun-watcher. Come, I'll enjoy your company on the walk."

Sternlight smiled weakly at the praise, kissed Night Sun's temple, and followed Dune up the stairs.

Night Sun shook her head at their retreating backs, relieved and more than a little confused. She turned to Ironwood, and he straightened as though anticipating her questions.

Their gazes locked, neither of them said anything for a time. The strain had etched deep lines around his eyes, and his tan shirt clung to his muscular body in damp folds. She could smell his musky sweat. He must have been terrified.

She rose to her feet and walked toward him. "Was any of that true?"

"Some."

Night Sun's brows drew together. As the fear seeped away, her strength went with it. She glanced at Cloud Playing, then Crow Beard, and grief and loneliness flooded her. "Oh, Ironwood, what will I do now? I feel so empty."

"You will do what you must. As you always have. Let me take you back to your chamber. You must be exhausted, too."

Night Sun crushed the blue fabric of her dress in nervous fingers. She walked closer to him, peering up into his handsome face. The fire cast an amber aura around them. Flickers of gold glimmered in his dark eyes. "Will you stay with me?" she asked. "To talk?"

"Night Sun," he said as if not wishing to answer that question. "I—I can't."

"Why?"

"It would make things harder. . . . For me."

She shook her head, denying some wordless inner warning. "I understand, but can't you just spend a hand of time with me? Surely you can stand that? I have no one else—now—and I need to talk. Please?"

His shoulders contracted and swelled against his buckskin shirt. First he shook his head, then he closed his eyes, and whispered, "All right. Just for a hand of time."

He gestured to the stairs, and followed her as she headed for the ladder that led to her fourth-story chamber.

Two hands of time later, they lay twined in each other's arms atop her sleeping mats. The night's chill slowly drained the heat from Ironwood's body, and he tightened his hold on Night Sun.

What have I done? Ironwood thought. *How did I let this happen?*

Night Sun had her head tucked beneath his chin. He stroked her bare back slowly, letting the softness of her skin ease his inner ache. Starlight fell in a cool veil over their naked bodies.

Tell her. Do it now. If the world is coming unraveled as fast as you fear it is, you might never have another chance.

"Night Sun?"

"Hmm?" she answered sleepily.

"I never stopped loving you."

She lifted her head and her long graying black hair tumbled around him. She'd never heard him say it before. Pain shimmered in her eyes; the intensity of it frightened him—as it had those long summers ago just before she'd told him she could never see him again. "Ironwood, I . . ."

When her voice faltered, he said, "You don't have to tell me you love me, Night Sun. I didn't expect that. I only wanted to tell you. I've said it so often in my dreams, I had to hear it aloud. Just once."

She brushed hair behind her ears and let out a breath. "The day that I say it, Ironwood, is the day we will have to leave Talon Town and give up the entire Straight Path nation. You realize that, don't you? We could never openly be together. Not here. Not anywhere among our people."

"Yes, I realize that."

"Are you willing to give up everything?"

He smiled. "I have nothing without you, Night Sun."

Slowly, she lay her head down again, and ran slender fingers over his arm, tracing the swells of muscles. In a bare whisper, she said, "Forgive me, Ironwood."

He stared at the starlight reflecting from the black creosote that coated the ceiling poles. It formed a weave of tiny shimmering diamonds.

He nodded against her hair. "I always have."

Thirty-Three

Sunlight poured through the eastern window in Night Sun's chamber, flashing from a cloud of iridescent flies that hummed in the warm spring air. She wandered the chamber aimlessly. She had been free for less than a day and had no notion of what to do first. Her gaze drifted over the room. It stretched two-by-three body-lengths. The Buffalo Thlatsina, with his curving horns and long black beard, stared at her from the south wall. On the floor below him stood a line of Green Mesa pots painted with exquisite black-and-white geometric designs. Herbs and roots for Healing filled the pots. As sunlight warmed the smallest one, the fragrance of dried mint rose. The Sun Thlatsina Danced on the north wall, his pink arms spread, one foot lifted. He wore a headdress of eagle feathers.

Everything lay exactly as she'd left it. Why did it feel unfamiliar? In her absence, had the chamber's soul fled? Her blankets, where she had held Ironwood, rested beneath the Sun Thlatsina, her most precious possessions in the large blue-and-white basket in the northwestern corner. Six hands tall, and four wide, the basket held her whole life.

Night Sun walked over and removed its lid. She gently took out the yellow blanket her grandmother had woven, then the first pot Cloud Playing had made, small and red, with her tiny fingerprints pressed into the surface. Night Sun touched each indentation, and a dazed sensation filled her—like forgotten terror suddenly reawakened by a word or a look. Her hand shook as she drew it back.

Her daughter was dead. She had seen the body, touched it,

and felt the cold flesh. But true belief, and with it acceptance, still eluded her. As though her soul insisted her eyes had played a trick on her, her memory saw Cloud Playing alive and smiling. What would happen when the truth finally sank in?

Night Sun peered inside the tiny pot, at the obsidian scraper Snake Head had given her in his seventh summer. He'd loved her then. Blessed gods, how had he come to hate her so? What could she have done differently?

Her hand hovered over the rare and precious turquoise knife from Ironwood. After they'd returned from that first trip together, he'd slipped it into her hands. They'd been in a crowd, at night, and no one had seen. He'd walked away without a word.

Night Sun picked it up and held it to her heart.

That trip had been joyous. For eight days, they had laughed and talked; every time he'd looked at Night Sun, her soul had soared. By the last night of their journey, she'd been desperately in love with him, and the knowledge had nearly broken her heart.

She lowered the turquoise knife and studied the polished surface, ground to shape by a master craftsman. The handle had been made from deer antler.

For seventeen summers, she'd kept Ironwood's laugh, and the look in his eyes, locked in a secret chamber in her soul. When Crow Beard insulted and embarrassed her, when he beat the children, those precious memories had kept her sane.

She gazed through the window. The rocky crest of Propped Pillar shone in the slanting morning sunlight. Golden eagles had built a huge nest of old juniper branches on top. The female sat in its midst with her beak tucked beneath her wing, sleeping in the warm sun.

What Night Sun would give to . . .

A shadow fell across her room, and she looked over her shoulder to see Ironwood standing in the doorway. A hollow ache grew within her. He smiled, but it was an uneasy smile. After last night, she didn't blame him. He wore a red shirt with black leggings and sandals. He'd pulled his graying hair away from his oval face and tied it back with a braided yucca cord.

He said. "I wanted to make sure you were all right."

Night Sun clutched the knife to her heart and turned to

him. When he saw it in her hands, he searched her face with warm eyes.

"I'm numb, Ironwood. I don't know how to think or feel. It's as if my wrists and ankles are tied, and I can't move very far in any direction."

"A lot has happened, Night Sun. You need time to sort it out."

She carefully tucked the knife between the folds of her grandmother's blanket in the blue-and-white basket and replaced the lid. "Even with time, I'm not sure I'll ever be able to do that. My husband is gone. I hate my son. My beautiful daughter is dead. And I don't know why someone would— would kill her." She rubbed her tight throat. "I've been trying to determine what is left of my life."

He took a deep breath, then apparently decided to say nothing.

Night Sun walked over and leaned her shoulder against the wall near him. "What is it?"

Ironwood's slanting brows plunged down over his flat nose. His pale golden skin looked flaxen in the wash of light. "Young Swallowtail returned last night, saying that Dune's apprentice, Poor Singer, is on his way with Dune's burial bundle. It should take a day or two for Dune to prepare Crow Beard's body." He probed her eyes. "Sternlight wanted me to ask if you wished to accompany the body on the journey south. Snake Head will be leading the procession."

Night Sun clenched her fists, as if the action alone could strangle her churning emotions long enough to see her way to the future. "And Sternlight thought I might not wish to spend four days on the sacred road with my son."

"It isn't necessary, Night Sun. Few Matrons ever go. And it might be dangerous. The procession will make a good target for raiders."

She massaged her forehead.

"There's . . . something else," he said softly.

Night Sun looked up.

"Do you remember that I told you when things settled down here, I was going to Lanceleaf Village to hunt for Cornsilk?"

"Yes."

As though he was struggling with himself, his lips parted,

but no words came out. He folded his arms tightly across his chest. It took several moments before he said, "I wanted to ask . . . would you like to go with me?"

Night Sun took a deep breath. Last night had stirred feelings that terrified her. But long ago she had crossed a line that could not be recrossed, and she'd run so far past it last night that she couldn't even see the line any longer. Go with him? Oh, if only she could. She wanted to go with him, desperately. Had she been thirty summers old, she would have packed her things now, this instant. But she just stood there, gazing at his tortured expression.

"Are you certain, Ironwood?"

With a weary smile, and wry crook of an eyebrow, he said, "No."

"But you asked anyway?"

"Yes."

"Because you feel sorry for me?"

"I think," he said through a long exhalation, "that you know me better than that. I asked because I need time alone with you. To talk. I have . . . ideas. But I can't discuss them with you in Talon Town." He stopped. "No, that's not right. The truth is, I don't *wish* to speak about them here."

Because he rightly fears that surrounded by First People I will feel obligated to say no?

"I understand."

"I had hoped you would."

Night Sun touched the sleeve of his red shirt. He watched her fingers intently as she bravely lowered them to rest on his forearm. "But I—I make no promises, Ironwood. I mean . . . about afterward."

"I ask for none."

In the long silence that followed, Night Sun heard the shrill cry of an eagle and the jingling of copper bells as someone walked by on the roof below.

"When did you wish to leave?"

"Four days. Maybe five. If that's all right?"

"I'll be ready."

Ironwood lightly touched her hand where it rested on his arm. Conflicting emotions danced across his face. The longer he touched her, the more his expression tightened.

A commotion rose outside and both of them peered through the doorway. Two people entered the plaza and stood looking around awkwardly. The young man wore a long brown shirt and the woman a pale green dress. Dusty and tired, they appeared to have come a long way. Slaves gathered around them, asking questions, poking and prodding the packs they carried.

"I must go," Ironwood said. "Dune asked me to keep a look out for Poor Singer."

"Do you think that's him?"

"It looks like him, but I can't tell from up here." He stepped out of her chamber onto the roof, and the wind caught his hem and sleeves and whipped them back and forth. He looked back and bowed respectfully to her. "If you'll excuse me, I need to find out."

"Until later, Ironwood."

She watched his broad back until he rounded the curve in the wall.

Go with him? She knotted her fists, sagging against the wall. *Oh, Night Sun, what are you doing?*

Ironwood crossed the plaza and approached Poor Singer and the young woman. Slaves crowded around them, asking questions. Poor Singer answered, while the young woman carefully appraised her surroundings. Her large dark eyes took in everything, scanning each of the five stories of Talon Town, lingering for a moment on the magnificent images of the Great Warriors, then moving about the plaza, noting each person.

Ironwood studied her. She had a warrior's gaze, though she carried her bow tied on top of her pack. Her broad cheekbones and pointed nose bore a sheen of sweat, and dirt streaked the front of her green dress. Black hip-length hair fluttered about her in the wind, shading blue when the light struck it just right. A pretty young woman. Ironwood doubted she could have seen more than sixteen summers.

As he neared, the slaves immediately stepped back and opened a path for him. The young woman eyed Ironwood with deadly intent, but Poor Singer just heaved a sigh and smiled.

Tall and skinny, Poor Singer had a narrow face and a thin hooked nose. His braid hung over his left shoulder.

"Good day, Poor Singer," Ironwood said in a friendly voice. "I hope your journey was safe and pleasant."

"Yes, War Chief, thank you. We had no troubles."

"I'm happy to hear that." Ironwood turned to the young woman. She watched him as a lioness would a mouse. Ironwood smiled at her. "And who are you?"

"Spidersilk," she said. "Silk for short. I'm from Turtle Village."

Ironwood's brows lowered. "Turtle Village? I heard that . . ."

An ache entered her large dark eyes. "My village is gone. My family is dead."

Ironwood nodded sympathetically. "I pray the thlatsinas keep them well. You are both welcome here. Please, if you will follow me, I'll take you to your chamber."

Poor Singer wet his lips nervously. "I think I should see Dune first, War Chief. He—"

"Poor Singer, I am no longer War Chief," Ironwood said with a forced smile. "You may call me Ironwood. Dune gave me strict instructions to show you to your room first, then, later, to bring you to the First People's kiva. You don't wish me to disobey the holy Derelict's orders, do you?"

"No. I'd never . . . I mean . . . Very well, then, thank you. I'm too tired to argue."

"Dune thought you would be. Tired, that is, and hungry." Ironwood led the way across the plaza, scattering turkeys as he walked. Gobbling and squawks marked their passage. The slaves had regrouped in the doorway that separated the eastern and western halves of the plaza, whispering. Ironwood wondered why they appeared so concerned. Perhaps it was just that they knew Poor Singer to be one of Dune's chosen Singers-in-the-making.

He stopped at the ladder to the first-floor roof. Silk was staring hard at Webworm, her jaw tight, fists knotted. The War Chief stood at his traditional post overlooking the entryway. Webworm, arms folded, had his eyes fixed on the roads and trails that traced the canyon bottom. Lanky and square-jawed, he wore a long red war shirt, a turquoise carving hung over his breast. Silk's attention had a breathless quality. A curious . . . power.

Ironwood turned to her, "Do you know him?"

The sidelong glance she gave him reflected pure hatred. "No," she answered in a voice that would have frozen a boiling hot spring.

Ironwood inclined his head agreeably and climbed the ladder. When he reached the rooftop, he waited for them to step off, then showed them to the ladder that led down into their chamber. "I hope this is adequate. If you need anything, please—"

"I am here, Ironwood," Mourning Dove called up from the chamber. "I'll tend to their needs."

Ironwood peered down through the hole in the roof and saw her plump chipmunk face staring up. She wore a faded brown dress. The rich scent of turkey and blue corn stew bathed his face.

Ironwood's brows drew together. Why would the Blessed Sun's slave be tending the needs of Dune's assistants? Was Snake Head keeping an eye on them? Why?

He said, "Thank you, Mourning Dove," and turned back to Poor Singer and Silk. "When you've eaten and rested, I'll return for you. Will two hands of time be all right?"

Poor Singer glanced at Silk, then shrugged. "That's fine, Ironwood. Thank you."

Ironwood waited politely as Poor Singer climbed down into the chamber. He'd expected Silk to follow, but she stood there with her long hair blowing, looking straight at him. Their gazes held. Almost as if their souls touched, he could sense the questions in her eyes. Many questions.

Ironwood cocked his head. "I don't know what you're asking me, Silk. Can you say it in words?"

She blinked, as though the fact that he'd read her eyes startled her—then backed carefully away from him. "I would like to talk with you . . . when your time permits."

"May I ask what about?"

She glanced at Webworm again, then back to Ironwood. "A-about Talon Town. I think I may have relatives here."

Ironwood sensed her grim determination. Perhaps the last family she has. Blessed Spirits . . . He smiled warmly. "Whenever you wish. We do have several people here from Turtle Village. I'll be happy to introduce you to them."

"Thank you." She turned then, and hurried down the ladder into the chamber.

Poor Singer said something to her, but Ironwood couldn't make out the words.

Ironwood fingered the deerbone stiletto on his belt. The girl's entire world had been destroyed. She must be feeling lost and lonely, looking for anyone who might be able to give her hope.

Unconsciously, his gaze lifted to Night Sun's door. As Father Sun climbed higher into the azure sky, the shadows retreated and the white plaster seemed to blaze.... Ironwood knew about loneliness.

To still the sudden ache in his chest, he walked to the ladder, climbed down into the plaza, and headed for his own chamber.

To pack.

Hope came in many guises.

Poor Singer sat with his back against the white wall, eating his bowl of stew self-consciously. The slave, Mourning Dove, laid out fresh clothing for them, then unrolled sleeping mats on the far side of the room and spread two red-and-black blankets over them ... as if Poor Singer and Silk would be sleeping together.

He could barely swallow his food.

He glanced at Silk, but she hadn't noticed. She ate her stew with her forehead furrowed and her gaze on the toes of her sandals—living inside her soul. She'd had a strange expression on her face when she'd climbed down the ladder. Why? He couldn't ask until the slave left.

He ate more stew and looked around. Two body-lengths square, the bright white walls fascinated him. They must replaster constantly to keep them looking this clean and fresh. Beautifully woven mats rested on the dirt floor. Red, yellow, and green designs covered them. A warming bowl filled with cheery red coals sat in front of him. The teapot stood on one side with a stew pot on the other. The slave woman had dipped up two cups of phlox petal tea and set them near the warming bowl.

Mourning Dove seemed to be taking an unusually long time fixing their bedding. A tiny, delicate woman, she wore a plain brown dress. Her eyes were bright, shining, her cheeks fat, and she kept glancing uncomfortably at Silk.

Poor Singer finished his stew and reached for one of the clay teacups. As he lifted it to drink, a sweet flowery fragrance rose.

"Please," Mourning Dove said finally. "I—I do not wish to be presumptuous, but . . ." She walked to stand in front of Silk, her eyes wide. "I heard you say that you came from Turtle Village. Is that true?"

Silk looked up. "Yes. Why?"

Mourning Dove wrung her hands anxiously. "There is a . . . a great Dreamer in this town. Her name is Featherstone. She saw you in a Spirit Dream."

"Me? She saw me?"

"Yes, I think so."

"What did she see?"

"Well, it wasn't very clear, but she saw you running away from a burning village and climbing onto the back of a huge bear. You rode the bear away into the darkness—and came to Talon Town."

Silk's shoulders tightened, and Poor Singer set his cup down with a loud *clack!*

He turned to Silk. "Blessed Ancestors, Silk! You're always having dreams about—"

She jerked up a fist to silence him, and Poor Singer clenched his jaws to stifle the bubbling questions.

Silk's gaze focused on Mourning Dove. "Did this Featherstone say why the bear brought me here?"

Mourning Dove swallowed hard. "Yes . . . she said you'd come to hurt her."

"To hurt her? Who? Who am I supposed to hurt?"

"The Blessed Featherstone. And everyone in this town."

"No." Silk exhaled and shook her head. "No. I'm sorry. I'm not the woman this Featherstone saw. There must be another coming. I don't know anyone here, and even if I did, I bear Talon Town no ill will. I lost all of my family when Turtle Village was attacked. The part about the burning village was correct. But I'm here, in Talon Town, hoping to find cousins."

Poor Singer felt suddenly lightheaded as he realized where he'd heard that name before. Young Swallowtail had mentioned a Featherstone—hadn't she been the cousin that Sternlight had witched so she would be captured by the Mogollon? The one who would have been Sunwatcher? Silk clearly hadn't connected the woman's name with Swallowtail's story.

Mourning Dove shifted uneasily. "You're not here to hurt Featherstone?"

"I told you, I don't even *know* her. Tell her I wish her no harm."

Mourning Dove seemed relieved. "That will make Creeper very happy. He was frightened when he saw you. He asked me to—"

"Who is Creeper?" Poor Singer asked.

"The leader of the Buffalo Clan." Mourning Dove smiled. "And someone who loves the Blessed Featherstone."

From her voice, Poor Singer figured that Mourning Dove cared deeply about Creeper. Disturbed, he picked up his tea again. Something wasn't right about all this.

Silk said, "Thank you for tending to our needs, Mourning Dove. The stew and tea were delicious. I think we'll try to rest before Ironwood returns to get us. We don't need anything else. You may go now, if you wish."

Mourning Dove left reluctantly, studying every line of Silk's face while she climbed the ladder to the roof.

Poor Singer waited until he no longer heard her steps, then he whispered, "What was *that* all about?"

Silk's head fell forward and her wealth of black hair tumbled around her, dragging the floor. "I don't know, Poor Singer. But it scared me. Why would anybody think that I—"

"Did you notice the name? Featherstone?"

Silk frowned at him, then her jaw dropped. "Wait! Isn't she the woman Swallowtail told us—"

"Yes! Sternlight's cousin who was taken slave by the Mogollon. I didn't think you remembered, or you wouldn't have been so calm."

"But why would she Dream about me?"

Poor Singer gestured lamely. "I don't think she did. But—

but it's strange that we should walk into Talon Town right after she had such a Dream."

Silk glared up through the roof opening at the dust that sparkled in the brilliant morning sunlight. "If one of the First People told such a vision to a Buffalo Clan elder, do you really believe he would have told a slave? And then asked the slave to ask us about it?"

Poor Singer frowned at the sitting mats and shook his head. "It doesn't sound wise, does it?"

"It sounds ridiculous . . . unless someone is trying to frighten us?"

"Why would anybody wish to frighten us? No one here knows us. Except Dune."

Silk tossed her long hair over her shoulder and reached for a cup of tea. She sipped it thoughtfully. "Dune doesn't know me. And he couldn't have known I'd be coming with you."

"Did anyone else know you planned to come here?"

"No one." Silk's fingers tightened around her cup. Her mouth pressed into a hard line. "Only my . . . my mother. She told me to come here if I was in trouble."

"But if your mother's . . ." Poor Singer halted at the hurt look she gave him. "Do you think her ghost came to speak to this Featherstone?"

"More likely her ghost would have visited Sternlight."

"The great Sunwatcher? Why?"

"She knew him . . . I think."

"How? Did Sternlight visit Turtle Village?"

Silk shook her head so subtly that he wasn't certain she'd done it. She turned the cup in her hands, then took a long drink before she set the cup on the floor near the warming bowl. "Poor Singer, there are things I haven't told you. But I—I think now that I should."

"You can tell me anything you want . . . or don't want. You're my friend, Silk."

Her jaw muscles worked under her smooth cheeks, and naked fear shone in her eyes. "I know that, Poor Singer. I think I've known it for days. But I just couldn't convince myself to speak about it—to you or anyone."

"Is it so terrible?"

"I'm scared. I may be in real trouble." Silk slid around and took both of Poor Singer's hands in a hard grip. "Sternlight may be my father."

"Your *father!*"

"Shhh! Not so loud." She glanced up at the doorway. "Yes. My father."

"But—but how could that be, Silk?"

"It's a long story." She heaved a breath. "And I only know pieces of it. Did you see the man standing watch over the town?"

"Up above the entry? Yes."

"His name is Webworm, and he's the new War Chief. *He* is the one who said Sternlight was my father. Or rather he—he accused Sternlight of being my brother's father, just before he killed my brother and the man I had always believed was my father."

Poor Singer swallowed down a suddenly dry throat. "I don't understand any of this, Silk. Does it have something to do with Featherstone's Dream?"

"It might . . ." Sweat beaded her broad cheekbones. "If my mother is really Night Sun."

Poor Singer leaned forward to stare into her eyes from less than a hand's distance. "Silk, this is all very confusing. Perhaps you'd better start at the beginning."

Thirty-Four

Ironwood rolled an extra shirt and tucked it into his pack. His chamber spread two by two body-lengths. Thlatsinas danced on each wall: Badger in the north, Buffalo in the east, Bear on the west, and Ant Thlatsina on the south. His sleeping mats lay against the west wall, beneath the ring of scalps that encircled the Blessed Bear Thlatsina. The long black and gray hair that hung from the scalps contrasted sharply with the white plaster. Every day he fed the scalps, sprinkling corn pollen over them to keep their souls contented, in the hopes that they would protect and nourish him in return.

The rest of the western wall glinted with a variety of weapons: obsidian-tipped lances, an intricately carved bow, bone stilettos, a buffalo hide helmet, and several beautifully woven shields.

A row of baskets and pots stood along the north wall.

Ironwood slipped a hafted chert knife into the pack. In about ninety hands of time, he and Night Sun would leave on their first journey together in over sixteen summers. His memory flashed with scenes from the past, precious moments that left his soul aching.

It would not, could not, be like that again. Not at their ages, and not after all that they'd been through. But just being alone with her for a few days would be enough for him. It would, perhaps, have to last him the rest of his life. He'd read the tone of her voice and seen the look in her eyes—she knew he was desperate, and she remained undecided.

Picking up a small pot of charred cotton for starting fires, he tucked it into the bottom corner of his pack.

"If she says 'no,'" he murmured as he stared into his half full pack, "I *will* go away. I—I don't know where. But I'll find a place."

With her son ruling Talon Town, Ironwood could not stay. While Crow Beard lived, they'd both had excuses. He could tell himself that, though she loved him, she could not leave her husband; the scandal would have shamed all First People. But now . . . if she rejected him now . . .

He jammed a bag of dried turkey into his pack and jerked the laces tight. Being cast off now would wound more than his heart.

He placed his pack against the wall and rose. An oval of sunlight shone through his roof entry and made a bright spot on the southern half of his chamber. Almost noon. Time to leave. Heaving a sigh, Ironwood climbed the ladder and stepped out onto the first-floor roof. The white walls gleamed with such strength he had to shade his eyes to see.

Webworm stood at his station overlooking the entry, talking to short, stocky Gnat. Webworm, tall and lanky, towered over his deputy. Both wore red warriors' shirts. Behind them, the irregular walls of the canyon gleamed a rich ruddy shade. The shadows of roaming Cloud People splotched the canyon bottom and sheathed distant Sunset Town, where it lay across the wash to the south; the shadows muted the bright gold blocks of rooms, turning the town a dull brown. The first faint greening of grass capped the southern rim above the pale sandstone slickrock. The wind smelled like warm sandstone. Planting ceremonies would be held soon.

And perhaps my own winter of the soul has almost passed.

As he climbed down the ladder, the slaves in the plaza began laughing, and turkeys squawked in rhythm to the pounding of feet. Women and children had drawn two lines, one at each end of the plaza, and were running foot races. It was a common practice, this midday break from chores to eat and play. Looms with half-finished blankets stood stacked against the northern wall, sporting red, tan, and green designs. Near them, cradleboards leaned. Blanketed infants mewed and waved tiny fists. Dogs slept in the cool shadows beside them. A flock of gobbling turkeys, heads bobbing, strutted around, trying to avoid being trampled.

Four boys, including young Swallowtail, stood at the starting line, their arms out like hawks preparing to leap from a cliff. Swallowtail stood two heads taller than any other boy in line. When Mourning Dove shouted, "Run!" the boys took off, legs pumping for the opposite line. Swallowtail came in first, but the ten or so slaves watching cheered all the competitors and slapped them on the backs.

When Ironwood followed the curve around the plaza, the races abruptly halted. They watched him with a mixture of awe and fear. His red shirt whipped around his black leggings. Except for the oldest slaves, he had led the raids that resulted in their captures, and none of them had a great fondness for him.

He'd never considered such things as a young man. But now, cut loose from those responsibilities, feeling the twinges of his age, a prickling of unease had invaded his peace.

As he neared the ladder, Poor Singer and Silk stepped out onto the roof. Had they seen him coming? Or just decided to wait for him? Poor Singer wore a fresh tan shirt with brown and green diamonds around the hem and sleeves. He had a pack slung over his shoulder. Silk looked lovely. Her yellow dress accentuated the blue-black tones in her long hair. Her oval face and full lips were enchanting, while those large dark eyes were wary and reserved.

Ironwood stood at the bottom of the ladder and called, "I appreciate your promptness."

Poor Singer gazed down at Ironwood with a curious expression of dread. "We didn't wish to keep you waiting."

Poor Singer started down the ladder and Silk followed, her hair fluttering in the wind. In contrast to Poor Singer's gangly descent—the pack bouncing loosely—she moved with an athletic grace, every movement controlled.

When they both stood before him, Ironwood asked, "Ready?"

"Yes, War Ch—Ironwood." Poor Singer reddened at his slip. The blush made his thin nose blaze.

"Come along, then. Dune will be waiting."

The races halted again, but Ironwood saw Swallowtail lift a hand to wave at Silk. She smiled and waved back.

Swallowtail called, "The bread was delicious! It lasted me all the way home!"

"I'm glad!" Silk yelled in return.

Ironwood slowed his pace to walk at Silk's side. "You gave Swallowtail bread?"

She gave him a sidelong glance. "Yes. He'd run very hard to get to us and left immediately after he'd eaten supper. I thought it would make his journey easier."

"I'm sure it did. Most people wouldn't have shown such kindness to a slave."

Silk shrugged.

Ironwood said, "The Sunwatcher, Sternlight, will be grateful. Swallowtail is one of his slaves."

Her steps faltered, ever so slightly, as though Sternlight's name unnerved her. Then she continued on, chin up, following in Poor Singer's steps.

"I've heard," she said carefully, "that Sternlight is a witch. Is it true?"

"No." Ironwood speculated about her boldness. Only someone very brave—or extremely naïve—would dare to ask. "He's just a priest, a very holy man. But you'll see. He's waiting in the kiva with Dune, and he's—"

Silk stopped dead. She wet her lips before turning to look up at Ironwood. "He's in the kiva?"

"He is." Ironwood studied her carefully, trying to see past her expression. "Does that bother you? You could wait in your chamber if you'd rather not—"

"No, no, I—I wish to meet him. I'll be honored to meet him." Her voice sounded forced. Resolutely, she started toward where Poor Singer had slowed to look back at them with uncertainty.

"He's a holy man, Silk," Ironwood said, hoping to allay her fears. "Nothing more."

She nodded, put her head down, and walked on.

Ironwood replayed her reaction, seeking the key to this mysterious young woman. Most of the distant villages gossiped about Sternlight—and all of the First People, for that matter. Who would have thought the outlandish stories were taken so seriously in Turtle Village? People often chattered, but usually it was just talk. Silk's fear was worrisome. Had the stories gained such a credibility?

You're no longer War Chief, he told himself resolutely. *You don't have to monitor such things anymore.*

As they neared the strip of rooms that divided the plaza, Ironwood walked ahead to the T-shaped doorway and ducked low to enter. The cool shadows of the altar room cloaked him. Dim firelight rose from the kiva below and lit the dangerous faces of the thlatsinas on the walls. Sharp beaks, furred muzzles, and glistening teeth shone.

When Poor Singer and Silk entered, they both stood with their eyes wide, studying the fierce masked gods.

"They're *beautiful,*" Poor Singer said, his voice hushed. He lowered the pack from his shoulder and tipped his head to look into each of their faces. "Who painted them?"

"Sternlight. The Great Warriors outside are also his work."

"His skill is astonishing." Poor Singer walked close to examine the bared fangs of the White Wolf Thlatsina. They glinted in the firelight.

Ironwood watched with amusement. "Sternlight breathes life into every image he paints. But come"—he gestured to the staircase that led down into the firelit womb of the kiva—"he can tell you himself."

Poor Singer sucked in a breath and his spine went rigid. His eyes met Silk's, and some secret passed between them. In a hoarse whisper, Poor Singer said, "He's down there?"

Ironwood cataloged the youth's reaction. This was more than just stories at work. Those wary old reflexes had him on guard, now, like a hungry dog with his nose to the wind. "Yes, come. I'll introduce you."

It took Poor Singer a few moments to gather his courage, but he squared his shoulders and went down the steps. Ironwood gestured Silk ahead of him and followed, alert for what, he didn't quite know.

A fire burned in the firebox straight ahead of them, all the way across the circular chamber. The four red pillars, the yellow, red, and blue bench levels, all seemed to waver and flutter with the leaping flames. In the thirty-six small wall crypts, the sacred dancesticks, rattles, and other ceremonial objects glistened orange.

Ironwood halted at the foot of the stairs and scanned the magnificently carved thlatsina masks that hung above the crypts. A strange chill prickled his neck. The masks seemed to be staring at Silk and Poor Singer with hollow, haunted eyes. As if of its own accord, his hand had wrapped around the handle of his deerbone stiletto.

Dune and Sternlight stood over Crow Beard's body, where it rested on the foot drum to the right, beneath a glittering turquoise-studded Death Blanket.

"Finally!" Dune said. Dressed in a long white shirt, his white hair and bushy white brows shining, he looked ghostly. His deeply wrinkled face twisted into a smile as he hobbled across the kiva to grip Poor Singer's hands. "It's good to see you, my boy. I had begun to fear Crow Beard might rot before you arrived."

Poor Singer's smile drooped. "Uh—well, we came as soon as we could."

"Yes, I know. Young Swallowtail told me the story. You brought my bundle?"

"It's right here." Poor Singer bent over his travel-stained pack. After unlacing it, he withdrew a small, beaded Power bundle and reverently handed it to Dune. "I hope this is it. I looked right where Swallowtail said it would be."

Dune took the bundle and cradled it lovingly in his arms. The turquoise, malachite, and coral beads sparkled in the firelight. "Yes, thank you for bringing it."

Dune shot a glance at Silk, lifted a white eyebrow, and then pinned Poor Singer with a questioning squint.

"Oh!" Poor Singer blurted, "Forgive me." He gestured to Silk. "Dune, this is Silk, from Turtle Village."

The lines in Dune's face seemed to deepen. He stood very still, his gaze probing Silk's.

Ironwood knew how uncomfortable Dune's scrutiny could be—he always felt like Packrat with Owl's talons embedded in his back—but Silk fearlessly returned the stare. Then a knowing smile bent Dune's thin lips.

After a short interval, Dune stepped forward and gently took one of Silk's hands. "It has been a long time," he softly said, "since I have seen such an infinity of open sky in any soul. Did you know it was there?"

Silk's full lips parted. She hesitated, then replied, "Yes, I think so."

Dune's voice turned serious. "You sail those skies often, don't you?"

"In my—my dreams."

"What bird is your Spirit Helper?"

Silk shifted her weight from foot to foot, and glanced uneasily at Poor Singer. "I'm not sure. Raven, maybe."

Dune rubbed his wrinkled chin and his eyes narrowed. "Yes, that would make sense. Especially since Poor Singer's Helper is Coyote. The two of you—"

"*How did you know that?*" Poor Singer cried, and winced at disrupting the sacred atmosphere of the kiva. Apologetically, he whispered, "Dune, I never told you—"

"You didn't have to tell me. You yip in your sleep. It was hard to mistake."

"I—I *yip?*"

Dune turned back to Silk. "Well, boy, if you had to bring a woman into my house, at least you picked a worthy one."

"Dune!" Poor Singer objected. "Dune, I would never . . . I mean, yes, Silk has been staying with me, but—"

"I wouldn't worry." Ignored until now, Sternlight walked forward. The grace of his movements always struck Ironwood.

Lean and tall, he seemed to float more than walk. His flowing black hair framed his serene face. His brown eyes shone with a warm light this afternoon. "You've told him about love, haven't you, Dune?"

Silk's posture reminded Ironwood of a deer surprised in a meadow, frozen in place, ready to flee at the first sign of trouble. And like a deer's, her eyes had that doelike mixture of fascination and fear.

"Certainly *not!*" Dune growled. "He wasn't ready to hear it."

"To hear what?" Poor Singer asked. "Dune told me to forget my body. That flesh was corrupt and would make me deaf to the voices of the gods."

Sternlight smiled serenely. "Well, that's true, if we're speaking about the love of the flesh, but there is more to love than the simple joining of bodies."

Poor Singer glanced at Silk, but her gaze remained on Sternlight alone.

Dune said, "Sternlight, it is a great risk to discuss love with someone his age. He doesn't even—"

"I was his age when you first discussed love with me," Sternlight gently reminded.

"You," Dune retorted, "were born holy. Poor Singer was born proud."

Poor Singer winced. "I'm not as bad as I used to be. I think I could hear about love now. I mean, if you wish me to know."

Silk watched Sternlight's every move: the twist of his lips, the way his hair fell over his broad chest, the twinkle in his brown eyes.

The young woman fascinated Ironwood. In some strange way, her facial expressions reminded him of Night Sun's: consciously bland, or calculated for effect. Rarely spontaneous. She kept any vulnerability hidden behind an impervious mask.

"You're not going to tell me, are you, Dune?" Poor Singer asked.

"If I tell you at this stage of your training, you'll think I'm giving you permission to walk about with a distended breechclout. You are not yet prepared to understand a love that is born in the soul and grows old in the soul. Trust me. I will tell you when it is time."

Poor Singer swallowed and nodded. "I trust you."

"Good!" Dune clapped his hands together. "Then let's get to work. Come along, Poor Singer." He hobbled away toward Crow Beard's body.

Poor Singer hurried after him. "What do you need me to do?"

Dune stopped in front of the turquoise-studded Death Blanket. "The first thing you must remember is that life itself is the most sacred ritual of all. As the caretakers of the dead, we are merely keeping order, assuring that things happen at the proper time—just as we do with all other rituals, planting, harvesting, renewing the world. Everything in the universe depends upon proper timing. Otherwise the places of humans, animals, and gods will be confused, and the world will fall apart. Now." He placed his Power bundle on the foot drum above Crow Beard's head. "We have much to do."

"And we"—Sternlight gestured to Ironwood and Silk—"must give them privacy to do it." He inclined his head to the staircase.

Poor Singer turned. "Silk, will you be—"

"I'll be fine." She gave him a confident nod. "I'll wander about the town, then return to our chamber. I'll wait for you there."

Poor Singer gave Ironwood a worried glance and stared pointedly at Sternlight. "I'll come as soon as we've finished here."

Ironwood followed Sternlight out into the bright sun of the western plaza and waited for Silk.

She left the altar room cautiously, her gaze searching the plaza before she stepped out fully.

A warrior in more than just her eyes. . . . Has she seen battle? Perhaps during the raid on Turtle Village.

Warm sunshine drenched her pretty face and flickered through her hip-length hair as she walked to join them. Ironwood's brows knitted. When he'd first seen her, from the fourth story, she'd been just a young woman arriving with Poor Singer. His eyes had almost skipped over her. Now he had to fight with himself not to stare at her. Something about her struck him as *familiar*, though he could not say why. The way she tipped her head, a gesture of her hand, the look in her dark eyes. He'd never visited Turtle Village. Never even ventured close, because of its proximity to Lanceleaf Village, so he couldn't have seen her before.

Then why am I so bothered by her?

She stopped a short distance away and lifted her pointed nose. Her nostrils flared as the fragrances of fresh spring grasses blew through the plaza. Or was she scenting for danger? He'd done that himself often enough, usually before battle, as if, by testing the wind, he could smell the locations of enemy warriors.

The slaves had returned to their duties, leaving the plaza empty and silent. Dust whirls bobbed and careened when Wind Baby gusted hard. Just watching her made Ironwood feel as if hidden eyes peered at them.

He scanned the roofs and doors. To Sternlight, he said, "Silk's village was destroyed by Tower Builders. She's come here looking for family."

Regret lined Sternlight's face. "I see." He held a hand out to Silk, inviting her to come closer. "Please tell me more about this. Perhaps I can help."

Silk came forward, but clenched her fists at her sides, as though bracing for a fight. "My mother always told me that I had cousins here. That they left Turtle Village many summers ago."

Sternlight appeared to ignore her defensive posture. "Do you know their names?"

"No, I—I never thought to ask. It didn't occur to me that I might need to know one day. But now . . ." She gazed at Sternlight and her control wavered. She clenched her fists so hard that her knuckles went white. "Now, I do need to know about my family. *Badly.*"

"I understand," he said softly. "Don't worry, Silk. If they are here, we will find them. Shall we sit down and discuss this?"

"I wouldn't want to bother you." She'd lowered her voice.

Sternlight turned to Ironwood, "Will you join us?"

"I was thinking I might talk to Silk later. I have duties to perform."

As if reading the strain on Ironwood's face, Sternlight gently said, "I understand."

Ironwood turned to Silk and her eyes narrowed, ever so slightly, but enough. "Until later, Silk."

Heart in her throat, Cornsilk watched Ironwood walk across the plaza. It had never occurred to her that she might be alone with Sternlight so soon after her arrival.

You can do this. Just be careful. You can't afford a mistake now. She gave him a careful scrutiny. His brown eyes seemed to see past all of her carefully built defenses and into her soul. The sudden sensation of vulnerability left her ready to run.

Sternlight said, "Why don't we sit outside where we can watch the canyon? It's very pretty today. Many of the first wildflowers are out."

She jerked a nod. "I'd like that."

Thirty-Five

Father Sun blazed over the canyon, bleaching the normally tan walls a rusty white and sucking the color from the sky. The pale sere blue sparkled with wind-blown dust. As Cornsilk followed Sternlight through the entry, she counted three whirlwinds careening drunkenly down the length of the canyon. Their swaying and bobbing looked playful, and for an instant, the sight eased her.

At dawn, when she and Poor Singer first peered over the rim of Straight Path Canyon, she'd been overwhelmed by how crowded it was. She'd never imagined the hugeness of the buildings, or the number of them. Fires had twinkled everywhere, glowing against the cliffs, dotting the bottomlands, lining the jagged wash, gleaming on top of the mesas. There had to be two or three thousand people living in this narrow canyon. They traded for almost everything, but where did they get their water in the summertime?

Sternlight turned right, his white shirt dancing in the breeze, and Cornsilk chanced a glimpse at Webworm, who still stood above the entry. He looked exactly as she remembered, square-jawed and lanky. His red shirt billowed in the wind. As they walked beneath him, Webworm frowned down and Cornsilk quickly lowered her head to watch her feet. He probably would not remember her, but she didn't wish to find out.

Green grass fringed the base of the white wall, and a pavement of coral-colored sandstone pebbles crunched beneath her sandals.

Sternlight turned right again and led her around the western side of the half-moon-shaped building, then followed a dirt trail through a maze of toppled boulders. Stones the height of tall men scattered the base of the cliff. Yellow and blue wildflowers thrived in the cool shadows cast by the boulders, their petals trembling in the wind. Behind the town, the sheer cliff rose two hundred hands into the faded sky. Beautiful paintings and rock carvings adorned the cliff face, telling the story of the Great Warriors' battle to save the First People after their emergence from the underworlds. Cornsilk's mouth opened as she tipped her head back to follow the spirals, handprints, and sun symbols that climbed the expanse of rock.

Sternlight sat down with his back against the cool stone, looking at the stunted trees clinging to the steep cliff. The gnarled junipers survived in patches of dirt no bigger than a handsbreadth across. Cornsilk knew, from the junipers that grew around Lanceleaf Village, that the trees would never get any bigger. They would remain miniature, their branches twisting and curling more every sun cycle.

Sternlight tipped his stunningly handsome face to peer at Cornsilk. "You'll find this a perfect place to talk. Father Sun keeps this spot warm all afternoon and long into the night."

Cornsilk eased down a body-length from him, her mouth dry, heart thumping. "Have you sat out here at night?"

"Often." An unearthly glow lit his brown eyes, as if one of the gods looked out at her. It made Cornsilk's spine prickle.

Lifting a hand, Sternlight pointed to the western mesa. The stone glowed a white-gold in the slant of sunlight. "I can tell you every place that Sister Moon, Father Sun, and several of the Blessed Evening People set over that mesa during the cycle, and at exactly what hand of time."

Cornsilk folded her legs under her and braced her shoulder against rock, facing him. "That's what you do, isn't it? As Sun-watcher? You chart the motions of Father Sun, and the other sky gods?"

"It's part of what I do, yes."

Cornsilk examined his smooth jaw, the curve of his lips, searching for some likeness between her face and his. The color of his eyes reminded her of a buffalo's, very dark brown, almost black, and he had a perfect, straight nose. *Nothing.* Her heart sank. She had been hoping so hard . . . but she saw no family resemblance. She wanted to run away and hide. This man was a stranger. All of the speeches she'd rehearsed in her head, the precisely imagined meeting between them, slipped away into the impossible fantasies they had really been.

"I'm sorry," she finally whispered, "I shouldn't have bothered you about this. You are one of the First People and I am just Ant Clan."

The crow's feet around his eyes deepened. "You are Ant Clan?"

Cornsilk nodded.

Sternlight cocked his head. "I thought Turtle Village was Coyote Clan."

Sick at her mistake, she frowned at the golden sand that mounded around her sandals. "Most were. My family was Ant Clan."

"I see." He seemed to let it go. He gazed between the boulders toward the steeply eroded banks of Straight Path Wash, where several slaves worked, watched over by a short burly man dressed in red. The kneeling women washed clothing. By pounding the wet cloth with stones, they loosened the dirt. They dipped the garment into a pot of warm soapy water and finally rinsed it in a pot of fresh water. Pine-pole drying racks fluttered with a rainbow of colors. The reds and blues appeared particularly bright in the noon sun.

"Tell me something about these relatives you seek." Stern-light asked. "We have many Ant Clan masons here—the best in the world, I think."

"My mother was a mason." Cornsilk lovingly studied the

massive white wall fifty hands away, wondering if her mother had laid the stones beneath the thin veneer of plaster. "She's dead."

"I'm sorry. There is so much grief these days."

"Sh—she was killed . . . in the raid." With sudden desperation, she cried, "I don't know *why* my village was attacked, Sternlight! We had done nothing wrong! Offended no one! Why do you think raiders would come to kill us?" Realizing how she must sound, Cornsilk swallowed and lowered her voice. "We didn't do anything wrong. I swear it."

Sternlight touched her fingers. "It's over. Let it go, and thank the thlatsinas that you escaped."

"It—it was an accident." She pulled her hand away from his and clenched it into a fist in her lap. "I should have died, too, but I hid in the brush on a hill above the village—no one saw me."

"Then you must have seen everything."

Cornsilk's tears welled before she could stop them. She looked up miserably into that handsome face, and saw kindness in his eyes. "I watched them kill my friends, my family. I saw them destroy everything I had."

Sternlight turned to sit cross-legged in front of her, his forearms propped on his knees, his long fingers steepled against his lips. For a time, he just looked at her. Then, in a comforting voice, he said, "You mustn't be so sad. It would hurt your family very much if they knew you were suffering this way. I know you miss them. But you will see them again."

"Are you certain?"

Sternlight gave her a confident smile. "Oh, yes, I am. I've been to the underworlds, and I've been to the skyworlds. I've walked among generations of our people. I *know* our relatives live."

Cornsilk stared at a sprig of grass beside her right sandal, thinking. She and Poor Singer had crossed a shallow trickle of water just after dawn, and mud clotted her yucca sandals and clung to the laces. "What do people do there? In the afterlife?"

Sternlight used his finger to shove around a flake of plaster that had cracked from the wall and been carried by Wind Baby to this nest among the boulders. "I once met an old man in the Soot World. He was a weaver. During his life on earth, he'd been an average weaver. No one had either praised or insulted his work. But after a hundred sun cycles in the Soot World, his weavings were highly prized. People spoke about him in hushed voices. You see, he had different fibers to work with in the underworld. He could pull a strand of purple from the tailfeathers of the Rainbow Serpent, and weave it together with a strand of Brother Sky's hair, and threads of the purest sweetest yellow, plucked from sage buttercup petals." Sternlight's eyes softened as though seeing those brilliant colors again. "I tell you truly, Silk, our families in the afterlives are very industrious and contented. They hunt and fish, and love each other, much as we do here."

The warmth of his voice affected Cornsilk's soul like cool salve on a fevered wound. With trepidation, she asked, "And the ghosts raid each other, don't they? Just like here?"

Sternlight raised his eyes to a hawk that sailed out over the canyon rim. "Yes, I saw wars. But they were not fought for vengeance, Silk. It must be hard, after what you have seen, to understand that there is an element of sport to war. In the Soot World, wars were played as games, just like hoop-and-stick, or the dice game, or throwing bones. Whichever side wins feasts the other after the battle."

Cornsilk pulled crusted mud from her sandal laces and dropped it onto the golden sand. "I hope the warriors who killed my family have to die over and over in the underworlds."

"The Blessed Bear Thlatsina. told me once that when a wicked warrior dies he is pursued across the face of the world by the Earth Spirits. They chase the warrior until they catch him and then may eat holes in his soul."

Cornsilk wiped her eyes with her hand. She tried to visualize ghosts with holey souls, and the thought made her frown. "And what happens to bad warriors in the afterlife?"

"They are tormented by the other ghosts who live there. The ghosts can tell, you see; from the holes in the warrior's soul, that he killed for spite, not out of duty, and they hound and ostracize him until he is reborn."

Cornsilk had been dreaming about killing Webworm and Gnat. The story gave her hope that if she failed, she might have another chance in a future life. "I hope those warriors are reborn as mosquitoes on my arm."

"Well"—Sternlight scratched his cheek thoughtfully—"everyone has their own idea of torture. I'd wish them reborn as bushy-tailed wood rats. Hunted by everything alive. Always scurrying in terror."

Cornsilk gave him a sidelong glance. "Thanks for the suggestion."

He smiled.

"Sternlight? You're being very kind to me, but I know you are the greatest priest alive, and—"

"I am?"

"Everybody says so."

"People say lots of things." He picked at a loose thread in the sleeve of his white ritual shirt, apparently uneasy with the praise.

Cornsilk hesitated for an uncomfortably long time, then said, "May I ask you something?"

"Of course."

"Well, it's"—she licked her dry lips—"it's an awkward question."

"I've heard awkward questions before."

She filled her lungs, in case she never got to take another breath. "Is it . . . true that when you were an infant all you had to do was point at birds and they would fall dead from the skies?"

Sternlight's head came up suddenly. After a moment, a soft laugh shook his shoulders. "That's one I haven't heard—and I thought I knew all the stories."

"You mean, it isn't true?"

Against the towering golden cliff, his wind-blown hair appeared as black as a raven's wings. "I'm afraid not. Power . . . well, my Power doesn't work that way. I could speak to the bird in its own language and ask it to fall to the earth and pretend to be dead. The bird might grant my request. But in the end, it would open its bright eyes and fly away, just as alive as before."

His openness had lent her courage. Suddenly very curious, she asked, "But there are witches who can kill with a glance, or a word—aren't there?"

A haunted look entered Sternlight's eyes. "Yes, there are."

"How do they do that?"

He drew up one knee and laced his fingers around it. "In all honesty, I don't know. Power is like a finely woven blanket where the warp is made up of strands of light and the weft is darkness. I've heard that witches boast they can pull out all the dark strands and weave the malignant Power around themselves like a cape of shadows."

Fascinated, Cornsilk asked, "Is that why they work at night? Because they can be invisible in their dark capes?"

"Maybe. Who can say? Witches are very clever."

Cornsilk scooped a handful of the warm sand and let it trickle through her fingers.

They sat in silence for a time, listening to the wind whimper around the boulders and rustle the wildflowers. As Father Sun descended in the west, shadows swelled by the rocks and stretched toward them, cool and dark.

"Did you understand what Dune was trying to tell you in the kiva? About your soul?"

Cornsilk dusted off her sandy hands. "Some of it. Poor Singer told me right after we met that I had a blue sky soul." She drew a halo around her torso. "He said he could see it glowing around me."

Sternlight gave her a thoughtful inspection. "Yes, it's very beautiful, but Dune meant more than that. A wild freedom lives in your soul, Silk."

"Freedom?"

"Yes. You see, most people never really know freedom, though they pretend they do because it eases the pain of their imprisonment. But you, Silk, *are* free. People could cage you and tie you up, and you'd still be free. The heart of your freedom doesn't beat in this world. It beats in the skyworlds. Dune was trying to tell you that you were born of the sky—not of the earth. And . . ." he said with a curious frown, "that is *very* strange."

Her forehead lined. "Why?"

Sternlight lifted his brows. "Only First People are sky born. That's why, after death, First People return to the sky."

"But what does that mean about me? Why would I have a sky-born soul?"

"I can't answer that. I've never seen a Made Person with a soul like yours." Sternlight pointed to the canyon rim where two golden eagles perched, their brown bodies dark against the dusty blue heavens. Their sharp eyes searched the canyon bottom for movement. "You must seek that answer yourself. But if you seek in the high places, where earth meets sky, the thlatsinas will help you."

Cornsilk squinted thoughtfully at the eagles. Behind them, billowing Cloud People followed the sky roads south, toward the homes of the Fire Dogs. She'd been wondering about many of the things Dune had said in the kiva—especially about Poor Singer being born proud, and how it was a great risk to discuss love with someone his age. Both had angered her. Poor Singer had acted selflessly the entire time they'd been together and always looked at her with warmth. Maybe Dune didn't know Poor Singer very well.

Bravely, Cornsilk turned to Sternlight. "What was it that Dune didn't wish to tell Poor Singer? About love?"

Sternlight smiled. Wind Baby flipped long hair over his eyes, and he tucked it behind his ears. "Oh, mostly that love is essential to any spiritual life."

"But I thought it was bad for Singers."

"No, no, Silk. Until love has quickened a soul, it is like an unfledged eagle. Only half alive. Filled with yearning. Believe me when I tell you that a soul that does not know the depths of love will never fly to the gods. A Singer's wings are woven from love."

"Poor Singer . . . he—he doesn't think it's good for him to be with me."

Sternlight's eyes seemed to go vacant for a time, as if lost in memories of another time, a tender time, filled with hopes and dreams.

"Silk," he said at last, "to love *is* to seek the gods. The first instant we feel love as little children, we set foot on that divine road. After that, every moment we spend loving is another step closer to the gods. Until the final moment, when we must leave the ground and fly."

"Then why can't Poor Singer know these things?"

He bowed his head. "When the time is right, Dune will tell him. Just now, Dune's trying to get Poor Singer to look beyond his body. That's the first step for a Singer, and it isn't easy at Poor Singer's age. Perhaps you shouldn't be together just yet.

But someday soon, he will need your love as desperately as he needs food, or water."

Cornsilk creased the fabric of her dress in anxious fingers. "I feel better knowing that. Thank you, Sternlight. I promise not to tell Poor Singer until after Dune has already done so."

He touched her hand to still its nervous movements. "I knew you wouldn't. Your sense of honor shows on your pretty face, Silk."

Cornsilk smiled. How odd that their conversation flowed so easily, like that of old friends. From down in the wash, laughter rose, and Cornsilk heard a child squeal with delight, then a dog barked.

"Well"—Sternlight gathered himself and stood—"let us start speaking to the members of the Ant Clan who live here. Perhaps we will find your family before another night falls, Silk." He extended a hand to her. His white shirt billowed around his tall body.

Cornsilk looked at those long fingers for a moment, thinking: *This man might be my father?* Then she placed her hand in his and let him pull her to her feet. As their gazes held, her heart ached. She had so many things to tell him, and to ask him. But she needed to be absolutely sure before she revealed her blanket, and herself, to him.

He gestured to the dirt trail. "Go ahead. I'll follow."

Cornsilk walked the worn path through the boulders with her eyes on the trail, and her soul floating in the past, seeing her mother's face. . . .

"Do not ask me, my daughter. I can tell you only that I believe he will help you."

Cornsilk glanced at him over her shoulder. He walked with his head down, his expression peaceful. His steps barely made a sound.

What favor did this great priest owe her mother? And when had he incurred the debt?

A very long time ago, probably, when her mother had lived in Talon Town.

As she rounded the curve of the wall, and headed left, due east toward the entry, she saw Webworm standing guard with a young man at his side. Certainly one of the First People, the youth wore a rich purple shirt decorated with copper bells. Each time the wind tousled his hem, the bells tinkled pleasantly. Across his chest glimmered gorgeous red, blue, and yellow macaw feathers.

Webworm turned to look down at them, and Cornsilk quickly lowered her head, like a woman with a purpose and a place to go.

Sternlight came up beside her and whispered, "If you can, Silk, try to avoid the man in purple."

"Why? Who is he?"

"He is the new Blessed Sun. His name is Snake Head."

"Why should I avoid him?" She looked up at Sternlight and saw how pale his face had gone, as though he *feared* the Blessed Sun.

Sternlight replied, "He is not known for his kindness to young women. Think of him as you would a scorpion."

A cold shiver ran down her back. "I see."

As they walked through the entry, Sternlight murmured, "Stay close to me, Silk. He's grown very bold of late."

Sternlight put a hand on her shoulder and guided her across the plaza toward a group of seated women who sorted and folded clothing. Neat piles of shirts, dresses, dance sashes, and cotton capes lined the wall. When the women saw Sternlight coming, they went quiet and grave. Like stone statues, they watched as Sternlight and Cornsilk neared them.

"A pleasant afternoon to you, Yellowgirl," Sternlight said to the oldest woman. Muscular, square-bodied, and in her forties, she had sallow cheeks and a thin face. Her short hair hung even with her chin.

"And to you, Blessed Sternlight," she responded without looking up to meet his eyes. "What may we do to help you?"

"This is Silk. She is of the Ant Clan and was born in Turtle Village. She is searching—"

"Sunwatcher?" a shrill edgy voice called. "Come over here!"

Cornsilk saw Sternlight's jaw clamp. He took a breath, whispered, "Stay here, Silk," and hastily walked across the plaza to meet the Blessed Sun halfway.

The Chief had his head cocked and a seductive smile on his face. Sternlight stood a head taller, which forced Snake Head to crane his neck to see Silk. The look he gave her made her stomach muscles clench. The women sitting against the wall looked Cornsilk up and down, and whispered behind their hands.

Yellowgirl said, "You do not look like a mason, child. Your arms are too skinny. And you should have well-muscled shoulders."

"I'm not a mason, but my mother was. She—"

"She was killed in the attack?"

"Yes. The Tower Builders—"

"What was her name?"

The questions fired at her one after another left Cornsilk feeling naked and vulnerable. She braced her feet and met Yellowgirl's hard glare. "Her name was Beeweed. She was not born in Turtle Village, but moved there f-from Lanceleaf Village." Surely that information could not hurt. "She married a man of the Coyote Clan, named Watertoad." In a shaky voice, she asked, "I am here looking for cousins who left Turtle Village long ago. Do you know of any?"

Yellowgirl shook her head. Her short black hair flipped over her sallow cheeks. "I am the master mason here, and I have never heard of any Ant Clan woman coming from Turtle Village. But we do have several Coyote Clan women who used to live in Turtle Village. Do you wish to speak with them?"

Cornsilk shifted her weight to her left foot. "No. If they are not Ant Clan, they're not my relatives. Thank you for your help, though. Would you pass the word around that I am searching for relatives?"

"Yes, child, I will, but listen to me." Yellowgirl leaned forward with her eyes narrowed. "If you wish the Made People in Talon Town to speak with you, you must stay away from the witch." She jerked her chin toward Sternlight.

Cornsilk turned. He still stood in front of the chief, blocking Snake Head's view of her. "Do you truly think he's a witch? He seems so kind."

Yellowgirl snorted derisively, and the other women laughed. "All witches do. That's how they lure their victims into their snares. If you do not wish to end up with corpse powder in your belly, *stay away from him!*"

Cornsilk folded her arms to hug herself. She stood uncomfortably, her gaze on the drifting Cloud People, until Sternlight returned.

He stopped at Cornsilk's side, gray-lipped, clearly upset, but his voice came out calm. "What did you discover?"

"Yellowgirl says there are no Ant Clan people here that came from Turtle Village. But she is going to pass the word around."

Yellowgirl lowered her gaze when Sternlight looked at her. He did not seem to notice this act, or if he did, he'd witnessed it so often, it no longer affected him. But it astonished Cornsilk. In her village, if a person refused to look at one of the holy people, it was a subtle accusation of witchery, implying the person feared the Evil Eye. The Evil Eye could cause miscarriages, illnesses, even death if the witch were Powerful enough.

"Thank you, Yellowgirl," Sternlight said, then added to Cornsilk, "There are others from Turtle Village here. Do you wish to speak with them? They might be able to tell you of Ant Clan members elsewhere who came from Turtle Village."

Cornsilk gazed up into his serene eyes. "Perhaps later. For now, I think I'd like to return to my chamber. It was a long journey. I'm very tired."

"Yes, I understand."

Cornsilk started to walk away, then turned back to Yellowgirl. "Thank you, Yellowgirl. I appreciate your help . . . and advice."

Yellowgirl gave Cornsilk a quick glance. "I'll let you know if anyone turns up who might be a relative of yours."

"You're very kind."

Sternlight said, "Let me walk you back to your chamber."

Cornsilk nodded, and kept her head down as they walked past the Blessed Sun, Snake Head. But she could feel his eyes upon her, probing, and her shoulders knotted. The image of a scorpion had lodged in her soul, one in human form, but heartless, deadly, and willing to prey on its own kind.

When they reached the ladder, Cornsilk gripped one of the pine rungs, and asked, "What did the Chief wish to speak with you about?"

Sternlight gave her that limpid gaze. "He asked about you, who you were, what you were doing here. Things like that." He paused. "Silk, if the Chief sends for you, do not go, and if he approaches you when you are alone, tell him you are here with the holy Derelict. Do you understand?"

"Yes, I—I think so."

"Not even Snake Head would dare to challenge Dune—I don't think." Sternlight put a friendly hand on her shoulder. "Rest for now. I will keep asking about your family. Perhaps we may yet find someone from Turtle Village who belongs to your clan."

Silk searched his face, trying, once again, to find any resemblance. For a moment she struggled with the desire to speak openly with him—but, in the end, merely nodded. "Thank you, Sternlight." Then she quickly climbed the ladder and headed for her chamber.

Poor Singer stood beside Dune, staring wide-eyed at the dead man. The magnificent blanket, studded with chunks of turquoise, had been folded at the bottom of the foot drum. The turquoise sparkled in the flickering firelight. Wispy gray hair clung to Crow Beard's scalp, contrasting with the rude stone cobble that protruded from the ruins of his face. The eyes had dried out and shrunk into the orbits, and the lids had drawn back over flat, lusterless lenses. The lips, too, had drawn into a mocking rictus, which, along with the rock, gave the sagging face a masklike appearance.

While the face had shrunk, Crow Beard's belly had swollen, and periodically made a gurgling sound. Poor Singer winced as he looked at it. The distended stomach pressed tightly against the cotton fabric of his blue-and-gold shirt like an inflated bladder. Despite the coolness of the kiva, the evil spirits of corruption had began to grow and thrive in the Chief's body. A faint sickly sweet smell taunted Poor Singer's nostrils.

Dune turned to Poor Singer, a bushy white eyebrow raised. "Here." He handed Poor Singer a small pot of white paint, chalk mixed with water. "I'll paint his arms if you will paint his legs."

Dune had rolled up the sleeves of his huge white ritual shirt so he could work, but the hem dragged on the hard-packed dirt floor.

Poor Singer wet his lips anxiously. "Paint them . . . how?"

Fatigue tugged Dune's wrinkles into a mass of criss-crossing lines, nearly burying his small round nose. The white hairs in his bushy brows stuck out at odd angles.

"Paint his legs with lines of white dots," Dune said, "representing his kinship to the Evening People. Paint all the way from the groin to the ankles, and try to keep your lines straight. We want the Wolf Thlatsina, who guards the entry to the skyworlds, to know that Crow Beard is sky born, like the stars."

Poor Singer nodded, dipped his forefinger into the paint, lifted the hem of Crow Beard's shirt, and pulled it up past the crotch. The penis looked like a newly hatched chick in a gray-frosted nest of pubic hair. The gasses of corruption had expanded the scrotum like an overgrown egg. A shiver went through Poor Singer when he touched the cold, clammy flesh; a queasy feeling slipped around his stomach.

In between painting dots, he distracted himself from the corpse by gazing at the magnificent ceremonial chamber.

Thlatsina masks hung over the small wall crypts, glittering with precious stones. Thirty-six in all, they wore brilliantly colored headdresses of blue, yellow, red, and deep black feathers. Tufts of pure white eagle down crowned many masks. Neck ruffs of buffalo, badger, rabbit, and other hides gave the appearance of beards. But Poor Singer's eyes lingered on the sharp fangs and polished beaks that glinted in the fire's amber glow. Poor Singer could *feel* their souls. Even in the empty eye sockets, he saw a strange, haunting light.

The circular kiva stretched at least a hundred hands across, supported by four red masonry pillars and encircled by three bench levels. Each bench had its own sacred color, yellow, red, and blue topped by white walls.

Another body rested on the opposite foot drum, covered completely by a beautiful Death Blanket. Poor Singer couldn't guess who it might be.

He finished one leg and started on the other.

Being more practiced than Poor Singer, Dune had already finished both arms. Leaning over the Chief's face, Dune frowned, and dipped his crooked finger in his paint pot. Over the left eye, he painted a crescent moon.

"What does that signify?" Poor Singer asked in a hushed voice.

"It will tell the sky gods that Crow Beard was a special man, a leader of renown, and deserves to be treated as such."

Poor Singer finished the right leg and set his pot down at the edge of the foot drum. "What do we do next?"

"I must take care of this next step. Just watch."

Dune's bundle sat above Crow Beard's head. He hobbled to it. The malachite, turquoise, and jet beads glittered as he rummaged through it and pulled out six feathers and a coil of cotton string.

Dune held them up for Poor Singer to see. "These will give him the ability to fly to the skyworlds."

He tied a feather to a wisp of Crow Beard's hair, one to each hand and ankle. Then he slipped the string around the dead chief's back and tied a feather over his heart.

"When Crow Beard reaches the top of the sacred Humpback Butte," Dune said, "these seed feathers will sprout and in a blink his whole body will be covered with feathers. He will have long pointed wings, just like Prairie Falcon, who gave the feathers."

Poor Singer clasped his hands before him, marveling. He had, of course, seen bodies after they'd been prepared for burial, but the ritual remained a secret. Only very holy people knew why things were done as they were. On the fabric of his soul, he could imagine the grand transformation and see the dead Chief sailing through the heavens.

"You may help me with this next part." Dune pulled a small leather bag from his bundle. It was painted with a red spiral and blue slash of lightning. "Open your right hand."

Poor Singer hurried forward and extended his open palm. Dune poured it full of cornmeal and draped a string over Poor Singer's wrist. "Fill Crow Beard's hands with meal, then tie them shut."

"Yes, Dune."

Poor Singer had to pry the Chief's stiff fingers open. He filled the right palm, forced the fingers closed around the meal, and held them shut with one hand while he looped the string with the other. He pulled it tight and knotted it.

While Poor Singer finished the left hand, Dune rubbed meal over the chief's face, dribbled some into the death-grinning mouth, and filled the sunken eyes. The yellow of the meal flashed golden in the fluttering gleam.

"Why did you fill his eyes with meal, Dune?"

"To cleanse them of any lingering taint he might have picked up in life. This way he may look upon the glories of the skyworlds with new eyes, eyes unpolluted by the horrors of this world." Dune pointed to the tied hands. "By your labors, you have given Crow Beard the ability to enter those worlds. You see, upon arrival at the first skyworld, Crow Beard will need to sanctify his path by sprinkling cornmeal to the six directions."

Reverently, Poor Singer whispered, "I understand."

Dune frowned down at the Bashing Rock. Finally, he sighed and tugged the rock loose, inspecting the stains on the smooth surface. "Normally I don't leave my Bashing Rock in, but Hard Snake needed the reminder."

Poor Singer leaned forward, uncomfortable with the need to correct Dune. "You mean . . . Snake Head?"

Dune set the Bashing Rock to one side and sprinkled corn meal into the crater where the nose had been. "Probably," he answered.

Next, Dune pulled a white cloth from his bundle and held it up to the light. Three holes pierced it. "And this," he said as he covered the Chief's face, "represents the billowy clouds that will hide Crow Beard's face when he returns to bring rain to our dry country."

Dune arranged the cloth so the holes fit over the eyes and mouth. Then, as though exhausted, Dune braced a hand on the foot drum and heaved a sigh. "There. That is all for Crow Beard today. Tomorrow morning, before dawn, we will finish the burial preparations. Now, we must care for ourselves. Take off your clothing."

Poor Singer slipped his shirt over his head. He knew that those who attended the dead had to take ritual baths afterward to cleanse themselves. Dune removed his shirt and laid it on the yellow bench, then led the way to the rectangular firebox. He looked like a walking skeleton. The large freckles visible beneath his thin hair looked black in the dim light.

Fresh clothing, blankets, and several pots rested near the fire.

Dune bent down with a grunt and picked up two small bowls. He handed one to Poor Singer. "Juniper needles were boiled in this water. There's a cloth soaking in the bottom. Squeeze it out and wash thoroughly."

Poor Singer wrung out the tan cloth and washed his arms and legs, then dipped and wrung it again to purify his chest and the rest of his body. The pungent fragrance of juniper encircled him. When he'd finished, he placed the cloth back in the pot and started to set it on the floor near the fire.

Dune thrust out a hand. "No, don't set it down. Hold it until I'm finished."

Poor Singer nodded while Dune rubbed his own juniper scented cloth over his face and neck. "Now, watch what I do." Dune raised the bowl high—and slammed it down to shatter on the hard floor. He turned to Poor Singer. "Break yours, too. These pots are tainted with corruption. No one may ever use them again."

Poor Singer raised his pot and smashed it. Angular sherds clattered across the floor.

"We have one final cleansing to undergo today." Dune picked up a blanket and handed it to Poor Singer, then crouched before a small pot to the right of the fire. He removed several crystallized globs of piñon pine sap and placed them on the glowing coals at the edge of the fire. As the sap sizzled and popped, it produced a haze of blue smoke.

"Place your blanket over your head"—Dune illustrated with his own blanket—"and lean over the smoke. Make sure it passes over your whole body. Smoke is a cousin to the Cloud People, who bring us rain and life. It will drive away any evil spirits who might have been clinging to the dead."

Poor Singer did as he was told, letting the sweet pine-scented smoke bathe him. It felt warm on his skin.

Dune walked a short distance away and returned with two new shirts. He shook out one with red and gold diamonds and handed it to Poor Singer. "This is yours."

Poor Singer gaped at the garment. "It's beautiful!"

Dune gave him a disgusted look. "You like that, eh?"

"Of course! Who wouldn't want such a—"

"I'll find you another shirt like your old one as soon as I can. Then you can give that one away."

"But why can't I keep this one?"

"Boy, if I could beat that pride out of you with a stick, I'd do it."

Poor Singer bit his lip, dropped his blanket on the floor, and slipped the new shirt over his head. The fine tight weave hugged his body. He smoothed it down over his narrow hips. "What will happen to my old shirt?"

"It will be burned, along with mine." Dune put on a blue-and-black shirt. It fit perfectly, as if it had been made specifically for him. "You must go straight back to your chamber now, Poor Singer. And maintain sexual abstinence for four days."

Poor Singer blushed. "I've never—been—with Silk, Dune. We are just good friends."

"Make sure that's *all* you are for four more days." Dune picked up the pine sap bowl again. He poured the remaining globules onto the fire. Orange flames leaped, and sparks whirled upward toward the hole in the roof. Dune stood and lifted the pot, letting it smash on the floor near the sherds of the other two.

Curious, Poor Singer narrowed his eyes at the little holy man. "What would happen if I weren't? If I broke the prohibition against abstinence?"

A toothless grin lit Dune's wrinkled face. "We maintain abstinence as a final precaution against roaming evil. If you break the prohibition, and some malingering spirit sees you coupling, it might just take that opportunity to crawl into your penis and live there. And then . . ." Dune lifted a finger and shook it.

Abruptly he walked past Poor Singer, heading for the stairs.

"And then . . . what?" Poor Singer trotted along behind.

They stepped out of the altar room into the pale lavender veil of twilight. The cliff had shaded purple; the sky had turned a luminescent slate blue. Bats flitted over the town, twittering and diving, and the reddish gleams from warming bowls inside the town's chambers flowed out to splotch the white walls with rosy glows. Conversations created a soft hum.

Dune took a deep breath, filling his lungs with the clean air. "You did well, my boy. I'm proud of you. Meet me here before dawn."

"I will. Thank you, Dune. I learned a great deal, but I wish you'd tell me—"

"Sleep well, Poor Singer." Dune grinned. "I'll see you at first light."

He hobbled off toward his chamber, and Poor Singer watched his back. Dune climbed the ladder, one rung at a time, and walked across the first-story roof. His white hair had a pale orchid glow. Poor Singer watched him until he stepped onto the ladder that led down into his chamber, and vanished.

Poor Singer turned in the direction of his own chamber, whispering, *"And then . . . what?"*

Sixth Day

I crouch on a narrow ledge overlooking a waterfall. It is fed by snowmelt. The water is icy cold as it cascades down the rocks, gurgling and growling its way to the small pool a hundred hands below. A meadow rings the pool. Two boys stand on either side, fishing spears in their hands. They must be around nine or ten summers. I've been listening to them laugh as they fish and leap from rock to rock. Tall pine trees dot the meadow. A red-tailed hawk sails just above the wind-blown branches. Her shadow flits across the pool and the boys' joyous faces.

Predators. We are all so much alike, perhaps because our food consists entirely of souls.

We kill animals. We pull up plants. All of these creatures that we strike down have souls, just like ours, souls that do not die when their bodies die.

One of the boys has speared a fish. He laughs at the big trout. It wriggles on the end of his spear as he pulls it out of the crystalline water.

And I wonder . . .

How many souls live inside my body? Hundreds? Thousands.

No one has ever told me much about these souls. What do they do inside me? Are they all asleep? Like eggs resting in a warm nest? Or have they woven themselves into the very fabric of my muscles and bones?

Three deer catch my attention. They prance across the south end of the meadow. They are quiet and placid until they spy the boys, then they bound forward like the wind. Deadfall cracks in their wake. The boys whirl to look.

And I blink thoughtfully.

When blood suddenly rushes in my veins is it the deer running?

Perhaps my growling belly is really Badger at play, and my fluttering heart a flurry of grouse wings?

I look down and gently touch my chest. I have become the guard-

ian of a thousand souls. Creatures who gave their lives so that I might live.

The boys are shouting to each other across the pond, gathering up their catches and packs, preparing to go home for supper.

I watch them trot merrily across the grassy meadow. They take the same game trail the deer did and meld with the forest shadows.

I dip my hand into the waterfall and drink. When the liquid reaches my belly, Badger runs around, perhaps shaking off the icy droplets.

I pat my stomach and reverently close my eyes.

Thirty-Six

Webworm sat on soft deerhides in his mother's chamber and ate a bowl of thick soup. Roasted chunks of squash simmered with dried currants, sunflower seeds, and beeweed made a delicious meal. The soup pot hung from a tripod over the bowl of coals, and beside it sat a warm pot of dried yucca petal tea. The gentle glow of the warming bowl dyed the walls and lit the gaudy faces of the Dancing thlatsinas.

On the opposite side of the chamber, Featherstone lay rolled in a red blanket, snoring softly. In her partly open mouth, Webworm could see the gap of her missing front teeth. Dark gray hair spread across her sleeping mats. She looked very peaceful, and the sight comforted him.

Creeper sat cross-legged near Featherstone, finishing his soup. The short fat man had a curious expression on his round face, as if he floated over a terrible battle, watching it unfold, unable to stop the slaughter. He wore a green shirt with the sleeves rolled up, revealing the thick black hair on his arms. Creeper spooned more soup into his mouth and chewed slowly.

Webworm used a corncake to sop up the rest of his soup and set his bowl aside. "What's wrong, Creeper?" he asked as he bit into the sweet corncake.

Creeper looked up as though the question had startled him from a dream. "Oh, nothing." He frowned down into his soup. "I saw Snake Head speaking with you this afternoon. What did he want?"

"To give me orders. He's such a fool." Webworm grimaced at his corncake. "He wants only five warriors to accompany the burial party on the sacred road to the Humpback Butte."

"Five?" Creeper's eyes narrowed in disbelief. "That will leave the party vulnerable."

"I told him that. He informed me it was none of my concern. As the Blessed Sun, it was his decision to make, and he'd made it. Five warriors. No more."

The order had ignited fury in Webworm. As War Chief, he would be responsible for the safety of the burial procession. How could he protect them with five warriors? The very idea was ludicrous.

Webworm looked over and found Creeper staring blindly into his soup bowl. He cocked his head. "That wasn't really what was bothering you, was it, Creeper?"

Creeper waved a hand, as if to dismiss Webworm's concern. "No, but . . . I mean, I *was* worried about Snake Head. He's such an arrogant youth, and I know you've been—"

"Tell me, Creeper. Please."

Creeper lowered his soup bowl to his lap. "I spoke with Mourning Dove earlier. She told me some things that distressed me."

Webworm took another bite of his corncake and chewed it, waiting for Creeper to elaborate. For many summers Mourning Dove had been Creeper's lover, though Creeper never spoke of the fact. Webworm knew because he had watched them together. The tender touches that passed between them could mean only one thing. The arrangement made perfect sense to Webworm. Most people, however, considered it shameful. A clan leader like Creeper could have had far more prestigious lovers. But he didn't seem to wish them. Mourning Dove served Creeper's physical needs, while Featherstone provided for his heart.

When Creeper said nothing else, Webworm asked, "What did Mourning Dove say?"

Creeper heaved a breath. "Did you see the young woman who came into town this morning?"

"Just for an instant. Why?"

"Mourning Dove said that she was from Turtle Village, that she had escaped the destruction and come here."

"Why?"

Creeper turned his clay cup in his hands. "In search of relatives. Apparently the rest of her family were killed in the raid by the Tower Builders."

Webworm ate his last bite of corncake, relishing the flavor before he swallowed it, and dusted the crumbs from his hands onto the hem of his red shirt. "Why does that worry you? It seems perfectly natural."

"Ordinarily, I would agree, but the young woman said many things that made no sense."

"Like what?"

Creeper took a final bite of his soup and put the bowl down on the hides at his side. "She told Yellowgirl her mother was a mason named Beeweed, who had married a Coyote Clan man named Watertoad. She—"

"That is strange." Webworm extended his long legs across the warm deerhides. "I visited Turtle Village several times, but I never heard of any Ant Clan women living there."

"Nor has anyone else, War Chief."

Their gazes held, and Webworm frowned. "What else did this young woman say?"

Creeper picked up his teacup and swirled the liquid, as if stirring up the fragments of boiled petals. He took a long drink. "She said her mother had moved to Turtle Village from Lanceleaf Village, and that—"

"*Lanceleaf?*" Memories flared . . . screams . . . the fire raging out of control . . . Beargrass' frantic voice . . . young Fledgling's terrified eyes.

"War Chief?" Creeper leaned forward and his thick black brows plunged down. "Are you well?"

Webworm closed his eyes, trying to banish the scenes. "She said her parents moved to Turtle Village. What else?" When Webworm opened his eyes, he found Creeper studying him worriedly. "I'm all right. Go on."

Creeper nodded, and continued softly, "The young woman's name is Silk."

"Silk?"

An icy tingle ran up Webworm's arms, as though his body had pieced the information together and was trying to force his stupid soul to understand. He shifted to sit cross-legged, peering intently at Creeper. "Silk. From Turtle Village. Originally from Lanceleaf Vill——" Understanding ran through his veins like fire. "Blessed Gods!"

"What is it? What's wrong?"

"I—I thought she looked familiar. I only caught a glimpse of her face as she walked beneath my guard station with Sternlight, but——"

"You know her? Who is she?"

Webworm stared unblinking at Creeper. The man's round face, framed with short black hair, had flushed.

"I think her name is really Cornsilk. She was the daughter of Beargrass and Thistle."

Creeper sat back against the wall. He didn't say anything for a time, then he murmured, "A girl. I *knew* it was a girl."

Webworm felt as though his stomach had fallen through the floor. "You mean, you think Cornsilk is Night Sun's daughter?"

Creeper's gaze wandered the chamber, idly searching the masked faces of the thlatsinas. "If she is, may the gods help us all."

Confused, filled with dread, Webworm said, "You mean because it will mean Night Sun's death?"

Creeper lowered his face and massaged the deep wrinkles in his forehead. "No, much worse. Don't you see? If this girl is Night Sun's daughter, it means that the holy Derelict, the great Sunwatcher, and Night Sun, plotted to deceive the Blessed Elders of the First People. And *did* it. If the truth comes out . . ."

Creeper didn't finish the sentence. He didn't have to.

Blood rushed so deafeningly in Webworm's ears that he could barely hear himself say, "It will mean all of their deaths."

Creeper got to his feet and paced nervously before the bowl of warming coals, his hands clenched at his sides. The folds of his green shirt shone orange in the gleam. "But this is bizarre. Sternlight and Night Sun might plot, but Dune? Why would the holy Derelict implicate himself in such a . . . ?" Creeper stopped pacing. He whispered, "Could it be?"

Webworm lurched to his feet. "What? Tell me what's wrong."

"I-I'm not sure, but I think—"

Featherstone rolled to her side, and they both went silent. Gray hair straggled about her ears. Tears beaded her stubby lashes.

"Oh, Featherstone," Creeper said gently. "Were we speaking too loudly? Forgive us. You should be sleeping. We didn't mean to wake you."

Creeper knelt and pulled the blanket over her shoulders again.

Jaw slack, eyes wide and vacant, Featherstone murmured, *"What's the matter with the two of you? They've laid a trap! Can't you see it?"*

Webworm's gut crawled. "A trap? . . . Mother? Are you awake? Here with us? Or is your soul flying?"

Drool spilled from the corner of her open mouth and trickled down her chin. She'd started to pant, as if running, running hard to get away from pursuers.

Creeper used the corner of the blanket to dab at the spittle. "Featherstone? Are you here with us?"

"Flying," she whispered, barely audible, "flying with the Meteor People."

Creeper gave Webworm a tender look and they both sank to the floor again.

Creeper's hand shook as he combed hair away from his eyes. "We had better keep this to ourselves." He ground his jaws, and added, "For now."

"Yes," Webworm agreed. "For now." But wondered how he should act if he happened to meet Beargrass' young daughter walking across the plaza? Should he pretend not to know her?

His belly soured. It would be very difficult. Now that he knew her identity, he longed to sit down with Cornsilk and talk. He *needed* to talk with her. If he explained why he'd killed her family, maybe she would tell him that it wasn't his fault, that, of course, he had to obey orders. Perhaps she would give him that heart-rending little girl smile he remembered so well and tell him she held him blameless.

Webworm laced his fingers in his lap and squeezed them tight. Or perhaps she would leap on him and tear him to pieces with her bare hands.

He expelled a shuddering breath. *It will be the first time in my life that I won't fight back.*

As Webworm frowned at his twined hands, a terrifying thought occurred to him. He glanced up at Creeper and found the little man staring back.

"Snake Head was very interested in Cornsilk today," he whispered. "You don't think he suspects the same thing we do—do you?"

Poor Singer had moved his blankets to the opposite side of the chamber. Curled on his side, he'd been lying there—wide awake—for two hands of time. His sole occupation consisted of watching Silk in the dim red gleam of the warming bowl. She slept fitfully, thrashing in her blankets, her black hair tumbling about. The soft sounds deep in her throat made him ache. Was she back home again? Seeing her village burning and her family dying?

The story she'd told him that morning had left Poor Singer floundering. What if Night Sun and Sternlight *were* her parents? Though the First People married amongst themselves, surely they would consider an aunt-nephew relationship to be incest? . . . If so, they would kill Silk as an abomination.

Poor Singer tugged his blanket up around his throat. He hadn't mentioned this possibility to Silk—but, smart as she was, she'd probably thought of it herself.

He frowned up through the roof entry at the Evening People. Against the indigo blanket of night, a few sparkled brilliantly, while others had the hazy quality of moonlit mist.

After mulling the details she'd told him, it made more sense that Silk's birth resulted from adultery. A powerful clan matron might dare to betray her husband, but surely she would never be foolish enough to commit incest. Not when she knew that such a heinous crime would result in the deaths of all concerned, herself included.

Poor Singer yawned and his breath condensed into a sparkling white cloud. The night had turned cold. He wished he'd thought to pull his cape from his pack. He could have used it as an extra blanket.

Silk slept on her back with one arm curved over her head. Her long hair spilled across the floor around her. The sight filled Poor Singer with worry and joy.

He feared for her. Until today, he hadn't realized the depth of his feelings. Dune had triggered the realization when he'd refused to say anything more about love. Poor Singer's embarrassment had caused him to turn away from Silk—ashamed of his feelings. Because he loved her. And because he knew that Dune thought it wrong.

How selfish you are. Silk may be in grave danger, and all you can think about is your own guilt?

He glanced at her again, and a hollow sense of dread tormented him. What would he do if someone in Talon Town tried to hurt her?

As Sister Moon climbed into the sky, a silver sheen poured down through the roof entry and lit the chamber.

His thoughts drifted.

The words of the Keeper of the Tortoise Bundle whispered in his soul: *"Study the ways of the coyotes. They are quick and smarter than humans believe. They watch from a distance, in silence, until they know it is time to move. Always be smarter than people think. Never take action before you are certain of your aim."*

He whispered to himself, "I must be smart."

Like Coyote in a cold den, he curled into a tight ball and breathed inside his blanket to keep warm.

Thirty-Seven

Night Sun stepped out onto the roof before sunrise. Her breath puffed white in the still, cold air. To the east, a turquoise band of light swelled over the dark canyon rim, but the arching dome of Brother Sky blazed with thousands of Evening People. The blocky silhouette of Kettle Town to the east was cast in deep blue, like a slumbering beast, where it crouched under the canyon wall.

A silver blanket of frost crystals covered Talon Town. Second moon weather could be very capricious, hot one day, freezing the next. Darkness usually brought deep cold.

Night Sun tugged her turkey-feather cape closed. The morning smelled of cedar fires. Slaves huddled around a bowl of glowing coals in the plaza, their hands extended for warmth. On the roof above the entry, Webworm stood guard, his black shape ghostly against the brightening sky.

Night Sun walked around the curving wall to the ladder that led up to the fifth story and Crow Beard's chamber. As she climbed, her long braid flapped against her back. Pale blue light sheathed her triangular face and flashed from the coral-and-jet bracelet she wore on her right wrist.

When she stepped off onto the roof, and stood before the low T-shaped doorway that led into Crow Beard's chamber, she took a deep breath. She hadn't entered his chamber since his death.

A leather curtain draped the doorway, but around the edges, red light shone. Snake Head, she knew, had ordered the chamber sealed from all but Sternlight, who tended the ritual warming bowl that kept the chamber lit for her husband's wandering ghost.

Night Sun ducked beneath the curtain and entered the chamber.

It seemed . . . benign.

For many summers she had entered that door with dread in her heart. How curious to feel no fear.

The thlatsinas Dancing around the walls filled her with awe, as they always had. The warming bowl sat in the middle of the floor and cast a crimson tint over fanged muzzles, huge open beaks, and bulging inhuman eyes. The gods watched her. Night Sun shivered. Was it her heart, or could she hear the eternal rhythmic thumping of their moccasined feet, as steady and faithful as the rising of Father Sun each morning?

She folded her arms beneath her cape and slowly walked about the room. Crow Beard's sleeping mats lay in the same place, the gold-and-red blankets neatly spread, as though he might return at any moment to rest in them. On the wall over his mats, the Wolf Thlatsina stood, bent over, one foot lifted, long gray ears pricked, as if eager for the next beat of the pot drum and another step. The multitude of turquoise wolf figurines that surrounded the thlatsina glowed with a faint lavender sheen. As First Wolf had done, these figurines guided people through the underworlds to the blessings of the afterlife. Each was priceless. Some, among the Made People, would kill to own one.

Night Sun stood at the foot of Crow Beard's mats and wondered what she should do with them. Though her son ruled Talon Town, she had the duty of distributing her dead husband's belongings. Perhaps she would distribute the figurines between the matrons of the other towns in the canyon. Or, better yet, give them to the leaders of the Made People clans.

Oh, Snake Head will love that.

Her gaze drifted over the pots and baskets lining the east wall to her right. Crow Beard kept his most precious possessions in the large black-and-tan basket in the northeastern corner. Night Sun walked toward it.

Strange, that the room felt so familiar. She had not slept with him in many summers, but she had routinely visited to talk about clan affairs, planting and harvesting, and about their children.

Our children.

For seven generations, the women of her family had been Matrons of Talon Town.

With Cloud Playing gone, who will follow me?

Night Sun rested a fist on top of the eight-hands-tall basket and stared at the white floor through blurred eyes. The whole world seemed to be unraveling around her. How could she even consider leaving Talon Town with no one to install in her place? So few First People remained. If their civilization were to continue, Talon Town *must* have a strong matron. Snake Head might rule, but he had no authority to make any of the decisions about building, planting, moving to a new village for the summer, harvesting, or other social affairs. He would, however, decide when to raid, and when to war, and she cursed the ancestors for that.

Spring equinox celebrations would start in less than a moon. Soon, perhaps today, runners from the outlying Winter Villages would arrive, asking her how many pine logs they should cut and haul in for new construction projects, how much firewood was needed, how much sandstone should they quarry, and did she wish extra turquoise for Traders? The Fire Dogs and Tower Builders had attacked several more villages, did she wish people to congregate in the canyon for safety? Or stay in the farming flats and raise their corn, beans, and squash? Perhaps they should all move north to the Green Mesa villages for the summer? The mountain cliffs would be safer. They'd done it in the past when no rains came to Straight Path Canyon. Why not for defense this time?

She leaned against the basket. *My people need me.*

In her soul, Ironwood's face and the light in his eyes beckoned. Blessed gods, how she feared it. What if they left Talon Town together? Sought out a new home far from the Straight Path nation? Could their love survive the dislocation, the loneliness for family and friends? Could *she*? Could Talon Town and the Straight Path nation lose both of them? No one else possessed Ironwood's knowledge of politics and warfare. What if the raiding erupted into outright war? Webworm would need Ironwood desperately.

But how could a strong and capable man like Ironwood subordinate himself to Webworm? And, if Ironwood offered advice, it would have to be in private, for Webworm could never allow it to be said that he leaned on Ironwood.

Whispers echoed through her soul. Stories told around the

Winter Solstice fires, about First People who'd stood up against the worst that life could bring: Wolfdreamer had led humans up through the dark underworlds and been forced to kill his own brother to keep them safe; Twisting Cloud Girl and Tusk Boy had climbed into the sky on the back of the Rainbow Serpent to gain Father Sun's aid in keeping back the terrible flood waters that threatened to swallow up the First People; White Ash and Bad Belly had braved the end of the world itself, to straighten the spiral of Creation so that humans might continue to live with Our Mother Earth.

All of those ancestors had stared defeat in the face, and refused to yield to it. They had not been crushed by loneliness, the hatred of their people, the arrows of enemies, or even the malignant wills of the gods. Fate might have broken their families and their bones, but it had never broken their spirits. They had not wandered about, moping, filled with self-doubts—at least, not for long. They'd stared defeat in the eye and fought back.

A faint smile softened her face. The heroic blood of those ancestors ran in her veins. Surely there must be something of them in her? If she reached down deeply enough, perhaps she could find the courage to give up everything she had known— Wolfdreamer had done it—and the nerve to let her people stand on their own feet without her—Twisting Cloud Girl had given her very life so that her people might have the strength to do exactly that.

Wind Baby flitted through the chamber, sniffing at the coals in the warming bowl; the red gleam wavered and danced. Night Sun ran her fingers over the fine weave of the basket lid, tracing the black lightning spirals that zig-zagged around the edges.

You don't know what the next half a moon will bring, but whatever it is, it will change your life forever.

Gripping the lid with both hands, Night Sun lifted it and started to set it aside, then gasped as if she'd been struck. The basket was empty! *Completely empty!*

"What happened to all the turquoise? The jewelry and rare pots? The blankets made by the . . ."

A soft laugh sounded behind her.

Night Sun whirled and saw Snake Head lounging against the wall by the door. He wore black leggings and a brilliant yellow shirt snugged at the waist with a black sash. He'd pulled his hair away from his handsome face and coiled it into a bun. His oval face with its large dark eyes shone orange.

"Did you take your father's belongings?" she demanded.

"They were rightfully mine, Mother. Regardless of who my father was—"

Enraged, she stammered, "H-how dare you!"

"Oh, please! Don't act innocent in front of me. I know you far better than you think."

Snake Head pushed away from the wall and walked toward her. Tall and broad-shouldered, he moved with the caution of a hunting animal, each step slow and deliberate. He stopped over the warming bowl and held out his hands.

Night Sun slipped the lid back onto the basket. "Return Crow Beard's belongings immediately."

"And if I don't? What?" He rubbed his hands together and gazed at her from the corner of his eye.

What, indeed? I can't accuse the new Blessed Sun of stealing his own inheritance. . . . Or can I? Was this the opportunity she'd been hoping for? A way out of this tangled disaster?

"If you don't," Night Sun calmly threatened, "I will call a meeting of the First People elders to discuss your fitness to rule Talon Town. Those things may have belonged to you, but not until ritually cleansed. And then it is my right to decide which items you receive. By taking them, you have disavowed all of the ceremonial teachings of the right of succession. Perhaps that act alone will cause the elders to find you unworthy of succeeding your father."

He turned to face her. "Perhaps you should use another threat. After all, if you reveal the sacred prohibitions I've broken, I might decide to do the same for you."

"What? I've broken no—"

"Did you know that I used to follow you?"

"Follow me? . . . When?"

"When I was a boy." He walked over to gaze up into the Wolf Thlatsina's haunting face. The fanged muzzle seemed to be grinning down with malevolent intent.

Night Sun stood silently, waiting. Why had he taken so many precious things and left the turquoise Spirit Guides? The figurines could have bought him status anywhere in the Straight Path nation, but the . . .

An icy tingle went up her back. Her heart started to pound. "Snake Head, where are the things you took?"

As though he hadn't heard, he reached out and ran his fingers down the lines of white dots on the thlatsina's left forearm. "Yes, Mother, I followed you everywhere you went seventeen summers ago. Every time you slipped off to couple with Ironwood, I—"

"*What?*" Fear—bright and hot—ran through her veins. *No, he can't know about those precious moments. It would taint them*—

"Why, indeed, Mother." His hand fell to his side and he looked at her over his shoulder. "I watched you thrashing around with Ironwood in signal towers, abandoned houses, rock shelters, and even, on occasion, out in the open in broad daylight. You were truly shameless." His eyes glowed. "And I *hated* you for it."

"I don't know what you're talking about."

"Really?" He gave her a look of mock surprise. "You don't recall any of those sordid meetings? Well, I do. I remember quite well, for instance, the time, during the Moon of Stone Cutting, when Ironwood spread a red-and-blue blanket out on that ledge of stone that juts from the canyon rim near TwoWay House. Why, Mother, the things you two did shock me even today when I think about them."

Night Sun's jaw trembled before she clamped it tight. *What a beautiful tender time that was. . . .*

"Why are you doing this?" she whispered.

"After all I witnessed, I have never been certain that Crow Beard was my father. Which—"

"Of course, he was your father!"

"Which means that I couldn't be sure you would actually give me any of his belongings. If he isn't my real father, you could have left me with nothing. So," he added with a smile, "I collected for myself, for all the summers I put up with the rantings of that foul old man."

"Snake Head, listen to me. He *was* your father, and I always intended—"

"Yes, well, that may be." He walked around Crow Beard's sleeping mats to stand no more than a body-length from Night

Sun. Hatred lit his eyes. "But I didn't wish to wait around to find out. Especially, Mother, since I'd hoped you'd be dead by now."

She propped a hand on the basket lid to steady herself. Hearing the words from her son's lips affected her like a blow to the head, leaving her dazed and sick to her stomach. "Sorry to disappoint you."

Snake Head's eyes narrowed. "Tell me something, will you, mother? How did you arrange that charade?"

"Everything that Sternlight and Dune said w-was true."

"Yes," he laughed softly. "I can tell by the confidence in your voice. Well, it doesn't matter now. At least . . . not for the moment. Did you also know that—"

"What do you mean, 'for the moment'?"

Snake Head shrugged. "I'm not sure. After all, I was the only one who saw your indiscretions. There aren't any witnesses to verify my words, though I have 'mentioned' your crimes to certain people—when I was a boy and didn't know any better. Still, the elders wouldn't believe me if I told them. But . . ." He paused. "I have considered openly talking about them anyway."

"That would tarnish you as much as me." *Who did he tell? Who would have listened to a boy?*

"No, I don't think so. As the Blessed Sun I could recover. You, however, would be ruined."

Angry, terrified, Night Sun slitted her eyes. "I'd make certain you didn't recover, my son. I'd—"

"Oh, Mother." He sighed as if pained. "I know you're already plotting to remove me with the least damage to yourself. Stop it. Right now. I might decide to call in people who could add to my stories in enough interesting ways that the elders would reconsider *your* fitness for being Matron of Talon Town."

Stunned, still weak from her imprisonment, she longed to sit down, but she dared not show vulnerability before him. Night Sun casually leaned her back against the wall and locked her shaking knees.

"My son," she said calmly, "no matter what rabble you convince to support you, you will have to fight me in the end. And, I assure you, you will lose that battle."

"Planning on murdering me, Mother?" He lifted a mocking

eyebrow. "Well, before you try, it might amuse you to know that I followed Crow Beard, too. Oh, yes, I did." As though delighted to hurt her, he leaned forward, and hissed, "I saw him couple with dozens of slaves. But all of them, Mother, were *your* slaves. I don't know why father did that, but he coupled with such violence, I assumed it was revenge."

Sounds rose from the plaza, coughs, babies' cries, soft conversations. Pots clacked against wooden paddles. The rich scent of frying corncakes drifted on the cool wind.

"Don't try me, my son. You may destroy me, but I will bring you down with me." She knotted a resolute fist. "On that, I give you my word."

She strode past Snake Head with her head high. As she ducked through the doorway and out into the pale pink dawn, she heard Snake Head call:

"I followed Webworm, too, Mother! Every time he coupled with Cloud Playing, I watched! And Sternlight—your nephew was the worst of all. You've no idea the sort of heinous crimes he's committed! Do you remember Young Fawn? Mourning Dove can verify my words! She followed me that day. She saw *everything. . . .*"

Night Sun scrambled down the ladder to the fourth-story roof and broke into a run, trying to get back to her chamber as quickly as she could.

Thirty-Eight

Thistle trotted along the trail ahead of Leafhopper. Their way threaded through the hills, cutting south from the holy road that angled southwest toward Humpback Butte and High Stone Village that stood at its base.

So much had changed, her yellow dress smudged with soot and dirt, her fine-boned face coated with dust. All of her life, she'd been so fastidious, much to Cornsilk and Fledgling's dismay. Now bits of grass and twigs clung in her black hair that hung in a single braid down the middle of her back.

Leafhopper didn't look much better, smudged, scratched, and hollow-eyed. The soot stains from the night Lanceleaf Village burned still clung to her clothing.

They had crossed the desolate sage-speckled flats south of Straight Path Canyon and now followed a winding trail southward through low buttes speckled with juniper and piñon. Dunes supported patches of sagebrush that gave way to halos of ricegrass higher than the greening junegrass and bluegrass. The squat buttes were capped by sandstones that covered tan, white, and yellow soils.

To the west lay Humpback Butte, while immediately to the south, across the broken terrain, they could see the rising silhouette of forested mountains, blue with haze, that marked the boundary between the Straight Path people and the Mogollon. Thistle's path would take her through the gap between those pine-covered ranges, and then south into the mountains controlled by Jay Bird's warriors.

The fiery face of Father Sun squatted just above the western horizon, casting long shadows over the irregular land. Radiant filaments stretched from his body and touched the delicate wisps of Cloud People that drifted across the blue, turning them molten. An amber glow flooded the rolling sage-covered hills.

The vista appeared so peaceful. How could such tranquility lull a country where the storms in peoples' hearts tortured the body and soul? Thistle bit her lip. She needed but to look inside herself to see the source of the ugliness.

Thistle heard Leafhopper stumble. Had she fallen again? Thistle slowed and looked back. Leafhopper's pudgy legs trembled and she weaved from side to side as she tottered down the dirt trail. Sweat drenched the young woman's green dress and matted the cotton fabric to her squat frame. Chin-length black hair straggled about her round face. Eyes glazed, mouth hanging open as she gasped for air, Leafhopper appeared ready to collapse.

Thistle had been running as though pursued by witches flying on rawhide shields. But she *could* run all day. She had been a mason her entire life, and despite her slim appearance, wiry muscles packed her body. Leafhopper, on the other hand, had spent her short life caring for children and grinding corn. Several times today, the girl had crumpled in the trail, and Thistle had been forced to turn back and coax her to continue.

Leafhopper looked up and saw Thistle watching. "Thistle?" she panted eagerly. "It's late. Shouldn't we make camp?" Leafhopper stopped and braced her legs. "Please?"

Thistle wiped the sweat from her fine-boned face. "If we just run a little longer, Leafhopper, we can make it to—"

"No! *Please*? My legs feel like boiled grass stems."

Thistle looked longingly southward, then, after a moment, nodded and walked back. She took Leafhopper's arm in a friendly grip. "I'm sorry. You've been doing so well." She pointed to a line of low hills just visible through the tops of the piñon and juniper. "How about making camp up there? On top of one of those hills, where we can keep an eye on the trail."

Leafhopper nodded. "Thank you. I couldn't run another step. I swear."

Thistle put her arm around Leafhopper's hot, sweaty shoulders and helped her toward the cluster of hills. Leafhopper's knees kept trying to buckle. "You've been very brave, Leafhopper. Not even Cornsilk"—she flinched, and continued more softly—"not even Cornsilk could have done so well today. I'm very proud of you."

The words seemed to soothe Leafhopper. She patted Thistle's hand.

Slabs of sandstone lay tumbled down the slopes beneath the fractured rimrock. In the fading gleam of sunset, pale blue light struck the flat faces at different angles, creating an iridescent mosaic of purple and lavender.

"I pick that hill," Leafhopper said, gesturing to the closest one.

Thistle smiled. "I think that will do nicely."

When they reached a narrow game trail that led up the face of the hill, Leafhopper climbed doggedly, setting one foot ahead of the other, probably anxious to get to the top so she could collapse. Sprigs of wild onion and biscuit root grew among the stones. Leafhopper plucked and chewed them as she edged around boulders and canted slabs.

Just as they crested the hill, Thistle caught a hint of movement from the corner of her eye.

"*Blessed gods!*" She tackled Leafhopper from behind, dragging her to the sandy ground.

"What—"

Thistle clamped a hand over Leafhopper's mouth with such strength that Leafhopper cried out and squirmed like a snared rabbit.

"Shh!" Thistle hissed. "Don't make a sound and *don't* move!"

Leafhopper silently peered at Thistle through frightened eyes. Thistle's gaze was riveted on the sheltered valley that lay cupped in the midst of the hills. Faint voices rose from the warrior's camp.

Thistle let Leafhopper look, then released her and crawled behind a tan boulder. Leafhopper did the same, craning her neck to see.

"Who are they?" Leafhopper whispered.

Dozens of men moved through the valley, packs, quivers and bows on their backs. Some carried shields. At some signal, they slowed, broke into groups and began twisting out sagebrush, snapping off juniper branches, and removing their packs. One young man immediately trotted for a high spot just to the east. A lookout, no doubt.

Thistle whispered, "*Fire Dogs.* See the short haircuts and the knee-length capes they wear, black on top, white on the bottom?" She pointed to a man standing by himself on the south side of the camp. "And look at the flat woven yucca hat he's wearing. They're Mogollon, all right."

Leafhopper paled. Now that she'd lain down, her whole body shook with exhaustion. "But—but what are they doing here? So close to the sacred South Road?"

"I don't know, but we should get far away from here. Come on, let's back down—"

"Oh, Thistle, please," Leafhopper begged. "Let me rest for a short while. I need a drink of water."

Thistle grimaced at the warriors. The men were rolling out blankets, taking cooking pots from their packs and building fires. She watched as a warrior walked through the camp, pointing to high points, and sentries were dispatched to keep watch.

"Just for a moment, Leafhopper. Then we must go." Thistle chewed her lip, frowning thoughtfully. This was a disciplined party, not just a group of men who'd decided to raid Straight Path lands.

Unslinging her pack, Leafhopper took out her gut water bag, and began gulping. Her arm trembled so badly that trickles spilled down her dress. She sighed, "Oh, I needed this."

Thistle untied her own water bag from her belt and took three swallows, just enough to wet her mouth and ease her stomach. She kept her eyes on the warriors. As twilight deepened, draping the hills like charcoal veils of mist, the warriors' cloaks blended with the night, turning them almost invisible.

Thistle started to take another drink and halted midway, the bag suspended before her chin. A man in a long red shirt walked across the camp. Short and stout, he wore a large coral pendant around his neck, and his long black hair hung in a braid down his back.

"That's . . ." Thistle's eyes narrowed. "That's a Straight Path warrior."

Leafhopper jerked around. "What? Where?"

"In the red warrior's shirt."

Leafhopper wiped water from her mouth with the back of her pudgy hand and pulled a bag of dried venison from her pack. "But why would one of our warriors be in a Fire Dog camp?" She gave Thistle a confused look.

Thistle ground her teeth, thinking. The Straight Path warrior walked right through the middle of camp. Even from where she sat, Thistle could see his tension. When he reached the base of the hill, he disappeared behind a jumble of boulders. Another part of the camp, hidden from view? Silently, Thistle counted warriors. *Forty-four.* Given the growing darkness, and the number of rocky niches, she'd probably missed several.

Leafhopper's fear had begun to outweigh her exhaustion. "I think I'm ready to go now."

Thistle touched her arm. "Don't move. With those sentries out, we can't leave here until it's completely dark."

Leafhopper's eyes went wide. "Will we be safe?"

Thistle examined the big rock they hid behind. "I think so. At least for another hand or two of time."

As night deepened, the six fires in the valley twinkled brilliantly, and the scent of burning sage drifted on the cool breeze.

Thistle murmured, "Why such a large camp?"

"Do you think they're massing to attack one of our villages?" Leafhopper asked through another mouthful of dried venison. The venison bag lay on a rock in front of her.

Thistle reached over and pulled out a piece. As she chewed, she tried to place the closest villages. High Stone was immediately north of Humpback Butte, but, living this close to the Mogollon, its brawling warriors had a reputation even the Fire Dogs respected. "Maybe, but raiding parties rarely have more than twenty or thirty members."

Beargrass' handsome face appeared on the canvas of her soul, serious, a hard glint in his brown eyes. Seventeen summers ago, they'd been sitting outside of Talon Town, Beargrass knapping out a fine chert arrow point, while she stirred a length of cloth in a vat of fermented prickly pear fruit juice. The cloth had been soaking for seven days and had turned a beautiful reddish brown. Beargrass frowned thoughtfully, and said, *"Ironwood told me this morning that a raiding party of more than thirty is almost impossible to control. He said that the more men you take, the more quarreling breaks out."* He gestured with his half-finished point. *"Someone always becomes dissatisfied. Men split up and choose leaders for their own clan groups within the party—then the trouble begins. . . ."*

Thistle clenched her fists, trying to forget his smile, and how very much she missed him. "No one would take this many warriors on a simple raid for slaves and food."

"Maybe they're planning on splitting up," Leafhopper suggested, "to dispatch two or three parties from here."

"It's possible. But who's that Straight Path warrior? Why is he walking free? The Fire Dogs should have killed him right off, or tied him up and tortured him, if nothing else. This doesn't make sense."

Thistle lifted her head to peer down. A golden halo of firelight swelled around the tumbled rock below; it silhouetted the tilted rocks and showed three men standing at the edge of the firelight. The Straight Path warrior stood among them, sipping a cup of tea. He had his head down, frowning.

"The other possibility," Thistle said to Leafhopper, "is that they need this many warriors not for an attack but to protect a very important person."

"Who?"

"That's what I must find out. I need to go down there, Leafhopper. I want you to stay here. If I'm not back in a hand of time, sneak down to the holy South Road and find a place to hide. I'll meet you. If you don't see me by dawn, run as fast as you can for Talon Town. Do you understand?"

Leafhopper's mouth trembled. "Let me come with you."

"It's too dangerous."

"But w-what are you looking for down there?"

"I need to see if this really is a raiding party, or some sort of escort. Then I'll be back. It shouldn't take long."

Leafhopper wet her lips. "Thistle, I—I'm afraid to go to Talon Town. I don't know anyone there, and I've heard that many witches—"

"Cornsilk is there," Thistle said, and cupped Leafhopper's chin to peer into her frightened eyes. "I'm almost certain of it. But I *will* be back in one hand of time, Leafhopper. Don't worry."

She nodded bravely.

Thistle said, "Remember, stay behind this rock, and don't move around too much or one of those sentries might see you."

"I promise, Thistle."

Thistle smiled at her, then started down the hill, sliding on her belly a few hands at a time. She fell into a watchful rhythm that Beargrass had taught her: slide, stop, look, listen, slide . . .

Blackness swallowed the dusk as Thistle crawled through the rocks and cactus that dotted the hillside. As she slithered to the sandstone rim, she saw that the caprock had been undercut, and the whole hillside had slumped and fallen, toppling square sandstone boulders down the slope.

Cupped in the midst of this cluster of low hills, the narrow valley made a perfect hiding place. Unless right on top of the camp, no one could see the fires, or hear the warriors' soft voices.

Pushing with her toes and pulling with her hands, she worked her way into the tumbled landslide of boulders, some as huge as small houses. The odors of packrat dung and urine rose strongly. When Thistle eased into the shadows between two tilted rocks, little feet scurried and tiny eyes peered out at her from a crack in one of the rocks. Thistle smiled at the packrat and tried to still her heavy breathing.

A man walked by, no more than two body-lengths away.

He unrolled his blankets at the base of the slide and returned to stand by the fire. Thistle edged forward. Five men now stood around the flames, talking quietly. A tea pot sat at the edge of the coals. Black-and-white cotton capes billowed around the mens' broad shoulders. One wore a turquoise plug that curved through a hole in his lip.

Her breathing went shallow. She'd never been this close to Fire Dog warriors.

The tallest man yawned and tossed the contents of his cup onto the fire. The flames sizzled and spat. He had an ugly, deeply scarred face. He said, "A pleasant evening to you. I think I'll—"

"Wait, Howler," the Straight Path warrior said. "I'm still worried. This must work perfectly or—"

"*How* can it go wrong? Hmm? Unless you're not telling us everything."

Thistle frowned. They both spoke the Straight Path language?

"Of course I'm telling you everything. If we make this happen, both of us will gain."

"I'm tired, Cone," Howler said, "It was a long day. We'll talk tomorrow."

"We're running out of time! The Chief's body is almost ready. We wouldn't have had this much time if old Dune hadn't had to send for his pack. There are things we must discuss tonight!"

Thistle edged forward another hand to get a better look. Short and stout, the Straight Path warrior had his back to her; she couldn't see his face, but that voice . . . she knew that voice. *No, no. It can't be.*

Howler propped his hands on his hips and the hem of his cape whipped and crackled. "Well, then, what is it?"

Cone tossed the dregs of his tea onto the ground. "I'm not sure we have enough men. Perhaps we should wait to attack. If we gather another twenty warriors, then—"

"Then we'll have eighty warriors, and far too many to make

a quick, clean strike! What's the matter with you? I thought you said your friend Snake Head is bringing only five warriors?"

"Yes, but, what if—"

"Stop worrying. Jay Bird knows what he's doing."

Jay Bird! Thistle edged closer. *But is he here, or still at the Gila Monster Cliffs?*

"I'm not so sure, Howler."

Howler gestured irritably. "Even if Snake Head brings fifty warriors, we have surprise on our side. Besides, didn't you say the new War Chief—what was his name?"

"Webworm," Cone murmured.

"Yes, Webworm. Didn't you say he was a weak fool? That he jumped at the sound of moth wings and did anything people told him? How could such a man refuse the orders of the new Blessed Sun?"

Cone turned toward the fire, and Thistle saw the round face, pug nose, and small eyes—she'd seen him the day he'd run into Lanceleaf Village with Wraps-His-Tail, bringing the news of Crow Beard's illness. *He was one of Ironwood's most trusted deputies. What happened?*

Cone frowned down into his empty cup and said, "I never told you that Webworm was a fool. I told you that he lacked imagination—and had no sense for politics. What if he smells the trap and decides to scout the road before the burial procession starts out from Talon Town? That's just the sort of thing he would do. I fought at his side for eighteen summers, Howler, I know how he thinks!"

"Your new Chief has said five warriors. That was his promise to us. Can't he control his own War Chief?"

Cone stared uneasily into the fire. "I hope so, for all our sakes."

Howler extended an arm and pointed across the valley to the largest fire, where more than twenty men sat. "Go and tell these doubts to Jay Bird—"

Thistle's head jerked in that direction.

"—I'm sure he will wish to know that his *well-paid* Straight Path rabbit is so frightened of his old friend he wants to go crawl into a hole and hide!"

Blood rushed in Thistle's ears as the twists of the maze became clearer. She didn't yet know why or how, but the gods had just shortened her journey by three days.

"You make a worthless warrior, Howler," Cone said contemptuously. "You don't have the head for it. My people should have kept you as a slave. Perhaps you'd like to go back and cut a little stone, eh? Or empty some piss jars?"

The thick scars on Howler's cheeks twitched. He took a threatening step forward. Two of the men around the fire leaped to their feet and grabbed him, holding him back, speaking to him in the strange Fire Dog tongue.

"That's right," Cone said. "Tell him that killing me before I can carry out my final duty is suicide."

Howler shook off their hands and glared at Cone. "My brothers tell me you are right, we still need you, but as soon as—"

"*What?* What will you do? Your Chief has promised me safe passage! Shall I inform Jay Bird you don't like his promises? That you would break them to salve your own petty pride?"

Howler's nostrils flared. He stood rigid a moment, then, in a low voice, asked, "Tell me something, rabbit, doesn't it hurt your conscience to betray your Chief?"

"Not a bit," Cone answered without hesitation.

Howler folded his arms. "And what about the others? The people who will be accompanying the burial procession? Perhaps some of your old friends will be there, eh? People you care about?" A cruel smile turned his lips. He leaned forward with his chin stuck out. "I hope so, rabbit. I truly do."

Howler stalked to his blankets on the north side of the fire and rolled up with his back to Cone.

The other Fire Dogs mumbled darkly to each other and walked for their own blankets, leaving Cone standing alone in the orange gleam of the flames.

Cone's mouth pursed, as though with disgust. He threw his cup on the sand by the fire and walked right in front of Thistle's face, so close she could smell his acrid sweat. He trudged up the hill a short distance and sat on a rock overlooking the firelit valley. For a time, he did nothing. Then, suddenly, he picked up a pebble and heaved it at nothing. A pained groan escaped his lips.

Thistle crept through the boulders and stood quietly in the

black shadows at the rear of the slide. Monstrous slabs canted at odd angles around her.

Cone sat ten body-lengths up the slope, his round face lit by the gleams of the fires. He chucked another pebble down the hill, then dropped his head in his hands.

Thistle swallowed, took a deep breath, and walked straight toward him, as though part of the camp.

When he heard her coming, he squeezed his eyes closed and demanded, "What is it?"

"Please don't call the camp guards," she spoke softly. "I must speak with you, Cone."

As if struck, he leaped to his feet. *"Who—who are you? What do you want?"*

She made a quieting gesture. "It's Thistle, Cone. From Lanceleaf Village. Remember me?"

"Thistle?" he whispered her name disbelievingly, and took a step closer to study her face. His eyes widened, and he glanced over the dark hillside. "Great Spirits, where's Beargrass? He's not *here*, is he?"

"No, Cone. I'm alone," Thistle said. "Please, listen to me. My husband is dead. Killed by warriors from Talon Town. *That* is why we must talk."

"Dead?" Cone asked softly. "Beargrass is dead?"

Thistle eased down on the rock where he'd been sitting. "The new Blessed Sun sent his warriors to kill Beargrass and destroy Lanceleaf Village. My husband is dead. My son is dead—and his head is in Talon Town. My sister and brothers are dead. My house is burned. I have nothing left."

Cone glanced over the hill again, still fearing a trap, then asked, "What are you doing here?"

"I was on my way to the Gila Monster Cliffs, to find Jay Bird."

Cone stared unblinking. "Because you wish to die? To join your husband in the underworlds?"

Thistle laced her fingers in her lap. In the dim firelight her yellow dress glowed a rusty orange. "Cone, we have very little time, so I'm going to tell you as quickly as I can. Sixteen summers ago, Sternlight gave Beargrass a baby and told him to take it and go far away, to hide the child forever."

"What child?" Cone asked. His brow furrowed.

"A little girl. She was the daughter of a slave named Young Fawn. I think her father was your good friend, Ironwood. You remember Young Fawn, don't you? She was killed about the same time Beargrass and I moved away from Talon Town."

Cone shook his head, then stopped and seemed to be thinking. "Yes, yes, Webworm found her body in the trash mound. Just after Solstice celebrations . . ." He came forward like a man walking through a field of rattlesnakes, and sat on the rock beside her. "Wasn't Young Fawn the daughter of Jay Bird?"

"Yes, Cone, she was."

"Thistle, are you telling me that you raised Jay Bird's granddaughter?"

"That's exactly what I'm telling you. And that's why Beargrass is dead, and my son is dead, and Lanceleaf Village is gone, and I—"

"Gone?"

"Burned to the ground, Cone. Webworm murdered everyone he could, old people, infants on cradleboards—"

"But that's crazy! Webworm would never—"

"He had orders from Snake Head."

Cone's eyes narrowed. He sat back on the rock and studied the six fires and the warriors who stood before them like black ghosts. "Snake Head ordered Webworm to find Jay Bird's granddaughter? That's it, isn't it?"

"Yes. I don't know how Snake Head found out, but he was willing to kill everyone in Lanceleaf Village to get her, and Cornsilk is now being held prisoner in Talon Town. Snake Head—"

"You mean he captured her? He—He didn't come to kill her? Snake Head sent Webworm to *capture* the girl?" He stared at her with huge eyes.

Thistle nodded.

Cone sat very still. "Blessed Ancestors! He's hedging his bets! Holding the girl in case Jay Bird breaks his promises! But I—I can't just walk over there and tell him! There have been too many delays as it is. Snake Head keeps changing things. Jay Bird is already suspicious of me. The trouble with being a traitor is that no one trusts you. What do you expect me to do, Thistle? After all Jay Bird's effort to lure Snake Head here, first of all, he'll think I'm lying about the girl, and second, he'll kill me!" Sweat beaded on Cone's pug nose. "And, anyway, why should I believe you?"

"Because if you don't," she said calmly, "and this attack results in the death of my precious daughter and Jay Bird's granddaughter, I assure you, I'll tell Jay Bird it was your fault. That I came to you begging help to save her, and you turned me away. You wouldn't even let me speak with him."

"If you're alive, Thistle." He tapped the deerbone stiletto on his belt. "I suggest that you—"

"No," Thistle said, and lurched to her feet. "Threats won't work, Cone, because I have only one thing left to live for: the daughter I raised and love with all my heart."

Thistle started walking down the hill toward Jay Bird's camp, and Cone leaped up to drag her back. "No! Thistle, wait. I'm sorry. I—I live my whole life in terror these days, and sometimes . . . I say and do things I regret." He released her arm and propped his hands on his hips. "Please, I'm sorry."

"What is this about, Cone? What are you doing here? I always thought you were dedicated to your people."

He took a deep breath, the muscles in his shoulders and arms flexing. "I am, Thistle. Listen, Snake Head cannot remain as the Blessed Sun. If he does, he'll destroy our people. Crow Beard was bad enough . . . but his son will be worse. If Snake Head is gone, captured and killed by the Mogollon as he carries his father's body down the south road, the Straight Path people will be unified in grief. Snake Head becomes a martyr instead of a despot. Night Sun can marry another, one more suited to rule."

"Yet, you work with Snake Head even as you betray him?"

"I'm working for my people, not Snake Head, and it's a dangerous game, one made more so by your presence here tonight."

Thistle folded her arms and shivered, thinking hard. She had to make this seem completely plausible, or these trained warriors would know she was lying. "Let me ask you this? Snake Head will be holding Cornsilk in Talon Town to use as a hostage, won't he? I mean, he wouldn't bring her on the burial procession with him, would he?"

"No. Never. He'd want her safe in Talon Town. Hidden away for that moment when he might need to use her."

Thistle nodded. "Good. I thought so."

Cone ran a hand through his black hair and squinted across the narrow firelit valley. "Well, help me to think. You're right. I must tell Jay Bird about Cornsilk. But how? That's the question. I have to find a way of doing it so that he doesn't kill me first and worry about whether or not I was telling the truth later."

"Cone," Thistle placed a hand on his, "I want to tell him. Since the day of Cornsilk's birth, I've been her mother. I love Cornsilk. I'm sure Jay Bird loved Young Fawn. Jay Bird *will* believe me. I promise you."

"If not," Cone whispered, "he'll suspect treachery, and we'll both be dead."

Thistle nodded.

Cone rose to his feet. "All right. But stay here for now. I'm not allowed to speak directly to Jay Bird. I must convince Howler to intercede for me."

Night Sun paced back and forth across Ironwood's small chamber. Her blue dress *shished* against her black leggings, and her copper bell eardrops made a soft tinkling sound. Her graying black hair swung in a long braid as she walked. Despite the evening chill, perspiration coated her face, and she kept blinking it away from her dark eyes. Since the altercation with Snake Head at dawn, she'd been hiding in her chamber, afraid to come out until darkness fell. When the plaza emptied, she'd hurried for Ironwood's chamber . . . only to find him gone.

He'll be back soon. He must come back soon!

Shaky, terrified, she did not know what else to do . . . who else to turn to.

Starlight streaming down through the roof entry lit the brightly painted faces of the thlatsinas Dancing on the walls, Buffalo to her left on the east wall, Ant in the south, Bear glaring down at her from the west wall, and Badger tall and stoic in the north.

Night Sun opened her soul and gazed imploringly into Badger's face, silently begging him to heal her wounded heart, to give her some way out of this. His black mask with the turquoise eye slits, the eagle-feather headdress, and long muzzle filled with sharp teeth, seemed to be peering down at her with vague curiosity about her presence. She had never been inside Ironwood's chamber—not even in the days when she'd risked almost anything to be with him. Now, she began to actually look around, to *see* his home.

His red-and-black blankets lay neatly rolled atop his sleeping mats on the west wall. Had he lain awake staring at the ceiling as often as she had over the past sixteen summers? Had he, too, slammed his fists into the walls, fighting not to think of her—as she had him?

Above the blankets, a ring of scalps encircled the Bear Thlatsina, the guardian Spirit of warriors. Ironwood had arranged the scalps so that black, gray, and silver alternated. A fine sheen of corn pollen sprinkled each scalp. Around the scalps hung an array of weapons: bows, lances, stilettos, four magnificent shields made from tightly-woven yucca fibers and decorated with zigzagging bolts of red lightning, and a buffalo hide helmet.

Baskets and pots sat neatly along the north wall to her right, and, in the corner, stood his pack. His *full* pack.

Suddenly weak, she sank down atop his sleeping mats and leaned back against the wall, hugging her knees to her chest. All day long she had been filled with wild thoughts, longing to flee before it was too late. Several times, she'd contemplated killing Snake Head to remove the threat, then she'd remembered the day he'd been born, and the joy in her heart . . . and knew she could never do it. No matter how much she hated the man he'd become, a smiling little boy lived inside her soul, and she couldn't manage to wish him dead. If only she could go back. . . .

Steps outside. The ladder creaked as someone climbed.

Night Sun stiffened, breathing hard.

Then rushing feet, and a man called, "Ironwood? A moment, please?"

Steps retreated back toward the ladder. Ironwood said, "Webworm? I didn't see you. What did you need?"

"I was hoping you might be able to give me some advice?"

Night Sun frowned. Webworm sounded worried, his voice tight. The roof creaked as the men moved. A shadow flitted over the roof entry and she looked up, but saw only brilliant stars twinkling and glittering.

Ironwood said, "Of course. Do you wish to come into my chamber?"

Night Sun's heart rose into her throat, but Webworm answered, "No, I don't need much of your time."

"Very well."

A pause, then Webworm murmured, "I am having a problem with Snake Head. He is so childish and headstrong! He cannot see reason!"

"What's he done now?" Ironwood asked through a tired exhalation.

"Day after tomorrow we leave with the burial procession for the sacred Humpback Butte, and we should take at least thirty warriors to guard the Blessed Elders who will be making the journey. You always took thirty. But Snake Head has ordered me to take no more than five."

"*Five?*"

"Yes. Even a pitiful war party could kill everyone in the procession, and I wouldn't be able to do a thing to stop them." The roof groaned as one of the men shifted. "I do not wish to disobey his order, Ironwood, but I cannot, in good conscience, follow it."

Ironwood didn't say anything for a time. Finally, he murmured. "No, you cannot. But you must appear to."

"I don't understand."

"Well, if I were you, I would take five warriors with the procession, just as the Blessed Sun ordered. But I would also send out scouts to provide an advance warning. And another party of twenty-five or thirty warriors following close behind who could rush up at a moment's notice. Your instincts are right, Webworm. It is your duty as War Chief to assure the safety of the elders. Just tell your warriors to stay out of sight, but within range. That way, you will be following orders, *and* carrying out your responsibilities to the people of Talon Town."

Webworm sighed. "Thank the Spirits, I feel so much better. I've needed to speak with you since yesterday, but only mustered the courage tonight. I—"

"Courage? To speak with me?"

"Yes, I—I know it was silly, but I feared that after Snake Head dismissed you so dishonorably you might think I had something to do with it."

Ironwood said kindly, "My fault. I should have spoken with you right after it happened. Webworm, if it had been my choice, I would have selected you to replace me. You were the finest of my warriors. I wish you nothing but success. If you ever need my advice, or my fighting, you have only to ask."

The roof creaked again. Softly, Webworm said, "You are my friend, Ironwood."

"Yes, now get some rest. You will need it for the journey south."

"Yes, I'm sure I will. Good night, Ironwood."

"Good night."

Ironwood crossed the roof again and started down the ladder into the chamber.

Night Sun watched him descend. His knee-length buckskin shirt accented the breadth of his shoulders and narrowness of his waist. The fringes on the sleeves and hem swayed in the starlight. He wore his gray hair in a bun at the back of his head.

When he stepped to the floor, Night Sun whispered, "Don't die of fright. It's just me."

Ironwood spun and stared at her wide-eyed. Then he glanced at the roof entry, to make certain no one could hear. "Night Sun? *What* are you doing here?"

"It seems everyone needs your advice tonight."

A frown lined his forehead. He walked across the room and knelt in front of her. Starlight sheathed his handsome oval face and reflected in his brown eyes. "Are you all right?"

"No. I'm not certain either of us is."

"Why not?"

Night Sun clasped her hands and held them together over her mouth for several moments, before answering, "I went to Crow Beard's chamber before dawn this morning, just to—to see it, and Snake Head found me there. He told me things that terrified me."

Her hands started to tremble, and Ironwood reached out and closed his fingers around them. "What things?"

"Snake Head knows about us."

Ironwood squeezed her hands. "I feared as much."

"You . . ." She lifted her head and stared at him. "You *knew?*"

"The night you were imprisoned, I went to see him, to try to convince him that holding you was foolish, that it would split the people apart. He told me that he'd never trusted me or my judgment. When I mentioned that his father had trusted me, Snake Head said, 'But he never knew about my mother's fondness for you.' It was the way he said 'fondness,' that convinced me." Ironwood placed a warm hand beneath her chin and his gaze went over her taut face. "Did he say how he knew?"

She nodded. "He used to follow us. Every time we—we were together, he . . ." She swallowed the lump in her throat. "And he relayed enough of the details of those precious times, Ironwood, that I have no doubt he did see us."

Ironwood did not move, but the crow's feet around his eyes deepened. "And what did you say?"

"I acted stupidly. I threatened him, told him if he told anyone that I'd make sure he suffered as much as I."

Ironwood released her and sank to the floor, sitting cross-legged. The fringes on his shirt brushed the hard-packed dirt. "Snake Head will have taken that threat seriously, Night Sun, and already be preparing to counter any charges you make against him."

"Yes, well, I'll be making plans, too. Ironwood I . . . I can't go away with you. I *must* marry again. You understand, don't you? This is the only way."

Ironwood tipped his face up, and seemed to be glaring at the Bear Thlatsina. He spoke very tenderly. "You can't win, Night Sun. Don't you see that? Yes, if you remarry you'll depose Snake Head, but he'll make certain you fall with him. He'll drag in every witness he can find or bribe. No matter what you say, the suspicion will be enough to doom you."

She searched his eyes. He was right. She knew he was right. But before she had time to think about it, her mouth said, "No. No, the elders would not condemn me based upon suspicions. They'll demand proof, and . . . and there isn't any. I'll be all right. I just have to marry quickly."

Ironwood took her hands and stared into her eyes. "Who will you marry?"

"I don't know. I was thinking about Blue Racer from Starburst Town. He . . ."

Ironwood bowed his head and clutched her hands so tightly they hurt. His arms shook. It took several moments before Night Sun realized he was suppressing tears, not rage.

She whispered, "I never meant to hurt you, Ironwood."

Thirty-Nine

Sister Moon rose over the hill behind Jay Bird's camp, a shining pearl in a star-spotted indigo sea, and a pale luminescent gleam flooded the rocky hillside. Every grass stem cast a shadow. The line of enormous standing stones on the hill at Jay Bird's back seemed to tilt, leaning over the camp with breathless anticipation. The assembled warriors shifted and whispered. Their moccasins kicked up a glittering haze of firelit dust.

Cone crouched on his haunches, his forearms on his knees. Thistle sat beside him. The guards had told them to remain outside the protective ring of twenty warriors surrounding Jay Bird, but through the tangle of bodies, Cone could see Jay Bird's face as Howler explained what Thistle wished to discuss. Jay Bird clearly didn't believe a word of it. The tall man had an air of utter self-assurance, a fierce dignity, that unnerved even the most valiant of men. As Jay Bird's thin face hardened, Howler started making more and more elaborate gestures.

Thistle sat with her knees drawn up, looking determined. By any man's standards, she was a beautiful woman. Tiny and delicate, she had a smooth, tanned face and long silky hair. She'd unbraided it for this meeting, and it hung down her back in blue-black waves. Her dark eyes slitted as she studied the warriors.

As if to lessen her own anxiety, she asked, "How come it was you who ended up here, Cone? I understand what you're doing, but not the why of it. You were one of Talon Town's most renowned warriors."

Cone plucked a blade of grass from the ground and awkwardly turned it in his hands. "It's a long story, Thistle. It began about a moon ago. Had I known then—"

"Before you came to Lanceleaf?"

"Just before, yes." He gestured with the green blade, feeling like a fool. How could he explain the complicated web of deceit? "Before I left Talon Town to come to Lanceleaf Village, Snake Head paid me to meet with one of Jay Bird's messengers."

"Near Lanceleaf?"

"No, on the way back, near Talon Town. Snake Head had been secretly speaking with this messenger for moons, and had set up a meeting just north of Center Place."

"Snake Head asked you, because he was too much of a coward to meet with the man himself?"

Cone nodded. "I see that you remember him well."

"Only as a wicked child. I haven't seen him in sixteen summers. Go on."

Cone ran the blade of grass over his fingertips. "Snake Head offered me so much wealth, Thistle, I just stood there with my mouth open. I thought, what's one meeting? Besides, he was to be the next Blessed Sun."

She turned to face him, and he saw kindness in her eyes.

It soothed Cone's lacerated soul.

"Wealth?" she asked. "But Snake Head couldn't have possessed many things."

"No, he rapidly ran out of his own goods. That's another story." He frowned at the ground, wishing he were anywhere but here. Beargrass had been his friend, and a loyal warrior to the Blessed Sun. Sitting here with Beargrass' wife made him acutely aware of his own perfidy.

Yes, perfidy, but one necessary to root out a terrible evil.

"Go on," Thistle said. "You were saying . . ."

Cone nodded. "I was supposed to meet the messenger, Howler, at midnight, the day before we arrived back at Talon Town. When Spider Woman climbed to the right place, I slipped from my blankets to go to the meeting place. Thistle, I swear, I didn't know that Wraps-His-Tail was following me.

You must believe me, he was my friend. I would never have . . ." His voice faltered. He crimped the grass stem with his thumbnail. A sweet fragrance rose from it. "Howler saw me being followed. There was nothing I could do. It happened so quickly. Howler leaped on Wraps-His-Tail from behind."

Thistle lowered her gaze. "I'm sorry. He was a good man."

"Yes. He was. He—he died in my arms. I kept telling him how sorry I was, that I never meant to hurt him." Cone's chest went tight. Wraps-His-Tail had stared up at Cone with forgiveness in his eyes.

Thistle pressed, "What happened next?"

Cone gestured with his grass blade. "We—Howler and I—carried Wraps-His-Tail's body to Talon Town and left it near the entry. I sneaked in and told Snake Head what had happened. I'm not sure what he did, but I heard that Snake Head went down and made the murder look like witchcraft. You know how Talon Town is. You mention the word witchcraft and everyone points at Sternlight. Any charge of witchery distracts people long enough that a real murderer can cover his tracks."

Thistle laced her fingers around her right knee. "But what was Snake Head trying to do, Cone? What messages were you carrying?"

Cone's mouth pursed with distaste. "It's almost too foolish to speak of. Snake Head wished to establish an alliance. Jay Bird laughed at it, and I told Snake Head so. But that didn't stop Snake Head. He wished to gain Jay Bird's trust, allay his fears so he'd drop his guard and Snake Head could slaughter the Mogollon. In that way Snake Head would make a name for himself among the Straight Path people as the greatest Chief ever."

"That's ridiculous! A man like Jay Bird *never* drops his guard. We've been enemies for too long!"

"Oh, I know it, and you know it, and most everyone else knows it, but it's a sign of just how poorly Snake Head is suited to the rank of Blessed Sun that he doesn't know it. The deeper I became involved in this, the more determined I became to destroy Snake Head."

"Couldn't you tell someone?"

"No. By then Crow Beard was dead, Ironwood replaced, and

Night Sun locked away in the Cage. Snake Head was in charge, and he kept badgering me to ask Jay Bird again, to try a new tack. It was very dangerous work, so I demanded more and more for my services."

"And he paid you?"

Cone tore the stem in half and glared at the pieces. "Oh, yes."

"But where did he get the goods?"

Cone squeezed his eyes closed. "From his dying father, Thistle. He was stealing Crow Beard's possessions while the old man's soul was floating about in the room."

"Blessed Spirits." Thistle's fists knotted in her dirty yellow skirt. "It must have been terrible for you when you found out."

Cone let the grass blade flutter to the ground and kicked dirt over it in frustration. "I didn't know until the very end. Right after Crow Beard died, Snake Head brought me a big pack of Crow Beard's most precious things. Exquisite Green Mesa pots. Turquoise nodules the size of two fists put together. Snake Head *boasted* to me of how he'd stolen them." Cone lifted his hands and opened them to the heavens. "Thistle, I—I just . . . snapped."

"That's when you switched sides?"

"No, no, not exactly. I'm still a Straight Path warrior. It's just that now I fight in a different way." He lowered his hands to his knees. "I hate Snake Head. I want to see him dead. And, as it happens, Jay Bird wishes the same thing."

Thistle bit her lip, as if fighting with something that she dared not say. "After the slaughter at Lanceleaf Village, Cone, I understand and share your hatred." She brushed at a patch of dirt on her yellow skirt, and her voice took on a deeper, graver note. "Snake Head's death will be the best thing for all of our people."

"I am convinced of it."

She looked up, and her cheek muscle jumped. "So you set up this plan to lure Snake Head here? To his death?"

"I did."

"And how did you manage to convince Jay Bird to come? Surely he could have sent his warriors to kill Snake Head. He didn't have to come himself."

"No, he didn't. But Snake Head demanded to meet with Jay

Bird and offered Jay Bird a reward he couldn't turn down." Just thinking about it sickened Cone. He swallowed the sourness in his throat and squinted at the sparkling fires in the valley below.

"What reward?"

"Snake Head promised that if Jay Bird came in person, he could have Crow Beard's corpse as a trophy to take home to the Mogollon. Can you imagine the prestige that will be Jay Bird's? He can say he *personally* captured the corpse and can parade Crow Beard's putrefying body from village to village, so that every Fire Dog for a moon's walk can spit upon our dead Chief. How could Jay Bird resist? Though it would have been better if Crow Beard's soul had still been in his body. Then Jay Bird could have made certain Crow Beard never reached the afterlife, but wandered the earth forever as a homeless ghost."

Thistle's brows drew together. "Crow Beard's soul isn't in his body?"

"No," Cone grimaced. "Despite Snake Head's promise to Jay Bird, apparently Dune smashed the dead Chief's skull to release it. That news disappointed Jay Bird, and he still hasn't gotten over it. It's another reason he doesn't trust Snake Head—or me, for that matter."

Thistle massaged her forehead. "This just gets worse and worse."

"Yes. I know."

Thistle looked at him. "I didn't mean that as an accusation. I'm praying with every bit of strength in my body that Jay Bird kills Snake Head. Tell me what I must do, and I will help you. I will help Jay Bird. I will help *anyone* who is trying to clean out the rot in Talon Town."

Wind Baby gusted through the valley, and Thistle's hair fluttered about her angry face. Cone longed to touch the silken strands. She had lessened his smothering guilt, and deep gratitude stirred his soul. "Thank you, Thistle. You have no idea how much it means for me to hear you say that. But . . ." He paused and scowled at the grass growing up around the rock where they sat. "You know, don't you, that if Snake Head has Cornsilk, he may be able to outwit Jay Bird. He can threaten to kill her—"

"*Stop it!*" A woman's hoarse scream rent the night. "*Let me go!*"

Cone whirled to stare. One of the guards strode downhill, shoving a young woman before him. Her face was round, her body pudgy, and limp black hair hung even with her chin. She might have been aged fifteen or sixteen summers. Like a rabbit, she gaped at the crowd of warriors with huge brown eyes.

"Oh, no," Thistle murmured.

"Who is she?"

"Leafhopper. Cornsilk's best friend. I told her to hide on the road until I returned. Apparently, the guards saw her."

When Leafhopper spied Thistle, she cried, "Thistle, help me!"

Thistle stepped forward and said, "Please? She is with me! She means you no harm. Please, don't hurt her!"

The tall warrior shoved Leafhopper to her knees near the fire. She stayed down, clasping her hands before her, gazing wide-eyed around the circle of men. Her mouth trembled with fear.

"Forget her for now!" Howler said as he pushed through the warriors, his hideously scarred face twisted. He gruffly motioned with his arm. "Come, woman. He's ready to see you—but you alone. He has ordered that Cone and I, and all the other warriors, stand at a distance."

"Does he speak—"

"He speaks your language better than you. Now, come, hurry."

Thistle rose and squared her narrow shoulders. Without a word, she patted Leafhopper's hair reassuringly, then walked past Howler and into the fire's glow. The warriors murmured, and some grinned lecherously.

Cone followed, shoving by Howler so he could see, but hard hands stopped him. Leafhopper studied his red shirt, and such hope lined her young face that it made Cone long to go to her, to comfort her. She looked at him as though he represented salvation itself—but he could do nothing. Not yet.

Jay Bird stood, and his long black-and-white cape fell around him in sculpted folds. His gray hair hung even with his shoulders and glinted orange in the firelight. Cone couldn't say precisely what made the man so formidable. Jay Bird wore no jewelry, dressed plainly, in common warrior's garb, and didn't even carry a knife at his belt. He stood there alone, pale, silent, dwarfed by the huge standing stones behind him. Yet Cone could not take his eyes from the man.

Thistle hurried forward, not like an enemy, but like a suppliant. She knelt before Jay Bird with her head bowed, lustrous black hair falling around her, and said, "Blessed Chief, I am honored to be able to speak with you. Who has not heard of the splendors of the Mogollon people and marveled at the stories of Chief Jay Bird's greatness? All speak of your victories, and the many kindnesses you've shown to the weary and wounded, even if they were among those you counted as enemies."

Cone lifted his brows in admiration. She had quickly moved to dangerous ground, acknowledging the hostilities between their peoples, then using Jay Bird's reputation for compassion against him.

And Jay Bird knew it. He smiled faintly. "How would a Straight Path woman know of such things?"

He had a quiet voice, drowsy, but drowsy like a lion's purr, promising quick death if displeased.

Thistle lifted her head and gazed up with wide beautiful eyes. "The Traders speak of these things, and more. Please, I know that much hatred lies between our peoples. But I have come here, at great risk to myself, to give you news that will surely bring joy and fear to your heart. For a short while, forgive me the crimes of my people. I promise I——"

Jay Bird stopped her with a soft, "Enough," then stepped forward and held out his hand. His warriors went silent, mouths gaping. The tension crackled.

Cone glanced around at their awed faces. Even he knew that Jay Bird rarely extended the hand of friendship to a stranger, and least of all to a woman of the Straight Path nation.

Thistle placed her thin fingers in his, and Jay Bird drew her to her feet. The top of her head barely reached his shoulders. As she looked up at him, Jay Bird stood quietly, looking into her eyes. Then he led her away from the fire, to sit with him on a flat rock at the base of the largest standing stone. The massive stone stood sixty hands tall and had a split top with a stunted juniper growing in the crack.

They made a strange sight. The tall graying elder, slender and dignified, seated next to the delicate raven-haired beauty in the dirty yellow dress.

Out of hearing range, Cone could only fold his arms and wait to see if she lived or died.

The fires in the valley threw faint multiple shadows over the low hills. Here and there the light fluttered on boiling bags hanging from tripods, wind-blown grass, and warriors rolled in blankets. Snores laced the cool night air.

Jay Bird considered the woman beside him and the remarkable claim she'd made. *In this web of deceit, what does this mean? Has she come here to trick me, or is she really driven by the need for revenge?*

He pulled his cloak tight, and turned to Thistle with hard unblinking eyes. She didn't flinch, but sat calmly, waiting for him to speak first. Dirt and grass stains streaked her yellow dress, and cactus thorns clustered on her left sleeve. She really did look as if she'd slid down the hill on her belly to get to him.

"You must know," he said, "that I believe none of this." Pain tinged his voice. He'd give anything if this woman spoke the truth . . . but how could he believe? She had shown up at just the right moment to distract him from his mission, and with the sort of news certain to throw him off balance.

"I ask only that you listen, Great Chief," Thistle said. "If, after I have finished, you still do not believe me, then I will submit myself to whatever punishment you choose, even if it means death, or worse, slavery and abuse by your warriors."

Jay Bird leaned forward, gazing down at the hands he held clasped between his knees. "Very well. Tell me your story."

"Let me start," she said, "with the day, almost seventeen summers ago, that Young Fawn came to me and told me of her pregnancy. I—"

"Why would she come to you? One of her captors?"

Thistle looked him straight in the eye. "I was her friend, Great Chief, not her captor. Young Fawn and I grew up together in Talon Town. Though our stations in life gave us different duties, mine as a mason, and hers as a slave, we often spoke and laughed together. You must know that slavery is a matter of degree. Young Fawn was Mogollon, but I am one of the Made People; we both served the First People. Neither of us meant much in the eyes of the rulers of Talon Town, and such things create bonds."

Jay Bird watched the firelight dance over her serious face. Search as he might, he could find no deception in her eyes. "Please, go on."

Thistle smoothed her fingers over the cold bumps on her arms. "When Young Fawn told me of her pregnancy, I feared for her. She had not asked her master's permission, and—"

"This was nine moons before the girl child was placed in your husband's arms?"

"No, Great Chief. Your granddaughter was born early. When Beargrass first brought the baby home to me, I believed she was about eight moons old. The child was very small and frail. I made sure she got extra milk, to give her strength. When my milk began to run out, I gave my own son to another woman to feed, and kept Cornsilk at my breast."

Jay Bird nodded, and she continued telling the story, but he barely heard her words. Memories coiled up from the locked chambers of his soul, and he saw again the beautiful little girl he'd loved more than life itself . . . and the attack where his wife, Moondance, had been shot through the belly, and his daughter stolen.

The attack had come as a complete surprise, superbly orchestrated by Crow Beard. Shrill war cries had torn that bright summer morning, making the very heavens throb. Flashing arrows had pocked the walls at Gila Monster Village. Jay Bird and most of his warriors had been cut off, separated from the village stronghold and unable to use its defensive location.

He and his warriors had fought desperately to advance along the canyon slope. Crow Beard's warriors, half of them commanded by a brilliant young warrior named Ironwood, had fought off Jay Bird's counterattack, while Crow Beard and the others plundered the village, murdered the elders, and took captives. Blessed gods, the Straight Path warriors had been brutal. When they'd finished and retreated down the wash, blood puddled on the rocks. As Jay Bird walked among the dead, crimson soaked the hem of his shirt. Once every twenty paces, he had to stop and wring it out before he could continue.

"*We were paid extremely well to care for her—*"

"By whom?" Jay Bird asked. "Who would have cared about a slave girl's baby?"

Thistle shivered in the cold wind. "The father, Great Chief."

"The father?"

"Yes. I believe the man that your daughter loved was War Chief Ironwood. He—"

"*Ironwood?*" He felt himself pale.

"Yes."

"How can you say she loved him?" Anger built under his heart, violent, edging toward a murderous rage. "More likely he took his pleasures from Young Fawn and she hated him!"

"No, not this time—though that is usually the way of things when slaves couple with their masters. Young Fawn told me she loved him, Great Chief, but even if she hadn't I would have known. A light shone in her eyes when she spoke of her lover."

Jay Bird remembered that light, and the way she had smiled her love at people. His mouth tightened as his heart throbbed. . . .

After the battle, he'd taken a straggling band of warriors and tried to rescue Young Fawn. Crow Beard had expected as much; he'd set up an ambush along the roads and butchered Jay Bird's war party. The few that escaped, Jay Bird among them, had limped back to the winding valleys and towering pines of Gila Monster Cliffs seeking solace for their wounds, both of body and soul.

But the realization that he had failed, that his daughter lived, and he could not save her from the torment of slavery, had almost killed Jay Bird. He'd holed up in his house built high on the cliff face. He'd petted his dog and told her to light the fire and get a pot of tea going. Asked the dog to put out the fire . . . and that's when he realized he'd gone mad.

"But tell me," he interrupted, pulling himself back to the present. "What makes you think that the child given to you by the priest Sternlight was Young Fawn's child? I know that

468 • Kathleen O'Neal Gear and W. Michael Gear

Sternlight said the mother was a slave, but might it not have been another slave?"

"There were no other pregnant slaves due at the time. At least not that I knew of . . ." She hesitated, gazing at him with trepidation and sadness. "Do you know your daughter's fate? What really happened to her?"

Jay Bird lifted his laced hands and propped his chin upon them. "I heard stories from Traders who attended that Solstice Celebration. They told me she had been murdered, her body found in a trash mound, but I know few of the details."

Thistle brushed long wavy hair over her shoulder, and folded her arms. "Great Chief, shall I speak plainly? I know this will not be easy for you, even after all these summers."

"I appreciate plain speaking, and I must hear it. Go on."

Thistle nodded. "Young Fawn had been stabbed in the heart, and the child cut from her body."

A hollow sensation swelled his chest. Voice tight, he said, "Cut from her body? What sort of madman would do something like that?"

"I can't say. The murderer was never found."

"Nor hunted for, I suspect."

"I heard that Ironwood did search for the murderer, but you know how solstice celebrations are; there were so many people at Talon Town, the task was just impossible."

Jay Bird's gesturing hand cast inky shadows over the ground. "So, you suspect Ironwood was the father of my granddaughter, and that Young Fawn loved him. You also think he is the one who sent payment to rear Cornsilk."

"I do."

"Well, I suppose it's possible. Men are curious creatures," he said with narrowed eyes. "If it is a child a man wants, he can get one from almost any woman, of high status or low. But no man would pay for rearing a slave's child unless he had loved the slave and felt a sense of duty to the little girl. That," he whispered, "says a great deal for the man."

"When you see Cornsilk, Great Chief, you will know the truth of my words. She has Young Fawn's beautiful eyes, and Ironwood's golden skin and slanting brows."

Ironwood! Of all men, why did it have to be him? The man had an uncanny, almost supernatural ability when it came to warfare. Over the years, Jay Bird had led his Mogollon in raid after raid, first in the attempt to rescue his daughter, and later, out of an unending desire for vengeance. While he might be able to inflict damage to the outlying villages, Ironwood had stymied his ability to strike at the First Peoples' rich towns in Straight Path Canyon.

He clenched his hands and tucked them inside his cape so that she could not see how much he wanted to believe her. After his wife's death, Moondance's twin sister had graciously taken Jay Bird for her husband. It was her right as the next clan matron, but not her responsibility. Downy Girl could have chosen any man she wished to rule at her side. By choosing Jay Bird, Downy Girl had placed the needs of their people above her own needs. She had brought him back from madness, given him a purpose. Jay Bird had tried very hard to love Downy Girl, but their togetherness had produced only sons. Without a daughter or granddaughter to take over as clan Matron, the succession would fall to Moondance's niece, Green Needle. She was a frivolous, selfish woman. Both Jay Bird and Downy Girl feared she would be the ruin of the Mogollon.

"Isn't it worth the risk," Thistle said, breaking into his thoughts, "to look upon Cornsilk with your own eyes, Great Chief? To see for yourself?"

Jay Bird turned away to study the shadows on the hills.

Ghosts haunted the hidden crevices of his soul. Moondance whispered, *"For both our sakes, my beloved husband, you must go and see. If she is not of our blood, she is not. But if she is . . ."*

Young Fawn's baby laugh rose. She peered up at him with shining eyes, and Jay Bird knew he could not chance that his granddaughter might suffer the way his daughter had. If Cornsilk were truly Young Fawn's daughter, and she'd been captured by the enemy, he had to rescue her, no matter the cost. Perhaps, in a small way, rescuing his granddaughter would make up for his failure to save Young Fawn.

He turned back and noticed that Cone had weaseled his way through the warriors to sit by the young Straight Path girl. They spoke in low tones, Cone with his brow furrowed, the girl looking very frightened.

"Tell me again, woman. Why are you doing this?" He examined Thistle with an eagle's alertness.

"Snake Head discovered what I have just told you. He sent Webworm, his new War Chief, to my village. There they murdered my husband and son, mutilated their bodies. Then they turned on everyone else, left no witnesses. They took Cornsilk away from me. Snake Head destroyed everything I ever loved, or lived for. The only thing I have left is my daughter—and he has her in his filthy grasp. I would rather see her die in a battle to save her than live as one of Snake Head's slaves."

"Do you hate your òwn Blessed Sun so much?"

He watched her face work, her shining eyes go hard. "He's not my Blessed Sun. He betrayed me and my family. He murdered my entire village! All of the old people, even the little children! Snake Head has corrupted everyone and everything he's ever touched. Only his death will ease my wounds." Her voice filled with revulsion. "Oh, yes, Great Chief, I hate him."

Yes . . . only the finest of actors could fill their voices with such passion. Jay Bird lifted a hand and motioned for Howler to come forward.

The ugly warrior trotted up, his eyes narrowed. "Yes, my chief?"

"Bring Cone."

Howler trotted back, spoke sharply to Cone, and returned with him. The short stocky Straight Path warrior stood erect, his red shirt flapping about his legs. His eyes darted back and forth between Thistle and Jay Bird, as though fearing what had happened.

"Cone," Jay Bird said, "it is critical that we get a new message to Snake Head."

"I can be there before dawn, Great Chief."

"How will you signal him at night?"

"I can't, Great Chief. But with the first rays of dawn"—Cone dug into the small bag he carried tied to his belt and pulled out a pyrite mirror—"I will use my mirror to send flashes through his window. The light blazes across his ceiling, and I guess it frightens his pet macaw. The bird always wakes him by squawking. What do you wish me to tell Snake Head?"

Jay Bird rose to his feet and scanned the faces of the warriors around his fire. They watched his every move, looking anxious, eager for a fight.

"Earlier this evening, Howler said you wished that we had

more warriors because you feared Snake Head might come prepared for an ambush, is that true?"

Cone swallowed hard. "It is. Webworm is soft-hearted, and too trusting for his own good, but he's not an imbecile. I worry that he might seek advice from Ironwood. Were I in his moccasins, I would. And if Webworm does that, Great Chief, we had better be prepared for battle."

Jay Bird turned to Thistle. "The same Ironwood?"

She nodded. "Yes."

Jay Bird frowned, bits and pieces fitting together as he considered the situation. "Let us give Ironwood no reason for suspicion, then. We wish him, and everyone in Talon Town, to feel quite safe during their journey south. Cone, you are to tell Snake Head . . . tell him that I worry his people will suspect conspiracy if he only sends five warriors to guard Crow Beard's body—and then it's stolen. Rather, let him send Crow Beard's body five bowshots in advance of the greatest procession of warriors he can assemble. Tell him that when I strike, and capture the corpse, his warriors will rush up. My warriors will engage his only long enough to skirmish. I will then withdraw my warriors and fall back. He will immediately recall his warriors into a defensive position, telling them he fears an ambush by a larger force." Jay Bird watched Cone's expression brighten. Indeed, any warrior would be happy with this plan. It didn't look nearly as ridiculous as Snake Head's first one.

Cone nodded warily. "So that it appears he won the battle."

"That will appeal to his vanity, won't it? And, Cone, he is bright enough to see the advantage of this plan, isn't he?"

"If he isn't, I'll explain it to him."

"Good. When he asks for your advice, tell him I am bringing perhaps forty warriors. You think he should bring eighty, just to be sure he can overcome my party if things get out of hand. Do you understand, Cone? We want him to bring as many warriors as he can."

Cone glanced at Thistle, silently asking questions, then returned his gaze to Jay Bird. "Great Chief, we're talking about warriors facing old enemies. What if Webworm loses control? You would be badly outnumbered."

"If Snake Head brings eighty warriors, how many will that leave in Talon Town?"

Cone lifted a shoulder. "Perhaps twenty, if . . ." His voice dried up as his eyes widened with understanding. He stammered, "You—you're going to—"

"Yes," Jay Bird answered. "I am."

Forty

Dawn resembled the inside of a seashell, pink and shining. Webworm sat in his place on the roof overlooking the entry to Talon Town and gazed out at the sunlit clouds sailing through the opalescent sky. They journeyed southwest, toward the arid lands of the Hohokam. Unusual in this land of westerly winds, a cool breeze flapped the hem of Webworm's tan cape and wiggled strands of his black hair loose from his braid, fluttering them around his square jaw and broad face. He inhaled deeply of the wet earthy air. Pools of mist filled the drainages. When the wind gusted, white tendrils twirled up and away like ghostly dancers.

At this time of the morning, the colors of the canyon took his breath away. The irregular rim gleamed a blood red, while the walls, still cloaked in shadows, shone purplish. Capped by the golden clouds and pink sky, the vista seemed too beautiful to be of this earth. Surely, it belonged to one of the shining skyworlds.

Cold and sleepy, Webworm huddled inside his cape and listened to the sounds of the waking canyon. Across the wash at Streambed Town, people moved through the plaza, lighting fires, and talking. Someone laughed. The lilting melody of a flute drifted along the canyon wall from Kettle Town, rising and falling on the wind. Talon Town slaves had already begun heading down to Straight Path Wash with empty water jugs. Two of the women carried cradleboards on their backs, secured by a tump line that ran across their foreheads. The infants squinted at the morning as they passed beneath Webworm's perch.

Webworm yawned. Gnat would be coming to relieve him soon. The past few days of preparing for the burial procession, and bickering with Snake Head, had wearied him. He thanked the Bear Thlatsina that he'd worked up the courage to speak with Ironwood. But he should have thought of taking a separate war party himself. Why hadn't he?

"Because you're not good at this," he whispered to himself. Breath frosted before him.

Politics had never been his strength. He was a *very good* warrior, but he had no skills for manipulation or clever deceit. Either act left him riddled with guilt, feeling soiled.

Get used to it. A War Chief is expected to do both, and do them well.

He saw Mourning Dove coming up from the drainage with a basket of clothing on her hip. He frowned. She'd been down washing clothing before dawn? In this cold?

Webworm suddenly felt ill. Why didn't he recall seeing her leave? She must have slept in Creeper's chamber last night and crawled out through the window in the pitch darkness—a crime punishable by death—unless she'd had Creeper's permission to go. Even if she had, it bothered him that he hadn't seen her leave. Despite his fatigue, he'd been watching very carefully. She must have taken great care to slip away when his head was turned.

Tiny, dressed in brown, her plump cheeks glowing red, she walked through the entry. She lifted a friendly hand to him and smiled. Webworm returned the gesture.

Mourning Dove walked across the western plaza, through the gate, and past the other slaves cooking breakfast. Then she climbed the ladders to Snake Head's chamber. Without even announcing herself, she ducked beneath the Chief's door curtain. For a moment, Webworm stared with his mouth open. What presumption! It wasn't like Mourning Dove to . . . *Fool. Snake Head must have been expecting her.*

Webworm heaved a sigh of relief and drew up his knees, tucking them inside his warm cape.

Snake Head ducked through his door and hurried down the ladders to the first-story roof. He wore a dark green shirt with red-and-black slashes across the chest. His long black hair hung loose, framing his oval face and large dark eyes. His breath puffed whitely as he walked.

Webworm stood up. The sky had turned golden, but Father Sun had not yet cleared the canyon rim. Talon Town remained in a cold well of shadow, its white walls tinted a pale blue.

Snake Head smiled as he strode up to Webworm.

"A pleasant morning to you, Blessed Sun," Webworm said with a forced smile.

"And to you, War Chief. How was the night? Anything unusual?"

"It was quiet, my chief."

Snake Head folded his arms across his chest and shivered as he scanned the brightening cliffs. An eagle circled over Propped Pillar, flapping lazily.

"I've been thinking about what you said, Webworm. About five warriors not being enough to guard the burial procession."

Webworm shifted. "Yes?"

"I've come to the conclusion that you were right. I regret not having seen your wisdom to begin with, but I'm certain of it now. Five warriors would leave us open to attack by even a small war party."

"Yes, my chief, it would." Elation bolstered Webworm. His arguments had worked!

"How many warriors do you think are necessary?"

"Thirty or forty would be a good number. That way if we run into—"

"If forty is good, then seventy or eighty would be better, don't you think?" Snake Head's brows lifted. Against the pale walls of Talon Town, his hair looked very black, and his dark eyes as inhuman as a weasel's.

Webworm shook his head. "No, my chief. I don't. First of all, there are only forty warriors in the Bear Clan. To get eighty I would have to send for our backup warriors in the other clans, and they are not really warriors at all. They are farmers, builders, and Traders. Their services are necessary when the town is attacked, but none of those people has ever been in a fight out in the open. They wouldn't know what to do. I think thirty or forty is plenty. We only need to make sure—"

"Well, I think we need more!" Snake Head's eyes suddenly

blazed with malice, as if Webworm's words had been an insult to his authority. "We're talking about the escort for *my* father. A man who was Blessed Sun—*your* Blessed Sun—for years. A leader of our people! Do you *dare* to stint on our final tribute to such a great man?"

"Snake Head, I meant no disrespect. I am your War Chief. It is my duty to advise you—"

"I've had enough of your advice, cousin. I've made my decision. We're taking eighty warriors. *See to it!*"

Snake Head spun and left.

Webworm rocked from foot to foot, his hands clenching as he watched Snake Head climb the ladders and return to his chamber. Great Ancestors, if it wasn't one extreme, it was another! How in the world could . . .

Less than twenty blinks later, Mourning Dove stepped out of Snake Head's chamber with the same basket of clothes. She climbed down and nonchalantly started across the plaza.

But this time as she neared the entry, Webworm stopped her. "Wait, Mourning Dove."

Webworm climbed down the ladder and gave her a hard look. She smiled nervously at him.

"What is it, Blessed Webworm?" Her chipmunk face had blushed, and he couldn't help but notice her rapid breathing.

"Where are you going?"

"To the drainage. I have clothes to wash."

Webworm stuck his hand inside the basket and felt the clothes. "These are wet. Didn't you just bring them up from the drainage?"

"Yes, but," she stuttered, "S-Snake Head was not satisfied with the job I—I'd done. He ordered me to wash them again."

Webworm frowned. "Mourning Dove, tell me the truth. What's going on? Why are you out washing clothes before dawn? And leaving town by windows?"

The color drained from her face. She looked faint. "Webworm, I—"

"I'm not going to tell anyone, Mourning Dove. I don't wish to see you dead. I just want to know what you're up to. Is this some task for Snake Head?"

She nodded miserably. "Yes, War Chief."

"What?"

"I—I can't say. Webworm, please, if he knew I was talking to you about this, he would *hurt* me." Mourning Dove glanced up fearfully at Snake Head's chamber, then whispered, "Please, let me go! I haven't much time!"

Webworm flicked his hand. "Go. But when you return, we *will* talk."

She ran through the entry and down the path to the wash, her brown dress flying. When she disappeared into the ravine, Webworm's shoulders tensed. All of the other slaves had gathered near the slave crossing. Why would Mourning Dove wash clothes alone? It didn't make any—

Steps sounded behind him, and Gnat said through a yawn, "Well, here I am. Ready for another day, War Chief. Are you ready for sleep?"

Webworm turned and scowled at the stocky, blunt-nosed warrior. He wore a turkey-feather cape over his red shirt and had twisted his black hair into a bun.

Gnat's bushy brows went down. "What's wrong?"

"I'll be back." Webworm slipped his bow over his shoulder. "In the meantime, *keep watch.*"

"Is something happening? Where are you going? What's—"

Webworm made a closed-fist gesture demanding silence. "Just do as I say, Gnat. Let no one enter town unless you know them. Understand?"

"Yes, of course."

Webworm walked through the entry and broke into a trot. His tan cape patted the backs of his knees as he ran. When he neared the place where Mourning Dove had disappeared, he dropped to a crouch and sneaked forward like Wolf hunting Mouse. The scent of damp earth rose strongly.

Straight Path Wash curved sharply at this point. Every spring huge chunks of earth cracked off and tumbled down, creating a narrow passageway for the water. Mist rolled in the bottom and boiled up over the lip. Webworm got down on his stomach and slid forward. Perfect beads of dew perched on the blades of grass. Fog coated his face. He eased forward and peered down into the drainage bottom. He could see Mourning Dove, but the man she spoke to had his back to Webworm.

He's a warrior. Dressed in red.

Why the secrecy? If Snake Head wished to speak with a

Straight Path warrior, why didn't he just call the man up to his chamber and do it?

Webworm cocked his head, trying to hear their soft voices, but they spoke too low. And within less than fifty heartbeats, the man left, never showing his face.

When Mourning Dove started up the trail out of the drainage, Webworm rolled to his back and lay very still. She didn't even glance his way, but ran up the path for Talon Town as fast as her legs would carry her. Webworm waited a short time, long enough that she—

"*Hello, old friend,*" a soft voice said, and Webworm rolled over with lightning quickness, scrambling to his feet and drawing his stiletto in one smooth move.

Cone stood before him, his arms spread, hands empty. "Don't kill me before we've had a chance to talk."

"Cone?" Webworm whispered in disbelief, scrutinizing the man's stocky body. "We thought you were dead! Where have you been?"

Cone walked forward, smiling. Dirt smudged his pug nose. His heavy moccasins were scuffed and travel-worn. The red shirt had seen better days; the hem hung in tatters. "Put away your stiletto, and I'll tell you."

"Oh," Webworm said with a laugh. "Sorry. You startled me." He tucked it back into his belt. He and Cone had fought side by side for many summers. That shared camaraderie . . . At that moment the image of Beargrass' face filled his memory, and a cold shiver slipped down his spine.

Cone's smile widened. "Blessed gods, it's good to see you." He stepped forward and embraced Webworm, pounding him on the back. "You are War Chief now, yes?"

"Yes," Webworm said as he pushed back. "But Cone, what are you doing out here? You had duties, responsibilities to—"

"It's a long story," he said. "And one I don't have time to tell you. Just know that I am working for the Blessed Sun, and my work is very important to the survival of the Straight Path nation."

"I know you are working for Snake Head. I just saw Mourning Dove come out of his chamber, and down to speak with you. What's going on, Cone? Is she carrying messages back and forth between you?"

Cone gave him a reserved look. "She is. No one pays much mind to the comings and goings of a slave."

Webworm cocked his head suspiciously. "Why don't you just come into town and deliver the messages yourself?"

"I can't, Webworm." Cone lifted his hands in frustration. "Snake Head doesn't wish people in town to know that I'm alive. It would ruin his plans."

"What plans?" Suddenly angry, Webworm said, "He may not wish our people to know, but I am War Chief! I should know what you are doing!"

Cone tilted his head. "Please, my friend, don't blame me. I am following orders, that's all. You know how that is. We are warriors. We must obey, whether we like the orders or not."

Webworm propped his hands on his hips, still haunted by Beargrass, Lanceleaf Village, and the past few days. He sighed, "Yes, I do know. But I don't have to like it."

"If it's any consolation," Cone said, and glanced around uncomfortably, as though fearing to be seen, "this will all be over in a few days. And, now, if you aren't going to kill me, I must be going." He grinned in that irreverent way of his that always made people laugh.

Webworm suppressed his smile. "The only way I'll kill you is if you don't tell me what this is all about when it's over."

"I will, I promise. Good-bye, old friend."

Webworm lifted a hand in farewell as Cone trotted down into the drainage and vanished in the swirling mist.

Webworm tramped back up the trail toward Talon Town. Why wouldn't Snake Head want people to know that Cone was alive? Wind whipped his cape about his tall body. What did it accomplish to have people think Cone was dead? People couldn't blame Cone for anything, or fear his actions. But what sort of secret task would be aided by such things? And why did it require leaving the War Chief in the dark?

Cone had disappeared while Ironwood was still War Chief.

Like a sparrow in a pond, Webworm felt as if he were floundering, completely out of his element.

If Cone had been telling the truth—and his work involved the survival of the Straight Path nation—Ironwood wouldn't have forgotten to tell Webworm. The man, no matter how distracted, wouldn't make a mistake like that.

Webworm growled to himself, blinking his tired eyes. He'd think about it later. For now, despite his head feeling as if it were stuffed with cotton, he had to begin the nearly impossible task of rounding up eighty warriors. Then, if he had the luxury, he'd speak with Ironwood.

I have a right to know what's going on. I'm War Chief!

Snake Head held his door curtain back just enough to watch Sternlight, Dune, and the two youths who'd been helping them walk across the plaza. He scrutinized the young woman. Slender, with broad cheekbones, a pointed nose, and full lips, she wore a beautiful pale green dress. Probably something Sternlight had given her. The fabric was too fine, the dye too rich, to be anything from the outlying villages. Her long hair hung to her hips and swayed gently as she walked.

Slaves filled the plaza, grinding corn, folding clothes, and two old men sat before looms, weaving. Children raced about, chasing each other through a flock of horrified turkeys. The squawks and squeals—along with a few loose feathers—carried on the morning breeze.

"What do you think?" Mourning Dove asked anxiously Since dawn, she'd asked to leave seven times. Her frustration had reached a fever pitch.

Snake Head let the curtain fall closed and turned to look at her. She sat against the wall by the macaw's cage, throwing sunflower seeds at the bird. The macaw gripped its foot pole and watched her with malevolent interest, as if eager to sink its talons into her bright shining eyes.

"It's possible," Snake Head said. He walked over to stand in front of her. Clots of mud hung from the hem of her ugly brown dress, and dust coated her fat cheeks. "Creeper really thinks she's my mother's misbegotten child, eh?"

"Yes, and Webworm remembers the girl from Lanceleaf Village. Her name is Cornsilk." Mourning Dove sounded tired. Snake Head had rousted her out of Creeper's bed very early. The leader of the Buffalo Clan had not been happy about it, but neither had he dared to complain. Instead, Creeper had dressed and left them alone together as Snake Head had ordered.

Snake Head chuckled. "I should have known. Sternlight told me it was a boy specifically so he could save a girl. But if true, it leaves my mother in a very bad position. She can't openly acknowledge the girl without risking her own life. Even more interesting, a true daughter of Night Sun would be the next Matron of Talon Town." Snake Head rubbed his chin in thought. "If the truth came out, it might well result in my mother's death, and the girl's installation as Matron."

"Matron? A woman with Made Person blood? She's tainted, Snake Head."

"No one would like it, that's true."

Mourning Dove studied the sunflower seeds in her palm as though she could read the future in their patterns and found it distasteful. "And what would you do?"

Snake Head smiled. "I don't know. Do you think I could rule side-by-side with my half-sister? She is a pretty thing, and perhaps she isn't opposed to incest. That would—"

"You won't rule together for long," Mourning Dove said spitefully. "The instant she marries, she can depose you and set up her husband as the Blessed Sun."

Snake Head's expression hardened. He walked over to his rumpled blankets and sank down, his gaze darting around the room. A warming bowl of fresh coals glowed in the middle of the floor, turning the white walls a pale red, reflecting with eerie brilliance in the macaw's sinister eyes. The bird's red, blue, and yellow feathers glittered.

"Even if the girl is mother's spawn, she'd never acknowledge her. She couldn't, after the deception she, Sternlight, and Dune pulled off in the kiva during her trial. Such news would outrage the Straight Path elders. They would certainly condemn them all to death—and Mother just wouldn't do that to her precious nephew, or that old liar, Dune."

Mourning Dove threw her handful of seeds into the cage and wiped her palms off on her dress. "Maybe not now, but Dune will be dead soon, and your mother and Sternlight are already old, over forty summers. They might live for another ten summers, but what will happen on your mother's deathbed? Have you thought of that?"

A tingle of fear went through him. By then, he'd have seen thirty-four summers, and would be revered as the greatest Chief the Straight Path people had ever known. It would be just like his mother to let him claw his way to the top, and then snatch it all out from under him by elevating a misbegotten daughter with a husband—or for herself to marry some drudge from a nearby town.

Snake Head folded his hands in his lap. He smiled at Mourning Dove. "That," he said in an intimate voice, "is why I keep you around."

Kneeling by the teapot, Cornsilk refilled her cup. The fragrance of flower petals rose with the steam. She tested the golden liquid, and when it burned her mouth, gently blew to cool it. Steam twisted away in angry patterns.

Her gaze drifted around the room, lingering on their packs and rolled blankets where they rested against the opposite wall. If only they could leave, return to the Derelict's little white house with its flaking plaster. If only, if only . . .

She closed her eyes, fighting the desperation that filled her. She hadn't even had time to still the aching grief over the death of her family. Talon Town frightened her. Only after arriving here did she realize just how alone she really was.

Who can I trust? Sternlight? He seemed nice. But how can I know for sure?

Perhaps she could trust Dune, and she definitely trusted Poor Singer, but he was just one young man.

Poor Singer was still at the great kiva. He'd told her that he didn't know what the final burial preparations entailed, but in Windflower Village they'd rarely taken more than three or four hands of time.

"Hello?" a voice called from the roof entry.

Cornsilk sat up straighter. "Hello. Who's there?"

The Blessed Sun climbed down the ladder into the chamber.

Cornsilk dropped her teacup on the floor and rose to her feet, staring. He was extremely handsome, with large dark eyes and long eyelashes, tall and broad-shouldered. The copper bells on his purple shirt clinked. He'd twisted his black hair into a bun.

"It's Silk, isn't it?" he asked.

She nodded.

"I'm Snake Head, the Blessed Sun of the Straight Path nation, and, of course, the chief of Talon Town. I welcome you. I've heard from the Made People that you're from Turtle Village."

"Was." She backed away from him. "My village was destroyed."

Snake Head smiled and looked her over carefully, studying the way her hips and breasts curved beneath the fabric of her pale green dress, the way her hip-length hair fell around her. "So I've heard. Yellowgirl also tells me that your parents originally came from Lanceleaf Village. Is that so?"

Cornsilk clasped her hands behind her back to hide their trembling. Her mouth had gone dry and thick. "Yes."

Snake Head watched her anxious movements, then gestured to the sitting mats around the warming bowl. "May I sit?"

"I—I was just preparing to go out. I don't mean to offend you, but . . ."

He sat cross-legged and pointed to the mat next to him. "Come and sit beside me, Silk. Let's be friends."

Cornsilk knelt across from him, as far away as she could get.

He peered into the teapot. "That smells very good."

"Please. Help yourself. There's a clean cup there by the warming bowl."

Snake Head poured out the last of the tea and lifted it to sniff the fragrance. "Sunflower, eh? Very nice."

Cornsilk laced her fingers tightly in her lap, waiting.

He swirled his tea. "Tell me, do you recall the War Chief of Lanceleaf Village? A man named Beargrass? His wife was named Thistle."

A sudden rush of blood flushed her cheeks and ran like fire through her veins. She shook her head. "I—I've never been to Lanceleaf. My parents just came from there."

He frowned down into his cup. "Well, then you wouldn't know if they'd had a boy named Fledgling and a girl named Cornsilk"—he looked up—"would you?"

Her heart pounded so hard she feared it might break through

her ribs. "No." She could barely hear herself answer.

"That's too bad. I've heard many interesting things about them. Especially the girl, Cornsilk. She was about your age."

"I—I'm sorry. Was there something else you needed, Blessed Sun?"

As though suddenly angry, he slammed his cup to the floor. Cornsilk jumped as the cup shattered and thin sherds clattered across the floor.

Snake Head narrowed his eyes, watching her the way a rattlesnake did a cornered packrat. "No. There's nothing else I need for the moment. I was hoping to speak with my misbegotten half sister. I think we have many things to talk about."

"I don't know anything—"

He lurched to his feet and loomed over her. "You should know that many people here once lived in Turtle Village. They've been talking about you and your family, and don't remember any of you. That's odd. Don't you think?"

Cornsilk just stared at him.

He gripped the ladder and snapped, "I am ordering that you are not to leave this place. Perhaps later, when your memory returns, we can talk. Until then, I want you to think about just where your interests lie. You can work for me, or against me. Beargrass worked *against* me."

He climbed the ladder with enough vigor to leave it rattling. His steps pounded angrily across the roof. She heard him yell at someone.

Breathing hard, Cornsilk stared up at the entry for a long time, then closed her eyes tightly.

Forty-One

Poor Singer tried to stop gaping at the First People's kiva. The sheer size of this circular ceremonial chamber, over a hundred hands across, left him humbled. The kiva in Windflower Village spread about half this size, and while beautiful, it could not compare with the majesty of this chamber. The yellow, red, and blue benches, topped by the white walls, engendered a sense of wonder in Poor Singer, as if, just by standing here, he had become part of the gods' world.

He lowered his eyes and sewed the shroud around Crow Beard's swollen body. Dune stood at his shoulder, watching with mild eyes. Across the way, a grim-faced Sternlight sewed on the shroud for Cloud Playing.

The small fire crackling in the rectangular fire box threw a wavering orange gleam over the thlatsina masks hanging above the thirty-six wall crypts. They seemed to be watching the final burial preparations with predator-like intensity. The sharp teeth and polished beaks shone, and Poor Singer could *feel* those hollow eye sockets gazing upon him.

He ran the thread through the last hole and tied the knot, then straightened, his bone needle in hand. "What should I do next, Dune?"

The frail little holy man lifted his chin, peering down his small nose at the stitching. Crow Beard had been totally encased. "I couldn't have done better myself. That's fine."

Sternlight glanced up from the turquoise-studded blanket that encased Cloud Playing's body like a cocoon. He smoothed and tucked the last strands of her hair into the blanket and began sewing it shut. "Crow Beard will be grateful for the work you've done, Poor Singer."

Rolling the bone needle between his fingers, Poor Singer

struggled with the sense of pride that tried to rise in his breast. Would it always be a battle like this?

Dune's thin white hair stuck out at odd angles around his deeply wrinkled face. He wore white, as Sternlight did. They'd all been working hard since before dawn, and sweat soaked their clothing, making Dune's shirt cling to his skeletal body like a second skin. His ribs showed through the fabric.

Dune turned away. "Now that that's finished, why don't you help me bless and purify the burial ladders?"

"I'd be happy to, Dune."

Poor Singer followed Dune around the foot drum to the fire-pit, where the two pine-pole ladders lay propped against the lowest, the yellow, bench. Four small pots of cornmeal rested in between the ladders. Dune reached for one and said, "Hold out your hands."

Poor Singer did, and Dune poured cool white meal into them, then set the pot down on the yellow bench and pointed to the ladder on the left. "Rub the cornmeal into the ladder. We are consecrating the wood for the journey, and appeasing any angry Earth Spirits who might have inhabited the tree we cut down to make the ladders. White meal signifies the blessed east, and purity. It will heal any hurt feelings."

Poor Singer bent over and began smoothing the finely ground meal on the long side poles of the ladder. "Shall I rub it into the sinew which ties the rungs to the poles?"

"You shall, and after you've finished with the white meal, rub on red cornmeal, then the yellow, and finally the blue. By joining the colors of the sacred directions we are bringing the Great Circle of life fully around, tying the ends together. The old is over and done. All hurts are forgiven. Crow Beard and Cloud Playing now have a chance for a new beginning." As he sat on the bench and worked white meal into his ladder, Dune sighed. "And the gods know, Crow Beard needs one."

Sternlight looked up and gave Dune a kindly glance. "Indeed, he does."

"I have heard," Poor Singer ventured with care, "that he did some unpleasant things during his life."

The wrinkles of Dune's ancient face rearranged themselves in contemplation. "Many. But all of that is over. We have cleansed his soul and cleared his eyes. He can see his errors now. The punishments he inflicts upon himself will be far worse than any we humans could impose."

Sternlight gazed at Poor Singer. "Crow Beard will spend the rest of eternity trying to make up for wrongs he did people. I think he will make a good rain god. He will want to take care of the people he hurt."

Poor Singer's gaze went to the sewn-up blanket on the foot drum in front of Sternlight. "And Cloud Playing? What will she do?"

Sternlight gently placed a hand on the body. "She had little to atone for. Everyone . . . almost everyone . . . loved her. She played with the children, cared for the sick, helped the elderly, fed the hungry. I know few people who gave as much as Cloud Playing did."

"Or suffered as much," Dune said as his eyes narrowed. "For a woman her age, she endured far too many blows. I can't understand why anyone would wish to murder her."

"She was *murdered?*" Poor Singer asked in a hushed voice.

Sternlight's handsome face tensed. "Yes, killed just beyond the walls of Talon Town by an unknown man. It happened right after her father's death."

Poor Singer finished applying the white meal and scooped out a handful of red. He began rubbing it over the ladder. In the muted gleam of the fire, the two holy men looked deeply sad, as though they missed Cloud Playing. But neither of them seemed to miss Crow Beard. That was intriguing. Poor Singer studied his companions from the corner of his eye.

Windflower Village received news from Traders and travelers, which generally meant they heard about the most dramatic events. Poor Singer knew that Cloud Playing had been the daughter of Night Sun and Crow Beard, but he'd heard very few stories about her. Crow Beard, however, had been a topic of constant discussion, almost all of it appalling. Poor Singer had never really listened to the terrible stories, because his mother had once told him that people in powerful positions, like Chief Crow Beard, got blamed for everything bad that happened, whether they were responsible or not. All of his life, Snow Mountain had taught Poor Singer to respect the Chief, and to love him for the good things he did for the Straight Path nation.

"I remember once," Poor Singer said, glancing first at Dune, then at Sternlight, "when Windflower Village ran out of food in the middle of the winter, Crow Beard and Night Sun opened the storerooms here at Talon Town and sent us corn, beans, and squash. I had only seen five summers, and I was very hungry. The deep sense of gratitude I felt still lives in my heart."

Sternlight smiled. "Yes, in that sense, they ruled well together."

"A man can be a good ruler, and a very wretched man," Dune said. "Which, the thlatsinas know, Crow Beard was."

Poor Singer frowned. "It's just like you to spoil a splendid moment of reverence, Dune."

"Well, I didn't want you to get the wrong impression. If you wish to see Crow Beard, then see him as he really was. Nearly every good thing he did, he did because Night Sun advised him to. Never forget, the Matron makes the decisions about who gets food and when. The Blessed Sun merely decides how best to carry out those decisions. How many men to send along to protect the food, which route to take. All of the terrible things, the brutal raids, the pillaging of villages, and slaughter of women and children—Crow Beard made those decisions alone."

"I hope I get to meet the great Matron," Poor Singer said. "I've heard many stories of her charity and goodness."

Dune's bushy white brows drew together. "You will meet her. Night Sun has needed privacy since she was released from the Cage. But soon—"

Poor Singer's hands stopped on the wood. "She was imprisoned? But who would dare?"

Neither of the holy men spoke for a time. They just stared at each other, as though some silent communication passed between them.

Very quietly, Sternlight said, "Dune, I'm finished here. I think that I will return to my chamber and eat something. I didn't have time this morning, and it's almost midday."

"Yes, of course. Go. We're almost finished, as well." He indicated the ladder with a waggling finger. "Providing Poor Singer keeps his mind on his sacred duties and continues sanctifying Cloud Playing's ladder."

Poor Singer winced and swiftly rubbed the red cornmeal over

the last rungs, then reached for the pot with the yellow meal.

Dune turned to Sternlight. "After the ladders are finished, Poor Singer and I will roll the bodies onto the ladders and leave them resting on the foot drums for the burial procession to take tomorrow. And then," he heaved a tired breath, "we, too, will be going home."

Sternlight pulled himself up, pressing his hands into the small of his back, as if it ached. "I have appreciated your help, Dune. And yours, too, Poor Singer." He hesitated, gazing at Poor Singer with those luminous eyes. "What will happen with Silk?"

"I don't know, Sunwatcher. She hasn't found any family here. She's alone. I think I'm her only friend in the world." He glanced uneasily at Dune. "I was hoping . . . perhaps . . ."

Dune arched both brows, and growled, "We'll discuss it."

Poor Singer smiled. "Thank you, Dune."

"If that doesn't work out, Dune," Sternlight said, "I'm sure we can arrange something here."

"Thank you."

Sternlight bowed slightly to Poor Singer and turned back to Dune. "Will you be taking supper with me this evening, Dune?"

"Yes, if you'd like."

"I would. I'd like one last conversation about the natures of the thlatsinas before you go."

"Gladly. I'll see you then."

Sternlight started across the kiva, his white shirt flashing in the firelight as he climbed the stairs to the altar room.

Poor Singer dipped up a handful of blue cornmeal and began carefully rubbing it into the sinews binding the rungs to the side poles. "He seems like a very holy man."

Dune scratched the back of his neck. "Most people think he's a witch. What do you see when you look at him?"

Poor Singer blinked.

"Keep rubbing," Dune ordered.

"Oh, yes, I'm sorry." As he rubbed, Poor Singer thought about how to put it. "I've heard people say he's a witch, but I just know he's a very good man. I *feel* it."

"Ah," Dune smiled toothlessly and his ancient head bobbed in an approving nod. "You've stopped looking with your eyes and started looking with your heart. You *are* improving." He flicked a hand. "Now, keep working. You'll have summers to improve your heart's vision, but only a day to get this done. Work, boy. Work."

Sternlight walked across the plaza. Rising against the background of buff-colored cliff, Talon Town's white walls possessed a blinding pearlescent gleam, and he squinted as he watched his sandaled feet. The hard-packed dirt glinted with sherds of broken pottery and shiny bits of chert, obsidian, and quartzite, the refuse of stone-tool making. Three slaves worked in the shadows of the five-story walls, making rattles for the upcoming Equinox celebration. Fist-sized gourds from last cycle's crops had been dried and hollowed out. The slaves sat in a row, each completing a separate task. Mourning Dove dropped pebbles into the hollow gourd, then Swallowtail applied sticky pine pitch to the small hole in the base and attached a wooden handle. Lastly, old woman Antelope Doll painted bird tracks and falling rain on the rattles.

As Sternlight passed, they all averted their eyes, and he sighed.

Two dogs rose from where they'd been sleeping and trotted to meet him, their tails wagging.

"Hello, Bright Moth," he said to the larger, black-and-white dog, and reached down to pat her silky head.

The smaller dog leaped up, dancing on her hind legs. Pure black, she had soft brown eyes.

"And you, too, Beanpod." Sternlight scratched her ears. "Thank you for coming to see me. You made me feel better."

He bowed reverently to the Great Warriors who peered down at him, their masks shining, before he climbed the ladders to his chambers. As he ducked beneath his door curtain, the scent of dried wildflowers struck him. He kept them in pots on the south side of his chamber, and on warm days like this, their fragrances rose sweetly into the air.

Sternlight gazed at the thlatsina masks on his walls, sixteen in all, sensing something. Not all messages came in words. He closed his eyes a moment, trying to find the source of the discomfort, then turned and looked at the White Wolf mask. It had its ears pricked, its fangs glinting in the light. Its furry face and long muzzle seemed to move faintly, as if . . .

"Sternlight?" a timid voice called.

He sucked in a breath and swung around. "Silk?"

"Yes, it's me. I—I was hoping I might be able to talk with you."

"Of course." He walked over, pulled up the door curtain, and draped it on its peg.

Silk stood outside, her long hair loose about her shoulders. What a pretty young woman. Her oval face with its pointed nose and dark probing eyes possessed a curious power. She carried a teapot in one hand and a pack over her shoulder.

"Please, enter, Silk."

She stepped inside and looked around, anxiously studying the thlatsinas. "Are you certain you aren't busy? I could return later."

Sternlight smiled. "The only business I have right now is with you. Won't you sit down?" He gestured to the willow sitting mats near the warming bowl. Last night's coals had burned down to ash that puffed up whitely when she knelt and set her pot on the floor.

As she unslung her pack, she said, "I know you've been working since very early. I thought you might be hungry and thirsty." She opened her pack and removed a small bowl of red corn cakes filled with piñon nuts, and set it beside the teapot. She looked up at him, fear in her face. "I didn't know when you'd return, so I made these two hands of time ago, but I've been keeping them warm. I hope they're all right."

"How very kind of you to think of me. As a matter of fact, I'm starving."

A sudden smile brightened her face, and it reminded him of spring sunlight in the canyon: breathtaking, fragile, and swiftly gone. "Preparing burials sounds like difficult work. Is it?"

Sternlight walked across the room, picked up two teacups and sat cross-legged on the mats opposite her. He lifted the pot and poured the cups full. "The really hard part is not the physical work, but looking into the faces of people you've loved, and knowing that they're gone. It drains a person's strength."

The ache in his voice surprised him. Over the sun cycles of handling the dead, he had learned a certain detachment, but Cloud Playing's death had wounded him deeply.

Silk nodded. "I understand."

Sternlight sipped the tea. "Oh, this is good, Silk. Did you blend flowers?"

"Yes, I brought dried sunflower and rose petals from Dune's house in the north." She placed the bowl of corn cakes between them. "Please, help yourself."

Sternlight took one of the cakes and eagerly bit into it. The sweet flavor tasted delicious. "These have a red color. You mixed prickly pear fruit with the cornmeal, didn't you?"

She nodded and her black hair fell over her shoulders. It was so long that its ends dragged the floor beside her. "Yes, my mother"—pain tightened her eyes—"she always made red corn cakes with fruit and nuts. I don't know any other way to make them."

"You don't need to know another way. These are perfectly delicious. I'll wager Poor Singer loves them, too."

Her eyes glowed. "Oh, yes, very much. But I think he likes anything I make."

"That's because he loves you, Silk, though I don't imagine he's told you that. But it's obvious."

She took a bite of her corn cake. "Is it?"

"Very. Every time he says your name he smiles. Haven't you noticed?"

Silk swallowed her mouthful, and took a sip of tea. "Well, actually, I have. Once or twice."

"I would have been surprised if you hadn't. I'm told that women know these things before men do."

She finished her corn cake and sat back on the mat. "I made the rest for you," she said, and pointed to the bowl. "I'm not very hungry." Fear flitted through her eyes as she looked around the room.

Sternlight picked up another cake and chewed slowly. "Poor Singer told me that you haven't found any family here, but you mustn't give up hope."

Tears suddenly filled her eyes.

Sternlight lowered his half-eaten cake to his lap. "Are you all right?"

Silk blinked the tears back. "Sternlight, I have something very important to speak with you about."

"I'd be happy to help if I can."

Silk glanced uneasily at the open doorway, as though fearing they might be overheard.

He gestured to the door. "Shall I lower the curtain?"

"Yes, if—if you wouldn't mind."

He placed his cake in the bowl, rose, and went to let the curtain fall closed. A bright outline of sunlight gleamed around it.

She lifted her head and watched him as he walked back. A glow lit her eyes.

He crouched on the mats to her left and said, "Now, what has you so frightened?"

She pulled her pack onto her lap and looked up at him as if he knew more than the gods themselves, and she feared him just as much. In a trembling voice, she said, "My mother told me that if I was ever in trouble, I should come to you."

"Your mother?"

Silk pulled a blanket from her pack. As she unfolded it, and he saw the red, blue, and black diamonds studded with the finest turquoise, his legs went weak.

He sank to the floor, staring at her unblinking, and saw for the first time the distinctive golden color of her skin, so exactly like her father's, and the pointed nose identical to her mother's. "Blessed thlatsinas," he whispered. *"Cornsilk?"*

She nodded.

Sternlight closed his eyes a moment, fighting the tide of emotion. He had helped bring her into the world, cut her birth cord, seen her take her first breath, and heard her utter her first cry. He looked at her again. "I don't know where to begin."

She shrugged lightly. "I know so little, any place will be fine."

On impulse, he reached out and touched her hand. "I'm so happy you're safe. We were very worried after the attack on Lanceleaf. We feared you might have been—"

"Why couldn't you stop the attack, Sternlight? You're very powerful. Couldn't you have ordered Webworm to leave us alone?"

He drew his hand back. "By then Crow Beard was dead, and

Snake Head had become the new Blessed Sun. Webworm had to follow his orders. My protests meant nothing. And your father was away at the time, I—"

"My father?" She searched his face. "You mean, you're *not* my father?"

He felt as if he'd been bludgeoned. He couldn't speak. Then a smile crept over his face. "No, but after hearing that hopeful tone in your voice, I'm sorry I'm not."

"Sternlight, please tell me who is? And my mother? I need to know their names."

Sucking in a fortifying breath, he said, "There are some things I wish to tell you first, about my part in all this. Then I will go and prepare your father. I suspect he will need a little time." He gently placed a hand on her cheek. "Your father has spent half of his life working to protect you, Cornsilk. He has placed himself at great risk more than once. When he sees you, he'll probably be terrified. Please, be kind to him."

She nodded against his hand. "I promise."

Sternlight tipped his face and frowned at the ceiling. "Hallowed gods, I've explained all of this to you a thousand times in my dreams. Why am I suddenly at a loss?"

"Sternlight? Please? Is Ironwood my father?"

He looked down into her frightened eyes and a curious pang tightened his chest. "Yes, he is. But let me start before that, Cornsilk. This story begins almost seventeen summers ago. Ironwood had been War Chief for less than a sun cycle, and Night Sun—"

"Wait." Cornsilk held up a hand. "Before you start, I should tell you that Snake Head came to see me. He—he climbed right down into our chamber without being invited, and he told me . . . he asked me about Lanceleaf Village and a girl named Cornsilk. I don't think he was certain, but he seemed to think I might be Cornsilk. He said he wanted to talk with his 'misbegotten half sister.' And then . . . then he made threats. Told me I wasn't to leave Talon Town."

Sternlight felt ill. He bowed his head and grimaced at the white-plastered floor. "Then I'd better hurry. . . ."

Ironwood took the rungs of the ladders two at a time on his climb to the fourth story. People, disturbed by his haste, rose from the plaza, shielded their eyes against the slant of the afternoon sun and watched him curiously, whispering. Yellowgirl walked out into the middle of the eastern plaza to frown up, probably wondering where he headed in such a hurry. Her blue dress whipped about her legs. Gnat, who stood guard over the entry, also turned to stare.

Blood rushed so powerfully in Ironwood's veins his whole body tingled. He hadn't the time to worry about what they thought.

As he sprinted across the third-story roof for the next ladder, his gaze scanned the canyon. The cliffs looked golden against the sere blue sky. A flock of piñon jays whirled over his head, trilling and uttering sharp *rack-rack-racks*. People sat against the exterior wall of Streambed Town, women grinding corn and men weaving multicolored blankets. Their laughter carried on the cool dust-scented breeze that swept the desert.

Ironwood halted outside Night Sun's door. She had the curtain lowered. He called, "Night Sun? Night Sun are you in there?"

"Yes," she replied. "Just a moment."

Ironwood spread his legs and clenched his jaw. Gnat and Yellowgirl continued to watch him with their brows lowered, but the others in the plaza gradually dispersed and went back to their chores. It seemed to take forever.

When Night Sun finally lifted her door curtain and draped it over its peg, Ironwood stared. She wore a long larkspur-colored dress and her graying black hair hung loose about her shoulders. She smelled of yucca soap and pine needles.

"I'm sorry to keep you waiting," she said. "I just finished my bath. What—"

"I need to come inside."

Night Sun saw the panic on his face and stepped back with a frown. "What is it? What's wrong?"

Ironwood entered, lowered the door curtain again and stood

in front of her breathing hard. Her dark eyes searched his. He said, "Night Sun . . . Cornsilk is here. In Talon Town."

Her face slackened in understanding. "She's *here*? Where? Where is my daughter? I want to see her." She headed for the door, and Ironwood reached out to grip her arm.

"I want you to listen to me first."

Night Sun glanced at his hard hand on her wrist, then said, "Go on."

Ironwood released her and took a deep breath. "The young woman who arrived with Poor Singer is our daughter. She escaped the Lanceleaf Village slaughter, but—"

"Thank the gods. Is she all right? What happened—"

"*But*," he said insistently, and lifted his fists to silence her, "before any of us knew who she was, Snake Head went to visit her. I don't know how he knows—*but he does.*"

Night Sun shook her head in confusion. "But how could he? If none of us realized—"

"That doesn't matter, Night Sun!" he shouted, and immediately regretted it. He closed his eyes a moment, calming himself, and forced himself to speak in a low voice. "He asked her questions about Lanceleaf Village and threatened her. Told her he suspected she was his 'misbegotten half-sister.' Do you understand what I'm saying? For the sakes of the gods, Night Sun. *He has the proof he needs to execute you! You must leave! It doesn't have to be with me, Night Sun, but you*—"

"Yes," she said, staring unblinking at him. "I understand."

Turning away, she slowly walked across her chamber to stare out the window. Propped Pillar sparkled with an amber brilliance in the afternoon sunlight. The eagle nest on the top was empty, the parents no doubt out hunting in the canyon. As she tipped her face to gaze up at it, long hair fell down her back, the gray strands glimmering whitely against her purplish blue dress.

Ironwood vented a halting breath and folded his arms tightly across his breast, giving her time to think it over.

"Your life is at stake, too," she said softly, without turning. "When are you leaving?"

"Tonight. I'll meet Cornsilk at dusk, then I'm grabbing my pack and getting out. I have no desire to face the elders. This time, they'll have no choice but to—"

"Ironwood." Night Sun turned. Her beautiful face was sheathed with sunlight, her dark eyes glimmering. A strange serenity had possessed her. "I don't want to live anywhere hot. Let's go north, to the mountains."

After a moment's hesitation, long enough for her meaning to sink in, Ironwood strode across the room and embraced her so hard it drove the air from her lungs. He held her in silence for a time, then said, "We must wait until it's completely dark to leave. Sternlight will distract Webworm when we're ready to go. I've already worked this out with him, though he thought it would be just Cornsilk and me, but—"

Night Sun pushed back from him. "Cornsilk could *stay*, Ironwood. She has the right. If she wishes to accept the position as Matron of Talon Town, my disgrace will not disqualify her."

Ironwood's gaze darted about while he thought. "I will speak with her about it." He looked down. "Night Sun, I would like to talk with her first . . . alone. I do not mean to—"

"Of course, Ironwood," she interrupted. "You have taken care of her for many summers. It is your right. Perhaps after you speak to her, you could bring her to my chamber? Or we could have supper together? Something?"

He nodded. "Of course, and then . . ."

Night Sun looked at him so sternly, Ironwood backed away in confusion. They stood six hands apart, their gazes locked. An odd expression creased her beautiful face.

"What's wrong?" he asked. "Did I say something—"

She steepled thin fingers over her mouth and gazed at him as though about to deliver a life or death ultimatum to an enemy chief. "You will *never* regret this, Ironwood. I know I've caused you much grief in the past, but I love you more than I could ever tell you. I *promise* I will make you happy."

He went still, staring at her.

When her jaw trembled, Ironwood stepped forward and clutched her tightly against him. It took several moments for him to realize the warmth in his hair was not her breath, but tears.

He gently kissed her temple. "As long as I'm with you, I can face anything. Now, let's talk seriously. We have to make plans. . . ."

Forty-Two

In a futile attempt to soothe himself, Ironwood let his gaze linger on the land. As the afternoon waned, shadows crept across the canyon, filling in the hollows, defining the drainages. A scalloped strip of sunlight hung like torn fabric from the cliff's rim, but the stone below had purpled with the coming of evening. From where Ironwood sat near a boulder at the edge of Straight Path Wash, he could see Sternlight and Cornsilk walking down the trail from Talon Town. He took a deep breath to steady himself.

At least Sternlight had managed to get her out of Talon Town. After Snake Head's warning, Ironwood had half worried that Webworm would refuse her permission.

He'd been preparing for this moment for more than sixteen summers, and now that it had arrived, all the practiced speeches sounded hollow.

For some time after Cornsilk's birth, he'd been too hurt and too afraid to even think about his daughter. But once Crow Beard returned and things settled down at Talon Town, he'd thought about her constantly. In his dreams, a little girl's bubbling laughter and the swift patter of childish feet echoed. Every sun cycle on her bornday, he'd sat alone in his chamber and tried to imagine what she must look like now, how she had grown. Did she have Night Sun's voice, or his own? Did she look like him or her mother? Frightened and lonely, the only solace he'd had was the knowledge that Cornsilk was safe and being raised by good, capable people. So often, so very often, he'd longed to sit with Night Sun and tell her that their daughter lived, that Cornsilk was three, or four, or five summers this cycle, and doing well. But when they passed in the plaza, Night Sun would deliberately lower her eyes, speaking to him only when she had to, and he'd known he would never lie in her arms, the arms of the mother of his child, and find comfort for his loneliness. . . .

Sternlight laughed, and Ironwood turned back to watch them coming down the trail. They were talking. Ironwood saw their mouths moving, saw Cornsilk smile, but couldn't yet hear their words. They both wore their long black hair loose, and a faint dust-scented breeze teased it around their faces. The sunlight slanting across the canyon turned Sternlight's white robe pale gold, and flowed into the folds of Cornsilk's yellow dress like liquid amber. What a beautiful young woman she'd become.

Absently, he noted that he'd twisted the tail of his best shirt into a wrinkled peak and tried to smooth it. He looked up at Brother Sky to calm himself. Among the clouds, black spots of eagles soared and dove, their shrill cries carrying. Sternlight had patiently explained to Ironwood all the things he'd told Cornsilk, and the many things he had not. *"She's confused and overwhelmed, Ironwood. Be gentle. Let her tell you how she's feeling. She has many questions."*

His heart thundered as they came closer. Perspiration dampened his flat nose. He'd worn his best shirt, the beautiful buckskin with porcupine quill chevrons across the breast and down the sleeves. The turquoise wolf pendant that Night Sun had given him hung around his neck, and his gray braid was tidy.

Less than fifty hands from Straight Path Wash, Sternlight stopped and nodded at the boulder where Ironwood sat.

Cornsilk glanced at Ironwood before turning back to Sternlight and saying something.

Sternlight placed a hand on her shoulder, nodded to Ironwood again, and walked toward Talon Town.

Ironwood rose to his feet. She had her back to him, watching Sternlight. A honeyed gleam lit the five stories of town and brightened the faces of the people who walked around on the roofs. To the west, where Father Sun still blazed, slaves climbed up from the wash with dishes and water jugs in their arms. Children followed behind, squealing and throwing sticks for barking dogs. Gray Wood, the slave master, brought up the rear. Though he did not have his bow nocked, it hung over his shoulder, and he carried an arrow in his hands as a warning. His red shirt flapped in the breeze.

Cornsilk turned, met Ironwood's eyes, and filled her lungs with cool damp air. She walked toward him.

Ironwood braced his feet. She had his own arching brows, and golden skin, but her pointed nose and large dark eyes belonged to Night Sun.

She stopped a few paces from him and said, "Hello, Ironwood."

"Hello, Cornsilk." A strange surge of emotion ran through him. He'd never called her by her name before, not to her face. He gestured to the patch of grass that encircled the boulder. "Will you sit with me for a time?"

She nodded and sat down a cautious ten hands from him. Her yellow dress spread around her, and her long hair touched the grass. Ironwood leaned against the tan boulder, which stood half as tall as a man.

"Did Sternlight have any trouble passing the guard?"

"No. It was Gnat. He didn't say anything."

"Good. I thought it better to talk out here, where we wouldn't be overheard. I'm glad that—"

"Ironwood," she interrupted, looking frightened, "let me say at the beginning, that I'm proud to be your daughter. You are a legend among many of the villages, and when my father—the . . . the man who raised me—spoke of you, he always smiled, and respect filled his voice. I know you are a good man, and you have taken good care of me. For that, I thank you."

Ironwood's heart might have been wound in rawhide. "Beargrass was the best warrior I ever knew, and a good friend to me. I knew you would be safe and happy with him."

Cornsilk cupped her hands over her knees. She seemed to be searching for the right words. "When anyone in our village said bad things about you, Beargrass always defended you. He said people could not possibly understand the pressures you faced, and that they should wait to see what happened in the end. He trusted you, Ironwood." She sucked in a nervous breath. "Because of that, I trust you."

He nodded. "And I trust you, Cornsilk, because you are Beargrass' daughter, in heart, if not in body." Ironwood forced himself to smile. "Sternlight said you had some questions you wished to ask me. I hope I can answer them."

She looked up at him with round eyes.

He waited.

"Ironwood, why did you send me away? You were War Chief, a powerful man. Couldn't you have kept me with you?"

He clenched his fists. A swallow went down his tight throat. "There is so much to say, and yet so little. Cornsilk, I—"

"Didn't you want me?"

"I wanted you with all my heart." He reached out and placed his right hand over hers. Her fingers felt cool and frail in his grip. "From the moment I saw your beautiful face, I loved you. But I had seen twenty-nine summers, and was the new War Chief, and I knew that if I kept you there was a good chance we would both be killed. I suspected, as well, that your mother would be condemned to death. I think Crow Beard would have demanded it." He lowered his hand. "And perhaps rightly so."

"Did you love her? My mother?"

Ironwood's face slackened as he searched Cornsilk's dark eyes. "I *still* love her. After you were born, she refused to see me. I understood and accepted her reasons, but it didn't change the way I felt about her. Crow Beard returned—" He paused and asked, "Sternlight told you about that? About Crow Beard's being gone for ten moons?" When she nodded, Ironwood continued, "After he returned, Night Sun and I passed each other every day in Talon Town, but neither of us spoke. We pretended nothing had happened. We had to."

"So no one would suspect about me?"

"Yes." He fought the urge to rise and pace back and forth. "Despite our care, there were still rumors. Fortunately, the rumors never reached the First People elders, or else they refused to believe them. I don't know which, and it doesn't matter now. What does matter is that you understand I had no choice. Cornsilk, I would have done anything to keep you with me— except risk your life or your mother's life." He shifted to sit cross-legged before her, gazing into her eyes. "The two most difficult things in my life were letting Sternlight take you from my arms the night of your birth, and seeing Night Sun every day for the next sixteen summers without being able to touch her. But at least I knew you were both safe."

Cornsilk watched him from beneath long eyelashes. "But, Ironwood, if you and Night Sun loved each other so much, why didn't you just run away together? Surely you could have found a safe place to live and raise me?"

"Duty, Cornsilk. Responsibility." An ache swelled his chest. The frail vessel of his heart had never been able to hold this emotion. He could stand face-to-face with death without blinking an eye, but not this—not this powerful mixture of grief and futility. Cornsilk watched him curiously. "I begged Night Sun to leave with me. But she is not only Matron of Talon Town, she is the Matron of the First People. The women in her family, the Red Lacewing Family, have guided and nurtured the First People for seven generations. Her other daughter, Cloud Playing, was three summers old at the time, too young to take over as Matron. Night Sun had no choice. Her first responsibility was to her people."

Cornsilk tucked a fluttering lock of hair behind her ear. "So, Night Sun chose her people over you and me?"

"No. She thought you were dead, Cornsilk. Night Sun chose her people over *me*." Ironwood picked up a pebble and tossed it into the drainage. It plopped into the muddy water and colliding silver rings bobbed toward the banks.

Cornsilk frowned at the grass. "Ironwood? I—I have something to ask, but it may offend you, and I don't wish to—"

"Ask. I'll tell you the truth, to the best of my ability."

She wet her full lips, then lifted her gaze to his. "I don't understand how it happened. Night Sun is the highest of the First People, and you are a Bear Clan man. How did . . . I mean, was I conceived here in Talon Town?"

He shook his head. "Not even I would have been so bold." A faint smile came to his face. "This is how it happened. Before Crow Beard left on the Trading mission, he ordered me to stay with Night Sun every moment, never to let her out of my sight. That meant that when she left on one of her Healing trips, to tend the slaves in the nearby villages, I had to accompany her."

"You went with her? *Alone?*"

"I had no choice. My Chief had ordered me to. Believe me, I would never have risked it without direct orders." Ironwood tipped his face to the dwindling sunlight. "On the seventh night of that first journey, we camped east of Spider Woman's Butte. We roasted a cottontail and shared it while we talked and laughed. It was such a wondrous time, almost unearthly.

After only a quarter moon alone with her, I loved her desperately, Cornsilk. I swear I think I would have killed if someone had tried to take her away from me then. We loved each other for the first time that night, and I've always believed that's when you were conceived. It might have been later, but I don't think so. I *felt* something that night, as if a new light had entered the world."

Cornsilk turned to look eastward. Father Sun had vanished beneath the canyon rim, but the last vestiges of his radiance threw a soft lavender halo over the cliffs. From this side view, Cornsilk looked all the more like Night Sun. Especially the Night Sun of his memories, in her twenty-seventh summer, with long black hair and a glint in her dark eyes.

Cornsilk bowed her head and creased her yellow dress with her fingernails. "I—I don't know what to do, Ironwood."

"What do you mean?"

"Does my mother know that I'm here? Sternlight says you and I are supposed to eat supper with her tonight, but has anyone told her who I am?"

"Sternlight and I have both spoken with her. She wanted to see you immediately, but I asked to speak with you first."

"Does she think of me as her daughter, or—or just someone—"

"You *are* her daughter," Ironwood said flatly. "In fact, when she thought she was going to die, she asked me to tell Cloud Playing to divide all of her belongings with you, including the lands around Talon Town. You are the only daughter Night Sun has left. And . . ." He hesitated. "That brings me to the last thing I must tell you."

"What?"

"Night Sun and I can't stay in Talon Town any longer. One way or another, word of this is going to get out. If Snake Head can prove you are Night Sun's daughter, he can order her killed, and the elders will back him up this time. Therefore, we are planning to go away together, tonight. Late. Do you wish to come with us? We could be a family, Cornsilk, for the first time. . . ." When she didn't answer right away, he went on, "On the other hand, by the customs of the First People, if Night Sun leaves Talon Town, you will become the new Matron."

Cornsilk's eyes widened. For a long while, she just stared at him. "*Blessed Spirits, I don't wish to be Matron of Talon Town!*"

"Don't make your decision too quickly. I know it must seem overwhelming now, but in a few days—"

"Ironwood, I was raised as one of the Made People. I wouldn't even know how to act among the First People! I would be an embarrassment to them! I—"

He put a hand over hers, speaking quietly, but with authority. "Take some time, Cornsilk. You may refuse the honor, but you owe it to yourself, and perhaps to Poor Singer, to consider it carefully."

"To Poor Singer?" she asked in confusion.

"You seem to care for him. If you were to marry him, you could proclaim Poor Singer the new Blessed Sun. I won't tell you that it would be easy. You're a hidden child, and I'm a Made man. A great many of the First People would resent that, but if you accept your mother's property, you control it, and Talon Town."

"Poor Singer's greatest dream," she said with a smile, "is to go home to Windflower Village and help his people."

"And you, Cornsilk? Do you wish to go with him?"

She gripped handfuls of her yellow skirt. "He hasn't asked me to, and I—I don't know if I would go even if he did."

"Well, let me pose another possibility." Ironwood propped his elbows behind him and leaned back. As evening settled, insects swarmed up from the wash, creating a glittering cloud over their heads. The sky had turned a gray-blue. "If you decided to stay here as Matron, you could name another man to rule. Sternlight, perhaps, or—"

"Sternlight? I could name Sternlight as the Blessed Sun?"

Ironwood nodded. "That would be your right, as Matron. I don't know that Sternlight would accept. I think he is contented to be Sunwatcher, but he might, and it would be a boon for Talon Town if he did."

She seemed to be thinking it over. Two upright lines formed between her brows. "But would that be wise, Ironwood? Many of the Made People believe Sternlight is a witch. I know it isn't true, but naming him as ruler would frighten many people."

"My daughter"—he smiled warmly—"you are thinking like a clan matron already. The people's needs first. You may be right. That isn't something I can advise you about. Myself, I'd choose Sternlight instantly. But he's my best friend, so I'm not a good judge."

"What about Snake Head? He'd make trouble, wouldn't he?"

"Ah, Snake Head . . ." he said through a long exhalation, and scowled at the sky. "He's a scorpion, a poisonous predator always willing to turn on his own kind."

Cornsilk smoothed her fingers over the soft spring grasses. "Ironwood?"

"Yes?"

Cornsilk pulled on the leather thong that encircled her neck and drew a small red bag out. Untying the laces on the bag, she poured a black object into her hand and held it out to him. "Do you know what this is? I found it inside my pack. Poor Singer didn't put it there, nor did I, so someone in Talon Town must have. But I've never seen anything like it before. Have you?"

Ironwood took the tiny black jet carving and scrutinized it in the poor light. The inlaid coral bead flashed, and he thought he saw a spiral serpent, but darkness cloaked the details. "No, I haven't. It's excellent workmanship, though, from what I can see. But I don't think it's Straight Path artistry. Looks more like Hohokam, or maybe even Fire Dog."

Cornsilk folded her arms tightly across her breast. "Ever since I found it, I've been having strange dreams."

"Dreams? About what?"

A shiver went up her back, and she gritted her teeth, as if to still it. "Dancing Badgers and blood-filled seas . . . and a—a young woman." She pinned him with a hard gaze. "What happened to Cloud Playing? I think I need to know."

Wind Baby gusted and black hair fluttered around her.

Ironwood handed the jet carving back to her, and Cornsilk put it in her pouch and tucked it inside her dress. He said, "She was murdered, Cornsilk. Cloud Playing was returning from Deer Mother Village. Someone caught her as she climbed up the wash, down there." He pointed to the broad hard-packed trail about two hundred hands to the east. "That's the main trail, the trail that Made People and First People take. But there is another trail about a thousand hands further east that is used by slaves. Cloud Playing tried to come up the main trail, but her murderer met her as she came out of the wash. I checked the tracks myself. He was a heavy man, a big man. His—"

"His tracks sank deeply into the sand?"

He smiled proudly. "Yes. Did Beargrass teach you that?"

She nodded. "So it was either a big man, or a man carrying something heavy. Like a pack? Or a—"

"Yes. Something like that. Anyway, Cloud Playing ran back down into the wash, and it must have occurred to her that she could take the lower trail, the slave's trail, because she headed for it. But cautiously. She stopped frequently as she walked the bottom of the drainage."

"And the tracks on the bank above? What was the man doing?"

Ironwood could see the images on his soul: tracks spinning, leaping . . . "Dancing. He was Dancing, Cornsilk. I can't explain it. It appeared to be some sort of mockery of our sacred ways. The murderer must have hated our beliefs, the thlatsinas, our rituals. Who else would be brave enough to mock them?"

"Someone like a Fire Dog?"

Ironwood lifted a hand uncertainly. "That's what it *looked* like, Cornsilk. I suspect that's what we were supposed to think. . . . But there's more to the story. About fifty hands from the slave trail, Cloud Playing broke into a dead run, apparently trying to reach the trail before she was cut off. She didn't make it. Her attacker came down the trail, Dancing. What happened next is confusing. They stood only ten hands apart at the bottom of the trail, and it seems they spoke, or he spoke to her. Cloud Playing began taking anxious steps, back and forth, in the same place. I counted over three dozen of her prints there. But her attacker just stood still, his feet braced. Then, Cloud Playing backed away and ran up the crossing as though being pursued by angry Earth Spirits. Her attacker followed slowly. Again, he was Dancing, spinning around, leaping from side to side."

"Is that when he killed her?"

"Yes. He knelt at the top of the drainage and shot her in the back. Cloud Playing fell to her knees, and her attacker crouched right in front of her. He used something sharp, either an arrow point, or a knife, to slit open her belly. Then he—"

Cornsilk put a hand to her lips. *"Blessed thlatsinas."*

"Even more interesting. This is a very curious murderer. After he'd killed her, he closed her eyes and rolled her onto her belly, presumably so her blood could drain out onto the ground, then he—"

"You mean," Cornsilk whispered. "As if bleeding out a freshly killed deer, sharing the feast with Our Mother Earth?"

Ironwood nodded, and his gaze searched the darkening landscape. He felt suddenly uneasy, as if they were being watched. Just the eerie story, probably, but his gaze sought movement in the growing darkness. "Suggesting that the murderer believed Cloud Playing's death somehow renewed the world." His gaze scanned the cliff tops and went over the drainage. "The strange thing is, the murderer also sprinkled her wounds with corpse powder."

"So a witch killed her?"

"Or someone wished us to think a witch killed her."

Cornsilk rubbed her arms. A frosty chill rode the night wind. The Evening People had begun to sprinkle the sky, flashing and glimmering. "She would have been the next Matron of Talon Town, wouldn't she?"

"Yes, she would have." Ironwood's ears pricked suddenly. He could hear voices. No, *one* voice, in the wind. Faint. He couldn't make out the words. Wind Baby? Speaking to him after all these summers? His heart pounded and he sat up straighter, listening.

"Cornsilk," he said softly. "I think we should be getting back."

Her yellow dress whipped around her long legs as she got to her feet. "All right."

Ironwood rose cautiously, studying the drainage and the trail to Talon Town. Firelight gleamed in the doors and windows. The Great Warriors seemed to be peering directly at them, their lightning bolt lances raised protectively, their magnificent masks shining.

He edged in front of her. "Walk behind me, Cornsilk. But stay close."

"Why, do you think there's something—"

"I'm just naturally cautious."

He'd taken three steps when a raven plummeted from the sky, its wings tucked. Against the slate gray sky, it looked blacker than pure jet. As the bird swooped over their heads, it let out a single spine-tingling *caw!* and soared into the sky again.

Cornsilk's mouth dropped open. "Where did it come from? It's night. Ravens don't fly at night!"

"It just dove out of nowhere."

The raven vanished into the well of darkness beneath the canyon rim.

Ironwood's nerves hummed. "Cornsilk, didn't you say you thought your Spirit Helper was Raven?"

"Yes."

He gripped her hand tightly. "Don't let go of me, you understand? I want you *very* close to me."

"I understand!"

She walked almost on his heels as they headed back toward Talon Town.

A dog growled, and a child let out a sharp yip, as if bitten. When a woman's voice scolded, "I told you not to tease the dog!" Webworm smiled. He crouched on the roof above the entry; he'd relieved Gnat less than a hand of time ago. The scent of cedar bark torches filled the night. Dusk had smoothed the canyon bottom, erasing the drainages and low hills, leaving a solid indigo sheet spotted with cooking fires. The orange sparkles blinked as people walked back and forth in front of them.

A lot of people were coming in for the burial procession. They would line the way out of the canyon, sprinkling cornmeal on the road, weeping and tearing their hair. Webworm had seen many of these things. The ridiculously huge party of dignitaries and warriors would pass by somberly, not saying a word to the mourners.

Webworm rubbed his face. Where had his elation at being chosen War Chief gone? Every day he grew less and less enthusiastic.

Deep weariness weighted his muscles. He had to remind himself that he was standing guard and could not afford such soul wanderings, but he had not slept in thirty hands of time. He'd spent every moment finagling, pleading, even offering to *pay* warriors from the other clans to join the burial procession. He'd managed to get sixty-eight, which should be enough to satisfy Snake Head. It would have to. He would leave five warriors on guard: four in Talon Town, and young Sawfly in the signal tower near Center Place. The only other warrior he had not approached had been Ironwood. He'd tried, but Ironwood had not been in his chamber all day. People said that Ironwood was with Sternlight, then with Night Sun, and finally Dune. Webworm had checked Ironwood's chamber one last time before he'd relieved Gnat at guard. Creeper had told Webworm that he'd seen Ironwood leave Talon Town just before sunset.

He had not returned, or Webworm would have seen him. What could he be doing out there? Had he gone to visit a nearby town?

As people began supper, the sounds of clacking cups and bowls rose. Webworm had gone to his mother's chamber long enough to speak with Creeper, kiss his mother's forehead, and gobble down a bowl of beans and onions. He felt better, though hunger still nibbled at his belly. Creeper had promised every able-bodied warrior the Buffalo Clan possessed, but several people were sick, one with a broken wrist. Badgerbow had cursed and told Webworm what foolishness it was to waste eighty warriors on a burial party, but he'd promised twenty men from the Coyote Clan. Yellowgirl had fussed about giving him fifteen. She considered her Ant Clan masons to be too good for warrior duty. Webworm agreed with her. A good mason was worth her weight in turquoise. A warrior was expendable.

He sighed.

Something caught his eye. Webworm had to look slightly to the side to see the person. Dressed in brown, he or she almost blended with the night. The person climbed out of Creeper's window and darted away into the darkness.

Mourning Dove? Where is she going this time? Another meeting with Cone? He rubbed his jaw as he considered, then sat down and brought up his knees so that he could prop his arms on them. At night, with no one to replace him, he didn't have the luxury of traipsing after her to find out what she was up to.

But, by Wind Baby's breath, this activity worried him.

Mourning Dove knew the penalty for going out at night. She wouldn't dare unless Snake Head or Creeper had given her permission. Would she? Webworm cocked his head. But if either had given her permission, why did she have to sneak out through the window? She could have walked out the entry under his nose.

For the same reason she did it this morning. Snake Head doesn't wish anyone, including me, to know she's out meeting with Cone.

He massaged the back of his neck. Cone had said his work was related to the "survival" of the Straight Path people. What did that mean? Securing more food to stave off famine? Creating alliances to better fight their enemies? Perhaps establishing Trade with the forbidden mound builders? Webworm had heard that they produced a magnificent black pottery and—

A sharp cry split the night down near the wash, followed by a man's hoarse scream.

Webworm lurched for his bow and quiver of arrows, then jumped to his feet, searching the darkness. His heart began to hammer when he recognized Ironwood running wildly for Talon Town, carrying someone, shouting, "*Sternlight? Sternlight!*"

Webworm slung his quiver and bow over his shoulder and raced for the ladder, climbing down three rungs at a time. When he lunged for the entry, he almost ran into Ironwood who dashed through with . . . *with Cornsilk!*

Webworm's mouth opened. She lay limply in his arms, her long bloody hair spilling down his side. A broken arrow protruded from her face. Blood dyed her yellow dress and the front of Ironwood's buckskin shirt.

"What happened?" Webworm demanded, nocking his bow and whirling toward the entry. "Are we being attacked?"

"I don't know." Ironwood placed the girl on the ground and knelt beside her, studying her bloody face.

"Who did this? Did you see—"

"I didn't have the time to search. My daughter's hurt too badly. I—"

"*Your daughter?*" Like broken potsherds reassembling themselves, the whole came clear in an instant, and he understood the terrible secret that Night Sun had been keeping from the other First People. In shock, he stared at Ironwood.

Rage twisted Ironwood's face. He lurched to his feet and shouted, "What's the matter with you? You're War Chief! Organize your warriors! Post guards around the town, and then form a search party! By morning the attacker will be long gone!" He made a sweeping gesture with his muscular arm. "*Move!*"

Unnerved, Webworm turned and ran for Gnat's chamber, which opened onto the plaza.

Behind him, Ironwood shouted, "*Sternlight! Night Sun!*"

Sternlight ducked beneath his door curtain and raced to the edge of the roof. Night Sun came out behind him, her blue dress shining in the firelight. People were lining the roofs, staring down, calling to each other in confusion.

"Ironwood?" Sternlight stood frozen. "What—"

"Sternlight, hurry! Night Sun, bring your Healing bag. Cornsilk is hurt. She's hurt badly!"

Webworm stopped outside Gnat's door and yelled, "Gnat? Get up!"

A groggy voice responded, "What's wrong? What's all the shouting?"

Gnat stumbled out into the cold air wearing only a breechclout, his black hair awry, his eyes glazed with sleep.

Webworm ordered, "Gather twenty warriors. Station ten on the roofs. I want the other ten with me. Tell them to bring torches. It may be a long night."

"But why? What's—"

"Someone tried to kill one of the First People. Hurry, Gnat! We've no time to lose!"

Gnat ran.

Webworm turned and sprinted past Ironwood and the wounded girl, heading for Creeper's chamber. He didn't know what to think or feel. It couldn't have been Mourning Dove, could it? No, no. He couldn't believe that. But if Mourning Dove had attacked one of the First People, and Creeper were guilty of allowing her to go in and out his window to do it. . . .

Never. Not knowingly.

Webworm stopped outside Creeper's chamber and called, "Creeper? Creeper, are you there?"

No answer.

Webworm threw back the curtain and peered inside.

Starlight streamed through the window, falling over the empty blankets piled in the middle of the floor. For a moment, he could not move, then it occurred to him that Creeper was probably still with Featherstone. They often spoke late into the night.

"Which means Mourning Dove used his window without Creeper's knowledge or permission." Webworm sank against the wall in relief, and wiped sweat from his eyes. "Of course. Creeper knew nothing about this."

A clamor rose in the plaza, people shouting and feet pounding. Webworm turned and looked. Ironwood's voice carried above the noise: *"Poor Singer, give me that blanket. Help me wrap her. Then I'm taking her to the First People's kiva!"*

"His daughter . . ." Webworm whispered, his eyes on the unconscious girl. Ironwood gently lifted her into his arms; her long hair dragged the ground. "I would have never believed it."

For the briefest instant, Webworm closed his eyes and said a soft prayer, begging the gods to help Ironwood escape before the wrath of the First People elders cost him his life.

He walked back out into the plaza. As he reached the edge of the crowd that had gathered around Ironwood, he saw Snake Head.

The Blessed Sun stood on the fourth-story roof, peering down, a torch held high in his right hand. It threw a wavering orange gleam over his handsome face, and Webworm could see the smile that twisted Snake Head's lips.

Confused rage surged through his veins. How could he smile? Did he have no heart?

Snake Head stood for several moments, then turned his back and ducked inside his chamber again. His door curtain swung closed behind him.

Gnat trotted across the plaza toward Webworm, his breechclout flapping. Cold bumps covered his muscular body. "I've wakened the warriors," he panted. "They're coming. In the meantime, I'll dress."

"I'll be waiting outside the entry."

Gnat nodded, said, "I'll join you shortly," and sprinted for his chamber.

Ironwood shoved through the whispering crowd, carrying Cornsilk toward the First People's kiva. Night Sun followed, her face pale, graying black braid patting her back. The youth,

Poor Singer, brought up the rear. Sternlight ran the opposite direction, toward Dune's chamber.

Webworm shouldered through the people toward the entry.

Dazed and numb, Poor Singer followed Night Sun and Ironwood across the kiva, past the red masonry pillars and the bodies resting atop their burial ladders on the foot drums. The empty eye sockets of the thlatsina masks above the wall crypts seemed to watch him as he passed, winking in the flickering firelight, as if alive.

Poor Singer wrung his hands as Ironwood strode to the rear of the dimly lit kiva, knelt, and gently placed Cornsilk's limp body on the yellow bench near the fire. The sight of Ironwood—shaking, his buckskin shirt covered with blood—unnerved Poor Singer even more.

"What happened?" Poor Singer begged as Ironwood got to his feet. The big man's oval face bore streaks of blood and dirt. "Will someone tell me now?"

"We were out talking, and I—"

"Ironwood, please," Night Sun said as she edged between him and Cornsilk, her Healing pack over her left shoulder, her blue dress swaying, "move back."

But at sight of Cornsilk, Night Sun faltered. A hand went to her throat. For a long moment, she just stared, her face growing pale.

"What is it?" Ironwood asked sharply. "What are you waiting for?"

Night Sun glanced at him, read the desperation in his eyes, and bent down beside Cornsilk. A touch as gentle as Night Sun's might have been reserved for the petals of a beautiful flower. She prodded the swollen flesh. "It's just that . . . she looks so much like Cloud Playing. I hadn't expected that."

Ironwood stepped away, and the expression of barely contained fury on his face made Poor Singer long to sit down, but he braced his legs and stood facing the big man. "You were out talking, and . . ."

Ironwood glared at him. "It happened so quickly, I never

even saw the arrow. Cornsilk jerked and cried out. I felt her fall." He lifted his bloody hand and stared at the palm, then clenched it into a tight fist and shook it. "She was *holding* my hand! I don't even know what direction the arrow came from!"

Night Sun studied Cornsilk, eyes wide, mouth working silently. Her blue dress spread around her sandaled feet as she marshaled herself and placed her Healing pack on the floor. Perspiration already coated her triangular face and pointed nose, matting her hair to her temples. The four black spirals on her chin had a blue tint in the firelight. Carefully, she pulled bloody hair away from Cornsilk's face and examined the broken arrow shaft protruding from the cheekbone.

Poor Singer felt sick. The arrow had struck at a downward angle, as if Cornsilk had glimpsed the deadly missile and tried to duck out of its path at the last instant.

Quietly, Night Sun asked, "How did the shaft break?"

The muscles in Ironwood's shoulders bunched. "It must have happened when she fell. I looked around her for the other half of the shaft, hoping to see some identifying marks or distinctive painting, but I couldn't find it."

Poor Singer folded his arms and tried to get a full breath into his starved lungs. *Cornsilk, you can't die. Don't die!*

Ironwood paced back and forth before the foot drum where Cloud Playing's body rested.

"Poor Singer?" Night Sun pulled several folded lengths of cloth from her Healing pack and placed them on the yellow bench beside Cornsilk. "Could you put on a pot of water to heat?"

"Yes, I—I can." He rushed to the masonry fire box, grateful to have something to do, hastily searched through the ceremonial pots and cups that sat around the rectangular base, and set out a large pot. He grabbed for one of the water jugs to fill it, and the jug slipped from his fumbling fingers and shattered on the floor. Water splashed the fire and steam burst up in a sizzling white gush.

Ironwood spun on cat feet, his hand going to the stiletto at his belt.

"Sorry, I : . . I'm sorry."

"Easy, Poor Singer," Night Sun said. "It'll be all right. It will."

He took a deep breath and tried to still his trembling hands, then reached for the other water jug. He couldn't help it; he kept shooting glances at Cornsilk's bloody face, and every time he did, he grew more light-headed.

Already the left side of her head had begun to swell and turn a purplish blue. Blood ran from her nose and mouth. It also seemed to be filtering underneath the skin, filling up the space beneath her eye, turning it a horrid black. Poor Singer managed to get the pot filled and set the water jug down before he dropped it. Then he pulled a stick from the wood pile and rearranged the coals. Scooping a pile toward him, he created a small indentation in the middle, where he set the boiling pot.

Ironwood turned to Night Sun. "Why Cornsilk? What's the *purpose*? Did he want to kill her because she's our daughter?"

Night Sun didn't look up, but her shoulders hunched. "You mean as a way to punish you and me where the First People elders failed?"

"I mean exactly that."

Night Sun rose, picked up one of the cloths, and went to dip it into the water.

"It's not hot yet," Poor Singer said.

Night Sun shook her head. "Doesn't matter. These are consecrated bowls. Their souls will seep into the water and chase away evil Spirits." As she squeezed the tan cloth out, she turned to Ironwood. "I can think of only one person bitter enough to want to kill our daughter."

A murderous glint entered Ironwood's eyes. In a quiet, deadly voice, he said, "So can I."

Poor Singer sank down on the bench near Cornsilk's head. "Who? Who would want to hurt her?"

Ironwood just turned away.

Poor Singer looked at Night Sun as she knelt in front of Cornsilk again. "Who?" he repeated.

"My son," Night Sun answered as she gently began washing Cornsilk's face. Blood soaked the cloth. "But he's too much of a coward to have done it himself. He must have hired someone."

"Or threatened someone." Ironwood paced slowly now, deliberately, as if tracking dangerous prey through a dense forest.

Poor Singer placed a hand over his aching belly. The Blessed

Sun had tried to murder his own half-sister? What sort of man . . . ?

Night Sun touched Poor Singer's knee. "She's going to be all right, Poor Singer. I've treated wounds like this before. Warriors returning from raids frequently—"

"I—I'm all right."

Night Sun nodded and began digging around in her pack, removing small bags—red, blue, yellow—placing them on the bench. Fragrances wafted up—sage, mint, and something pungent that Poor Singer couldn't identify.

He soothed himself by stroking Cornsilk's hair. "It's all right, Cornsilk," he whispered. "You're going to be all right." The blue vein in her temple throbbed as swiftly as a bird's, but she barely breathed.

Leaning down, close to her ear, Poor Singer murmured, "I love you, Cornsilk. Don't leave me. Please, don't leave me."

Night Sun gave him a measuring sidelong glance, then cleaned around the broken shaft. Bright red blood oozed.

"Why would someone wish to hurt her?" Poor Singer pleaded. "You two seem to know, but I can't understand—"

"*I can*," Dune said. He descended the staircase, his sparse white hair shimmering orange, and hobbled across the kiva. Sternlight followed behind him, carrying an armload of blankets.

"Why?" Poor Singer asked as the panic rose again.

Dune walked past Crow Beard's shrouded body and braced a hand against the southeastern pillar to steady himself. His white shirt gleamed faintly coral. As he examined Cornsilk, his deeply wrinkled face turned grim. "The same reason Cloud Playing was killed."

Poor Singer glanced at the body encased in the gorgeous burial shroud. "I don't understand."

Sternlight lowered his armload of blankets to the yellow bench at Cornsilk's feet and sat down beside them. When he gazed at Cornsilk, his face slackened. *As though one of the Earth Spirits had leaped up and grabbed his soul.*

Only Poor Singer seemed to notice.

Ironwood propped his hands on his hips. "Well, we drew the murderer out, Dune. Our plan worked. But he's apparently smarter than we are. He's still free."

"Drew him out?" Night Sun asked.

Dune leaned his shoulder against the red pillar. Firelight shadowed his deep wrinkles, making him look a thousand summers old. "Yes, that's why Ironwood has been staying so close to you the past two days. We suspected the murderer might target you. But he targeted Cornsilk, instead, and now we know *why* he's been killing."

Night Sun asked, "Why?"

"Someone did not wish Cornsilk to become the next Matron of Talon Town. Nor did they wish Cloud Playing to."

Night Sun stared at Dune. "Are you saying—"

"Of course that's what I'm saying. That is the only thing that Cloud Playing and Cornsilk had in common. But who would be hurting so much—"

"I don't believe it." Ironwood shook his head and walked toward Dune. As he passed the fire, his gray braid shimmered. "I think they were killed for different reasons, Dune. Cloud Playing because she was going to return and deny Snake Head his inheritance. And Cornsilk . . . he wished to kill Cornsilk to punish Night Sun and me. He couldn't do it at the trial, so he tried tonight." He gestured at Cornsilk with his fist. "Why, he threatened her only this morning!"

Dune hitched his way over to the bench and sat down beside Sternlight. He pinned Ironwood with his gaze. "Well, I'll grant you that it's possible you're right. But why, then, didn't he try for Night Sun? And how do you explain Young Fawn? Snake Head was just a boy at the time."

Ironwood waved a hand. "Young Fawn . . . that was so long ago, I'm not sure they're connected."

"Young Fawn?" Night Sun looked up, her cloth hovering above the broken arrow shaft. The carefully polished wood reflected the fire like a mirror, spattering Cornsilk's bloody face with wavering orange light. "Snake Head mentioned something about her. When he—he threatened me."

"He *threatened* you?" Dune asked.

Night Sun nodded. "Yesterday. At the very end, when I was leaving, he said . . ." She lifted her eyes to Sternlight and a swallow went down her throat.

Poor Singer watched in fascination. What kind of spiderweb had he and Cornsilk walked into? If only he could take Cornsilk and flee back to Dune's little house! Anything to be away from Talon Town with its plots.

It seemed to take an act of will for Sternlight to pull his gaze away from Cornsilk. "It's all right, Night Sun. What did he say?"

Her fist tightened on the bloody rag until crimson ran in a stream between her fingers. "It horrified me so much, I even hate to speak of it. He—he told me that he used to follow us, Ironwood and me, Webworm and Cloud Playing. Sternlight, he said I had no idea what sort of crimes . . . you had committed . . . and he asked if I remembered Young Fawn. Then he said that Mourning Dove could verify his words, because she'd followed him that day and had seen everything. I didn't know what he meant by that."

Sternlight tucked his hands beneath his arms, but not before Poor Singer saw them shaking. Who was Young Fawn and what had happened to her that would so frighten the great priest?

"What's the matter with you, Sternlight?" Ironwood demanded. "Didn't you hear Night Sun? Snake Head accused you of murder—"

"I . . . I've seen her." He used his chin to point at Cornsilk. Ironwood glanced at Cornsilk, but swiftly returned his gaze to Sternlight, silently questioning. Sternlight did not look at his friend. He said, "I've seen her *here*. Lying on this very bench, just as she is now. With all of us around her. The gods . . ."

The fire leaped suddenly, splashing the kiva's white walls and illuminating the mouths and eye sockets of the thlatsina masks. Poor Singer's stomach muscles tightened. He could feel their gazes drilling into his soul, could almost hear those frozen mouths crying out. As if in warning.

"In a Spirit Dream?" Dune asked. "You saw her here in a Dream?"

Sternlight nodded. "Yes. I—I saw Cornsilk here, in the kiva. And Cloud Playing was Dancing with the Badger Thlatsina . . . and there was a fiery blue cave filled with black water. And I think the answer to all this madness lies there."

Poor Singer's flesh crawled. He glanced from Dune to Sternlight and back. "You mean . . . the turquoise cave? I *know* that cave."

"What cave?" Dune asked with his bushy brows lowered.

"The turquoise cave! The Keeper of the Tortoise Bundle lives there. It's beautiful. I traveled there with my father—"

"Your father?" Sternlight said. "Who—"

"Wait!" Dune said and held up a hand. "We'll discuss all of this later. Let's pry that arrow out of Cornsilk first." He pointed to the pot on the coals. "Ironwood? Is that pot of water boiling yet?"

Ironwood peered over the edge of the steaming pot. "Almost. A little longer."

"Good." Dune slapped his knees and rose to his feet. "What do you wish me to do, Night Sun?"

She reached for the blue bag she'd placed on the bench and handed it to Dune. "Add some sage and some phlox." She dug around in her pack, pulled it out and handed it to him. "Thank you, Dune."

As he headed for the pot, he stopped beside Ironwood and looked up seriously. "Regardless of which of us is right, my friend, there's still someone out there who wishes Cornsilk dead. We must be vigilant."

"Yes, we must." Ironwood strode the length of the kiva and propped one foot on the bottom step of the staircase, keeping guard.

Night Sun was staring at Cornsilk again, a terrible longing in her eyes as her gaze traced Cornsilk's features. That wounded expression touched Poor Singer.

The killer is still out there. Waiting. It chilled Poor Singer's very bones. Had Cornsilk heard any of this, or did her soul walk in the underworlds? Blood still oozed around the embedded arrow, trickling down her throat and onto the yellow bench. There it formed a glistening pool, before spilling onto the dirt floor.

"It's all right, Cornsilk," he whispered. "Everything is all right."

"It's boiling," Dune announced.

Night Sun nodded. "Let it steep. The tea must be strong. Cornsilk will need to drink all of it when we're done. Sage and phlox heal."

Dune walked back to Night Sun. "Where's your knife? Let's pry that point out before the evil Spirits smell the blood and decide to make a home in her marrow."

"And," Sternlight added softly, as he leaned forward to brace his elbows on his knees, "before she wakes."

Dune and Night Sun both gazed at Poor Singer. He swallowed down a dry throat, seeing the question in their eyes. So, this was the awesome responsibility that went along with being a Healer.

What a silly fool I've been. He'd only seen the glory, the adulation of his people for his skill and Power. He glanced at Cornsilk, more frightened then he'd ever been in his life. What if he failed? What if this woman he loved with all his heart died? How could he bear that?

He rose on trembling legs. As he wiped his sweaty palms on his green shirt, he heard himself ask, "Just tell me what you need me to do."

Night Sun picked up her slim obsidian knife. *This is my daughter. . . . I'm about to cut open my daughter.* The haunting cries of the infant she'd thought dead came back to her now. *My only daughter. . . .* Fear built inside her like a tempest in a black storm cloud.

When she glanced at Poor Singer, she hesitated. The boy's eyes had gone glassy. *Is he ready for this?*

"Poor Singer," she said, "I'm going to cut next to the shaft. You'll need to pull the skin apart. It will be slippery. Can you do that?"

"Yes, I—I can." The youth bent over and wrapped his hands around Cornsilk's face in preparation.

Dune walked closer to stare over Night Sun's shoulder. With his back to the fire, shadows flowed into his wrinkles, making them appear cavernous.

"Keep the cut as small as possible," Dune advised.

"I know."

Night Sun worked the sliver of obsidian through the skin and muscle under the cheek bone. A new rush of blood, streaked with clear liquid, welled from the incision. By feel, she followed the shaft down, encountered the binding sinew, and then the point where it was embedded in bone.

Poor Singer dutifully pulled the wound open with blood-reddened fingers. He had his jaw clamped, and perspiration formed a sheen on his narrow face.

Night Sun glanced up at Dune. "The point is embedded in the upper jaw, just above the teeth. It's obsidian."

Dune nodded thoughtfully. "Better to just snap it off."

Night Sun took a deep breath to ease the suffocating band that had tightened around her chest. "We won't leave a hole in the bone that way. Evil won't be able to slip inside. We can always lance the cheek and drain infection, but if it enters the bone . . ."

"I know many warriors who are alive today because we left the point in their bones," Ironwood said as he came over to study the wound. "Do you want me to snap it off?"

Night Sun shook her head. "No, I'll do it. But I'll need both you and Poor Singer to hold her head still."

"I'm going to come around behind you, Poor Singer," Ironwood said, and wrapped his muscular arms around the young man's. His hands tightened on Cornsilk's skull, while Poor Singer held her jaw firmly.

Night Sun slid her fingers down the shaft, compressing Cornsilk's cheek in the process. She needed to snap it off sideways, to break the tip of the point off flush with the bone.

I'm sorry, my daughter. Night Sun swiftly jerked the shaft sideways and felt the brittle obsidian snap. With care, she eased the shaft from the wound, using her incision to keep the sharp stone from doing even more damage.

Poor Singer fumbled for a rag to wipe up the blood, and Night Sun ordered, "Let it bleed."

He put the rag down and sank back against the bench. "Why?" he asked feebly.

"We want it to drain as much evil out as it can."

"Then she'll be all right?"

"The point snapped even with the bone, but we must wait to see, Poor Singer," Night Sun said as she studied the shaft.

Cornsilk groaned softly, coughed, then went still again.

Ironwood said, "Let me see the shaft."

Night Sun handed it to him, and stared at her daughter's face again, trying to memorize every feature. If infection didn't set in and corrupt her flesh, she'd live.

Oh, my daughter, why did you have to come to me now?

Night Sun rose and went to stand beside Ironwood. He kept turning the short length of shaft in his hands, over and over. His handsome face looked haunted.

"Any markings?" she asked.

"No," he murmured. "It's *exactly* like the one that killed Cloud Playing."

Forty-Three

Steps padded in the altar room above the kiva. Moccasins on dirt, soft. Ironwood straightened, studying the pale blue gleam of dawn that filtered down the stairs. Webworm came into view. He bowed to the thlatsinas on the walls. His red-and-black cape hung in dirty folds about his lanky body, and dust streaked his broad face and black braid. He started down the stairs, but when he saw Ironwood his steps faltered. Awkwardly, he asked, "Is Cornsilk all right?"

"For now. I take it you didn't catch—"

"No," Webworm answered shortly. He finished climbing down, his movements shaky, and braced a hand against the wall beside Ironwood to steady himself, his gaze going around the kiva.

Night Sun, Dune, and Sternlight slept fitfully on the benches to the left, while Poor Singer sat by Cornsilk in the rear, just beyond the fire box. He'd been up most of the night, feeding the low flames, speaking softly to Cornsilk.

Ironwood frowned at Webworm's bloodshot eyes. "How long has it been since you've slept?"

Webworm sank down on the yellow bench. He smelled of sweat and juniper smoke. "Two days."

"Blessed Spirits, Webworm," Ironwood whispered harshly, not wanting any of the sleepers to hear. "You can't lead a war party on an extended march—"

"I haven't any choice. Snake Head has risen. The burial procession and accompanying war party are assembling in the plaza. I'll rest tonight."

Had Ironwood known last night that Webworm had been up for so long, he'd have led the search party himself. "Forgive me for putting you in that position last night. I didn't know—"

Webworm waved a hand dismissively. "You were right. I am War Chief. I have responsibilities. I shouldn't have needed you to tell me to post a guard and organize a search party."

"You were exhausted."

Webworm gave him a grateful look and peered around the red pillars to where Cornsilk lay beneath her blankets in the back. Her beautiful face had swollen and blackened. Poor Singer sat with his hand on her shoulder.

"You got the arrow point out?" Webworm asked.

"Yes. It hadn't embedded very deeply. Either the person who shot wasn't very strong, or he shot too quickly, before he'd pulled the bow all the way back. We might have surprised him."

Webworm nodded and braced his chin on his hand. "I noticed you didn't take the trail. You walked through the shadows near the rocks, staying out of the light cast by Talon Town and Streambed Town."

"And the attacker? What was he doing?"

Webworm's eyes narrowed. "He must have used the rocks, Ironwood. Walked across them and shot down at you from the top. We found no tracks at all, except in the drainage bottom. He ran through the water to hide his trail when he fled. Only a few sandal prints marked the mud."

"A big man? Heavy?"

Webworm nodded, and reached inside his cape to pull something from his belt. "I found this near where Cornsilk fell." He handed the broken arrow shaft to Ironwood. "It's like the one that killed Cloud Playing." Webworm's eyes softened as he glanced at her shrouded body.

Ironwood turned the shaft in his hand. "No markings. Nothing to tell us who the man might have been or where he came from."

Gaze still on Cloud Playing, Webworm said, "This killer is very smart, Ironwood. He knows every stone, every patch of grass, every place to hide in Straight Path Canyon. I think, my friend, that he has lived here for a very long time."

Ironwood's soul perched on the verge of understanding, but couldn't seize it. He walked over and sat on the bench beside Webworm. The hem of his gore-encrusted shirt draped over the yellow bench. "What are you thinking?"

Webworm lifted a shoulder. "Cloud Playing and Cornsilk were both Night Sun's daughters. It may mean nothing. But I wonder."

Ironwood lowered his head and massaged his temples. "On the march . . . watch Snake Head."

"Oh, I don't trust him, either. Especially not after the strange orders he's been giving me, and this business with Cone—"

"Cone?" Ironwood blurted. His gaze searched Webworm's. "What are you talking about? Cone is *alive?*"

Webworm's mouth pressed into a bloodless line. "So . . . you didn't know anything about it, either. I had thought, since you were War Chief before me—"

"About what?"

Webworm leaned back against the wall and stared at the pine poles criss-crossing the ceiling. "It's a long story. Before dawn, yesterday morning, I saw Mourning Dove going back and forth between Snake Head's chamber and the wash. It looked suspicious, so I followed her. She was delivering messages between Cone and Snake Head."

The weariness in Ironwood's muscles vanished in the painful rush that washed his veins. "Did you speak with Cone?"

"Yes. He said he was working for the Blessed Sun and that his work was very important to the survival of the Straight Path nation."

Ironwood gripped the arrow shaft. "This doesn't make sense. If he's working for Snake Head, why doesn't he—"

"Just walk in and out of town? Yes, I asked him the same thing. Cone told me that Snake Head does not wish people to know he's alive. That such knowledge would spoil Snake Head's plans. Cone said he was just following orders." Webworm let out a frustrated breath. "I was hoping that you knew about this secret task and had just forgotten to tell me. With everything else going—"

"What secret task?"

Webworm's head fell forward so that his chin rested on his chest. "Only Snake Head would send a warrior out without advising the War Chief."

"The man is a fool. He'll be the death of us all. If he——"

Feet pounded in the altar room, and soft voices echoed. Ironwood placed the shaft on the bench.

Night Sun woke, sitting up in her blanket, her graying black hair loose about her shoulders. Her blue dress was splotched with Cornsilk's blood. Sternlight and Dune sat up next.

"They're coming," Night Sun said. She threw off her blanket and stepped down from the bench, going to stand over Cloud Playing. "I will see you soon, my daughter," she whispered, and bent to kiss Cloud Playing's blanketed face. "I love you."

Dune sighed as he slipped from the bench and marched over to Crow Beard. He fumbled with something, then Ironwood saw him sprinkling Crow Beard's shroud with the mixture of blue cornmeal and ground turquoise, to purify him for the journey. Next, he went to Cloud Playing.

Webworm remained sitting, but Ironwood rose as the burial procession descended the stairs: four warriors, specially dressed in red shirts with green sashes around their waists, then Badgerbow, Creeper, Yellowgirl, and finally, Snake Head.

The Green Sash Men split, two walking down each side of the foot drums. Night Sun and Dune moved out of the way, giving the burly men room. They stationed themselves at the head and foot of each burial ladder, then lifted the ladders onto their muscular shoulders and stood waiting.

Snake Head wore a magnificent blue shirt covered with red and yellow macaw feathers. A huge turquoise wolf pendant dangled around his neck, and a wooden headdress adorned his head. Consisting of three terraces, all painted white, the headdress symbolized rain clouds. Tall and handsome, he gazed over the ceremonial chamber as though he found everything distasteful. He had not yet deigned to look at Ironwood.

"Blessed Sun," Ironwood said, provoking the confrontation, "I understand you have been meeting secretly with Cone. Would you tell me for what purpose?"

Snake Head slowly turned, but his gaze glanced off Ironwood and landed on Webworm. Webworm shivered, as if with a sudden chill. "Get up, War Chief," Snake Head ordered. "We have a long walk today."

"Yes, my chief." Webworm rose.

"Are you afraid to answer me, Snake Head?" Ironwood pressed. "Why? What are you—"

"Hurry it up!" Snake Head motioned for the slaves to carry the ladders out.

They marched by and headed up the stairs. Snake Head glared at Ironwood before following in a whirl of blue shirt. Badgerbow and Yellowgirl walked behind him, and lastly Creeper.

The short pudgy leader of the Buffalo Clan halted and scanned Webworm's bleary face. "Are you all right?"

Webworm forced a ragged smile. "Fine. Is Mourning Dove with Mother?"

"Yes, she'll be watching over her while we're gone."

"Come, then, we have duties to perform." Webworm gestured to the stairs. Creeper reluctantly started up.

But Webworm did not follow. He stood beside Ironwood with his head bowed. After a moment, he gripped Ironwood's forearm and pulled him close. "Please. Be gone when I return."

Ironwood thought of all the battles they'd fought together, the campfires and laughter they'd shared. When the First People elders ordered his imprisonment, and they would, it would be Webworm's duty to try and take him, and one of them would die.

Ironwood nodded. "I will, old friend."

Webworm searched his face one last time, as if memorizing Ironwood's features, then loosened his grip and climbed the stairs.

Sawfly stood guard, as he did every day from dawn to dusk, in the small square signal tower overlooking the holy South Road. Fifty hands tall, the tower was a single body-length across. It had been constructed of large sandstone blocks, and had walls six hands thick. Perched forty hands above the ground on a narrow juniper platform built into the top of the signal tower, he had an expansive view of the countryside. Four windows, one for each direction, surrounded him. The sacred mountains filled the frames, hovering like pale blue ghosts over the horizons.

He propped his moccasined foot on the south-facing window. The only way in or out of the tower was by ladder. After he'd entered, he'd drawn it up and slid it down into the tower below him. The ladder's base rested between the dead coals in the fire pit and the wood pile.

Yawning, Sawfly tipped his pointed chin into the morning breeze that gusted around the tower. It cooled his triangular face and tousled the shoulder-length black hair around his jutting ears. In the distance he saw the burial procession heading down the road.

Blessed gods, he was glad to see them go. He'd been born in the northern Green Mesa villages twenty-three sun cycles ago and only moved to Talon Town the summer before last. He didn't understand any of this First People lunacy. One instant they leaped for each other's throats, and the next they huddled together like a pack of wolves to decide the fate of the world. Only this morning Snake Head had sent a runner to Center Place to inform the Blessed Weedblossom that his mother's "misbegotten daughter" lay prostrate in the First People's kiva in Talon Town. And everyone knew what that meant. Before the day was through, Night Sun would, once again, be in the Cage, along with her lover, Ironwood.

Sawfly shook his head. People of his clan, the Bear Clan, married for love, coupled for pleasure, divorced when they had to, and life went on. The First People seemed to marry for status, couple for children, and keep spouses they hated for their entire lives. And they thought this behavior set a moral standard for the Made People?

Sawfly's wide mouth quirked at the irony.

Yesterday, Mourning Dove had passed the news that Snake Head believed the young woman from Turtle Village to be his half sister. Then, last night, as Sawfly stood guard on the walls—which he rarely did—the Made People had scurried around in the darkness like packrats, going from chamber to chamber, carrying the news that Ironwood had called the young woman from Turtle Village his "daughter." It didn't take a Spirit Dreamer to hook the two together.

Beyond the north window, a hazy veil eddied and spun across the greening highlands. Wind Baby had been fickle the past few days, leaping and playing, or holding his breath. Sawfly studied the veil as it swept up into the air, whirled around, going higher and higher. He squinted at the last spinning wisps . . . and heard the sound of a moccasin across stone.

Reaching for his bow and quiver, Sawfly drew them into his lap and leaned out the south window. A beautiful woman stood below, looking up at him. She had a thin, fine-boned face, with long dark hair. They gave her an air of innocence, especially when she smiled, as she did now.

"Hello!" she called up.

"Hello."

"I'm sorry to disturb your watch, but I'm trying to reach Starburst Town, and I seem to have lost my way. Could you tell me where it is?"

Sawfly leaned further out the window, pointing to the right, toward the western end of the canyon. "Over there. You need to follow the road that runs—"

The impact of the arrow knocked him out of the window and sent him crashing to the ground. He landed hard, his body tangling up like a loop of dropped yucca cord. Sawfly blinked up at the sky in terror. He couldn't feel his body! It had gone completely numb below his neck! . . . *The arrow must have struck my spine. Oh, thlatsinas, no!*

A tall man wearing a black-and-white cape straddled Sawfly. He had a hideously scarred and *familiar* face. The man drew his chert knife from his belt with a smile. As he knelt, lowering the blade to Sawfly's throat, he said, "Remember me, Straight Path dog? I used to be a slave in your town." He bent forward to peer into Sawfly's horrified eyes from less than a hand away. *"Now you pay for what you did to me!"*

The sharp blade stung as it sliced through Sawfly's throat. He struggled to move, but only his head responded, thrashing back and forth as blood filled his mouth. A gray mist fluttered at the edges of his vision, closing in, shading blacker and blacker. . . .

Cone furiously hurled a rock over the edge of the canyon and watched it fall. His belly churned. His tattered red warrior's shirt flapped around his stout body. As Father Sun rose toward noon, sweat beaded his pug nose and ran along the jaw of his round face. He wiped the moisture from his eyes and squinted at the burial procession moving away to the south along the sacred road. The people had become faint black dots in the rolling red-and-gold landscape punctuated by long ridges and eroded buttes.

He twisted to look northward across Straight Path Canyon. The white half-moon shaped towns shone brilliantly against the massive golden cliffs. The smaller villages, blocky splotches, would start planting crops in less than a moon, repairing and constructing new additions to the buildings, quarrying turquoise, malachite, and jet. The bravest Traders would run the roads bargaining for coral and seashells, copper bells and macaws, buffalo robes and dried meats. In spring, the Straight Path world came fully alive. How he loved the sights of spring, the greening grass, the tufted clouds in a pristine blue sky, the way the sun lay on the land, drawing the colors out of the soil.

"Look well, my eyes. You'll never see it again."

Cone took a weary breath. The ache in his chest expanded.

By now, Howler would have taken the signal tower, and Jay Bird would be stealthily approaching Talon Town. If the Mogollon did it correctly, it would take them the rest of the day. Jay Bird's warriors would slowly filter down the roads, one or two at a time, so as not to arouse suspicion. Then, when they were all in place, Jay Bird would strike fast and hard.

Cone stared at the rust-colored sandstone beneath his moccasins. Tired, empty, he no longer knew how to think or feel about anything. In all the time he'd carried messages between Jay Bird and Snake Head, he'd believed he was helping to save the Straight Path nation from the wickedness of its new Blessed Sun. Removing Snake Head was the only way to secure his people's future.

Yet Snake Head would live, because he would be away when

the town came under attack. He would survive and live on as Blessed Sun. No one would know that he'd plotted with the Fire Dogs, living among them like a scorpion in their garden.

Everything I did has come to naught. Snake Head would live, while Wraps-His-Tail, Beargrass, and so many others were dead. Snake Head's plotting had just led to more dishonor.

"I'm a fool," he whispered harshly. "I did this!"

He had counted about seventy people in the burial procession, which meant Talon Town had only old men, women, and some children to defend its walls. Perhaps a few sick or injured warriors had remained.

Like nerves shocked into senselessness by the blow of a war club, his despair—despair he'd carried for two days—opened an abyss in his soul.

Thistle had reasons for wanting to hurt Talon Town. The First People had ordered the destruction of her village and family. They were holding her foster daughter. But he . . . he had no reasons. None at all.

"Those are my friends down there."

Killing Snake Head was one thing. He had believed in that, and still did. But attacking Talon Town when most of its warriors were gone was a cowardly act!

Cone kicked at a pebble and dust puffed in front of him. When Cone had told Jay Bird he could not, would not, be party to attacking a defenseless town, the aging Mogollon Chief's eyes had narrowed. He'd said, "Then go. I give you your life for the work you have already done, but do not let me find you fighting against me—*or I will reclaim that life, warrior.*" He'd made the slit-throat sign with his hand and walked away.

Cone had run.

Smarter, wiser men would have headed for a place where no one knew them, but Cone had come straight back to the only home he'd ever known.

And here he stood, like a soulless rock, unable to convince himself to go, knowing he could not stay.

Billowing Cloud People sailed through the blue sky, trailing patchwork shadows across the canyon. Cone gazed at Talon Town and swallowed convulsively.

He ought to be down there.

Fighting.

The old people and children needed him. The sacred duty of the Bear Clan had always been protecting those who couldn't protect themselves.

As though a ghost had whispered to his soul, Cone slowly turned and looked back along the sacred South Road. The burial procession had become a dark blur.

"Blessed First Bear," he whispered. "I'll have to hurry!"

He raced down the sandstone slope and bounded for the road. He could still do something for his people. Then, perhaps, he could take himself to his ancestors with some sense of honor.

Seventh Day

My feet barely make a sound as I kneel on the hill overlooking Orphan Village. Laughing children play in the plaza. It is a tiny village, one story, maybe seven rooms, held in the tree-veined palm of rolling grass-covered hills. Turkeys squawk and strut. Dogs lie in the shadows, their tails wagging when the children dash by.

But I have eyes only for the hawk. A passing stranger told me about her. She clings to the willow bars of her cage in the northeastern corner of the plaza. It is a large cage, a full body-length tall and two wide. She is a truly beloved pet. Most owners would not prepare such a lavish cage; they would merely tie her legs and tether her to a post, throwing her food when necessary.

Feathers cling to the willow bars, marking all the places she has beaten her wings against the wood.

In the summer, the Chief of this village robs a fledgling from its nest and brings the bird home. It is part of his Spirit vision. It is said that his Helper is Packrat, and that by caging one of Packrat's greatest enemies, the Chief pacifies and gains the blessings of his Spirit Helper.

The hawk beats her wings, and striped feathers flutter through the warm sunshine. Her sharp eyes focus on the turkeys strutting arrogantly in front of her cage.

I understand her desperation. . . .

Though she has never been free, never soared through crystalline skies, or dived for prey, the hunger lives in her heart. With every flap of her wings, she is hunting, hunting . . .

Like me.

A wild creature lurks in my soul, and it longs to sail free through endless skies. Yet I have spent my life building my own cage. I tie each stick into place as if my life depends upon it. My mother taught me, and her mother taught her, and her mother taught her.

It is what we do. Humans cage things. Dogs, turkeys, and hawks. We domesticate corn, beans, and squash. Any wild strain is promptly plucked out and killed.

Especially if the strain grows in our own hearts.

Wildness is dangerous.

So we line the deserts with roads. That way no one ever strays from the path. We build huge houses to separate ourselves from earth and sky, then paint our walls with majestic images of mountains and rainstorms, and ask, "Don't they look real?" We busy ourselves making lamps and torches, and boast that we're not afraid of the dark.

But in our hearts, we are afraid.

For all our efforts, the pretty cage is not safe. A desperate hunter beats his wings against the bars, longing for a leap from a towering cliff, or to dive through rain-scented storm winds.

The hawk below me screams again. The shrill desperate cry echoes from the hills, and in my soul.

I know how she feels.

Inside the cage, the hunter can only hunt himself.

Forty-Four

Thistle dug her fingers into the dirt of Straight Path Wash and pulled herself up beside Jay Bird to peer over the bank at Talon Town. Swirls of dark gray cloud painted the evening sky, and owls *hoo-hooed* as they sailed over the cliffs. She'd braided her long hair and coiled it into a bun at the back of her head. Despite the chill, her tattered yellow dress clung damply to her slender body. Scents of wet earth and grass filled her nose.

Four guards. They stood on the walls, their faces gleaming orange in the soft light coming from the chambers.

Hatred swelled. These people, perhaps these very men, had murdered Beargrass and Fledgling! They'd burned her village and slaughtered her clan. They'd taken *everything* from Thistle! . . . Everything except Cornsilk.

She fought back the tears of rage that blurred her eyes.

Cornsilk? Where are you?

Leafhopper crouched in the bottom of the drainage, along with about sixty warriors, waiting instructions to move. In the growing darkness, her squat frame and short hair made her look like a boy. All afternoon long, as they'd stealthily traveled the canyon, Leafhopper had talked about seeing Cornsilk again. It had warmed Thistle's heart, because Thistle had been having terrible nightmares that Cornsilk had never reached Talon Town, that her daughter lay in some patch of sagebrush, dead.

Jay Bird's thin face had taken on a predatory alertness. He wore the red shirt that Howler had stripped from the dead signal tower guard. Thistle had rinsed it in the drainage, but it still smelled of blood.

She took a deep breath. The very air seemed to pulse with fear. And they had good reason to be afraid. Straight Path Canyon's huge towns had been organized and built for defense. If one person screamed an alarm, within half a hand of time every town and village down the length of the canyon responded with an outpouring of warriors. *That* was their strength. They could push an enemy war party back against the canyon walls and literally shoot them to shreds.

Thistle ground her teeth as she scanned Talon Town. She had helped to build those impenetrable walls. Ten hands thick in places, they could not be battered down or scaled—though she had watched very brave warriors throw up ladders in an attempt to do so. The Straight Path archers atop the walls had laughed as they picked them off.

Jay Bird looked at Thistle and tapped the dirt with his forefinger. "Draw it for me. We will have perhaps one finger of time to do this. I must know exactly where the First People's chambers are."

Thistle sketched the half-moon shape in the soil, drew the line of rooms that divided the plaza, and said, "Remember that I have not been here in almost sixteen summers, Great Chief. I expect their chambers will be in the same places, but they may have moved."

"I understand. Go ahead."

"Here, on the fifth floor at the very back, was Crow Beard's chamber. Over here on the right, the east side, Night Sun's chamber sat just beneath Propped Pillar"—she tapped the sketch—"and Sternlight's chamber was a short distance away

... here. Close to the front, on the first floor, Ironwood used to live here. Featherstone's chamber—"

"She is the elderly demented woman?"

"Yes."

"Never mind. She would slow us down too much. And if the First People are not in their chambers, where else might they be?"

Thistle made a dimple in the line of rooms separating the halves of the plaza. "Here, Jay Bird. This is the First People's kiva."

Jay Bird looked back and forth from her map to Talon Town, as if memorizing the critical locations. A strange gleam had entered his eyes.

He turned to Howler, and the tall ugly warrior wet his lips nervously. Jay Bird said, "I think it's dark enough. Pick three men to follow us. They'll have to get as close as they can to their targets and kill as silently as possible. They will have only one chance."

"I understand," Howler replied.

"Do you?" Jay Bird made a gesture to the left, indicating the people walking around Streambed Town, talking and laughing. Then he gestured to the right, toward the bright glow of Kettle Town. "One wrong move, Howler, and the warriors from these towns will join forces and leap upon us like wolves on field mice."

Howler nodded. "I've already told our people they cannot make a sound, or even 'accidentally' set a fire, that anything which alerts the other towns will bring a thousand warriors down upon us and guarantee we do not make it out of the canyon alive."

"Good. Make sure they also understand that by first light tomorrow the Straight Path dogs will have mounted a war party. We will need to run as far and as fast as we can tonight."

"I'll tell them."

"Go, then. Get them into position while I speak with Thistle."

"Yes, my chief."

Climbing back down into the wash, Howler silently ran through the lines, tapping certain men on the shoulders. Three rose and dispersed, walking separately toward Talon Town. Their gray shirts blended with the twilight.

With the silence of spring mist, Jay Bird crawled over the lip of the drainage and lay flat in the grass, eyes squinting.

Thistle followed his gaze, knowing he must be searching for the warriors he'd sent ahead. She could see nothing in the dusk, but he seemed to be monitoring someone's movements. His eyes tracked to the left.

She ground her teeth. She had no weapon, because they did not yet trust her. She had only her hands to defend herself. But they *would* trust her. Soon.

After another finger of time, Jay Bird whispered. "It is time, Thistle."

She scrambled over the bank and stood up, her heart jamming against her ribs. "I'm only sorry Snake Head isn't here so I could kill him myself."

"That will come, good woman. Especially if this night's raid succeeds." He slowly rose to his feet, checked the bow slung over his right shoulder and the quiver over his left. It held ten beautifully fletched arrows. He untied the war club from his belt and tested its familiar weight.

"You're sure the warrior on guard over the entrance is called Gnat?"

"Yes. That's him."

"All right, let's go."

Ironwood ducked out of the altar room and looked around the plaza. Night had fallen, and bats flitted in the faint orange glow that came from the town. No one walked the plaza. The Made People had retreated to their chambers to cook supper, and the slaves had been confined. Soft voices drifted on the wind.

Gnat stood guard over the entry, his stocky body silhouetted against the slate-gray sky. Three other warriors crouched on the fifth-story roof. Ironwood nodded approvingly. With only a handful of real warriors left in town, wariness was imperative. Gnat had done well.

Ironwood started across the hard-packed dirt, and Wind

Baby ruffled his graying hair and whipped his buckskin sleeves. The scent of Cornsilk's blood rose from his stained shirt. He needed to change clothes. A hand of time ago, Weedblossom had sent word that she wished to speak with Night Sun tomorrow morning. Both of them knew what the summons meant. As an act of charity, Weedblossom had given Night Sun time . . . to prepare a defense, to get rid of the evidence— meaning their daughter—or to leave.

Night Sun had already brought her pack to the kiva in preparation. As soon as they could, the three of them would go, even if Ironwood had to carry his daughter every step of the way. If she woke before dawn, they would ask whether she wished to go, or remain as Talon Town's Matron. If she didn't wake, they would simply take her.

He climbed the ladder and walked across the roof toward his chamber, inhaling the cedar smoke that rode the wind. The sweet pungency coated the back of his throat. Hundreds of fires sparkled across the canyon bottom, like topaz beads sewn on a cobalt velvet background.

Ironwood climbed down into his chamber.

The white walls reflected the dove-colored light pouring through the roof opening. He stood for a moment, letting his eyes adjust to the dimness, then went to the pile of folded shirts at the head of his bed. He would need something warm and sturdy. He slipped his soiled shirt over his head and tossed it to the floor. He put on a plain doeskin shirt, tanned to a golden brown. The fringes on the sleeves and hem danced.

He closed up his pack and slung it over his shoulder, then reached for his quiver of arrows and his favorite bow.

His eyes traced the fierce images of the thlatsinas, and went over each weapon on the wall. The water and seed beings that lived in the scalps whispered to him, their voices like whimpers of wind, but he couldn't make out any of their words.

"Good-bye," he said softly.

He lifted a hand and smoothed his fingers over the ornately carved bow presented to him by Crow Beard after the battle at Gila Monster Cliffs. The world had changed that day. He'd changed.

At Gila Monster Cliffs he had proven his value, not just to his chief, but to himself. For the first time since the deaths of his precious wife, Lupine, and their little son, he'd known who he was.

"Now I'm taking a new road. I pray the gods help me to find my way."

One last time, Ironwood looked around, reliving every memory brought forth. Then he swiftly turned and climbed the ladder, fleeing before the sadness overcame him. He stood silently on the roof, fingering his bow.

An owl hovered over Propped Pillar, its wings tipping as the wind gusted. Evening People glittered across the sky.

Gnat crouched over the entry, a blanket around his shoulders.

Ironwood climbed down to the eastern plaza and headed for the First People's kiva, his moccasins whispering on the dirt.

Inside him, exhilaration mixed with melancholy, creating a strange emptiness. He didn't understand it, not fully. He would be with Night Sun. And, perhaps, their daughter, Cornsilk. He had been praying for this day for almost half his life. Why wasn't he dancing? Sixteen summers ago, he would have.

You're an old man now, Ironwood. Too soul weary for such foolish displays.

He neared the doorway to the altar room and, beside it, the gate that connected the halves of the plaza. Just before he ducked inside, he heard an unknown man's voice. . . .

Gnat drew his blanket tightly around his shoulders. The shadows of evening were fading to night, the western horizon glowing with the last pale blue light. As hot as the day had been, night would bring a bone-numbing chill.

Gnat rubbed his eyes and craned his neck around. Fatigue had combined with worry to nibble at his senses. Talon Town was his responsibility. Now he finally understood why Webworm had been so jumpy and irritable over the last moon. Gnat's own nerves were strung as tight as a sinew bowstring.

He could remember that last meeting with Webworm. "This is crazy! You're leaving me four warriors? *Four?* I couldn't guard a corn granary against a pack of children with that few men!"

Webworm had given him the dull, flat-eyed look of a man weary to the point of dropping and pointed across the plaza at Snake Head in his funeral regalia. "Do you want to go complain to the Blessed Sun?"

"No," Gnat had growled. "But I'd give anything to have Crow Beard back." And then his gut had knotted, fearing that he'd insulted Webworm and his position as War Chief. To his relief, Webworm had just smiled, said, "Me, too," and strode off to take his place at the front of the procession.

Gnat turned to inspect the rising bulk of Talon Town, the white walls now ghostly in the gloom. Wisps of smoke carried from warming bowls and cooking fires. The whole place was eerily quiet. Too quiet.

Gnat knew Ironwood and Night Sun would be facing hard questions when Snake Head and the clan elders returned. And then what? If the elders ordered their deaths, did this young Cornsilk become Matron?

Gnat tried to see the way of it all. Cornsilk would depose Snake Head, or at least, he hoped so. Anything would be better than Snake Head's lunacy. *Leaving me four warriors to guard Talon Town!* Of course, if the need arose, he could call out all of the old men and women. Most of them could use bows, if poorly.

He turned uneasily, watching the shadowed flats. At least the decision to strip Talon Town of warriors had come so suddenly neither the Fire Dogs nor the Tower Builders would have had a chance to respond to the opportunity.

"Nothing's going to happen," Gnat said to himself. "It's only for four days. No one can organize a party of warriors that quickly."

He grumbled and tucked his blanket tight again. Coyotes yipped in an eerie racket up on the cliffs. Well, good hunting to them. Rumor had it that people in the small villages had even been putting mice into their stews to extend their meat.

Gnat shifted uneasily. From the moment of Crow Beard's death, it seemed the threads of the Straight Path world had started to unravel. As if a madness had possessed the people.

I could just leave. He cocked his head at the thought, as if listening to a Spirit voice. *Would that be so bad?*

And to think that only a few days ago he'd thought of becoming War Chief. Now he wouldn't take the job if it were offered to him. He actually pitied Webworm.

He conjured images of the Green Mesa villages, of the rough-hewn mountains that rose just to their north. He could see the clear rivers running down from those pine-and-spruce-covered heights to water fertile valleys.

They'd readily take a warrior of his reputation. Maybe it was time to marry into a family that owned good fields and a sturdy house. There'd be fighting aplenty with the Tower Builders, good hunting up in the mountains.

No more raids like Lanceleaf. No more worry about Snake Head's lunacy, or weird murders, or whether Sternlight was a witch. No more plots!

He rubbed his fingers down the handle of his war club. *I'll do it! I'll just up and go.* He'd walk to his room, throw his few things into a pack, roll his blanket, and walk out. Just Go. Tonight. Right now!

He stood up, tempted, and made a face as he glanced up at the rising levels of Talon Town. A sinking sense settled on his heart. No, he owed it to Webworm to see this through. *But just as soon as the War Chief returns, I'm going north.*

He took a deep breath, relief flooding him. Then he heard footsteps in the darkness below the entrance. From long experience, he figured them as two people, both trotting.

"Who's there?"

"A warrior, and a woman of the Ant Clan," a man called back breathlessly, as though they'd been running hard. "We bear news from the Blessed Sun!"

Gnat winced. What had happened now? "Well, then, enter and come up here to tell me about it."

He stretched his back muscles as the man and woman passed through the entryway and climbed the ladder. Despite the darkness, Gnat could see that the man was gray-haired, wearing a warrior's shirt. A bow and quiver hung over his back, while he gripped a war club in his right hand.

Gnat didn't recognize him, but then, with the Blessed Sun calling up so many for the funeral procession, it was no wonder. Take off the man's red shirt and dress him in a weaver's smock, and maybe his face would tug a memory.

The woman looked vaguely familiar. He squinted at her in

the darkness. "All right, tell me. What kind of idiocy has the Blessed Sun thought up this time?"

"You won't like it," the man said as he walked close and gave Gnat a grim smile. No, this was no weaver, but a true warrior. Why didn't he recog—

"You remember Lanceleaf Village, Gnat?" the woman asked hollowly. "You were there. You helped to kill Beargrass, and my son."

"Beargrass?" Gnat started, swinging around to face the woman. "Thistle? Is that—"

He barely heard the whistle of the war club before it crushed his skull.

Jay Bird caught Gnat's body as he slumped and eased him to the plastered roof. He took a moment to gauge Thistle's response, but even in the darkness he could see her steely eyes as she stepped forward and peered at the warrior's body. No doubt about it, this woman hated.

"Grab his other arm." Together, he and Thistle propped the corpse up and crouched around him as if the three of them were talking. Then, looking out at the night, Jay Bird hooted in the soft imitation of an owl's call.

A moment later shadows moved in the darkness. Howler's three picked men slipped through the entryway and pursued their separate courses to silence the remaining guards, who stood gazing down at the roads. This was the most delicate part of the operation. If an alarm was to be given, it would come now. Still, none of them expected an assault from within their own walls.

All these summers, I have waited for this. Jay Bird filled his lungs with the cool night air, hoping to calm his pounding heart. The dead left in Crow Beard's wake, Young Fawn's captivity and death, all those wailing ghosts, would be avenged here, tonight, at Talon Town itself.

Jay Bird took a moment to be awed by the very size of the building. Five stories tall! It was huge! What talent it took to build walls capable of bearing so much stone and plaster!

"How did they ever build this?" he wondered aloud.

"One day, Great Chief, I'll tell you. My own hands helped to raise the eastern walls." Thistle paused, voice dropping. "In another world. Another life."

A low whistle carried on the quiet night. One guard dead. Then, another, and—

"*What?*" the man on the eastern wall shouted. "*Who are you! What do you—*"

Jay Bird clenched a fist and looked up. His warrior had knocked the man flat. In the starlight, he could see them wrestling on the rooftop, rolling over and over. Finally, the sound of club against skull split the night, then a groan, a whistle, and all went silent again.

Jay Bird turned and motioned. Thirty warriors flowed through the entryway in a smooth stream. They moved with such silence, only the grating of sandals on the ground marked their invasion of Talon Town.

Jay Bird and Thistle hurried down the ladder to meet the warriors, motioning them into the shadows of the line of rooms that divided the plaza.

Thistle pointed to the upper stories in the eastern tier of the town. "Those are the rooms of the First People. That's where you will find Night Sun. Her chamber is there, that T-shaped doorway."

Jay Bird translated her words to his warriors, and motioned the first party of ten to get moving. They trotted across the plaza and charged up the ladders beside the Great Warriors. In the dim light the gods appeared to be glowering down with malignant intent.

"The slaves are locked in the circular chambers over there," Jay Bird told Howler, and waved to the rooms. "You'll need to drop a ladder down to them and remind them to be quiet as they make their escape."

Howler nodded and took the second group of ten warriors.

"That doorway next to the gate leads to the First People's kiva." Thistle led Jay Bird and the remaining warriors along the strip of rooms dividing the plaza and toward the door.

At that moment, a man shouted, then came scuffling noises and groans.

"What's happening?" Jay Bird called softly. Two of his warriors dragged a big, gray-haired man through the gate. It took both of them to hold him. Jay Bird instinctively clutched his war club, dropping into a crouch. He could hear his warriors drawing nocked arrows against bowstrings.

A war club was raised to dispatch the struggling man when Thistle called out, "Wait! It's Ironwood!"

"Stop!" Jay Bird called out in his own tongue. "We need him."

"We found him scrambling up a ladder, trying to warn the guards," the tall warrior, Foxbat, whispered.

"Ironwood," Jay Bird said with a frozen smile. "It's been such a long time." Jay Bird reached out, offering his hand.

To his surprise, the Straight Path warrior looked around at the men surrounding him, then nervously accepted Jay Bird's hand, asking, "Who are you? Why—"

Jay Bird yanked him close, drew his stiletto from his belt, and jammed the sharpened tip against Ironwood's neck. "Make no sound, War Chief, or I drive this point home. Now, listen closely. Do you know Cornsilk? A girl from Lanceleaf Village? Tell me this instant, or you and a great many people will die."

"Who are you?" Ironwood hissed between clenched teeth.

"Her grandfather!"

Ironwood shook his head in confusion. "What?"

Thistle stepped forward, close enough that Ironwood could see her clearly. She said, "I've come to save my daughter, Ironwood. Where is she? The Cage?"

Jay Bird felt Ironwood swallow, his throat working against the point of the stiletto. His eyes widened as he gazed down at Thistle. "No. She's . . . she's in the kiva, Thistle. Why are you *doing* this?"

"Because she's all I have left, Ironwood. Come on, this way!" Thistle hurried forward.

"Foxbat!" Jay Bird shoved Ironwood to the two warriors who'd captured him. "Quickly! Bind his hands and tie a cord around his neck so you can choke him down if he tries to scream."

He and his warriors trailed along after Thistle into the splendidly painted altar room, and then descended the stairs into the great kiva with its four red masonry pillars and stunning array of masks.

"Cornsilk!" Thistle cried, running toward a knot of people gathered around a prostrate young woman.

A tall woman rose to her feet and gave Jay Bird a wary look. The three men stood up one at a time, whispering uneasily to each other.

"Surround them!" Jay Bird gestured to each side. "Search this place. Take anything that looks valuable." Then, as his warriors scattered, scooping offerings from the wall niches and pulling down sacred masks, Jay Bird stepped toward the waiting people, his heart in his throat.

Thistle knelt at the unconscious girl's side. Was this his granddaughter? For the moment, he could see little beyond the dark ugly bruise, the swelling on one side of her face.

"What happened here?" he demanded.

The woman, a slender hard-eyed beauty, spoke. "She was shot in the face with an arrow. An attempted murder. Who are you?" She scanned the warriors. "What do you want?"

Jay Bird raised his eyes, reacting to the tone of command. No one had ever addressed him like that. He met her stare, read her growing alarm as she watched his warriors stealing the most precious artifacts of her people. One of his men threw a magnificent Green Mesa pot to the floor, where it shattered and spilled its contents across the dirt. The warrior gleefully scooped them up.

"That's enough," Jay Bird ordered his men. "We may have only moments left before someone sounds the alarm. Stuff what you have in your packs and surround these people. They're coming with us."

He turned to the tall woman. "What is your name? And don't lie to me, or you'll be dead."

"I am Night Sun." At that instant, she gasped and took a running step forward. Jay Bird looked where she did and saw Ironwood being shoved in ahead of Foxbat, bound and gagged.

Jay Bird caught her arm and jerked her backward. "And these people?" He nodded to the old man, the curiously tranquil priest, and the youth who watched him with wide, disbelieving eyes. The boy had twined a hand in Cornsilk's blood-soaked yellow sleeve.

The white-haired elder with the deeply wrinkled face stepped forward. "I am Dune, called the holy Derelict. Beside me is Sternlight, Sunwatcher of Talon Town. The young man is my assistant, Poor Singer. Apparently, you already know Cornsilk. What is it you wish from us, Great Jay Bird?"

At the name, Night Sun and Poor Singer reacted as if slapped. Sternlight only stared, an odd light burning in his eyes. He did not seem to see the kiva, crawling with mortal enemies, but gazed into another world.

"How is Cornsilk?" Jay Bird asked. Thistle was holding the girl's hand. "Will she live?"

"Of course she will," Night Sun said. "I tended her wounds myself. Now I demand to know . . ."

Ironwood shook his head, and Night Sun caught it. She shot him a quick look, and whatever she had wished to demand, she decided against it. She squared her narrow shoulders and leveled a glare at Jay Bird.

Jay Bird lifted an eyebrow. "As much as I would like to linger and enjoy the hospitality of Talon Town, I simply haven't the time. I do, however, look forward to getting to know all of you. At Gila Monster Cliffs. Within the walls of my own village we will have fewer interruptions." He gestured threateningly with his stiletto. "The first one of you who resists, or seeks to impede our progress, will force me to take my displeasure out on Night Sun." He searched their eyes, one by one—especially Ironwood's. "Do you understand?"

Even the War Chief nodded.

"Let's go!" Jay Bird turned toward the exit.

"Great Chief?" Foxbat asked. His lean feral face had tensed. "What of the old man? I don't think he could walk across the room, let alone make the march back to Gila Monster Cliffs. Should I kill him?"

"Kill the holy Derelict? No, my friend." Jay Bird gripped his warrior's arm. "He's worth too much to us. We'll carry him and Cornsilk. When we get outside, take some ladders. They'll serve just fine for litters."

"Yes, my chief." The man trotted for the stairs.

Jay Bird knelt by Cornsilk and scrutinized her. Wrapped in three blankets, she looked warm. Her breathing came in quick shallow gasps, but she seemed to be sleeping soundly. Very gently, Jay Bird slipped his arms beneath her shoulders and knees, and lifted her. "Howler? Take everyone else ahead of me and make certain the plaza is secure. I'll carry my grand-daughter myself."

"I understand."

Howler gestured to one of the warriors who held Ironwood. "Black Quill, throw your cape around Ironwood, and take him out first, just in case someone gets excited and decides to shoot before they look."

"Yes," Black Quill removed his black-and-white cape and tied it around Ironwood's shoulders. The big man glared defiantly as the warriors shoved him toward the stairway.

With a practiced efficiency, Howler directed the departure of the rest of the people. "Take the priests next, then the youth and the woman."

Jay Bird waited, clutching Cornsilk to his chest, until the last warrior had trotted up the steps, then he carried his grand-daughter out and into the cool night. Talon Town had turned a pale blue in the moonlight. Someone cried out . . . then screamed. A dog barked. Dark figures, many calling out in the Mogollon tongue, hurried across the plaza for the entry, escaping into the darkness.

Foxbat and Howler ran up carrying a ladder and a coil of yucca rope.

"Good," Jay Bird said. "Place it on the ground."

They did, and Jay Bird carefully lowered Cornsilk to the pine rungs. The blankets would cushion her body, but her right ear rested on a bare pole. Jay Bird removed his cape, folded it and tucked it beneath her injured head. "Tie her down and let's be off."

"Yes, my chief."

Jay Bird stood, cupped his hands to his mouth, and made a shrill whistle, recalling the warriors inside the walls. As they trotted past, Jay Bird turned to the two men who carried Corn-silk. She lay on the ladder wrapped in blankets. Jay Bird gazed at her swollen face with his heart thumping, searching, searching for some resemblance to his daughter. He saw nothing, but perhaps later he would, when the swelling went down. "Be very careful with my granddaughter."

"It's our honor, Great Chief." From the tone, he knew she'd be coddled like a fragile pot.

Two warriors held Sternlight in hard hands. They rushed

him past toward the entry. He looked like a man caught in a horrifying snare, ready to chew off his foot to escape. One by one warriors trooped out, some bloody, all carrying sacks of loot over their shoulders, or prodding captives before them, mostly young women who had dared to look out of their chambers when they heard the racket. A hollow wailing pierced the night.

The holy Derelict passed, riding a ladder carried by two burly warriors, clutching the rungs as if for dear life, a sour, humiliated look on his face.

Two more warriors shoved Night Sun forward, her hands bound, a thong about her neck. Her eyes were those of a woman seeing her world die.

Look well, Matron, for after this night, the Straight Path people shall never be the same.

To Jay Bird's surprise, Ironwood tried to touch Cornsilk as her ladder rushed by, but Foxbat pulled him back and choked him into submission.

Ironwood staggered, coughed, then struggled to turn to Jay Bird, calling, "Jay Bird? Listen to me!"

"What is it?"

"You and I, we know each other." Ironwood fought for breath, wheezing. "If you will treat Night Sun well . . . I—I'll do whatever you wish of me. Do you understand? Anything."

Jay Bird heard the desperation and found it . . . interesting. Then he caught the look Ironwood and Night Sun exchanged. Jay Bird nodded to himself. "Yes, I think I do understand."

The lowly War Chief loved the great Matron of Talon Town? A brave man, indeed. Perhaps, for that reason, Jay Bird would take Night Sun as his consort—as Ironwood had taken Jay Bird's daughter.

As they rushed out through the entry and into the night, they passed Gnat's dead body, crumpled in a black heap beside the wall.

Jay Bird turned one last time, pride swelling inside him as he gazed upon the great stronghold of the Straight Path people—a stronghold that had fallen to his cunning. *What a raid! It shall be talked about by my grandchildren's grandchildren. My only regret is that I can't leave it in flames!*

The slaves raced ahead down the road like thirsty beasts

scenting water. Hushed weeping mixed oddly with joyous whispers.

Jay Bird, in his ring of warriors, sprinted after them.

The other villages had wakened. People rushed around the roofs of Streambed Town, gasping, pointing.

"Come on!" he yelled, waving a fist over his head. *"Run! Run hard!"*

Forty-Five

Wind Baby blew through the darkness, spinning along the hillsides as though frantic before flying to the sagebrush. Amid the shrieking wind and flailing plants, Cone's movements were barely audible.

He slithered on his belly around patches of cactus, edging closer to the firelit camp where Webworm, Snake Head, Creeper, Badgerbow, and Yellowgirl sat hunched against the wind, eating their supper. Webworm's red shirt contrasted sharply with the white worn by the elders and Snake Head's gaudy blue. In the dancing firelight, the red and yellow macaw feathers sewn to the chest of Snake Head's shirt glimmered and flashed as the wind tugged at them.

The sounds of low voices and horn spoons clacking against clay bowls rose and fell with the gusts. Dust sparkled faintly in the orange gleam, whipped up by Wind Baby. The seventy warriors had separated into ten groups, each with its own fire. Cone scanned the dark rolling hills. Six lookouts stood on the highest points, little more than black silhouettes against a starry sky.

Webworm had made camp one thousand hands from the sacred South Road, where enough brush still grew to feed their cooking fires. Burning sage and roasting venison taunted Cone's nostrils. He'd had nothing to eat since breakfast, and hunger knotted his belly. He forced it from his thoughts. He had to concentrate.

He inched closer, his bow and one arrow gripped in his right hand. His quiver and eight more arrows rested against his left shoulder blade—but he'd better not miss. With all these warriors, he wouldn't have a second shot, and the very survival of his people might depend upon him this night.

The thought left him shaken and sick to his stomach. Cone's eyes blurred. *It doesn't matter what happens to you! Someone has to do this!* He had, in his own way, been hoping that Jay Bird would do it for him. But that was not to be.

He silently inched his way to a six-hands-tall sagebrush and squinted at the camp. Snake Head's insidious laugh carried, high and shrill, like that of a cruel child tormenting a helpless animal.

"That's because you're a fool, Creeper," Snake Head said. Across the fire Creeper looked like a whipped puppy, his round face taut. "If you knew anything about the Mogollon, you'd know they were worthy of being our allies. If we had them on our side, we—"

"But, Snake Head!" Creeper objected. His short, plump body strained against the fabric of his white shirt as he leaned forward. He wore his black hair in a short braid. "The Mogollon have never been trustworthy! What makes you think that suddenly they—"

"Because *I* am dealing with them. That's what. My father was a fool—" his gaze fell on each of the elders sitting around the fire "—all of you knew it! Don't try to look as though you don't know what I'm talking about! Crow Beard didn't have the skill to manage such an alliance, but *I* do."

Creeper glanced around the circle and lowered his gaze. His hands fluttered restlessly in his lap. "Well, if you think you can do it."

Badgerbow shifted, and the scalped side of his skull gleamed in the firelight. He glowered distrustfully at Snake Head. "You are the Blessed Sun," Badgerbow said gruffly, "and I must respect that. But before you dive into such negotiations with our enemies, I recommend you seek the advice of the elders. I will be happy to call a council to hear you out."

Snake Head's spine stiffened. His handsome face turned

stony. "I'll let you know if I require such a meeting, elder."

"You listen to me, boy!" Badgerbow glared, his jaw set askew. "If you do not consult with the elders of our people before you place us all in jeopardy—"

Snake Head lurched to his feet, towering over the fire. His blue shirt snapped and billowed in the wind. "Don't tell me what to do!" he shouted. "I am the Blessed Sun! I tell you what to do, Made man! You do not ever—"

Cone drew back his arrow, sighted on Snake Head's back, and smoothly let it fly. His arrow struck Snake Head squarely between the shoulders, lancing through at least one lung.

Snake Head staggered, gaping at the people around the fire. Then a hideous scream broke his lips. "I'm shot!" he shrieked. "Oh, dear gods!"

"Webworm!" Creeper shouted. "Go—"

But the War Chief was already on his feet, running toward the darkness. Snakehead's stagger made it impossible for Webworm to tell exactly where the arrow had come from. Cone watched him race off to the northeast, shouting to his warriors to follow.

Snake Head's knees went weak. He sank to the ground and clawed at the bright black point that protruded just beneath his right breast. "Help!" he cried. "Help! Help me . . . ?" Blood bubbled at his lips. "Somebody . . . save me!"

The elders gathered around him, studying the wound, shaking their heads. Snake Head coughed up more blood, choking on it, his eyes bulging.

With the stealth of Rattlesnake, Cone crawled backward through the sage, praying the whining gusts of wind would cover his retreat.

When he reached the deep darkness at the base of the hill, he got to his feet and ran with all his might, swerving around the hill and running flat out across the desert.

He heard arrows hissing. One landed in front of him, missing by a body-length. The next slapped him in the side like a thrown rock. He stumbled, winced at the fiery pain in his kidney, and trotted unsteadily forward, clutching the brightly feathered shaft.

Feet pounded behind him; another arrow slammed into his back and sent its terrible sting through his breast. Cone wobbled, lost his footing, and tumbled to the ground, his face in the sand. He brought up his knees, struggling to crawl. . . .

A moccasined foot brutally kicked him over onto his back. Cone stared up at the glistening Evening People and the shocked faces of his one-time friends: Webworm, Toehold, Little Rat. . . .

"*Cone?*" Webworm cried, and fell to his knees at Cone's side. The expression of stunned horror on his face left Cone feeling hollow. "Cone, what are you doing out here? Why did you do this? I would never have thought—"

"Come closer, old friend."

Webworm leaned over him, studying Cone's twisted face and the blood that ran warmly over his chest.

"Listen," Cone gasped as he struggled to grip Webworm's red sleeve. He twined his fingers tightly in the fabric. "Snake Head . . . betrayed our people. I've been carrying messages between him . . . and Jay Bird."

"*Jay Bird!*"

"Yes, and . . . Jay Bird tricked Snake Head . . . into bringing eighty warriors—"

"Why was Snake Head talking to Jay Bird?"

"Snake Head . . . trying to establish alliance . . . behind the backs of the elders."

"I understand," Webworm said as his eyes searched the darkness. "Where is Jay Bird now?"

Cone tugged weakly on his shirt. The arrow had struck the bottom of his right lung, and he could feel it filling with blood, swelling his chest, cutting off his air. Soon, the warm liquid would rise into his throat, and his other lung would fill. "Jay Bird . . . he's . . . at Talon Town. Attacking Talon Town."

Webworm bowed his head and Cone saw him clench a fist. "Gods, forgive me. We have to get home! I've left the town—"

"Too late . . . for that. You can try . . . to cut Jay Bird off . . . on the southwestern trail . . . probably has . . . captives."

Cone coughed, and frothy blood poured from his lips. He felt tired, so tired, as though all of his strength had drained away. "Webworm," he said, trying to hurry. "Glad . . . you'll be next Blessed Sun . . . Mourning Dove knew. She . . . she wanted you to rule. Me, too. Sorry . . . I won't . . . be there."

His hand suddenly went numb. His fingers loosened and his arm thumped to the ground.

He felt like thistledown borne on the wind. *I should be afraid.*

Despite the gray fog at the edge of his vision, Cone saw Webworm's mouth moving. The War Chief must be talking, but he couldn't hear anything, not even the ferocious wind that whipped Webworm's hair around his square-jawed face. A terrible weight pressed down on Cone's chest. For an instant, when he realized he wasn't breathing, panic surged through him, but it rapidly melted into a sublime sense of acceptance. Cone closed his eyes against the darkening mist and let himself drift away . . .

Heart pounding, Webworm rose on shaking legs and looked down at his friend. He allowed himself a moment to feel the hollow sense of loss expanding in his gut, then spun and tramped back for camp. Cone's blood had been hot as it spilled. Now the wind turned it icy cold, sticky and clotted on his fingers.

Creeper saw him coming and stood up from where he crouched over Snake Head. Blood splotched his white shirt. A large red stain spread over his belly. The other elders halted their efforts around the Chief and breathlessly waited for Webworm.

He stopped by the fire, his jaw clenched, fists trembling. "It was Cone. He shot Snake Head."

"But why?" Creeper said.

Warriors crowded around them, staring at Snake Head with curious eyes, whispering to each other. The scent of dust filled the air.

"He said that Snake Head had betrayed us. Our Blessed Sun has secretly been meeting with Jay Bird for at least a moon, and he—"

Badgerbow gasped and rose to his feet. "Jay Bird? The Great Chief himself? But that's *insane*!"

A stinging sensation built in Webworm's heart and filtered to his fingertips. He realized that Snake Head was dead. Bitterly tired, barely able to concentrate, he fought to work out what must be done next. If only Ironwood were here! He'd know what to do—and perhaps together they could see the correct path. He massaged his forehead. *You only have yourself. You must choose a course of action. . . . And the Blessed thlatsinas help you if you're wrong!*

Creeper came to Webworm's side and squeezed his arm gently. "Where is Jay Bird? If he's been meeting with Cone—"

"Jay Bird"—Webworm took a breath—"has apparently tricked Snake Head, Creeper. Tricked him into pulling out most of our warriors, then Jay Bird ran straight for Talon Town. By now, he's attacked and is scurrying for home."

Yellowgirl glared down at Snake Head with loathing. "Blessed thlatsinas," she murmured. "Our families may be dead."

"Or taken as slaves," Badgerbow reminded.

Yellowgirl's mouth puckered. She was muscular, with sallow cheeks and black hair that hung even with her chin. An expression of pure hatred strained her thin face. She spat upon Snake Head's body and slowly rose to her feet to pin Webworm with her gaze. "What should we do now, War Chief?"

Webworm swallowed down his tight throat. "Split our forces." He turned. "There's no time to waste. I must try to cut off Jay Bird's retreat, and you, Creeper, must see that the bodies of Crow Beard and Cloud Playing are properly buried, so they can ascend to the skyworlds. When that's done, Snake Head must be taken back to Talon Town. If I leave you twenty warriors, will that be enough?"

Creeper searched Webworm's face. "It will have to be. If you're planning what I think you are, you'll need the rest."

Yellowgirl stepped forward and cocked her head knowingly. "You're going after them?"

"I am. Cone said we might be able to cut them off if we ran cross-country to the southwestern trail." He extended his icy hands to the warmth of the blaze and shivered lightly. Cone's blood had caked on the backs and under the nails. "I have to try. This . . . this is my fault. If I hadn't listened to Snake Head and pulled out so many warriors—"

"This is *not* your fault!" Creeper snapped in the harshest voice Webworm had ever heard the little man use. Creeper stepped forward and glared up at Webworm. "You were obeying the orders of your Chief! That's all there is to it! Your duty now is to try and gain the release of the slaves Jay Bird's taken." His voice softened, and he tenderly patted Webworm's arm. "We will all be looking forward to your return, War Chief. We wish you a speedy journey."

As Creeper started to walk away, Webworm gripped his shoulder. "When you get home . . ." Webworm whispered, and glanced around uncomfortably. All eyes were upon him. "I'm afraid for Mother. If they took her with them as a slave, she'll never make it to Fire Dog territory. We both know that. She's too frail. But if they didn't take her . . . you know that when she goes 'vacant' she can't care for herself. And, well, Mourning Dove may not be there—"

"*What?* But why wouldn't . . ." Pain laced Creeper's voice. Apparently it had not occurred to him until now that she might have been released during the raid. Webworm could see Creeper's face change as the truth dawned. "But of course, you're right. It's just that . . . I had not thought . . . she's always been so loyal."

"This was her chance for freedom, Creeper. I wouldn't blame her if she took it."

Creeper lowered his gaze to the sand. "Nor would I."

Webworm glanced up at the other elders. They stood silently by the fire, staring at Snake Head's corpse. The Blessed Sun lay on his back, eyes wide and disbelieving. Clotted blood had leaked out of his mouth and down his cheek to shine blackly in the wind-whipped firelight. Badgerbow scowled while Yellowgirl glowered at the flames, as if by looking she could snuff them out.

What have you done to us, Snake Head? Webworm struggled with an urge to kick the corpse, to beat the dead flesh with sticks and rocks.

The rest of his warriors stood about uneasily, bows in hands, quivers over their shoulders—as if fearing the Earth Spirits might rise up and swallow them whole.

"Creeper," Webworm said hoarsely, "I must sleep for a few hands of time. Will you wake me at midnight?"

"You can't leave in the middle of the night! What purpose would it serve? Get a good night's rest, then—"

He shook his head. "I must leave as quickly as possible. If Cone was telling the truth, Jay Bird may have attacked earlier today and will have a good head start on us. Wake me at midnight."

Creeper looked away, but nodded. "Yes, of course."

"Thank you." Webworm gripped Creeper's shoulder, then strode toward the other campfires, already sorting men in his mind, idly wondering what Cone had meant about him becoming the new Blessed Sun.

Featherstone sat in the plaza with her eyes closed, her gray head in her hands, listening to the reedy voice of Weedblossom speak to Moon Bright and fidgety old Whistling Bird. She'd never met with these esteemed elders. Oh, she knew them all right. Each of the First People knew the others. But what would such elders wish with her? They had always spoken kindly to her when they passed, but hurried away, as though worried Featherstone might suddenly go vacant on them, and they'd have to look into her empty eyes, or touch her soulless body. So why did they sit here today with frowns on their withered faces?

"*I cannot agree!*" Whistling Bird shouted. "What if she loses her soul at some critical moment? Do you have any idea what kind of devastation—"

"Our kinship system was established just after the First People emerged from the underworlds, Whistling Bird!" Weedblossom said sternly. "Shall we abandon it because you now think it's inconvenient?"

"Not inconvenient, Weedblossom. Dangerous!"

Featherstone opened her blurry old eyes and looked at them. When she'd been a child and flown on the back of Dragonfly, she remembered looking down upon Center Place with awe. Weedblossom had always been the greatest of the elders to her. Ever kind, she was considerate to those of low status, and a very great Singer. All of the homeless ghosts who came to Weedblossom, begging her to help them reach the afterlife, went away feeling joyous. Featherstone knew because she often felt the ghosts' emotions as they trotted past Talon Town.

Brilliant sunlight fired the white plaza, making Featherstone squint. The slaves had run away. Made People wandered about soberly picking up refuse, trying to piece their lives back together. Several of the children had been hauled off as captives, young Toadboy from the Buffalo Clan, Red Spark from the Ant Clan . . . she ached for them all, remembering how the brutal Fire Dog, Crooked Lance, had hurt her.

"We have faced danger before, Whistling Bird," Weedblossom said.

"But never from the inside! Don't you understand? This"— he gestured to Featherstone—"could be the greatest threat the Straight Path people have ever faced!"

Featherstone frowned. The elders had come to Talon Town at dawn, surveyed the damage caused in the raid, then called out Featherstone. So, here they sat, on willow-twig mats, Moon Bright to Featherstone's left, Weedblossom to her right, and Whistling Bird directly in front of her. Because they were in mourning after the deadly raid, they all wore long red robes belted at the waist with white sashes: red in memory of the bloodshed, white to cleanse the hatred from their grieving hearts.

Featherstone gazed methodically around the circle. Hunchbacked Moon Bright nervously smoothed her fingers over the dirt of the plaza. Her silver hair blew in the warm breeze that swept Talon Town. Deep wrinkles lined her face, reminding Featherstone of a winter-killed buffalo carcass, shrunken and brown. Moon Bright didn't seem to know what to think. The diminutive Weedblossom, on the other hand, looked determined. Her knotted fingers rested on her knees like sharp talons. She wore her white hair in two short braids. She kept glancing at Whistling Bird with fury in her eyes. Whistling Bird didn't seem to notice. He stared unblinking at Featherstone, as if evaluating her fitness. His bald head gleamed golden in the sunlight.

"Featherstone?" Whistling Bird asked. "Do you think you can do it?"

Featherstone blinked and frowned. "Do what?"

Whistling Bird shook his head. "See? What did I tell you?

She doesn't even know what we've been speaking about! How can she possibly—"

"Featherstone?" Weedblossom tenderly patted Featherstone's cheek. "Try to listen. We're discussing something very important."

"What?"

Moon Bright wet her lips and leaned closer, as though proximity might help Featherstone understand better. "You, Featherstone, are the last female member of a once great family. Seven generations of Red Lacewing women have ruled Talon Town. If Night Sun does not return, and we think it likely, *you* have the right to claim the position of Matron of the First People. What will you do? Do you think you are fit to rule?"

Featherstone sat back, stunned. "Hallowed rain gods," she whispered. "*I* am next in line?"

"You are the *end* of the line, Featherstone," Weedblossom said gently. "Which is why I think that, no matter the risks, you should take your place."

"Well," Whistling Bird said sullenly, "she is old. Perhaps she will not rule long enough to cause any—"

"Hush!" Weedblossom snapped. "Have you no heart?" Then she turned back to Featherstone. "Would you like to rule, Featherstone?"

As though awakening from a long sleep, Featherstone suddenly understood what they were trying to tell her. She pulled herself up straight, looked Weedblossom in the eyes, and said, "It's my duty to serve, Weedblossom. My wishes are of no concern. Besides, I'll have my son to help me. I—I pray." Off and on throughout the morning, she'd cried, terrified for Webworm and Creeper. "My son is all that I need to rule well."

Weedblossom peered at Moon Bright and Whistling Bird. "Which of you dares to deny a Red Lacewing woman the right to rule her people?"

Moon Bright said, "Not I."

Whistling Bird threw up his arms. "All right! I can't fight all three of you!"

Forty-Six

Evening poured through tattered clouds, streaking the sky with pale lavender light. Long shadows crept across the rolling desert. Out in the sagebrush a fox yipped. Ironwood sat on the ground beside Cornsilk, his muscles aching, and listened. As the Fire Dog warriors went about setting up camp, lighting fires, throwing out bedrolls, they laughed and talked. He knew how they felt, heady with the giddy rush of triumph. The scent of roasting jackrabbit spiced the air. Ironwood's empty belly groaned. Would Jay Bird feed his captives tonight? They always received breakfast, to give them the strength to run all day, but Jay Bird had not yet deigned to offer them a supper.

Just at the edge of camp he could see young Red Spark's body where it lay trussed to a pole like a deer carcass. The girl had broken and run in a futile attempt at escape. One of the Fire Dogs had nocked an arrow and nonchalantly shot her down. Ironwood could still see that deadly sliver as it arced and drove the vicious point through the girl's back.

But why didn't Jay Bird leave her where she fell? Why carry a worthless corpse for a whole day?

Anger and humiliation vied inside Ironwood. He hated himself for allowing this to happen. How could he, the great warrior and legendary War Chief, have walked straight into the arms of his enemies? He should have scented the danger and been able to shout a warning to the guards on the walls. Instead, he'd been wallowing in his own guilt and pain, and completely ignored the scratching of carefully placed sandals, the faint pungency of fear sweat on the night wind . . . until too late.

Fool! So many mistakes.

He glanced around at the six men with nocked bows who surrounded the prisoners. Including himself, fifteen people—counting hapless Red Spark—had been captured. They slumped in various positions, most already asleep after the brutal run. Only he and Sternlight remained awake. Sternlight sat cross-legged at Poor Singer's feet, watching the camp. Poor Singer curled on his side next to Cornsilk. Before he'd fallen asleep, he'd gently rested his hand on a lock of Cornsilk's long black hair. Night Sun lay to Ironwood's left, breathing deeply, her beautiful face slack. Dune lay flat on his back on his blanket-covered litter ten paces away. He'd been too exhausted from the jostling ride to move. As Ironwood's gaze moved over the captives, he silently named each one: *Four Fingers, little Cottonwood Boy, Greenshoot Woman . . .* His gaze shifted to Thistle. She roamed the camp freely. But why shouldn't she? Her treachery had allowed the disaster to take place. She would be a hero to Jay Bird and his people.

Ironwood looked down at Cornsilk. Despite what Thistle had done, he could not find it in his heart to hate her. She had raised his daughter as her own. At Ironwood's request, she had arranged it so that Cornsilk's litter was left near him for a short time each night, so that Ironwood could look at her and make certain she still breathed.

He reached out and stroked Cornsilk's limp hand.

To his surprise, her eyes fluttered open. She had wakened often in the past three days, but had gone right back to sleep. Her face was still swollen and hideously bruised. For a long moment, she stared curiously at the sky, as though not certain where she was, then turned and looked at Ironwood.

"What—".

"Shh," he whispered. "The guards have forbidden me to speak to anyone. If they hear us, I'll be punished. Talk in a very low voice and don't look at me when you do. Focus on someone or something else."

Cornsilk swallowed hard and let her gaze drift to where Thistle stood, speaking with Jay Bird. The elderly Mogollon Chief looked as ragged and tired as Ironwood felt. His filthy shirt hung in tatters; his gray hair and thin face bore a coating of red dirt. He stood four hands taller than Thistle. She had to tip her head back to look Jay Bird in the eyes.

Cornsilk let out a sigh, as if the sight of her "mother" eased her soul. She whispered, "What happened?"

Ironwood watched Swallowtail roaming the periphery of the

camp. For over a hand of time, the tall boy had been circling Cornsilk, getting as close as he dared, trying to catch a glimpse of her face. Ironwood did not know why. Perhaps Swallowtail just wanted to make certain she was all right—Cornsilk had, after all, been kind to him. Ironwood murmured, "It's a long story, my daughter. You were shot in the face. We removed the arrow, and then Talon Town was attacked. Thistle led Jay Bird and his warriors into the plaza. Many were killed. It all happened very fast. We were taken prisoner. Jay Bird spared you because he believes you are his granddaughter."

Cornsilk's gaze shot back to him, questioning, then returned to Thistle. "But I'm not. Am I?"

"No. But Thistle never knew for certain who your parents were. I wished it that way—to protect you, Cornsilk. She must have guessed that I was your father and assumed your mother was the slave Young Fawn. She was Jay Bird's daughter."

Cornsilk seemed to be taking this in. "What will he do when he discovers I'm not his granddaughter?"

"You will be safe. Thistle will make certain of that. She loves you very much, and Jay Bird will grant Thistle whatever she wishes. Thistle helped him pull off the greatest raid of his life. He knows how much he owes her."

Cornsilk shifted to look at Poor Singer. The tall, skinny young man snored softly. Dirty black hair fell over his shoulder. Dread tensed Cornsilk's features. "And what will happen to Poor Singer and the rest of you? If my mother asks, will all of you be allowed to go free, too?"

"I don't know. He will certainly want me dead."

"Dead?" Cornsilk asked feebly. "Why?"

One of the guards cocked his head and peered at Ironwood suspiciously. Ironwood shifted, bracing his hands behind him and leaning back to stare up at the stars twinkling through the charcoal puffs of clouds. The guard studied him a time longer, then turned to sniff in the direction of a roasting rabbit.

Very softly, Ironwood answered, "Jay Bird has good reasons."

When she didn't answer, Ironwood glanced at her. Tears trickled from her eyes, streaking the dust that covered her bruised face. His heart went out to her. "Do not grieve for me, Cornsilk. Unlike most men, I have lived to see my greatest dream come true, to see my precious daughter grow to womanhood. My life has been full and mostly happy."

"But there must be something—"

"I think our time is up," Ironwood said when he saw Thistle push through the camp with two warriors at her sides. "I'll try to speak with you more tomorrow."

Thistle called, "Cornsilk? Are you awake?" and anxiously trotted forward.

Both guards nocked their bows and aimed them straight at Ironwood's chest. He sat placidly while Thistle knelt beside Cornsilk and smoothed dirty hair from her wounded face.

"Oh, my daughter," Thistle said, and bent to kiss Cornsilk's dirty forehead. "I'm so glad to see you. How are you feeling?"

Cornsilk reached out. Thistle took her hand and clutched it tightly. "I'm hungry, Mother."

"I'm sure you are." Thistle gestured to the warriors. "Please, carry her to Jay Bird's fire." She stood and backed away, glancing only perfunctorily at Ironwood.

As the guards lifted Cornsilk's litter, she lowered a hand toward Ironwood, the palm open in a gesture of need, and gazed down through wet eyes.

He dared not reach back, but he watched as they carried her away.

Webworm had long ago lost any sense of his body and staggered more than trotted after White Stone, the best tracker of the Bear Clan. White Stone's body wavered on the trail ahead, like one of the heat Spirits that haunted the distances.

The way led inexorably south, across the rolling hills, over the flats with their grassy sand dunes, and into the rolling juniper forests that slanted up to the Gila Monster Cliffs—the forbidding stronghold of the Mogollon.

If we don't catch them before they reach the mountains, it'll all be over. We'll never have another chance like this. Webworm tried to swallow, his mouth burned dry. How long since he'd drunk? Last night? That morning?

Almost two days since he'd slept. *Run! You can do this. Run,*

Webworm. Find them. Avenge yourself and your people. You can sleep later . . . forever, if necessary.

He tripped over a scraggly saltbush, teetered, and stumbled to a halt, hands braced on his shaking knees as he bent double and panted for breath. Every muscle burned and quivered; his stomach cramped. He straightened, leery of resting too long, and looked back. His warriors were strung out across the flats for as far as he could see, their red war shirts tattered and dust mottled.

He turned after White Stone and stumbled forward again, pushing himself just a little farther. The world had come undone, and it was partly his fault. A War Chief accepted responsibility for his mistakes.

If it kills me, I'll find Jay Bird. That, at least, he could do with the same dedication Ironwood would have shown. But then, Ironwood would never have allowed Snake Head to strip Talon Town of adequate defenses.

But I'm not Ironwood. I never have been. I only fooled myself into thinking I could do his job. One disaster had piled on another, until Webworm worried his senses had gone as rubbery as his legs.

Flickering images appeared in his fevered mind: Beargrass' innocent eyes . . . the fear in young Fledgling's expression . . . Cloud Playing's dead body sagging in his arms, her half-open eyes staring into his . . . Night Sun's face when Crow Beard accused her of bearing a child in secret and hiding it away . . . the blood dripping from Cornsilk's nose and mouth . . . Snake Head's shock at being shot . . . Cone's weary relief as eternal night drifted down . . .

Blessed thlatsinas, it all haunted him, goaded him ever onward toward the rising blue mountains beyond the southern horizon.

You should regroup your warriors. They're too strung out. Yes, yes, he should. But out here on the flats, he'd have plenty of warning before the Mogollon could counterattack. He blinked, trying to clear his fuzzy vision. To close up ranks, he'd have to slow down. Slowing meant the Fire Dogs would be that much further ahead. *And, if I lose them . . . if I don't get the prisoners back, or punish the raiders . . . I'll live the rest of my life in disgrace.*

Better to run himself into the ground in pursuit than see the loathing gaze of his family and clan.

White Stone had slowed as the trail led between two low sandstone buttes. Webworm reeled forward, legs shaking almost too badly to hold him up. He steadied himself by grabbing White Stone's arm.

"You're ready to drop flat on your face, War Chief," White Stone said. He glanced uneasily behind them. "And the others need time to catch up. We should rest."

"What . . . what have you found?" Webworm asked.

White Stone pointed to the headlands. "I was afraid they'd come this way. This valley narrows to the south. The way this caprock overhangs the valley, we can't scale it. Anyone headed south must pass through this defile—and I don't like the looks of it."

"Can we go around?"

"It'll take at least a day, maybe two." White Stone shook his head. "If the Fire Dogs set up an ambush here . . ."

Webworm squinted southward. The valley was like a large funnel, and the weathered sandstone caprock dominated the heights. For a long time, he just stared.

"Here, War Chief, drink some water. You need it."

White Stone lifted the skin bag to his lips. The first rush of water was like a blessing from the thlatsinas. It burned down his raw throat and lanced a cold stream into his hot gut. Webworm sucked down another greedy swallow, and then another, until White Stone pulled the nearly empty water bag away.

Webworm wiped his lips, finally able to take a deep breath. Several of his warriors had caught up and stood bent over, panting. "Thank you, White Stone."

"You are pushing too hard, War Chief," White Stone murmured, and turned to study the caprock again.

"Tell me, old friend," Webworm asked, "were you running in my sandals, what would you be doing?"

"Pushing just as hard." White Stone's lips twitched. "I thank my ancestors that I'm only a scout."

The water, with the power of lightning, had given his rubbery muscles another charge. Webworm scowled at the string of staggering warriors coming across the plain. Had he truly run so hard they couldn't keep up?

"All right, let's move. Stay close. White Stone, you go ahead. At the first sign of a trap, call out."

They moved forward, slowly entering the valley. Anxious eyes searched the caprock for a bobbing head, a startled bird, anything out of the ordinary.

Webworm glanced back across the flats at his straggling warriors. How could the Fire Dogs, with their captives, have covered such a distance so quickly?

Because they were rested, well fed, and hadn't run for a day south with the funeral procession, and a day due west to catch their enemy's trail, and finally headed south for another two days.

Webworm prayed the Fire Dogs hadn't anticipated their rapid pursuit, and that they'd pushed ahead for the sanctuary of the distant mountains rather than lingering here at the gap.

From the tracks, it looked as if the Fire Dogs had fifty or sixty warriors, and perhaps thirty more people taken from Talon Town. The distinctive prints of Straight Path–made moccasins and sandals made it easy to separate out the tracks. He could only guess that about twenty of the Straight Path prints belonged to freed slaves. The rest had to be captives.

Webworm halted, staring at the way ahead. It became a rock-lined slit. The perfect place for an ambush.

I can't make a mistake. . . .

"White Stone? Wait." Webworm trotted up to where his scout gazed anxiously at the rocks and brush. Around him were no more than fifteen of his best warriors. The others would take half a hand of time to catch up. "I need a volunteer. Someone must go through alone, see if the way is clear, and shout it out."

"I will." Twinstar came forward. He, too, looked to be on his last legs, but he grinned. Short and skinny, his two front teeth were gone, and the others, yellow and worn, likely to be so in the near future. "No Fire Dog has made an arrow yet that can find my flesh."

"May the thlatsinas go with you, my friend." Webworm patted him on the back. As Twinstar darted into the gap, the rest of his warriors dropped into weary squats, just out of bowshot of the high canyon walls.

Webworm lowered himself to a half-buried rock and rested. One by one, stragglers caught up and flopped down to rest.

A finger of time later, young Twinstar came trotting out of the narrow defile. With a groan, Webworm rose to his feet and plodded forward.

"They're gone," Twinstar told him. "I went through the narrows, climbed the sandstone steps beyond, and saw a body out in the basin. They killed a captive. Red Spark, a youngster from the Ant Clan."

"How long has she been dead?"

Twinstar shrugged. "A day at least. Her eyes are dried out, and she's started to swell."

Webworm sighed, relieved no ambush awaited them, but ever more frustrated at learning the Mogollon were even further ahead than he'd feared. How could they make such rapid progress? Were they being carried by eagles? "But if they made it this far, this fast," he thought aloud, "they might slow down, believe themselves safe, and camp at the Cottonwood Springs just this side of the mountains."

"They're carrying at least two people on litters," White Stone pointed out. "And the captives can't travel that fast. Red Spark must have been slowing them down too much. She's the first they killed, and the only one, so far. The others will be on their last legs."

"Yes, they will. Come on. Let's go. I'll feel better when we're on the other side of this gap."

He followed White Stone and Twinstar into the cool confines of the defile, glancing up nervously. Sheer rock walls topped with brush closed in around them. Anyone caught down here would be unable to fight back. What a place for a massacre. Webworm's eyes darted about like a man walking through a ghost-filled room, expecting invisible hands to attack him.

Past the narrows, he scrambled up the humpbacked layers of sandstone, all worn smooth by the endless torrents of water during the rainy season, and crouched down over Red Spark's body. She'd been shot in the back with an arrow—no doubt as she broke and ran in an attempt to escape. Webworm prodded her body and sniffed. Definitely dead for over a day.

Something nagged at him, and not just the revulsion of seeing the flies crawling on the girl's dried skin. Shot in the back . . . through the lung. Just like Cloud Playing.

The flashback of her limp body in his arms, the sodden weight of her cold flesh, the blood draining out of her and onto . . .

Red Spark was shot through the lung . . . so, where's the blood? The sand beneath her was dry, unstained.

Perplexed, he rose to his feet . . .

And the first deadly arrow cut the air, slicing through Twinstar's body. He screamed and fell, and a second arrow ripped through Webworm's sleeve, then one pierced White Stone's shoulder, the force throwing him to the ground.

Webworm screamed, *"Run!"*

Shouts and whoops rose on the still air as the Fire Dogs leapt up from behind the low sagebrush.

His warriors dashed by as Webworm clawed for his bow with one hand and tried to drag White Stone to his feet with the other. The scout was losing blood fast. Too fast! It drenched the front of his shirt and flowed down his legs. Hideous shrieks split the air as men went down around Webworm, wounded or dying, some shot through with as many as three arrows.

Horror ran like fire through his veins.

"Come on, White Stone! You have to run. I can't carry you! Go!"

His face a mask of pain, White Stone stumbled forward.

Mogollon warriors seemed to be rising right out of the ground. Some raced around the sides, heading for the high points controlling the defile. Webworm's only escape was back that way—and if any of them were going to survive, they had to run for it *now*.

"Hurry! Back! Run for your lives!" Webworm shouted, shoving White Stone before him as he charged for the gap. Already he could see Fire Dogs taking position.

With a curious detachment, he considered his certain death. *Thank the thlatsinas the other warriors didn't catch up. . . .*

He leaped down the sandstone ripples and half dragged the stumbling White Stone into the defile. The feathered shafts of the Mogollon arrows clattered on the rocks around him and thudded into the soft sand of the wash.

"Go back!" he shouted at the warriors coming up the defile. "It's a trap! Go back! *Run!*"

Forty-Seven

Hands and feet bound, Poor Singer sat in front of the fire. High overhead, sullen clouds blotted the afternoon sky and piled over the peaks behind them. Lightning flashed silently in the distance. Raindrops made an eerie hiss on the burning logs. It had been raining for about one hand of time, long enough to soak his tired body to the bones. His every muscle ached. He feared that if he had to stand on his wobbly legs anytime soon, they might just snap in two. The desperate run had siphoned his strength and shredded his brown shirt. The sleeves had big rips, and the hem hung in pieces.

On all sides, his fellows sat, tied with thongs around their necks, heads down, hair plastered against their skulls, and looking every bit as miserable as he felt. Beyond them, the ever vigilant warriors kept watch, arrows nocked in bows.

Gila Monster Cliffs Village sat in the flats at the base of a fragrant pine-whiskered mountain. What a beautiful place: to his right, a shallow river gurgled, the water crystal clear and delicious. Large smooth cobbles filled the channel, but sandy gravel spread over the banks. Enormous bare-branched cottonwoods and oaks crowded the river bottom. They swayed and whispered in the cool storm winds.

Poor Singer glanced around. Guards stood about a hundred hands away, six of them, equally spaced around the fire. Closer, to Poor Singer's right, Cornsilk lay, her head pillowed in Thistle's lap, her black hair spreading over her mother's legs. She'd awakened earlier, but the instant they'd stopped she'd gone right back to sleep. Poor Singer's gut wrenched when he looked at her. The bruise had turned a hideous shade of purplish yellow, and a thick ridge of scar tissue had begun to form. But the swelling had gone down.

What will Jay Bird do to her when he discovers she isn't his granddaughter? And Poor Singer was almost certain she wasn't. Would he kill her in rage? Enslave her? Perhaps return her to Thistle as a reward for Thistle's help in the Talon Town raid?

Night Sun and Ironwood sat side by side, next to Thistle, whispering intimately to each other—though Ironwood had been forbidden to speak to any of them on the run, the guards made no moves to stop him now. Every so often, Ironwood reached out and stroked Cornsilk's hair, then briefly talked with Thistle. Sternlight and Dune sat to Poor Singer's left. Their white shirts had turned a grimy brown in the past eight days. The other captives had immediately been taken to the village, where they would begin serving Mogollon families.

Poor Singer blinked against the windblown raindrops. The village was smaller than he'd expected. Perhaps one hundred people lived here. The houses had been built on the first terrace above the river, the walls constructed from round river cobbles, cemented with mud mortar. A long time ago, they'd been plastered with gray clay, but most of that had cracked off, revealing the crude masonry beneath. The village looked dingy and primitive in comparison to the glorious towns of the Straight Path nation.

He gazed back at the river. Water purled over rocks and about green tufts of moss. Head-high berry and currant brambles choked the banks. Poor Singer squeezed the fingers of his bound hands. It was very beautiful here. If he had to be a slave, this would be better than many other places.

When the breeze blew, spatters of silver light flitted across the dark river bottom like disembodied moth wings. Poor Singer bit his lip and watched them while he contemplated his fate.

The warriors had been chuckling about defeating the war party of Straight Path dogs . . . but could it be true? Did that mean they would never be rescued and would spend their lives as slaves? He'd asked Ironwood, and the big man had smiled faintly and answered, "The rest of you might. I once raided this village, Poor Singer. I killed people, took captives, including Jay Bird's daughter. I doubt he will show me the kindness of slavery." At that point, Night Sun had leaned her shoulder against Ironwood's and they'd stared into each other's eyes for several moments.

They'd had almost no time to talk on the run. The Mogollon had kicked them awake before dawn and forced them to run until long after dusk. They'd eaten and drunk whatever their captors saw fit to give them, then collapsed into dead sleeps.

At least that part of the journey had ended. Some detached part of his brain noted that the rain had finally stopped, though the sky carried the heavy threat of more.

Huge cottonwoods arched over Poor Singer's head, their branches thick with new leaves.

Ironwood shifted to look over his shoulder at Jay Bird and Mourning Dove. They walked down the path toward the river. Both had bathed. Jay Bird's thin face and gray hair shone, and he wore a clean tan shirt. Mourning Dove had braided her black hair. A tiny, delicately built woman, she smiled radiantly, as though happy for the first time in her life. Her plump cheeks glowed pink. She wore a fresh orange dress with two black stripes around the hem, sleeves, and neckline. Mourning Dove stopped two body-lengths behind Dune and Sternlight, as if not wishing to be too close to the renowned holy men.

Poor Singer didn't blame her. Dune had been giving people lethal looks. Every guard who passed near him lifted a hand and made the sign against the Evil Eye, which seemed to please Dune. Despite the fact that he'd been carried the entire way, his old body had grown scrawny and now it looked as if barely enough skin clung to his bones to keep them from falling apart. His white hair dangled in dirty strands about his deeply wrinkled face.

On the journey, Dune had routinely tried to speak with Poor Singer, but the guards never allowed it, and Dune seemed disinclined to say anything to Poor Singer that might be overheard. Poor Singer had longed to speak with him, too. He could tell by the look in Dune's faded eyes that he had important news.

Jay Bird walked around the circle and stood between Thistle and Poor Singer, his eyes fixed on Cornsilk's sleeping face.

Oh, Cornsilk, whatever is going to happen is going to happen now. I wish I could fix this for you.

But he couldn't, not this time.

Jay Bird inhaled a deep breath, exhausted, still flushed with victory, but nonetheless afraid of what this night would bring. After all these years, here he stood, at an ending he'd dreamed of and longed for—at a beginning he couldn't quite comprehend.

He noted the positions of his guards, six around the camp, another ten posted on the high points around Gila Monster Cliffs Village. Then he surveyed the faces of the captives. Dune the Derelict and Night Sun stared at Jay Bird defiantly, while Ironwood and Poor Singer seemed to have accepted whatever the future might bring. Sternlight sat with his dark head bowed, refusing to gaze at Jay Bird, and that caught Jay Bird's attention. A man only refused to look at his enemy when he feared what he might see in his enemy's eyes—or feared what his enemy might see in his own.

I need to watch this man. He had learned that most of the people at Talon Town believed Sternlight to be a witch. All through his long life, Jay Bird had fought a relentless battle against sleep-makers and their foul ways.

Mourning Dove sat warily behind Dune. Over supper, she'd told Jay Bird many things and skillfully kept many to herself. By the way she avoided his questions, he could tell she'd held back a dark powerful secret. Perhaps to use later, if she needed to? But she'd also openly told him that she wouldn't be staying at Gila Monster Cliffs. Though her mother had been Mogollon, she considered the Tower Builders her people. Strange, since she'd shared his prayers before their meal and bowed reverently to his house gods. Apparently, Mourning Dove lived with one foot in each world. She had carefully selected traditions she liked from both the Mogollon and the Tower Builders, and then blended them into a whole that satisfied her. Perhaps that was just her way of surviving childhood—her mother must have been telling her one thing, her father another. Children had curious abilities to make ideas work together, even if they appeared complete opposites to adults.

His gaze shifted. Thistle looked worried. She nervously

stroked Cornsilk's hair. He had offered to have his slaves pour her a bath and give her clean clothing, but she said she would rather wait until Cornsilk woke, so they could enjoy such luxuries together. Thistle loved Cornsilk very much. Of that, Jay Bird had no doubt. But as to everything else . . .

"Let us begin," Jay Bird said, bracing his feet, hands clasped behind his back. "I wish to know the truth. Who will be the first to tell me?"

The captives glanced uneasily at each other, then Dune gave Jay Bird a questioning look. "Which truth?"

"Don't play games with me, holy Derelict! I will have you flayed and burned alive!"

"The question was not a game, Jay Bird. I merely wished to know which story you wanted to hear? About Cornsilk or—"

"Of course, I wish to hear about Cornsilk! Why do you think I rescued her from Talon Town and carried her all the way here?" His angry face softened when he gazed down at Cornsilk again. "Is she my granddaughter? That is what I wish to know. I don't see it in her face. Thistle has told me she believes Cornsilk is—Mourning Dove has told me she's certain Cornsilk is not." Jay Bird lifted his eyes and looked from Mourning Dove to Ironwood. "What do you say, War Chief? Are you this child's father?"

Ironwood took a deep breath, nodded, and said, "I am."

Jay Bird frowned at Cornsilk. "I see you in her. The brows, the shape of the face, the skin. But I do not see Young Fawn in her."

Sternlight propped his bound hands on his drawn-up knees and leaned forward. Wet strands of black hair fell limply over the front of his filthy ritual shirt. "I was present at Cornsilk's birth, Great Chief. I brought her into this world with my own hands and, that same night, delivered her to Beargrass, Thistle's husband. Ironwood is her father. I know this to be true."

Jay Bird rubbed his chin and considered the implications. "And her mother?" Jay Bird's heart pounded with hope. "Was her mother my daughter, Young Fawn?"

Sternlight glanced at Ironwood, Night Sun, and Dune, before shaking his head. "No, Great Chief. Young Fawn was not Cornsilk's mother."

Thistle sucked in a disbelieving breath. "You lie!" She would have shouted it, but she clearly did not wish to wake her daughter. The accusation came out a hoarse whisper. "Right after you gave her to us, Young Fawn's mutilated body was found in the trash mound! Who else could have been the mother?"

Night Sun took a breath. Streaks of dirt and sweat covered her blue dress. Her graying black hair had come loose from its braid and straggled about her triangular face. The four black spirals tattooed on her chin shone in the firelight. "Me."

"You?" Jay Bird demanded sharply. "You mated with the lowly War Chief and didn't induce a miscarriage when you discovered your pregnancy? Ridiculous! Any thinking member of the elite—"

"I tried everything, Jay Bird," she said calmly. "Mugwort leaves, black nightshade berries, cottonroot bark, a mixture of juniper needles and berries. I'm a Healer. I know *exactly* how to induce a miscarriage. But . . ." She sighed and smiled sadly down at Cornsilk. "My daughter insisted upon being born. I conceived Cornsilk when my husband, Crow Beard, was away Trading with the Hohokam. I was terrified, because I knew he would kill her when he returned. And"—she gazed tenderly at Ironwood—"I knew Crow Beard would kill the only man I've ever loved."

Jay Bird glanced around the circle, judging the truth in people's eyes. One by one he read them. No, there was no deceit here. Mourning Dove gave him an "I told you so" look.

Disappointed, he locked eyes with Thistle. "These people say she is not my granddaughter. Did you deliberately mislead me? So that I would attack Talon Town and avenge the wrongs done to you and your clan?"

Thistle shook her head, looking uncomfortable with this disturbing information. "I truly believed Cornsilk was your granddaughter, Jay Bird. But I do not deny that I wished to avenge the deaths of my family. I felt great joy during the raid."

Jay Bird had shared that joy. Because of Thistle, he had pulled off one of the greatest raids in Mogollon history. His name would live in legends. Even if Cornsilk were not his granddaughter, he owed Thistle a great deal. And, yes, from her defiant expression, from the narrowing of her eyes as she spoke, she hadn't purposely deceived him.

He glanced at Cornsilk, resting peacefully on Thistle's lap.

Not my granddaughter. A twinge of pain speared his soul. By the Spirits, he'd prayed for it to be true. But perhaps this disappointment was simply the price of victory. The gods never gave a man all he wanted. He knew that better than most. Besides . . . if Cornsilk were Night Sun's daughter, then Jay Bird had truly taken out his vengeance for the abduction of Young Fawn. A daughter for a daughter.

Thistle sat quietly, now frowning at Sternlight, as if assessing his words.

"Well, then," Jay Bird said, and smiled grimly at Ironwood. The man knew what was coming. Jay Bird could see it on his face. "My only task is to decide what to do with each of you. I—"

"I think," the Derelict said with a tilt of his ancient head, "that you need to listen for a time longer, Jay Bird."

The authoritarian tone rankled. "To *what*, old man?"

Dune smiled, and firelight flickered over his toothless mouth. "To the story of your grandson."

Jay Bird stared. From the corner of his eye, he saw Mourning Dove nod, and he remembered Thistle's story of how Young Fawn's stomach had been slit open, the child stolen from her womb. "This is the 'other' truth you mentioned?"

"It is."

Sternlight started to shake. As he bowed his head, his wet hair straggled around his face like shiny black serpents. He squeezed his eyes closed.

Jay Bird said, "Tell me."

Dune's eyes never wavered. "Young Fawn mated with Crow Beard. Crow Beard loved her desperately. You might say, obsessively."

Night Sun's head suddenly came up and she stared at Dune in a way that made Jay Bird think the news surprised her. It also made him think it might be true. He looked at Thistle and saw her face slacken in understanding.

Ah, here it comes. . . .

"That's why Young Fawn couldn't ask Night Sun's permission for the mating," Thistle said. "That's why she couldn't tell *anyone* about her lover! Blessed Spirits, of course!"

Quietly, Night Sun said, "He loved her, Dune? Are you certain?"

"With all his heart—as much heart as he had, anyway. I think that's why he treated you so badly. He truly wanted to marry Young Fawn and put her in your place."

Night Sun's fists knotted in the fabric of her dress. She closed her eyes.

Jay Bird lifted his chin to Dune. "Go on."

"When Crow Beard discovered Young Fawn was carrying his child, he nearly went mad. You see, despite the fact that he loved Young Fawn, he feared your people's legends more."

"About the child born and hidden away?" Jay Bird said. "The child who would one day return to destroy the Straight Path nation?"

Dune gestured with his bound hands. "Right after Young Fawn told him about the baby, Crow Beard called Sternlight and me into his chamber"—Sternlight nodded—"and asked us to tell him what to do."

"And did you?"

"We tried." Dune shifted, extending his bound legs out in front of him. "He was the Blessed Sun. He wouldn't listen to us. He decided, in a fit of rage and despair, that both the mother and the child had to die." ·

"*What?* He ordered you to kill them *both?*" Jay Bird winced with distaste. *I can't believe it! What is wrong with these Straight Path people?* If he had lain with a slave, he would have willingly adopted the child into his household. "Why?"

"Crow Beard feared that if Young Fawn lived she would someday whisper the story to the wrong person and it would get back to Night Sun."

Jay Bird turned to her. "And what would you have done?"

The cottonwoods behind Night Sun swayed in a gust of wind, creaking and moaning, and shadows danced over her taut face. What a stately, elegant woman. Even days of running had not diminished her beauty.

She said, "I refused to allow my own daughter, Cloud Playing, to marry Webworm because he was half Mogollon. His mother had been taken as slave by your people when very young. I would never have allowed such a birth to take place. My duty would have been clear. I would have divorced Crow Beard, and probably I would have ordered Young Fawn's death, as well as her child's. *I* fear the legends, too."

Dune continued, "Sternlight and I suspected that. It took two days, but we talked Crow Beard into letting Young Fawn and the child live—with the promise that they would both be sent away after the child's birth."

"Why would you wish your enemies to survive?"

Dune's brows arched. He kicked sand with his bound feet. "Because I don't believe your prophecies. And, though the child was barely a moon old inside Young Fawn's womb, I *sensed* something extraordinary about him. I suggested to Crow Beard that he leave until after the child was born so that the rumors would die down. By the time he returned, we promised him that both Young Fawn and the baby would be gone. He'd never have to hear of or see them again."

Sternlight paled. "Though on his deathbed, Crow Beard ordered the child killed. It was his last order."

Jay Bird nodded. The news did not surprise him. Crow Beard had been a ruthless adversary, and proud of his ability to murder without remorse. Jay Bird had despised him for it. "What did he say?"

"He called the boy 'Jay Bird's brood.' In the end, I think Crow Beard feared your prophecies more deeply than any of us realized."

Jay Bird spread his feet to brace himself. "And?"

Is the boy alive, or did they obey Crow Beard's order?

Dune and Sternlight looked at each other. Jay Bird noticed that Ironwood sat forward, listening intently.

Through a tired exhalation, Dune said, "The boy is alive. After his birth, Sternlight gave the infant to me. I, in turn, gave the boy to a Trader named Sitting-in-the-Sky, to take to a very old friend of mine named Black—"

"*Me?*" Poor Singer asked in a whisper. His soft brown eyes had gone huge and vulnerable. He wet his chapped lips. "*Are you talking about me?*"

Dune nodded calmly. "I'd planned on telling you. Eventually."

Mourning Dove put a hand to her throat as if to ease a pain there, and said, "It was only a matter of days after the youth's arrival that Talon Town was attacked and the slaves freed. The prophecies . . . they came true!"

Jay Bird lowered himself to the sand beside Poor Singer and

studied his thin face and beaked nose, his tall, skinny frame, and long black hair. Could this . . . And then it came to him. "Blessed gods," he murmured. "You don't look anything like Young Fawn . . . but you do look a great deal like—like *me* . . . forty summers ago."

Poor Singer's open mouth trembled before he clamped it shut. He searched Jay Bird's eyes, not certain what to say or do. He, too, saw the resemblance. "Dune?" he begged as he turned. "Why didn't you ever tell me? Why didn't Black Mesa tell me? Did my mother, Snow Mountain, know?"

"Yes, of course, she did. But we all wanted you alive. If the truth were known—even by you, Poor Singer—there was a good chance you would be killed. If not by Crow Beard himself, by one of the other First People. They would have been just as frightened of you as Crow Beard was."

"You could have told me!" Poor Singer yelled. "It's my life we're talking about!"

"Exactly my point!" Dune snapped. "Your life!"

Poor Singer deflated and looked around the fire. He winced at the sight of Night Sun's lowered brows and hard stare.

Tentatively, Jay Bird reached out and placed a hand on Poor Singer's shoulder. "Is it true? Are you my grandson?"

Poor Singer stared at him open-mouthed. "If . . . if Dune says so. I believe him. I'm just very confused. My mother always told me that Sitting-in-the-Sky was my father. No one even hinted to me that . . . though mother never said a bad word about Crow Beard. She'd always insisted that people who did were just misinformed or bitter. She did everything she could to make me think well of Crow Beard."

Poor Singer squeezed his eyes closed and kept silent for a long time.

Jay Bird's grip on his shoulder tightened. The boy *did* look like him. And deep inside he felt the truth of Dune's words. This was Young Fawn's child. His daughter had given him a grandson. It didn't help with the succession, but a member of his family had come home. A flood of warmth went through Jay Bird. He reached for the hafted knife on his belt. As he sawed through Poor Singer's bonds, he said, "Don't be afraid, Poor Singer. At least, no more afraid than I am."

Jay Bird stood and signaled to his guards. The six men closed in around the fire. Howler had a worried look on his scarred face, as if skeptical of the truth of the story. "Help Thistle and her daughter to one of the guest chambers," Jay Bird ordered. "Take all the others and lock them in the western pen. I will decide what to do with them after consulting more with my grandson."

Howler nodded stiffly. "Yes, my chief."

"Poor Singer, if you will come with me, I will introduce you to—"

"May I stay for just a few moments?" the youth asked. "To speak with Dune?"

Jay Bird glanced at the ancient holy man. Dune had his forearms propped on his knobby knees, and a glint shone in his watery eyes. "Of course, Poor Singer. When you are ready, Howler will show you to my chambers."

Jay Bird walked around the fire, feeling a deep sense of longing. He needed time. And needed to hear Downy Girl's thoughts. Her wisdom had guided him for more than twenty-five summers. She would be as astonished as he that Young Fawn had left a son.

He started up the trail for the village.

Darkness hugged the rolling hills, but starlight gleamed from the pines that whiskered the mountain behind the village. Tears blurred Poor Singer's eyes as he looked at Dune. "I had a *right* to know, Dune!"

Dune didn't respond. He sat watching the guard saw through the yucca cord binding his hands and wrists. Once the guards had finished, Dune grunted to his feet and hobbled over to take Poor Singer by the arm. He led him down to two large rocks by the side of the river.

"Here," Dune said softly. "If we talk in low voices, the sound of the river will cover them. Sit down, Poor Singer."

Poor Singer lowered himself to the cold rock.

Mourning Dove hovered in the background like a wounded ghost, her gaze fixed on Poor Singer as though her very life might depend upon him.

Poor Singer whispered, "Why didn't you tell me, Dune? Why didn't my mother tell me?"

Dune eased down atop the other rock, and a faint smile turned his toothless mouth. "The time hadn't come," he said gently. "Black Mesa and I had decided that I would tell you after you had completed your Singer's training. Unfortunately, I never had a chance."

"Oh, Dune." Poor Singer flapped his arms. "I don't know what to say. I feel . . . lost."

"Well, don't. You've just been found. By your real family. And," he said, and squinted at the muscular guards in their black-and-white capes who were cutting the bonds of the other captives, "if I live through this, I'll gladly finish your training. That is, if you still wish me to be your teacher."

Poor Singer tugged a blade of grass from where it grew in a crack in the rock and tore it in half, then in quarters. "Dune, I don't know what to do. My whole world has been turned upside down. I don't know anything about my real mother. My real father was a—a monster! I even lost my nation tonight. I can never go home. You know that, don't you? If anyone were to find out that I was Jay Bird's grandson . . ." He couldn't finish it. His throat constricted with grief. "And I miss my mother and Black Mesa, Dune. I *want* to go home."

Dune let out a breath and frowned at the river. Sparkles of firelight reflected from the black surface. "I'm sorry, Poor Singer. At least you are alive, and you—"

Howler tramped across the sand toward them. "Are you finished talking?" he asked Poor Singer.

Poor Singer glanced at Dune. "I guess so. For now."

"Then come on, old man," Howler said, and gestured to the group of captives ringed by guards near the fire. "Let's go."

Dune patted Poor Singer's arm, and said, "We will speak more of this later," slid off the rock, and walked toward the fire.

Howler called, "Mousetail? Carry the injured girl. Show her and her mother to the southern guest chamber. Foxbat, you and your men take the rest to the western pen. I'll bring up the rear, and show the boy to Jay Bird's rooms."

Mousetail knelt by Cornsilk, and Thistle said, "Be gentle, please!"

Mousetail carefully lifted and carried Cornsilk up the trail with Thistle walking closely behind him.

The remaining guards, arrows nocked, closed in around Dune, Sternlight, Ironwood, and Night Sun, and herded them up the hill. Ironwood kept glancing around, as if seeking an opening for escape.

Poor Singer couldn't convince his legs to move. When he finally did, his knees almost buckled. He caught his balance and walked across the sand with Howler ten paces behind him.

As he neared the trailhead, Mourning Dove met him. Her eyes shone like stars. She glanced back at Howler, then gripped Poor Singer's arm and hissed, "*Ask Sternlight about your mother. He murdered her! I saw it all! He stabbed her in the chest and cut you from her womb! Ask him! Ask!*" Then she raced up the trail with her orange dress flying about her legs.

Numb, his pulse pounding, Poor Singer watched her blend into the darkness, then he sat down in the middle of the trail and dropped his head in his hands.

Howler stopped beside him. "What's the matter?"

"Nothing, I just . . . I wish to stay down here for a time. Is that all right?"

Howler gave him a distrustful look, dark and boding ill if he tried anything suspicious. "Yes. But not for too long. I'll help Foxbat with the captives, then I'll return for you and take you to Jay Bird's chambers." He paused. "You won't run off, now, will you?"

Poor Singer shook his head. "No. I won't. I just need time to think."

"Very well."

Howler's steps faded as he climbed the trail toward the dingy village.

Poor Singer ran his hands over the damp soil of the trail. Fragments of the conversation wheeled through his head.

Everything he had once believed about himself was false, his family, his village, even his people—and the men and women who had deceived him were his most trusted loved ones. He couldn't reconcile the two facts. They tugged at his soul until he feared they might rip it in half.

In a hoarse whisper, he said, "Blessed thlatsinas, who am I? *What* am I?"

Forty-Eight

Hummingbird is the Creator, Poor Singer," Jay Bird said and pointed to the painted bowl in the rear of the chamber. The lavender glow of dawn streamed through the window to Poor Singer's left and threw a long rectangle across the gray stone floor. The beautiful animals painted on the bowls that lined the wall seemed to spring to life, especially the black wings of Hummingbird. "Every beat of her wings gives breath to the world, and if her wings ever stop beating the world will suffocate. That is why we pray to her and offer her corn pollen, to give her strength."

"Thank you for telling me, Grandfather." Poor Singer listened inside his heart for some resonance of the story, some hint that his soul was Mogollon, but he could find only a confused Straight Path youth. On the wall above the Hummingbird bowl, an array of baskets hung in shadow. They rattled as Wind Baby sniffed about the room.

Poor Singer took another bite of bread. He sat across the fire from Jay Bird, finishing his morning meal of roasted venison and toasted squash-seed bread. At home, in Windflower Village, they rarely had venison. It should have tasted particularly sweet and rich to Poor Singer, but he'd lost his appetite.

Downy Girl sat to Jay Bird's right. She'd been fawning over Poor Singer, stuffing his skinny carcass with food, forcing him to drink bitter willow-bark tea, just in case some of the evil Spirits from the Straight Path lands lingered in his body. She'd even given him a magnificent new red-and-green shirt to wear. As he ate, Poor Singer looked down at the soft cloth. Two hands of time ago, he had bathed in the river. His long black hair gleamed, and his deeply tanned skin had a glossy sheen. But despair lived in his heart. He kept trying to smile as he ate, but his soul floated somewhere outside his body, looking down upon this strange new world.

A frightening wrongness pervaded everything. Like icy wind, it whispered in the depths of Poor Singer's soul, warning of disaster to come, promising horrors much worse than any he had yet witnessed. He couldn't shake off the sensation.

Jay Bird leaned back on his deerhide and sipped from his cup of dried gooseberry tea. Downy Girl, her long gray hair coiled on top of her head, sat beside the Chief. She wore a black cape about her gaunt shoulders. She looked very old. Her cheeks, which once must have been pink and full, had gone hollow. A white film covered her brown eyes. She suffered from the aching joints disease. All night long, she had moaned in her sleep.

Downy Girl's wrinkled mouth drew down in disappointment when Poor Singer set aside his half-finished bowl of venison and bread and picked up his cup of gooseberry tea.

"You well? Yes, Poor Singer?" she asked in her broken Straight Path tongue.

"I'm just full, Downy Girl. It was a delicious breakfast. Thank you." He frowned at the green-and-red geometric designs on his shirt. They looked bright against the gray floor.

Jay Bird turned his teacup in his hands. "You look sad, Poor Singer."

He lifted a shoulder. "Not sad. I feel hollow. The people I loved most lied to me. All of my life, I believed my mother was Snow Mountain. The man I respected most in all the world—Black Mesa—told me stories about my dead father, claiming he'd been a Trader." He sipped his tea and swallowed. "I know they must have thought they were doing the right thing, but they weren't, Jay Bird. I just don't understand how they could have deceived me for so long."

Downy Girl reached out and placed a hand gently on Poor Singer's shoulder. "We not lie to you, Poor Singer. I promise."

Poor Singer smiled weakly. "You've been very kind, Downy Girl, but I feel like an outsider here."

"Not long. Today we send word to all villages that grandson has come home. Then, on Summer Solstice, we make you formally a member of clan. You be surprised to know how many cousins you have. Each wish to speak with you, to welcome you to their hearts."

A sick qualm of dread filled him. "I don't even speak their language, Downy Girl. They'll whisper about me behind their hands, and I won't be able to understand a word of it."

"You learn." She gently patted his arm. "Six moons, perhaps a little more, and you speak well enough. You see."

Poor Singer bowed his head and his black hair fell over his shoulders. He toyed with his cup. "I'm sorry. I'm not sure I can stay here. Not if . . . those captives outside are my friends. Some of them, I love. If something happened to them . . ."

Jay Bird's face fell. Poor Singer saw it from the corner of his eyes. Jay Bird had been elated about the perfectly executed raid and the capture of Talon Town's most esteemed citizens. But Poor Singer had to try to save his friends.

Tersely, Jay Bird said, "They are slaves now, Poor Singer, part of the spoils of war. You understand this?"

Poor Singer finished his tea and set the cup on the stone floor in front of him. "Yes, but what's going to happen to them? Have you decided?"

Jay Bird's brows drew together at the hurt in Poor Singer's voice. "Not yet. I'll treat each differently. But I assure you, none of their fates will be pleasant."

Poor Singer jerked a nod of acceptance, and Downy Girl reached out and touched his arm. "Perhaps, something might be worked out for a few of them." She winked. "This old woman; your grandmother, she's pretty important around here."

Jay Bird scowled at her. "*Which* few?"

If Mogollon society worked at all like Straight Path society, the fate of captives was ultimately decided by the Matron. Jay Bird looked uneasy about the sentimental way Downy Girl gazed at Poor Singer.

She lifted gray eyebrows. "I think this new grandson, he be able to help you make this decision. We talk afterward, Jay Bird."

"Very well." Jay Bird pulled a stick from the wood pile and savagely prodded the low flames. Sparks shot out and smoke billowed toward the soot-coated roof.

Poor Singer shoved his empty cup around with his forefinger.

Jay Bird had probably been looking forward to watching all of them die slow deaths in retribution for the deaths of his own people at Straight Path hands.

Jay Bird gave him a measuring sidelong glance. "What were you thinking, Poor Singer?"

Poor Singer looked up. "What will happen to Cornsilk? And Thistle?"

He had gone to see Cornsilk half a hand of time ago and found her curled asleep in red-and-blue blankets, her black hair streaming around her. The run had been especially hard on Cornsilk. With all the bouncing and jostling, she'd gotten little rest. She needed all she could get now. But Poor Singer felt almost desperate to speak with her.

"Downy Girl and I discussed that early this morning while you were out bathing. They may go free, if they wish," Jay Bird replied. "Though I doubt they will."

Poor Singer blinked. "Why not?"

Jay Bird made a sweeping gesture with his arm. "By now word of Thistle's treachery has spread far and wide. She can't go home. Not ever again. She and Cornsilk are much safer here with us than among the Straight Path dogs. Oh, Thistle might be able to find some outlying village that would take her. But within a few moons, the First People would hear of her presence and they would certainly kill her."

Poor Singer clutched his cup hard. He hadn't thought of that. "Yes, I'm sure that's true."

Downy Girl glanced at Jay Bird, then at Poor Singer. Her head tilted. "You like Thistle and Cornsilk to stay here, Grandson?"

"I know that this may not please you," Poor Singer said with trepidation. "You have, perhaps, already been thinking about young Mogollon women who might be suitable for me. But I wish you to know I love Cornsilk. Wherever she is, that's where I want to be."

Downy Girl sighed, as if she *had* been thinking about suitable matches, but she forced a smile to her wrinkled face. "Then I hope she choose to stay here with us. And what of other captives, Poor Singer? What you wish done with them?"

Jay Bird prodded the fire again, his jaw stuck out at a hard angle.

Poor Singer said, "G-Grandfather, what do you recommend?"

Just being asked for his advice seemed to soothe Jay Bird's ire. The dignified, white-haired Chief looked up, and the set of his jaw eased. "The only one I will not give up is Ironwood. I will leave it to you to decide the fate of the others, but—"

"Oh, thank you, Grandfather! I—"

"*Wait.*" Jay Bird held up a hand. "I caution you to make your choices wisely. Hear me. I have done you no favor, Poor Singer. Night Sun, as Matron of Talon Town, was involved in every decision to attack us, including the attack where your mother, Young Fawn, was taken slave, where your grandmother was brutally murdered, and where the loved ones of many others in this village died. If you free her after the misery she has caused, it will be very difficult for people here to forgive you."

Poor Singer thought about that, then nodded. "I understand."

"And, as Sunwatcher, Sternlight must have known and blessed many, if not all, of those raids. Dune, on the other hand, is our most valuable captive. If we offer to trade him back to the Straight Path nation, we might be able to gain fifty, or even a hundred, of our own people in return. There are many here at Gila Monster Cliffs who would give their very lives to see those family members again." Jay Bird paused to gauge Poor Singer's response. Poor Singer just gazed back in misery. "Think wisely, Grandson. The decisions you make will cling to your hands like boiled pine pitch. Provided, of course, that Downy Girl approves them."

Poor Singer drew up his knees, propped his arms across them, and braced his forehead. He felt empty. If he asked for Night Sun, Dune, and Sternlight to be released, as he must, then he would have no home here. His own cousins, aunts, uncles, perhaps even his grandparents, would despise him for it. In revenge for the loss of their loved ones, a few might consider murdering him.

But he couldn't go home to his mother, either. Eventually, the truth of his birth would come out, and if the drought went on too long, or the corn withered on the stalks, hateful eyes would turn his way. He might be the death of everyone in Windflower Village, while Thistle would be a hero here at Gila

Monster Cliffs, and Cornsilk would be accepted because of Thistle. No haven existed for Poor Singer. No one, anywhere, would take him in. Oh, Dune might, but Poor Singer wouldn't put Dune in such a dangerous position.

He toyed with the hem of his shirt, creasing it with his fingernails. He desperately needed to speak with Cornsilk.

And with Sternlight. I must confront him about what Mourning Dove said. I don't believe it, but . . .

Poor Singer sucked in a breath. "Grandfather, would you tell me about my mother? What she was like? How she died? No one has told me these things. Perhaps if I knew more, I would be able to make decisions more clearly."

Downy Girl patted Jay Bird on the leg and rose to her feet, her knees crackling, and her face tensing with pain. "You two should speak alone. I be close, in next room, if you need me." She hobbled through the northern door into a splash of sunlight. Her white hair sparkled, then she vanished from Poor Singer's view.

Jay Bird leaned forward, dipped his teacup into the pot to fill it and gave Poor Singer a stiff-lipped, almost hurt, look. "Young Fawn was captured when she was six summers old, Poor Singer. All I remember is a bright-eyed little girl with a smile that melted my heart. Her favorite game was hoop-and-stick, and her best friend was named Pollen."

A frail smile came to his elderly face. He drew an imaginary circle around the room. "They used to chase each other around and around in here. I remember because Young Fawn was prone to breaking things. If she handled something, there was a good chance it would wind up shattered on the floor. If she ran, she frequently tripped and fell. She was awkward for her age, but a very beautiful child. She used to . . ." His smile faded. "She used to go to sleep at night, cradled in the crook of my left arm while I finished supper."

Jay Bird closed his mouth and his jaw set again. Hatred filled his eyes. Hatred for a people and nation that Poor Singer loved.

Poor Singer smoothed away a bead of tea that clung to the lip of his cup. "Could you tell me how she died?"

"I heard she was murdered, stabbed twice in the breast, her child—you—cut from her womb. Her body was discovered in a trash mound outside of Talon Town. That's all I know, Poor

Singer. Thistle told me most of those things. Perhaps you should discuss this with her or Mourning Dove. They will certainly know more than I do."

"Grandfather, who would wish to kill my mother?"

"Any Straight Path dog who knew she was my daughter." Jay Bird's brow lined. "Thistle said that War Chief Ironwood hunted for the murderer, but couldn't find him. It happened so long ago, I doubt anyone knows now."

Poor Singer laced his fingers around his right knee. *Mourning Dove claims she does, but is this some game I don't understand?*

Jay Bird said, "I tried to rescue Young Fawn, Poor Singer. You must believe me. I tried four times. I just . . . couldn't. Ironwood, always Ironwood." His eyes slitted at those defeats.

"Thank you, Grandfather, for sharing your memories. They mean more to me than I can tell you. All I have of my mother is a vision of her through your eyes. I hope you will not mind me asking you a thousand questions over the next few sun cycles."

"I suspect I will come to enjoy that very much, Poor Singer."

Poor Singer shoved his cup across the floor with his thumb. "Grandfather, I would like to speak with my fr—with your prisoners. If that would be all right?"

Jay Bird went still, as if he feared treachery, but when he gazed into Poor Singer's face, he sighed. "They are your friends. Of course you may speak with them."

"Thank you. I promise I will—"

"Jay Bird?" Downy Girl called as she ducked through the doorway, her wrinkled face taut. Light reflected oddly from the white film over her eyes. The orbs resembled frozen ponds. She spoke in a rattle of Mogollon.

Poor Singer knew very little Mogollon, but enough to recognize Jay Bird's question when he asked, "Who?"

"Mourning Dove and her son."

Poor Singer got to his feet and bowed respectfully to Jay Bird. "I will return later, Grandfather. Thank you, again."

"I look forward to more discussions, Grandson," Jay Bird said, and shifted to a cross-legged position, straightening his shirt and sighing, then speaking wearily in Mogollon.

As Poor Singer neared Downy Girl, she placed a hand warmly on his shoulder and gestured for him to duck through the doorway first. He smiled, and did, and saw Mourning Dove standing with Swallowtail. They had the same plump cheeks and brown eyes, though Swallowtail stood three heads taller than his mother. His father must have been a tall man.

"Good morning," Poor Singer said.

Mourning Dove didn't answer. She just stared at him. Swallowtail smiled and said, "Good morning, Poor Singer. I hope you are well."

"Yes, thank you, Swallowtail," he answered, and stepped out into the sunlight, onto the trail that led in front of the buildings and down the slope to the pen. Poor Singer hurried away.

Mourning Dove's words last night had left him floundering, unable to sleep. Despite his exhaustion from the long, tortuous run, he'd squirmed in his blankets, trying to convince himself to forget about it, that she must be lying, but he couldn't find a reason for such dishonesty. What did she have to gain by telling him that story? Did she just wish to wound his soul?

The sun-speckled trail snaked its way toward the gurgling stream and the pen. Two women with large baskets on their backs passed him, smiling politely but warily. Three children scampered at their heels. They whispered and pointed at Poor Singer with crooked fingers.

Poor Singer took the left fork in the trail just before the stream and carefully used the stones to cross, his arms out for balance. Crystal clear water gurgled and cascaded around his feet. This lush place was so green, with its trees and berry bushes and tumbling water! Thinking back to Windflower Village's buff sandstone and the brooding Great Warriors, it was like stepping into another world. The scents of water and mud encircled Poor Singer as he walked down.

Four warriors guarded the pen, one on the roof and three around the base. Howler stood in front, his body cloaked by the dappled shadows of a huge cottonwood tree.

The pen, built partly into the side of the stream terrace, had neither windows nor doors. A circular hole in the roof provided entry, but a person needed a ladder to get down into the chamber. Poor Singer looked around and spied the ladder resting against a tree ten paces away.

Howler squinted at Poor Singer, and his ugly facial scars

twitched. Poor Singer watched him blandly. He wore a brown shirt with fringes on the hem.

"Good Morning, Howler. My grandfather has given me permission to speak with the prisoners. Please lower the ladder."

Howler ground his teeth as though doubtful whether he actually had permission, but as he scrutinized Poor Singer he seemed to decide that it didn't matter.

Isn't it nice to know that nobody considers me a threat? The thought made Poor Singer sigh.

Howler nodded to one of the other warriors and issued a sharp command in the Mogollon tongue. The warrior leaped to obey, grabbing the ladder, and tossing it to the man on the roof, who promptly dropped it through the entry. Murmurs rose from inside when it thudded on the ground.

Poor Singer thought he could make out Ironwood's deep voice, and a tingling pain shot through him: *"The only one I will not give up is Ironwood."* Poor Singer had seen on the journey how very much Night Sun and Ironwood loved each other, and he wondered what would happen to Night Sun when Ironwood . . . when he . . . Poor Singer swallowed hard. If he couldn't even think it, how could he stand by and watch it happen?

The guard watched Poor Singer through slitted eyes, but Poor Singer ignored him. His damp sandals barely made a sound on the plaster as he headed for the ladder. He stood for a moment, looking down through the hole into the shadowed interior, his heart thumping. The scent of sour sweat rose.

What would he do if Sternlight admitted to killing his mother? How could Poor Singer ask his grandfather to free his daughter's murderer? How could he find it in himself to want to ask?

Poor Singer gripped the side poles and stepped down to the first rung.

Jay Bird calmly sipped his gooseberry tea as Mourning Dove and her tall skinny son settled on the opposite side of the fire. They both wore fresh tan clothing, simple but clean. They looked rested. Which was more than Jay Bird could say for himself. His eyes had a puffy look, and his muscles trembled when he exerted the slightest effort. Swallowtail's shoulder-length black hair framed his moonish face and beak nose. Mourning Dove's plump cheeks shone with perspiration.

"What is it you wish to see me about?" he asked, resting his teacup on his right knee.

Mourning Dove leaned forward. "Great Chief, I came to tell you that my son and I will be going home soon. In a few days."

"To the northern Tower Builders?"

"Yes, but first, I wished you to know all that we have done these past sun cycles for you and your people."

Jay Bird sighed. He knew that tone. It meant: "And after I tell you, I expect a reward." "Go on."

Mourning Dove placed an arm around the back of her son. The boy's eyes had an inhuman gleam, like a predator bird about to strike. "Because my mother was born of your people, I have always believed in your prophecies of a savior, a child born and hidden away, a boy who would grow to a man and destroy the Straight Path nation. For many summers, I have been diligently working to make that prophecy come true. I did not know of Poor Singer. I believed the savior to be Webworm. He—"

"Webworm? The new War Chief of Talon Town?"

She nodded. "Yes, he is half Mogollon, you see. And though my mother was Mogollon, I believe it is correct to trace ancestry through the male—as my father's people do. That made Webworm the most likely man to fulfill the holy prophecies. I realized this at a very early age. Though I could have escaped many times during my youth, before Swallowtail was born, I didn't, because I—"

"Well, it doesn't matter now. I suspect Webworm's dead, and all of your efforts have come to naught. So why are you telling me this?"

Mourning Dove wet her lips nervously and glanced around the chamber for a few moments, as if collecting her thoughts. "Great Chief, I worked very hard to depose Snake Head. I convinced him that he had to kill his own mother and sister to make sure he was not deposed! Not that it took much effort. He hated both of them. But I did these things so that Webworm's mother would become the Blessed Matron of Talon Town, and her son would rule—"

"Mourning Dove, I—"

"Are you blind?" she blurted. "Even if Webworm is dead, his mother will be ruling Talon Town, and she is demented! Now is the time to attack the whole canyon! When I return home to my people, I will tell them this same thing. Neither of our peoples alone could do it, but together—"

Jay Bird cringed. "You wish *me* to ally myself with the Tower Builders?" They were barbarians. Primitive and savage.

Mourning Dove's spine stiffened. She lifted her chin and eyed him severely. "Perhaps you would rather wait until the Straight Path dogs recover from your raid and decide to attack you?"

Jay Bird swirled his tea and watched the pale green waves wash the sides of the cup. "No. I wouldn't."

"Then allow me to set up the alliance! I worked with Cone, carrying messages between him and Snake Head. I am *good* at manipulating people."

"I'm sure you are, but a warrior would be far more suitable for such a position."

"Then send a warrior, too! But allow me to coordinate between your warrior and the Tower Builders. I speak the Tower Builders' tongue. Do you have a warrior who knows their language?"

Jay Bird watched her thoughtfully. Were the Straight Path people such fools that they hadn't seen this woman's intelligence and cunning, this deadly spider in their midst? "Allow you to coordinate? The answer is no, and since you believe yourself a Tower Builder, I shouldn't have to explain why. Your people trace ancestry through the men. Having a woman as my go-between would weaken my position."

She glanced at her son. "Great Chief, I will be honest with you. I need to return to my people with something to offer. I have spent almost my whole life as a slave. My son was born in slavery. No one there will remember or care about us. But if we return to the Tower Builders as your emissaries, bearing an offer of friendship, and a plan to join forces to attack—"

"Mourning Dove," Jay Bird said with an irritated sigh, "these are your problems, not mine, or my people's."

Swallowtail whispered, "I told you."

Mourning Dove's jaw set. She nodded. "Great Chief, we feared you might say something like that. Then let us offer you something in return."

Jay Bird shifted restlessly. What was this all about? What more could she, a former slave, possibly offer? "I have a very busy day ahead of me, Mourning Dove, I—"

"Yes, I'm sure you do." She sighed, and her round face tightened.

Her son smiled, as though happy about this twist of events.

Mourning Dove turned back to Jay Bird and a dark fire entered her eyes. She bent forward. "Great Chief, if you will allow me to act as your go-between with the Tower Builders, I will tell you the name of your daughter's murderer."

Forty-Nine

Poor Singer stepped to the hard-packed dirt floor of the chamber and gave his eyes time to adjust to the dimness. Despite the warmth outside, this room remained cold. As his vision cleared, he saw that it spread about two body-lengths square. In front of him, Night Sun sat beside Ironwood, his muscular arms around her. Her blue dress had rips everywhere, on the sleeves and skirt, across the stomach, where brown skin showed through. Her graying black hair hung in tangles around her triangular face. Ironwood's tan doeskin shirt was filthy, stained with soot, dirt and sweat, but it looked intact. Dune and Sternlight sat against the wall to Poor Singer's left. Their long white robes had turned a dirty gray-brown that blended with the shadows.

Night Sun straightened at the sight of Poor Singer. "Did you bring any food? Or some water?"

"No. Haven't you been fed?"

"Not since yesterday at noon." She sank back against Ironwood and let out a disappointed breath. "I'd give anything for a big cup of water."

Ironwood kissed her dirty temple. "Soon. Jay Bird is known for his kindness to prisoners."

"Besides," Dune said grimly, "he doesn't want us to die today. He wants us to live, so he can kill us slowly before the entire village."

Ironwood actually smiled, and Poor Singer wondered where he found the strength, knowing as he must, what was to come. He looked up, and Poor Singer let his gaze drift over that calm oval face, noting the flat nose, slanting brows, and pale golden skin—so much like Cornsilk's.

Ironwood asked, "Has he told you his intentions?"

"He told me that . . . that I could decide the fate of everyone . . . except you, Ironwood."

Ironwood lowered his head and nodded. "He is more generous than I would ever have expected." Sincere gratitude laced his voice. He tightened his arms around Night Sun. "You will, I hope, see that everyone else goes free?"

"Yes, of course."

"Thank you, Poor Singer!"

Night Sun closed her eyes and buried her face against Ironwood's broad chest. Her shoulders shook. Ironwood stroked her back, murmuring inaudibly against her hair, and at the soft sound of her cries Poor Singer's soul went cold.

He turned to Sternlight. The Sunwatcher met Poor Singer's eyes. Long black hair fell over his grimy robe, but the light had gone from his dark eyes. He just looked weary.

"What is it, Poor Singer?" Sternlight asked.

"Did you kill my mother?" Poor Singer hadn't planned to blurt it out, but now that he had, everyone in the room went deathly silent.

Sternlight's face slackened. He stared at Poor Singer nakedly. "Who told you—"

"That doesn't matter. Did you do it?"

"No, of course, he didn't!" Ironwood snapped. "How could you believe such malicious gossip? Sternlight has never hurt anything, or anyone, he—"

Poor Singer made a chopping gesture with his hand to silence Ironwood. "Answer me, Sternlight."

The wrinkles around Dune's eyes deepened. He let out a tired breath. "It's time he knew the truth, Sternlight."

Sternlight nodded and gripped handfuls of his long black hair as if to remind himself that he was awake and not lost in some terrible nightmare. Very softly, he replied, "Please, listen to me, Poor Singer. Before Crow Beard left for the lands of the Hohokam, he told me he had changed his mind. He was not going to keep his word to Dune that both you and your mother could live. He said he would let you live only at the cost of your mother's life. It was either you or her. If Young Fawn lived, he could always deny he'd had anything to do with her. There wouldn't be any proof, since you'd be dead. And what was a slave's word against that of the Blessed Sun? Crow Beard had grown wild and frantic. He feared Night Sun was planning on divorcing him and leaving him with nothing. He didn't know what was right any longer—if he ever had known."

Ironwood released Night Sun and sat forward. "What are you saying?"

Sternlight hesitated, then his gaze focused solely on Poor Singer. "I—I was not in this world, Poor Singer. For sixteen days I'd been walking and talking with the gods. The day your mother died was the day the thlatsinas first visited me. They appeared in a pillar of light and walked at my side down the sacred Turning-Back-the-Sun trail. I didn't want to believe the things they told me, but I—"

Poor Singer spread his feet to brace himself. *"Did you kill my mother?"*

Dune put his gnarled hands over his eyes. Ironwood and Night Sun sat deathly silent.

"I—I begged the thlatsinas to take the responsibility away from me. To save me from having to choose between you and your mother. But they told me I had to do it. The Wolf Thlatsina revealed a Dream to me. In it, I saw that Young Fawn's life would assure that the Straight Path nation would die a lingering death of decay and corruption—" Sternlight reached out to Poor Singer with both hands. "—but that your birth would be the beginning of a new age. A time when the old would be swept away and a clean bright future would unfold for those who dared to seek it. It would require a different way of life, yes, but—"

"So . . ." Tears clutched at Poor Singer's throat. He fought to keep his voice steady. "You killed my mother?"

Sternlight's extended hands trembled. He drew them back and tucked them beneath his arms. After a time, he nodded. "Yes."

Dune said, "And he saved you, Poor Singer."

Poor Singer couldn't find any words. He tipped his face toward the ceiling and closed his eyes.

Ironwood said, "Sternlight, why didn't you tell me? I would have found a way to help you. We could have gotten both mother and child away. I don't know how, but I would have figured something out."

"You were carrying enough burdens at the time, Ironwood. I had to make the decision alone."

As if that beautiful tormented voice conjured within Poor Singer the visions Sternlight saw himself, he had a momentary glimpse of a handsome young man moving in the gods' shadows, trying to deny what the divine voices were telling him, knowing he couldn't.

Would I have had more strength than Sternlight? Could I have told the gods that I didn't believe them? That there had to be another way? That even gods couldn't possibly know everything?

Hoarsely, he asked, "Dune, did you know about this?"

"Not until the night that Sternlight placed you in my arms. I was in Talon Town at the time, for the Solstice celebrations. He told me then what he'd done . . . and *why.*"

Night Sun said, "How like Crow Beard to saddle you with the duty, Sternlight. He was such a coward!"

"All that is past now." Dune's sandals scraped the floor as he shifted. "Poor Singer?"

He lowered his head and gazed at Dune. The old man's sparse white hair glowed in the dim light streaming down through the roof entry. "What is it, Dune?"

For the first time, Dune spoke to him as though he were an adult, an equal. "Remember, all that matters is love and charity. I think, after what you have gone through in the past moon, you can now understand the meaning of those words. Let your soul guide you."

Sternlight braced his forehead on his drawn-up knees, as though awaiting judgment. Black hair fell around him.

Poor Singer looked from person to person, seeing their dread, their love for Sternlight. His heart ached. He clenched his fists into tight balls. "I will do my best to see that you are freed, Sternlight."

Poor Singer turned and hurried for the ladder, gripping the rungs, just as four warriors flooded down. They shoved Poor Singer back against the wall and stationed themselves around the room, war clubs in their hands, cruel smiles on their faces.

Poor Singer blurted, "Grandfather?" as Jay Bird came down the ladder, his elderly face flushed, eyes alight.

Jay Bird blinked at the dimness, then fixed his gaze on Sternlight, and ordered, "Hold him."

Two of the warriors grabbed Sternlight by the arms and dragged him to his feet. Sternlight's throat worked, and Poor Singer saw the sweat running down his jaw. "What do you want?"

"Why did you do it?" Jay Bird choked. "Did you kill my daughter because we had captured both of your sisters? Because we'd worked them to death quarrying stone?"

"You—*you* killed my sisters?" Sternlight asked in surprise.

"I didn't kill them. They died! They were pampered First People. They couldn't stand the hard work!" Jay Bird's face contorted with rage. He took several deep breaths, as if to steady himself, then he regripped his stiletto. His tan shirt looked gray in the light.

Sternlight's eyes softened. "Great Chief, the ways of Power are mysterious. It draws people together however it can, and for its own reasons." He glanced around the room, his gaze stopping on Ironwood long enough to give him a confident, reassuring look, then he met Jay Bird's eyes again. "Tell me. What is it you want from me?"

"*I came for my daughter's murderer!*"

As the Chief lunged forward, Sternlight wrenched violently against the granite arms of the guards, throwing himself back against the wall, kicking out with his legs. Jay Bird's polished stiletto flashed once, twice.

"*No!*" Ironwood shouted, and scrambled to his feet. The two remaining guards leaped on him like dogs, knocking him to the floor, smacking him on the head and back with their clubs. They seemed to get a perverted joy from his hollow grunts. One of the warriors smiled broadly as he brought his club down hard on Ironwood's temple. The big man jerked, seemed confused, and flailed his arms as if blind.

"Enough!" Night Sun yelled in a commanding voice. *"That's enough!"*

The guards halted and looked up in surprise.

Ironwood rolled to his knees and vomited onto the floor. Night Sun rushed to his side and held his head, giving the guards a steely look. "Go on! Get away!"

The warriors glanced at Jay Bird, who stood over Sternlight's crumpled body, breathing hard. His gaze had fixed on the hot wet blood that smeared in his hand. His mouth moved, expression oddly vacant in contrast to the fire in his eyes.

Jay Bird turned to Poor Singer. His narrow, wrinkled face looked strangely younger, like the warrior he had once been. He pointed to Sternlight with his bloody hand. "This man— this filthy *beast*—killed your mother."

Dune knelt beside Sternlight, surveying the blood that soaked his chest and bubbled at his lips. Sternlight choked and red poured from the corners of his mouth. Dune sat down and pulled Sternlight's head in his lap, whispering, "The thlatsinas will be coming for you, Sternlight. Don't worry."

A smile twisted Sternlight's lips, then his muscles loosened and his arms slid to the floor. The life seemed to fade from his eyes gradually, as though it took the soul time to separate completely.

Poor Singer could only crouch there, frozen, his knees shaking as he took in the blood, the tormented faces, the warriors' lingering smiles. His stomach cramped against the bottom of his heart.

In a daze, he climbed to his feet and scaled the ladder as fast as he could, emerging into the sweet air with its clean scent of pine and bright sunlight. A voice echoed in his soul, deep and soft, *"The next time you return here, Buckthorn of the Coyote Clan, your world will be dying all around you. Be prepared to make an offering . . . "*

Stumbling through the village, Poor Singer raced for the trail that cut a winding line up the side of the mountain. He would have to fast and pray for several days, then he would go to her. Beg her to . . .

Behind him, Jay Bird shouted, *"Poor Singer? Poor Singer, come back!"*

Hot wind gusted through Gila Monster Cliffs Village, tousling Swallowtail's hair about his tanned face. He stood with his antler tine poised over a half-finished arrow point. The stone lay on a square of leather in his left palm. He positioned the tip of the tine on just the right spot, applied pressure, and a long flake of stone popped off and spun to the ground. The edge would be deadly in another finger of time. That pleased him. He smiled and, surreptitiously, glanced up at Cornsilk.

She knelt beside Thistle, fifty paces away, stuffing jerky into her pack, talking and pointing up at the mountaintop. A long thick braid hung down her back. Her dress clung to the curves of her body in a way that made Swallowtail's blood warm. Despite the ugly scar on her cheek, she was a beautiful young woman. He ran a tongue over his dry lips as he thought.

"Swallowtail?"

Sandals scraped on stone, and he turned to see his mother coming. Mourning Dove stopped and followed his gaze. Her plump face had sunburned on the long run and begun peeling yesterday. Pink spots of new skin dotted her forehead and cheeks. She asked, "The girl is going after him? Jay Bird's given her permission?"

"Yes."

Mourning Dove wiped her sweaty palms on her dark green dress. "Well, it won't matter. By the time she returns with Poor Singer, Ironwood will be dead. Jay Bird just sent his guards to drag him out of the pen so they can begin torturing him. Ironwood is old. He won't last more than two or three days."

Swallowtail didn't answer. Ironwood had captured his mother those many summers ago, and she hated him almost as much as she'd hated Snake Head. She deserved her revenge. Swallowtail nonchalantly pressed down with his tine and flaked off another long sliver of obsidian. "Do you plan to stay and watch?"

"I'm not leaving until Ironwood lies dead and I've had my chance to spit upon his corpse."

Swallowtail nodded to himself. *That will give me a few days.*

Mourning Dove frowned. "What's the matter? What are you thinking?"

"Just wondering." He continued flaking his arrow point. Black bits of stone fell atop the small scatter at his feet. From the time he'd turned three summers and first heard his mother tell the story of Young Fawn's death, he'd been convinced that the First People were not human but evil Earth Spirits who roamed about killing and witching others. "Do you think there's a chance that Cornsilk might go back to Talon Town? That she would ever decide to accept the position as Matron of the First People?"

It took a moment for her to answer. "Are you asking me if she might return, and depose Featherstone?"

He held his point up to the sunlight, checking the flake scars, admiring the fine workmanship. The Straight Path people had taught him well. He'd become a master flint knapper, the best in Talon Town. Every animal he'd butchered to feed his masters' bellies had been a study for him. He'd learned how the tools worked on bones and muscles, how soft the liver was, and how the internal organs were connected. Stone and flesh were closely related, like cousins, or perhaps brothers.

"Yes, Mother, that's what I mean."

Mourning Dove searched his face. She had never understood him. She never would. A woman like her, so good and loving, could not conceive of the depths of the hatred that coiled inside him like a serpent in the brush, ready to strike.

"I doubt it," she said, "but it's possible. Why? Do you think—"

"I think," he said as he lowered the point, "that she may need 'company' on her journey to find Poor Singer."

"You mean you will escort her?"

Swallowtail smiled. "Yes. She *needs* me, Mother."

Fifty

Creeper smoothed his red shirt down over his belly and tried to concentrate on Weedblossom's droning voice. She, Featherstone, and Whistling Bird stood on the east side of the grave dug into the floor. They wore white, and Featherstone's dark gray hair glimmered in the light streaming through the window behind her.

Webworm stood on Featherstone's left, at the head of the grave. The fine clothing looked regal on his lanky body. He wore a long tan-and-blue shirt with copper Trade bells dangling around the collar. They tinkled when he moved. He'd pulled his black hair away from his broad face and twisted it into a bun at the back of his head. A magnificent bone hairpin, inlaid with turquoise, coral, and malachite, held it in place.

Badgerbow, Yellowgirl, and the new War Chief, White Stone—his wounded arm bound in tan cloth—stood in the row beside Creeper. They all wore red, the color of mourning and death. Two warriors stood near the pile of dirt at the head of the grave. No one looked happy. Creeper forced his gaze back to the shallow hole in the floor.

Snake Head lay in the bottom, facedown. No one had washed his body or combed his hair. He still wore the bloody shirt he'd died in. Tainted possessions taken from his room had been tossed around him: turquoise beads, shell bracelets . . .

"From this moment," Weedblossom said, and raised her gnarled hands to the ceiling, "Snake Head, the traitor, will be locked in darkness here in Talon Town. He will hear his own people curse him, feel them spit upon his grave, and be able to contemplate his arrogant foolishness."

Weedblossom nodded to the warriors behind the dirt pile, and the men lifted a large slab of sandstone. Everyone backed away to give them room. The warriors walked forward and dropped it over Snake Head, taking care not to break his skull.

Creeper anxiously twisted his hands. He had hated Snake Head, but this punishment turned his soul cold. After Snake Head's body had been returned to Talon Town, the elders had searched his chamber and, to their horror, discovered a jar of corpse powder. They'd begun questioning the Made People and other First People, and heard dozens of stories of his wickedness. The next day the elders had officially condemned Snake Head as a witch. Weedblossom had said that the speck of dust in his head had become a whirling dust devil, blasting anything in its path, and that he deserved to wail for all eternity for the crimes he'd committed.

"Good, now cover him up." Weedblossom nodded to the warriors.

The two men returned to the dirt pile and began shoving soil back into the hole.

The elders filed out, then Webworm followed, and finally the clan leaders turned to go. There would be no sacred Songs, no Dances to celebrate his life. No one would weep or cut their hair in grief.

Snake Head was truly alone now.

Creeper walked out last, ducking through the low doorway into the bright noon sunlight. Talon Town sparkled whitely, and the canyon had a pale orange hue, as though washed out by Father Sun's brilliance. Warm wind gusted across the plaza.

Webworm and the First People elders stood in a small group, talking in low voices, and the Made People went back to their daily duties. Badgerbow lifted a hand to Creeper before he disappeared through the gate that separated the eastern and western plazas. Creeper waved and headed for the ladders that led to Night Sun's old chamber—now Featherstone's chamber.

As he climbed to the fourth floor, sweat beaded on his cheeks and ran down his chin. The days had grown very warm. Wildflowers created a yellow and blue patchwork across the highlands. The canyon seemed too silent, though, as if people were still in shock from the raid.

Creeper shook his head. The very fact of the raid had the First People rushing about like dogs with the foaming-mouth disease. The next morning the elders decided that they had been too indolent and arrogant, believing themselves invincible. Changes were quickly instituted. Talon Town no longer had a front entryway. Nor were there exterior windows, or even tiny slits for ventilation. Featherstone had ordered them all walled up. The only way in or out of town now was by ladder. At night, those ladders were drawn inside. The new War Chief, White Stone, stood over the front, as always, but nine other warriors stood around the walls to help him keep watch.

They all vowed it would never happen again, but as Creeper gazed across the crowded canyon, at the huge towns and hundreds of small villages, he knew the time would come when they would not be able to protect themselves. A good War Chief with enough warriors could box this canyon tight, kill the Trade, and cut off access to wood, water and food. It might take moons, but in the summertime during a drought . . . Creeper shuddered. The Straight Path people considered themselves a nation of glorious warriors. Surrender was unthinkable.

He walked across the rooftop, ducked through the doorway into the chamber, and returned to his former activity: arranging Featherstone's chamber for her. Early that morning he'd set out the pots along the southern wall, to his right, and stacked the baskets in the northwestern corner. He'd laid out sitting mats around the fire bowl, making certain everything was easy to reach. Featherstone's eyes had worsened in the past few moons. Often, these days, she couldn't see her teacup when it sat right in front of her.

Creeper knelt beside the fire bowl and spread the legs of the boiling tripod, then hung the pot in the center. The soot-coated clay pot swung gently.

Though Night Sun's things had been removed and ritually buried beneath the floor of the plaza—to keep their depraved taint from causing illnesses or deaths—this chamber still *felt* like Night Sun. Creeper's gaze drifted between the Buffalo Thlatsina on the south wall and the Sun Thlatsina on the north wall. The Buffalo seemed to be tossing his shaggy head, his long black beard flying as he Danced, while the Sun god had his pink arms spread, and one foot lifted. Through the window in the eastern wall, Propped Pillar leaned toward Talon Town. Two eagles, male and female, perched near the nest on the top of the stone tower, their heads cocked, searching for movement below.

Weedblossom had come in yesterday and ritually smoked the chamber to cleanse it of evil Spirits, and the faint fragrance of cedar clung to the walls. Despite such precautions, Creeper felt a sadness here.

He hadn't realized until recently what a frustrated life Night Sun had led, and he sympathized with her. He couldn't find it in him to hate her for loving one of the Made People. Though he had spent much of his life hoping to see Featherstone one day become the great Matron of the First People, Creeper wished she were just an ordinary old woman from the Coyote Clan. The past few days he had been very lonely. He missed Mourning Dove. They had shared a kind of intimacy that he would never have with Featherstone, no matter how much they cared for each other. Mourning Dove had been his *friend.* They had helped each other as much as they could given their circumstances, and had lain awake late into the nights just talking. He ached for that closeness, for the sensation of her sleeping in his arms.

She's gone, you fool. Let her go.

Creeper crouched beside Featherstone's rolled sleeping mats and spread them across the floor, then placed two folded blankets at the foot—the soft red-and-white one on top, as she liked it to be.

"Creeper?"

"Yes, I'm here." He swiveled toward the door.

Webworm entered, carrying two small sacks. His blue-and-tan robe, woven of the finest cloth, shimmered in the light.

"What do you have in the sacks?" Creeper asked.

"Sandhill Crane cleaned out the slaves' chambers. The slaves ran so fast none of them had time to take their belongings. These came from Mourning Dove and Swallowtail's spaces. I thought you might wish to go through them." Webworm tilted his head awkwardly. "I know how much you miss Mourning Dove. It occurred to me that a keepsake, something she loved, might help."

"Thank you, Blessed Sun."

Webworm came forward and held out the sacks. Creeper took them and set them on the floor near the fire bowl. As he untied the laces, he said, "Mourning Dove would have been very happy to see you as the Blessed Sun."

Webworm walked to peer out the eastern window at Propped Pillar. "I still can't believe the story you told about how she saw me as the fulfillment of Fire Dog prophecies."

"But she did."

Creeper turned over Mourning Dove's sack and gently poured it onto the floor. What a pitiful collection: a crudely made pair of sandals; a piece of broken pottery that had been sanded to a round shape and hung on a cord as a pendant; a brown dress, tattered and worn thin on the elbows; a beautiful red dress—the one Snake Head had given her. Creeper picked it up with two fingers and dropped it a short distance away. *He* had touched it. A few other things completed the collection, none of them important. Creeper tenderly ran his fingers over the pendant. He'd seen her wear it many times. Slipping it around his own neck, he arranged it over his heart.

"Yes," Creeper said, "she believed. I think she spent her whole life working to make certain you became the Blessed Sun."

The words seemed to make Webworm uncomfortable. He shifted his weight from one foot to the other. "I don't know how to take that. I feel so incompetent, I'm afraid she might be right."

"That you will destroy the Straight Path nation?" Creeper chuckled. "I don't think so. It may take you some time to get used to the position, but you will do very well, Webworm. You have the heart of a great leader. And Featherstone will help you, as much as she can. I have always prayed that the two of you would one day lead this nation."

"Did Swallowtail believe I was the fulfillment of the prophecies? I never knew him very well."

"I can't say. But I do know he hated Snake Head. Swallowtail would have done anything to bring Snake Head down and put someone else in his place. That poor boy watched his mother abused over and over, and because he was a slave there was nothing he could do about it. It wounded him deeply. As a child, Swallowtail used to beg me to tell him that I was his father. Of course, I couldn't."

"Do you think Snake Head was his father?"

Creeper shrugged. "Mourning Dove would never tell me, but the boy looked like Snake Head. He had the same tall body and dark eyes, and I know that Snake Head gave her permission to bear the child. I just assumed . . ."

Creeper's voice faded as he emptied Swallowtail's sack onto the floor. Several small bags rolled out, then a fine obsidian blade, the one he used for butchering, a beautiful jet figurine, and a cord-wrapped tube of fabric. "What a strange collection."

Webworm crouched opposite Creeper and frowned down at the figurine. "He must have stolen that." As he picked up the exquisite jet, his brows arched. "This is such fine workmanship, I'm sure it comes from the Hohokam."

"Swallowtail did pester the Traders who came through from that region. He had a curious obsession with Hohokam stonework, but he could never have purchased such an item. You must be right. He stole it."

Creeper loosened the ties on one of the small bags and smelled it. "Mugwort leaves. What's in that one close to you?"

Webworm lifted the small red bag and took a good sniff. His nose wrinkled. "Goldenweed. These are Healing herbs. And good quality. Expensive."

Creeper picked up the cord-wrapped tube of fabric. "I wonder what this is?"

He untied the knot and removed the cord. When he shook the fabric pack out, he noticed that four black spirals decorated the bottom. "I don't understand. Only women from the Red Lacewing family are allowed to use this symbol. I wonder where—"

"It can't be!" Webworm sank to the floor. His square-jawed face went pale; he held out his hand. "Give it to me."

Creeper handed him the pack.

Webworm turned it over and over, studying the weave of the cotton thread, the yucca ties, the four perfect black spirals. Tears beaded his lashes. He lowered the pack to his lap. "This is Cloud Playing's pack, Creeper. She always carried it when she went on the Healing trips with her mother. . . ." Webworm's gaze went to the small bags of herbs, and his lips parted with words that wouldn't come. Finally, he whispered, "Blessed gods."

A tingling numbness ran through Creeper. "You mean, you think . . . Night Sun said Cloud Playing was bringing her pack, but . . . no, Webworm, I can't believe it! Swallowtail was a good boy! I sat with him around supper many times. I think I would know if a murderer—"

"Would you?" Misery lined Webworm's face. "You said he hated Snake Head, that Swallowtail wanted to destroy him. He may not have believed in the Mogollon prophecies, but it didn't take a genius to know that if you killed Snake Head's female relatives, he'd be toppled as the Blessed Sun."

"Then why didn't he try to kill Night Sun?"

"Perhaps he thought she was out of the way when Snake Head imprisoned her, or that she was so old she would die naturally soon enough and save him the trouble."

"But Swallowtail was gone when Cloud Playing was killed," Creeper insisted. "I remember because I bid him good-bye myself. I packed food for him, and—"

"And he came back two days late, didn't he? That's what I heard. Who's to say that he didn't hide down in the wash for a couple of days, waiting for her? Maybe even track her from Deer Mother Village?"

"But she was killed with a bow and arrows! Swallowtail had no such weapons!"

Webworm tenderly smoothed his hand over the wrinkled pack. The copper bells on his shirt clinked. "The boy had access to stone tools. He could have refashioned any of them into arrow points, and making a crude bow requires only a piece of wood and a string." Webworm hesitated. "We must decide what to do about this, Creeper."

Creeper prodded the fine jet figurine with his fingertip while he thought. It resembled the curious witch pellet that Mourning Dove had seen Lark spit up—some sort of a stylized serpent. Creeper remembered laughter and joy, and many afternoons spent soothing Swallowtail after Mourning Dove returned from a brutal coupling with Snake Head. The boy had gazed at his mother's bruises, at the blood on her clothing, an insane rage behind his eyes. Swallowtail *had* been crazy enough to kill. But did he have the cunning to destroy Snake Head and his family from the inside out? Perhaps Mourning Dove's obsession with the prophecies, with assuring that Webworm became the Blessed Sun, had given Swallowtail the idea.

Creeper's blood turned to ice. Could Creeper have lived and

loved the boy for so long and not had the slightest notion of how his soul worked?

"Where is Featherstone?"

Webworm gestured toward the door. "She's in her old chambers. I was helping her pack. She was talking about Night Sun and how much she missed her, and Mother just drifted off. You know how she is. I spread a blanket over her and thought I'd go back and check in half a hand of time."

"Webworm, this news will be very hard on Featherstone. She loved Cloud Playing. If it were true that Mourning Dove's son was the one . . ." His voice tightened. "I think Featherstone has forgotten all about Cloud Playing's death. I'm not sure what such knowledge will do to her."

Webworm carefully rerolled the pack and tied it with the cord. "You mean it might be best to keep this to ourselves?"

"There's nothing we can do about it anyway. Is there?"

Webworm cheeks reddened, then anger, bright and hot, lit his eyes. "Not at this instant, but may the gods help that boy if I ever have a chance to make war on the Tower Builders."

Creeper lowered his gaze to the scatter of precious tools and herbs. His heart thumped a slow steady cadence. "I pray with all my heart that Mourning Dove is gone when you do."

Eighth Day

I lie on my back staring up at the swaying Ponderosa pine branches above me. The needles are long and curved. Moonlight coats them, turning them a ghostly silver. Through the filigree of twigs, the Evening People shine.

My body has gone numb. My soul is floating, barely tied to my flesh.

I am ready, I think. I did not feel ready until tonight, but I have done what I can to cleanse and purify my heart. Either she will accept my offering now, or she never will.

I only know that I must try.

I close my eyes, and listen to the wind soughing through the pines. The branches creak and groan. The air smells sweet with the scent of mountain wildflowers. I fill my lungs and hold it for as long as I can, then slowly let the breath out. I am tired, very tired . . . one last thing to do.

The Dream stole Poor Singer's soul away.

He ran as Coyote, his padded feet parting the newly green spring grass and the first delicate wildflowers. From this height, he could see across the infinity of dark mountains that layered the distances. Each range etched the horizon in a lighter shade of hazy blue-gray. Behind him, buttes and mesas carved the lowlands. Ahead of him, jagged peaks punctured the bellies of the Cloud People. His breath puffed whitely. As he bounded higher, the air grew colder, burning his lungs.

He crested the hilltop and loped down a steep slope, scattering gravel and ducking under deadfall. He wiggled through a thicket of brush, leaped a narrow brook, and bounded up the next slope, his paws silent on the soft green grasses. His ability to see in the darkness amazed him. Mice darted through the grass in the meadows, and packrats skittered in the jumble of rocky outcrops. Their sight and scent stirred hunger in his empty belly.

He loped through a patch of wildflowers so tall they brushed his golden muzzle, then ran alongside a grove of aspen trees. Their white trunks glowed in the starlight. Eyes glinted from the densest part of the forest. He tipped his nose and smelled the air. *Elk.* Three of them: two cows and a calf. They watched him pass, then calmly went back to foraging.

The first sliver of Sister Moon's face blazed over the shining peaks. Poor Singer hurried.

Racing up an icy slope, paws slipping, he stood on a windy knoll and slitted his eyes against the freezing gale. His fur ruffled up and down his back. He searched the jagged snow-covered peaks, until he thought he knew the right one, then headed for it.

Why doesn't this look familiar? I know these are the right mountains, but this isn't the trail I followed with my father. Am I lost?

He swerved around a lightning-struck stump and loped higher up the slick side of the mountain, his eyes on the lofty summit. He didn't see the cave. . . .

Panic threaded his muscles, turning them shaky, making his breath come in shallow gasps. *This has to be the way. It has to.*

Snow had gathered in the fur of his paws and melted to clumps of ice that spread his toes until they hurt, but he refused to take the time to chew them out.

Poor Singer bulled through a snowdrift taller than his head, leaping and struggling to climb the steep incline. After the long days without food, he could feel what little strength he had draining away, being devoured by his trembling muscles. When he clawed his way up, he stood on a rocky ledge and shook snow from his coat. A haze of glittering white surrounded him. As it cleared, he looked up.

A tingle eddied through his veins. This *was* the peak. He could not be mistaken about that. It looked like an ice spear, white and jagged.

Poor Singer scrambled up the rocky ledge, and when he struck a shallow meadow, he ran with all his heart, his pink tongue dangling from the corner of his mouth. His muscles prickled now, as if starved for blood, but he charged up the last slope. Above him, the peak turned to solid rock. Snow filled every crevice, and a fog of windblown ice crystals haloed the summit.

There!

He almost missed it. Since the last time he'd been here, the creeping barberry bushes had grown up, covering half the entry—or disguising it. The holly-shaped leaves reflected the starlight with blinding intensity. No wonder he hadn't seen the dark hole. Now it blended with the snowy slope.

Poor Singer shouldered through the bramble, his fur catching and tugging painfully. He left a trail of golden tufts on the branches. This time the narrow tunnel was pitch-black and foreboding.

He walked deeper, then broke into a trot, racing down the slope, calling, "Keeper of the Tortoise Bundle? Where are you? I used to be Buckthorn, of the Coyote Clan. I—"

"I know who you are, Poor Singer."

Her voice came from everywhere, echoing off the walls, resonating in his soul.

Poor Singer licked his muzzle nervously and slowed to a walk. The air grew warmer, and he could hear the plopping of water as it dripped into the dark pool below. He edged forward, one breath at a time, his claws tapping the moist stone, creating a staccato like arrows upon rock.

His padded paws slipped into the water-filled hollows in the floor, soaking his feet, melting the ice between his toes. The cave smelled curious. He knew that odor; it clung to tumbled stone walls and dusty crevice burials: the scent of ancient destruction.

"Where are you?"

"Come closer. I'm here. Down here."

Poor Singer edged forward, searching the blackness. The *plop, plop* of water grew louder. How close was he to the pool? He couldn't be more than—

Like an explosion, silver light poured through the entrance, and the cave burst into blinding waves of blue flame. He collapsed on his haunches. Brilliant turquoise sparks tumbled and winked, surging across the roof and flowing down the walls to coat the floor of the cave. The wondrous pool turned luminous. Poor Singer focused on it, trying to still his hammering heart.

The water looked so calm. In the midst of this blaze, it provided the single still point. Had he noticed that last time? Or had he been so stunned that fear had devoured his senses?

He saw her.

She walked from a hidden fissure in the rear of the cave, her long black hair draping around her, the folds of her red dress shining with a purple hue. Poor Singer's whiskers quivered in awe. So . . . there was another chamber, the entrance perfectly hidden by the seamless appearance of the turquoise walls. She followed a narrow path around the curve of the pool and came to stand over him, her midnight eyes wide, her gaze penetrating. The fire in the cave surrounded her like a effervescent halo.

"What have you to offer me?"

Poor Singer inhaled a breath of the warm, damp air. "Myself."

"In exchange for what?"

"The life of a man called Ironwood."

"Your grandfather wishes to kill him?" she asked as she gracefully walked to the opposite side of the narrow tunnel and sat down, her back against the stone. The conflagration had turned so blinding Poor Singer had to slit his eyes and tip his muzzle to see her.

Was she human? Or a god? "Yes, and I—I can't let that happen."

Her gaze bored into him. *"You would give up Cornsilk? You would sacrifice her happiness as well as your own?"*

Poor Singer's forelegs had started to shake so badly, he had to lie down on the warm floor. "I love her, Keeper. I love her very much, but she is young. She will find another."

The Keeper just stared at him. *"Why would you give up your life for a man you barely know?"*

Poor Singer swallowed down his tight throat. "I just . . . I can't see any more of them die. Please. This isn't their fault. Don't you understand? If I hadn't been born, none of this would have happened! But I was. And these things have happened because of me. This is my responsibility!"

"Do you know how many innocent men and women Ironwood has killed? How many children he has taken as slaves? What makes you think his life is worth more than yours? Are you guilty of any of these crimes?"

Poor Singer lowered his muzzle to rest on his paws. "No, no, I'm not. But what does that matter?"

"*It matters a great deal to the gods. They are fanatical about justice.*"

"But Keeper, many of the gods were warriors. They are also fanatical about duty and responsibility. Ironwood is a good man. He was only doing his duty to his people and his Chief. And I am doing mine now."

She drew back her head as if in disbelief. "*You consider dying for no reason to be your duty?*"

"But it isn't for no reason. I'm offering my life for Ironwood's because I believe the world will be better with Ironwood in it. So many have already died because of me. Please, let me do this?"

The magnificent blue fire began to subside. The walls went from a blazing azure to pale blue, and finally to an icy gray-white.

The Keeper's black eyes seemed to grow in that tarnished gleam, huge as an owl's, and just as wary. She asked, "*Do you now understand what it means to have the heart of a cloud?*"

Poor Singer's mouth went dry. He bent to lap water from the floor, cooling his hot throat, calming his nerves. The moisture tasted sweet and warm. He licked his muzzle to dry it.

"I believe," he answered through a long exhalation, "that the heart of a cloud is tears, Keeper. I've been thinking a lot about it. We often speak of the Cloud People shedding tears for us, to give us life. Rain is their tears."

A bare smile touched her face. "*And walking upon the wind? Do you know what that means?*"

Poor Singer shifted uncertainly. He had been worried about this one. His tail brushed the stone wall as he thought about it. "If I lived in the heart of a cloud, I would be able to look down upon the world from high above the chaos, to see it more clearly. I think that's what it means. If I could live inside the tears of others, I would see life more clearly."

As though she found the rounded pits in the stone floor fascinating, she thoughtfully smoothed her fingers over them. When she looked up again, her dark eyes seemed to fill half of her beautiful face. "*Your offering tonight proves you have grown the heart of a cloud. You are a Singer. Your people need you.*" She rose to her feet and her red dress swayed about her tall body. "*Now go and walk upon the wind. Tell your grandfather what you did here. What you saw here. He will understand.*"

She started back for the trail that skirted the dark pond, and Poor Singer sat up. "But, wait! What about my offering? Do you accept it? Will you help me to save Ironwood's life?"

The Keeper of the Tortoise Bundle bowed her head. "*If you will do as I told you, you will be a very great Singer one day. Make your life an offering, Poor Singer. It will save far more people than your death. Someday, when you are able, return here. I will teach you what I know of clouds and tears.*"

She walked around the trail and vanished into the crevice in the cave. The pond wavered from the breath of her passing, and fragments of light danced over the walls.

Poor Singer stood on weak legs. He started back up the tunnel, his head hanging low, feeling numb.

"*Poor Singer?*"

The call was faint. He turned to look into the maw of the cave, but saw only darkness.

As he pushed through the tangle of barberry and out into the bright moonlight, he felt something, like a hand upon his shoulder. Frightened, he whirled around, breathing hard, scanning the snowy meadow and the glistening peaks, but . . .

"*Poor Singer?*"

He jerked awake, gasping, staring wide-eyed at the coral gleam of dawn. Charcoal clouds drifted on the eastern horizon, their bellies clothed in the palest of golds. Cornsilk knelt beside him. She wore a clean black-and-white cape and buckskin moccasins. A thick black braid draped her left shoulder. Her wound had healed, but an ugly yellow bruise remained around the raw pink scar high on her cheek. His gaze drifted from the scar to her full lips, pointed nose, and the oval line of her jaw. He sat up and hugged her fiercely.

Heartsick and weary, he cried, "Oh, Cornsilk, I'm so glad to see you." The feel of her slender body against his soothed him.

She slipped her arms around his waist and hugged him back.

"I half-expected to find you spinning around and flapping your arms like a moth."

"This time . . . well, I had to learn to be a cloud."

She gently pushed back and looked him over in detail, as if checking to see what injuries he'd sustained during the transformation. Apparently satisfied he was all right, she unslung a small pack from her back and unlaced the ties. "I knew you'd be starving. Can you eat now? Did you learn to be a cloud?"

He nodded, feeling curiously floaty, and cold, terribly cold, deep down. "I'm starving. What did you bring?"

Cornsilk sat beside him on the gray limestone and pulled out two bags. "Your grandmother, Downy Girl, gave me venison jerky and ricegrass-seed bread." Cornsilk's dark brows drew together as she searched his face. "But you've been fasting for many days, Poor Singer. You'd better just eat a little. You might throw up."

"I'm willing to take that chance."

Cornsilk handed him a length of jerky and pulled out a gut water bag. "Drink this first, Poor Singer. It will cushion your empty stomach."

Poor Singer took three sips and handed the bag back. "Thank you, that tasted good." He wiped his mouth with the back of his hand and took a small bite of the jerky. His stomach squealed and cramped.

Cornsilk watched him closely. Behind her an eagle soared through the morning sky. Its long wings flashed gold as it dipped into the wind and sailed westward. She said, "Are you all right, Poor Singer?"

He took another small bite. "So far."

"Good. We have a long walk back to Gila Monster Cliffs Village."

"We do?"

"Poor Singer," she said with a frown, "it took me four days to find you. Fortunately you left a trail clear enough that a five-summers-old child could have followed. But, in your condition, it will take us at least three days to get back." Cornsilk's expression turned contemplative. "And I think, Poor Singer, that we should get back as soon as possible. Jay Bird is very worried about you."

"I'm surprised he didn't send ten men to drag me back."

"Both Dune and I asked him not to."

Poor Singer's brows raised. "And he listened?"

"Dune had that look in his eyes, you know the one I mean? It's like a shout, telling you that all the evil Spirits in Creation will be loosed upon you if you don't obey?"

He nodded, and sighed. "Boy, do I know that look."

"I pleaded with Jay Bird to let me search for you. He watched me for a long time with his eyes squinted. Then he nodded and said he trusted me—because you loved me. He gave me permission to find you."

Poor Singer reached out and took her hand. Her fingers felt thin and delicate in his grasp. "Cornsilk, I do love you. I want to be with you always. If . . . if you want to be with me?"

She gave him a sad smile that broke his heart. "I want that more than anything in the world, Poor Singer." And her smile faded. She turned away. "But I don't know where we'll ever find a home. My mother—Thistle—has decided to stay here, at Gila Monster Cliffs. But I can't, Poor Singer. Nor can I go back to the Straight Path nation, and my father . . ."

Poor Singer lowered his jerky to his lap and frowned. *He must be all right. The Keeper said . . . seemed to say . . .*

"Cornsilk? What's happened while I've been away?"

She shoved a rock out of the way and slid over next to him, as if needing his closeness. "Your grandfather regrets that he killed Sternlight in front of you." She frowned at the ground. "I didn't know Sternlight well, Poor Singer, but he was kind to me. I will miss him."

"So will I."

"Even though he murdered your mother?"

"I didn't know her at all, Cornsilk." Poor Singer took another bite of jerky. She clearly didn't wish to speak about her father yet. He chewed slowly, giving her more time. The jerky had a tangy flavor he didn't recognize, like cedar bark smoke mixed with phlox blossoms. "I'm still uncertain how to feel about Sternlight killing her to save me, but I know he did what he thought he had to. There is honor in that." He glanced at her and found Cornsilk scooping the pine needles between her feet into a pile. "And the others?" he asked cautiously. "What has happened to them?"

"Your reaction to Sternlight's murder seemed to temper Jay

Bird's anger. He freed Night Sun and Dune, though guards follow them wherever they go in the village." She paused, her mouth open.

Fear charged his drained muscles. "And your father? Tell me about Ironwood."

She sat quietly for several moments, watching the sky turn from pink to a rich shade of amber. Sunlight struck the highest peaks first, and the pockets of snow seemed to burn. Then, as Father Sun's face peeked over the horizon, light flooded the lowlands, chasing away the last vestiges of night.

"Cornsilk." His gut twisted. "Is your father still alive?"

"I don't know." She shook her head. "When I left, he was still locked in the pen. But I'd heard rumors that Jay Bird was planning on sending guards to drag him out." She knotted her fists. Cool fragrant breezes blew up from the meadow below them, tearing strands of black hair loose from her braid and fluttering them about her pretty face. "To begin torturing him."

Poor Singer dragged her pack over, tucked the remaining food back inside, and tied the laces. Then he slipped his arm over Cornsilk's shoulders. "Could you help me up? We need to leave now, and I'm not very strong."

Cornsilk put an arm around his waist and hugged him tightly. "I'll carry you all the way back, if necessary."

Poor Singer rose on weak knees, and they began picking their way down the trail.

Fifty-One

Nauseated, trembling, Ironwood sagged in the arms of the guards who dragged him down the rocky trail. His knees raked the ground, leaving blood trails. They threw him into the plaza, facedown, and left him lying there. It took several moments before he could muster the strength to turn his head. Mogollon Fire Dogs crowded around him, forming an irregular circle. He couldn't see them very well, except for their clothing. They had dressed in their finest for this grand event. The red, yellow, and blue fabrics tinkled with shell bells and glittered with polished stones. Ironwood blinked to clear his blurry vision. The crack on the skull he'd received just before Sternlight's death had left him blind for . . . *for how many days?* Five? Six? His sight was returning slowly—not that it mattered. He would only need his physical eyes for a short time longer.

Rolling to his side, he tried to breathe. His entire body had become an open wound. They'd taken turns. Some of the villagers had stabbed him with sharp sticks; others had tied him down and used their stone knives to slowly slice open the muscles in his legs, arms, and on his face. Jay Bird never let them go too far. If the blood flowed profusely, he ordered it stanched with glowing stones. If Ironwood appeared thirsty, Jay Bird personally held a water jug to Ironwood's lips. They'd kept him well-fed, to fortify his strength. They wanted him to live and suffer for as long as possible, believing that his pain would comfort all the friends, husbands, wives, and children whom Ironwood had killed.

He bowed his head and gazed at the tight leather thongs binding his bloody hands and feet. He did not fear death, not really. He had seen too much of it to be afraid. He knew its course, and its character. Indeed, at this point, he would see death as a friend.

He feared only the aftermath.

The Mogollon would make certain his soul did not reach the afterlife—just as they had with Sternlight's. Jay Bird had forced Ironwood, Night Sun, and Dune to watch the burial. And though he hadn't been able to see, Night Sun had told him what followed. The Fire Dogs had thrown Sternlight into a hole, covered him with a stone slab, and laughed. The news had withered Ironwood's heart. All of his life, Sternlight had stood by him, helping him, covering for his errors. Sternlight had deserved better.

Neither of them would sit with their ancestors and discuss the old times, or hunt and fish to their hearts' content. Jay Bird would assure that Ironwood's soul remained locked in the earth for eternity, too, lost and wailing. He who had spent his life seeking the companionship of others, longing for it, would never enjoy it again.

But it's a punishment I deserve. Sternlight did not.

An odd burning filled his chest. He lifted his eyes and tried to find Night Sun through the blur of shapes and colors. *There.* Standing tall and straight. Jay Bird stood on one side and Dune on the other. Two guards flanked them. She must know he did not have much time left, yet she made no sound. She would not shame the Straight Path people by begging for Ironwood's life when she knew already it was lost. Nor would she give the Fire Dogs the satisfaction of seeing her weep.

Pride welled inside Ironwood. Though he could barely see her, he gave her a smile.

Ironwood heard the guards coming, closing in around him, their sandals scuffing the ground. Blurry figures loomed against the blue sky.

He cocked his head. "What now?"

They didn't understand his language, and wouldn't have answered if they had. Their gazes were riveted on Jay Bird. The Chief slowly walked through the crowd, his black shirt with white designs swaying around his legs. Jay Bird knelt and gripped Ironwood's chin, twisting his mutilated face up so that he could peer into his eyes. Ironwood could make out the Chief's thin face and black splotches of eyes. The elder's hair resembled a fuzzy gray halo.

"Are you seeing better?" Jay Bird asked.

"A little."

"Good."

"Why?" Ironwood asked hoarsely. "What is it you wish me to see?"

Jay Bird got to his feet and stood over Ironwood like a wrathful god. "I wish you to know the moment the world goes completely dark."

Ironwood braced himself. "Is it time to die?"

"No, my old enemy. It is time for you to walk the lances."

"The . . ." Ironwood swallowed. He had heard of it from warriors who'd been forced to watch their comrades do it. The Mogollon formed two parallel lines. Each person lifted an obsidian-tipped lance and held it poised to strike as the enemy captive was shoved down the corridor. The game was to see who could blind the prisoner first.

"Let's get it over with," Ironwood said, and struggled to rise, but he couldn't seem to get his feet under him.

The guards dragged him up. Ironwood saw people moving across the plaza, getting into position. His legs trembled badly. A pang of fear went through him, fear that he might not be able to meet this last challenge. The Fire Dogs would roar with laughter if he failed, and then they would treat him as a coward. So far he had been accorded the torture worthy of a great warrior, but if he weakened, they would stuff his mouth with dry dung, force it down his throat, then heap it around him and set it afire.

It will be said that War Chief Ironwood died screaming like a frightened child. The Traders will carry the story everywhere. The men and women who fought at my side will hate me for humiliating them and all Straight Path warriors.

Ironwood fixed his blurry eyes on Night Sun, locked his knees, and lifted his head. *I can do this. Just a little longer. If I stay on my feet for another hand of time, they will reward me with death.*

The guards cut Ironwood's bonds and he spread his shaking legs to brace himself up. Jay Bird turned and marched away, going to the head of the two lines of warriors.

"*Walk!*" one of the guards ordered, and shoved Ironwood into a shambling trot.

As he entered the gauntlet, he heard Night Sun let out a small cry, and glimpsed the lance from the corner of his left eye. Ironwood instinctively flung up his arm to deflect the blow, and the onlookers exploded with shouts and cheers. The crowd surged forward, laughing and stamping their feet. The acrid odor of their sweat filled the air. Ironwood stumbled on down the line, desperately trying to pick out lances in the gyrating multicolored smear . . .

The *game* had begun.

Poor Singer stopped on the winding mountain trail, panting, his legs rubbery. Exhaustion weighted his limbs. What should have been a three-day trip had taken them only a day and a half—and he felt it in every strained muscle. Propping his hands on his hips, he gazed out across the basin. It looked almost flat, like a smooth green blanket rumpled around the edges. Jagged blue peaks hovered above the ground in the east, but the Thlatsina Mountains in the west had vanished. Poor Singer frowned. A hazy band of smoke stretched across the northern sky. It had grown darker and even more ominous since yesterday.

Cornsilk came up beside him, her pretty face stained with perspiration. "Do you think it's a forest fire?"

"Maybe. But it's early for a fire so large. The grass is still green. Snow covers the mountains. What could be burning?"

Wind Baby sighed through the trees around them, carrying the scents of juniper and sage buttercup. A small herd of deer trotted through a meadow below, white tails up, signaling danger.

"They must have seen us," Cornsilk whispered.

"Or scented us. Wind Baby is blowing right down our backs."

Poor Singer watched the deer lope into the forest and disappear without a sound, then he turned his gaze back to the thick black smoke. "Perhaps the thlatsinas are trying to tell us something, Cornsilk."

She exhaled tiredly. "Probably that we need to push ourselves even harder. Come on. The village can't be more than a finger of time away. It's just down there at the base of the mountain."

"You go ahead. I need a little longer to catch my breath."

She squeezed his shoulder, said, "I'll wait for you at the bottom of the meadow," and headed on down the slope.

Poor Singer stared out across the basin. An odd sensation tingled his stomach. As if . . . as if somewhere deep inside he knew the ground was getting ready to split wide open and swallow everyone and everything that meant anything to him, and there was nothing he could do to stop it.

"You're being foolish," he whispered. "The Keeper told you that if you talked with your grandfather, told him what happened in the Dream, that he would—"

He cocked his head when he heard a voice. It seemed to ride the wind like a falcon, soaring and diving over the slope—a low voice, the words indistinct.

"Cornsilk?" he called, and gazed down the trail she'd taken, squinting through the weave of sunlight and shadow that made up the juniper grove. "Did you say something?"

A sharp cry rang out . . .

And was suddenly silenced.

Poor Singer's heart thundered. "*Cornsilk?*"

He ran with all his might, swerving around the twists in the trail, rushing headlong through the trees, his arms up to protect his face from the overhanging branches. "*Cornsilk? Cornsilk, where are you?*"

Swallowtail kept his left hand clamped over Cornsilk's mouth as he shoved her before him into a dense growth of currant bushes that clustered between four tall junipers. The branches scratched his arms and her face as he forced her to the ground. He knelt behind her with the tip of his knife pressed to her silken throat. He could feel her heartbeat pounding against his wrist, and his distended manhood strained at the fabric of his shirt. The excitement of the chase, the thrill of catching her completely by surprise, all of it had stoked an insane *need* to hurt her.

Poor Singer thrashed through the forest no more than twenty hands away. Swallowtail fought to still his breathing.

Poor Singer cried, "Cornsilk? Cornsilk, answer me? Where are you? Are you hurt? Cornsilk!"

She squirmed, and Swallowtail hissed, "*Don't!*"

As a warning, he pricked her throat with his blade. Cornsilk jerked to look at him, her dark eyes terrified, and he smiled as her blood ran warmly over his fingers.

"*Cornsilk? What happened? Where are you!*" Poor Singer shouted and flailed his way down the trail, out of sight.

Swallowtail could follow his path from the loud cracking of branches and the snapping of deadfall. When Poor Singer had run far enough, Swallowtail lowered his knife and wiped the bloody blade on the shoulder of Cornsilk's dress. "If I remove my hand from your mouth, will you promise not to cry out? I just want to be inside you, Cornsilk. You are one of the First People, and I *need* to be inside you."

He could feel her jaw tighten as understanding dawned.

She hesitated, and Swallowtail ran his hand down her arm, caressing it. "I will do it anyway. The only difference is this: if you cry out and Poor Singer comes running, I'll shoot him dead before he can get near you. Do you understand? I will kill him. And then," he added with a smile, and kissed her hair, "I will have to kill you to keep you from telling Jay Bird that I murdered his grandson."

Cornsilk started shaking and it made Swallowtail chuckle. She nodded against his hand.

"You promise?" he said. "You will not cry out?"

She nodded again.

Cautiously, Swallowtail removed his hand. Cornsilk turned to face him. Red spots, left by his fingers, marked her face. They were exciting.

"Swallowtail," she whispered. "Why are you doing this? I have never hurt you! Why—"

"Lie down and get ready for me!" he ordered. "And remember—" he slipped his bow and quiver of arrows from his back and laid them on the forest duff, within easy reach "—if you make a sound—"

"I—I won't. I won't, Swallowtail. Just don't hurt Poor Singer. Please, I—"

"Do as I say!"

Cornsilk lay back on the soft cedar-scented ground and pulled up the hem of her green dress, revealing long brown legs.

Swallowtail pulled up his hunting shirt, eagerly crawled forward and shoved her knees apart. She was dry, and tight, when he forced himself inside. The only other woman he'd been with had been Cloud Playing, and she'd been so close to death that all of her muscles had been slack. Cornsilk's body held him like a firm hand. He stretched out on top of her and placed his knife against her throat again.

Hatred burned in her eyes, and he smiled. He would wait. Savor each moment of this. Then, just before ecstasy overtook him, he would kill her and watch the life drain from her eyes while the semen drained from his body—just as he'd done with Cloud Playing.

"Move," he ordered in a hoarse whisper. "Move!"

Cornsilk made a feeble attempt, and he thrust violently against her hips.

"Blessed gods," he whispered, "keep moving. Move faster!"

He felt the first prickling in the root of his penis—more quickly than last time, the sensation overpowering him, as if he were a hawk swooping through fire, soaring, ablaze! He pressed the knife against Cornsilk's throat and gazed directly into her horrified eyes. The thrill nearly made him laugh out loud. Just a moment longer, not long now, and he'd slash through that thin veneer of skin . . .

Something struck the side of his head, the force strong enough to blast lights through his eyes and knock him sideways, off of Cornsilk. Swallowtail scrambled to his knees. *"Who—"*

He heard as well as felt the sickening *thunk* as a rock slammed into the back of his skull. Dazed, in shock, he knew he had to get to his feet to fight. He dragged himself up, staggering, and looked into the horrified face of Poor Singer. The youth stood in front of him with tears streaming down his narrow face and a huge round rock gripped in both hands. Swallowtail roared in angry defiance and lunged for Poor Singer . . .

Cornsilk kicked his legs out from under him. Swallowtail toppled to the ground, rolled, and grabbed for Cornsilk, but Poor Singer fell upon him, screaming, *"Don't you hurt her! Don't you ever hurt Cornsilk!"*

Swallowtail heard, more than felt, the next blow. His skull cracked, and lights, like a thousand splintered stars seared his vision. Lights . . . fading into the grayness . . .

Powered by terror and rage, Poor Singer barely realized it when Swallowtail slumped to the ground like a clubbed dog, his limbs twitching. Poor Singer kept beating, lifting the rock and bringing it down hard, screaming, *"I won't let you hurt her!"*

Swallowtail's body had grown flaccid, but the rock came

down again, and again. With each blow, the boy's rubbery limbs shook and flopped.

"Poor Singer? *Poor Singer!*"

Poor Singer blinked. He vaguely heard Cornsilk, but he kept grabbing up the bloody rock and bashing it down. Killing Swallowtail for what he'd done! He—

"*Poor Singer!*"

Cornsilk tugged the rock out of his hands and threw it into the forest, where it rolled and thumped against a tree trunk. Poor Singer sat with his fists suspended in midair, trembling, crying like a child. He looked up into Cornsilk's face and saw the blood trickling from her throat.

"I—I had to make him s-stop." Then he glanced at Swallowtail. Only red pulp and bone fragments marked the place his nose had been. The boy's shirt was still pulled up, twisted around his torso to expose the wet penis, like a dead slug across his thigh. "Cornsilk, I . . . oh, gods . . ." He squeezed his eyes closed, trying to blot the sight from his soul. "I can't believe I—"

Cornsilk knelt and embraced him, drawing Poor Singer against her as if she would never let go. "He was going to kill me, Poor Singer," she said in a shaking voice. "I could see it in his eyes. He wanted to kill me."

"But why! Why would he attack you? He had no reason! You hardly even knew him!"

Cornsilk pushed back and gazed into his blurry eyes. "I don't know why. But he wanted me dead. The . . ." She swallowed. "The rape . . . I think that was just an afterthought."

"You mean, you think he came up here to kill you?"

Her shaking was getting worse, as if now that it was over, the truth had begun to sink in. Cornsilk released Poor Singer to rub her arms. She clamped her jaw to still her chattering teeth.

"Oh, Cornsilk." Poor Singer stroked her hair. "It's all right, Cornsilk. You're safe now. Everything's going to be all right. Do you hear me? I won't let anybody hurt you. *Not ever.*"

"If you hadn't c-come when you did, I—"

"But I did come," he said, and thought about how he'd almost missed Swallowtail's trail. The boy had been very careful. His moccasins had barely scuffed the dust. When Poor Singer saw the faint prints, he'd immediately whirled and started back up the trail. That's when he'd heard Swallowtail's voice . . . and panicked.

"Are you all right, Cornsilk?"

She wiped the tears from her face and smeared the drops of blood. They streaked her cheeks in ghoulish patterns. "Let's hurry," she said as she scanned the forest. "I won't feel really safe until we're out in the open—away f-from here."

Poor Singer went to pick up Swallowtail's bow and quiver of arrows. As he slipped the quiver over his left shoulder, he looked again at the dead boy. Poor Singer had never killed a human being before. He had killed animals for food and hides, but this . . . Flies crawled hungrily over Swallowtail's crushed face. What should have sickened him left only a hollow sensation in the pit of his gut.

Clutching the bow in his right hand, he walked back, placed his left arm around Cornsilk, and hugged her as they headed downhill.

Night Sun forced herself to watch, her heartbeat sickeningly loud in her ears. *Watch! So you can tell the story . . . someone must tell the story.*

Ironwood stumbled, and fell to his knees. The crowd went wild. They rushed forward, jeering and throwing stones at him. He futilely lifted his arms to protect himself, but the rocks battered his bloody flesh. Soft grunts escaped his lips as he groped about, seemingly in a daze. Then his hand curled around a stone, and with a quick pitch, he lobbed it back at his tormentors.

An agile warrior ducked, but the stone thumped hollowly against an old woman's breast, toppling her backward amidst shrieks of pain.

Some of the Mogollon roared, relatives of the old woman, no doubt. Others hooted in approbation of a warrior who still fought back.

Night Sun couldn't breathe. As Father Sun rose toward noon, he poured a harsh white light upon the plaza. *How long has it been? Two hands of time. More? Blessed Ancestors, let this end!*

"Get him up!" Jay Bird shouted, and gestured to the guards. The elderly Chief's eyes had taken on a monstrous gleam of delight. He was smiling. "Howler! Drag him to his feet! And be mindful of the stones he throws!" Jay Bird gripped his own lance, ready to deliver the final blow when the time came.

Howler and another warrior broke from the line and hauled Ironwood to his feet. He braced himself on wobbling legs and wearily lifted his gray head to face his executioners.

Night Sun looked into that tormented face and the whole world died around her. She was remotely aware of the shrill laughter and war whoops, of the stench of sweating bodies, the coppery odor of Ironwood's blood . . .

Her throat went tight. One of his eyes had swollen shut from a nearly fatal lance thrust. The rest of his body looked worse. Every time he'd deflected a blow downward, the lance point had driven into his chest, stomach, or legs. Blood drained from *dozens* of punctures and gashes.

Dune took Night Sun's arm in a frail grasp, as if he needed something to hold on to. His voice came with difficulty. "How can he stand? How?"

She lifted her head and stiffened her spine. "He's showing them how a Straight Path warrior dies. *Never let anyone forget.*"

"So long as I live, the story will live."

The guards spun Ironwood around and shoved him down the corridor again. Shrieks of joy rose from the Fire Dogs. They leaped and danced and struggled to get close enough to see what was happening.

Howler's lance flashed, and Ironwood let out a small, wretched cry. He staggered, holding both hands over his left eye. Another lance shot out, striking him in his right cheek . . . his legs went weak. Ironwood collapsed. But this time, he did not try to rise. He lay on his side in the dirt, his chest heaving.

Night Sun's eyes burned with tears. She lived his every heartbeat, his every breath. Images flitted: laughing together . . . loving each other . . . the pain that had lived in his eyes all those summers. A thick band of rawhide had tightened around her chest. No matter how much air she drew into her lungs, they felt starved. Panic gripped her. Would his pain never end?

Night Sun glanced at the two guards. One stood to her left. One to Dune's right.

Night Sun strode forward, her sandals sinking in the sandy plaza. The guards shouted at her in the Fire Dog tongue, but she didn't stop. She headed for Jay Bird.

"*End it!*" she shouted. "Ironwood has proven himself! It is time you acted like a *Chief*, Jay Bird! Be done with this!"

A guard ran up and gripped her arm, jerking her backward so hard he almost pulled her off her feet. Without thinking, Night Sun backhanded him. The guard's head snapped back, and the crowd roared, half cursing, half laughing.

The humiliated guard tore the stiletto from his belt, and came at her . . .

"*Stop it! Stop!*" a terrified voice cut through the din. "*Grandfather*, make him *stop!*"

Poor Singer shoved through the crowd and ran toward Night Sun, his black hair flying. Cornsilk came through behind, started to follow . . . then saw Ironwood. She let out a cry and rushed to her father's side.

The guard glanced between the two youths, hesitating, his stiletto hovering above Night Sun as she glared at him.

Jay Bird threw up a hand and shouted something in Mogollon. The guard scowled, cursed her, and lowered his weapon.

Poor Singer stopped in front of Night Sun. "Are you all right?"

"Yes. Thank you." Night Sun hurried by him, chancing that she would have one last opportunity to see Ironwood.

Poor Singer caught up and kept pace with Night Sun, escorting her across the plaza. As they approached, the villagers shoved each other out of the way. Wide eyes examined them. People whispered behind their hands.

Cornsilk had thrown herself over Ironwood. He lay unmoving. Blood rushed in Night Sun's ears. She knelt beside Cornsilk, but looked up at Poor Singer. "Please, speak to your grandfather. Perhaps you can convince him—"

"I'm going!" He ran, shoving through the crowd.

Night Sun cataloged the wounds leaking the very life out of Ironwood, and whispered, "Hold on." She took his bloody hand in hers. "Hope just walked into camp."

His left eye was a blood-clotted hole. He looked up at her through his right eye, and a fleeting smile crossed his face. "Too late . . . I think."

Cornsilk wrapped her arms around Ironwood's gory chest and wept. "Don't die! Don't die, Father."

Ironwood smiled weakly and struggled to look at Cornsilk. The effort seemed to drain his last reserves. His face contorted as he slowly sank back to the ground. He heaved one final deep breath, and his head rolled to the side, his eye closing.

"No!" Cornsilk wailed.

Frantically, Night Sun reached for the big artery in his neck . . . and found a pulse. Weak, but there. "He's asleep . . . or unconscious. But he's alive."

She spun as a roar went up from the crowd and people began shuffling back, opening a lane for Jay Bird. The Chief tramped down it with his eyes blazing, Poor Singer running at his heels.

As Jay Bird raised his spear over Ironwood, Poor Singer leaped in front, and knocked it aside. "I *must* speak with you!"

"Move! I've an old score to settle, and I've waited too long to—"

"Just a few moments! That's all I'm asking!"

"To say *what?* To beg for his life?" Jay Bird yelled. His elderly face glowed bright red. "I told you days ago that I would *not* release Ironwood. And I will not. How dare you run in here and demand that I stop this! Can't you hear the souls of your murdered ancestors calling for his blood!"

"Grandfather, *please.*" Poor Singer spread his arms in a gesture of surrender. Tears streaked his face. "I must speak with you. Just let me speak with you. I bring you news."

"News? From whom?"

Mustering all of his courage, Poor Singer said, "From the gods."

Jay Bird's enraged face tightened. "What do you mean?"

"I had a vision, Grandfather. The god who spoke to me gave me a message for *you.*"

Jay Bird shoved him aside. "This is a trick. You are telling me this to keep me from killing Ironwood, and I have already made it clear—"

"As the gods are my witness, Grandfather, I *swear* to you this is not a trick! I'm telling you the truth! If you will only give me some time to explain—"

"No!"

Jay Bird lifted his lance again, and Poor Singer leaped, slamming into his grandfather so hard that Jay Bird stumbled sideways. Spinning in rage, Jay Bird lifted a fist to strike Poor Singer.

The instant seemed to freeze.

The crowd went deathly silent. Jay Bird's furious face turned to stone.

As if his entire life had been leading to this moment, Poor Singer shouted, "You would refuse to listen to the words of the gods? What sort of leader are you? All of my life I have heard stories of the great Jay Bird, and now I find a man who considers himself above the gods."

"If the gods wished to send me a message, why would they not come in person to tell me? Why send a skinny youth—"

"*I am a Singer, Grandfather!* And, before these people, I tell you, you *will* listen to me!" He turned then, raising his hands to the gawking Mogollon. He cried, "I bring word from the gods! They are angry at this foolishness!"

Howler and some of the other former slaves translated the words, and they passed through the assembly like a hissing snake. Some of the Mogollon spat at Poor Singer. Others eyed him fearfully.

Jay Bird grabbed Poor Singer's arm and spun him around to glare into his face. "I'll deal with you later, boy. For now . . ." His words abruptly dried up as his eyes shifted. He searched the crowd and then the heavens. "Do you hear that?"

"What?" Poor Singer cocked his head at the distant roar, like a violent thunderstorm out over the desert . . . except it seemed to be growing louder, riding the very air.

"Kill Ironwood!" Howler shouted. "Let us get this over with!"

But Jay Bird didn't move. He stood listening. Finally, he whispered, "Blessed gods . . ." threw down his lance, and grabbed for Poor Singer's arms.

At first, Poor Singer did not understand what was happening. Then the thunderous roar struck like a mountain falling down around them. One of the Mogollon guards screamed and threw himself to the quaking earth, his arms protectively covering his head.

A sick, lightheaded feeling overcame Poor Singer. He struggled for balance, began to stumble, his feet weaving, and grabbed for Jay Bird to keep standing.

Jay Bird shouted, "Why are the gods angry with *me?* They should be venting their wrath upon the Straight Path dogs for all they have done! Not me!"

Yells and shrieks split the air as dust seemed to dance out of the earth of its own will. Frightened dogs yipped shrilly and darted between the buildings.

As the shaking grew more violent, Jay Bird lost his hold on Poor Singer, careened sideways, and toppled to the ground. Poor Singer fell backward, desperately clutching sprigs of grass, as if they could save him. In the sky above, the Cloud People bounced around like hide balls thrown against rock.

Roof timbers cracked in the village. Dirt cascaded down, and a wall of dust gushed over the plaza. People crawled across the shuddering earth, trying to get to the collapsing houses where children wailed.

The roar grew to deafening booms, like the footfalls of giants. Poor Singer closed his eyes and prayed. . . .

Then, suddenly, the roar dropped to a grumble, and the ground stilled.

Stunned silence held the village. Then someone shouted, and people began running across the plaza, heading for the line of rooms that had collapsed. A new roar rose as people pawed through the wreckage, screaming and calling out the names of loved ones.

Poor Singer sat up. Ten hands away Jay Bird braced himself on his elbows. They stared at each other. His grandfather looked like a man who had just seen the Creator, Hummingbird, dive out of the heavens and alight before him.

"Let us go somewhere and talk, young Singer," Jay Bird said, breathing hard. "I will hear your message."

Fifty-Two

Jay Bird sat with Poor Singer on a grassy rise overlooking the stream that meandered at the base of Gila Monster Cliffs Village. The newly leafed trees added a bright spring green to the clusters of junipers. Puffy tumbles of cloud sailed across the blue vault of sky, but the air had a curious unfamiliar odor, a bilious, metallic tang.

"So, you killed Swallowtail?"

Poor Singer looked down at the blood on his hands, dried now, flaking off his skin in irregular patterns. "Yes. I did, Grandfather."

Jay Bird pondered the story of the Keeper and the turquoise cave, and the horror of finding Swallowtail raping Cornsilk. Clots of blood matted Poor Singer's black hair to his cheeks. Jay Bird leaned forward and propped his forearms on his knees. That sense of serenity, of growing Power, hung about the boy like a mantle.

"I offered my life in exchange for Ironwood's," Poor Singer said.

"You would have given your life to save him?"

"I wanted to very much."

"And what did the Keeper of the Tortoise Bundle say to this?"

Poor Singer turned his deeply tanned face toward the speckles of sunlight falling through the trees. They glittered in his hair and reflected from his soft brown eyes. "She knew that you wished to kill him, and she—"

"She *knew?*"

"Yes, I don't know how."

A sharp pain lanced Jay Bird beneath his left breast. He lifted a hand to massage the spot. "Doesn't matter. Holy people often know such things, sometimes before we know them ourselves. I was just surprised. Go on."

Sorrow crinkled the lines around Poor Singer's young eyes. "The Keeper asked me why I would give up my life for a man I barely knew. I told her I couldn't stand to see any more of my friends die, that all of this was my fault. If I hadn't been born, if Sternlight had let me die, none of this would have happened."

Jay Bird lowered his hand to his lap and laced his fingers tightly. He didn't know what to say. His grandson must love these Straight Path people very much.

Poor Singer shook his head and continued. "She asked me if I understood what it meant to have the heart of a cloud."

". . . The heart of a cloud?"

"Yes. A Spirit once told me: 'You must have the heart of a cloud to walk upon the wind.' I didn't understand back then."

"And do you now?"

Poor Singer frowned. "Some of it. I told the Keeper that I thought that the heart of a cloud was tears, and 'to walk upon the wind' meant to be able to look down from high above, to see more clearly." He turned to face Jay Bird, and his eyes were moist. "I think the teaching means that if I live inside the tears of other people, I will see life more clearly."

Jay Bird sat back. For a man Poor Singer's age to understand the nature of shared pain was rare. How many old men, men in their seventieth summer, had yet to learn that truth? "What did she say?"

"She said, 'Tell your grandfather what you did here. What you saw here. He will understand.' " Poor Singer frowned at Jay Bird, as if wondering if he did.

Jay Bird smoothed his hand over the grass at his side. The new blades felt soft and delicate. "Did she say anything else?"

Poor Singer nodded. "Yes. She told me that if I spoke with you, I would be a great Singer one day, and that I should make my life an offering. That it would save far more people than my death."

An odd throbbing pain built above Jay Bird's heart. This wise woman of the mountains had hidden a message for him alone in those words. *She is warning me that my grandson will be a very great holy man. That is, if I don't kill his soul by killing his friend.*

But to let Ironwood go free! His wife's dead eyes stared out at him from the depths of his soul. How could he let her murderer go? Or turn his back on the loss and abuse of his daughter? Could he simply forget the terrible suffering and grief?

Jay Bird shook his head. "I can't let him go, Poor Singer."

"He was following the orders of his Blessed Sun, Grandfather, as your War Chief follows yours. You are punishing the tool for allowing itself to be used."

"But his death will strike terror into the hearts of our enemies, Grandson. I must—"

"They are already afraid, Grandfather." Poor Singer's nose wrinkled at the strange odor carried on the western breeze. "The gods have their own sense of justice. I . . ." He frowned. "Like an old tree, the Straight Path nation looks massive from the outside, but the center of the trunk is rotting, dying. They do not have much time."

"How do you know, Poor Singer? Did the gods tell you this?"

Poor Singer folded his arms tightly across his chest. "No . . . but I know it to be true."

Jay Bird's brows lowered at the glow in Poor Singer's eyes. For long moments, he stared into those eyes, seeing the promise of the future, the pain of the past. Justice was such a tenuous thing, the balance so precarious. How could he believe? Poor Singer was barely a man. Could Jay Bird trust his vision?

Jay Bird closed his eyes. "Sometimes," he whispered, "a man must be willing to forego the satisfaction of vengeance and place his faith in his family."

Poor Singer straightened. "What does that mean?"

Hatred curled like an angry snake in Jay Bird's belly. "It means I . . ." He could barely get the words out. "I will free Ironwood."

Poor Singer embraced Jay Bird so hard the hug drove the air from his lungs. A warm sensation spread through him—the same sort of elation he used to feel when Young Fawn hugged him. Jay Bird smiled wearily and patted his grandson's back.

"But *you* must tell him," Jay Bird said. "If I look upon him again, I will surely kill him."

"I'll tell him!"

Jay Bird shoved back. "Then go. Do it now, before I have time to reconsider. We will talk more later."

Poor Singer leaped to his feet and ran, his legs pumping as he took the trail toward the pen.

Jay Bird struggled to calm his writhing gut. All those years of brooding, the suppressed rage, had carried him as wind does a feather. Now, his soul had come to ground. The arms of the breeze had failed him.

Is this the price for all that pain? He had grown sentimental in his old age. But perhaps it would all work out. Poor Singer would have to repeat his vision to the entire community. Everyone would wish to hear it. *And it might be the only thing that saves me from my people's wrath.*

Not that it mattered. He had endured their wrath before, and this one act had given him the grandson he might otherwise have lost. The warmth of Poor Singer's embrace lived in his heart.

He squinted after the youth. Sunlight slanting through the clouds threw a golden veil over Poor Singer as he climbed toward the village.

"Keeper, I pray I am doing the right thing. If I'm not . . ."

The earth shook again, a tremor that took Jay Bird by surprise. And then, off to the west, the Rainbow Serpent glittered to life. She rose majestically over the mountaintop behind Gila Monster Cliffs Village, and stretched across the sky like a many-colored bridge of light.

The billowing thunderheads seemed to part before her, retreating to the edges of her glory.

Awed, Jay Bird whispered, *"This time . . . I hear you."*

Creeper stood beside Webworm in a shower of falling gray ash, watching the stream of people climbing over the walls, down the ladders, leaving Talon Town. Packs wobbled on their backs as they headed toward the wash to fill their jars with gray water one last time. An ominous buzz of conversation stirred the quiet.

Creeper folded his arms and hugged himself. The ash settled

over the canyon like a smothering blanket, turning the town's white walls gray. Nearly four hands had built up in the plaza. A weaving pattern of trails cut through the windblown drifts. Creeper turned and squinted northward. He could barely make out the towering sandstone wall behind Talon Town. Patches of golden rock appeared and disappeared through the thick veil of whirling ash. Traders had been coming through, and they told horrifying stories. The massive quake, they said, had been felt for ten days' run in any direction.

Webworm let out a deep sigh. He wore a red cape with the hood pulled up to shield his face, but ash coated his black hair and clung to his eyelashes. He had his jaw clenched. "A Hohokam Trader came through this morning. He told me that fiery rivers are pouring out of the Thlatsina Mountains, burning everything in their paths. He said forest fires are consuming the whole world. His people are terrified, too."

Creeper gazed up at the sky. It glowed an eerie shade of yellowish purple, as though the skyworlds had been battered and bruised by the gods' wrath. Smoke stung his nostrils with every breath.

"What did we expect?" he said in a low voice. "First the Matron is disgraced, then Talon Town is raided, and she, the holy Derelict, and the Sunwatcher are captured. After that the Blessed Sun is murdered and buried as a witch—"

"The gods must hate us."

Tenderly, Creeper placed a hand on Webworm's shoulder. He would not repeat the other whispers he'd heard late at night, whispers that made his heart beat painfully in his chest: *"Look at what has happened to us! The new Blessed Sun is half Fire Dog, and the new Matron is a demented old woman! We are doomed! Let's go before it's too late!"*

Webworm tugged his hood more closely about his face and frowned at the latest group of people to descend the ladders. Their bright capes, reds, yellows, and one a pale purple, contrasted with the ashen ground. Family by family, they were heading for the outlying villages and kin who would take them in. "If this keeps up, Creeper, I will rule over silence. Talon Town will be abandoned."

"We cannot stop them. They are free people."

"That Trader," Webworm murmured, "he told me that just

before the rivers of fire spurted from the earth, the ancestors in the underworlds grew so angry that the shaking ground cracked wide open, swallowing rivers and villages, then one of the mountains exploded—the entire top blew off, Creeper! Huge molten boulders flew through the air like birds! He said—"

"Hallowed Ancestors!" Creeper gasped, "*Sternlight predicted that the gods would hurl huge fiery rocks to split the Fifth World apart!*"

Webworm turned to peer at Creeper with his frightened soul in his eyes. "Do you think . . . can this really be the end of our world, Creeper?"

Creeper gazed down at the stream of people vanishing into the gray haze. Somewhere out there, a child sobbed.

"Who's to say, Webworm?" he answered gently. "Only the gods and very great Dreamers know such things."

Fifty-Three

Sun Cycle of the Dragonfly, Moon of Fledgling Robins

Ironwood led the way up the winding game trail, taking Night Sun by the hand as they walked along a narrow precipice. To his right, the sheer cliff fell away, ending hundreds of hands below in a huge pile of worn and broken boulders. Magnificent mountain peaks jutted through the haze around them. Snow still veined the deepest cracks, but a warm wind flapped the fringes on his buckskin shirt. He loved these alpine meadows. Wildflowers turned the slopes into a mosaic of blue, yellow, and white. Thunderheads crowded the blue high above. It had been raining off and on, settling the ash that still rose in plumes to the southwest.

In the past two moons, his body had mostly healed, though

walking still pained him. The empty left eye socket ached all the time, but the steady leakage of pus had tapered off to a yellow crust. He adjusted the patch he wore over it and looked down at his arms, at the intricate tracery of whitening scars. Pink ridges of tissue criss-crossed his face, too, but his chest, legs, and back were worse.

When they reached the crest of the hill, he stopped and looked down the trail. Cornsilk, Poor Singer, and Dune walked a short distance behind. Dune had picked up a walking stick and used it to gesture with, as well as for support. He was stabbing it at Poor Singer. The two had been arguing about this trip for days. Poor Singer claimed he had to find out if the Keeper of the Tortoise Bundle was real. To which Dune replied, "Real where? In this world, or another?"

Ironwood smiled.

Night Sun turned to follow his gaze. "Are they still at it?"

Ironwood's gaze caressed the graying black hair that fluttered about her beautiful face. Poor Singer had talked his grandmother into providing new clothing for them, and Night Sun wore a red dress with black lightning spirals around the hem. She looked lovely. They'd left Gila Monster Cliffs Village as soon as Ironwood could walk, but they hadn't gone far—just up into the mountains. They'd spent a full moon in a wondrous little canyon filled with currant and berry bushes, surrounded by tall pines and oaks.

Since then, they'd been slowly making their way north through the ash-coated deserts. They didn't have the strength for rapid travel, and with raiding warriors and refugees on the trails, care had to be taken. They'd adopted a leisurely pace, stopping often to let Dune rest, to hunt or fish—for none of the villages would have welcomed them. Besides, since they didn't know where they were going, it mattered little when they arrived. Up there, in the far northern mountains, they would find a home.

Ironwood grinned. "Poor Singer maintains this is the way, and Dune says he's lost his senses. That no one with any brains would live in this cold country."

Night Sun laughed, and the sound melted Ironwood's heart. It had been a long time since he'd heard her laugh with true joy.

Dune waved his walking stick at Poor Singer and the youth skipped sideways with a yip. Cornsilk grinned at their antics. Despite her rich tan, an irregular splotch of white scar tissue marred her cheek.

We all have scars. Cornsilk's and mine are just easy to see.

"I must admit," Night Sun said, sighing, "I really love these cool mountains. The pines, the streams, the abundance of game. I could be very happy here, Ironwood."

Ironwood grasped Night Sun's hand and held it tightly. "As soon as you want to stop, tell me. I'll start cutting stones for a house."

She slipped her arm around his waist and pulled him close. "Do you think the rumors are true? That the Mogollon joined forces with the Tower Builders to attack Straight Path Canyon?"

"The Trader who told us said he'd heard they were going to attack the canyon, not that they had. I'm sure Webworm has heard the same rumors. He'll be taking the proper precautions." Ironwood tenderly smoothed loose hair behind her ear. "Do you miss home so much?"

Night Sun looked away, her gaze roaming the pines and quaking aspens. "One does not forget a lifetime of responsibility. In a sense, I always will be Matron of Talon Town. But being worried about them doesn't mean I want to go back, my husband. I don't. I only regret that you and I haven't found our place yet."

"We will. I want to keep going north, far away from Straight Path country."

Night Sun rested her head against his chest and tightened her arms around his waist. "So do I."

As Dune, Poor Singer, and Cornsilk came closer, Ironwood heard Dune say, "You don't search for gods, boy, the gods search for you. And usually, after they've found you, you wish they hadn't."

Poor Singer shook his head. He wore a blue shirt and had tied his hair in back with a length of cord. The style accentuated the narrowness of his face and the size of his dark eyes. "I don't think she was a god, Dune. I think she was a woman. A human being."

"Human beings don't live in turquoise caves, you imbecile. Gods do."

Ironwood looked southward. Far away, on the other side of those jagged peaks, sat Fourth Night House, and the turquoise mines of the Straight Path nation. Could such a cave truly exist? Ever since Poor Singer had told the story of the Keeper, Ironwood had been trying to imagine where the cave might be. Large veins of turquoise were very rare and precious. Even if they found it, the cave might be heavily guarded. On the other hand, the Keeper might have enough Spirit Power to keep the cave hidden from probing eyes.

"But she looked real, Dune," Poor Singer insisted. "I swear it."

"Well," Cornsilk said, "the only way to know is to keep searching."

Ironwood heaved a sigh. "Do you still think it has to be one of these peaks, Poor Singer?"

The youth lifted a hand to shield his eyes from the glare of the sunlight and scanned the splintered granite pinnacles. "They look different without the snow, and the meadows have greened, the aspens are all leafed out, but I'm almost certain."

"Good enough," Ironwood replied, and took Night Sun's hand again. "I'll lead."

They climbed the game trail, passing through a whispering grove of aspens, and emerged into another alpine meadow. This one sloped downhill. A fringe of barberry bushes ringed the tall grasses.

When rain began to fall again, the thick-muscled man stopped stacking firewood to catch his breath and caught sight of five people climbing the game trail. He frowned at the bobbing line of heads, wiped his sweating brow on his elkhide sleeve, and flexed his strong hands. His broad, tattooed cheeks and gray hair glistened with dampness. Scars from old battles puckered his flesh. He glanced at the gnarled war club where it lay propped against a tree, the copper spike gleaming.

He turned and called, "Nightshade?"

She shoved the brush aside and ducked out of the narrow cave entrance, standing tall, her red sleeves billowing in the stiff mountain wind. It still surprised him that she insisted upon wearing red, for the tradition came from a people they had both long ago abandoned.

Lifting a hand to her forehead, she examined the visitors climbing through the meadow. Their laughter echoed. As though in response, Thunderbird roared and the drizzle turned to a downpour. Rain cascaded down the sides of the mountains, making the granite shine. Nightshade smiled.

"At last, Badgertail. It took them long enough."

He said, "Were you expecting them, my priestess?"

Off to the side, where willows were fed by a seep, came the thrashing sounds of children playing. Three shapes moved through the pines, their laughter joyous.

"Yes, my kidnapper." Nightshade lowered her hand and smiled. "I've been expecting them for a long time."

Bibliography

Acatos, Sylvio, *Pueblos: Prehistoric Indian Cultures of the South-west*, translation of 1989 edition of *Die Pueblos*. New York: Facts on File, 1990.

Adams, E. Charles, *The Origin and Development of the Pueblo Katsina Cult*. Tucson: University of Arizona Press, 1991.

Adler, Michael A., *The Prehistoric Pueblo World* A.D. 1150–1350. Tucson: University of Arizona Press, 1996.

Allen, Paula Gunn, *Spider Woman's Granddaughters*. New York: Ballantine Books, 1989.

Arnberger, Leslie P., *Flowers of the Southwest Mountains*. Tucson: Southwest Parks and Monuments Association, 1982.

Baars, Donald L., *Navajo Country: A Geological and Natural History of the Four Corners Region*. Albuquerque: University of New Mexico Press, 1995.

Becket, Patrick H., ed., *Mogollon V*. Report of Fifth Mogollon Conference. Las Cruces, New Mexico: COAS Publishing and Research, 1991.

Boissiere, Robert, *The Return of Pahana: A Hopi Myth*. Santa Fe: Bear & Company Publishing, 1990.

Bowers, Janice Emily, *Shrubs and Trees of the Southwest Deserts*. Tucson: Southwest Parks and Monuments Association, 1993.

Brody, J.J., *The Anasazi*. New York: Rizzoli International Publications, 1990.

Bunzel, Ruth L., *Zuni Katcinas*. Reprint of Forty-seventh Annual Report of the Bureau of American Ethnography, 1929–1930. Glorietta, New Mexico: Rio Grande Press, 1984.

Colton, Harold S., *Black Sand: Prehistory in Northern Arizona*. Albuquerque: University of New Mexico Press, 1960.

Cordell, Linda S., "Predicting Site Abandonment at Wetherill Mesa." *The Kiva*, 40(3): 189–202.

————, *Prehistory of the Southwest.* New York: Academic Press, Inc., 1984.

————, *Ancient Pueblo Peoples.* Smithsonian Exploring the Ancient World Series. Washington, D.C.: Smithsonian Institution, 1994.

Cordell, Linda S., and George J. Gumerman, eds., *Dynamics of Southwest Prehistory.* Washington, D.C.: Smithsonian Institution Press, 1989.

Crown, Patricia and W. James Judge, eds., *Chaco & Hohokam: Prehistoric Regional Systems in the American Southwest.* Santa Fe: School of American Research Press, 1991.

Cummings, Linda Scott, "Anasazi Subsistence Activity Areas Reflected in the Pollen Records." Paper presented to the Society for American Archaeology Meetings, New Orleans, 1986.

————, "Anasazi Diet: Variety in the Hoy House and Lion House Coprolite Record and Nutritional Analysis" in *Paleonutrition: The Diet and Health of Prehistoric Americans.* Southern Illinois University at Carbondale, Occasional Paper No. 22, Sobolik, ed., 1994.

Dodge, Natt N., *Flowers of the Southwest Deserts.* Tuscon: Southwest Parks and Monument Association, 1985.

Dooling, D.M., and Paul Jordan-Smith, eds., *I Become Part of It: Sacred Dimensions in Native American Life.* San Francisco: HarperCollins Publishers, 1989.

Douglas, John E., "Autonomy and Regional Systems in the Late Prehistoric Southern Southwest." *American Antiquity,* 60:240–257.

Downum, Christian E., *Between Desert and River: Hohokam Settlement and Land Use in the Los Robles Commnity.* Tucson: University of Arizona Press, 1993.

Dunmire, William W., and Gail Tierney, *Wild Plants of the Pueblo Province: Exploring Ancient and Enduring Uses.* Santa Fe: Museum of New Mexico Press, 1995.

Ellis, Florence Hawley, "Patterns of Aggression and the War Cult in Southwestern Pueblos." *Southwestern Journal of Anthropology,* 7: 177–201.

Elmore, Francis H., *Shrubs and Trees of the Southwest Uplands.* Tuscon: Southwest Parks and Monuments Association, 1976.

Ericson, Jonathan E. and Timothy G. Baugh, eds., *The American Southwest and Mesoamerica: Systems of Prehistoric Exchange*. New York: Plenum Press, 1993.

Fagan, Brian M., *Ancient North America*. New York: Thames and Hudson, 1991.

Farmer, Malcom F., "A Suggested Typology of Defensive Systems of the Southwest." *Southwestern Journal of Archaeology*, 13: 249–266.

Fewkes, J. Walter, J.J. Brody, ed., *The Mimbres: Art and Archaeology*. Albuquerque: Avanyu Publishing Inc., 1989.

Fish, Suzanne, K., Paul Fish, and John H. Madsen, eds., *The Marana Community in the Hohokam World*. Anthropological Papers of the University of Arizona, No. 56. Tucson: University of Arizona Press, 1992.

Frank, Larry, and Francis H. Harlow, *Historic Pottery of the Pueblo Indians: 1600–1880*. West Chester, PA: Schiffler Publishing, 1990.

Frazier, Kendrick, *People of Chaco: A Canyon and its Culture*. New York: W.W. Norton, 1986.

Gabriel, Kathryn, *Roads to Center Place: A Cultural Atlas of Chaco Canyon and the Anasazi*. Boulder, CO: Johnson Books, 1991.

Gumerman, George J., ed., *The Anasazi in a Changing Environment*. New York: Cambridge University Press, 1988.

———, *Exploring the Hohokam: Prehistoric Peoples of the American Southwest*. Albuquerque: University of New Mexico Press, 1991.

———, *Themes in Southwest Prehistory*. Santa Fe: School of American Research Press, 1994.

Haas, Jonathan, "Warfare and the Evolution of Tribal Polities in the Prehistoric Southwest" in *The Anthropology of War*. Jonathan Haas, ed. Cambridge, England: Cambridge University Press, 1990.

Haas, Jonathan, and Winifred Creamer, "A History of Pueblo Warfare," Paper Presented at the 60th Annual Meeting for the Society of American Archaeology, Minneapolis, 1995.

———, *Stress and Warfare Among the Kayenta Anasazi of the Thirteenth Century A.D.*. Chicago: Field Museum of Natural History, 1993.

Haury, Emil, *Mogollon Culture in the Forestdale Valley, East-*

Central Arizona. Tuscon: University of Arizona Press, 1985.

Hayes, Alden C., David M. Burgge, and W. James Judge, *Archaeological Surveys of Chaco Canyon, New Mexico*. Reprint of National Park Service Report. Albuquerque: University of New Mexico Press, 1981.

Hultkrantz, Ake, *Native Religions: The Power of Visions and Fertility*. New York: Harper & Row, 1987.

Jacobs, Sue-Ellen, "Continuity and Change in Gender Roles at San Juan Pueblo" in *Women and Power in Native North America*. Norman, OK: University of Oklahoma Press, 1995.

Jernigan, E. Wesley, *Jewelry of the Prehistoric Southwest*. Albuquerque: University of New Mexico Press, 1978.

Jett, Stephen C., "Pueblo Indian Migrations: An Evaluation of the Possible Physical and Cultural Determinants." *American Antiquity*, 29: 281–300.

Komarek, Susan, *Flora of the San Juans: A Field Guide to the Mountain Plants of Southwestern Colorado*. Durango, CO: Kivaki Press, 1994.

Lange, Frederick, Nancy Mahaney, Joe Ben Wheat, Mark L. Chenault, and John Carter, *Yellow Jacket: A Four Corners Anasazi Ceremonial Center*. Boulder, CO: Johnson Books, 1988.

Lekson, Stephen H., *Mimbres Archaeology of the Upper Gila, New Mexico*. Anthropological Papers of the University of Arizona, No. 53. Tucson: University of Arizona Press, 1990.

Lekson, Stephen, Thomas C. Windes, John R. Stein, and W. James Judge, "The Chaco Canyon Community." *Scientific American* 259 (1) 100–109.

Lipe, W.D. and Michelle Hegemon, eds., *The Architecture of Social Integration in Prehistoric Pueblos*. Occasional Papers of the Crow Canyon Archaeological Center No. 1. Cortez, CO: Crow Canyon Archaeological Center, 1989.

Lister, Florence C., *In the Shadow of the Rocks: Archaeology of the Chimney Rock District in Southern Colorado*. Niwot, CO: University Press of Colorado, 1993.

Lister, Robert H. and Florence C. Lister, *Chaco Canyon*. Albuquerque: University of New Mexico Press, 1981.

Lomatuway'ma, Michael, Lorena Lomatuway'ma, and Sidney Namingha, Jr., *Hopi Ruin Legends*. Edited by Ekkehart Malotki. Lincoln: University of Nebraska Press, 1993.

Malotki, Ekkehart, *Gullible Coyote: Una'ihu: A Bilingual Collection of Hopi Coyote Stories*. Tucson: University of Arizona Press, 1985.

Malotki, Ekkehart, and Michael Lomatuway'ma, *Maasaw: Profile of a Hopi God*. American Tribal Religions, Vol. XI. Lincoln: University of Nebraska Press, 1987.

Malville, J. McKimm, and Claudia Putnam, *Prehistoric Astronomy in the Southwest*. Boulder, CO: Johnson Books, 1993.

Martin, Debra L., "Lives Unlived: The Political Economy of Violence Against Anasazi Women." Paper presented to the Society for American Archaeology 60th Annual Meeting, Minneapolis, 1995.

Martin, Debra L., and Alan H. Goodman, George Armelagos, and Ann L. Magennis, *Black Mesa Anasazi Health: Reconstructing Life from Patterns of Death and Disease*. Occasional Paper No. 14. Carbondale, IL: Southern Illinois University, 1991.

Mayes, Vernon O., and Barbara Bayless Lacy, *Nanise: A Navajo Herbal*. Tsaile, AZ: Navajo Community College Press, 1989.

McGuire, Randall H. and Michael Schiffer, eds., *Hohokam and Patayan: Prehistory of Southwestern Arizona*. New York: Academic Press, 1982.

McNitt, Frank, *Richard Wetherill's Anasazi*. Albuquerque: University of New Mexico Press, 1966.

Minnis, Paul E., and Charles L. Redman, eds., *Perspectives on Southwestern Prehistory*. Boulder, CO: Westview Press, 1990.

Mullet, G. M., *Spider Woman Stories: Legends of the Hopi Indians*. Tucson: University of Arizona Press, 1979.

Nabahan, Gary Paul, *Enduring Seeds: Native American Agriculture and Wild Plant Conservation*. San Francisco: North Point Press, 1989.

Noble, David Grant, *Ancient Ruins of the Southwest: An Archaeological Guide*. Flagstaff, AZ: Northland Publishing, 1991.

Ortiz, Alfonzo, ed., *Handbook of North American Indians*. Washington, D.C.: Smithsonian Institution, 1983.

Palkovich, Ann M., *The Arroyo Hondo Skeletal and Mortuary Remains*. Arroyo Hondo Archaeological Series, Vol 3. Santa Fe: School of American Research Press, 1980.

Parsons, Elsie Clews, *Tewa Tales*. 1924. Reprint, Tuscon: University of Arizona Press, 1994.

Pike, Donald G., and David Muench, *Anasazi: Ancient People of the Rock*. New York: Crown Publishers, 1974.

Reid, J. Jefferson, and David E. Doyel, eds., *Emil Haury's Prehistory of the American Southwest*. Tucson: University of Arizona Press, 1992.

Riley, Carroll L., *Rio del Norte: People of the Upper Rio Grande From the Earliest Times to the Pueblo Revolt*. Salt Lake City: University of Utah Press, 1995.

Rocek, Thomas R., "Sedentarization and Agricultural Dependence: Perspectives from the Pithouse-to-Pueblo Transition in the American Southwest." *American Antiquity*, 60: 218–239.

Schaafsma, Polly, *Indian Rock Art of the Southwest*. School of American Research, Albuquerque: University of New Mexico Press, 1980.

Sebastian, Lynne, *The Chaco Anasazi: Sociopolitical Evolution in the Prehistoric Southwest*. Cambridge, England: Cambridge University Press, 1992.

Simmons, Marc, *Witchcraft in the Southwest*. 1974. Reprint. Lincoln: University of Nebraska Press, 1980.

Slifer, Dennis, and James Duffield, *Kokopelli: Flute Player Images in Rock Art*. Sante Fe: Ancient City Press, 1994.

Smith, Watson, with Raymond H. Thompson, ed., *When is a Kiva: And Other Questions About Southwestern Archaeology*. Tucson: University of Arizona Press, 1990.

Sobolik, Kristin D., *Paleonutrition: The Diet and Health of Prehistoric Americans*. Occasional Paper No. 22, Center for Archaeological Investigations. Carbondale, IL: Southern Illinois University, 1994.

Sullivan, Alan P., "Pinyon Nuts and Other Wild Resources in Western Anasazi Subsistence Economies." *Research in Economic Anthropology* Supplement 6: 195–239.

Tedlock, Barbara, *The Beautiful and the Dangerous: Encounters with the Zuni Indians*. New York: Viking Press, 1992.

Trombold, Charles D., ed., *Ancient Road Networks and Settlement Hierarchies in the New World*. Cambridge, England: Cambridge University Press, 1991.

Tyler, Hamilton A., *Pueblo Gods and Myths*. Norman, OK: University of Oklahoma Press, 1964.

Underhill, Ruth, *Life in the Pueblos*. 1964, Bureau of Indian Affairs Report. Reprint. Sante Fe: Ancient City Press, 1991.

Upham, Steadman, Kent G. Lightfoot, and Roberta A. Jewett, eds., *The Sociopolitical Structure of Prehistoric Southwestern Societies*. San Francisco: Westview Press, 1989.

Vivian, Gordon, and Tom W. Mathews, *Kin Kletso: A Pueblo III Community in Chaco Canyon, New Mexico*, Vol. 6. Globe, AZ: Southwest Parks and Monuments Association, 1973.

Vivian, Gordon, and Paul Reiter, *The Great Kivas of Chaco Canyon and their Relationships*. Monograph No. 22. Santa Fe: School of American Research, 1965. Vivian, R. Gwinn, *The Chacoan Prehistory of the San Juan Basin*. New York: Academic Press, 1990.

Waters, Frank, *Book of the Hopi*. New York: Viking Press, 1963.

Wetterstrom, Wilma, *Food, Diet, and Population at Prehistoric Arroyo Hondo Pueblo, New Mexico*. Arroyo Hondo Archaeological Series, Vol. 6. Santa Fe: School of American Research Press, 1986.

White, Tim D., *Prehistoric Cannibalism at Mancos 5MTUMR–2346*. Princeton: Princeton University Press, 1992.

Williamson, Ray A., *Living The Sky: The Cosmos of the American Indian*. Norman, OK: University of Oklahoma Press, 1984.

Wills, W.H. and Robert D. Leonard, eds., *The Ancient Southwestern Community*. Albuquerque: University of New Mexico Press, 1994.

Woodbury, Richard B., "A Reconsideration of Pueblo Warfare in the Southwestern United States." *Actas del XXXIII Congreso Internacional de Americanistas*. II: 124–133.

———, "Climatic Changes and Prehistoric Agriculture in the Southwestern United States." *New York Academy of Sciences Annals*. Vol. 95, Article 1.

Wright, Barton, *Katchinas: The Barry Goldwater Collection at the Heard Museum*. Phoenix: Heard Museum, 1975.

At its pinnacle in A.D. 1150 the Anasazi empire of the Southwest would see no equal in North America for almost eight hundred years. Yet even at this cultural zenith, the Anasazi held the seeds of their own destruction deep within themselves....

On his deathbed, the Great Sun Chief learns a secret, a shame so vile to him that even at the brink of eternity he cannot let it pass: In a village far to the north is a fifteen-summers-old girl who must be found. Though he knows neither her name nor her face, the Great Sun decrees that the girl must at all costs be killed.

Fleeing for her life as her village lies in ruins, young Cornsilk is befriended by Poor Singer, a curious youth seeking to touch the soul of the Katchinas. Together, they undertake the perilous task of staying alive long enough to discover her true identity. But time is running out for them all—a desperate killer stalks them, one who is willing to destroy the entire Anasazi world to get to her.

Tom Doherty Associates, LLC
www.tor.com

0 37145 00799 1

ISBN 0-812-51559-5

51559

UPC

S

Printed in the USA